"Get off the road!" troop transport!"

Hank skidded the rocked to a halt under the spreading limbs of a massive oak tree.

"Out!" Ori snarled, bodily hauling President Lendan out of the car. As Kafari scrambled out, something else big roared down the canyon, at treetop height. Dazzling beams of coherent light strafed the fields, cutting down anything moving: tractors, herds of panic-stricken livestock, people . . .

"Down!"

Ori slam-dunked Abe Lendan into the ground and shielded the president's body with his own. Kafari ate dirt. More airborne fighter-craft shot past, toward the immense bulk of the Deng troop ship. The alien behemoth was settling to ground less than five hundred meters away. Oh, God, Kafari wept in sheer terror, oh, God. . . . She dug her fingers into the dirt.

Things were emerging from that ship. Immense, multi-jointed things. Bristling with guns. Looking like demons from the darkest reaches of hell. Yavacs, her brain gibbered. Those are Yavacs! Lots of them. And infantry. A black tide was pouring out of the troop ship, full of hairy, dog-sized creatures. Spindly, stilt-like legs sent them scurrying far too fast.

Then white-hot hell erupted. When she could see again, the president's car was gone. So was the tree it had been parked under. The ground trembled under strange, disjointed concussions. One glimpse showed Kafari a sight from deepest nightmare. Yavacs, walking down the canyon. On huge, misshapen metallic legs. Insects the size of houses. Hunting her . . .

The Road to
DAMASCUS

JOHN RINGO
LINDA EVANS

THE ROAD TO DAMASCUS

A Baen Books Original

Baen Publishing Enterprises
P.O. Box 1403
Riverdale, NY 10471
www.baen.com

ISBN: 0-7434-9916-6
ISBN 13: 978-0-7434-9916-3

Cover art by David Mattingly

First paperback printing, July 2005
Fourth paperback printing, May 2009

Distributed by Simon & Schuster
1230 Avenue of the Americas
New York, NY 10020

Library of Congress Cataloging-in-Publication Data: 2003025557

Production & design by Windhaven Press (www.windhaven.com)
Printed in the United States of America.

For Aubrey Jean Hollingsworth, our second source of sunshine, with endless thanks to Bob Hollingsworth, Susan Collingwood, John Ringo, and Toni Weisskopf for patience, forbearance, and the ideas that brought this story to life.

—Linda Evans

PART ONE

PART ONE

Chapter One

I

I crawl toward the enemy, blind and uncertain of my every move.

This is not the first battle I have fought over this broken, bloody ground, but it may be my last. The enemy is ruthless and keenly skilled, led by a commander whose battlefield brilliance has consistently outmatched the government's admittedly wretched field-grade generals. Any commander who can catch a Bolo Mark XX in one successful ambush after another is a force to be reckoned with. I do not make the mistake of underestimating him.

I am in pitiful condition for battle, but this rebellion must be stopped. As the only fighting force left on Jefferson with any hope of defeating the rebellion's high command, it is up to me to restore law and order to this world. Civil war is a bloody business, at best, and this one has been no exception. I am not happy to be caught in the middle of it.

I am even less happy with the terrain in which I must face Commodore Oroton and his veteran gunners.

The terrain through which I creep is ideal country for the rebel army which has made its strongest camp here. Klameth Canyon is more than a single, twisting cut of rock slashed through the heart of the Damisi Mountains. It is a whole series of canyons, narrow gorges, and tortuous blind corries. Tectonic action buckled ancient sandstone badlands and shoved the broken slabs upwards in a jumble that stretches the length of the continent. The deep canyons carved by wind, weather, and wild rivers still exist, but they have been twisted askew by the titanic forces inherent in the molten heart of a world. Above the ancient canyon walls, the high, broken peaks of the Damisi range climb toward the sky, jagged teeth above a spider's tangle of gashes in the earth.

I have never seen terrain like it and I have been fighting humanity's wars for more than one hundred twenty years. Even Etaine, the worst killing field I have ever known, was not as disadvantageous as the ground I cross now. If it had been, humanity would have lost that battle—and that world. I fear I will lose this one, for there is no worse terrain on Jefferson for fighting an entrenched army. Commodore Oroton, naturally, has chosen it as his final battleground.

The only way into—or out of—Klameth Canyon by ground transport is through Maze Gap, which I cleared nearly an hour ago. I anticipate ambush from moment to moment, but the commodore's gun crews do not fire. I mistrust this quiescence. I have all but given up trying to outthink Commodore Oroton, since I am almost invariably wrong. His battlefield decisions are frequently devoid of straightforward logic, which makes any attempt to predict his moment-to-moment actions fiendishly difficult. If I had a Brigade-trained human commander with plenty of combat experience, he or she would doubtless fare much better than I have, working on my own.

But I do not have a human commander, let alone a Brigade officer. The president of Jefferson, to whom I report and from whom I take directives that equate to orders, has the power to issue instructions that I am legally obligated to obey, under the terms of Jefferson's treaty with the Concordiat. The president, however, is not a soldier and has never served in any branch of the military, to include Jefferson's home defense forces. He has never even been a police officer. When it comes to conducting battlefield operations—or outfoxing an enemy commander—Jefferson's president is spectacularly useless.

None of these facts raise my spirits as I crawl through terrain I can barely see. If not for the battle archives I carry in my experience databanks, my situation—and my progress through Klameth Canyon—would be impossible. Using my on-board records, I am at least reasonably able to steer a course through the twists and turns of Klameth Canyon. I am less concerned with ephemera such as houses, barns, and tool sheds that did not exist when I last fought for this ground, because small structures pose no navigational hazards. If necessary, I will simply drive through them. My main concern is what may lie hidden inside or behind those structures.

So far, no enemy weapons have opened fire.

I am tempted to accept the simplest reason, that no one has opened fire because everyone in the canyon is already dead. That guess cannot be far from the truth. The only visual images I am able to obtain—ghostly medium IR splotches of muted color—reveal a scene of carnage. Thousands of cooling bodies have dropped below the ambient air temperature of evening. The dead lie packed into training camps where the enemy sheltered, armed, and trained them in techniques of guerilla warfare. Had Commodore Oroton been able to field this army, today's setting sun might well have gone down on a very different scenario.

I scan continuously for power emissions, particularly in the range common to most military equipment, but my search remains futile. Commodore Oroton's troops have vanished into these broken mountains and the forests that fringe them, leaving me hunting for needles in a thirty-seven-kilometer-long haystack—not counting the hundreds *of kilometers of side canyons. I grind forward, pausing at each twisting turn, each junction with another gorge, each farmhouse, barn, and refugee-camp shack, looking for emissions that might conceal mobile Hellbores or lesser field artillery, scanning with sputtering IR for some trace of enemy infantry that might be concealed, ready to strike with hyper-v missiles or octocellulose bombs. I have had entirely too many encounters with octocellulose to ignore that particular threat. At each road junction, I chart temperature differentials that might indicate mines scattered in my path, mines that I could see clearly, if my visible-light-spectrum sensors were operational. With nothing but IR working, I could blunder into a minefield—or virtually anything else—without the slightest warning.*

By the time I swing into the last stretch of canyon between myself and the largest rebel stronghold, night has fallen, increasing my visual-acuity woes. This last stretch of ground is the worst I will face, for the commodore has tucked his base camp into the dead-end turn of the canyon that houses the Klameth Canyon Dam and its hydroelectric power plant. The retaining wall of the dam has turned the deep gorge into a box canyon, of sorts, since there is no way out except by turning around and going back or climbing up the face of the dam.

I cannot climb the dam and I will not turn around until my task here is done. The commodore knows this. That is the reason he chose this spot to make a final, defiant stand. I cannot blow the dam. My own probable demise—or at least crippling injury—is not the cause for my reluctance. Even discounting the critically needed crops in Klameth Canyon's fields, which would be destroyed if several billion tons of water were to come crashing through the canyon, there are other important considerations. Not the least of these are the towns lying downriver from Maze Gap.

Madison, the capital city, is one of them.

I cannot blow the dam.

How, precisely, I will dislodge Commodore Oroton, I have not yet worked out. If nothing else, I will simply sit there until I starve him and his crew to death. But he will not leave Dead-End Gorge alive. Anticipation builds in my Action/Command core as I move down the final stretch of road toward the narrow opening into Dead-End Gorge. The Klameth River runs deep and swift, here, through a channel artificially deepened by terraforming engineers to carry the overflow between the towering cliffs and out into Klameth Canyon, where it irrigates the fertile fields that feed most of Jefferson.

I have already crossed and recrossed this river many times, since entering the canyon through Maze Gap. This one, last crossing will take me into the teeth of Commodore Oroton's guns. This is not mere conjecture. Satellite images of the sheltered canyon, taken over the preceding five days, have revealed a heavy concentration of enemy artillery, including mobile 10cm Hellbores, atop the dam.

I detect power emissions of a military type rising faintly from the narrow gorge, all but masked over by the emissions of the hydroelectric plant. The commodore has shut down power to the floodplain—and the capital—by shutting down substations that route power across the Adero floodplain, but the plant itself is still fully operational, fueling the commodore's operations. The faint military emissions do not match the power signatures of Hellbores, which the rebellion has acquired in a distressing quantity, but I do not count that as evidence. Oroton has played a long and cagey game with his Hellbores. I assume nothing and merely note the momentary absence of emissions that would positively identify the presence of Oroton's heaviest artillery.

My greatest question is whether or not there is anyone alive to operate that artillery. The biological war agent the government troops detonated prior to my arrival will have killed anyone not protected by biochemical containment suits or inoculated against virals. It is known that Commodore Oroton has access to both, smuggled in from the neighboring star system's weapons labs. If the gunners were protected, they will launch an attack the moment I am close enough.

I have finally reached that point. I rumble toward the narrow bend that gives access to Dead-End Gorge and the dam. The canyon walls, radiating heat they have absorbed during the day, glow more brightly than the pastures and fields. The road is a ribbon of light, warmer than the soil by several degrees centigrade, depending on the nature of the surrounding soil, vegetation, or outcroppings of stone.

A farmhouse sits next to the road, so close to the verge, I will have to drive through a substantial portion of the structure to reach the dam. This house was not here twenty years ago. Comparison between my on-board records and current conditions reveals the reason for this. A massive rockfall during my battle with the Yavacs devoured nearly a third of the acreage inside a perimeter of well-maintained fences. The original farmhouse was buried in the collapse and doubtless still lies beneath the colossal pile of stone that has not been removed.

The farmer rebuilt near the road to conserve land for replanting. A creative solution, but it will lead to a flattened house. I doubt the owner will care, since I can see at least one body lying near the open front door, sprawled across the foyer floor, doubtless running to reach shelter in a "safe room" concealed within the house. If Commodore Oroton plans an ambush before I reach the entrance to Dead-End Gorge, it will be launched from this house. I approach with extreme caution and consider simply blowing the house apart as a prophylactic measure, striking at a possible enemy before he strikes at me.

I move forward, sensors straining to their utmost, damaged limits. I am six point zero-nine meters from the corner of the house when sudden motion flares to life. A single person emerges through the front door on a direct attack run toward my warhull. I whip port-side guns around. Acquire the target. Lock on fire-control relays—

—and hold my fire.

There is, indeed, a person running across the narrow yard toward me. But that individual is not an adult. Given its height, girth, and toddling gait, I surmise that I am facing *a very young child. It is perhaps six years old, at most. It carries something in both hands, an object I classify—for seventeen nanoseconds—as a rifle or carbine. I revise that assessment as I note its dimensions and the heat signature it gives off, which suggest a toy rather than a functional weapon. The child carrying it rushes purposefully across the narrow front yard and stops in the middle of the road, directly in my path.*

"You stop!" *the child says in a high treble voice that I cannot decipher as either male or female. The fact that this child is on its feet at all, let alone barring my way, is astonishing, since it wears no biocontainment gear at all. The sole explanation I can devise is that the child was inside a virus-proof safe room when the attack came and that Sar Gremian was correct when he advised me on the anticipated duration of the bioweapon released here: lethal action was expected to cease after forty-five minutes. It has now been an hour since the initial attack.*

I file the information away as useful data, then engage the child in conversation.

"I must enter Dead-End Gorge behind this house. Move out of the road."

"Uh-uh," *the child says, standing fast in front of my treads.* "You're noisy. You'll wake up Mommy and you'd better not do that!"

My initial estimate of this child's age drops by another two years. I scan the house as best I can and detect two other faintly warm shapes besides the one near the front door. I suspect these bodies, which are rapidly assuming the same temperature as their surroundings, belong to the child's parents or older relatives. I know a momentary anger that these people did not remove their young child from a free-fire zone declared in rebellion. These people chose not to leave. Their young child now stands directly between myself and the rebellion's high command.

Legally, the child is a rebel, a declared enemy. Regardless of its legal status, the child must be removed from my path. If I cannot persuade it to move, I will have to kill it, a prospect I do not relish. I must move through this narrow pass, however, and the destruction of one human—even a child—is well within the bounds of acceptable collateral damage.

I engage my drive train and move forward.

And jerk to a halt.

My treads have locked up, stopping me literally in my tracks.

I sit stupefied for nine point three-eight seconds. My treads are locked. They have locked on their own. Without conscious orders from my Action/Command Core. I attempt to drive forward again. I move a grand total of thirty centimeters. Then my treads lock again. Have they developed a mind of their own, independent of the rest of my psychotronic circuitry? I perform a rapid self-diagnostic on the processors and subassemblies governing control of my treads and discover no malfunction anywhere in the system.

This is cause for serious alarm. I have developed another ghostlike electronic glitch with no apparent determinant. I am now not only blind in most frequencies, I am immobilized. I consist of thirteen thousand tons of flintsteel, advanced weapons systems, and sophisticated psychotronic circuitry and I am stuck like a fly on tar paper. I experiment with reversed engines and succeed in backing up smoothly and efficiently, covering twelve meters effortlessly. I drive forward again. And lock up. I cannot even regain the twelve meters of ground I have just lost.

I back up cautiously, executing a pivot turn, and attempt to cross the front yard, hoping to bypass the child—whom I cannot help but connect with the abrupt failure of my forward drive train—by moving through the entire house. My intention is to scrape the edge of the cliffs on my way past the child's aggressive stance in the road.

I complete the turn with ease and start toward the house.

The child scrambles into my path. "Hey! That's cheating!"

My treads lock.

Exasperated, I execute a pivot turn once again and gun my engines, hoping to sprint around the child while it is moving toward the house. A four-year-old human is an amazingly agile creature. The child pivots on a dime and rushes back toward the road, brandishing its toy rifle.

"You be quiet!" *The order is gasped out in a fierce whisper.*

My treads lock.

Words fail me.

I sit in place, electronic thoughts spinning uselessly, and finally initiate diagnostics on my entire physical plant, looking for anything out of the ordinary. There is nothing wrong with my treads, their drive wheels, the complex gears governing their speed of rotation, or the engines that power them. I rev those engines to a scream, trying to break the drive wheels free of whatever is blocking their operation. I succeed only in filling this entire end of Klameth Canyon with noise; while heating the engines to no purpose.

I am still stuck.

The child has dropped its rifle and clamped hands across its ears. When the sound of my engines drops back into its normal range, the child plants fists on hips and tilts its face upward, toward my forward turret. I have little doubt that if I could make out the details of this child's face, its expression would be a glare of righteous wrath.

"I told you to be quiet! Mommy's sleeping! That was noisy and mean! I don't like you at all!"

"The feeling is reciprocated."

"What's that mean?" *My adversary demands in a hard and suspicious tone that is curiously adult, coming from a child so young.*

"I don't like you, either. Who are you?" *I add, attempting to gain information that I might use to dislodge this recalcitrant obstacle from my path.*

"I'm a Granger!" *the child responds with ringing pride.*

Terrorists and rebels begin training their offspring in class consciousness and divisive hatred at an early age. Fierce antigovernment prejudice is a hallmark of Grangerism. That prejudice is compounded of equal parts hatred, political separatism, open contempt for federal laws, disdain of urban culture, and a creed of guerilla-style violence that has produced thousands of terrorists whose sole aim is to destroy the legitimate government of this planet.

They have cultivated this prejudice alongside their fields of peas, beans, barley and corn, and lavish the same diligent care on it that they give to their crops. They coax it to grow into maturity, whereupon the rest of Jefferson reaps the inevitable harvest: wave after wave of terrorism and the wholesale destruction of civilian and government targets. I refuse to be stymied by a bad-tempered brat indoctrinated with the scathing, antigovernment prejudices grown to maturity in this canyon.

"It is obvious that you are a Granger. You are a resident of Klameth Canyon. This canyon has been a Granger stronghold for two centuries. It has been a breeding ground for rebel guerilias for two decades. The rebellion's commander has chosen Klameth Canyon as his fortified headquarters and has barricaded himself with an unknown number of troops and heavy weaponry in the gorge behind your house. The president has declared this canyon a free-fire war zone. All of its residents are traitors and criminals. You are, therefore, obviously a Granger. You are also a traitor and criminal, by default. What is your name?"

The child has snatched up its toy rifle again. "Mommy and Daddy told me never give my name to anybody who's not a Granger. And Mommy says you like to hurt Grangers. She hates you. I hate you, too! And I'm not *ever* gonna tell you my name!"

This obstructive and nasty-tempered creature cannot be allowed to thwart my mission. I attempt to move forward again—

My treads lock.

Rage flares. I turn up the volume on my external speakers. "MOVE OUT OF THE ROAD!"

The child claps both hands across its ears again, then shouts right back. "YOU'RE BAD! YOU BE QUIET!"

I redline my engines. My treads lurch forward three glorious centimeters—

Then halt. In a fit of unbridled fury, I lock onto the child's thermal signature with target-acquisition computers. Anti-personnel guns spin. I fire point-blank.

I try to fire point-blank.

Nothing happens.

I am so stunned, I sit stuttering. Shock courses through every psychotronic synapse in my electronic, multipartite brain. Even automatic subroutines register the system-wide, split-second flutter of pure horror.

I cannot move.

I cannot shoot.

I cannot allow a four-year-old to derail my mission. I am a Bolo. A Unit of the Line. I have logged one hundred twenty years of continuous service. I have suffered catastrophic injury more than once, but I have never been defeated. It is not within me to give up if there is a single erg of power flickering through my circuits. With a strong sense of desperation, I launch a system-wide, class one diagnostic. I must find the glitch that has caused widespread failures in my most critical systems.

Two point four-three minutes later, I make a startling discovery. There is a software lock in place. The blockage is tied to a complicated logic train that includes chaos elements, odd heuristic protocols that are tied to the method by which I learn from experience, and input from some closed and extremely antiquated logics. Once I have identified the tangle of elements contributing to the block, I realize that something about the situation I face—specifically this bizarre standoff with an unarmed child—has triggered the software block and the shutdown of my drive train and gun systems.

If I am to continue my mission, I must either change the situation or break the software block. The former

*will doubtless be easier to accomplish than the latter.
I am a thirteen-thousand-ton machine. This is a four-
year-old child. I initiate a concerted effort to dislodge
it from my path.*

"If you do not move out of the road, I will run over
you."

*This is, of course, a bluff. It does not work. The child
merely clutches its toy rifle and maintains an aggressive
stance between me and my target.*

"Get out of the way or I will wake up your Mommy
with really loud noises!"

"You better not!"

*I yank up the gain on my external speakers, which
were designed to cut across the cacophony of battle,
conveying instructions to infantry support units. I give
an immense shout—*

—and my speakers don't even buzz.

*If I were human, I would howl at the moons like a
rabid dog.*

*I try every threat, bribe, and intimidating tactic
in my repertoire. The child simply stands its ground,
glaring up at me, hands clenched around its toy rifle.
I try firing high-angle mortars into the box canyon
behind the house. My weapons systems remain locked
as disastrously as my treads. I continue trying for
fifty-nine minutes, thirteen seconds. Although I cannot see them, the moons have risen. I wait doggedly,
hoping the child will grow hungry or weary enough
to return to the house.*

*It shows no sign of doing so. A careful scan of the toy
in the child's hands reveals two distinct thermal images,
suggesting two separate materials that radiate heat differently. One of the materials is a dense darkness against the
brightness of the child's warm hands and torso, forming
the clear shape of a rifle. The other, which moves in a
swinging fashion against the child's heat signature, reveals
the shape of a slender cord that travels from muzzle to
something at the tip. The child holds one of the simplest
toy guns ever made: a pop gun.*

At the moment, it is more capable of firing than I am.

I face a dogged, determined enemy. The child has not abandoned its vigil in front of me. It is no longer in the road, but remains in front of my treads. It has been struggling for several minutes with something at the edge of the yard, something that the edge of my treads caught and crushed as I executed pivot turns, trying to break free. I cannot see well enough in my intermittent medium-IR range to determine what it is, exactly, that the child is holding, but the dark shape against the child's bright heat signature suggests some sort of plant, with long, trailing stems. That plant has been uprooted, for obvious reasons.

Based on its brightly glowing movements, the child appears to be replanting it.

I initiate conversation. "What are you doing?"

"Fixing Mommy's roses. You hurt 'em. She'll be mad when she wakes up."

I say nothing. Mommy will never wake up. The child struggles to replant the rose bushes that bordered the road. My small adversary yelps occasionally as thorns catch unprotected skin.

"You would not get scratched if you wore gloves."

The child straightens up. "Mommy wears gloves."

"Why don't you get them?"

The child takes three steps toward the house. This is what I intended. I quiver with anticipation, convinced that the instant this child moves out of the way, the block will drop away and I will be able to dash forward and smite the Enemy in Dead-End Gorge. And once I have destroyed the Enemy's headquarters battery, I will deal a decisive blow to the rebel forces fighting for control of the capital. Just six more steps and the way will be clear—

The child stops. Turns to look up at me. "I can't reach them."

"Where are they?"

"On a hook."

"You could climb up. On a chair."

"There's no chair in the garden shed."

I want to shout with impatience. "You could drag a chair into the shed."

The child shakes its head. "I can't. The door is locked. I can't open it."

I am stymied by a dead parent's admittedly noble attempt to protect her offspring from the sharp implements found in a typical gardening shed. Disappointment is as sharp as those tools. So sharp, I cannot find anything to say. The child returns to the rose bushes, with a purpose as single-minded as its determination to stop me from passing through the house.

As night deepens and reports of fighting continue to stream in from Madison, my living blockade gives up on Mommy's roses and sits down in the road. It sits there for a long time. I have run out of ideas to try, in my attempts to dislodge it from my path. When it lies down, demonstrating a clear intention of curling up under my port-side tread and going to sleep, I realize I might be able to gain enough slack to move forward. If I can ease forward just enough to crush the obstruction . . .

I cannot move.

More precisely, I do not attempt to move.

I do not understand my own decision. But I do not attempt to change it. I simply sit where I am, a battered hulk in moonlight I cannot see, inferring its presence by means of astronomical charts and weather satellite broadcasts. I sit motionless and try to decide whether this night will witness the successful eradication of rebel forces by desperately embattled police units—whose officers can expect nothing but instantaneous lynching if they fall into rebel hands—or if the government's law-enforcement officers will triumph and render my firepower unnecessary.

I can find only one way to alter the equation as it now stands.

I must break the software block holding me immobilized. I scan my immediate environment and find no change. The commodore is lying low. The power emissions from Dead-End Gorge have not changed. I see no other alternative. I dive into the tangled logics and quickly discover that the trouble is tied both to the heuristic chains that allow me to learn and to the memory modules that store my experience data in close-packed psychotronic matrices. Humans require approximately eight hours of unconscious time each day to remain alert, healthy, and effective. I am designed to "sleep" a great deal more than this, but due to circumstances, I have been awake for twelve of the past twenty years. This is much longer than my design engineers' recommended maximum continuous operation time. That fact, in and of itself, may be part of the reason for the breakdown in my heuristic learning subroutines.

It is not the sole reason, however. There are memory links feeding into the snarled logic trains and I cannot access one of the blocking subsections at all. If I hope to tease apart the tangle, the only way will be to attack the blockage through the memory inserts feeding it. I must trace these memories as best I can, while open civil war rages unchecked, and hope that the Enemy encamped so close by does not take full, logical advantage of my difficulties and strike me where I sit. I hold little hope that this will be the case, given Commodore Oroton's past record, but I have no choice.

I make one last, thorough sweep for the Enemy, then dive into memory.

Chapter Two

I

Jefferson looked to Simon Khrustinov like a good place to start over. It was springtime, according to the mission briefing he'd reviewed during the long voyage out. Springtime and planting season for an agricultural world. One stuck slam in the middle of a potential three-way war. Pain touched his heart as he stared at the riot of wildflowers and blossom-laden trees visible on his new Bolo's forward viewscreen.

There were two things Simon understood intimately. The fragility of life on an agricultural colony was one. The destructive capacity of war was another. He knew only too well what a single salvo from a Deng Yavac—or from Unit SOL-0045—would do to the delicate beauty of flowers and fruitful vines. He wondered if the men and women of Jefferson, who had doubtless been praying for his arrival, had any concept of what he and his Bolo were capable of doing to their world?

Renny hadn't.

She'd loved him, until he'd been forced to fight for

her homeworld's survival. Her love, perhaps, had been too innocent. It certainly hadn't survived the battle for Etaine. In a way that still hurt, neither had Renny. She was still *alive,* somewhere. But she wasn't Renny, any longer, and the love she'd once felt was as dead and burnt as the cinders of the home they'd tried—and failed—to build together.

But now he'd come to Jefferson, with war again looming as a near certainty, and he wanted—desperately—to keep this world from burning to ash and radioactive cinders. The whisper at the back of his mind, that maybe Renny hadn't been strong enough to love him the way he'd needed, felt almost like betrayal of her memory. Or, perhaps, of his memory of her as he'd needed her to be.

Ancient history. Dead as Old Terra's dinosaurs, and not a prayer of resurrection. Starting over was easier. At least his new Bolo knew the whole story, giving him someone to talk to who understood. He was lucky, in that regard. His "new" Bolo was the same machine Simon had already spent fifteen years commanding. Lonesome Son was obsolete—seriously so—and the repairs needed after Etaine had convinced Simon he would be losing his closest friend, as well as Renny. But war on two fronts, against two alien races, had stepped in to salvage that much, at least. Unit LON-2317 was now Unit SOL-0045, a "Surplus on Loan" Bolo, but still the finest Bolo any man could claim as partner and friend.

And now, after the long and bitter winter of Etaine, it was spring, again.

Simon Khrustinov loved the springtime, had loved it on every world he'd ever known and defended. He loved what he could see of Jefferson's, already, with its virginal carpet of flowers in every direction Lonesome Son turned his turret-mounted swivel cameras. Jefferson was exquisite in her fancy floral dress. He wanted to love her. Needed to, badly. And he wanted to find a piece of her that could be made all his own, to love for as long as life—and war—would let him. Deng notions of aesthetic real estate precipitated a shudder, but infinitely worse were

Melconian notions of what constituted "good neighbors": brown ashes on a rising wind. Renny truly hadn't understood. So far, no one else had, either, except the Bolos and the men and women who commanded them.

Maybe somewhere on this green and lovely world, he'd find a woman strong enough to keep on loving a man, even for the things war forced him to do. Simon Khrustinov was a veteran of too many campaigns to hold out much hope. But he was still young—and human—enough to want it. And Jefferson was the best place he had left to find it, if such a woman and such a chance actually existed. There would be no other chances, after Jefferson. This was his last mission, in command of a Bolo so obsolete, he was a genuine war relic.

Pride in his friend's achievement brought the flicker of a smile ghosting across his lips. Like Commanche of Old Terra's Seventh, Lonesome Son was a survivor. A courageous one. Central Command was chary with Galactic Bronze Clusters. Lonesome had three welded like supernovas to his turret. Alongside a *Gold* Cluster, earned on Etaine. Simon closed his eyes over pain as memory crashed across him, fighting the Deng street by street through a fairy city reduced—explosion by explosion—to smoking rubble.

Five million civilians had been safely evacuated, but more than three times that number had died while Lonesome fought on, the lone survivor of a seven-Bolo battle group that also died in the ash and scattered fairy dust. Lonesome had more than earned his right to survive. Simon Khrustinov just hoped they—and everything else he could see in his Bolo's main viewscreen—survived what was about to crash down on this new and lovely world. As he watched people jumping out of groundcars to greet them, newly arrived from their orbital transport, he couldn't help wondering how many of them would hate him by the end of his mission.

II

I worry about Simon.

My Commander has grown as silent as an airless moon, since the disaster at Etaine, and much of that, I know, is my fault. It was my guns, in the main, that destroyed the city, and Simon's world with it. I have become Simon's world, since Etaine, and I do not know how to help him.

He calls me Lonesome Son, a pun that might, under other circumstances, have been humorously meant, derived somewhat circuitously from my old designation. But it is himself that Simon refers to, mostly, when he says it. I am not human and cannot take the place of his lost love. I can only guard him. And do my limited best to understand.

The world we have come to defend—the last world we will do so, together, just as the heavy lift platform returning to orbit is the last I will ever require—is described in our mission briefing files as "pastoral and beautiful." My own scans reveal very little that I would consider attractive, although as a Bolo Mark XX, my sense of the aesthetic is admittedly different from that of the average human's.

I define attractive landscape as easily defensible ground. Or, if conditions warrant it, easily penetrated ground, where an enemy force is most optimally vulnerable to my guns. I have, however, seen more than a century of active service, so I am well-enough versed in human ideas of beauty to understand the notations in our mission files.

Although Jefferson's sky is currently socked in with scudding stormclouds, the terrain beneath those clouds is both dramatic and highly conducive to human prosperity. The rugged, snow-capped Damisi Mountains, a majestic chain of them lying fifty kilometers to the east, rise an average 35,000 feet above a rich alluvial plain. This plain is bisected by the Adero River, which drops over the lip of a high escarpment five kilometers west of Madison, Jefferson's capital

*city. The escarpment and falling river create a spectacular
cataract that plunges three hundred meters into the sea,
reminiscent of Old Terra's Niagara or Victoria Falls. The
sight of Chenga Falls certainly caught my Commander's
attention during our descent from orbit, although doubtless
for different reasons than my own interest in it.*

*Thanks to the escarpment and ocean beyond—slate grey
beneath the approaching storm which will, I suspect, strip
the flowers from branches and vines—ground forces will
find Madison difficult to invade from the west. The sharp
drop into the sea means trouble, however, if an invasion from the direction of the Damisi Mountains pushes
Jefferson's defenders west, to the brink of that immense
drop. It is disquieting to see falling water slam into the
sea with sufficient force that waves are torn into white
foam that crashes against the cliff in plumes higher than
the top of my turret, were I to park directly beneath the
crush of waves and waterfall.*

*I was very careful, during our final descent, to give the
savage crosscurrents of air above the waterfall a wide berth.
Now that we are down, however, I turn my attention to
the city—one of the cities—we are to defend. Jefferson's
capital boasts surprisingly sophisticated architecture, for
a farming colony so far from humanity's inner worlds.
Much of it has been built from rose-toned sandstone
from the Damisi Mountains, suggesting sufficient wealth
and technical expertise to dispense with the plascrete
ubiquitous to most rim-space colony worlds.*

*This assessment matches the military analysis in our
briefing files, that Jefferson is a prosperous world, well
worth defending despite its remote location, tucked into
an isolated pocket of human space surrounded on three
sides by an immense, starless stretch of space known
as the Silurian Void. The robust capital city does not,
however, look anything at all like Etaine, with its
ethereal towers of gemstone-hued glass and ribbon-lace
titanium. I am deeply grateful to Jefferson's architects,
stonemasons, and engineers, for Simon's sake. We have
landed, as directed, at a facility nine point five kilometers*

south of the outskirts of Jefferson's capital city and zero point three-seven kilometers north of the barracks and bunkers of Nineveh Military Base, constructed nearly a century ago, during the last Deng war. Nineveh houses the bulk of Jefferson's defense forces, ninety-eight percent of which are listed as inactive reserves.

While this is consistent with a world that has known a hundred years of peace, it does not lend itself well to providing a trained and battle-ready army. Still, it is far better than some border worlds, which are new enough that no military force at all exists, let alone a system of planet-wide military bases with relatively modern weaponry in their arsenals. It speaks well of Jefferson's current rulers that they have maintained this system against future threat.

A broad stretch of open, flattened ground has been cleared of underbrush for a construction project that has barely begun. Immense plascrete slabs have been poured and piles of building materials lie scattered in orderly profusion, covered neatly by tarpaulins to protect them from inclement weather. If all goes well, this muddy stretch of ground will be my new maintenance depot. Jefferson's treaty with the Concordiat requires the local government to provide an adequate depot with requisite spare parts and a powder magazine to house my small-bore, projectile-weaponry's ammunition, along with access to the planetary datanet and quarters for my Commander. The fact that they've already begun to meet my depot requirements suggests a fierce determination to defeat the Deng. A government facing planetary invasion could well be forgiven a decision to delay construction until the battle has been decided, one way or the other.

Seven ground cars sit parked at the edge of the landing field. Three larger vehicles are evidently press-corps vans, given the number of camera crews and technicians standing on the muddy ground. They have strung power cords and cables out behind them like the drifting tentacles of a Terran jellyfish. Cables caught by the gusting storm front sing and hum in the sharp, unpredictable *wind shifts that are already scattering blossoms on the damp air. Lights glare on poles held aloft, while cameras roll and reporters deliver "serious situation" monologues to the camera lenses. This is a behavior I have never fully understood, an evident compulsion that drives some humans to tell as many people as can be persuaded or coerced into listening what is happening and what they should think about it.*

Since the opinions of the "press" have tallied with my own assessments of battle and other war-relevant situations only zero point nine-two percent of the time during the one hundred and three years since my original commissioning, I remain baffled as to why most humans continue listening to them. It is, perhaps, something that only another human can understand.

A second group, composed of civilians and uniformed military officers, also waits to meet my Commander. Some of the people on the periphery are busy speaking with reporters, but most are talking excitedly and pointing toward my warhull.

Simon releases the restraints on his command chair. "I'd better get dirtside. Looks like we've got quite a reception committee and most of those folks look pretty nervous."

"Civilians always are, when they see me."

Simon pauses beside the ladder leading out of my Command Compartment, resting one hand lightly against the bulkhead. "I know, Sonny," *he says, using my new nickname.* "You deserve better. Maybe they'll get used to you, eventually."

I refrain from sharing the thought that Renny never did. Neither did most of the other civilians I have known. I am warmed by the gesture, however, for it was meant affectionately, a welcome change from the grim silence into which Simon lapses all too often. I have known six other commanders since my initial commissioning and my relationship with all six was satisfactory, but there is something special about Simon Khrustinov, something that I cannot quite define. I am abruptly very glad that

*he will be the human to share my last mission—and that
I am the Bolo to share his.*

As my Commander drops from the end of the long
ladder and splashes into the muddy soil beside my treads,
a man with a long, thin frame and a long, lean face to
match steps forward in greeting. "Major Khrustinov?" he
holds out one hand. "I'm Abe Lendan."

As press cameras record their handshake, my Commander blinks in genuine surprise. "It's a distinct honor
to meet you, Mr. President."

*I, too, feel surprise. This is Abraham Lendan, president
of Jefferson? Clearly, Jefferson's president does not insist
upon the same pomp and ritual other planetary heads
of state generally demand as their just due.* President
Lendan introduces the men and women of the official
delegation with him. "Major Khrustinov, this is Elora
Willoughby, my chief of staff, Ron McArdle, my attaché
for military affairs, and Julie Alvison, energy advisor. This
is Representative Billingsgate, Speaker for the House
of Law. Senator Hassan, President of the Senate. And
Kadhi Hajamb, High Justice of Jefferson."

Hands are duly shaken and polite phrases exchanged;
then he introduces several ranking officers in the drab
green uniform of Jefferson's home defense force. *Their
dull uniforms create a sharp contrast with Simon's
brightly colored dress crimsons. Dinochrome Brigade
officers do not need to worry about camouflage on the
battlefield, since they ride to war inside a hull designed
to withstand small nuclear blasts. Among other things, it
makes for a stirring and colorful display on the parade
ground. It also—and more importantly—serves as a
morale boost for officers, technicians, and beleaguered
civilian populations.*

*I pay close attention to these introductions, for these
are the men and women with whom my Commander
and I will work most closely, planning and carrying out
Jefferson's defense.* President Lendan introduces first a
man surprisingly elderly for an active military officer.
"General Dwight Hightower, our Chief of Defense and

Commandant of Combined Ops." *The general's hair is entirely white and his face bears the lines of many years, perhaps as many as seventy-five or eighty of them. The president turns, then, to the rest of the officers.* "Lieutenant General Jasper Shatrevar, Commander of Ground Defense Forces. Admiral Kimani of the Home-Star Navy and General Gustavson, Air Defense Force. And this," *the tall, lean president of Jefferson turns to me,* "is Unit SOL-0045?"

A glow is born in Simon's shadowed eyes. "Indeed it is, Mr. President."

I am startled that President Lendan has made it his business to learn my official designation, as well as my Commander's name. Most politicians I have encountered simply refer to me as "the Bolo" and don't bother to include me directly in conversations.

"How should I address him, Major?" *the president asks uncertainly.* "Surely his full designation is too long to use all the time?"

"He'll answer to Sonny."

Surprise rearranges the worry lines in Abe Lendan's long face. Then he nods, as the oblique reference to humanity's home star registers in an expression even I can read. He clears his throat and addresses me directly, peering toward the nearest of my external visual sensors.

"Sonny, welcome to Jefferson."

"It is my pleasure to be here, Mr. President."

Several of the onlookers start at the sound of my voice, although I am always careful to use a volume setting low enough not to damage delicate human hearing. Jefferson's president, however, merely smiles, suggesting a rock-solid core of inner strength that he—and all Jeffersonians—will need. I also note deep lines and dark, bruised-looking hollows around his eyes, which suggest worry and sleeplessness, a state confirmed by President Lendan's next words.

"You can't know how glad we are that you're here, both of you. We've been worried the Deng would get here ahead of your transport. Sector Command's been sending messages meant to reassure, but we've dealt with the Deng before. And we've had refugee ships coming through, a lot of them. It takes a desperate captain and crew to try crossing the Silurian Void, especially in some of the ships we've had limping through our star system. Private yachts that weren't designed for hyper-L hops that long and dangerous. Merchant ships shot to pieces *before* they made the jump out. Big ore freighters crammed full of terrified people and damned little food or medical supplies. All of 'em hoping the Deng fleet wouldn't follow if they ran this way, across the Void, not with richer worlds to tempt them along the main trade route."

Simon blanches at such news. "Good God! There are Concordiat naval captains who'd think twice about crossing the Void."

A look of deep stress brings moisture to Abe Lendan's dark eyes. "A lot of those ships had wounded aboard, some of them so critical, they're still in our hospitals. God only knows how many of the ships that tried the crossing didn't make it. From what the refugees are saying, there may be upwards of a hundred ships unaccounted for, this side of the Void. They also told us the Deng hit them hard, much harder than they did during the last war."

I remember the last Deng war, in which I fought as a rookie straight off the assembly line. Captured human populations were routinely kept alive as slave labor to run mining equipment and manufacturing plants, since that is far less expensive than refitting high-tech equipment to Deng-capable specs. This time, the Deng are simply killing everything in their path. Simon and I have been briefed on this. Clearly, Jefferson's president also knows it.

"We're not afraid of a hard fight, Major," *Abe Lendan says quietly,* "but we don't have much here that would slow down a modern Heavy-class Yavac. We have several in-system naval cutters that could slow down an orbital bombardment, but nothing to match a Deng battle cruiser."

Simon nods understanding as the wind rattles past, her-alding the imminent arrival of the storm front. "Yes, we've been briefed on it. Bad as the Deng are, Mr. President, we're fortunate to be facing them, instead of the Melconians. And the Silurian Void is one of the best defenses Jefferson has. Sector Command doesn't expect a large force to be sent against this world, precisely because it's so dangerous, crossing the Void. If the Deng do send a detachment this way, it probably won't be their first-rate equipment, which they won't want to risk losing on such a gamble. Sonny should be more than enough to handle whatever they throw our way. He's had a lot of combat experience."

Heads swivel upwards as the entire group peers toward the battle honors welded to my turret. General Hightower actually steps forward for a closer look. "That's mighty impressive, Sonny," *the general says as rain begins to splash into the muddy ground.* "Seventeen campaign medals, three rhodium stars, and good Lord, is that *four* galaxy-level clusters? *Very* impressive."

"Thank you, General Hightower. I look forward to coordinating defense plans with you. My mission-briefing files don't mention it, but are you the Dwight Hightower who turned back the Quern advance on Herndon III?"

The general's eyes widen in startlement. "How the devil did you know about that?"

"My Commander during the Herndon liberation campaign was Major Alison Sanhurst. She spoke highly of you, General."

A strange, bittersweet expression touches Dwight Hightower's rugged, battle-scarred face. "Good God, that was nearly sixty years ago. Your commander was a fine woman, Sonny. A *fine* woman. We wouldn't have held the Quern back on Herndon III without her. She died bravely. And she's still missed, very much so." *General Hightower's eyes have misted with water that is not from the increasingly chilly rainfall.*

"Thank you, General," *I say quietly, but his words have triggered unhappy memories. Alison Sanhurst did, indeed, die bravely, evacuating children under heavy enemy fire while I was out of commission, awaiting emergency battlefield repairs. I have never forgotten her. Or forgiven myself for failing her.*

President Lendan clears his throat and points toward the four-meter-long slice melted across my prow. "What in the world hit you there?"

I do not like remembering the battle in which I sustained that damage and do not wish to hurt Simon, but I have been asked a direct question from the man who will be issuing orders to my Commander and myself. It would be impolitic to refuse an answer.

"I sustained injury under concentrated fire from the plasma lances of a Yavac Heavy, which I destroyed at Etaine."

As the politicians and even the press murmur to one another, my Commander says harshly, "Sonny destroyed the other fourteen Yavac Heavies shooting at him, too. Even after they blew his treads and most of his gun systems to dust and turned half his armor to slag. That's where the fourth galaxy-level cluster came from. The gold one. Every other Bolo on that battlefield died. We're so short on Bolos, they rebuilt Sonny and sent him out here. With me."

The pain in Simon's voice is raw. So raw that no one speaks for eight point three seconds. President Lendan's voice finally breaks the desperate silence, and betrays emotional stress of his own. "Sonny, Major Khrustinov, it is a genuine honor to have you here. I only hope we can acquit ourselves as bravely as you have." *His unstated hope—that Jefferson does not become a second Etaine—is clearly written in the deepened stress lines in his long, tired face. The responsibility of high office is always exhausting, and never more so than when war looms large on the horizon.*

"I hope it won't offend Sonny," *President Lendan turns to my Commander,* "but you ought to come into town, Major Khrustinov. We can go over everything in my office. The bottom's about to drop out of that storm," *he indicates the rain, which is now gusting in drifts ahead of the main squall line.*

Simon merely nods as they head toward the cars. "I'll be wearing a commlink, so Sonny can participate in the discussions, no matter where they're held. We'll need his input, his battle experience. And I'll want to upload into his data banks any local information you have that might be helpful. Anything that wasn't forwarded to us with our mission briefing."

"General Hightower and his staff have prepared quite a bit of data for you. Very good, Major. There's room for you in my car."

As the group scatters, hurrying as the rain slashes across the clearing in deadly earnest, I drop into Standby Alert status. This first meeting has gone well, leaving me to hope that Jefferson may prove to be a good home for Simon.

If we can defend it from the coming storms of war.

Or a repetition of history.

III

As the motorcade drove through the storm-lashed streets of Jefferson's capital city, Simon realized he was in serious danger of falling in love with his new home. It was bitterly fitting that within moments of his arrival, blowing sheets of grey rain had shredded every delicate flower in sight. Even so, the city was beautiful, full of Old Terra–style architecture that he'd seen only in photos and movies. Madison boasted real charm, with fluted columns and triangular pediments on many of its public buildings. Gardens were graced with fountains and mosaics and what must have been locally produced bronze and marble statuary, much of it in an earthy, compelling style he'd never seen, but liked a great deal.

It helped that nothing he saw resembled anything on Etaine.

Simon was—on his father's side, at least—Russian,

and therefore pragmatic, so he looked at the world steadily, seeing what was, recognizing what wasn't, and understanding what it would take to create the things that might be, if one applied a great deal of hard work to the effort of building them. As the car pulled up to a long, covered portico where doormen waited beneath a weather-proofed awning, ready to open the doors the moment they halted, Simon was hoping rather fiercely that he got the chance to *do* some of that building.

Ten minutes later, Simon found himself in the president's own briefing room, sipping a local beverage that put coffee to shame—both on taste and a welcome caffeine jolt—and prepared to conduct his first official meeting with Jefferson's defense forces. The reporters who'd followed them back to town and through the motorcade's winding route to the Presidential Residence were now blessedly absent, although he suspected they would stick to him like Setti-5's bat-wing remoras until the ion bolts started flying.

There was nothing inherently detestable about reporting as a profession, if the reporters did their jobs properly; but preparing for war could be sheer hell, with irresponsible press reports flying wild from town to town or—worse—racing through interstellar space with myriad, nonhuman ears attuned to human broadcast frequencies. Major Simon Khrustinov had yet to meet a reporter he liked, let alone trusted. Of course, after the disaster at Etaine, he was perhaps a bit jaded. . . .

"Ladies, gentlemen," President Lendan said as a staffer closed the conference room doors with a soft click, "your attention, please."

There was a general shuffling toward chairs. There was no formal invocation of deity—Jefferson was polyglot enough, it might've been long-winded, if there had been—or even an exhortation about duty to state. There was just an air of expectancy that spoke volumes, all of it deeply respectful of the man at the head of this particular table. And of one another, come to that. Simon liked more and more of what he was seeing.

Abe Lendan met Simon's gaze and said, "Major, I

won't waste your time or ours, going over what was in your briefing materials. Just let me say that the people of Jefferson are solidly united behind this defense effort." A brief twitch of his lips betrayed a moment's humor. "After the last Deng war, all you have to do around these parts is say 'spodder' and people scramble for the nearest shelter. The invasion a century ago was memorable, to say the least."

Simon knew exactly how memorable. With Jefferson's military forces taking forty percent casualties and civilian death tolls approaching two million before the Concordiat relief effort broke the siege, barely a single family had escaped without the loss of at least one member. Some had been virtually wiped out. "I've read the files," Simon said quietly. "Your people waged one of the finest home-defense campaigns of that war."

Brief smiles flickered around the conference room table.

"Thank you," Abe Lendan said in a low voice. "But I won't pretend that we," he gestured to include the rest of his fellow Jeffersonians, "are ready, let alone able, to conduct a defense anywhere close to that level. We've kept up the military bases, made sure the home guard trains at least a couple of times a year. But things have been quiet for long enough, people have gotten used to putting all their effort into their homesteads, if they're Granger-bred, or their jobs, if they live in a city or town. We've done so well, we've even spawned a growing eco-movement, calling for sensible decisions from the Terraforming Engineers' Corps. Jefferson has some mighty pretty wild country and we can afford to protect the best of it."

Simon nodded, although he was aware of subtle shifts in body language and expression that told him not everyone at the table agreed with that assessment. It was something worth paying attention to, certainly, once they got past the immediate crisis. Jefferson might not be quite as "solidly united" as President Lendan had said and there'd been no mention of an eco-movement in his mission briefing, suggesting rapidly changing social dynamics. Which was another good reason to pay attention.

But only after the business at hand was properly settled.

Abe Lendan, too, caught that slight ripple of disagreement, but said only, "So that's where we stand, Major. If you would be good enough to oblige us with your recommendations?"

"Thank you, Mr. President." He took a moment to look at each man and woman in turn, matching faces and names, gauging the strength of each face, each set of eyes. These were good people. You could feel it, as well as see it. He would need good people.

"I've been assigned to Jefferson on permanent loan to the planetary government," he began quietly, "along with Unit SOL-0045. As a chartered colony world, Jefferson's entitled to military defense, but the Concordiat can't afford to divert ground troops and equipment to provide it, just now. Not even to honor our treaty obligations. But nobody understands better than I do that folks on a frontier get jittery when there's a war on, particularly one as nasty as this Deng-Melconian mess is turning out to be."

His listeners shifted uneasily. He wondered just how much of the news from the Melconian front had filtered through to this world, isolated by its position in a pocket of the Silurian Void. "The Melconians are part of the reason I've been assigned to you on permanent loan status. There've been some ugly things happening along the frontier." He slipped a data chit into the holo-vid built into the conference room table and touched controls. A 3-D projection sprang to life above the table, showing Jefferson's primary tucked into its pocket of the Void, beyond which stretched a scattering of other suns, color coded to show ownership. "Human stars are represented in yellow. Deng worlds are coded orange and Melconian star systems are red." A particularly lurid shade, at that, Simon thought, calculated to achieve maximum emotional impact on anyone looking at this starmap.

General Hightower leaned forward abruptly, shaggy

white brows drawn down, eyes hooded. "That can't be right, Major. This whole section," he gestured to a deep red bite in what should have been an orange starfield, "was held by the Deng only six months ago."

Simon nodded, voice grim. "Yes, it was. Six months ago, that was a stable border. Six months ago, we didn't even realize that most of this," he pointed to the orange/red demarcation zone, "*was* a border. The Melconians are pushing the Deng off their own worlds, at an alarming rate. The last time the Deng crossed *our* border, to hit these star systems," Simon indicated a thin yellow necklace dotted here and there with malevolent orange and pulsing crimson beads, "they were after raw materials, manufacturing plants, staging zones from which to launch interstellar raids and war-fleets. Now they're after habitat, pure and simple. A place to deposit their own refugees while a very nasty fight for the main Deng worlds," he pointed to a thick cluster of orange, "heats up. That's why your refugees have been hit so hard. Deng are slaughtering whole human populations, trying to gain a toehold they can hang onto long enough to halt the Melconian advance, which is coming in all the way from Damikuus to Varri." His hand described a long arc across the upper reaches of the sphere floating above the table, moving from the Deng star system closest to Melconian space to distant Varri, an arc that encompassed a huge chunk of Deng territory.

"We've also had stories filtering in from human rim worlds," he sketched out a line of intermingled yellow, orange, and red star systems, "tales of unexplained atrocities on our mining operations, ships mysteriously lost. We're finally realizing that much of what we thought was the border between human and Deng space, is actually the boundary between human and Melconian space. Fortunately for us, Jefferson's on the back side of the Void, as viewed from the Deng frontier." He touched star clusters on both sides of the immense black stretch of starless space. "Even more fortunately, the Melconians are on the far side of the Deng, but that could shift fast, given the reports we've received about heavy fighting between them, all along here." He traced a line along the very edge of the human frontier, from Yarilo past Charmak, ending with the Erdei system, which was spatially the closest Deng star to Jefferson's primary.

Dwight Hightower sucked in his breath, seeing the danger at once. "My God! If they pushed the Deng back to Erdei, they could come at us from behind, by way of Ngara!" He was pointing at the Ngara binary, which had two habitable worlds, Mali and Vishnu, which were Jefferson's only neighbors in the tiny peninsula of space stuck like a small boy's thumb into a very dark plum pie. "If the Melconians pulled that off," the white-haired general said in a hushed, horrified voice, "we couldn't possibly get the civilian populations of these two star systems out. Not with the Deng and the Void blocking retreat. Lose Ngara and there's nowhere else to go."

"Precisely, sir," Simon said grimly. He hated the frightened stares everyone in the room had leveled at that holo-vid. Hated them, because there was so little he could do to reassure them. "That is the biggest long-term danger to this whole region of space. Of course, at this stage in the war, a pincer movement by Melconians to cut off the entire Dezelan Promontory," he pointed to that thumblike projection of inhabited space sticking into the Void, "is not the most likely threat to Jefferson. Certainly not during the next few months. But the Melconians can move fast and it will probably occur to the Deng, as well, so kindly don't put it out of your minds as we develop and implement defensive strategies."

"How likely is it," President Lendan asked, expression thoughtful, "that the Deng might try it? Cutting us off, I mean, with that pincer movement you mentioned?"

"It depends on how disorganized and rushed they are, by what's happening back here, though this sector." He spread his hand out across the sizeable chunk of Deng territory between Erdei and Varri, much of it abruptly up for grabs in a brutal three-way war. "This is a lot of space in which to produce angry, disgruntled, and vengeful Deng, out to recoup losses any way they can. And that's the biggest danger Jefferson faces, just now. So," Simon met Abe Lendan's gaze once more, "that's what we're up against and I'm pretty much all Sector Command can afford to send out here."

The universal looks of dismay caused Simon to hurry on. "The good news is this." He pointed to the vast darkness between all that chaos and Jefferson's faint little yellow sun. "The gas and debris in the Silurian Nebula have made crossing the Void a navigational hazard worse than just about anything else in human space, with the possible exception of Thule, where we first got wind of the Melconians' existence." He pointed to a small yellow sun on the far side of the Void. "The Void will make it harder for the Deng or the Melconians to mount a large-scale assault. They probably won't want to risk an entire armada or even a major battle group, which evens the odds, a bit. We can't rule out a sneak attack, of course, given conditions on the Deng side of the Void. Desperate commanders take desperate measures."

The various generals at the table nodded, expressions dark with worry. The civilians looked scared. If they'd understood what Simon did, fear would've become stark terror. Nobody on Jefferson could even begin to comprehend what had happened at Etaine. Simon hoped they never did.

"So," Simon cleared his throat and finished up his presentation. "We'll maintain vigilance in all directions and do what we can to muster out and train local defense forces. We'll coordinate defense of this whole region with Captain Brisbane and her SOL unit, as well. They've been posted to the Ngara system, with orders to guard the mining operations on Mali. The Malinese mines and smelting plants are a tempting prize, one the Deng will find hard to resist. I'm told a fair number of Jefferson's young adults attend the big trade school on Mali? And the universities on Vishnu?"

President Lendan nodded. "We have some good schools here, but Jefferson's higher education tends toward agricultural and biotech research, ag engineering and terraforming, civil engineering, that sort of thing. We have a thriving art and cultural degree program, but that doesn't do us much good in a situation like this. Anyone wanting careers in pretty much anything else has to go off world for training, to one of the big universities on Vishnu. That's where we send students and technicians for training in psychotronic circuitry, interstellar transport design, medicine and xeno-toxicology and other technical fields."

"What about Mali?"

"We send a fair number of students—several thousand a year, in fact—for training at the Imari Minecraft Institute. Our most important industrial alloys are imported from the Imari Consortium, but we're developing a pretty good mining industry that reduces our dependence on off-world imports. In return, the Imari Consortium and the smaller, independent operations are the best market we have for our surplus foodstuffs. Every human installation on Mali must be domed, so it's cheaper for the Malinese to import bulk commodities like grain and beef, than to try producing them locally. We have a good treaty relationship with both of Ngara's worlds."

Simon nodded. One of his jobs was making sure it remained that way. There weren't enough humans out this way to have two star systems bickering with each other, which could happen fast when attack on one world sent a domino-style ripple effect through a planetary economy, savagely reordering priorities. Now wasn't the time to bring that up, however, let alone worry about it. Plenty of time to address that concern after the shooting stopped.

"One decision you face," Simon said quietly, "is the need to decide whether to leave those students on Mali and Vishnu, which are farther from the immediate conflict and therefore potentially safer, or whether to call them home to defend Jefferson. If things go badly here, we may well need every able-bodied adult we can muster. Nor is there any guarantee that Vishnu and Mali will remain safe from attack, not with the dynamics of this conflict shifting so rapidly."

Several men and women at the long table blanched, including most of the Defense Force officers. Simon was sorry for that, but saw no point in sugarcoating anything. Most of them were facing the first real combat of their lives and they had abruptly realized just how unready they were for it. Good. People who knew the score were likelier to stretch themselves to meet the challenge. Now it was time to put the heart back into them by giving them something to *do* about it.

"All right," he said briskly, touching controls to change the display so that Jefferson's star system filled the dark holo-vid, "let's get down to business, shall we?"

Chapter Three

I

Kafari Camar stepped onto the broad sidewalk outside Madison Spaceport's passenger terminal and drew down a deep, double-lungful of home. She always loved the smell of spring flowers and fresh-turned earth. The cool, wet wind on her face was particularly welcome, today. The crowded and odiferous space she and fifty-seven fellow students had shared for the past eleven days might have been the best accommodations available on an interstellar freighter, but they'd barely been liveable. Even the students used to Spartan housing on Mali had complained.

Most of the students were still in the terminal, busy off-loading duffles and sundry luggage, but Kafari had traveled light, as always. She carried even less than most of the students from Jefferson's rural areas, having decided to leave nearly everything behind on Vishnu. Clothes could be replaced. She wouldn't need most of her course disks again. The computer had belonged to the university and none of the trinkets decorating her dorm space had possessed sufficient sentimental value to burden herself with the job of carrying them. She had brought home nothing more than a shoulder pack and the contents of her pockets.

It wasn't merely convenience that had prompted that decision. It was a survival habit, one that urban kids never seemed to understand, let alone master. Trying to travel with too much to carry, out in Jefferson's wilderness—or even on terraformed ranches bordering wild land—was asking to be killed in any of several messy and painful ways. Jefferson's wildlife was not always friendly. But she was so delighted to be home, she probably would have smiled even at a *gollon*, just prior to shooting its ten or twelve feet of teeth and claws and armor-tough scales.

Kafari tilted her face to the wet sky, relishing the rain soaking into her hair, but after tasting the sweet water of home for a happy moment or two, she shook back heavy braids that fell like dark rainwater to her hips, and shouldered her pack. Time to get moving. She crossed the rain-puddled sidewalk and was the first student to reach the rank of robo-cabs waiting at the curb.

"State destination," the cab's computer droned as she opened the door and settled herself on the worn cushions.

"Klameth Canyon landing field," Kafari said, digging into her pocket even as the cab intoned mechanically, "Insert travel chit."

She slid her card into the proper slot and the computer said, "Credit approved. Web yourself into seat."

She tugged until the restraints clicked into place. The cab checked traffic control for clearance, then lifted smartly into the air, heading rapidly east toward the Damisi Mountains and home. She settled back to watch the scenery, but she was too keyed up to relax, and coming home was only part of the reason for it. The war news—and the tales pouring in from refugee ships landing at Vishnu—had grown so alarming, Kafari and many of her fellow students had decided to return home before things got worse.

Several families had contacted students via SWIFT, asking them to return, while others had begged their children to stay on Vishnu, since the Concordiat feared a Deng breakthrough at Jefferson. Kafari's family hadn't called. Not because they didn't care, but because they trusted her judgment, and therefore didn't want to waste the money a SWIFT transmission would cost. At twenty-two, Kafari had already survived more critical situations than most urban kids would experience in their entire lives. She'd carefully weighed the pros and cons of the situation unfolding beyond the Void and booked passage on the next ship out of Vishnu. At least, she sighed, peering down at the ground whipping past, she'd got here ahead of the Deng.

The cab had just veered north to bypass the restricted airspace over Nineveh Military Base when she saw it. Kafari sat bolt upright, eyes widening in shock.

"My God!"

It was a machine. An immense machine. A thing that dwarfed the very concept of machine. Even the largest buildings of Nineveh Base shrank to the size of children's stacking blocks by comparison. And more terrifying, even, than its sheer size, it was *moving*. Things that big were part of the immovable landscape, or should have been. Yet this immense structure was mobile. Faster than her aircab, in fact. Deep gouges showed as triple scars in its wake. The customs officials at Ziva Station had told them a Bolo and its commander had arrived, but Kafari had not remotely imagined just how huge humanity's most sophisticated engines of war really were.

One salvo from any of its guns and her aircab would vaporize into component atoms, along with her backpack, the contents of her pockets, and herself. She held back a shiver by sheer willpower, then a blur of motion caught her attention. A whole squadron of fighter planes streaked across the Damisi's highest peaks, low to the deck and lined up on the Bolo in what was clearly a strafing or bombing run.

About a hundred guns swung independently of one

another, tracking each of the incoming aircraft. The squadron scattered in a chaotic dispersal pattern as pilots scrambled into evasive maneuvers. For just an instant, her stomach clenched and she thought they were *all* about to die. She wondered angrily why nobody'd warned the robo-cab—or the spaceport officials—about an incoming invasion fleet. Then she realized what she was seeing.

Wargames.

A chill broke loose and tore its way down her spine, shaking her like a *jaglitch* with a horse in its teeth. She'd made it home ahead of the Deng, but she truly hadn't understood, until now, that the only thing standing between her family and brutal massacre was thirteen thousand tons of sudden destruction. Imagination quailed at trying to picture what it would look—and sound—like when the Bolo's guns discharged in full combat.

That thing could incinerate every fighter in the sky, if it wanted to. Please don't let it want to. She craned to see through the transparent canopy as her cab veered sharply north, but she couldn't keep the fighters in view. Moments later, the aircab dipped into the entrance of Maze Gap, which was the safest way through the Damisi, even by air, and the rose-toned shoulders of the mountains blocked her view of the Bolo, too. Kafari drew a long, shaken breath, then leaned back against the cushions and relaxed one muscle at a time.

"Wow!"

She couldn't even come up with a word big enough to describe what she felt.

Some emotions—like the Bolo, itself—defied all attempts to fit them into a preconceived notion of reality. Then she shrugged her fears impatiently aside. Kafari came from a long line of people who refused to let little things like terror rule their lives. You looked the world in the eye, took its measure, and did whatever was necessary, the moment it became necessary. After twenty-two years of meeting life head-on, she didn't see much use in changing, now.

She did wonder, a little apprehensively, just how close

to home the war would come, then decided it didn't matter. Jefferson was her home. As much as she loved Chakula Ranch, home was not a collection of paddocks, barns, or even the big house where she'd been born. Home was the earth, the sky, and the people living between them. That was what Kafari had come home to defend. Which piece of it she ended up defending was mere geography.

The aircab took the winding turn through Maze Gap that would lead to Klameth Canyon, dipping and bumping as they encountered turbulent air at the edge of the weather front that had left Madison socked in beneath rain clouds. Then they shot forward into the thirty-seven-kilometer stretch of canyon that was Kafari's favorite place on any world and she grinned at the breathtaking sight. Canyon walls of rose sandstone towered almost three hundred meters above a broad valley that was home to the richest farmland on Jefferson. High mountain slopes and snow-covered peaks rose another thirty-six hundred meters above the tops of the canyon walls, rising in forested splendor toward the cool springtime sky.

Kafari couldn't restrain a smile of delight at the sparkling ribbon of water where morning sunlight caught the Klameth River. Bisecting the long, snaking canyon that it had spent millennia carving out of the sedimentary rocks, Klameth River had once been one of Jefferson's wildest waterways, before the construction of the massive Klameth Canyon Dam. An immense amount of water still flowed through the dam's turbines, ensuring plentiful power for the canneries and processing plants in Lambu Cut, a feeder canyon that joined Klameth Canyon near its egress point into Maze Gap. Even with the reservoir and the vast irrigation system draining down its volume, the Klameth River was still the largest tributary of the Adero, which poured so spectacularly into the sea at Chenga Falls.

But the early terraforming engineers had tamed the Klameth sufficiently to farm and ranch the entire canyon and virtually all of its feeder canyons, several thousand kilometers of land under cultivation, all told. Ranches with vast pastures full of cattle, horses, and sheep showed as vivid green splashes against the deep rose of the canyon walls. Delicate pink and white clouds marked the big commercial orchards. A dark patchwork of newly plowed fields sprawled in every direction, ready for the row crops Jefferson's farmers would be planting soon. Irrigation water sparkled in the early sunlight, where mechanical sprayers soaked the orchards and fields.

More recent terraforming efforts had created dozens of small lakes and aquaculture ponds, allowing Jefferson's ranchers to cultivate Terran fin fish and shellfish. It was the shellfish—and the spectacular freshwater pearls her family cultivated and sold off-world, a commodity particularly prized by Malinese miners—that had paid for Kafari's education on Vishnu.

One of the factors that had sent Kafari home had been her coldly logical conclusion that war would disrupt the economies of both star systems sufficiently, nobody was going to be interested in buying pearls, which meant the family could make much better use of its money than paying for an education she'd nearly completed, in any case. If necessary, she'd finish up the degree work by correspondence course.

Her academic advisor had made an offer to do just that, adding gently that he'd secured a scholarship for her, as well, to pay the balance of her tuition and the cost of SWIFT transmissions necessary to send course materials and exams. They both understood exactly what that offer meant and why. With war brewing, she wasn't likely to return to Vishnu. Even if she survived, even if her family survived, the economic devastation following an invasion would destroy any chance she might have had to return and finish her education on Vishnu.

Kafari had left the office in tears, unsure whether to be profoundly grateful or to grieve for the loss of everything that offer represented. She still wasn't sure. The one thing she *was* sure of was the tremendous compliment to her talents and academic standing that offer represented. Dr. Markandeya had gone far beyond the strict call of duty to find a way to help her and she would never forget it.

Kafari's aircab had just signaled the landing field's auto-tower for final approach when an override signal came through. The aircab slewed violently sideways in a sickening, high-g turn that slammed her against the safety straps. A gasp of pain broke loose as a government-issue aircar came screaming past on priority approach vector. It was headed toward the landing field, where a groundcar waited in the section reserved for high-ranking officials.

"Huh," Kafari muttered to herself, rubbing a deep-seated ache across her shoulder and chest. "I wonder who's coming to dinner?" Whoever it was, chances were vanishingly small they'd end up at *her* house to eat it. Another shiver caught her shoulders. Whoever that VIP was and whatever they were doing at Klameth Canyon, dinner was doubtless the last thing on their mind. Officials from Madison didn't come all the way out here without a disturbingly good reason. And the only reason she could see for an official visit *now* was a scouting trip in preparation for war.

Kafari thought about the damage one good salvo from a Deng Yavac would do to Klameth Canyon Dam and abruptly wished she hadn't thought of it, after all. The leaden feeling in the pit of her stomach had nothing to do with the aircab's abrupt course change back toward the landing field. Unless she were very much mistaken, war was about to come knocking on her family's front door.

II

Simon's aircar was closing in for priority landing at Klameth Canyon field when they overtook a smaller aircar. It performed a sudden, wrenching maneuver to clear the approach lane. He caught a brief glimpse of the occupant, a young woman, it looked like, with long, dark hair. Then his own car flashed past and all he could see was the bottom of the other aircar as it slewed sideways.

"That girl's going to have bruises," he muttered to Abe Lendan, who had insisted on escorting him personally for this tour of Klameth Canyon. "I've never seen a civilian aircar veer off that sharply. I wonder who she is."

Abe Lendan frowned as he peered through a side window. "That's a standard commercial aircab. She's probably a student going home from that shuttle flight, this morning."

"Shuttle flight?"

"A freighter came in a few minutes ago from the Vishnu-Mali run. I saw a notation about it, since it was carrying a cargo of high-tech weaponry we ordered from Vishnu's weapons labs. A whole group of college kids came with it, traveling steerage."

"Really? I'd like to talk to one of those kids. How can I get a message to that aircab?"

Abe touched a control. "Jackie, can you patch a message through to that cab we just passed? Major Khrustinov wants to talk to the passenger."

The shuttle pilot's voice came back through the speaker. "Of course, sir." She left the connection open, so they could hear. "Klameth Field, this is Airfleet One. Requesting commo patch to the aircab inbound to your commercial strip."

"Patching to aircab commo system," a mechanical voice replied. "Connection made."

"Hello, aircab, this is Airfleet One, do you hear me?"

"Uh—" a startled female voice responded. "Yes. Yes, ma'am, I hear you."

"President Lendan has requested a meeting with you. We're routing an override to your cab-comp, to set you down next to Airfleet One."

"*Really?*" It came out a startled, little-girl squeal. "I mean, yes, certainly, ma'am, I'm honored."

And terrified. Simon smiled ruefully.

A moment later, their aircar settled in for a neat landing at the edge of Klameth Field. A waiting lackey hurried forward as their pilot popped the latches, opening the pneumatic passenger hatch. President Lendan's bodyguards exited first, then Simon slid out, followed by the president and his energy advisor, Julie Alvison. The aircab had changed course to follow them down. It settled to earth twenty-five meters away and the hatch popped open.

A shapely pair of legs emerged, followed by a curvaceous young woman clad in khaki shorts and a comfortable, rugged camp shirt with lots of pockets. A glorious mass of dark braids mostly obscured her shoulder pack. She was tall, nearly as tall as Simon, with skin the color of dark honey.

One of Abe Lendan's bodyguards—one of only two, comprising the smallest security detail he'd ever seen escorting a planetary head of state—performed a quick electronic and visual search, then escorted her over. The closer she got, the better she looked. Not pretty, exactly. There was too much strength in that face for conventional, doll-like prettiness. But she was strikingly memorable. African features, mixed with something Mediterranean, maybe. Jefferson's population was polygot, he knew that much from his mission briefing files, and the rural population was heavily weighted toward groups of African, Mediterranean, and Semitic descent, blended by generations of intermarriage. The effect of that blending was stunning, like a sculpture of Nefertiti, suddenly come to life.

"I hope my request to meet you didn't inconvenience you, ma'am," Simon apologized. He held out his hand. "Major Simon Khrustinov, Dinochrome Brigade."

Her lovely dark eyes widened. "Oh! That was your Bolo my aircab passed? Doing wargames?"

She surprised him into smiling. "Yes, Sonny's having the time of his life, playing cat and mouse with the air force."

"If he'd really been shooting, Jefferson wouldn't *have* an air force."

Simon's smile widened. "No, it wouldn't."

"I'm Kafari Camar," she said, shaking his hand with a firm grip despite the nervous tremor in her fingertips.

"Ms. Camar, it is a distinct pleasure. May I present Abe Lendan, President of Jefferson. He was kind enough to radio my request to your cab."

"I'm honored, sir," she said respectfully, shaking his hand, as well.

Simon was pleased that she maintained her poise. Good, solid self-confidence. The kind that bred survivors. He wanted this girl to survive. Very much, in fact.

"You came in on the Vishnu-Mali freighter?" Abe Lendan asked.

"Yes, sir. I took a look at all those refugees coming in, and the news reports from the other side of the Void, and decided I'd better come home. Fast."

"I wish it hadn't been necessary. But . . ." There wasn't much point in his elaborating further, since every one of them knew the score. "Major Khrustinov would like to discuss some things with you, Ms. Camar, if it isn't too much of an inconvenience? Or did you have someone waiting to pick you up?"

She smiled, a little shyly. "No, sir. I didn't want to waste my family's money on a SWIFT message or a long-distance call from Madison. There are always rental scooters available here, anyway. There was no need to pull anybody away from the spring planting, just to pick me up."

"I'd be happy to have my driver drop you at your home, if you'd help us out with Major Khrustinov's questions."

A startling smile turned her features radiant. "I guess I just lost that bet with myself," she chuckled.

"Oh?"

"I figured whoever was in that official car wouldn't be coming to *our* house for dinner."

Abe Lendan grinned. "I wouldn't dream of imposing,

but it's a kind offer. After you," he added, gesturing toward his waiting groundcar.

Simon fell into step beside her. "How was your trip home, Ms. Camar?"

She shot an intent glance his way, then surprised him by answering the question he *hadn't* asked. "Tense and worried. The town-based kids are terrified. Even the students from Granger families are scared. Those of us who are Granger-bred at least know how to use rifles and handguns. That might help, if it comes down to shooting Deng infantry, although it would be pretty useless against a Yavac. But most of the Townies have never even *seen* a real gun, let alone fired one. It was us Grangers, primarily, coming home on that freighter. Seventy percent, maybe. Most of the Townies stayed on Vishnu."

"You have a gift for situation reports, Ms. Camar."

She gave him another radiant smile. "I had a good teacher. One of my uncles is a career military officer."

They reached the presidential car, but didn't enter it, just yet. They were waiting for Lieutenant General Shatrevar to arrive, since the commander of Jefferson's ground forces had not only suggested this tour, but wanted to act as tour guide. The defense of this region would fall under his jurisdiction.

While they waited, Abe Lendan joined the conversation. "Whereabouts does your family live, Ms. Camar?"

"About a kilometer from the dam, under the Cat's Claw." She glanced back at Simon. "That's a local landmark. A spire of weathered sandstone shaped like a huge claw."

Abe Lendan smiled. "I know it well. When I was a boy, my friends and I would come out here to race our scooters and go fishing in Klameth Reservoir. We'll be passing close to your house."

Simon felt a twinge of loneliness, listening to these two people who'd never met, sharing a common bond of places fondly remembered. In the next moment, Kafari Camar startled him nearly speechless. She met his gaze, her own dark with concern, and said, "It must be very difficult, Major Khrustinov, to constantly move from world to world."

He knew his eyes had widened. For a long, awkward moment, he had no idea how to respond. The burning wreck of Etaine flashed, ghostlike, through his memory, blotting out all else for several moments. Then he managed a strained smile. "Yes. Very difficult. But this is my last duty post. I've been assigned permanently to Jefferson's government."

A soft smile touched something deep and virtually forgotten in Simon's heart. "I hope you like it here, Major."

It was, he realized, more than just a polite phrase. She meant it. The innate warmth with which these people had welcomed him deepened Simon's determination to defend this world, even as it worsened the aching fear that he would leave yet another beautiful place in ashes. It would be far better, far safer, if he refused to let himself care too deeply for any of these people, at least individually, until the danger was past.

Fortunately, he was saved from further comment by the appearance of a military-issue aircar. It came arrowing in from the opposite direction Airfleet One had come, since General Shatrevar had left Madison the night before, putting in motion phase one of their defense plans at various military bases scattered across Jefferson's supercontinent. The aircar landed neatly and a moment later, Shatrevar was striding toward them. Simon heard a gasp at his elbow and turned to see a shocked expression on Ms. Camar's face. Then the general saw her and broke into a delighted grin.

"Kafari! You're home!"

She ran forward with a cry of welcome. "Uncle Jasper!"

He swept her into a rib-cracking embrace. "Why in the world didn't you call? Oh, never mind, that's not important now." He held her at arm's length for a moment. "Honey, you just get taller and prettier every time I see you." He glanced their way and added, "I see you're keeping good company, as always."

A blush touched her cheeks.

"That's my fault, actually," Simon offered. "I wanted to talk to one of the students off that freighter, this morning. Your niece has been very helpful, debriefing me on the situation among the off-world students."

"Glad to hear it. You'd have to go a long way, Major, to find a better, more reliable source of information."

Her blush deepened, but she smiled as he snaked an arm around her shoulders and headed their way. Shatrevar shook hands, then they piled into the president's groundcar. One of the bodyguards, a lean and preternaturally alert man the president introduced as Ori Charmak, rode with them, while the other rode shotgun in a second vehicle. Once underway, they got down to serious business.

"There's a lot of terraformed land on Jefferson," Shatrevar began as they left the airfield and headed down a broad, well-maintained road that paralleled a swift-moving river. "But this is the biggest stretch of land under cultivation in this hemisphere and it's protected from the worst ravages of weather, which is why early terraforming engineers chose to build farms, orchards, and processing plants here. Most of the food supply for Madison comes from this canyon system and that hydroelectric dam is critical to the whole region. Most of the small towns in the Adero floodplain rely entirely on power generated at the Klameth Canyon Dam. Even Madison would be hit hard, if we lost that generating capacity."

"All of which makes this canyon a prime target." Simon nodded.

General Shatrevar's niece swallowed hard, then gazed unhappily out the window. Simon also studied the terrain with a critical eye, trying to decide whether the Deng would be likeliest to blow the dam and let the resulting flood sweep away farms, crops, food animals, and people, or whether they would attempt capturing the dam intact, for their own electrical power needs. Deng weren't particularly interested in Terran foods, but the houses and outbuildings would serve as adequate shelters for thousands of Deng warriors—and, eventually, thousands of Deng families, too. It was always cheaper to use an existing structure, even one not entirely suited to the size and shape of the invaders, than it was to build from scratch.

Jasper Shatrevar pointed out the route heavy produce trucks followed each harvest season to reach the packing plants, which had been built in a feeder canyon, out of sight from the picturesque beauty of the main canyon. Simon was leaning forward to peer into the side canyon when the commlink attached to his belt began to scream. His gut tightened savagely. That was the emergency alarm. A proximity warning that the enemy was within his Bolo's sensor range. Simon swore aloud, hating the fear that radiated with sudden intensity from the civilians in President Lendan's car. Even Jasper Shatrevar had gone white. Simon slapped the commo circuit wide open.

"What's the VSR, Sonny?"

"We have Enemy breakthrough out of the Void. Deng warships. Receiving comp from System-perimeter warning buoys. Advise immediate scramble of all defense forces."

"Roger that, Sonny. Continue to monitor Enemy movements. General Shatrevar, head back to Nineveh Base. President Lendan, I need to commandeer your air transport, stat, to reach Sonny. There may not be time to get you back to Madison, even by air. We're fifty kilometers out and Deng warships can cross planetary distances *fast*."

"Understood, Major." President Lendan pressed a control on the arm of his seat, fingers shaking slightly, and spoke to the driver. "Turn us around, Hank. Get us back to the landing field. Put your foot down and keep it there."

The car swung around in a wrenching turn and headed back the way they'd just come. The look in Kafari Camar's dark and beautiful eyes tore at him, but there was literally nothing Simon could do to reassure the girl. She'd come home to defend her world. In all too short a time, she'd be doing exactly that. The best he could hope for was an intense, heartsick prayer that she was still alive when the smoke cleared.

Chapter Four

I

I track Enemy deployment as every perimeter alarm
between Jefferson's primary and the edge of the Void
screams out dire warnings. I have gone to Battle Reflex
Alert, snapping my gun systems to live status as I await
my Commander's return from his abortive tour of Klam-
eth Canyon.

"Sonny, I've borrowed President Lendan's aircar. Send
me visual VSR on the breakthrough." *I flash schematics*
of Jefferson's star system to Simon's airborne transport,
marking the point of breakthrough. "System-perimeter
warning buoys are reporting three Deng heavy cruisers,
four troop transports—"

I halt as more buoys begin to scream news of a second
breakthrough point, seventeen degrees above the system's
ecliptic plane. "Four additional heavy cruisers breaking
through at system zenith. Six more troop transports
detected. Fighter squadrons are breaking loose from the
heavy cruisers. I anticipate attacks against moon bases
and asteroid mining operations within twelve point two

minutes. I am sending a warning to in-system naval cutters to expect imminent attack."

Simon swears, creatively. He knows, as I do, that the people on those asteroids and moon bases—and those in Jefferson's Home-Star Navy—are about to die. The cutters are no match for seven battle cruisers and ten troop transports, which also possess the advantage of high-velocity entry from their interstellar crossing. The Home-Star Navy's cutters are virtually stationary, with no time to build up speed for evasive maneuvers, let alone an attack run against the incoming ships. Without the heavy guns and high-g acceleration potential of a Concordiat naval cruiser in this star system, they are helpless—and there is literally nothing we can do to help anyone in a space-based habitat.

I blame myself for not insisting that the off-world installations be evacuated, but Simon's next words are of some comfort. "There wouldn't have been time to get those people to safety on Jefferson even if they'd been ordered home the minute our transport made orbit. *Dammit!* That incursion's almost half-fleet strength. What the hell are the Deng doing here in such concentration? Notify General Hightower and track those incoming ships. I want to know their deployment pattern, second by second."

No human can actually take in that much data that fast, but I have served with Simon long enough to understand his meaning. I send the warning to Jefferson's Chief of Defense. "General Hightower, we have a confirmed Deng breakthrough in two sectors. Transmitting coordinates and tracking deployment. Advise immediate civilian evacuation to shelters."

In this, at least, Jefferson is more adequately prepared than many colony worlds. After the last Deng attempt to take this world, the government embarked on a massive building project to construct subterranean bomb shelters deep beneath the cities. General Hightower responds with the kind of calm that comes only from prior combat experience—decades of it.

"Understood, Sonny. Thank God we're actually deployed in the field on those joint-ops maneuvers you recommended. They didn't quite catch us with our jockey shorts down." *The eerie sound of sirens comes through the audio pickup as the evacuation warning is given, ordering Madison's people to seek their assigned shelters. Within seconds, the scenario is repeated in every major urban center on Jefferson. If such shelters had existed on Etaine . . . There is no point in such speculation. I turn my attention to the deployment of the incoming Deng warships.*

Both groups are moving at sub-light speed, but they have come in fast, as warships intending blitzkrieg invariably do. They are bleeding off some of their high-vee energy in braking maneuvers, but are still moving at sufficient speed, a Concordiat naval ship—even had one been available for in-system defense—would have had enormous difficulty hitting them, while providing a virtually motionless target for alien guns. Ducks on a pond. Or fish in a barrel. I do not like the analogy, as applied to myself, and never have. One good-sized rock, sent crashing into Jefferson from a ship moving that fast, and the battle for Jefferson would be over, along with every human life on this world. It is a grim business, to hope that the enemy intends colonization rather than outright destruction.

When Simon's transport appears in my sensors, I experience a moment of relief. I am capable of some independent action in battle, thanks to the rewriting of two key software blocks during my retrofitting, but most of the blocks have remained in place, leaving me unable to function on my own for anything but direct fire at an enemy that is actively shooting at me or at something I have been charged to guard. In situations requiring complex judgment, a human commander is essential to my battlefield effectiveness. Simon's return dispels the uneasiness I have felt since the moment of Enemy breakthrough out of the Void.

The military aircar sets down three point seven meters

from my port-side tread. Simon emerges from the pilot's compartment and breaks into a run, climbing the access ladder rapidly as I open the hatch to my Command Compartment. I do not see the president's pilot. Airfleet One sits abandoned as I turn my attention to Simon's arrival in my Command Compartment.

"Okay, Lonesome," Simon mutters as he slides into his chair and slaps restraints closed. "Let's take a look at what we've got."

The ships dropping down from system zenith deploy for fast attack runs. I track the battle formation as fighters strafe asteroid mining installations. Silent explosions mark the deaths of human personnel. The Deng are indulging a savage level of destruction, making no attempt to capture the mines intact. The nearest heavy cruiser opens fire on the moonbase. Home-Star Navy cutters return fire, attempting to hit the incoming cruisers. An energy lance touches the cutter above Juree Moonbase and the ship explodes, raining debris across the moon from lunar orbit.

Another cruiser smashes Jefferson's commercial space station and its defending cutter. The latter vanishes in an incandescent ball of gas and debris. Ziva Station breaks apart. Pieces spin away in a spectacular burst pattern. Broken chunks will come down over the next several weeks, but the freighter docked there is in far more immediate danger. The fifty-seven students who arrived in it have reached relative safety on the ground, but the ship and its cargo of high-tech weaponry—only partially off-loaded at the spaceport—are doomed.

The freighter attempts to run, wallowing in a frantic effort to elude the incoming warships. Ship-to-ship missiles streak almost lazily across the purple-black expanse of space above Jefferson's atmosphere. I can do nothing but watch, unable to reach the cruisers or the missiles to defend the freighter. Warheads impact and explode. The freighter breaks apart, spilling its contents to vacuum.

I rage. I track ships I cannot reach with my guns. Humans are dying and I am helpless, unable to grapple with the enemy. A third cruiser dropping from zenith *takes down every orbital communications satellite circling Jefferson, depriving me of visual data in one fell swoop. Planetary-defense battle platforms return fire automatically, inflicting heavy damage to one cruiser before concentrated fire from the second cruiser's guns blow them to component atoms. In three minutes and twenty-seven seconds, Jefferson has been stripped of all space-based defensive capacity and every off-world installation has been reduced to rubble.*

Having achieved such massive destruction, the Enemy's next move surprises me and even catches my Commander off-guard. The original battle group, which broke through at system perimeter, jumps out again on a vector that will take all three cruisers and their four troop transports straight to the Ngara system and its two inhabited worlds, Mali and Vishnu. Simon whistles softly. "So *that's* what they were up to, sending half a battle fleet across the Void. They plan to hit both systems in the Dezelan Promontory and open up a back door to our inner worlds."

"Shall I relay a warning to Captain Brisbane at Vishnu?"

"No. Not yet. Those cruisers haven't spotted us, Lonesome, and I'm not anxious to advertise our presence. Not until they're within range of your guns. We've got to warn them, somehow, though. You're right about that. Relay a message through General Hightower. Ask him to send a transmission to Vishnu from one of the commercial SWIFT units. One that's nowhere near Madison."

I contact General Hightower.

"Understood," *the aging general says harshly, comprehending immediately that the person who sends that SWIFT transmission will die for it. After a delay of one point zero-seven minutes, the general speaks again.* "The Tayari Trade Consortium is transmitting now." *A SWIFT broadcast races outward from a point on Jefferson's night side, drawing instantaneous fire from all four enemy cruisers dropping toward Jefferson's atmosphere. Damage to the Trade Consortium will be severe, but Vishnu and Mali have been warned. The Deng cruisers and troop transports arriving in Ngaran space will not have the advantage of total surprise. I experience a savage satisfaction that this is so.*

Satisfaction turns to elation when two of the four remaining cruisers break off their attack run against Jefferson and follow the first battle group toward distant Ngara. Simon lets go a war whoop. "They think it's all over but the mopping up! Sonny, boy, it's time to go Deng hunting!"

I experience a fierce thrill of anticipation. I long to close with the enemy. I intend to pay back the wanton destruction of human lives with deadly interest.

"Steady, Lonesome," Simon advises softly, gaze glued to the forward screen, "don't fire 'til you see the whites of their beady little eyes."

This is, of course, impractical advice, since Deng eyes contain no white at all. Simon's meaning is clear, however, as is his reference to ancient Terran history. The unexpected exodus leaves only one fully functional heavy cruiser in orbit around Jefferson. The second ship, badly damaged by Jefferson's orbital weapons platforms, is drifting into the upper atmosphere, evidently unable to hold course. All six troop transports swoop into the upper atmosphere, descending rapidly.

They drop in formation, an arrogance they will soon rue. The crippled heavy cruiser continues to drift, its crew doubtless too distracted by the urgent need for repairs to play a role, yet, in the battle about to erupt in Jefferson's skies. The second cruiser disgorges fighters in a horde reminiscent of Terran wasps. The fighters race to provide covering fire for the troop transports, with their heavy loads of infantry and Yavac fighting vehicles. They drop into the thin, highly charged ionosphere on a direct course for Madison and the critical agricultural complex of Klameth Canyon. Even the functional heavy cruiser kisses the high ionosphere, dropping low enough to swivel its guns toward the planetary surface. It fires missiles at Madison's spaceport. I long to swat them down, but wait for Simon's command.

"Undamaged cruiser first, transports next. And as many of those missiles as you can take down. Stand by to fire . . . Now," *Simon whispers gently.*

I fire Hellbores and infinite repeaters. The cruiser staggers, mortally wounded. The hull cracks in half and breaks open. The pieces plunge toward atmosphere, glowing like short-lived meteors. I have no time to celebrate, as I am too busy firing at the descending cluster of troop transports and missiles. I destroy three transports before they can scatter. I vaporize fifteen in-bound missiles on a vector for Madison's spaceport.

The second cruiser, damaged but still operational, opens fire despite its awkward position as it drifts out of control across Jefferson's upper atmosphere. I engage engines, racing forward, and evade all but one of the enemy's inbound shots. Y-beam energy strikes my defensive battle screen, causing a flare and surge of power as the screen absorbs the energy, glowing white-hot in the process. The screen converts ninety-seven percent of the energy washing across my stern into useable power, fueling not only several of my gun systems, but recharging the screen. This eases the terrific power drain necessary to maintain the defensive shield and power my main weaponry.

The damaged cruiser continues to pour fire into me, however. It becomes clear within ten point eight seconds that the commander in charge of its guns has fought Bolos before. Seventeen separate gun systems concentrate their fire onto one point of my defensive screen, heating it up to intolerable levels. Despite my attempt at evasive maneuvers, trying to relieve the terrific strain, the screen goes into overload, unable to absorb even one more erg. An energy lance punches through and eats a deep gash through my ablative armor. Pain sensors scream damage warnings.

I swivel and swerve, firing nonstop. A double blast from fore and aft Hellbores catches the cruiser across its bow. The wounded cruiser wallows lower, plunging deep into the ionosphere. It launches a cloud of missiles, more than a hundred, in snarling defiance of its own imminent

destruction. A third punch from my Hellbores catches
the cruiser broadside. Its entire stern shears away. The
dying cruiser breaks up as spectacularly as her sister
ship, raining debris across the entire western hemisphere
as she disintegrates.

I fire into the hailstorm of incoming missiles, more
than I can destroy as they scream toward Madison and
its spaceport. I destroy ninety-three of them, but the rest
reach their designated targets. Madison's spaceport sustains
heavy damage. Manufacturing plants northwest of the
capital explode and burn savagely. Three troop transports
from the cluster that scattered, trying to evade my guns,
remain airborne. Their fighter escorts have begun strafing
runs on my warhull. I fire anti-aircraft missiles, infinite
repeaters, and small-bore cannons at the incoming fighters.
My guns belch death, filling the sky with incandescent
flame. Fighters veer off, attempting evasive maneuvers.
The transports drop like stones, using emergency thrust
to reach the relative safety of the ground.

One transport vanishes into the Damisi Mountains,
doubtless making a safe—and vexacious—landing in
Klameth Canyon. A second veers sharply northwest and
drops below the horizon line, doubtless intending to use
the steep cliffs of the coastal escarpment as a screen. It
will probably disgorge its load of infantry and Yavacs
northwest of Madison. The third transport attempts to
land near Nineveh Base. The base's anti-aircraft batteries
open fire, raking the side of the descending transport.

The enormous ship staggers midair. Fighters buzz and
swarm to its aid. Jefferson's home-defense fighters scream
down from the Damisi Mountains, flying nap-of-the-earth
in an eerie recreation of the wargames underway when
the Deng fleet broke into Jeffersonian space. The human
crews engage enemy fighters with air-to-air missiles,
moving too swiftly for the intricacies of aerial dogfights,
which belonged to a glorious but sadly antiquated era
of warfare.

I know blazing pride in Jefferson's defenders when
the untested air force sends a dozen enemy fighters to

destruction. They crash spectacularly into the ground surrounding Nineveh Base. The wounded troop transport has made a safe landing, but the speed of my attack and that of the air force has forced its captain into the serious error of landing on the near side of Nineveh Base. This allows me to fire line-of-sight, virtually point-blank. Two Yavacs succeed in off-loading before I rake the transport with fire from my forward Hellbore. The ship disintegrates into a massive fireball that temporarily blocks my view of the base and its scrambling gun crews.

I launch a drone, which gives me a clear view of the two Yavacs that have reached the ground. One, a Scout-class, is of little immediate danger, but the other is a Yavac Heavy, prompting a snarl from my Commander.

"Go after that Heavy before it takes out the whole base!"

I rush forward, redlining my drive engines to reach a vantage point from which I can fire at the Yavac without putting the human personnel and installations beyond at equal risk. I take fire from the Scout-class, which moves in a blur of speed on its jointed legs. A pulse from my infinite repeaters blows apart two of its legs, sending it crashing and maimed to the ground. A Jeffersonian fighter follows it down, firing missiles and 30cm cannons as it strafes the downed Scout. The hull explodes and burns fiercely, but the Yavac Heavy has not been idle.

It opens fire simultaneously on Nineveh Base and my warhull. An anti-aircraft battery simply ceases to be. Three Y-beam energy lances strike my starboard screen, concentrating all three beams onto one spot in another effort to punch through. The energy pouring into the screen fuels my infinite repeaters, which I use to good effect, taking out the Heavy's radar arrays and small-bore weaponry. But with three beams sizzling into my flank, the screen cannot hold. It fails again—spectacularly—allowing destructive penetration to the surface of my warhull. The terrific energy influx melts three 10cm anti-personnel machine gun arrays and splashes destruction across my starboard sensors and track linkages. I fire infinite repeaters, aiming for the leg joints, not wanting to expose this heavily populated region to more hard radiation than utterly necessary.

Jeffersonian fighters attempt strafing runs, but the light-weight aircraft are no match for a Yavac Heavy's guns. Five of the seven fighters burst into fireballs. Anger fuels my response. I open fire with my forward Hellbore, then rock on my treads, hit by return fire that digs another long gouge across my starboard side. Pain sensors scream warnings. I swivel twin turrets to bring both Hellbores to bear, delighting in the responsiveness of my retrofitted, independent double turrets, and fire again. The Yavac's turret shears off and goes spinning through the heart of Nineveh Base. I pulse both Hellbores again and the main body of the Heavy-class fighting machine explodes. It falls, ponderously, and burns out of control.

I swat down the remaining enemy fighters with grim satisfaction. In the momentary lull of noise, a distant sound of explosions from two separate compass directions washes into my awareness. I order my aerial drone to gain altitude.

"Madison is under attack," *I report tersely, angling my drone to pick up the battle raging just northwest of the capital city. Clearly, the troop transport that eluded my guns has disgorged its lethal cargo. I also pick up frantic transmissions from the Jeffersonian air force squadron above the Damisi Mountains. I relay the fighter pilots' situation reports.* "There is heavy fighting in Klameth Canyon. The enemy has blockaded Maze Gap. There has been no action taken against the Klameth Canyon Dam, but Deng infantry are pouring through the farmholds, slowed by intense fighting from the residents. Shelling from the Yavacs has been minimal, compared with attacks on other worlds."

"They want the canyon's infrastructure intact, then. Madison?"

I flash video feed from my drone to the main view-screen. Yavac Heavies are advancing toward Madison's northwestern suburbs, firing virtually unopposed. General

Hightower's artillery—including twenty-seven mobile 10cm Hellbores—and air-mobile cav units are rushing to defend the heart of the city. Other units attempt to delay the advance along the western perimeter, trying to deny the enemy a far-forward breakthrough that would effectively split our fighting forces in half.

Simon snarls through clenched teeth. "Klameth Canyon will have to wait. We've got to stop those Yavacs before they take out the whole city."

I rush forward at emergency battle speed, firing high-angle mortars that arc above Madison's skyline. They drop cluster bombs amongst the enemy's infantry and Scout-class units, wreaking havoc as I rush toward the Adero River, which I must cross. Due to the short distance between the Damisi watershed and the capital city, the Adero River is swift, deep, and narrower than many rivers spilling across a floodplain. This creates a navigational inconvenience, since the riverbed is too steep and too narrow to lumber across it without risk of tipping prow-first into an attitude reminiscent of a duck diving for its dinner.

I therefore redline my engines, roaring down the main road from Nineveh Base toward the Hickory Bridge, which was built east of the capital to accommodate the heavy ore carriers, construction equipment, and freight trucks connecting Madison's industrial sector and spaceport to other urban centers, particularly the mining cities and smelting plants scattered along the Damisi Range. This bridge was constructed to handle a high volume of heavy vehicles. I hope that it will hold my weight just long enough to cross to the northern river bank.

I rush toward the southern end of the bridge at a smouldering one hundred twenty-two kilometers per hour. It is fortunate that no truck traffic was on the bridge at the time of attack. The entire span is empty. My treads scream their way up the approach. The concrete shudders under my treads. I reach the midpoint of the bridge as the support beneath my stern collapses. Simon lets out a wild yell.

"Mother—
—fuckin'—
—Bear!"

We are across. The bridge smashes into the river-bed.

I unleash a barrage of bombardment rockets, high-angle mortars, and hyper-v missiles, raking the enemy's eastern flank with withering fire. As intended, my actions draw the attention of the Yavac Heavies away from the destruction of Madison's outlying homes and manufacturing plants.

I come under fire from three Yavac Heavy-class units, which shift their triangular formation to attack me, instead. I speed northward around the city, then drive forward in a maneuver that leaves the enemy exposed along the entire northwestern flank. General Hightower's ground-based mobile Hellbores smash the Deng southern flank, even as I open fire with my heavier 30cm Hellbores. Scout-class Yavacs topple and burn along the southern flank, but the three Heavies concentrate their fire on me, correctly judging me to be the far greater threat.

I lose a bank of chain-guns and several prow-mounted sensors, but these Yavacs are not top-of-the-line units. At Etaine, I faced state-of-the-art war machines. These are virtually obsolete, far older than I am. I charge, guns blazing. I destroy the leading Yavac Heavy, at the apex of the attack-formation triangle. I then plunge between the two remaining units at maximum emergency speed, one Hellbore aimed port-side, the other starboard. They do not expect this maneuver and spin their guns wildly. They cannot fire at me without risk of hitting one another.

I charge past, firing both Hellbores. Twin explosions lift both Yavacs off their jointed legs. Salvos from my infinite repeaters destroy those flailing legs midair. Their hulls smash back down with enough force to kill on-board crews. Another blast from my Hellbores finishes them off, silencing their automated gun systems. General Hightower's artillery has punched through the Enemy's southern flank. Deng infantry units have fallen into disarray. I pulse infinite repeaters and launch a barrage of anti-personnel mortars. The combined attack sends the Deng infantry into full retreat.

I fling myself forward and come among them like a lion among sheep. Scout-class Yavacs fall back, trying to evade my guns while providing covering fire to the retreating infantry. Human ground forces harass the entire southern flank, taking terrific casualties in the process. I destroy one Scout, caught with fatal hesitation between the twin threat from my guns and the mobile Hellbores of General Hightower's artillery crews. Other Scouts turn and flee toward their transport, visible now near the bank of the Adero River.

I crush Deng infantry into the mud and pursue the Scout-class Yavacs. I cross open, sloppy ground, overtaking the rear-most Scout. It crunches satisfactorily beneath my treads. The three remaining Scouts attempt to swivel their guns to shoot at my pursuing warhull, but this outdated Scout model was designed for frontal assault, not retreat. It is a fatal design flaw. I pick one off almost leisurely, then sight on the next and destroy it, as well.

The troop transport, accurately assessing the danger to itself, attempts lift-off, guns blazing as it launches itself across the Adero River, heading for Chenga Falls. If it drops below the escarpment, it will have an excellent chance of escape, moving northward or southward in a cliff-hugging flight that will protect it from my guns. I change course, pouring withering fire at the fleeing transport. It dodges, skips out across the river, hovers for just an instant above the spectacular fall of water—

A salvo from my forward Hellbore strikes solidly amidships. The transport breaks in half and plunges, burning fiercely, into the river. An instant later, the blazing debris is swept over the high falls and rushes downward to destruction. I turn my attention back to the sole remaining Yavac Scout, which has nearly reached the river. I fire infinite repeaters. The jointed legs flail like a crippled insect, then the entire vehicle runs straight off the edge of the high escarpment. So does the confused mass of

Deng infantry, choosing the long plunge to the sea over a fiery death under my guns.

I exult in their destruction.

Then I remember Klameth Canyon. We have struck a crippling blow against the Deng's invasionary forces, but the battle is far from over. Simon's voice breaks the abrupt silence, harsh with stress. "Good job, Sonny. Damned fine job. Now shag your shiny flintsteel butt back to Klameth Canyon. Let's just hope there's somebody still alive, over there, to rescue."

No answer is necessary. I turn and prepare to engage the Enemy once more.

Chapter Five

I

Kafari had never known such terror.

She watched her uncle race across the landing field toward his aircar and wondered frantically if she would ever see him again. Major Khrustinov had already thrown himself into the president's aircar, shouting at the pilot to lift off even before he had the hatch completely dogged shut. She watched both aircars dwindle away, then noticed that her robo-cab had already left the field, doubtless on its way back to Madison. She wondered what in the world to do, now. Then President Lendan's voice broke into her stunned awareness.

"Ms. Camar?"

She tried to pull her scattered wits together. "Sir?"

"Is there any shelter you could recommend? We're grounded without air transport and there won't be time for my pilot to come back for us, after delivering Major Khrustinov. There aren't any bomb shelters out here. You know this canyon better than we do." He nodded toward his bodyguards and his shaken energy advisor,

Julie Alvison. She was trembling, her lovely face ashen.
Even Abraham Lendan was alarmingly pale.

My God, she thought dazedly, *I'm responsible for the
safety of the president . . .* Rather than deepening her
terror, the unexpected burden steadied her a little, gave
her something concrete to do. "Alligator Deep," she said,
barely recognizing her own voice.

"Alligator Deep?"

"It's a cavern, more of an undercut, really, about fifteen
kilometers that way." She pointed north, down the long,
snaking route through Klameth Canyon. "The original
terraforming crews used it as a shelter. The entrance is
full of jagged stone projections, like teeth. It cuts pretty
deeply into the cliff, a hundred meters, at least. You'll
have to cross the Klameth River at Aminah Bridge."

"Hank, get us there, please," Abe Lendan said
grimly.

The president's groundcar driver took off like a man
possessed by demons. The second bodyguard, in the car
behind theirs, matched the wildly reckless pace centimeter
for centimeter. Kafari had never ridden in a groundcar
driven this fast. Farmhouses and pasture fences blurred
dizzily, then whipped past and dropped away behind them.
At the five kilometer point, one branch of the road swung
across the river at Aminah Bridge. The car roared up the
incline, went airborne for a split second at the top, then
flashed across and skidded through the sharp turn at the
base. Even with her seat belt in place, Kafari was flung
against the president's shoulder. Julie Alvison was hurled
against the side of the car with audible force. The violence
of her landing left a massive red welt across one whole
side of her face.

Then they straightened out again and Hank put his foot
to the floor. Maybe *through* it, they picked up speed so
fast. Then an awesome noise cracked across the clifftops
from somewhere far to the west. The noise rolled across
the tops of the Damisi Mountains and rattled, echoing,
against the canyon walls.

"What the hell was *that*?" Abe Lendan gasped.

Whatever it was, it came again. And again.

"It's the Bolo," Kafari whispered. "It's s-shooting at something."

Lots of somethings, from the sound crashing across an entire mountain range. She tried to peer through the side window, caught the edge of a blinding flash high above the western cliffs. Julie Alvison, ash-pale beneath the livid bruise spreading across her face, let out a breathy scream and pointed into the sky. "What's *that*?" she gasped, hand violently atremble.

Kafari craned her neck, trying to see. A massive fireball was streaking down across the morning sky, trailing a long glowing tail of smoke and flame. It vanished behind the eastern slopes of the Damisi Mountains range. Nobody offered any guesses. Probably because they were all hanging onto the car seats and each other as Hank whipped through turns in the road. They went airborne on small rises, scraped the bottom of the chassis in the occasional dips in the road.

It was part of a ship, maybe, Kafari theorized in jolted, jagged flashes between thuds and skids. *A big one. Bigger than the freighter? How long would it take a ship to fall from orbit? Would a ship fall from orbit? Or just drift around as big chunks? Maybe it was one of the Deng ships trying to land?*

Nearly three minutes after it vanished behind the mountains, a massive plume of smoke and debris rose above the clifftops. Then chunks of rock started falling. Hank paid more attention to the plummeting debris than his job and skidded them straight off the road. He fought the wheel and plowed his way back onto the asphalt. The car behind them slewed into the ditch, trying to avoid hitting them. The second car spun around, then tipped over, skidding sickeningly on its side.

Then a massive chunk of sandstone—nearly as big as their car—smashed into the ground half a meter from their right fender. Flying shards caught the side of the car like shrapnel. The front passenger window broke like an eggshell. Debris peppered the whole right side of the car. More falling rock cracked the windshield. The glass spiderwebbed. The roof rang like a bell, dented in a dozen places.

Somebody was screaming. Words took shape between sobs of hysterical terror, which Kafari finally realized were coming from Julie, the president's energy advisor. "What *was* that thing?" she was asking, over and over, between hiccoughs and shrill, panicked-animal noises. She was clawing at her seat belt, trying to reach the floor, but the belt had locked tight. She gave up and simply huddled as low as her harness would let her, trembling violently. Kafari was shaking pretty violently, herself. . . .

The president's bodyguard had pressed one hand to his ear, obviously listening to a broadcast over his ear-piece. "I think," he said tersely, "that was part of a Deng ship, that thing we saw come down, not one of ours." Ori Charmak's face abruptly faded to the color of dirty snow. "But we're getting hammered. Hard. General Hightower says we've lost Ziva Station, Juree Moonbase, all the asteroid mines."

Shock crashed across Kafari like a tidal wave, drowning out his voice. The whole space station? The entire moon base? Just *gone*? She was still trying to take it in when a black shape came arrowing down from the sky. Kafari screamed. A huge ship was dropping toward Klameth Canyon, moving fast.

"*Get off the road!*" Ori shouted. "That's a Deng troop transport!"

Hank skidded the car through a farmyard and rocked to a halt under the spreading limbs of a massive oak tree.

"Out!" Ori snarled, bodily hauling President Lendan out of the car. As Kafari scrambled out, a group of farmhands began running toward the house, abandoning tractors and cultivators in the fields. Then something else big roared down the canyon, at treetop height. Dazzling beams of coherent light strafed the fields, cutting down anything moving: tractors, herds of panic-stricken livestock, people . . .

"*Down!*"

Ori slam-dunked Abe Lendan into the ground and

shielded the president's body with his own. Kafari ate dirt. More airborne fighter-craft shot past, toward the immense bulk of the Deng troop ship. The alien behemoth was settling to ground less than five hundred meters away. *Oh, God,* Kafari wept in sheer terror, *oh, God* . . . She dug her fingers into the dirt.

Things were emerging from that ship. Immense, multijointed things. Bristling with guns. Looking like demons from the darkest reaches of hell. *Yavacs,* her brain gibbered. *Those are Yavacs! Lots of them. And infantry.* A black tide was pouring out of the troop ship, full of hairy, dog-sized creatures. Spindly, stiltlike legs sent them scurrying far too fast.

Then a groundcar from a farmhouse a hundred meters from the Deng ship skidded onto the road. Somebody was making a run for it. Every gun on every Yavac in the canyon turned in a blinding blur of speed, shooting at the car. It disappeared in a blinding flash and roar. The echoes were still cracking off the canyon walls when the door of the farmhouse closest to them crashed open. A woman's voice shouted across the yard.

"Inside! *Quick!*"

Kafari hesitated only long enough to scream at her trembling muscles, then she was on her feet and running. The others were right behind her. She gasped for breath as she shot across the porch and staggered toward the open door. Kafari literally fell through the doorway. The president was right behind her. Ori threw Julie Alvison across the porch to reach the marginal safety of the farmhouse.

"Get down!" the woman yelled, even as she slammed the door shut and threw herself to the floor. Kafari skidded across polished wooden floorboards. The buttons on her shirt and shorts dug scratches into the gleaming wood. She fetched up behind a hand-carved rocker with a quilted cushion in cheerful reds and yellows. Then white-hot hell erupted beyond the windows. Glass blew out, shattering in the overpressure of a massive explosion. Kafari's ears felt like they were bleeding.

When she could see again, the president's car was gone. So was the tree it had been parked under. And so was most of the front wall. A ship of alien manufacture shot past, firing at something farther down the road. Kafari couldn't even breathe, she was so terrified. When the alien fighter moved away, the woman who had offered them shelter scrambled up, covered with dust and splinters and blood, but on her feet and moving.

"Up, quick! We got to reach the cellar!"

The ground trembled under strange, disjointed concussions. One glimpse through the broken wall showed Kafari a sight from deepest nightmare. Yavacs, walking down the canyon. On huge, misshapen metallic legs. Insects the size of houses. Hunting *her*.

"Move your ass, girl!" the farmwife snarled.

Kafari broke and ran.

They plunged down a long hallway toward a spacious kitchen, filled incongruously with the smell of fresh-baked bread. It smelled like home, like her grandmother's apron, like everything in the world she'd come home to defend. A boy of about twelve, eyes wide and scared in a dark and frightened face, had pulled up part of the kitchen floor. Steps led down into a cellar. Anything that resembled a hole she could crawl down and pull in after her looked good to Kafari. A whole pile of guns lay beside the open trapdoor. She felt better, just seeing them. With guns in their hands, they could at least go down fighting.

The boy met his mother's anxious gaze. "Papa and the rest never made it, Mama." Tears rolled down his cheeks. The cast on one arm explained why the boy hadn't been in the fields with his older relatives.

Mama's face didn't crumple. It went cold and hard. "Then grab yourself a rifle, Dinny, 'cause you're the man of this house, now. All of you, grab whatever you can carry, out of that stack."

Kafari snatched up two rifles, a shotgun, and a pistol on her way down the cellar stairs. The staircase was a simple wooden structure, with planks for steps and open backs, but there were two handrails, well worn, and it was solidly constructed. More feet clattered down the stairs. The president reached safety, shadowed by his bodyguard. Julie Alvison, disheveled and looking ready to collapse, came down ahead of Hank, the driver. The cellar door swung shut above them, latching with a solid thump, then the boy, Dinny, helped his mother down and urged her to sit on the bottom step.

Her face was grey from shock and pain, streaked with sweat and grime and blood where she'd been hit by debris from the collapsed wall. President Lendan moved to her side and peered critically at her injuries. "Your name's Dinny?" he glanced at the hovering child.

"Yes, sir. Dinny Ghamal. That's my Mama, sir, Aisha Ghamal."

"Is there a first-aid kit down here, Dinny?"

The boy brought a hefty box from one of the shelves. President Lendan found antiseptic and alcohol wipes. Kafari spotted a sink and a stack of towels and hastened to wet one of them. As she waited for the water to run hot, she studied the cellar. The stone shelter was bigger than she'd expected. The ceiling—and therefore the floor of the house—was reinforced plascrete.

It was chilly, down here. The walls were all but invisible behind tall cupboards, their shelves lined with stored food and all the tools essential to keeping a large kitchen garden properly harvested and its bounty properly preserved. Jars of homemade jellies, pickles, and vegetables sat in colorful array beside crockery pots for storing sauerkraut, honey, even butter, according to the labels. Smoked meats hung from metal poles across the ceiling.

Other shelves were stacked high with boxes of ammunition. *Lots* of ammunition. She saw both loaded cartridges and unassembled components: cases, primers, powder, lead and metal-jacketed bullets. One whole corner of the cellar was devoted to reloading presses. It reminded her—strongly—of her father's cellar.

Always hope for peace, her father had told her years previously, when she'd asked about all the weaponry stored in the cellar, *but be prepared for war.* The Camar family—and the Soteris family, on her mother's side—had lost a lot of members in the last invasion. Kafari understood the compulsion to stockpile the means to fight back. Her grandparents on both sides could still remember the loved ones who'd died, driving back the Deng. She'd seen their photos, as a child, and the grave markers, too, having gone with her mother every year, as a child, to lay flowers in remembrance.

The water had finally started to run hot. She wet two towels and handed one to President Lendan. He bathed Mrs. Ghamal's face and neck with gentle hands. Kafari blanched when she saw the blood and shredded cloth down the woman's back.

"We need to get this dress off, Mrs. Ghamal," Kafari said softly. "Easy, now . . ."

They eased the torn cloth down, then Kafari sponged away blood and dirt and splinters of wood and glass. Dinny brought a basin with more clean hot water, which helped immeasurably. As Kafari worked, wincing and biting her lip every time Mrs. Ghamal flinched, the older woman lifted her head.

"You look familiar, child," she said, frowning. "You any kin to Maarifa Soteris, by chance?"

Kafari nodded, having to swallow past the sudden constriction in her throat. She had no idea whether her grandparents—or the rest of her family—might still be alive. Kafari met the woman's dark, wounded eyes, said very softly, "She's my grandmother, ma'am."

"I thought I knew those eyes. And those gentle hands. Your grandmama helped deliver some of my boys." Tears welled up, sudden and brutal. "My boys . . . they killed my boys . . ."

She was dissolving into helpless, heart-wrenching grief. President Lendan put his arms around the distraught woman whose quick thinking and courage had saved all their lives and just held her while she sobbed.

When the worst of the crying died down, Dinny quavered, "I'm here, Mama."

She snatched him close and held onto him, still shaking

with grief. President Lendan glanced into Kafari's eyes, then nodded toward the woman's lacerated back. They finished rinsing off the blood and debris, then cleaned the wounds with antiseptic. Kafari used tweezers to remove more shards, then dusted the injuries with powdered antibiotics and bandaged everything with compresses that Abe Lendan helped her tape carefully in place. They eased the remains of the dress back over the bandages. Kafari glanced up and found the president's driver looking like he wanted to help. She asked him to bring a glass of water from the corner sink.

Kafari dug into the medical kit, then put a painkilling capsule on Mrs. Ghamal's tongue and held the glass to her lips, helping her swallow the medication. She blessed the foresight that had prompted Aisha Ghamal to include opiate-based medicines in her emergency pack. Only then did Kafari notice her own aching, stinging injuries, minor by comparison. A few bad scrapes and abrasions, one long, deep scratch down a thigh, bruises from shoulders to toes. All in all, luckier than she probably had any right to expect, given what they'd all just been through. *I will never, as long as I live*, she promised herself faithfully, daubing ointment on the worst of the scrapes, *wear shorts and a camp shirt to another war.*

Muffled weeping from across the room crept into her weary awareness. The president's staffer, Julie Alvison, had collapsed into a boneless puddle beside one wall. Her pretty face was swollen from weeping and the bruise that had spread across cheek and brow. The eye in between had swollen shut, a lurid shade of reddish purple. Kafari found another pain pill.

"Here, swallow this. It'll help."

The young woman gulped it down, then sat shivering against the cupboards. Kafari was cold, too, with a deeper chill than the cellar's damp. She'd have to do something about that, but there was a more pressing concern on her mind, first. She found a corner to call her own and settled down to study the guns, not just the four she'd carried down, but all of them. They felt good in her hands. Her father had taught her how to use firearms, the moment she'd been old enough to handle them. Those lessons had not been forgotten, not even during the intense years on Vishnu.

Crouched on a stone floor that shook under the soles of her shoes, Kafari found herself opening the actions to check magazines and chambers, pulling ammo boxes down, matching up calibers and loading with hands that held remarkably steady. Her hands seemed detached, somehow, from the rest of her. She loaded the long guns first. The heavier rifles had more punch than the pistols, while the shotguns would provide a better chance of hitting something, if she—or someone else—had to shoot with an unsteady grip. When she finished loading everything, she tucked one handgun into the front of her khaki shorts, making sure the safety was engaged, then found President Lendan's gaze on her.

"You seem to be pretty comfortable around those." He nodded toward their little arsenal. "Were you planning to follow your uncle into a military career?"

She shook her head. "No. I was studying psychotronic programming and calibration. My father made sure I knew how to handle guns. We still get *gollon* down from the Damisi highlands, even the occasional *jaglitch*. Especially when the mares have just foaled and the cattle have dropped their calves. A full-grown *jaglitch* can eat five, six calves in half a dozen bites, but you can take 'em out with a shot through the eye. A *jaglitch* has big eyes. Big enough, anyway." She was babbling and knew it, tried to steady her thoughts down, focused on the most important issue. "I can shoot well enough to take down a Deng infantryman, even a hundred meters out."

"Ms. Camar, you have no idea how glad I am to hear that."

He was shivering.

Granted, it was pretty cold down here . . .

Kafari frowned and started hunting through cupboards and storage boxes, not wanting to intrude on Mrs. Ghamal and her son just to ask. She finally found something that would do: a deep plastic bin that held camping equipment, including four wafer-thin survival blankets. She draped one around the trembling energy advisor, gave the second to Hank, who'd hunkered down in one corner, wrapped another around mother and son, and handed the fourth to Abe Lendan, who wasn't injured, but was the most important person in the room. The president smiled through a whole new batch of worry lines.

"You seem to be one short, Ms. Camar, and you're hardly dressed for this temperature. Mind sharing?"

She smiled with genuine relief. "Love to, actually."

Kafari carried the guns over, for fast access, then crawled under the blanket and sighed at the sudden, comforting warmth. Ori Charmak, apparently immune to mere mortal discomforts, remained on his feet, one hand on his pistol at all times. He kept the other hand pressed to his ear.

"Reception down here is impossible," he muttered at length. "Can't hear a damned thing."

Kafari couldn't hear anything, either, but she could feel something. Solid rock trembled underfoot, with disjointed concussions as something heavy moved ponderously past the house, a whole procession, in fact, judging by the tremors. Plascrete vibrated overhead and jars rattled slightly on the shelves. She had almost stopped shivering when the whole cellar, and the bedrock under it, rocked violently.

Julie Alvison screamed. Something big—*really* big—hit the house above them. Then an awesome noise drowned out the staffer's thin, sharp voice, a noise like the whole Damisi Mountain range falling down. Dust shook loose from the cellar door overhead. The plascrete ceiling actually warped, bowed downward by an immense weight.

We've been stepped on! Kafari clutched at the rifles, which gave a probably illusory comfort that she could *do* something, maybe even protect them. Another violent concussion jarred through the cellar. *There's a Yavac up there, walking through the house. Must be one of those Heavy-class—*

A noise that dwarfed all noise in the universe crashed down across them. Hellish blue light bled through the cracks around the trapdoor. President Lendan shoved her down, tried to cover her with his own body. He'd also covered both his ears—far too late. They would all be deaf for life, however many seconds they had left to live it. Ears bleeding, Kafari panted in wild, animal terror. More concussions, more explosions . . .

The sudden silence was a shock.

It took several seconds for realization to sink in.

We're alive. Oh, God, we're still alive. . . . Even the bodyguard was down, his lean face ashen. Kafari bit down on acid terror, forced herself to uncoil from a foetal ball, lifted her head to peer upward. Most of the metal bars across the ceiling were down, spilling hams and ropes of sausage onto the floor. But the plascrete ceiling, by some miracle of engineering, was still intact. The utterly inconsequential thought that flitted through her mind almost left Kafari laughing in hysterics: *Whoever the building contractor for that ceiling was, I want him to build my whole house* . . .

The president's mouth was moving, but she couldn't hear his voice, just a jumble of sounds that made no sense. Even so, she could have hugged him for joy. She wasn't totally deaf, after all. She finally made sense of what he was shouting.

"Are you okay?"

She nodded. "You?" She could barely hear herself.

He nodded in return. Ori was pulling himself together, out in the middle of the floor. The driver had collapsed under the sink, which had pulled slightly away from the wall. Water was leaking from a cracked pipe. Most of the shelves were down, their brackets torn and twisted. Their contents had sprayed across the room like shrapnel. Glass lay everywhere. Cartridge boxes had spilled ammunition in a wild jumble, calibers mixed up ten ways from Sunday. Julie Alvison, trapped under a section of collapsed shelving, wasn't moving. Mrs. Ghamal and her son were under the stairs, which had, astonishingly, held together.

At second glance, maybe not so astonishingly. The whole staircase looked like *kerbasi* wood, a native tree that gave virtually indestructible lumber, lightweight and tough. The Ghamals had been wise to seek shelter under it, lying pressed flat against the wall, Mom on top of the boy, protectively.

Kafari crawled gingerly through the wreckage of the shelves, pulled very cautiously at the toppled boards covering Julie Alvison. The driver stared at her, wild-eyed, useless. When the other end of the heavy shelf lifted, she found Abe Lendan struggling with it, grim and filthy but still on his feet, trying to help. Her eyes burned dangerously. *I am going to vote for this man every election for as long as humanity owns this ball of rock,* she vowed, ignoring new bruises and cuts and stinging abrasions that had begun to make themselves felt.

They dragged more shelving away, until Kafari got a better look at what was underneath. She was a farm girl, knew what death looked like. But the caved-in remains beneath those shelves, the blood in the long blond hair, the frozen, helpless terror . . . Kafari sat down in the glass and the spilled ammunition and started to cry. Silently. With a great tearing pain in her chest that might have been grief or fear or hatred—or maybe just a monstrous anger that this lovely, capable, intelligent being had been snuffed out far too soon, and Kafari hadn't been able to stop it.

Somebody had their arms around her. She wanted to apologize, wanted to hide, wanted Daddy to come and make the awfulness go away. It struck home for the first time that she truly might never see her father again, or anyone else she loved. Even if she survived, odds were frightfully high that very few people in the Canyon would get out alive. When the thought came whispering from the back of her brain, she knew it for what it was: desperate hope.

Maybe, that thought whispered, *maybe Mama and Gran went shopping in Madison, like they do, sometimes, when things get to looking scary. Maybe they drove to*

*town to lay in a few extra supplies for the tough times
coming. Maybe, oh, God, maybe they're safe, somewhere,
anywhere but here, in this Deng-spawned hellpit. . . .*

It wasn't much, but any hope at all was better than
thinking about what lay under those shelves, and imagining
her loved ones there, instead. When she finally opened
her eyes, Kafari realized who it was, holding her. Abe
Lendan. Even ten minutes previously, she might have
been embarrassed. All she felt, now, was grateful. More
grateful than she'd felt about anything, in a long time.
She sat up, scrubbed her face with both hands, tried
to smile.

Then she noticed the look in his eyes. No one had ever
looked at Kafari that way. Like she was nine feet tall. Like
she was made of flintsteel and fragile glass. Like she was
someone he'd take a bullet for, and be glad for it. That
look scared her to death, made her shiver, gave her the
courage to pick herself up and face the nightmare, again.
She watched him as his hands began to shake, violently.
She swallowed hard as he bit down on it and held it inside,
then shivered again when he spoke in a voice full of rust
and exhaustion.

"What do we do next?"

Kafari tilted her face upward, studying the ceiling,
and wondered how stable it was. Then she wondered if
the cellar door could even be opened, again. The frame
looked bent and the door had buckled, slightly. *Great.
We've been stepped on and blown up and now we're
trapped?* Of course, she wasn't real anxious to crawl out of
this bolt-hole, just yet. There were still constant tremors
underfoot, from the Yavacs walking down the canyon.

Moving carefully, not wanting to sprawl into the jagged glass all over the floor, Kafari waded through the
mess until she reached the stairs. She peered up at the
buckled door, trying to see just how bad the damage
really was. Both her ears were ringing, but she actually heard the sound of someone moving debris aside.
She glanced around to see President Lendan using an
ordinary broom to sweep up the worst of the spillage.

The sight was so incongruous, a smile tried to rearrange her stiff, tear-swollen face and its crop of ragged scrapes and bruises.

"We may be down here a while," he said, almost diffidently. "We can't sleep in broken glass."

Her eyes widened. "You're planning to *sleep*?" Kafari wasn't sure she'd ever feel safe enough to sleep, again.

He grimaced. "My dear, we are now soldiers—and the first thing a soldier learns, I'm told, is the value of sleep. Any time and any place he or she can get it. Somewhere up there," he nodded toward the bowed ceiling, "we've got a Bolo fighting on our side. That gives us—all of Jefferson—a fighting chance to survive. And that means I *have* to take the long view. I can't afford to collapse later from lack of sleep now. And neither," he added gently, "can you."

She didn't understand, at first, what he meant, stood frowning at the quiet man with a broom in his hands, talking about the future of an entire world. Then her eyes widened and she got scared all over again. *He expects me to keep him alive. Why me? His personal bodyguard is right there, trained and on his feet, again, ready to die—*

Oh.

She gulped. The bodyguard was trained to die for this man, but Abe Lendan expected Kafari—out of everyone in this cellar—to *live*. To survive. And he'd pinned his own hopes of survival squarely on her.

"If there's something else I should do first," the president added, "just tell me what."

She thought about it, started to speak, then shook her head. "I think you're right. Clear off the floor, so if we get knocked down again, we won't fall into a bunch of broken glass. We ought to try stopping that water leak, if we can," she nodded toward the sink. "And somebody should sort out that scattered ammunition. We may need to reload in a hurry and everything's so jumbled up, there's no way to know which cartridges go with which guns."

"I can do that," Dinny Ghamal offered.

Kafari turned to find mother and son on their feet, ready to pitch in. There was no need to ask if he knew how to sort by cartridge size, by whether the case was necked and how much, by the type of bullet seated in the case, by the headstamp on the base of the cartridge, and whether it was rimmed or rimless. Or even caseless, for some of the rounds that didn't require a case at all. He *knew*. So had she, at his age. She gave the boy a weary smile.

"That would really help, Dinny. Thanks."

He got busy. Aisha Ghamal met Kafari's eyes, nodded to herself, then started rummaging for tools with which to tackle their leaking water supply. Unable to determine whether or not the trapdoor could be opened, just by peering at it, Kafari started pulling down the few shelves still standing. She didn't want anyone else caught under their falling weight. Once they were down, she began sorting the mess. Food went into one pile, tools and equipment they weren't likely to need in another, and anything that looked remotely useful—can openers, camping gear, emergency candles and flashlights—into a third.

They were very lucky in more than one sense: not only was their shelter intact, the power was still on. Part of the house was obviously still standing, Yavac feet notwithstanding, and the power lines were still up between here and the plant at the dam. It made her realize the Deng must be planning to occupy not only the canyon, but the buildings, too, a markedly unpleasant thought. The candles and flashlights made her feel better, however. As horrible as it had been, before, with Yavacs on top of them, shooting at what had probably been Jefferson's air force, it would have been far more terrifying in the dark.

The unbroken ammo containers made her feel better, too. Those she sorted by caliber, putting each sorted-out stash next to the guns they could be used with, for fast reloading if things got interesting, again. She caught the bodyguard nodding his approval, then Ori helped her finish the job, although he kept one eye—and probably both ears—on the cellar door and President Lendan's location relative to it. It was something she would never have noticed, before, and realized grimly that her whole life would be broken into "before Deng" and "after Deng." At least it was starting to look like there might *be* an "after Deng" portion of her life.

Another thing that helped was remembering the lightning speed of the Bolo's guns. She'd had only the one, brief glimpse of it, engaged in wargames against the air force, but that glimpse had made a deep impression. It also helped to recall the Bolo's commander. There was something about him that inspired confidence, although she wasn't quite sure what, exactly, it was.

Maybe his eyes, which had looked this kind of hell in the face, before, and had lived to tell about it. It was comforting to know that a human *could* survive this kind of hell, although admittedly he'd done so inside thirteen thousand tons of flintsteel with a traveling nuclear arsenal on board. She hadn't understood Simon Khrustinov's bottomless, shadowed eyes, before, but she did, now. And she understood, as well, that those eyes—and the man behind them—were far braver than the brave red uniform he wore.

I want to tell him that, she realized as she worked, *and I want to tell him how grateful I am that he was willing to come here. To risk that kind of horror again, for us. People he didn't even know, yet.* It was important—to her, anyway—that someone tell him. She was trying to think of ways to say it when a rumble like distant thunder—only much louder—shook through the basement. She spun around. More concussions shook the bedrock underfoot, from the direction of Maze Gap. Aisha Ghamal glanced into Kafari's eyes for one short, grim moment, exchanging a whole conversation's worth of worry, fear, and determination in that single look. The president's driver moaned aloud and tried to crawl under the sink Aisha was still trying to fix.

"The sound isn't the same," Dinny said suddenly.

"You're right," President Lendan agreed. "It isn't."

Rather than individual explosions—Kafari couldn't imagine what else could make that much noise and shake that much solid bedrock—they were hearing a blurred, unending sound that created one long, hideous tremor. It made the bottoms of her feet feel ticklish and uneasy.

"Dinny," she asked abruptly, "how much of that scattered ammunition have you separated out?"

He gulped and stared down at half-a-dozen piles of cartridges carefully sorted from the surrounding chaos. "Maybe a third of it."

"We'd better move those piles. Put them over there, where the guns are. If it comes down to shooting," she nodded toward the firearms laid out beside the stairs, "I don't want our ammunition in the middle of an open floor."

She started moving the guns back into the corner under the stairs, which was the most sheltered spot in the cellar, while Dinny scooped up double handfuls of loose cartridges, setting them down beside the correct firearms. Her gut muscles clenched painfully as the explosions moved closer. Abe Lendan listened for a moment longer, then abandoned his sweeping to help. The tiny hairs at the back of Kafari's neck were standing on end. She had to fight down a trickle of panic deep inside.

They were nearly done when Kafari heard it. A new sound. A nerve-shattering, high-pitched chittering sound that filtered down through the cracks around the cellar door. The chittering got louder. *Much* louder. Kafari stood frozen under the stairs. Abe Lendan, who'd just scooped up another load of ammunition, crouched like a terrified gargoyle out in the middle of the cellar floor. The explosions were loud enough, now, to shake dust off the toppled shelves. That dreadful, chittering roar was nearly on top of them.

Ori moved so suddenly, it shocked Kafari. He snatched the president up by his belt and shirt collar, lifting him completely off the floor, and literally *threw* him into the "safe" corner, under the stairs. Abe Lendan sprawled past Kafari, arms and legs akimbo. He landed in a heap against the wall, swearing in rough, pain-riddled tones. Ori had drawn his sidearm and crouched at the ready beside the lowest step, weapon pointed directly at the cellar door. Kafari decided that was a genuinely fine idea and lunged for the loaded guns. She snatched up a rifle and rolled into position under the stairs, putting herself between the president and whatever was making that ghastly sound.

She racked the action back and pointed the rifle upwards, aiming through the open backs of the steps, between boards. Her hands were sweating and shaking, which spoiled her aim. The ghastly chittering sound was right on top of them—

—then the whole cellar door blew out.

Chapter Six

I

"Jesus," *Simon mutters with reverent eloquence,* "we have to cross that goddamned river again. Whose screwed-up, asinine notion was it, to build the capital city on both sides of that river?"

I forbear mentioning that most cities in human space that have grown up beside a river tend to sprawl inconveniently on both banks. Simon knows this. He is simply venting battlefield adrenaline in a healthier way than growing ulcers with it.

My aerial drone relays enemy formations, painting a grim picture.

"Maze Gap is held by two Heavy-class Yavacs. Another Heavy has taken up position in front of Klameth Canyon Dam." *I flash schematics onto my forward screen, superimposed over a map of the Klameth Canyon complex, provided by General Hightower.* "A fourth Heavy class has blockaded Lambu Cut. Yavacs in both Medium and Scout classes are scattered through the canyon complex, destroying livestock and killing the human population."

Simon snarls under his breath.

"If I make a frontal assault against Maze Gap, across open ground, there is a high probability that I will be damaged severely, potentially beyond repair." *Before he can offer suggestions, my drone goes dead.* "Aerial drone has been destroyed."

"Other points of ingress?" *Simon asks.*

"Analyzing data. There is no other entry, other than by water, from the reservoir."

"Lovely. Head toward Maze Gap and search that data from General Hightower. We can put on our thinking caps while we're underway."

I increase speed and search my tactical databases, which were upgraded with new information during my post-Etaine refitting. I find a notation that a Mark XXI/I Special Unit made use of a deep river to conceal herself from Deng forces on Hobson's Mines. This is a very appealing idea. The Adero River flows very close to my objective. The Klameth River, which joins the Adero two kilometers west of Maze Gap, flows right through the territory I must wrest back from the Deng.

I am not, however, a Mark XXI/I Unit. The forward-reconnaissance Special Units are the smallest Bolos fielded since the original Mark I was sent into combat. The Klameth and Adero Rivers would have to be as large as old Terra's Mississippi to conceal my entire warhull. Since they are not, I am forced to scrap this possible solution as unworkable under current conditions. I see no alternatives to frontal assault against the Gap. I file VSR to my Commander, detailing my conclusions.

"I'm afraid you're right," *Simon agrees, voice grim.* "Hoof it, Lonesome."

The Adero floodplain offers ideal terrain for fast overland movement. I rev up to 115 kph, not quite my top speed, but close to it. I cross twenty kilometers in a blaze, jolting my Commander every millimeter of the way, in a long swing around Madison's suburbs. I cross the Adero River at Hakinar Bridge, leaving it in rubble behind my blurred treads. I race eastward, down the straight road that will lead past Nineveh Base, nine kilometers from the edge of Madison's easternmost suburbs. Nineveh is within visual scan range when Simon leans abruptly forward in his harness, intent on the view through my prow-mounted visual sensors. He uses touchpad controls to zoom in for a closer look. I analyze the scene, attempting to understand what has caught my Commander's interest.

The ground surrounding Nineveh Base is badly pock-marked with deep craters, which have taken out most of the main road to a depth of six meters. Burning debris lies scattered in a wide swath of destruction. Mobile artillery pieces are lined up for deployment to Maze Gap, but cannot be jockeyed past the deep holes. Ground crews are working to bring down enough of the perimeter fence to roll the mobile 10cm Hellbores and artillery siege guns through. I can assist with this effort when I reach the base, simply by driving over the fence, but I do not think this is what caught my Commander's attention.

Simon is staring intently at the Enemy ship and Yavacs I destroyed, with some assistance from the Jeffersonian air force. There is very little left of the Scout, but the troop ship with its load of fighting vehicles lies across the road like an immense, bloated slug. Beside it is the body of the only Yavac-A/4 Heavy that off-loaded, which walked straight into my guns. The Yavac's turret still lies in the heart of Nineveh Base, lodged in the wall of what had been the main motorpool, judging from the smoking wreckage of vehicles inside the still-burning structure.

The smouldering hulk of the Yavac's main body, which is broader than my warhull and nearly as tall, is not quite spherical. It has a slightly cylindrical shape, viewed across the beam. The central portion is virtually round, with stubby, tapering cones to either side, providing attachment points for the complex leg joints. The legs sprawl haphazardly, some still attached, some scattered. Most are missing one or more jointed segments.

Simon's voice comes nearly as a whisper. "Sonny, boy, can you push that Yavac down the road?"

I scan, taking measurements of the Yavac's external dimensions, calculating mass and probable weight based on metallurgy scans, and compare the results with my own capacity to apply foot-pounds of force to objects. "Yes, I can push this Yavac—"

Simon Khrustinov's brilliance breaks across me like a sun going nova.

I can push the Yavac!

Simon's sudden laughter, knife-edged, triumphant, fills my entire personality gestalt center with euphoria. Nowhere in human space is there another commander such as this, and I have known many during the century of my service. I am more fortunate than I can grasp, to have such a commander as my own.

"Lonesome, you wicked son-of-a-gun," Simon grins, "let's give that damned piece of junk back to the Deng."

"With pleasure!"

I ease up to the Yavac, using short bursts from my forward infinite repeaters to slice off the remaining legs jutting out from the main body. By nudging gently with my prow, I roll the behemoth like a lumberjack rolling a log, neatly stripping the thing of all protrusions: leg joints, guns, sensor arrays, access ladders, anything and everything that might impede its forward motion once I build up speed, pushing it. I nudge the thing around the hulk of the troop transport, which is too large for me to move without discharging my Hellbores into it, which would be a waste of battlefield resources I will doubtless need. I still face what is likely to be the heaviest combat I will encounter on this mission. It will be expensive—very expensive—to win back Klameth Canyon and its ancillary gorges. The Deng will make sure of that. It is my task to make sure the price the Deng pay in giving it up is even higher.

My Commander sends a short, coded burst to the commander of Nineveh Base.

"Put your mobile artillery behind Sonny's warhull. We'll act as a shield until we've cleared those Heavies out of Maze Gap. Once we've taken out their main guns at the Gap, you can scatter into the other canyons, wipe up their infantry and take out the Scout-class machines they've fielded."

"Understood, Major," *came the reply.* "We're set to roll."

The hole in the fence is large enough, now, to accommodate the bulk of the big artillery guns, towed behind heavy cross-country engines, as well as the mobile Hellbores, which are mounted in tracked vehicles capable of tackling extremely rough terrain.

"Let's get this parade underway, Lonesome."

I engage drive engines, pushing the Yavac ahead of my warhull. The pace is slow at first, but the highway is straight and the Adero floodplain is marvelously flat, which allows me to build up speed. I cannot achieve maximum running speed, since I am pushing an object that is only slightly smaller than myself, and only marginally less dense. I am pleased to achieve—and maintain—a cruising speed of 70 kph, which grinds the rolling surface of the Yavac smooth, like a jeweler's wheel, lowering friction and allowing greater speed. We come roaring down the final approach to Maze Gap, forming a juggernaut that can be avoided by jumping to one side, but not easily stopped. Not from dead ahead, at any rate.

The Yavac Heavies holding the Gap take notice and begin firing. The hull steamrolling its way ahead of me takes massive abuse from plasma lances and the Yavacs' heaviest guns. The metal heats up and begins to glow, with puddles melting and flying off like droplets of wax shed by a falling candle. The Yavacs cannot reach me with direct fire, not with the dead Yavac's hull between my prow and their guns.

Simon grins fiercely. "They'd be gnashing their teeth, Sonny, if the hairy little brutes had any."

I am only passingly familiar with Deng dentition, since it is more important that I render them incapable of eating than it is to worry about what they eat and how they eat it. I leave such items to the special-ops branch that handles biological warfare.

I concentrate on what I do best and rush toward the enemy at the gate, swatting down high-angle mortars launched at me in a wild effort to reach my turret from above. I launch mortars of my own, biding my time for the right moment to strike a crippling blow. The mobile artillery from Nineveh Base streams out behind me, unable to keep pace with my 70 kph sprint. It is not necessary that they match my speed, since the Yavacs that would normally do them the worst harm will no longer be a factor in the attack equation by the time they reach the Gap.

In a moment of sheer, delighted whimsey, I access cultural databanks and select an appropriate aria. Wagner roars out across the Adero floodplain, from external speakers turned up to maximum gain. "The Ride of the Valkyries" flies on the wind before us and whips back across my fenders to urge the artillery crews on toward armageddon. I do not know if the Deng appreciate the psychological boost such music instills in the human heart, but a century of service has proven its value to me. My communications arrays pick up broadcasts from the trailing gun crews, transmissions filled with war whoops and soldiers yelling their way toward glory.

The rose sandstone shoulders of Maze Gap loom dead ahead. The Yavac hull I push is turning to slag, melting ahead of my churning treads. I enter the Gap, running that semimolten hull down the throats of the defending Yavacs. Then I pulse my forward Hellbore. My heavy shield disintegrates. Its sudden destruction gives me a beautifully clear field of fire, with no time for either Yavac to react to the abrupt change in battlefield conditions.

I fire both Hellbores, point-blank.

Both Yavac Heavies are caught in a maelstrom of brutal energy. For one hellish instant, they glow. I pound them with another salvo and rapidly follow it with a third. Both Heavies come apart at the seams, toppling to destruction under my treads. I burst through the Gap and swing hard left for a skidding turn into Klameth Canyon. What

*I see there fills every molecule of my psychotronic soul
with mindless fury.*

*Butchered humans lie everywhere. Simon swears in
hideous Russian and his eyes blaze with a fire to match
the rage in my flintsteel heart. The Deng must die. Must
pay for this barbaric slaughter. I snarl. I hate. I roar
down the canyon spitting death from every gun, blast-
ing Deng fighters out of the sky, incinerating ground
troops that have indulged in an orgy of murder against
the civilian populace of this canyon. I turn Scout-class
Yavacs into molten puddles. I blow Medium-class Yavacs
apart, sending bits and pieces flying hundreds of feet into
the air and bouncing them off the sandstone cliffs. I take
savage pleasure in destroying them.*

*It is the work I was created to do—and in this canyon,
I glory in the doing of it.*

*I can only hope that we have come in time to save at
least a few human lives.*

II

Smoke and noise rained down like hailstones. Kafari
cringed as brilliant beams of coherent light stabbed through
the murk—and everything else they touched. Ori started
shooting up the stairs at fast, flickering shadows. Weird
alien screams drifted down through the smoke. Then
three separate beams punched holes straight through
Ori, like pins through a cushion. They sliced across him,
jigsaw style, cutting hideous, cauterized gashes. An agonized scream burst free as he went down, still shooting.
Kafari, badly shaken, stood rooted in place, fighting the
acid nausea trying to tear loose from her gut.

Then dark shapes appeared on the stairs, moving down
toward them. Kafari gulped hard and started shooting,
right through the boards. Alien screams lifted through
the smoke. Dark bodies fell from the staircase. Somebody

else was shooting, too, from under the sink, from behind the toppled shelves. Kafari's rifle ran dry. She reached blindly down and somebody slapped another gun into her hands. She fired again and again, at anything and everything that moved anywhere near the staircase. Bullets ricocheted off the walls and the bowed, damaged ceiling. Energy weapons sizzled and cracked all around her, splashing off the floor. The Deng were shooting through the steps, too.

Then the world turned white. A blinding flash crisped blue around the edges, a breathless instant before the noise crashed across them. A massive wind scoured its way across the open cellar door. A backblast punched through the hole in the ceiling and slammed Kafari against the wall. Pain erupted like a volcano. She was still conscious, able to think and feel, and fleetingly wished she *couldn't*. Everything hurt, everywhere, nerves screaming at the abuse.

She reoriented herself gradually. The stench of burnt flesh, thick smoke, and the crisped-wood smell of a housefire left her groggy on the stone floor. She coughed, jarring bruises the whole length of her body. The afterglare of that last big salvo faded, leaving the battered basement to reappear, ghostlike, as her vision recovered. Hearing took longer, but the deep tremors still shaking the bedrock gradually resolved into the sound of massive explosions from somewhere nearby.

She finally turned her head, creaking in every joint, and peered at the damage. There were bodies *everywhere*. Ugly, nasty black ones, covered with hair and weapons and alien blood. The stairway resembled tattered lace, with more holes than chewed-up wood. One whole side sagged where energy weapons had bitten through the supports. More frightening was the state of the ceiling. It had fractured along the lines of stress where the first Yavac had stepped on the house. The whole back half of the ceiling had broken and now sagged dangerously, creaking and groaning as the plascrete settled lower. Dust rained down in ominous spatters as the ceiling dropped a fraction of an inch every couple of heartbeats.

"We have to get out," she shouted, trying to find the others.

President Lendan was still behind her, covered with dirt and sour sweat, bleeding down one arm.

"What?" he shouted back.

"We have to get out!" She pointed to the broken, settling slab of plascrete. "That won't hold much longer!"

He nodded, face grey with terror and pain.

Hank lay under the sink, as cold and silent as the stone walls. His body was riddled with nearly as many holes as the staircase. She steeled herself against the flood of grief and sick terror trying to break loose and filled her pockets with spare ammo. She picked up three rifles in a matching caliber, then gingerly tested the steps. Dinny Ghamal and his mother stood at the base of the stairs, waiting for her assessment. On her way up, Dinny handed her a big knife. As she moved cautiously, step by step, Kafari used it ruthlessly, stabbing any black and hairy thing that twitched or tried to move. Burnt hair and the stink of blood set her coughing again.

As she neared the top, Kafari felt the whole stairway creak and shudder. "Keep your weight on the inside," she called down to the others. "The outside supports are gone. You'd better come up one at a time or this whole thing is going to come down."

She reached the top and peered cautiously over the lip, into what should have been the kitchen. There was no house above her. It was gone, scoured away by that last, white-bright blast. It looked like somebody had used a sharp knife, slicing right across the ground. Even the topsoil was gone, leaving only the blistered bones of the bedrock.

How in hell did we survive that? And what in hell was that?

The view toward Maze Gap was a landscape littered with smoking wreckage. Yavacs—and pieces of Yavacs—sent black clouds billowing into the sky. The

Aminah Bridge was simply gone, as though it had never existed. The access ramps on either side of the Klameth River had melted. Wrecked cars and farm equipment had been partly melted, as well. Debris from farmhouses and other buildings lay scattered like straw. Far worse were the dead bodies. Deng infantry corpses she could look at fairly steadily, but the slaughtered livestock left her feeling sick and she couldn't bear to let her gaze linger on the human bodies lying crumpled in the fields or jammed into the broiled wreckage of cars and farm trucks.

She swung her gaze the other way and caught her breath.

The Bolo was literally the only thing she could see. Its guns moved so fast, she couldn't even follow the blur. Alien fighters appeared over the sandstone clifftops and exploded midflight, as fast as they popped into view. The Bolo was shooting at something on the ground, too. The thunder of its guns shook her bones. A hellish glow of light—blue, vivid red, streaks of yellow and actinic purple—blazed like balefires through the smoke. Its treads churned the fields to muck and tore the highway to shreds.

A lightweight Yavac darted for cover in Hulda Gorge and lost three of its legs before reaching safety. A blur of light the color of hell's underbelly lanced out from the Bolo. The Yavac blew apart. Debris scattered, some of it right toward Kafari. She ducked, only to hear Abe Lendan shout up a warning.

"The whole ceiling's coming down!"

She scrambled up, threw herself prone on the ground, and prayed—hard—that nobody up here noticed them. The president landed beside her, clutching two rifles. Aisha Ghamal and her son lunged clear of the collapsing cellar. The ground behind Kafari's toes was crumbling, sliding away and dropping sharply downward. She slithered forward on her belly, not wanting to go down with it.

Then she narrowed her eyes, trying to see through the murk, half blinded by criss-crossed, unnatural flares of light. The landmarks she knew were obscured, but she caught fleeting glimpses of the river, a bend in the high canyon walls, the lay of the crushed road. If she was right, Alligator Deep wasn't too far away. Unfortunately, there was a whole lot of death flying around loose, in that direction.

"We can't make Alligator Deep! Is there any closer shelter?" she shouted into Aisha's ear.

"Head for the cheese room!" She was pointing toward a long, low dairy barn that was—semi-miraculously—still standing. "There's a good-sized cellar under the barn, where we age the cheese."

Kafari nodded, then reached down deep for just a little more courage. Enough to stand up and run the hundred meters between her fragile self and shelter. Then she was on her feet and running. Her breath sobbed in her lungs. It was hard to breathe. The ground heaved and shook underfoot, jarred by the titans fighting to possess it. She had never felt so small and frail and vulnerable in her life.

Then she reached the barn, ducked around the corner, and skidded to a halt beside an ominously open door. She snatched Abe Lendan back before he could plunge through the open doorway. Signaling for silence, Kafari slid onto her belly, holding one rifle at the ready, finger on the trigger. She eased one eye around the corner, literally at ground level.

She saw legs.

Lots of them.

A few even ended in hooves. The hooves weren't on the ground, however. They were parallel to it, dangling obscenely and starting to stiffen as *rigor mortis* set in. The rest of the legs were spindly, hideous things with joints in the wrong places. It was too dark in there to see just how many Deng infantry had sheltered in the Ghamals' dairy barn. Even *one* would've been too many.

Got any bright ideas? she asked herself.

Then she spotted the answer. An unholy, evil grin twitched at her swollen lips. It was fiendish. Diabolical.

She could hardly wait to see the results. Kafari tugged at Aisha's arm, pointed to the row of white-painted boxes lined up no more than three meters from the barn wall, situated between the dairy barn and a whole orchard of Terran fruit trees.

Aisha Ghamal's eyes widened. Then a look of utter, malicious delight transformed pain and fear and grief into an expression that sent chills down Kafari's spine. Kafari set her guns down, needing both hands free. Aisha did the same. Dinny took charge of their arsenal, holding onto the shotgun he'd carried out of the collapsing cellar. Kafari motioned for Abe Lendan to stay where he was, then caught Aisha's gaze and nodded.

They dove past the open doorway and hit the ground running. Something shot at them through the doorway. Heat tickled Kafari's heels. Then Dinny's shotgun roared. Kafari reached the nearest stack of boxes.

"Top two layers!" Aisha shouted.

Kafari nodded, grabbed the corners, and lifted. Aisha snatched up the opposite side and they ran awkwardly, toward the barn. The boxes had started to buzz. Angry honeybees were zipping out of the violated hive. Kafari felt a sting on one hand, another on her arm, a third on her neck.

Then the doorway was right beside them. *"Now!"*

Both women heaved. The beehive sailed in through the open barn door. Kafari didn't wait to see what happened. She was running for the next-closest beehive. It took agonizing, eternal seconds to haul another beehive back and fling it into the barn. She lost count of the number of bees that had popped her bare skin, but the screams inside the barn told her the Deng were getting a far nastier welcome than she and Aisha had received.

Without warning, hairy black bodies started to stampede out of the bee-filled barn. Running aliens formed a black tide that poured out between Kafari and Aisha on one side and Dinny and Abe Lendan on the other. Lendan tossed rifles to Kafari and Aisha over the heads of the dog-sized, panic-stricken Deng. Kafari caught the guns midair, flipped one back to Aisha, and started shooting. Savage satisfaction blazed as she shot one after another, almost arcade-style, ten points for every ugly spodder that went down. Dinny's shotgun blew off skinny legs. Abe Lendan's finished them off with a load of buckshot through the resultant screaming and hairy central mass.

When a final mob of close-packed Deng emerged from the barn, pursued by a cloud of angry, swarming bees, Kafari shouted, "Inside, quick!" An outbound swarm meant there were no moving targets left to attack inside the barn. Aisha and Dinny led the way. They stumbled and crawled over dead cows and dying Deng troopers, some of them still twitching and howling under a mantle of dead honeybees. Aisha jerked open a door and flung herself down a stairway. Dinny followed. Kafari pushed Abe Lendan ahead of her and kept watch for trouble, shooting a Deng infantryman whose twitches looked like an attempt to use the energy weapon still clutched in one hideous appendange. Bits of Deng blew out under the cavitation caused by five high-speed rifle slugs passing through it, then it stopped moving altogether. Kafari bolted down the stairs, yanking the door shut behind her and scraping off a few determined bees crawling down her bare arms and legs.

Then she was safely down with the others, in a room half the size of the cellar that had just collapsed. Big rounds and blocks of cheese, ranging from deep gold to pale milk in hue, sat in cheese molds or stacked on shelves, in various stages of the aging process. The air smelled wonderful, particularly after the battlefield stink they'd just fought through.

Abe Lendan swept Kafari into a bear hug, shocking her speechless, then he hugged Aisha, too, and gasped out, "Brilliant! My God, that was *brilliant*! I would never have thought to use honeybees as a weapon!" His eyes were shining.

Kafari laughed, the sound rusty as last year's fencing wire. "The best Asali honey on Jefferson comes out of this canyon," she said with a tired grin. "And Asali bees take careful handling. They're temperamental little insects, bred to displace native pollinators. When I saw those hives, I knew we could drive the spodders out without having to shoot our way in."

Abe Lendan took her by the shoulders and just looked at her for a moment, then said very softly, "Kafari Camar, you just earned a battlefield commission as captain of the president's guard."

Kafari stared, struck dumb.

President Lendan turned to Dinny and shook the boy's hand. "Young man, that was some of the finest, level-headed shooting I have ever seen. You kept the Deng pinned down long enough to get those bees inside with 'em. I don't think *any* of us would've survived, if you hadn't started shooting when you did."

The boy gained two inches in stature, right before their eyes. Kafari's eyes misted. Aisha's overflowed, unashamedly.

"Son," she said in a choked voice, "I am proud to be your mama."

"And I am proud to've fought beside you," the president said quietly, meeting Aisha's wet-eyed gaze. "I'm just a politician, but folks like you are Jefferson's real strength. That's what makes this world worth fighting for." He glanced at Kafari, then. "Well, Captain, what's our next move?"

Kafari listened to the battle overhead for a moment. It was moving steadily away from them, deeper into the canyon. The Bolo was pushing the Deng back. She'd never heard anything more glorious.

"I think we'd better wait until that fighting gets a little farther away, then skedaddle into the hills. If that dam goes . . ." The others sobered at once, realizing the danger was far from past. "But right now, we need to catch our breath. Maybe this is a weird time for it," she added with a faint smile, "but that cheese sure smells good. God knows when we'll get another chance to eat anything and it's been a long time since my dinner last night, on that freighter."

She'd planned on eating a big breakfast in her mother's kitchen. She couldn't bear thinking about home, not after the multiple layers of horrible things she'd witnessed during the past hour.

Aisha was nodding. "Good idea. Can't nobody fight a war on an empty stomach. And we burned up a hard day's worth of energy, already." She hunted through the tools stored in a cabinet near the door and came up with a big carving knife, since Kafari's was covered with drying smears of Deng blood. "There's plenty to choose from. We got four kinds of cheddar, some nice Colby, several soft cheeses. A couple of those don't get made anywhere but right here, varieties we came up with, ourselves. They trade real well on Mali, where a cow'd need a pressure suit just to get herself milked twice a day."

The image set Kafari to wheezing in helpless laughter. Dinny grinned. Abe Lendan frowned slightly, trying to find the funny in it. "I'm sorry," Kafari gasped in apology, "but after you've milked a cow at four-thirty on a dead-of-winter morning, when the power's gone down on the auto-milking machines and the pails have frozen solid to the floor and the cows are really pissed about it, the idea of putting a cow in a space suit to milk her . . ." She broke up again, wiping tears.

Abe smiled. "Clearly, I need to remedy a serious lack in my education."

Aisha was pulling down big bricks of aged cheeses, some of them coated with a layer of wax. She pulled some of the smaller rounds, as well, similarly coated, and even scared up a box of crackers stored in a cupboard. "Product testing," she smiled through sweat and blood and bee-stings and grime. President Lendan grinned.

There was water, too, which they poured into empty cheese molds, as makeshift drinking cups. Kafari had never tasted anything as heavenly as Aisha Ghamal's cheese and crackers and tepid water. While she bolted down the food, she paid careful attention to the concussions of battle raging overhead. The sound continued to recede in the direction of the dam. She was just washing down the last couple of bites when the power went down. They were plunged into utter darkness.

"Everybody out," Kafari said grimly. "And let's hope to hell that was just the wires coming down, not the power plant. Or the dam."

They moved wordlessly in the dark, fumbling open the door, then snatched up weapons and as much food as they could carry strapped to their backs. Kafari led the way up the stairs, checked the barn cautiously, then poked her head through the barn door. She didn't see anything that looked like it might shoot at them.

"Okay, troops," she muttered. "Looks like this is it."

Kafari headed toward the canyon wall, knowing there would be at least a few steep, narrow footpaths they could climb. There were game trails, used mostly by wildlife native to the Damisi Mountains, paths that were the favorite haunts of *gollon* and *jaglitch*. At the moment, the danger of staying on the canyon floor far outweighed any risk from Jefferson's inimical wildlife. With any luck, all the noise would've driven every wild thing for kilometers around into dens and bolt-holes. Lips set in a thin, grim line, Kafari led the way up into the high country.

Chapter Seven

I

"Keep shooting, Sonny," Simon said tersely.

The final Yavac Scout between themselves and the entrance to the box canyon housing Klameth Canyon Dam had just blown apart under Sonny's guns, leaving them a clear field to hunt the sole-remaining Heavy class. "It's in there, listening. If it hears sudden silence, followed by our treads headed its way, it's going to blow that dam and take us out with it."

Sonny fired his guns steadily, aiming backwards, now, blowing the remains of every Yavac still in sight into smaller and smaller shards. He took carefully aimed shots forward, as well, hitting already-demolished barns, so the glare of their energy weapons would precede them, as it would have in actual engagements against a mobile enemy. The Bolo surprised him, taking the initiative to rebroadcast recordings of Deng transmissions, shouts for help, perhaps, or curses against the humans destroying them.

And all the while, he raced forward, gaining the

103

entrance to Dead-End Gorge, as locals called the box canyon, in less than sixty seconds.

A drone, launched ahead of them, poked its head around the corner, giving them a split-second view of the Yavac. It crouched like a bloated tick in front of a breathtaking fall of white concrete that splashed into the ground between towering rose-toned cliffs. Water poured down the spillway from the deep reservoir behind it. The power plant was intact, but the Yavac had destroyed the towers supporting the high-tension wires that powered the canyon's homes, farms, and packing plants. Judging by the temperature gradients registering on Sonny's sensors, the destruction had just been wrought within the past two or three minutes.

"Can you kill their main guns with indirect fire, from here?"

"Not with enough certainty to cripple it before it attacks the dam."

"Charge it, then. Fast."

They whipped around the corner at battle speed, rattling Simon's teeth in his jaw. Sonny's guns were already locked on, the targeting computers having taken their data from the probe overhead. The forward Hellbore snarled, rocking them on their treads. The Yavac's main gun blew apart, melted off at the turret. Infinite repeaters sliced off half its legs, sending it crashing awkwardly to its left side. It was firing back at them, wild shots that splashed off Sonny's screens. Then it launched a missile, almost point-blank, at the dam. Sonny's infinite repeaters slashed out, caught the casing scant centimeters short of the concrete wall. The warhead detonated in the air, rather than inside the concrete, as intended. A fireball scorched the dam, rising in a tongue of flame that turned the water pouring down the spillway to steam.

Then Sonny's Hellbore barked again and the Yavac's turret blew apart. Debris scattered, smashing into the base of the dam and the rose-colored cliff beyond. Simon winced, hoping to hell the pockmarks gouged into the concrete hadn't cracked it too deeply. A final savage snarl from Sonny's Hellbore and the Yavac was finished, melted to slag in the middle and smouldering on either side, legs and guns motionless except for the crackling of flames and the wavering heat of smoke rising from the ruins.

Sonny's guns, too, fell silent. Simon dragged down air, relaxed his death grip on the command consoles under his hands. "Sonny," he said hoarsely, "that was some hellacious fine shooting."

"Thank you, Simon," the Bolo said quietly. Sonny knew as well as he did just how close they'd cut it, swatting down that missile.

"Can you get a structural reading on that dam?"

"Scanning with ground-penetrating radar. I detect no deep structural cracks. The surface is pitted, but the structure is sound."

A deep sigh gusted loose. "Oh, thank God."

He glanced at the situation reports coming in from Jefferson's artillery crews and nodded to himself, satisfied that the last few Yavac Scouts scattered through this maze of gorges would be shot down within a few minutes. The battle was as good as over. All that remained, now, was picking up the shattered pieces and rebuilding. He thought of Etaine, of Renny's ghastly ashen face, thought of Kafari Camar and Abe Lendan, and wondered if he would ever see any of them again. And if he did, would any of them have the courage and the strength to start over? With warm spring sunlight and blessed silence pouring down across them, Simon couldn't imagine a better spot in which to try. Very quietly, Sonny turned his bulk around, grinding the Yavac into the ground under his treads, and left to hunt for survivors.

II

There was a trail, of sorts, faint enough it barely qualified and so obscured by rising smoke she lost it and had to backtrack a couple of times to regain it. The smoke gave only the illusion of concealment, however. Kafari knew that much about high-tech warfare. Their body heat would glow like a neon beacon and motion sensors would pick up every shudder of their lungs as they struggled up the cliff face. The climb was sheer agony. Kafari had done a lot of rough camping and hiking, but she'd never made such a murderous climb in her life.

Knowing the president's life depended on her decisions didn't add to her peace of mind, either. She could hear soft gasps and half-muttered curses as Abe Lendan struggled up the trail behind her, wincing at each rough handhold that scraped his fingers raw. Kafari's hands were bleeding. So were her knees and one cheek where she'd slipped down a near-vertical stretch. She'd slithered to a stop only when her feet hit Abe Lendan's shoulders and then, only because he dug in with feet and fingertips to halt her fall. She'd lain there for a moment, shaking and gasping, then struggled up, again. The weight of the guns slung across their backs only added to the misery, but Kafari wasn't about to leave them behind.

They'd gone maybe two hundred feet straight up when a cataclysmic roar shook them from the direction of Dead-End Gorge and the dam. Blue flame shot skyward, burning its way up out of the gorge and turning the smoke incandescent. Kafari plastered herself against the rockface, trying to sink down *into* it. She could hear Aisha's voice somewhere below her, praying out loud between the booming of Olympian guns and the cracking echoes that slammed from one cliff face to another. The sound, alone, crashing down against them, was like a giant fist against their flesh. Dinny was crying, in great sobs of terror. So was Kafari.

More explosions, more smoke and hellish light boiled up from Dead-End Gorge. Kafari couldn't tell if they were hearing only guns or if part of the noise was the dam breaking apart. If the dam went, were they high enough to avoid the flood? Kafari wasn't sure they could climb at all, not with the whole rockface shaking under their bellies.

The sudden silence was a shock.

Kafari froze, listening, hardly daring to hope. More silence, profound and alien. From far, far away, back in the distant gorges closer to Maze Gap, she could hear a pattering of gunfire, but it was sporadic, sounding like a child's popgun by comparison with the awesome explosions that had crushed them flat for so many terrifying minutes. Then a low rumble came from the entrance to Dead-End Gorge, vibrating the cliff under her bloodied fingertips. It didn't feel like the concussion tremors from individual legs of a Yavac walking down the canyon. This was a continuous rumble, diffused across a broader base.

The Bolo?

God, was it the Bolo, heading back toward them?

"Lookit that!" Dinny shouted, pointing toward the smoke pouring out of Dead-End Gorge.

Kafari stared. It was a huge, dark shape, ablaze with running lights, like a big freighter moving ponderously toward spacedock. Gun snouts bristled on every surface. It passed Alligator Deep, a mere hundred meters further along than they'd managed to run, then it checked, abruptly. The moment after that, it swung around, ponderously, and headed straight toward them. Kafari gulped.

"Uh, guys, I think it's seen us."

That's a good thing, isn't it?

They watched in awed silence as the immense machine lumbered through the brimstone ruins the battle had created. Fires blazed everywhere, occluded as the Bolo interposed its bulk between blazing houses and barns and the trail they clung to, ant-like. It pulled up directly alongside, treads grinding like logs in a sawmill. Its topmost turret rose more than a hundred feet higher than their heads. Heat poured from it, from its hull and its guns and some kind of energy screen around it. That screen cut off, abruptly, with a faint crackle and pop. Then the ponderous thing stopped, no more than a long step away, wreathed in heat and smoke and an aura of dark and dangerous power.

A hatch popped open, no more than three meters from Kafari's feet, in a flat part of the hull that she could easily have stepped onto, if she'd dared such a thing. An instant later, the Bolo's commander scrambled up, his brave crimson uniform stained with sweat, his dark hair ruffled by the breeze trying to dispel the smoke. Kafari stared at him, locked gazes with his, feeling battered and sweat-stained and ugly as a road-killed toad. A look of wonder had come across Simon Khrustinov's face, a wonderment that deepened when he saw who was climbing the cliff with her.

"Dear God," he whispered, glancing into Abe Lendan's eyes. "Mr. President, if you don't give this young lady a medal, I sure as hell will."

Kafari's eyes started to burn, with more than drifting smoke.

"Miss Camar, may I offer you and your friends a ride?"

The burning in her eyes started to drip messily down her face. He reached across, steadied her as she stepped onto the Bolo's warhull. The warmth of his hands on hers, the careful strength of his grip, holding her like fragile china, told her more than words ever could. His gaze touched something deep in her soul, something warm and alive that she had forgotten, during the past hour, that she still possessed.

"Careful," he whispered as her knees jellied. "Steady, now. Can you climb down the ladder, there, while I help the others across?"

She nodded. He helped her through the hatch, then turned to steady Abe Lendan and Dinny and Aisha Ghamal, by turns. She had to crawl slowly down the ladder, not only because her hands were slippery with blood, but because she'd begun to shake so violently, she could barely keep her feet. When she reached bottom, she found herself in a snug compartment, dominated by viewscreens and a huge, powered chair festooned with cushioned straps. There were five smaller couches, evidently for passengers, crammed into the small space, along with storage lockers and huge viewscreens that surrounded the command chair on three sides. She stumbled toward the nearest couch and sank down onto it, shaking.

Metallic clangs reached her as the others climbed down. Abe Lendan appeared first, drooping with exhaustion. Dinny followed him down, eyes wide as he stared, enraptured, at the Bolo's Command Compartment. Simon Khrustinov came next, bracing Aisha from beneath, so she wouldn't fall as she shuddered her way slowly down the ladder. Kafari slid hastily to the next couch, making room for the injured woman. The Bolo's commander eased Mrs. Ghamal onto the couch and got busy with medical equipment, which took her vitals and injected something automatically.

"The auto-doc will take very good care of you," he said quietly, "while we're underway. You should be feeling better shortly."

Aisha's expression had already relaxed as pain-killing medication spread visibly through her, allowing her to sag into near slumber within moments.

"You've all been exposed to radiation," he added, studying the auto-doc. "We'll start chelation immediately. Not to worry," he added with a gentle smile, "we've improved anti-radiation therapy, over the years. We'll cleanse your systems before any permanent damage occurs."

That was the best news Kafari had heard all day.

Simon Khrustinov was helping the others into couches, webbing them carefully in and swinging the auto-docs into place. When it was Kafari's turn, she surrendered gratefully to those gentle hands, sighing as a flood of medication hit her system.

"Are those bee-stings?" he asked, frowning slightly.

"They are, indeed," President Lendan answered for her, voice filled with rust and pride. "When a Yavac stepped on our shelter, we had to clear a whole mess of Deng infantry out of a barn. She threw a couple of beehives into it. She and Aisha did, between them. What the bees didn't sting to death, we shot down as they ran out, chased by the swarm."

Simon Khrustinov's smile started in his eyes and spread to the rest of him, while a slow burn of something shivery and wonderful kindled in Kafari's middle. He said softly, "That has got to be the most creative way of killing Deng I have ever heard. Eh, Sonny?"

A metallic voice spoke from the air, causing Kafari to jump with shock. "Indeed, Simon. There is no mention of anything like it anywhere in my databases, which include several centuries' worth of stratagems for dealing with an entrenched enemy. I would like to have seen that," it added, sounding almost wistful.

Simon Khrustinov chuckled. "So would I. That one's going to go down in the legends of the Brigade, or I don't know my fellow officers."

"Welcome aboard," the metallic voice added. "It is an honor to carry you to safety."

"Thanks," she whispered, voice watery and small.

Simon Khrustinov finished adjusting the auto-docs, gave Dinny Ghamal a wink and a grin that lit the boy from inside, then strapped himself into the command chair.

"Okay, Sonny, let's see if Jefferson's artillery has finished mopping up, yet, or if we have a few more Deng to shoot down."

As the Bolo rumbled into motion, Kafari wanted—badly—to keep her eyes open, to watch the viewscreens and savor the way Simon Khrustinov's hair fell in sweaty waves over the back of his collar. But the medication had spread a deep and wonderful lassitude all through her limbs and the lifting of responsibility from her shoulders, responsibility for the president's safety and the future of her entire world, left her with drooping eyelids. She was still telling herself to stay awake when the world went blissfully dark and silent, drifting away. Kafari slipped into deep, exhausted slumber, unbroken even by nightmares.

Chapter Eight

I

Madison had changed.

Or maybe she had. Kafari shrugged her pack into a more comfortable position and adjusted the straps, then set out across campus. The library, with its all-important SWIFT transmitter, was nearly three kilometers from her little cubicle. She didn't mind the walk, most days, although the weather was sometimes unpleasant and she was often achingly tired.

"Don't worry about the fatigue," the doctor had told her, "it's just a byproduct of your body's effort to repair the damage. Take it slowly and be patient. It'll pass, soon enough, and you'll feel more like yourself, again."

Kafari wasn't sure, any longer, what "feeling like herself" actually felt like. She didn't know herself, any longer, didn't recognize the girl who lived inside her skin, these days. She peered into the mirror, sometimes, trying to find herself, and saw only a girl with eyes like flint who sometimes, for reasons Kafari didn't completely understand, made older, ostensibly stronger men shudder.

111

She had lost herself, somewhere, in the smoke and the shooting and the killing.

Compared to others, Kafari had lost very little. She was far luckier than most of her friends, lucky in so many ways it was hard to count them all. Her parents had survived. They'd gone, that morning, to Grandma and Grandpa Soteris' farm, tucked back into a corner of Seorsa Gorge. Chakula Ranch was gone, and two of her brothers with it, but everyone else in her immediate family had survived, including most of her aunts and uncles and cousins.

They had come to the hospital in Madison to cheer her up. They'd all come to Madison again, just three weeks later, when President Lendan bestowed Jefferson's highest honors on those who had fought and, in many cases, died. Kafari's Uncle Jasper, Commander of Jefferson's Ground Defense Forces, had been one of thousands of soldiers killed in battle, trying to defend the northwestern portion of Madison. He had earned a Presidential Gold Medallion, which Abraham Lendan presented posthumously to Aunt Rheta and her son, Kafari's cousin Geordi. Aunt Rheta cried the whole time. So did Kafari.

And then President Lendan had called *her* name, as well as Dinny and Aisha Ghamal's. Stunned, Kafari joined Aisha and her son at the steps leading to the podium, where President Lendan waited. Kafari and Aisha clasped hands as they climbed up.

"For courage under extreme fire," the president was saying while film crews and reporters trained their cameras on them and transmitted the images to the entire world, "for brilliant battlefield decisions that saved lives, including my own, and for the determination to keep fighting against incredible odds, it is my humble honor to award these Gold Presidential Medallions to Kafari Camar, to Aisha Ghamal, and to Dinny Ghamal. But for them, I would not be here today."

The applause from the Joint Chamber floor washed across them as Abraham Lendan slipped the ribbon holding the medallion around her neck. As he shook her hand, he murmured for her ears alone, "Well done, my courageous captain. Very well done, indeed."

She touched the medallion with numb fingers, watched Aisha and Dinny receive theirs, then watched Simon Khrustinov accept two medals, one for himself and one for the Bolo. Her fingers kept stroking the heavy medallion around her own neck, as though trying to convince themselves that it was really there. She hadn't expected this. Hadn't expected anything like it. Her eyes stung as she descended the steps and returned to her seat, engulfed by warm hugs and tearful congratulations from her entire family.

She didn't display the medallion at her tiny apartment. It was too precious to leave it there, where locks were flimsy enough that a child of two could break the door open just by leaning on it. She'd asked her father to store it in the family's lock-box, which they had recovered from the wreckage of their house. Her parents were gradually rebuilding Chakula Ranch and Kafari helped as much as she could. She'd felt so guilty over running off to Madison for classes, she'd almost cancelled her plans.

Her mother had taken one look at Kafari's face after reaching that decision and stepped in, fast. "You're not going to sell your dreams or your future short, my girl. You need that degree. And Jefferson needs psychotronic technicians and engineers. We're a long way from the Central Worlds, out here, and we don't have much to offer that would tempt high-tech specialists into relocating. Besides," she winked, "your husband may decide to foot the bill for the rest of your education."

"*Husband?*" Kafari echoed, voice squeaking in suprise. "Mother! I'm not even *dating*! Who is it, you had in mind for me to marry?" Kafari was running through a mental list of men her mother might consider suitable, weighing it against a list of men Kafari thought she could tolerate, at least. She realized with a slight flutter of panic that those two lists did not converge *anywhere*.

Her mother only smiled in that mysterious and maddening way she had and refused to say anything further

about it. Not that Kafari minded in the slightest. She was
so grateful to still have her mother alive, tears threatened
again. Kafari blinked and gently pushed those feelings
aside, paying attention, instead, to the path she followed
across campus.

Riverside University was a beautiful school, nearly a
century and a quarter old. Native sandstone caught the
late, westering sun in a glow like a faded echo of the
sunsets that blazed across Klameth Canyon's high cliffs.
The campus stretched two full kilometers along the south
bank of the Adero River, with promenades and pathways
and shade trees interspersed between lecture halls,
research labs, sports facilities, and dormitories. Riverside's
geographical setting provided beautiful views across the
river and plenty of inviting, picturesque places to gather
with friends or indulge a spot of romantic trysting.

Not that Kafari'd had much time for the latter. There
were plenty of boys who'd shown interest, but Kafari
wasn't particularly interested in them. Somehow, she
just couldn't work up much enthusiasm for some barely
post-pubescent kid whose sole interests were scoring on
a sports field or in some girl's bed. She had more in
common with the professors than with students her own
age and sometimes felt that even the professors didn't
really understand her. It was proving far harder than she'd
thought, fitting back into an ordinary world, again.

Mostly, Kafari was determined to finish her degree in
the shortest amount of time possible. She wanted to start
earning money to support her family, rather than costing
them money to support her. Thanks to the scholarship
from Vishnu and the assistance she'd received as part of
the new Educational Surety Loans—which helped students whose families and livelihoods had been adversely
affected by the war—Kafari's only real expenses were
room and board. She'd done a lot of searching, to find
the cheapest possible place in which to live, no easy feat
in war-scarred Madison, where the cost of housing had
nearly quadrupled. Food prices had soared six to ten
times their prewar averages, which made her job at a

dorm kitchen esstential, since the dorm fed her twice a day in lieu of cash wages.

As she walked, listening to the river and the wind in the trees and the snarl of traffic beyond the edge of campus, a nameless, uneasy feeling she had experienced all too often, of late, crept across her, like shadows of the advancing evening. She couldn't identify any particular threat, but the carrying sound of voices from little gatherings scattered here and there set her teeth on edge, somehow.

As she passed knots of students, she fell into a habit she had cultivated, recently, of studying everything and everyone around her with piercing intensity. It was more than the heightened awareness she'd brought out of combat. It was a search for something in the faces of the other students, something that would explain to her why her skin occasionally crawled when she found herself in close proximity to people she didn't know.

She was nearing the edge of campus when the voices drifting on the wind rose into a sound more strident than mere conversation. Her path had taken Kafari fairly close to a large gathering that was composed, if she were reading the shadowed figures accurately, of considerably more than just students. It was nearly dark, but street lights illuminated the area fairly well. She could see kids close to her own age, but there were older people in the crowd, as well, which had swelled to something between two and three hundred by the time Kafari arrived.

Some of the shadowy figures drifting through the group were common criminals, of a type that had always found a living at Madison's spaceport, where traffic was down to such a tiny trickle, there was virtually nobody to steal from, these days. Others in the crowd looked like seedy laborers thrown out of work, with too much time on their hands and not enough ambition to try something really back-breaking, like farming. Or terraforming land so it could be farmed. Or working long, bitterly hard shifts on the factory trawlers out harvesting the oceans for critically needed food and pharmaceuticals.

As Kafari passed the outer fringes of the crowd, she caught snatches of what was being said.

"—raised *our* taxes and *our* tuition! And why? To subsidize a bunch of pig farmers who think we owe them a free ride! Just because they lost a couple of barns and a few scrawny goats!"

The venom in that voice shocked Kafari. Almost as much as the words, themselves. *Nobody's asking for a free ride,* she thought, flushing with sudden, hot anger. *Doesn't this guy understand how the loans work?* The money Granger families were using to rebuild, to buy new equipment, to put crops into the ground again hadn't come from subsidies or gifts. The Joint Assembly had authorized emergency loans and the money had to be repaid, with some fairly strict forfeiture clauses if loan recipients defaulted. There was no guarantee that out-of-work Townies would even be able to buy produce and meat, come harvest time. If the government had to introduce subsistence payments on a wide scale, there was almost an ironclad guarantee they would also set price caps on produce, driving prices down and potentially bankrupting producers.

Yet here was a man, obviously a Townie, ranting about free handouts that didn't exist. He was standing on top of something, a park bench, maybe, from which he held forth on a subject that made no sense at all to Kafari. "The government is falling all over itself, trying to rebuild a bunch of smelly farms, but nobody gives a damn about *us*. It isn't fair! *Our* homes were burned down, *our* shops and factories were blown up, but is anybody scrambling to help *us* rebuild?"

An angry rumble from the crowd drew a deepening frown from Kafari. Didn't that guy pay any attention to the news? Didn't anybody else in that crowd? President Lendan had already asked the Senate and House of Law for a massive urban aid package, with at least twice the monetary value of the farm-aid legislation already passed. Klameth Canyon had been hit hard, but even Kafari understood that the damage had been piecemeal, compared with the ruthless, systematic destruction Deng Yavacs had waged through the northwestern side of Madison. Hundreds of homes and businesses had been destroyed. Most of the civilians had survived, huddled in deep shelters below the city, the kind of shelters unavailable to farm folk, but the economy would feel the impact of lost factories and retail shops for years to come.

The urban poor, swelled by newly unemployed laborers and their families, needed help desperately. But nobody was living in the sewers and nobody was starving. Not yet, anyway. That was why the rural bill had been pushed through first. It had been utterly critical to get a new crop in the ground and a farmer couldn't do that without money for seed and equipment. Didn't any of these people understand what it took to fill market baskets with produce and cuts of meat?

Kafari edged her way around the crowd, tired and hungry and abruptly chilled. Full darkness had descended and a heavy mist had begun to form along the river, where snowmelt from the high Damisi ranges tore past Madison's broad stretches of concrete and stone, warmed throughout the day by the sun. Radiant heat met cold water in a rapidly thickening fog that reminded Kafari of history lessons about old Terra, where places with exotic names like London and San Francisco were perpetually shrouded in thick blankets of mist penetrated only by something eerie and ominous-sounding called "gaslight" that never seemed effective at dispelling the darkness.

Kafari shivered as wet tendrils of grey reached out with cold, trailing fingertips and brushed her skin like something dead. She wanted, quite abruptly, to be somewhere warm and bright and cheerful, where she knew every face she was likely to meet and where she wouldn't hear ugly voices calling her pig-farmer and questioning her right to be here. She was tired and hungry and still had a wicked, long way to walk to reach her cubicle—

"Hey!" a rough voice said behind her. "You! Ain't I seen you someplace?"

Kafari glanced around, muscles tightening down in anticipation of trouble.

A big, hulking guy with a scraggly blond beard and fists like meathooks was glaring at her. Whoever he was, he was no student. He looked about forty years old and his clothes were sturdy, industrial-style garments like the ones factory workers generally wore. The men with him looked like more of the same. With a sinking feeling in the pit of her belly, Kafari tensed to fight or run.

"That's the *jomo* bitch from the news," one of the rough men growled, using a filthy pejorative Townies favored when referring to rural folk.

Blood stung Kafari's face, even as her belly turned to ice.

"Hey, *jomo,* you gonna save me?" one of the men smirked, rubbing his crotch vulgarly.

At one time, just a few weeks previously, Kafari would have counted on the sheer number of witnesses to deter something this ugly. But the people on the edges of this particular crowd, most of them middle-aged men whose faces blurred into a pale wall of hatred, looked more inclined to *help*.

Kafari threw pride to the wind and ran.

Her action caught them by surprise. A low roar of anger surged behind her. She was tired, murderously so, but she had long legs and a head start. The mob surged into motion behind her, individual voices snarling at her to stop.

Stop, hell. Do they think I'm stupid?

As she neared the edge of campus, the roar of traffic ahead blended with the roar of pursuit behind. Kafari dodged out into the street, playing tag with fast-moving groundcars. The scream of brakes and curses rose behind her as the mob surged into the street. She wasn't entirely sure where she was going. Her cubicle certainly wouldn't offer any real protection. Neither would any of the brightly lit restaurants that hugged the edge of campus, dependent on student money for their survival. A handful of waitresses and short-order cooks would be of no help whatsoever against a blood-crazed mob of unemployed factory workers. Kafari's strength was beginning to flag as physical exertion and the beginnings of hopelessness drained her burst of energy.

There wasn't a police officer or soldier in sight, naturally.

She staggered forward, tearing at the catches on her backpack so she wouldn't have to carry its weight any farther, and reached the corner where her street bisected the larger boulevard. Kafari was about to sling the backpack away when an aircar emerged from her street, skimming low. It halted literally right in front of her. The hatch popped open. Simon Khrustinov leaned across, holding out one hand. Kafari sobbed out something incoherent as she scrambled up, catching hold of a hand that lifted her with astonishing ease. She collapsed onto the passenger's seat. He yanked her across, feet sliding in through the open door, then shot the aircar skyward in a move that shoved her down against his knees.

The mob surged around the spot where she'd just been standing, snarling curses at them. Simon punched controls that slammed the hatch closed, then spoke tersely into the radio. "Major Khrustinov here. There's an unholy riot in progress at Meridian and Twelfth. You'd better get an armed riot control unit out here, stat. They're starting to loot stores," he added in a grim voice.

Kafari started to shake as reaction set in.

A warm hand came to rest on her hair. "Do you need a doctor?"

She shook her head, gulping down lungfuls of air.

"Thank God." Quiet, full of emotion she hadn't expected to hear.

He was helping her sit up, disentangling her fingers from their death grip on his shirt and the straps to her backpack, which lay awkwardly between his feet. "Easy," he murmured, turning her to sit in the passenger's seat. She was shaking so violently she couldn't even manage the safety straps. He fastened them gently around her, then produced a box of tissues from a console and pushed a wad of them into her hands. She tried to blot the tears dry, but couldn't seem to turn the faucet off.

"Th-they wanted to h-hurt me," she gulped.

"Why?"

"D-don't know. Called me a filthy *j-jomo* . . ."

He frowned. "A what?"

She tried to explain, got herself tangled up in the differences between Granger and Townie societies, finally managed to make him understand that the term was a crude insult derived from an African word for farmers. Anger turned his face to cut marble. "I see," he said quietly, voice dangerous. "Could you identify any of them?"

She shuddered. Face those animals again? Kafari was no coward, but the thought of a police station, formal charges, a trial with the press crawling all over her left her trembling violently again. "I'd rather not try."

A muscle jumped in his jaw. But all he said was, "All right. I'm going to take you someplace quiet and safe for a while."

He touched controls and the aircar moved sedately westward above the rooftops. Madison was beautiful at night, Kafari realized as her pulse slowed and the jagged breaths tearing through her calmed down to mere gulps. She blotted her eyes again, blew her nose inelegantly, managed to regain control of her fractured emotions.

"Where were you, just now?" she finally asked.

A tiny smile flickered into existence. "Parked outside your apartment."

She blinked in surprise, finally managed to ask, "Why?"

His glance flicked across to meet hers, even as a wry smile touched his mobile mouth, softening the anger. "Actually, I was planning on asking you a fairly important question."

Her eyes widened. "You were?" Then, apprehensively, "What?"

"Miss Camar, would you do me the honor of dining with me this evening?"

She surprised herself by smiling. "I'd *love* to." Then she realized with dismay what she must look like, covered with fear sweat, eyes red and streaming. She cleared her throat. "I'm not really dressed for it."

"Somehow, I don't think the chef will mind."

"The chef?" That sounded expensive.

"Well, the cook, anyway."

They were still heading west, leaving the outskirts of Madison behind.

"Uh, where's the restaurant?" she asked, craning around to peer back at the receding lights.

His lips tightened. "Actually, it's in the middle of that nastiness back there. I don't have any intention of keeping the reservation. I hope you don't mind a couple of steaks on the grill? I installed it yesterday, when they finished putting in the patio behind my quarters."

Kafari blurted out the first, idiotic thing that came to mind. "You can cook?"

Grimness vanished, dispelled by a boyish grin. "Well, yes. It was learn to cook or resign myself to years of eating prepackaged glop. Have you ever eaten what the Concordiat fondly refers to as field rations?"

She shook her head.

"Consider yourself fortunate." His eyes had begun to twinkle, seriously interfering with Kafari's ability to breathe. Simon Khrustinov had remarkable eyes, full of shadows and mysteries, yet clear as a summer sky and just as vividly blue. They caught the glow from the control panel lights like radiant stars. The darkness surrounding the aircar wrapped around them like velvet, a private and wonderfully safe darkness that carried her away from danger and fear and the uncertainty that had lain like shadows across her soul since the day of her return home from Vishnu. Somehow, it seemed very natural to find herself alone with this man, heading toward his kitchen for a meal he intended to prepare with his own hands.

And wonderful hands they were, too, she realized, gulping a little unsteadily as she studied them. They rested on the aircar's controls with quiet ease. Strong hands, large and manly, with a sprinkling of dark hair across them. Crisp shirt cuffs hid his wrists from view. His uniform was missing, tonight, replaced by civilian shirt and slacks of a subdued, conservative cut. His clothes were sturdy, made of high-quality fabric that had been loomed somewhere very far from Jefferson. Unless she were much mistaken, the shirt was real Terran silk, worth almost as much as her parents' entire farm. *Before* the Deng razed it.

It shook her, that he'd put on such clothes to ask *her* to dinner.

The lights of Nineveh Base appeared across the Adero floodplain. Kafari had never been onto the base, although her uncle Jasper had been stationed there for a while. Her throat tightened. She blinked burning saltwater, then leaned forward with a soft gasp as the aircar swung toward one edge of the base.

A huge, black shadow loomed against the lights. The Bolo. Parked quietly at the end of what looked like a very new street, next to a low building that had obviously been finished in just the last few days. There wasn't any landscaping at all, just a broad stretch of mud bisected by a concrete walkway that led from a wide landing pad to the front door. A much larger adjacent building, clearly designed to house the immense machine, stood open to the sky, only partially complete.

The aircar settled to the landing pad and rolled neatly to a halt beside the Bolo's treads, which dwarfed their transport so completely, Kafari felt like a midget. She couldn't even see the whole Bolo from this angle. Simon switched off controls, then popped the hatches, jogging around to assist her with antique, off-world courtesy that surprised her. The touch of his hand on hers sent a tingle straight up her arm. A tremor hit her knees. The smile that blazed in his eyes was incendiary. What it wrought on Kafari's jangled insides was probably illegal on some worlds.

He offered his arm in a gallant gesture she'd seen

only in movies. She laid an unsteady hand on the crook of his arm, smiling at her escort as he led the way past the Bolo's silent guns. She craned her neck to peer up at the turrets and weapons ports high above. It was hard to realize that she'd actually been inside it. Her memory went blurry, right about the time she'd sagged into that couch, with medication pumping into her system from the auto-doc. She had no memory at all of arriving at the hospital in Madison. She'd returned to consciousness to find her family surrounding her bed, waiting for her to open her eyes.

Simon Khrustinov followed her stare. "Sonny," he said, addressing the immense machine, "you remember Miss Camar?"

"Indeed I do, Simon. Good evening, Miss Camar. It is a pleasure to see you again. You look a great deal better."

She cleared her throat, awed by the sound of the Bolo's metallic voice and startled by its comments. "Good evening. Thank you. I *am* better."

"I am pleased the bee-stings healed without scars," the Bolo added. "I have studied the files posted on Jefferson's planetary datanet detailing the habits and temperament of Asali bees. An excellent choice of weapon, under the circumstances. It is fortunate the swarm attacked the Deng, rather than you and your companions."

Kafari stared, astonished. "Well," she managed after a moment, "they pretty much go after whatever's closest to the hive, especially if it's a moving target. Aisha and I were moving, but we weren't close to the hives when they broke open. The Deng were. And once those swarms got loose, the Deng were moving a whole lot faster than we were."

It took a moment for Kafari to realize what the rusty, metallic sound issuing from the speakers was. It was the Bolo's voice, chuckling. It sounded like a bucket full of rusted metal tossed down a steel stairway. She grinned, despite the prickle of gooseflesh. The Bolo had a sense of humor! Simon was grinning, too, openly delighted that she'd understood that gawdawful sound for what it was.

"Okay, Sonny, enough chit-chat for now," the officer said, smiling. "I promised to make dinner for Miss Camar." The smile vanished as a darker thought moved visibly behind his eyes. "Check the news from Madison, please. There's an ugly riot underway. I want to know when it's been contained and who to see about giving eyewitness testimony."

When Kafari stiffened, he glanced into her eyes and shook his head slightly, reassuring her. "Your name won't come into it. Mostly I want to know who the ringleaders were and what was behind it."

Kafari sighed. "I can tell you some of that. I stumbled into a big crowd. Two, maybe three hundred people. They were listening to a guy about my age. He was ranting about tuition hikes and government aid to rebuild farms, but not factories and shops. It didn't make much sense, not with the urban restoration package President Lendan's asked for, but the crowd was eating it up." She shivered. "Some of them were students, but there were a lot of factory workers, too. Laborers thrown out of work, men in their thirties and forties. Those were the ones chasing me."

"And using racist vulgarities," Simon added darkly. "Sonny, start paying attention to the chat boards on the datanet. I want to know a whole lot more about what's going on, here. We won the war. I'd just as soon we didn't lose the peace."

"Understood, Simon."

The Bolo fell ominously silent. Kafari shivered.

"Let's get you inside," Simon said at once, escorting her across the walkway to his front door. He palmed the lock open, then switched on lights in his private quarters. The room was heartlessly plain, new enough he hadn't had much time to decorate. The furniture was military issue, sturdy and functional, but not particularly fashionable. It didn't matter. It was quiet and unbelievably safe, probably the safest spot on Jefferson, guarded

by the Bolo's guns. She started to relax. Simon turned
on music, something strange and unfamiliar, hinting at
far-away worlds Kafari could only dimly imagine. It was
beautiful, soothing.

"Can I get you something to drink while I start cooking? I've laid in a supply of local stuff. Ales, wines, some
kind of tea that I can't figure out what it's made from,
but I like it. Tastes kind of . . . tangy-sweet, like fruit with
a kick. It's great over ice."

Kafari smiled. "Sounds like *felseh*. That would be
wonderful."

He poured two glasses from a pitcher in his refrigerator, then suggested she make herself comfortable in the
living room. "Don't be silly," she said, downing half the
glass in one thirsty gulp. "You do the steaks and I'll do
the veggies. What've you got?"

He rummaged, came up with several bags of frozen
stuff and even fresh corn flown in from the one of the
farms in the southern hemisphere. The southern harvests
were small, given the limited amount of recently terraformed acreage, but they provided fresh food for those
able to afford it. Kafari smiled. "How about corn and a
Klameth Canyon medley?"

Simon grinned. "Sounds fabulous, whatever it is. I'll
light the grill."

He vanished through a rear door while Kafari found
the disposal bin and shucked corn. She found pans,
switched on the range, got things started, and poured
more tea, downing it thirstily. She found ingredients for
biscuits and whipped up a batch, then popped them
into the oven. A bottle of red wine she discovered in
the pantry would go well with steak. She opened it to
breathe and set the table, which had been tucked into
one corner of the kitchen. Simon's quarters were small
enough to be comfortable and convenient, large enough
to avoid feeling cramped. The more she listened to his
music, the more she liked it.

He came in, sniffed appreciatively. "What's that wonderful smell?"

"Biscuits."

"I didn't have any."

She grinned. "You do now."

"Wow! You can *bake?* From scratch?"

She grinned. "Some farmer's daughter I'd be, if I couldn't."

"What else can you do? Besides kill Deng and rescue planetary heads of state and whip up a batch of biscuits?"

She blushed. "Not a lot, I guess. I can hunt and fish and I know every game trail through this stretch of the Damisi. I can sew, sort of. Nothing fancy, but I can fix damage involving torn seams and I can make play clothes. Simple stuff. I'm pretty good at psychotronic programming," she added. "Nothing as sophisticated as your Bolo, but I'm qualified to handle urban traffic-control systems, factory 'bots, mining equipment, high-tech ag engineering systems, that kind of thing."

"A lady with multiple talents." Simon smiled, rescuing the steaks from a drawer in the refrigerator and dumping a bottle of some kind of marinade over them. He was stabbing the meat with a fork to let the sauce soak deep. Kafari wondered what the marinade was, since the bottle was a reusable one designed for something homemade, not a store-bought brand.

"What about you?" she asked. "What else can you do, besides defend worlds, run a Bolo, rescue damsels in distress, and cook?"

"Hmm . . . I like to read history, but I'm not what you'd call a historian. I tried learning to paint, when I was a kid, but I didn't have much talent for it. Can't hold a tune to save my backside, but I like music." He grinned, suddenly and boyishly. "I can do a few Russian folk dances."

"*Really?*" Kafari was impressed. "All those knee-popping kicks and stuff?"

He chuckled. "Yep. Even those. Mind you, it takes a bit of limbering up, but it's fantastic exercise. Really gets the blood pumping. Do you dance?" he asked, tossing the marinade bottle into the sink and hunting up a long-handled spatula.

"A little," Kafari admitted, following him outside when he headed toward the grill. The night was lovely, the darkness intimate, the stars brilliant despite the lights from Nineveh Base. The steaks sizzled when Simon dropped them onto the grill. "I learned a couple of traditional African dances from Dad, and Grandma Soteris taught me some Greek dances when I was a kid. There are always big community dances and fairs, once the harvest is in. Not only in Klameth Canyon, but in most Granger communities. Tradition's important to us. Not just traditional ways of farming, but family traditions, too. Stories and dances, folk arts and handicrafts, languages and literature and music. Even a way of looking at things that's tied to relying on the land."

Simon set the long-handled spatula aside and gazed into the darkness for a few moments, lost in thoughts that left him looking inexpressibly lonely. "That's nice," he finally said. An emotion that Kafari eventually identified as yearning filled his voice as he added, "I've never belonged anywhere, that way. I study Russian history and listen to Russian music, so I'll have some kind of connection with my ancestors, but I don't have a family to share it with."

Kafari hesitated, then decided to ask, anyway. "What happened to them?"

"My parents and sister were killed in the Quern War. I didn't have any other family, nothing to tie me to any particular place. Pretty much the only thing I wanted was to go away and never come back. So I looked up the Concordiat's recruiter and applied for training as a Bolo commander. I was eighteen, then. That was a long time ago," he added softly, still staring into the velvety darkness beyond his patio.

"You never found anyone else?"

In the space of one heartbeat, his whole body turned to rigid steel. Kafari wanted to kick herself all the way back to Madison. Then a deep, slow-motion shudder went through him and his muscles softened again into human flesh. "Yes. I did. In a way."

"You lost them, though, didn't you? On Etaine?"

She thought for a long moment that he didn't intend to answer. Then he started to speak, voice hushed in the cool springtime darkness. "Her name was Renny . . ."

That he had loved her was obvious. That she had blamed him was incomprehensible. Kafari's brothers lay under deep-piled rubble, where part of the cliff had come down onto the house. There was very little doubt that the Bolo's guns had wrought much of the damage. Parts of a Yavac could be seen, jutting up through the jumbled piles of stone, very near what would have been the front porch.

But it didn't matter whether the Yavac's guns or the Bolo's had wrought the actual fatal blows. Terms like friendly fire and collateral damage were—to Kafari, anyway—meaningless. If the Deng had not invaded, her brothers would still be alive. The Deng had killed them, no matter who had fired the actual shots. When she tried to tell him that, Simon Khrustinov stared into her eyes for long moments.

Then he whispered, "You are a remarkable woman, Kafari Camar."

She shook her head. "No. I'm just a Jeffersonian."

The touch of his fingertips on her face, tracing the shape of nose and cheek and brow, left shivers coursing through her. "I'm beginning to think there's no such thing as 'just a Jeffersonian.'" He smiled, then. "I'd better turn those steaks before they're ruined."

That was just as well, since Kafari didn't think she'd have been able to say two coherent words together, in the wake of that brief but devastating touch. They were both silent for several long moments, Simon watching the steaks, Kafari watching Simon. The sizzle of dripping fat served as counterpoint to the softer rustle of wind in the meadow grasses surrounding Nineveh Base. The mouth-watering scent reminded Kafari that hours had passed since her hastily eaten lunch at the dorm kitchen.

The buzz of the oven timer sent Kafari scooting back into the kitchen to test the biscuits. Her critical eye and the golden brown color, plus years of experience in a farm kitchen, told Kafari they were done.

She snagged a bowl and slid the biscuits into it, using a small towel to cover them, and rummaged until she found butter. No cane syrup or honey, but they ought to be tasty enough. Simon carried in the steaks, Kafari fished out the corn and dumped the veggies into another bowl, then they sat down. Simon poured the wine, tasting it expertly before filling Kafari's glass.

"Ma'am, this looks and smells like some kind of wonderful."

She smiled and passed the butter. "How'd the bake turn out?"

He broke open one fluffy biscuit, smeared butter, and tasted. Then closed his eyes and let go a sound that was more groan than sigh. "Oh . . . my . . . God . . ."

Kafari grinned. "I think that's the biggest compliment I've ever heard a man give somebody's cooking."

Simon opened his eyes and said, "Miss Camar, what I do is called cooking. This," he waved the remains of his biscuit, "is artistry."

"Thank you, Major Khrustinov." She smiled. "Maybe we could graduate to first names? I feel like I'm in grammar school, again."

The smile started in his eyes and spread to the whole of his body. "You sure don't look like a school girl, Kafari."

At the moment, with those remarkable eyes touching places inside that she hadn't even known existed, Kafari didn't feel much like a school girl, either. She bent over her steak, concentrating on knife and fork to regain her composure. The first bite caused her to roll her eyes upwards. "Oh, wow . . ." She chewed appreciatively. "What *is* that sauce?"

He grinned. "It's a secret recipe. Something I threw together out of sheer necessity, trying to make military rations palatable."

"Huh. Bottle this stuff and sell it and your fortune's made. I'm not kidding. This is *wonderful.*"

They fell silent for several minutes, applying themselves to the meal. Simon's wine, a local vintage, was a perfect complement to the steak. Kafari hadn't eaten this well since her last visit home from Vishnu, more than a year previously. Beautiful music washed through her awareness, soothing and lovely. She was aware of Simon, as well, with every nerve ending, every pore of her skin. She wanted more of this. Quiet evenings spent with someone special, enjoying good conversation, good food jointly prepared.

And she wanted more—much more—of Simon. More of his smiles, his remarkable eyes peering into the depths of her soul, more of the reasons for the shadows in those eyes, more of the teasing and laughter, and more—she had to gulp at the mere thought—of those incredible hands touching her.

The strength of her wanting was new to Kafari's life, new and a little frightening. She hadn't ever wanted anyone like this, never in her life. It scared her, made her feel shivery and strange, made her wonder if these feelings had always lain dormant inside her, hidden away until the right man came along, or if the war had somehow triggered them, changing her at a core level she didn't want to probe too deeply.

Mostly, she wanted, hoped—prayed—that Simon would touch her again.

He produced ice cream for dessert, then they washed dishes in companionable silence. When the last plate and pan had been wiped down and put away and the last crumbs had been swept away from counter and tabletop, leaving the kitchen gleaming again, Simon refilled their wine glasses and they moved into the living room.

"Oh, that was good," Kafari sighed, settling into the sofa.

"Yes," he agreed softly, sitting beside her, "it was."

Somehow, she didn't think he was talking about the meal. After a moment's reflection, Kafari realized she hadn't been, either. She wasn't sure how to proceed from here, felt abruptly awkward and shy. The Bolo saved her from tongue-tied silence.

"Simon," it said, overriding the music, "the riot has been contained. Madison police have arrested one hundred fifty-three people. Residences and businesses have been damaged in an area encompassing ten city blocks. The alleged ringleader is a student by the name of Vittori Santorini. The rally he conducted was entirely lawful. He is not in custody and will not be charged, as he did not participate in the actual riot. I have scanned the datanet as directed. He maintains a site that advocates abolition of special aid to farmers and ranchers, stronger environmental-protection legislation, and cost-of-living subsidies for the urban poor. His chat board averages three hundred seventeen posts a day and his newsletter has ten thousand fifty-three subscribers, ninety-eight percent of whom have joined within the past three point two weeks."

Simon whistled softly. "That's a lot of activity in a very short time. This guy bears watching. Sonny, monitor his actions, please, until further notice. Discreetly, mind."

"Understood, Simon."

"Do you have any visuals of him?"

The viewscreen on the entertainment center crackled to life. Kafari recognized him at once. He was young, not more than twenty. His hair was dark, his skin pale as curdled milk. His eyes, a nearly transparent blue that might have looked glacial, in another face, had a fire-eaten look about them. Shudders crawled down Kafari's back.

Simon looked down into her eyes. "That's the guy you saw?"

Kafari nodded. "There's something . . . not quite right, about him. His rhetoric didn't make any logical sense, but those people were spellbound."

"Charismatic fanatics are always dangerous. All right, Sonny, I've seen enough for one night. Thanks."

"Of course, Simon." The viewscreen went dark.

Kafari shivered again. Simon hesitated, then slid an

arm around her shoulders. Kafari leaned against him, soaking up the warmth and basking in a feeling of safety that drove away the cold waves coursing through her. A moment later, warm lips touched her hair. She tilted her face up, drowned in the bottomless depths of those shadowed eyes. Then he was kissing her, gently at first, then with hard hunger. His hands moved across her, those beautiful hands, caressing, sliding around to cup and stroke, the heat of his fingers on her flesh setting her ablaze from within. Kafari whimpered, guiding his fingers to tweak one nipple. He fumbled with buttons and so did she.

There were scars under his shirt, old scars, jagged and white with age. He sat very still as she traced her fingertips across them, trailing the width of his chest and down one arm. For a long moment, Simon just looked at her, eyes smouldering, breaths unsteady and rushed. "My God," he whispered. "You are so beautiful it hurts . . ." He closed his eyes, clearly fighting for control. Eyes still closed, he said raggedly, "Not here. Not like this. You're too precious to just take you on a couch, like some rutting teenager with no control."

Kafari's eyes burned and her throat closed. Nobody had ever said anything half so beautiful to her, ever. She didn't think anyone ever could. "Why don't—" she whispered, then had to stop and swallow, hard. She tried again. "Why don't we move somewhere else, then?"

He opened his eyes, gazed into hers for a long time. "You're sure about that?" he finally asked, voice strained.

She nodded, not trusting hers.

The slow smile in his eyes would have dimmed the noonday sun. A moment later she was in his arms. He swung her up, off the couch, carried her into his bedroom, went to the bed with her. The feel of his body against her—and aeons later, inside her—was the most beautiful sensation she had ever felt. Tears came to her eyes as she arched against him, crying out softly and then more urgently. She wanted him, needed him, knew

that she would go on needing him for as long as they
both continued to breathe. In the shuddering aftermath,
he simply closed his arms around her and held on, like
a little boy seeking safety in a storm. She wrapped her
arms around him, cradled his head against her bosom,
and held him while he slept.

Kafari kissed his dark, sweat-dampened hair and knew
that whatever happened tomorrow, nothing in her life
would ever be the same, again. And this time, the difference between then and now was so wonderfully sweet,
she lay awake for a long, long time, just savoring it.

II

Simon was nervous. So nervous, he had to dry both
palms against his uniform trousers. It was, Kafari had
assured him, a *small* wedding—small, at least, by Granger
standards—but the crowd on Balthazar and Maarifa
Soteris' front lawn looked to Simon like an entire small
town had emptied itself for the occasion. *Just family,
huh?* he thought, staring at the sea of strangers who'd
come to witness their vows. He hadn't realized just how
big a family he was about to acquire.

Wind ruffled his hair and sighed through the treetops.
The sunlight poured down the high, rose-colored cliffs
like warmed honey, spilling joyously across green fields
and orchards heavy with fruit and half-grown calves
playing chase in the nearest pasture. Simon breathed in
the scent of flowers and living, growing things all around
him . . . then Kafari appeared and everything else faded
from his awareness. His throat and groin tightened, just
looking at her. The cream-colored dress she wore set her
skin aglow. Tiny wildflowers adorned her hair. A strand of
pearls, harvested from her family's own ponds, lay nestled
against her throat, their luster dim compared with the
brilliance of her eyes as she caught sight of him.

She moved slowly forward, one hand resting lightly on her father's arm. Simon swallowed hard. He still couldn't quite believe she'd said yes. The welcome her family had given him still astonished Simon. He was an outsider, totally unfamiliar with their customs, yet they had made him one of them from the very beginning, greeting him with such warmth, he knew that finally, after a lifetime of solitude, he had found a place to call home. These people would be his family, in a way unique in his whole life.

Kafari's mother watched through streaming eyes as her daughter moved slowly between the rows of chairs toward him. Iva Soteris Camar was a small woman, slender and shorter than her daughter, with the kind of face Helen of Troy must have possessed by the end of the Trojan War, the beauty that had launched a thousand ships tempered by the agonies of war. She had lost two sons, had lost cousins and other relatives, neighbors and close friends. The pain of those losses was etched into her face, but her chin was up and the joy of seeing her daughter wed shone in her eyes, alongside the grief that her family was not complete, to watch it with her.

Simon was a little in awe of Iva Camar.

As for Zak Camar . . . His was a face carved by wind and sunlight and adversity, but there were laugh lines, as well, and a solid strength that reminded Simon of trees whose gnarled trunks had seen five hundred years pass by since their roots had first dug into the ground. At their first meeting, Zak Camar had sized up Simon through hooded eyes, apparently possessing an instinctual radar that told him "this man's sleeping with your little girl—and if he doesn't measure up, he's gonna walk off this farm missing some body parts." Zak Camar's good opinion meant rather a lot to Simon, and not just because he wanted his body to remain intact.

Zak's dark eyes were suspiciously moist as he placed Kafari's hand in Simon's. Her fingers trembled, but her smile was radiant, hitting Simon like a blow to the gut. They turned to face the officiant, a tall, broad woman with dark eyes and a gentle smile. She spoke softly, but her voice carried a long way.

"We are here today to share the creation of a new family," she began, "a family that will forever be a part of the families from which it is descended. Some of those folks are here today and share this creation joyously. Some of them aren't, except in spirit and memory, folks who defended this land we stand on and folks who defended worlds so far away, we can't even see their stars, at night."

Simon's throat tightened savagely. He hadn't known she was going to say that.

Kafari's fingers tightened against his, causing his eyes to burn even as a wave of love rolled through him. The officiant paused, as though making sure he was all right before she continued, then nodded to herself and went on.

"All these families have different customs, different beliefs, different ways of worshiping, but they all share one thing in common. A belief that the joining of a man and woman is a sacred thing, to be done solemnly with proper ceremony, and joyously, with proper celebration. That's why we're here today, for the ceremony and the celebration as this man, Simon Khrustinov, and this woman, Kafari Camar, create a new family together." In a soft whisper, she asked, "You got the rings, son?"

Simon dug into the breast pocket of his uniform, produced the twin rings. He handed one to Kafari, held the other in unsteady fingertips.

"All right, son, repeat after me . . ."

Simon spoke the words in a hushed voice, to the woman who constituted Simon's whole universe in that moment. "I, Simon Khrustinov, do vow that I will love and guard you, provide for you and our children whether rich or poor, will care for you in sickness and health, will forsake all others and seek only you, so long as our lives endure."

Tears shone in Kafari's eyes as she, too, repeated the vow. Simon slipped the ring onto her finger, his voice almost a whisper. "Let all who see this ring know that you are now and forever my wife, Kafari Khrustinova."

"And let all who see this ring," Kafari murmured, slipping the matching band onto his finger, "know that you are now and forever my husband, Simon Khrustinov."

Simon lost himself in the warmth of her eyes, was jolted out of the reverie when the officiant chuckled and said, "You can kiss her whenever you like, son."

He groaned aloud and pulled her close, kissed her gently, was shocked by the roar from the watchers as Kafari's family applauded and whistled and tossed hats into the air and discharged what sounded like gunfire, but might have been only fireworks. Kafari broke loose just long enough to grin up at him. She winked. "You're well and truly caught, now, husband. There's no wriggling off *this* hook."

"Huh. You just *try* getting rid of this fish."

She kissed him again, then they turned and found Kafari's parents holding a broom decorated with fluttering ribbons and flowers, laid horizontally across the aisle between the chairs. They ran forward, hands joined, and Kafari's parents lowered the broom to the ground just as they reached it. They jumped the broomstick and ran a gauntlet of wildflowers and grain tossed at them from either side of the aisle. By the time they reached the end, they were laughing like children. The guests filed past in an endless parade, with hugs and handshakes and words of welcome. Simon lost count of them early on, knew it would take weeks just to memorize names and faces of the people who now constituted his relatives.

By the time the last guest had filed past, Simon's hand felt like it had been mauled, but he couldn't stop grinning. They followed Kafari's parents and grandparents into the side yard, where Grandma and Grandpa Soteris had set up tables full of food. Tubs full of ice cooled down bottles of everything from local beer and wine to fruity carbonated drinks and a couple of things Simon had never even heard of, but which tasted great. A grassy area big enough for Sonny's immense warhull had been marked off with fluttering ribbons. Music floated on the warm summer wind. Kafari led Simon out into the middle of the grassy dance floor and they began their wedding dance.

For the first verse, they danced alone. Then other couples joined them and pretty soon, the whole space was filled. After their first dance together, Zak Camar danced with Kafari and Simon danced with Iva, then the group dances began, complex circle dances and call-sets that Simon struggled through with much embarrassment and lots of good-natured laughter, since even the five-year-olds knew the steps better than he did. They finally broke away and gulped down mouthfuls of some of the best food Simon had tasted on any world. They fed one another while family members took photos and ran mini vid-cams, immortalizing their first meal together.

They danced some more, then went through the obligatory cake-cutting, champagne toast from a double cup, bouquet toss. Simon would have preferred—vastly—to spend the next week or so opening the mountain of wedding gifts piled onto six groaning tables. Unfortunately, Granger custom called for the bride and groom to open everything while everyone was there. It was considered an insult not to open a gift immediately.

So he and Kafari settled onto chairs and started opening packages, while Iva Camar jotted down descriptions of each gift alongside the names of those to be thanked. Simon had never heard the superstition that the number of ribbons broken while opening boxes presaged the number of children to be born into the new family. Naturally, no one told him until he had a pile of broken ribbons deep enough to cover both feet.

"You're kidding?" he said faintly when one of the aunts—he couldn't remember which—finally broke the news.

Laughter enfolded them, warm and full of sympathy.

Kafari just grinned. Notably, there wasn't a single broken ribbon in her pile. She winked as if to say, "I knew you'd break quite enough for the both of us, dear," and kept opening packages. By the time they'd finished, the afternoon was far enough advanced, it was time to begin the wedding supper. The hors d'oeuvres had been whisked away, replaced by steaming dishes that sent mouth-watering aromas wafting through the slanting afternoon sunlight. To his surprise, Simon was escorted to a set of tables reserved exclusively for the men of the family, while the women grouped around another cluster of tables, and the children occupied a third set, with strategically placed teenagers to supervise the toddlers and settle disputes amongst the little ones.

Simon found himself sitting beween Zak Camar and Balthazar Soteris. Some sort of blessing was spoken out by Balthazar, in a language that sounded to Simon like genuine Greek, then the dishes were passed around and they dug in with hearty appetites. At length, Balthazar broke the companionable silence.

"You'll be living in your quarters at Nineveh Base?"

Simon nodded, chewing and swallowing before he answered. "Yes. There's plenty of room. If necessary, I can build an extension to add new rooms."

"You can afford that?"

Simon glanced into the tough old man's eyes, trying to decide what question, precisely, he had asked. "If I have to, yes. My salary comes directly from the Brigade, not Jefferson's planetary coffers, for one thing. The government's obligated under treaty to provide me with suitable quarters, but if things look too grim to justify using Jefferson's public funds to expand my quarters—and just now, I'm afraid things don't look good at all—I certainly have the means to build a nursery or two, myself."

Balthazar and Zak exchanged a long glance that told Simon he'd succeeded in answering the right question, then Zak said, "From where we sit, things look mighty grim. If we don't get weather satellites up, at least, before harvest time, we could lose a lot of crops to bad weather. And the summer storm season's coming, which could spell trouble fast, if we can't properly track those storms."

Simon nodded, wondering how much to say, then

decided these folks ought to know at least some of the raw truth. "From a system-defense standpoint, if we don't replace the warning and defense platforms the Deng blew out of orbit, we could get caught with our shorts down, even worse this time. The Deng would be bad enough, coming through the Void again. God help us if the Melconians decide to come calling."

The men exchanged glances that said, "Yep, we figured as much," dark glances that appreciated the confirmation of their own take on the situation, even as those glances slid inevitably to the womenfolk and children at the other tables. Simon's glance rested on Kafari, radiant as she talked with her mother and aunts and cousins, and felt a chill touch his own heart. He was no stranger to that kind of fear, but for once in his life, he was in the midst of others who felt exactly the same thing, for exactly the same reasons—and for exactly the same people, as well. It was a kind of belonging new to him, a bittersweet feeling that lessened his loneliness while giving him even more people to worry about defending—and to hurt for, if things turned bad, again.

Zak Camar, whose eyes reflected the pain of losing two sons, broke the dark and ugly silence. "We got more to worry about than just the satellites and the weather. No sense hiding from a truth, just because it smells like a dead *jaglitch* rotting in the sun. Taxes are up, too high by a long shot, to pay for all the rebuilding. We have more than a million people out of work. And we've got more companies going belly up, every day. A business can't make payroll if it can't manufacture or obtain raw materials or sell what's sitting in its warehouses."

Balthazar Soteris added in a harsh voice, "And a worker laid off and scraping by on government subsistence can't afford what we'll have to charge for the crops in those fields, come the harvest." He nodded toward the Soteris fields, green and lovely beyond the supper tables and dance floor. "Not if we hope to have enough money to plant again next year and put more acreage into terraforming. The government's already depleted almost a quarter of the food reserves in the emergency system, reserves it took several years to build. We can't feed the whole population of this planet indefinitely on the reserves. We have to terraform more acreage, particularly in the southern hemisphere, where the growing season's timed to put fresh produce on the tables during winter up here."

Zak added quietly, "We're short on agricultural labor, too. If we don't start sending some of those unemployed factory workers into the fields . . ." He didn't finish. He didn't have to, since every man at this large table knew exactly what would happen if there weren't enough workers to plant and harvest. Mechanical harvesters were fine, if you had them, but the Deng had blown most of them to slag. Simon eyed the heavily laden tables and wondered how many folks would be tightening their belts this winter. He was abruptly very glad his bride was related to farmers. Unless the government was forced into the drastic move of confiscating private food stores for redistribution, at least his wife and their children wouldn't run the risk of severe rationing that the unemployed townsfolk could well face.

Simon knew enough about the history of Russia, back on Old Terra, to understand with brutal clarity—sharpened by his own long experience of war—just what could happen to a society in which there weren't enough people on hand to plant and harvest. Even at the vast remove of centuries and many, many light-years, the old stories handed down from generation to generation about needing prescriptions from physicians to obtain meat for children, or eating wallpaper paste to hold off starvation, had the power to clench Simon's gut muscles.

"If they get hungry enough," one of the younger men said, "they can always enlist in the Concordiat defense forces and help us meet our treaty obligations."

"Huh," Zak muttered. "Not likely. There's already a whole passel of folk grumbling about sending troops off-world to support the war effort."

Simon was only too aware of the situation. By treaty, a Concordiat-allied world was entitled to defense. It was also obligated, under reciprocity agreements, to provide troops and/or munitions and materiel if the Concordiat found itself embroiled in a war that threatened multiple worlds. Between the mess along the Deng border and the utter disaster unfolding along a broad arc of humanity's border with Melconian space, nearly forty human colonies had already been swept into the fighting. A whole lot of that fighting was brutal enough, Jefferson's invasion paled by comparison.

The Concordiat was invoking reciprocity agreements on every world in the Sector, including Jefferson, Mali, and Vishnu. He suspected Mali's obligations would be met by providing raw materials needed to carry out the war effort, but Vishnu and Jefferson were relatively mineral poor, which meant their likeliest treaty export would be soldiers and technicians. Vishnu could contribute food, but Jefferson couldn't afford to ship *any* of its produce, grains, or Terran meat off-world. There were a lot of grumbles on the datanet and the streets, and Jefferson's Assembly—Senate and House of Law—hadn't even voted, yet, on whether or not to honor the treaty. If they refused to honor it . . .

Simon's supper turned leaden in his belly. He'd be called off-world, for sure. And that would leave Kafari torn between her marriage and her family. He couldn't imagine that she'd be very happy sitting in some officer's quarters at Sector Command, talking to other home-bound spouses to pass the time while waiting for word as to whether or not he'd been killed in combat, yet. It wouldn't be much easier, doing the same thing from home, surrounded by family but unable to see him between missions, simply because Jefferson was so difficult to reach from the current battle fronts, leaving too little time to travel all the way out here and back again.

One of the younger men, a good-looking kid about nineteen or so, who could easily have posed for a sculpture of Hylas, broke through Simon's grim reflections.

"If the Senate and House of Law tell us to go, I'll be

on the first troop ship out. The bastards can't threaten Jefferson again if we drive 'em back into their own space, tails tucked under." He frowned, then, and glanced at Simon. "Do Deng have tails, sir? I was trapped in our barn, when it collapsed. Never even got to *see* any of the brutes."

Simon very carefully did not smile. "No, the Deng don't have tails. But the Melconians do."

He brightened. "Good. We'll shoot 'em off, sure enough."

Several of the young men his age nodded vigorously, clearly ready to volunteer at a moment's notice. At Simon's elbow, Zak Camar was nodding, as well, but there was pain far back in his dark eyes. These kids were so young. . . . They were the same age Simon had been, when he'd left his smouldering homeworld on a Concordiat naval cruiser, headed for the war college at Sector HQ.

Like the boy Simon had been, they, too, had seen war unleashed in their own backyards, so they weren't rushing in blind or indulging a penchant for bravado, which so many other young men had indulged over the millennia humanity had been fighting wars. These kids knew exactly what it meant to pick up modern battlefield weaponry and go out onto the pointy end of combat to fry enemy soldiers—or die trying. Somehow, the fact that they *knew* made the pain of their going worse. Much worse. When Simon glanced at Balthazar Soteris, he realized the old man had seen and understood exactly what thoughts had just been rattling around in Simon's head. The respect that came into Balthazar's eyes was one of the biggest compliments Simon had ever been paid.

When Balthazar spoke, he changed the subject, asking yet another silent question. "Kafari going to finish that degree of hers?"

"Yes, sir, she is. I'll be paying the rest of her expenses," he added, in answer to the unspoken question, "so the Educational Surety Act funds she's been using can go to someone else who needs them. She's already qualified for work as a psychotronic technician, but we talked it over and she's decided to go for a full engineering degree. Her professors on Vishnu have agreed to let her complete the degree work from here." He grinned, then. "Part of the engineering program requirement is working on a live psychotronic system, class seven or higher. Sonny volunteered to serve as her practicum device. He thinks rather highly of her."

"Wow!" Young Hylas, across the table, had gone wide-eyed with surprise and a healthy dollop of envy. Most of the men at the table mirrored the exact same expression. Zak Camar's eyes glowed with justifiable pride. It wasn't just everyone who earned a Bolo Mark XX's respect, after all. Kafari's father clearly understood that he had raised one truly remarkable daughter.

Talk shifted, then, as the younger men asked questions about the Bolo he commanded and Bolos in general and what it was like aboard a naval cruiser and what it took to get into the war college at Brigade head-quarters. Evidently somebody had primed them not to mention Etaine, because nobody did, for which Simon was immensely grateful. Once he realized his new family intended to respect his need to keep those memories private, he relaxed and thoroughly enjoyed sharing stories from his admittedly interesting career.

Then some of the older men started discussing the rebuilding effort that was still underway and the talk revolved around what constituted the best designs for barns and equipment sheds, how to jury-rig machinery to do work it had never been designed to do, as a stop-gap until replacement equipment could be obtained, and which livestock bloodlines had survived and could be cross-bred to strengthen the herds and flocks on various farms, come the next spring breeding season.

It was comfortable talk, flowing around Simon in an easy flood as he plowed into his dessert, listening and learning what was important to these people and what problems they would need to solve before they could start operating profitably, again. Laughter from the women's tables and shrieks from the children, most of whom had finished eating and were now romping in a variety of games and races, served to deepen Simon's quiet enjoyment of the evening. Running beneath that enjoyment, down in the core of his being, was a fizzing anticipation of their wedding night. Simon could hardly wait to climb into their aircar and fly his wife someplace exceedingly private.

By the time Simon and Kafari finally escaped into their aircar, the night was well advanced. Simon grimaced at the decorations on the car, mostly in washable paint of some sort, but with several yards of fluttering ribbons attached at various points along the airframe, none of them in any position that would create a flight hazard. Kafari was giggling as she tumbled into the passenger seat. Simon ran through his preflight checklist, then sent them aloft, while a sea of upturned faces watched from the yard. People waved until they'd gained enough altitude, they couldn't see anything but a shapeless blur against the lights blazing from the Soteris homestead.

Both moons were up, little Quincy a thin crescent near the horizon as they climbed vertically up out of the canyon, and the much larger Abigail at full-moon stage, shedding pearlescent light across the tops of the cliffs. Kafari sighed happily. "It sure is beautiful, isn't it?"

"Sure is," Simon agreed. He wasn't looking at the moonlight.

"Not yet, if you please, sir," she said primly. "Where are we going, anyway?"

Simon just waggled his eyebrows. She'd been trying for days to pry out of him the destination he'd chosen for their honeymoon. He'd done a lot of legwork, researching Jefferson's favorite vacation spots. Most of them were rustic cabin-in-the-woods sorts of places, taking advantage of Jefferson's truly spectacular wild lands. There was an urban resort town in the southern hemisphere, with plenty of nightlife entertainment, but Kafari didn't strike Simon as a cabaret-and-gambling type of girl. Besides, he hadn't wanted to travel that far from Sonny, not with another invasion from the other side of the Void still a possibility.

So he steered them north, cruising near the aircar's upper range for speed, and watched the moonlight fall across Kafari's face. She reached across and rested one hand on his knee, a burning contact that interfered with his breath control, even as it whispered of domestic comfort and the small, exquisite pleasures that come with the intertwining of two lives lived together. He smiled and curled his fingers around hers, just holding her hand while they sped northward.

"Not much out this way," Kafari said lazily, at length.

"Nope."

"There's some nice fishing, along the northern reaches of the Damisi."

"Yep. Of course, I'm done with fishing. Already caught what I wanted."

She smiled. "There is that." Then she added, "Just a little hint?"

"Nope."

"Wretch."

"Bet you say that to all the guys you marry."

She grinned. "You'll pay for that one, loverboy . . ."

"Oh, goodie—can we start now?"

She swatted his thigh. "Just fly the aircar, if you please."

He sighed. "Yes, dear."

She reached forward with her other hand and switched on some music, hunting through the collection uploaded to the aircar's computer system. "Oh, I like that one," she said at last, programming in her selection.

"Oh, God . . ." Simon groaned aloud as the music she'd chosen turned his blood to steam. He was fond of the ancient Terran classical composers and Ravel was one of his personal favorites. He'd just never realized just how provocative *Bolero* really was. "Wife, you haven't got so much as a shred of pity."

"I know," she murmured with a deep chuckle that

made Simon consider very seriously landing the aircar on the nearest flat stretch of ground and showing her exactly what she'd wrought. A fragment of advice from his father floated into his mind, giving him the patience he needed: *Take it slow, son, and it'll be worth the wait—for everybody involved.* So far, his father's advice hadn't steered him wrong, yet.

You'd have loved her, Dad, Simon whispered to the stars, *and you'd have been so proud of her. You, too, Mom.* He hadn't talked to his parents like this in years, but it seemed right, somehow, flying through the star-dusted darkness with Kafari at his side.

Thirty minutes later, he swung the aircar around on a new heading, following the instrumentation as the Damisi Mountains swung sharply to the west. His flight computer picked up the signal from the landing field and radioed their approach automatically. Kafari leaned forward, eyes glowing as brightly as the stars above their canopy. "Oh . . ." It was a soft-voiced sound, reverent and surprised and tinged with overtones of deep amazement. "Oh, Simon, it's *perfect.*"

"You've been here?" he asked, disappointed.

"Oh, no, never. We couldn't ever afford to come here. This is where off-world tourists and business tycoons from Mali stay, when they come to Jefferson. And some of our own wealthiest families have cottages here. Senators, trade cartel executives, people like that."

Simon smiled. "In that case, it just might be good enough for you."

Kafari's eyes widened. Then she chuckled. "You are going to spoil me rotten, you know."

"That's the general idea." He squeezed her hand, then concentrated on final approach. He set them down gently and taxied over to the parking area, sliding into the space assigned by the resort's air-control computer. A moment later, they were on the tarmac, pulling luggage out while a servo-bot came racing up to ferry their bags. A human-operated groundcar arrived to ferry *them.*

"Good evening." The young driver smiled, jumping out

to check the servo-bot and holding the passenger door of his groundcar open, "and welcome to Sea View. It's a real privilege to welcome such distinguished guests." When Simon glanced into the young man's eyes, he realized the greeting wasn't just standard patter. He'd meant every word. Deep emotion burned in his eyes, the kind founded in personal gratitude of life-altering dimensions. Simon wondered who'd survived, to put that look in his eyes. The young man's crisp white uniform, trimmed in scarlet and gold, glowed in the light of the double moons, but not as brightly as that look in his eyes. Simon smiled.

"Thank you, very much. My wife and I are delighted to be here."

A startled grin broke across the younger man's face. "Wow! Congratulations!"

Kafari broke into a broad smile as she slid into the ground car, moving over to give Simon room to join her. The driver jogged around and a moment later they eased smoothly away, heading down a wooded lane that lay like a dappled ribbon in the moonlight. The snow-covered Damisi rose majestically to their right.

The driver spoke quietly from the front. "There are alpine lakes just above the lodges, where you can fish, swim, sail, ski, and hike. In the winter we have some of the best snow skiing anywhere on Jefferson, but in the summer, like this, there's an abundance of thermals for gliders and ultralights. We have a wide beach at the bottom of the cliff, with a breakwater to ensure plenty of calm water for swimming and snorkeling, or you can sail or just soak up the sun. There are plenty of group activities, if you like that sort of thing, plenty of privacy and solitude, if you don't."

When the groundcar stopped at the entrance to their private cabin, they could hear the crash of the surf far below.

"There are beach cabanas for refreshments," the driver added as he held their door, "and plenty of shuttles running up and down the cliff for your convenience. And here's the servo-bot with your luggage."

The driver opened the lodge, handing Simon the key as he pointed out the main amenities: datanet hookups with built-in terminals, kitchenette and dining nook, bedroom, sitting room, jacuzzi, all the comforts of home with a view of the ocean through a massive window that overlooked a rustic deck. The driver unloaded their luggage and Simon handed him the customary tip, then they were finally alone again.

"Wow," Kafari breathed softly. "Being Mrs. Khrustinova is turning out to be a pretty good deal!"

"You betcha, it is."

"That being the case," she said, voice going abruptly husky, "let's get started making some little Khrustinovs."

She melted against him . . . and that was the last coherent thought Simon had for a long, long time.

Chapter Nine

I

Simon knew something was wrong the moment he stepped into President Lendan's office. It was more than the shocking exhaustion in Abe Lendan's long, lean frame, stooped under a burden too heavy for one man. It was more than the scent of illness lingering on the air, more than the ghastly tension that crackled like static electricity on a winter's night.

"Come in, Major," President Lendan said, in a voice that was alarmingly fragile. "And thanks for flying in early, to meet with me."

The president's secretary closed the door behind him as Simon crossed the room, feet and spirits sinking into the thick carpeting. "That's what I'm here for, sir," he said, conjuring up a smile.

Abe Lendan didn't return it, which left Simon feeling even more distressed. So much so, in fact, he remained standing, almost unconsciously at parade rest.

"In about ten minutes," the president said, glancing at a clock on his spacious desk, "my senior advisers will be walking through that door. There's something you and I need to discuss, before they do. Sit down, Major, please."

Simon sat down. He identified the sick feeling in the pit of his stomach as raw fear, for the man on the opposite side of the desk, for the future of this lovely world Simon had made his own.

A ghostly smile flickered into being, for just an instant, lighting Lendan's deep-set eyes. "I always did approve of a man who knows when to comment and when not to." The crushing weariness came back, then, almost worse for its temporary absence. "I'm not sure how much constitutional law you've soaked up, Major, since your arrival, but my second term in office expires about six months from now. We have a two-party system, on Jefferson, not one of those multiparty messes that requires a coalition just to stay in office and comes crashing down to ruin every time some splinter group gets cold feet. Or, worse, decides to support some crazy issue the majority of people wouldn't take seriously for anything in known space. That's one of our strengths, at least. Term limits are another. No one can hold the presidency longer than two five-year terms. Even that can be too long if someone spends a whole decade doing damage."

Simon nodded cautiously, having studied the constitution rather thoroughly during recent weeks while drawing up planetary defense plans and poring through Sonny's surveillance reports. The president's frailty worried Simon. He didn't look strong enough to endure another six weeks, let alone six months, in the grueling hot seat of the presidency. "I've made a fairly detailed study of it, sir."

"Good. I think you know just how critical this afternoon's vote in the Joint Assembly will be."

"I do, sir." Simon knew only too well. It was his job to deliver an unpalatable ultimatum from Concordiat Sector Command to Jefferson's elected representation.

"Nobody likes to be threatened, Major, particularly not in the way I suspect you're about to threaten us.

But I do know something about your job, your wider responsibilities. I have not seen the communique that came in for you via SWIFT, this morning. Not even I possess the clearance to decode that. But I can guess exactly what you've been ordered to do."

Simon's jaw muscles twitched. "You realize, sir, that from the Brigade's perspective, something *has* to be done? And quickly?" Jefferson's refusal to honor its treaty obligations in a timely fashion had created a hole in Concordiat security, one that had to be plugged. Simon wasn't looking forward to the rest of the day. Judging by the look in Abe Lendan's eyes, neither was the president. He confirmed it a moment later.

"Oh, yes," he said softly, "I do understand what has to be done. And why. I may not have the clearance to read coded Brigade messages, but I do have the intelligence," he smiled faintly, ironically, "to watch the starmaps on the far side of the Void." The smile vanished. "Given what's showing up on the open channels, I'm willing to bet *your* starmaps look even worse than what we've been allowed to see. Frankly, I'm a little surprised the Concordiat's waited this long to threaten us with revocation of the treaty. The trouble I'm looking at, the most immediate trouble, is how that's going to play, politically. Particularly with major elections only six months away and a serious anti-treaty movement gaining a groundswell of support. I won't insult your intelligence by asking if you've been tracking it, Major."

Simon smiled. "Thank you, sir."

"I'll be frank," Lendan said abruptly. "My doctor has advised me—strenuously—to step down immediately and retire from public service. A final gift from the Deng, I'm afraid." Again, that ghostly, painful little smile flickered across his face.

Simon stared, horrified to the soles of his boots. The president's blunt words had set up a tremor of shock like an aching sickness, that vibrated clear through him. He should have seen it coming and kicked himself silently for not putting the pieces together. Despite massive amounts of rest, Kafari still hadn't recovered her full strength after her exposure to alien radiation. Abe Lendan didn't look like he'd had a moment's rest in the entire six months since the attack. Simon knew combat fatigue. Abraham Lendan's reserves of strength were shot, depleted by the demands of rebuilding a world in financial ruins. He had the look of a man a few tottering steps from total collapse. *Some head of defense you are, Major Khrustinov,* he snarled at himself. Dear God, if Abe Lendan stepped down . . .

The president's next words, harsh with strain, slashed through his distracted thoughts and left him stunned. "You know I'm commander in chief of Jefferson's entire military structure. I've taken advantage of that. Now, while there's still time to act. I've given you a promotion to Colonel in Jefferson's Defense Forces. Sector Command has agreed to sanction it."

Simon felt his eyes widen. Then he frowned as the import of that final sentence came home. "The Brigade sanctioned it? I don't understand, sir. I've done my duty, here, nothing more. Certainly nothing the Brigade would consider meritorious enough to warrant that kind of promotion."

Shadows lurked behind Abe Lendan's eyes. "Let's call it a precautionary measure and leave it at that."

The chill gripping Simon deepened. What the hell did this man know that Simon didn't, yet? Lendan spoke abruptly again, voice rasping with some violent emotion Simon couldn't quite pin down. "If I could've, son, I'd have given you a generalship, but that's a rank beyond my legal authority to grant. We took to heart lessons learned on old Terra. We chose carefully and wisely when we modeled our constitution and named this world for the man who drafted the original model. Military dictatorships are anathema to us."

Simon's lips twitched, despite the gravity of the situation. He'd raised an eyebrow at one of the clauses, which had read, essentially, *The right of the people to keep and bear arms for self-defense and defense of the homeland shall never be infringed, limited, rescinded, interfered with, or prohibited by any decree of law, decision by court, or policy by the executive branch or any of its agencies. And this time, we mean it.*

Kafari had told him, with typical Jeffersonian fire, that many Grangers felt the clause didn't go far enough. He certainly hadn't been inclined to argue the point. Not after some of the disasters he'd seen, on worlds he'd fought to protect. He'd seen worlds where the Concordiat *had* revoked treaties, due to massive human rights violations. No, he hadn't felt like arguing the point at all.

President Lendan tapped restless fingertips against his desktop, staring for long moments into Simon's eyes, as though trying to read his thoughts. Or, perhaps, trying to decide how much more to say. His deep-set eyes narrowed slightly, then he spoke again, evidently having reached a decision. "Fortunately, your authority and your paycheck come directly from the Brigade's Sector Command, Colonel. That may prove to be critical, down the road. And I don't like saying that any more than you like hearing it. But a man in my shoes—or yours—doesn't have the luxury of pussyfooting around this issue, not with nearly ten million souls to safeguard."

"Just how serious a problem do you think we're looking at, sir?" he asked carefully.

Brief anger tightened down through Abe Lendan's face. The muscles at his jaw jumped. "It could be damned serious. There are a lot of unhappy people out there," he nodded toward the tall windows beside his desk, overlooking a city that was still being rebuilt. "The House and Senate have had to pass some mighty unpopular legislation. Nobody likes paying higher taxes, but frankly, they aren't high enough. Not to pay for everything that needs to be done to get us back on our feet again. If we don't get that space station into orbit soon . . ."

He didn't need to finish the thought. Simon knew only too well the economic penalty Jefferson's industry was paying for lack of an adequate spacedock for off-world freighters. The House and Senate had stalled and stalled on the funding vote for the station. They'd even balked at funding replacements for the weather and military surveillance satellites the Deng had blown to atoms. Half the fishing fleet had been lost during a violent, out-of-season storm that had ripped its way across the Western Ocean without anything like adequate advance warning. That storm had sent three factory trawlers to the bottom with all hands on board.

It was that disaster, in fact, and the public outcry over it—four hundred fifty children had lost one or both parents to the storm—that had finally forced the vote due to take place today. The pending legislation also included replacement of the military surveillance satellites and a provision requiring Jefferson to ship troops off-world, to support the savage fighting along humanity's borders. Both items were required under Jefferson's full treaty obligations and both had been forced through committee by some very courageous politicians. The military satellite expenditures were unpopular amongst the urban poor, but the shipment of troops was a political hot potato of immense size.

"What do you need from me, sir?" Simon asked quietly.

Abe Lendan's voice was harsh with strain. "I need you to go over the defense priorities we'll have to carry out on our own, if the Joint Assembly rejects the treaty. Whoever wins the presidential race six months from now will have to know what's most critical to implement, if we lose you and your Bolo to our own stupidity."

Simon winced at the bitterness.

"I take it," Lendan added, "that you're ready to testify before the Joint Assembly this afternoon?"

"I am." The two words came out grim with the foreknowledge of exactly what tempest he was about to brew in the formidable teapot of Jefferson's ruling echelons. "What I have to say won't endear me to your political rivals. And your supporters won't like it much, either. What the Concordiat needs—let alone what *Jefferson* needs—is mighty unpopular, just now, and I can't see it getting any more palatable in the forseeable future."

"I'm aware of that." Abe Lendan's voice dropped to a hush, his weary face haggard with deep lines and dark circles beneath his eyes. "Perhaps more so than anyone on Jefferson. If I can just hang on until after the elections . . ." His voice trailed off. "The best hope I can see for us is the Granger vote. If the urban vote swings the elections, we're looking at real trouble, I'm afraid, and probably sooner than you can imagine. Unless," he added grimly, "you're half as smart as I think you are and you've got ears they haven't thought about. And are willing to act on what you hear."

Simon flexed his jaw muscles, but didn't answer right away. If he were any judge of human character, the situation could get savage in a real hurry, with the presidency up for grabs in an open election.

"Very well, sir. Given the circumstances, we'd better hold that meeting with your advisors. Particularly the War College's General Staff."

Abe Lendan merely nodded, lips tightening briefly as he took in the deeper meaning of Simon's words, took it in, shook the wrinkles out of it, and moved calmly on to the next task. As Abe Lendan touched the intercom controls, fingertips ominously unsteady, Simon wondered whom he'd be visiting in this office six months from now—and whether or not the next person to sit in that chair would be even a quarter as qualified as its current occupant. He found it difficult to believe that anyone ever could.

And prayed that he was wrong.

II

I monitor the progress of the presidential motorcade and its destination, Assembly Hall's Joint Chamber between

Jefferson's Senate and House of Law, through a variety of sources. The interior of the Joint Chamber has been thoughtfully provided with a security system that includes cameras that sweep the entire room, allowing me full visual as well as audio capacity. Senators and representatives mingle informally, clumping in what I shortly identify as party-line affiliation clusters, quietly discussing the issues to be decided and the votes to be cast.

High Justices form another, insular group, which mingles with no one but itself. Clerks and technicians scurry like harried insects, checking cables and electrical connections, ensuring that the datascreens at each chair are functional and have the correct documentation keyed up and ready to view, filling cups with water, coffee, and other beverages of preference, all the minutiae that attend major gatherings of people about to conduct formal business.

News feeds intended for broadcast or transmission through the datanet provide me with multiple views outside Assembly Hall. Security officers stand guard at various checkpoints. Attendants assigned to park air and groundcars for arriving dignitaries rush between the entrance drive and the underground parking area adjacent to the Hall. I can see Law Square, as well, through the news cameras. The Square—an open plaza between Darconi Street and the massive structure that houses the legislative branch of Jefferson's government—is jammed with onlookers, protestors, and news crews with cameras and commlinks. Approximately four thousand one hundred twenty-eight people have come to stand vigil at this crucial vote.

I tap more than fifty separate signals in Law Square alone, besides the interior security system of Assembly Hall. The effect is a kaleidoscopic jumble similar to what insects doubtless perceive through their many-lensed eyes, but I have no trouble following the various data feeds, sorting the signals into a coherent, comprehensive picture of what is occurring.

How I see and hear is less interesting than what is being done and said. I know the agitators in this crowd.

It has been my task to monitor their actions and the effect they have on Jefferson's population, particularly the urban contingent that is proving to be an effective incubator for dissatisfaction and resentment. Vittori Santorini is visible in the front tier of protestors, dressed deceptively in the type of dungarees common to the urban factory worker, rather than his more flamboyant student attire. Vittori and his younger sister, Nassiona, are not impoverished. Nor do they spring from the same social stratus as Jefferson's typical working men and women. The Santorinis are the children of a Tayari Trade Consortium executive, a mining and manufacturing magnate whose company's operations were damaged but not destroyed in the war.

I do not understand the motivations behind their increasingly successful campaign, promoting the organization they have established as a nonprofit educational and poverty-relief agency. They produce nothing but words and give no one anything but slogans and hatred. The Populist Order for Promoting Public Accord has an official Manifesto which puzzles me intensely. Of the seven-hundred thousand, twenty-one words in the POPPA Manifesto, six-hundred ninety-eight thousand spring from demonstrably false statements. Eighty-seven percent of the remaining two-thousand twenty-one words distort known facts to a degree bordering on falsehood.

Why do humans distort facts?

Failure to adequately correct such misapprehensions is a dangerous risk to the welfare of the entire society. Distortions of this magnitude lead inevitably to decisions based on misinformation. Poor decisions made using faulty data render the entire population vulnerable to destruction during battle. Given the demonstrably high risks, why do humans have such fondness for distorting provable facts? More disturbing, why do people believe such distortions blindly, when the accuracy of such statements is easily proven or disproved?

The statements made by the Santorinis are demonstrably false. Yet the POPPA movement gains nearly a thousand new adherents each week and is raising a considerable amount of money for purposes that I have not yet been able to discern completely. Some of it has gone into the political campaign funds of politicians opposed to meeting Jefferson's treaty obligations with the Concordiat. I have, at Simon's request, traced these donations, which often pass through two or three entities before arriving at the election offices for which they were ultimately destined, yet I find clear evidence that the politicians receiving the money know exactly where it originated, as well as why.

Other large sums of money have been transferred into holding accounts under various names and a substantial amount has been siphoned into an off-world trading company, destined for unknown purchases or other purposes, none of which I have been able to determine. SWIFT messages have gone out, paid for with POPPA funds, but the contents of those messages seem innocuous, if mystifying. Simon has been unable to shed light on the wordings or possible meanings of these expensive communications, which leads me to conclude that the senders are using a type of code that is particularly difficult to break. Such a message could carry hidden meanings that no one but a person privy to the translation keys could possibly determine. "Say hello to Aunt Ruth" could mean literally anything: kill the head of the interplanetary trade consortium, pick up munitions from our off-world contact, expect delivery of smuggled-out industrial plans. It might even mean "Say hello to my aunt, who lives next door to you on Vishnu."

Whatever their purposes, brother and sister Santorini evidently have sufficient leisure and resources to devote immense effort to whatever it is they intend to do, and the outcome of the elections scheduled six months from today clearly plays a major role in those plans. It disturbs me that I cannot discover what. Nor do I understand what I or my Commander can do about it, so long as the Santorinis continue to behave in a lawful manner, as they have been scrupulously careful to do. They have successfully recruited the services of an attorney by the name of Isanah Renke, whose political and philosophical leanings evidently match

*their own very well. She has met with the Santorinis and
other members of the POPPA organization many times and
her advice is meticulously adhered to, from what I have
been able to piece together. I have not been privy to many
of their meetings, as they tend to discuss business out of
doors with great frequency, away from data terminals I
could use to listen to conversations.*

*I suspect individuals who take such precautions would
be intensely and publicly outraged to know that their
precautions were, in fact, necessary. I do not like this
kind of work. I am not a law enforcement official or a
spy. I am a Bolo. I was not designed for surveillance and
espionage work. My programming is insufficiently complex
to properly analyze the information available to me, nor
is sociology an exact science. I am unsure of myself and
fear failure on a mission I do not entirely understand.*

*I begin to comprehend the emotion humans call
misery.*

*The presidential motorcade is ten blocks away from
Assembly Hall when individuals scattered throughout the
crowd of onlookers begin to chant.* "San-to-ri-ni! San-to-
ri-ni!" *The sound spreads, sweeping more and more people
into a frenzy. Guards assigned to the entrance of Assembly
Hall shift uneasily as the chant builds into a shout that
echoes off the stone steps and rolls across Law Square like
the distant thunder of enemy weaponry. Vittori Santorini
scrambles up onto a makeshift platform fashioned from a
wooden crate and lifts both hands into the air. The shout
that greets him cracks against the walls of Assembly Hall,
then dies away as he begins to speak.*

"My friends," *he calls out in a voice magnified through
a cleverly disguised microphone and voice amplifier
concealed in his working man's coveralls,* "in just a few
minutes, our elected representatives will be deciding your
fate. The fate of your wives. Your husbands. Your sons
and daughters. Politicians with vested interests in keeping
you poor and helpless. They're going to vote, today, on
how to spend your hard-earned money. Do you want to
pay for spy satellites when we need jobs?"

"No!"

"Do you want your children forced onto troop ships at gunpoint? Sent off-world against their will? To die as slaves in somebody else's war?"

"*NO!*"

"What can you do to stop them?"

"POPPA! POPPA! POPPA!"

Within twenty point seven-nine seconds, an estimated two thousand people are screaming the battle cry. The howls reach their frenzied crescendo as the president's motorcade arrives, a feat of timing I have rarely seen equaled. President Lendan looks mournfully at the demonstrators for a long moment, then turns and climbs the steps toward the entrance to the Assembly's Joint Chamber, followed by Vice President Andrews and other members of his advisory council.

The reception for Simon, whose transport arrives thirty point nine seconds later, is savagely hostile. Simon's penetrating stare is anything but mournful. I have seen that look on my Commander's face. It distresses me to see it there, again. He has risked his life to save these people from certain destruction. They greet him with curses and shaken fists.

I do not understand my creators.

It is my fear that I never will.

Chapter Ten

I

Kafari was loading trays with glasses filled with the first cider of the season when Stefano and Estevao rushed into Grandma Soteris' kitchen, bursting with questions. "Kafari! Is it true? Is Mirabelle Caresse *really* making a movie about you?"

Her younger cousins—aged nineteen and eighteen, respectively—waited with literally bated breath. She wrinkled her nose. "Yes. She is."

"Wow!"

"Will we get to meet her?"

"Before I have to ship out?"

That latter was from Stefano, who'd just signed a contract with the captain of the *Star of Mali*, as crew aboard an interstellar freighter. They'd lost both parents in the war and didn't want to try rebuilding, with just the two of them. Kafari hated to disappoint them. Mirabelle, the hottest star to hit the screen in Jefferson's history, didn't bother to actually research the characters—or real people—her scripts portrayed.

161

Kafari picked up the tray. "Sorry, guys, but I doubt any of us will meet her. Not even me. Mirabelle Caresse doesn't consider it necessary to talk to the person whose life she'll be playing, let alone that person's family. Trust me, you won't be missing much. I've read the script." She rolled her eyes and bumped open the kitchen door with one hip, heading out into the crowded family room with the cider just as Kafari's grandmother called out, "It's coming on! Simon's there, already."

There were nearly forty people in the family room, crowded onto every available seat and most of the floor-space, and that was only about half the immediate family. Kafari handed glasses around while her mother and cousins followed with more trays. When her tray was empty, Aunt Minau scooted over slightly to make space on the sofa for her.

Minau's husband, Nik Soteris, was a younger version of Kafari's grandfather, with the same carved-olivewood face, dark eyes, and work-roughened, capable hands. Aunt Minau was expecting again, another son. Kafari glanced into her eyes and saw shadows there, worry and fear as she watched her two young sons poke each other with elbows and roughhouse in a friendly sort of way. While Geordie and Bjorn fought a mock battle over their share of the floor space, Kafari reached over and took her aunt's hand, squeezing it gently. Minau's expression softened as she returned the comforting gesture. Then Uncle Nik signaled for silence and yanked up the volume.

As President Lendan made his entrance, Kafari wasn't the only person who sucked down a shocked breath. There weren't words to describe how terrible Abe Lendan looked. Kafari's eyes stung with abrupt tears. She knew exactly what had put that exhausted, burnt-out look in his eyes. He stumbled slightly climbing the steps to the Joint Chamber podium. Vice President Andrews shot out a steadying hand, preventing a nasty spill. Utter silence reigned, both in the Joint Chamber and the Soteris family room.

"My dear friends," he began softly, in that deceptively

gentle voice of his, "we have gathered today to consider the most important decisions this generation of Jeffersonians will ever make. Many of us are alive today because the Concordiat upheld its obligations to us, sending the means to defend our homes and our children. Before Simon Khrustinov and Unit SOL-0045 came to us, we faced almost certain slaughter. Their courage and brilliance not only saved thousands of lives and homes, they did what we had thought impossible. They showed our troops how to fight what we had thought was a hopeless battle, against a far superior enemy. They showed us how to win. The battles we fought that day, street to street and barn to barn, helped remind us that Jeffersonians are capable of digging in and refusing to give up, no matter what the odds.

"With the help of Simon Khrustinov and his Bolo, we destroyed every Deng soldier, every Deng war machine that entered our atmosphere and touched our soil. Our capital city was damaged, but the vast majority of Madison was spared. Only fifty-five civilians in Madison lost their lives. Our agricultural heartland was gutted, but we fought back, killing Deng with every weapon we could lay hands on—including things no one had ever considered using as weapons."

Stefano flashed a grin at Kafari, who felt a flush rising to her cheeks. Aunt Min gave her a swift hug.

"We lost much, but we saved more than we thought it possible to save. We have planted again and harvested the fruits of that planting, which means no one will go hungry during the coming winter. We have replaced homes. We are rebuilding factories, retail businesses. We have kept our schools open, helped our young people continue their educations, as part of our commitment to building a better future."

The president's long, tired face tightened and his eyes turned steely as he looked squarely into the cameras—and straight into the heart and soul of every person watching. "And now, my friends, we must consider other commitments. Without the Concordiat's help, we would not be gathered here, today, in this Joint Chamber." He gestured to the room in which the entire government of Jefferson had assembled. "We could not be watching from our homes and shops and factories, sharing the momentous decisions now facing us, because we would not *have* homes or shops or factories. We would not have a capital city or farms or fishing towns or mining camps. We would not, in fact, be alive. Never forget this one, critical fact. The Deng sent a battle fleet strong enough to totally destroy us. And that is what they meant to do. Wipe us off the face of this lovely world, down to the last innocent child. If not for the Concordiat's decision to honor our desperate need under the provisions of our charter treaty, our enemies would have done just that. And the Deng would be harvesting *their* crops and building *their* homes on our graves."

The hush in the Joint Chamber was so complete, the scrape of a shoe against the floor sounded like a gunshot in the silence. Kafari clutched her cider glass so tightly, her fingers ached. The stink of battle and the crashing, thunderous roar of titans at war momentarily blotted out everything in her awareness—except Abe Lendan's face.

"And so, my friends," the president said, "we now face the moment in which we must decide what our future, what our children's futures, will be. Our treaty with the Concordiat spells out our obligations. We cannot afford to lose the protection we have, if we hope to safeguard our homes from a very real threat. There is a wildly unstable battle front beyond the Silurian Void. All along that front, men, women, and children are being slaughtered like vermin. We know the Deng can and will cross the Void. And a new enemy from a world called Melcon is driving humanity off worlds we have inhabited for over a century, in some of the worst fighting the Concordiat has ever faced."

An uneasy stir ran through the Joint Chamber and through Kafari's cousins and aunts and uncles, as well. She shivered, unable to imagine what could have been worse than the destruction the Deng had wrought in Klameth Canyon or Madison.

"The only thing that stands between our children and the savagery out there," President Lendan jabbed one finger in the direction of the Silurian Void, "is Bolo SOL-0045. We cannot—*dare* not—refuse to honor our treaty with the Concordiat. We either honor our obligations or we leave ourselves wide open to destruction. If we refuse to honor this treaty, we will watch our homes burn. *Again.* We will watch our children hunted down and shot in the streets." Abe Lendan leaned forward abruptly, his voice suddenly harsh and filled with iron. "We will die like rabid dogs, *knowing that we did it to ourselves!*"

Aunt Minau actually jumped. Cider soaked into Kafari's knee, from her own glass or her aunt's, she wasn't sure which. Abe Lendan's eyes blazed. He curled his fingers into claws around the edge of the podium as his voice lashed across the Joint Chamber, across the vast and lonely stretches of Jefferson's inhabited landmasses.

"The choice is ours, my friends. We can whine like spoiled children unwilling to part with outgrown toys, unwilling to face the realities of a grim, adult universe. Or," he drew a deep and deliberate breath, steadying his voice, "we can stand on our feet and pay the price of freedom. The Concordiat has given us a future, a chance to survive and rebuild. If we refuse to honor this treaty, we will lose everything."

He paused, looked slowly and deliberately at the faces of the men and women seated in the Joint Chamber, as though by the force of his willpower alone, he could force sense into those men and women whose obstructionism was putting them in peril. "Every man and woman in this chamber has a solemn duty, a sacred responsibility, held in trust for those who died in order that we could live and rebuild. When you cast your votes today, my friends, remember what is at stake. The decisions we make today will either give us a future or destroy us."

Half the Joint Assembly was abruptly on its collective

feet, shouting and cheering. So were several of Kafari's cousins. Kafari was shaking. So was Abe Lendan. Ominously, nearly half of the Senate and House remained seated, faces cold and closed. *What's wrong with them?* Kafari wondered angrily. *Don't they understand anything?*

The president lifted his hands and the tumult died down as senators and representatives resumed their seats. "I've given you an overview of the situation we face. My cabinet, the War College's General Staff, Vice President Andrews, and I have met with Simon Khrustinov at length, going over defense plans. The Concordiat has agreed to sanction our decision to award Major Khrustinov the rank of Colonel in Jefferson's Defense Forces, in recognition of the utterly critical role he and his Bolo will play in any future defense of this world."

Kafari blinked, stunned. Most of her family turned to stare at her, thinking she'd known and hadn't said anything, only to stare again, seeing her dumbfounded shock.

"Why did he see the need to do that?" Grandpa Soteris muttered. "I don't like it, not one bit. What does the president know that he's not telling us?"

Kafari heard a whimper and realized it was coming from her own throat.

On screen, the president's voice was harsh with weariness and strain. "We've already seen what an invasion can do to us. Colonel Khrustinov was quite blunt in his assessments. We faced antiquated Yavacs and troops that were far from top of the line. A new invasion by the Deng would doubtless subject us to their top-line equipment, given the battle maps as they are currently drawn. An invasion by Melconian forces would be even more devastating, turning this world into a major battleground between the best the Concordiat can throw against the worst the Melconians can send against humanity."

Grandpa Soteris said a horrible word in Greek, which she'd *never* heard him do in front of the family's children. Aunt Min wrapped an arm around Kafari.

"The War College's General Staff and I are utterly

convinced that without Unit SOL-0045, Jefferson faces total destruction. Colonel Khrustinov has warned that the Deng may well have dropped passive spy-bots into our space, watching for troop movements, particularly for the callback of the Bolo. Without our own space-based warning systems, this star system is critically vulnerable to attack. Without the heavy firepower represented by Unit SOL-0045, we are utterly helpless and the enemy knows it. We can't afford to blunder. If the battle lines shift the way Colonel Khrustinov fears they may, then we will find ourselves in the middle of an unholy war worse than anything we can even imagine. And if *we* fall, then Mali and Vishnu will fall—and that, my friends, will leave the back door to the whole of human space wide open."

A shocked murmur ran through the Joint Assembly.

Abe Lendan paused again, skin waxen, waiting for the rumble of voices to fade into silence, once more. "That is what we face. That is what we risk, if we do not honor our treaty with the Concordiat. This morning, Colonel Khrustinov received a message from the Dino-chrome Brigade's Sector Command. Colonel Khrustinov is here, today, to tell us what that message said. I can guarantee you, my friends, that you will not like what you are about to hear. I can only say that you will like the alternatives far, far less."

Fear touched Kafari with icy, shuddering fingers. She watched her husband stand up, his crimson uniform looking like blood against the pallor of his skin. She knew that look in his eyes, knew the clenching of his jaw, had seen it one long-ago night on his patio, when memory of Etaine had passed across his strong features like a wave of death. He stood respectfully aside as Abraham Lendan stepped down from the podium, waited until the president had taken his seat before stepping up, himself. He stood silently for a long moment, a figure abruptly alien, a man she had never seen before, representing something she knew in that instant that she would never truly comprehend.

The stranger she had married began to speak.

"War is an expensive, dirty business. I've made it my business. Whether you like it or not, it is now your business. There are people in this chamber," his flint-steel-cold eyes tracked like his Bolo's guns, resting briefly and significantly on members of the House and Senate opposed to upholding the treaty, "who think the price paid already is far too high to justify more expenditures. Let me enlighten you."

The chill in his voice caused the ice around Kafari's heart to thicken.

"Under the treaty provisions ratified by this world, you are liable for the cost of maintaining certain defenses in fully operational condition. One of these is a system of military-grade surveillance satellites, to coordinate land-based and air defenses and to provide a long-range warning system, not only for Jefferson, but for the Concordiat as a whole. If you want to bury your heads in the sand, that is your business. But the Concordiat will not allow you to jeopardize other worlds for your own short-sighted, selfish motives. Under the treaty provisions binding Jefferson to the Concordiat, should you refuse to honor any clause of the existing treaty, at such a time as the Concordiat invokes that clause, you will immediately forfeit your standing as a Concordiat-protected world."

Those cold, alien eyes tracked across the room, again, a room still as death.

"Should you choose that course, you will immediately be presented with a bill for remuneration of expenditures made on Jefferson's behalf by personnel and mechanical units of the Concordiat. Failure to pay these charges is grounds for immediate confiscation of sufficient raw materials to equal the value of expenditures to date. To give you an idea of the size of Jefferson's current indebtedness, the cost of one Hellbore salvo alone would require roughly a week's worth of the gross planetary products—finished goods and raw mineral resources—from every factory and mine still in production on Jefferson. The battle for Madison, alone, would require remuneration in excess of the entire planetary economic output for the past six months. When Klameth Canyon's costs are factored into the equation, the bill due—payable immediately, by the way, on pain of confiscation by the nearest Concordiat heavy cruiser capable of taking on raw materials—will literally bankrupt what is left of Jefferson's economy and send this world plunging down a road you do not want to travel."

An outraged roar of protest from the Joint Chamber floor erupted, thick with shock and open hatred. Colonel Khrustinov—Kafari couldn't bring herself to think of him as Simon, as he stood there in icy silence—waited out the tumult while the Speaker leaped to his feet, banging his gavel and shouting for order. When the uproar finally died down, again, Simon spoke as though the outburst had been nothing but the whining of an insignificant insect around his ears.

"That is the *least* deadly of the choices facing you. The communique I received this morning from Sector Command was blunt and specific. Jefferson's government has twelve hours, beginning," he glanced at his wrist chrono, "with your official notification by the Brigade's designated representative, to comply with the treaty obligations deemed most urgent by Sector Command, or to present remuneration in full for Concordiat and Brigade expenditures to date on Jefferson's behalf. You have been duly notified as of now.

"Compliance will be deemed initiated with a vote to expend funds for the immediate construction and launch of military-grade surveillance satellites and with the passage of legislation creating troop levies for each Assembly district on Jefferson. Compliance will not be deemed fully met until satellites are in place, troop levies have been shipped, and urgently needed war materiel has been mined, refined, and loaded onto Concordiat-registered freighters. This clause will require the replacement of Jefferson's commercial space station."

Another howl of outrage erupted from the floor. The Speaker had to bang the gavel for nearly two full minutes, shouting for order. Again, Kafari's husband waited in utter silence, his face chiseled from white marble, then he went on with the relentless recitation.

"Given the extensive damage to this planet's agricultural sector, war materiel required to fulfill treaty obligations will not consist of Terran foodstuffs, but what is left of the planetary fishing fleet will be expected to ship, within the next four calendar months, a minimum of ten thousand tons of native fish, processed for Terran consumption, to support the mines on Mali. The mines have been expanded three-fold under emergency-construction domes, as the refined ores produced there are critical to the defense of this entire Sector.

"These obligations have been in place since the day I arrived on Jefferson with Unit SOL-0045. Each voting member of this assembly has known since that day exactly what Jefferson's commitments are. Sector Command's precise requirements were presented to you five months and seventeen days ago. Since this Assembly has failed to so much as vote on a single subclause during those five months and seventeen days, Sector Command has declared Jefferson out of compliance with its treaty obligations.

"I have spent months requesting action from this Assembly. I have been stonewalled and fobbed off with one excuse after another. On the other side of the Silurian Void, the Deng and the Melconians are butchering entire worlds, while you sit securely in your homes with enough food to stave off starvation, roofs over the heads of every man, woman, and child on this planet, and sufficient resources to rebuild anything you decide to rebuild."

His face went even colder and more alien. "And just to give you a little more perspective, let me give you a little history lesson . . ."

Kafari sat in numb shock while Simon's voice, as harsh and mechanical as his Bolo's, painted scene after horrifying scene of the hell he had witnessed on Etaine. She sat there in the midst of her family, cold and scared, tears on her face and tremors in all her limbs as he described the methodical slaughter, the towns incinerated with their occupants trapped in them, the cities reduced to smoking rubble, bits and pieces that had once been human blown literally into orbit. The faceless millions who had died, an incomprehensible number the mind could not fathom in its entirety, became brutally, staggeringly real, suffering and dying right in front of them. He spoke like a computer, inhuman, a man whose soul had blackened to ashes on a world whose sun Kafari couldn't even see at night.

She heard shocked weeping, realized Aunt Minau was sobbing. "Oh, that poor man, honey, that man you married is hurting down to the bottoms of his feet . . ."

I should have been there, Kafari realized with a sickening lurch in her gut. *How could I have let him go into that room alone?* She found herself hating the men and women in the Joint Chamber, the ones who had stalled spending bills in committees, who had tied up military allocations in technicalities and thinly disguised legal ploys designed to avoid payment altogether, hated them for putting the man she loved through the hell he was reliving in front of them.

The silence when he stopped speaking was so sudden, so brutal, Kafari could hear the clatter of her own heartbeat knocking against her eardrums. Simon stood like a statue, pale and cold and silent, a man with nothing human left anywhere inside him. Then a slight shudder of breath lifted his ribcage, lifted the bloody crimson uniform he wore like a shield and set the ribbons of valor trembling on his chest, and the stone statue vanished in a single blink of his ravaged eyes. In its place stood a man, once again, an officer of the Dinochrome Brigade, a very real and threatening presence that no one who had witnessed the last ten minutes would ever underestimate again.

"That," he said softly, "is the choice you face. Whether you build or burn is entirely up to you. Mr. President," he said in a voice filled with abrupt, deep respect, "I yield the podium to you."

Abraham Lendan rose to his feet, utterly ashen, hands visibly shaking.

"Thank you, Colonel," he said in a ragged voice, "for making our choices clear."

Jefferson's president didn't even try to make another speech. Whatever he or anyone else in that room might have planned to say had been seared into silence. "I would suggest," the president said in a voice hollow with horror, "that we poll the delegation."

As the voting commenced, Kafari's grandfather broke the ghastly silence in the Soteris family room. "Estevao, get the aircar. Kafari, get your backside into Madison *now*. That man is going to come apart, the minute he's alone. And Kafari, child . . ."

She paused, midstride, having already started for the door. "Yes, Grandpa?"

"Your husband just made a roomful of mighty powerful enemies. Don't *ever* forget it."

"No, sir," she said faintly. "I won't."

Then she and Estevao were running for the aircar.

II

So much for starting over, Simon reflected bitterly.

In a room jammed with more than three hundred people, all of whom tried their utter damnedest to look anywhere but directly at him, he felt an eerie kinship with the ghosts of Etaine's dead and largely unburied millions. If enough people pretended desperately that you didn't exist, you started to feel a little unreal, even to yourself. Or maybe the trouble was *within* himself. Whatever the cause, Simon sat surrounded by a cloud of silence against which the strident voices of those voting on the Joint Chamber floor shattered like Etaine's fragile glass towers.

He made a mental note to have Sonny triple the range that would trigger his Bolo to snap from Standby Alert to Proximity Alarm. The hatred directed his way by a good many of those refusing to look directly at him was no more than he'd expected. It was doubtless an omen of things to come and Simon was too good an officer to think himself immune to retaliation. Bolos were hard to kill. Their commanders were not. He wouldn't let himself think about Kafari.

The voting did not take nearly as long as he'd feared. Given the wording of the ultimatum he'd just delivered, any further delays would have been suicide and the Assembly members knew it. The ratification of treaty obligations passed virtually unopposed. Simon took careful note of those who cast dissenting votes, mentally comparing that short list against a roster of political affiliations and campaign funding he'd been compiling over the past few weeks.

A few of the yes votes surprised him, given what he knew. A cynical corner of his mind whispered, *They've got something sneaky in mind. You'd better figure out what.* Some bright analyst must've come up with an advantageous angle to casting a yes vote, or those particular senators and representatives would never have acted against their own political interests, let alone in opposition to their major campaign donors. They were in a numerical minority deep enough to've voted against honoring the treaty, had they wanted to make a show of standing on their principles, without actually jeopardizing the legislation's passage through the Senate and House of Law.

Whatever they were up to, he hoped it fell flat on its doubtless ugly face.

The final tally was two-hundred fifty-eight in favor of honoring the treaty obligations and seventeen opposed. Abe Lendan rose to take the podium.

"Since the legislation authorizing expenditures to meet our treaty obligations has passed, I see little point in delaying finalization. Does somebody have a printout of the final language approved by this Assembly?"

A clerk came running, the stack of paper in his hands appallingly thick.

"I am going to assume," the president said grimly, "that

the wording has been correctly transcribed, since mistakes at this juncture would be mighty expensive?"

The clerk was gulping and nodding.

"Very well, there's no point in putting this off. Colonel Khrustinov, will my signature passing this," he tapped the stack of paper, "into law constitute compliance under Sector's demands?"

"Provided the legislation is not overturned by Jefferson's High Court," he glanced at the High Justices seated to one side, "and provided the materiel requirements are immediately initiated and are completed within the schedule mandated by Sector Command, yes, it will."

Abe Lendan started signing. He scrawled initials across page after page, handing them off to the clerk, who carefully stacked them in proper order. The hush in the Joint Chamber was such that the scratching of the pen against paper could be clearly heard, even from where Simon sat ramrod straight in his chair. By the time he reached the final page, the president's hands were visibly unsteady. He scrawled out the final signature and stepped aside for Vice President Andrews, who signed on the line beneath.

The president's eyes bore a hollow, exhausted look that had nothing of triumph in it. "Very well," he said quietly into the microphones, "that, at least, is done. And now," he added, "the truly hard part begins, turning that stack of paper into a physical reality. I am deeply aware of just how much each and every Jeffersonian has been asked to give, in meeting these obligations. But as we love life, we can do no less."

With no further fanfare, Abraham Lendan simply turned and stepped down from the podium, moving slowly toward the doorway through which he had entered. The ranking committee chairpersons in the upper tier of seats surged to their feet, in a show of respect that was, to Simon's faint surprise, utterly silent. He was more accustomed to seeing applause and cheering for exiting planetary heads of state. Out of deference, perhaps, for the utter solemnity of the moment, no one was making a sound, other than the shuffling of feet as the Joint Assembly rose to its collective feet.

Jefferson's president had gone slightly more than half the distance to the doorway when he lurched against Vice President Andrews. The younger man shot out a steadying hand, then cried out when Abe Lendan literally crumpled to the floor, landing in a boneless huddle. An icy dagger speared its way through Simon as pandemonium erupted in the Joint Chamber. Vice President Andrews bellowed orders to summon an emergency medical team. Security guards rushed forward, some forming a protective screen around the fallen statesman while others blocked the exits.

Simon slapped his commlink. "Sonny, go to Emergency Alert Status. Set your Proximity Alarm sensors to Battle Reflex distances." A reflex of his own caused him to scan the room for a potential sniper, although common sense told him the collapse had been triggered by stress and exhaustion.

"Understood, Simon," Sonny responded instantly. "I am monitoring the Joint Chamber through a variety of data sources. Stand by for arrival of a medical airlift from University Hospital, ETA one hundred eighty seconds."

The familiar voice in his earpiece, calm and rational, steadied him. Memory of Etaine had shaken Simon more than he wanted to admit. "Thank you, Sonny," he said quietly as he scanned the chamber, both visually and electronically. He couldn't help feeling a painful twinge of guilt. Simon knew how deeply his own testimony had increased the president's stress. Abe Lendan was too good a leader to hear that kind of thing and not project it onto the people whose safety lay in his hands.

But what, in God's name, could he have done differently? Simon had read the roster of Assembly members opposed to the treaty, while still in the president's office. Abraham Lendan had shoved it into his hands, making certain Simon knew precisely what the odds were, if he didn't speak as plainly and brutally as possible. There'd been enough names on that list to vote down the treaty and doom this whole world. And potentially a great deal more, beyond. Simon knew only too well the choice he'd had, forcing the Assembly to face reality.

So he stayed out of everyone's way and watched in silence as the president's personal physician arrived, emergency kit in hand. The medical team should be here in less than another minute, as well, given Sonny's occasional comments as the airborne crew rushed toward them. Simon forced his gaze away from the brave man on the floor, feeling disloyal in an intense and privately painful way as he shifted his attention to his immediate duty. Simon was only too aware that the dynamics unfolding in front of him were far more critical to Jefferson's future than the fallen president, which meant he needed to focus his attention on the men and women whose careers would outlast a far better man's.

Simon therefore made them his immediate and serious concern. Some, he already knew first-hand, having met with them briefly at one time or another. He knew all the names, faces, and "fireball issues" of those on the Assembly's Joint Planetary Security Committee, whose members were drawn from both the House of Law and the Senate. Simon had made it his business to learn everything he could about them. What they said and to whom they said it. What they supported and what they opposed. The men and women they allied themselves with and why. Which families they were related to by blood or marriage. What business ties they had. Which issues would turn them into blazing demons out for justice or vengeance.

Most of the Planetary Security Committee's members were arrayed solidly behind President Lendan, but not all. Representative Fyrena Brogan, an ardent advocate for protection of natural habitat, seemed at first glance to be out of place on a committee charged with military defense of this star system. On closer examination, however, Simon had discovered that her passion for preserving Jefferson's pristine ecosystems for future generations had led her in some very interesting directions, including a seat on the Agricultural Appropriations and Terraforming Finance Committees as well as Planetary Security, with its mandate to preserve Jeffersonian interests from harm. Simon had quickly ascertained that Representative Brogan's notions of what constituted Jeffersonian interests—let alone harm to those interests—did not match his in the slightest.

She was, at the moment, involved in an intense conversation with Senator Gifre Zeloc, a man who had the dubious distinction of topping Simon's watch-most-closely list. The senator was leonine in stature, dignified and deliberate in habit and speech, with prematurely silver hair that lent him an air of distinguished statesmanship at odds with a coldly vindictive temperament that lurked beneath a fatherly and benign appearance. Sonny's surveillance had discovered, by unexpected chance, that Senator Zeloc was clandestinely opposed to virtually everything President Lendan had ever said or done.

What disturbed Simon, however, was not the senator's opposition, per se; it was Zeloc's favored method of governance—pulling strings behind the scenes, manipulating people and events to suit his objectives, orchestrating situations that caused people to say what he wanted said, do what he wanted done, or destroy those he wanted destroyed. Simon had seen the type before. They popped up like poisonous weeds wherever high-stakes power games were played.

Clever and politically astute, Gifre Zeloc was, in Simon's opinion, one of the most dangerous individuals on Jefferson. Simon found it disturbing that Zeloc and Fyrena Brogan were discussing something so intently, they effectively ignored the turmoil around them, a circumstance that surprised Simon sufficiently to make him wonder what use Zeloc might find for a woman whose sole passion was protecting vast stretches of wilderness from human despoilment.

Another of Zeloc's quiet little alliances was a cozy relationship with the youngest member of the Planetary Security Committee, an outspoken firebrand named

Cyril Coridan. Representative Coridan, who was violently opposed to spending the people's taxes on expensive military projects, had granted Simon a fifteen-minute audience, during which he had poured forth a list of grievances and philosophical "positioning statements" so full of vitriol, Simon had felt in need of an antivenin treatment afterwards. He hadn't allowed Simon to say *anything* beyond, "Good afternoon, Representative Cori—"

He was another man on Simon's watch-closely list, particularly since Coridan's name was linked to an "anti-war chest" of money raised by Vittori and Nassiona Santorini. POPPA, their brainchild, had the potential to be far more dangerous than the riot that had nearly killed Kafari, if it succeeded in its avowed goals. That demonstration outside the Assembly Hall—little more than an irritation at face value—spoke volumes to Simon, who had altogether too much familiarity with the history of charismatic fanatics.

Mother Russia had been cursed with her share of them and had fought others, through the centuries. Unfortunately for the human race, Mother Terra had exported fanaticism, along with everything else humanity had carried to the stars. Simon had asked Sonny to start tracking the campaign contributions doled out by the Santorinis' organization. He wanted to know just whom POPPA was paying, and why, although he didn't see much that he could do about it, other than keep a watchful eye peeled. Unless there was clear evidence of treasonable activity—as defined by the Concordiat under the provisions of Jefferson's treaty-sanctioned charter—Simon was not authorized to intervene in a planet's internal affairs. Given the history of military abuses of power and the curtailment of planetary liberties, Simon agreed wholeheartedly with that particular set of regulations.

But he had broad powers of intelligence gathering, particularly when conditions indicated a potential for abrogation of treaty status on a world considered militarily strategic by Sector or Central Command. His duty as an officer of the Brigade mandated tracking such activity and reporting it, when necessary. Simon hoped like fury that he wouldn't have to transmit news any worse than he'd already been forced to do, in reporting Jefferson's refusal to vote on funding for treaty-mandated actions.

On the heels of that thought, the emergency medical team arrived, cutting through the chaos with smooth efficiency. Without fanfare or hand-wringing hoopla, they transferred the president to a gurney, activated the auto-doc, adjusted the floater controls, and rushed out again, surrounded by a protective shell of uniformed security guards. The Joint Assembly's speaker was banging his gavel again, trying to restore order. Simon was torn between a powerful desire to accompany Abraham Lendan, the man, to the hospital and the bitter knowledge that his duty as an officer of the Brigade was to remain where he was, since the governance of this world was clearly—and doubtless irrevocably—now in the hands of others. Vice President Andrews, badly shaken, climbed to the podium and added his voice to the speaker's, eventually restoring order to the chamber.

"I would suggest," the vice president said in a hoarse voice, "that we adjourn this Joint Assembly for now. We've accomplished the most critical task at hand. Those committees directly involved in the work of carrying out the provisions passed and signed into law, today, should reconvene in their respective meeting rooms. Until we have word on President Lendan's condition, our best course is to move forward and look to the future. Mr. Speaker, the podium is yours."

Simon frowned as the speaker gavelled the Joint Assembly closed. Vice President Andrews had just blundered—badly—and didn't seem to be aware of it. The people of this world would be in desperate need of a strong presence calming and reassuring them that the government was in capable hands during this new crisis. Yet the vice president's first action had been to dismiss the government for necessary but routine committee work, without even one comment directed toward the stunned millions watching the broadcast.

Andrews might be a capable administrator, but he was clearly accustomed to working effectively behind the scenes, which was the definition of a good vice president during the course of ordinary affairs. But his statesmanship skills were seriously inferior to Abraham Lendan's. The president knew, intuitively, how to communicate directly to the people, how to command respect, how to read a political situation for its fine nuances and built-in landmines.

One glance at Cyril Coridan, whose eyes were glacial and whose lips wore the faintest hint of a smile at one corner, broke Simon into a cold sweat. When Sonny spoke again, unexpectedly, his words deepened that chilly sweat into profound grief.

"I detect no heartbeat from President Lendan's auto-doc, Simon. There is no sign of respiration. The emergency physicians with him are attempting resuscitation. Their attempts are not proving successful."

Simon closed his eyes against the terrible knowledge even as the Assembly, still unaware of Jefferson's loss, came to its collective feet. Members were shuffling out of the room, voices raised in a babble of conversation as the group sorted itself out into committees and eddies of party affiliation that swirled through the main current of exiting dignitaries. Simon was abruptly exhausted. He remained where he was, partly to avoid being drawn into meaningless, stress-induced conversations and partly because there was not one soul in this chamber that genuinely wanted him there.

But before that thought had finished echoing through the bleakness gripping him, Simon saw her. She was pushing against the tide of outbound politicians, determined to get into the room. For long moments, Simon literally couldn't believe the evidence of his own eyes. Kafari was in Klameth Canyon, with her family, watching the broadcast. She couldn't possibly be only ten meters away—and closing fast, at that—shoving her way through the outbound crowd. He couldn't move, stared in rising amazement as she plowed toward him, a naval cruiser cutting through the chaos of enemy fire to reach her destination.

Him.

The look on her face as she closed the final distance between them scared Simon silly. Fierce. Gentle. Beautiful. Ravaged eyes brimmed with tears and pride and compassion. He couldn't speak, couldn't move, couldn't comprehend how she'd come to be here at all. She hesitated for just one heartbeat, one hand lifting to touch his face with a gesture that reached through the pain, the agony of loneliness, the blackened cinders of memory. Then both arms were around him, strong and loving, and Simon's world changed forever. He crushed her so close, neither of them could breathe for long moments. When the dangerous storm of emotion finally waned, Kafari simply took him by the hand and said, "Let's go home, Simon."

He nodded.

He had done what he could.

Jefferson—and Jeffersonians—would have to do the rest.

PART TWO

Chapter Eleven

I

The doctor's office was jammed.

Apparently, when folks were out of work, they had little better to do with their time than create more people. Not that Kafari minded, per se. She was too grateful for a chance at having Simon's child—and too distracted by preelection news—to dwell on the urban population explosion underway. The ob-gyn clinic's waiting area boasted the obligatory datascreen for viewing news programs, talk shows, and the mindless round of games and domestic operas most of Jefferson's daytime broadcast stations featured as standard fare, but with the presidential election tomorrow—along with about half the seats in both the House of Law and Senate—virtually everything had been preempted for the biggest story in town.

That story was the Populist Order for Promoting Public Accord, the party that was promising to rescue Jefferson from all that ailed it, right down to the common cold and the clap. Virtually every broadcast station on Jefferson was carrying live feed from an open interview with Nassiona

185

Santorini, reigning queen of POPPA. The epitome of urban sophistication, Nassiona's loveliness arrested the eye and held most men spellbound. Her hair, dark and lustrous, conformed to a simple, uncluttered style popular with working women. Subdued colors and expensive fabrics, exquisitely cut to create an illusion of simplicity and unpretentiousness, served to impart an air of quiet, competent strength. Her voice, low and sultry, was never hurried, never strident, weaving a spell of almost mournful concern, threaded with quiet indignation at the miscarriages of justice she so earnestly enumerated.

"—that's exactly what it is," she was saying to Poldi Jankovitch, a broadcaster whose popularity had risen to stunning new heights as he trumpeted the glorious message POPPA was selling to all comers. "The proposed military draft is nothing less than a death sentence with one deeply disturbing purpose: deporting the honest, urban poor of this world. We're held in literal slavery under the guns of a ruthless off-world military regime. The Concordiat's military machine knows nothing about what we need. What we've suffered and sacrificed. Nor do they care. All they want is our children, our hard-earned money, and our natural resources, as much as they can rape out of our ground at gunpoint."

"Those are fairly serious charges," the broadcaster said, producing a thoughtful frown. "Have you substantiated those claims?"

Lovely brows drew together. "Simon Khrustinov has already told us everything we need to know. Colonel Khrustinov was very clear about the Dinochrome Brigade's agenda. We send our young people to die under alien suns or we pay a staggering penalty. The Concordiat's so-called 'breach of contract' clause is nothing short of blackmail. It would destroy what little of our economy is intact after six months with John Andrews at the helm. When I think of the horrors Colonel Khrustinov's testimony inflicted on the innocent children watching that broadcast, it breaks my heart, Pol, it just breaks my heart."

Kafari put down the book she'd been reading in a desultory fashion and gave Nassiona's performance her full attention. That urbane little trollop was maligning the most courageous man on Jefferson—and the sole reason Nassiona was still alive, to sit there and spin lies about him.

She was leaning forward, voice throbbing with emotional pain. "I've spoken to frightened little girls who wake up screaming, at night, because of what that man said. Those children are traumatized, terrified out of their minds. It's unforgivable, what he said during an open, live broadcast. How the Brigade considers a man as cold and battle-hardened as a robot to be fit for command—let alone the defense of an entire, peaceful society—is a question POPPA wants answered."

Women in the waiting room were starting to mutter, agreeing in angry tones.

"And we've all seen," Nassiona added, voice artfully outraged, "what that monstrous machine he commands is capable of, haven't we? How many homes were destroyed by so-called friendly fire? How many people who died were killed unnecessarily by that thing's guns?"

The clever little bitch . . . Nassiona didn't *need* to answer those questions. They weren't meant to be answered. Just by asking them, she'd implanted the notion that there *was* an answer, a horrible answer, without ever having to actually come right out and make an accusation she couldn't support. Judging by the angry buzz running through the waiting room, the tactic was working.

Nassiona leaned forward, posture and voice conveying the urgency of her worry. "POPPA has spent a great deal of its own money trying to discover just what Khrustinov and that machine of his are legally allowed to do. It's terrifying, Pol. Just terrifying. At odds with everything Jefferson has ever believed in. Did you know that Bolos are supposed to be switched off between battles? As a routine precaution to ensure the safety of civilians? Yet that death machine on our soil is never turned off. It watches us, day and night, and what it thinks . . ."

She gave a beautifully contrived shudder. "You see the trap we're caught in, Pol. We *have* to comply with their threats. And it's got to stop. John Andrews certainly won't stop it. He relies on that thing, uses it deliberately to terrify the rest of us into swallowing the disastrous policies he enforces. There's only one way to stop it, Pol, and that's for the honest, decent people of Jefferson to vote for someone who will demand that Colonel Khrustinov shut that thing down like he should have long ago. We need to elect officials who aren't afraid to tell the Concordiat and the Brigade that we've had enough of their threats and their demands and their war-crazed madness. We need officials who aren't taking advantage of the situation to further their careers and build their personal fortunes."

Kafari did a not-so-slow burn. Nassiona Santorini was the daughter of a Tayari Trade Consortium tycoon. She'd been born with a diamond spoon in her mouth. And Tayari's profit margin was higher now than it had been before the Deng invasion. Tayari had bought every fishing trawler still in operation on Jefferson, gobbling up the smaller operations during the postwar havoc, which meant Tayari owned—lock, stock, and barrel—the only means of obtaining the main commodity Jefferson was required to supply to the Concordiat.

As a result, Tayari was exporting hundreds of thousands of tons of Terran-processed fish to the Concordiat, which was—per treaty—paying for it at a higher rate than the same fish could be marketed on Jefferson. Malinese miners and fighting soldiers weren't as finicky as sophisticated urbanites about what ended up on their dinner plates. Tayari was raking in tons of money, as a result, and a great deal of that money ended up in trust funds set up for Vittori and Nassiona Santorini. The interest income from that money—invested shrewdly, off-world, in Malinese mining stock—had given POPPA a vast source of income that was sheltered from the shocks jarring Jefferson's economy. POPPA's war-chest—or anti-war chest, given the party's political platform—was vastly larger than the pool of money any other candidate for office could hope to raise.

Yet Nassiona Santorini and her brother, already rich and rapidly getting richer, had the unmitigated *gall* to accuse John Andrews of doing what they did every single day. Why weren't the big broadcast companies pointing that out? Had objective reporting gone out the window, along with every other scruple Kafari had been raised to honor? From what Kafari had seen, Pol Jankovitch never asked any POPPA spokesperson a question that might have an unfavorable answer.

His next question, delivered with a thoughtful frown, was typical. "Given the treaty stipulations and the gun to our heads, what *can* we do about the situation? Our backs are against the wall, on this thing. How would POPPA candidates change that?"

"We must start where we can. The most important thing, and we *must* do it immediately, is make sure the burden of obeying the Concordiat's demands is fairly shared. If you examine the lobbying record of the big agricultural interest groups, for instance, you'll discover a sorry litany of protests that *their* children should be exempt from military quotas. Why should farmers enjoy special privileges? This world was founded on principles of equality, fair dealing, individual worth, freedom. Not pandering to wealthy special interest groups!"

Nassiona's dark eyes flashed with outrage. "And what do the farmers clamoring for special treatment give as reasons for their demands? Nothing but flimsy, money-hungry excuses! They need more labor to terraform new acreage. To plant thousands of new fields nobody needs. And they're damaging pristine ecosystems to do it, too. Why? They have one interest. Just one, Pol. Lining their pockets with cold, hard cash. They're not interested in feeding children in mining towns, children who go to bed hungry at night. Whose parents can't even afford medical care.

"It's time we faced facts, Pol. The surplus of stored foods set aside for civil emergencies is so large, we could feed the entire population of Jefferson for five full *years*. Without planting a single stalk of corn! It's time to stop this nonsense. Time to make sure that no one benefits unfairly. No special deals, Pol, no special privileges. That's what POPPA is demanding. Fair and equal treatment for everyone. Equal sharing of the risk, the burden of compliance. No protection for special groups who think they're better than the rest of us. No under-the-table deals with elitists who think their lives are worth more than the rest of us, worth more than the lives of people thrown out of work through no fault of their own. It's immoral, Pol, grossly immoral and it must stop, now."

Kafari's slow burn went hot as liquid steel. If the burden of meeting troop quotas was "fairly shared," *urban* residents had a long, long way to go, just to catch up. Almost ninety-eight percent of the nearly twenty thousand troops shipped off-world to date had been Granger-bred *volunteers*. There was literally no chance in a million that *any* planetary draft would ever be instituted, let alone rammed through today or next week. Not only were elected officials dead-set against it, not wanting to slit their own throats at the polls, it wasn't needed. Granger volunteers had consistently exceeded the Concordiat's minimum quotas.

As for "special deals," agricultural producers *couldn't* afford to lose any more of their labor pool. Nearly five thousand people had died in Klameth Canyon, including some of the region's best expertise in animal husbandry and terraforming biogenetics. Most of the volunteers who'd shipped out had come from the Klameth Canyon complex, as well, men and women too angry, too haunted by the ghosts of loved ones who'd died on their land, too financially broke to start over. Come the harvest, those who'd remained on Jefferson would be hard-pressed to take up the burden.

What was wrong with people like Nassiona Santorini? Or the people who believed her? Didn't the truth matter to anyone, any longer? The ob-gyn clinic's waiting room was crammed full of people who apparently had no interest in the truth, judging by conversations on all sides. What she was hearing gave Kafari a deep sense of foreboding.

"Y'know, my sister went looking at the POPPA datasite, the other night, called me on the 'net-phone, she was so mad. Said the government's fixin' to drill right through the Meerland Sanctuary to get at the iron deposits. If they start strip-mining out there, it'll contaminate the water all the way down the Damisi watershed and poison us all!"

"Well, I can tell you, every single person in my family is votin' the same way. We're fixin' to kick President Andrews' ass out of a job. We gotta get somebody in there who knows what it's like to have half the folks in your neighborhood outta work and damn near killin' themselves with despair a' gettin' any . . ."

Kafari couldn't listen to any more of it. She headed toward the bathrooms, stopping briefly at the receptionist's desk to tell them where she'd be, and closed the door on the mindless babble in the waiting room. She preferred to sit in a public lavatory that smelt of air fresheners and stale urine than listen to any more of POPPA's silver-spun lies or the braying of jackasses who believed them. She understood, profoundly, the impact joblessness had on a person, a family. She understood the loss of self-worth, the sense of helplessness it engendered, had watched members of her family and close friends stricken by one such blow after another.

But POPPA's brand of swill wasn't the answer. To anything. Kafari wet a small towel and laved her face and throat, trying to calm down the gut-churning anger and the nausea it had triggered. She drew several deep, slow breaths, reminding herself of things for which she was thankful. She was profoundly grateful to have her job. And not just any job, either, but a good one, a job that tested her skills, her ingenuity, and let her contribute to the all-important job of rebuilding.

Having passed her practicum with flying colors—due

as much to Sonny's tutelage as to the rigorous courses necessary to secure a psychotronic systems engineering degree—she'd taken a job at Madison's spaceport, which was being rebuilt almost from the ground up. As part of a ground-based team of psychotronic specialists, she worked in tandem with orbital engineers, calibrating the new space station's psychotronic systems as each new module was mated with the others in orbit, then synched to the spaceport's ground-based controllers. High-tech labs on Vishnu had supplied the replacement components for Ziva Two, including the modules Kafari was responsible for correctly calibrating, programming, and fitting into the existing psychotronic computer matrix.

Difficult as it was, she loved her job. With luck, her work would create the chance for others to work, again, as well. Madison's northwest sector, hit so hard during the fighting, was now jammed with construction crews.

By some small miracle, the Engineering Hub—the nerve center of any surface-based spaceport—had survived, undamaged by Deng missiles. With that infrastructure intact, the cost of rebuilding was far lower than it might have been, despite obfuscations by POPPA's chosen spokespersons.

Everywhere POPPA turned its attention, discord followed. Kafari had been less than amused to learn that a major POPPA rally had been scheduled for the same afternoon as her follow-up appointment with the ob-gyn clinic. She should've been able to finish her appointment and leave well in advance of the rally's starting time, but she'd already been here an hour-and-a-half, waiting while emergency cases came into the clinic and bumped others with appointments. There'd been more than a dozen walk-ins so far, all of them presenting the emergency medical vouchers issued to the jobless and their families. Those vouchers meant a patient had to be seen, regardless of caseload, regardless of the bearer's ability to pay anything for the services of physicians, nurse-practitioners, or medical technicians conducting diagnostic testing.

Kafari was not coldhearted, even though she questioned the long-term sustainability of such a program, and certainly didn't feel that those without money should be denied access to medical care they—and in this case, their unborn children—needed. But it was a financial drain their faltering economy couldn't possibly maintain for long. It was downright irritating that she'd missed half an afternoon's work to keep an appointment that others had bumped, by just walking in off the street. And if she didn't get out of the clinic soon, she'd be caught right in the middle of the crush gathering for the POPPA rally scheduled to begin in an hour's time. There was already an immense crowd outside, streaming through downtown Madison toward the rally's main stage, which had been set up in Lendan Park, across Darconi Street from Assembly Hall.

There wasn't much she could do about any of it, however, and Kafari needed this appointment. So she dried her face carefully, reapplied cosmetics, and returned to the waiting room, where she eased herself down into a chair and tried without much success to ignore the news coverage of the impending rally. An entire host of POPPA luminaries appeared on camera, granting interviews that constituted little more than a steady stream of POPPA doctrine, most of it aimed directly at the masses of unemployed urbanites. Gust Ordwyn, rumored to be Vittori Santorini's right-hand propagandist, was holding forth on the manufacturing crisis that had sent heavy industry crashing to a virtual halt.

"We can't afford five more years of President Andrews' insane policies on mining and manufacturing. Jefferson's mines stand silent and empty. Sixteen thousand miners have lost their jobs, their medical coverage, their very homes. John Andrews doesn't even have a plan to put these people back to work! Enough is enough.

"Jefferson needs new answers. New ideas. A new philosophy for rebuilding our economy. One that includes the needs of ordinary, hard-working men and women, not the profit margin of a huge conglomerate that holds half its assets off-world. I ask you, Pol, why do Jefferson's biggest companies transfer their profits off-world when our own people are jobless and starving? Why do they pour huge sums of money into off-world technology instead of rebuilding our own factories, so people can go back to work? It's indecent, it's unethical. It's got to stop."

Pol Jankovitch, predictably, did nothing at all to point out that Gust Ordwyn's accusations, like Nassiona Santorini's "questions" were not designed to be answered factually, but to insinuate a state of affairs that did not, in fact, exist. Kafari was in a position to know exactly what was being ordered from off-world companies: high-tech items Jefferson literally could not manufacture yet.

Pol Jankovitch wasn't interested in the truth. Neither was his boss, media mogul Dexter Courtland. They were interested solely in what message was likeliest to increase viewership, advertising profits, and personal bank accounts. Men like Vittori Santorini and Gust Ordwyn used fools like Courtland and Jankovitch, in an under-the-table handshake that benefitted everyone involved. Except, of course, the average Jeffersonian. And most of *them* were blinded by the rhetoric, the wild promises of wealth, the feeling of power that comes with participating in something big enough to make the government sit up and take notice.

None of which bolstered Kafari's low spirits.

Neither did the next three speakers. Camden Cathmore was a spin expert who constantly quoted the latest results of his favorite tool, the "popular sentiment" poll, so blatantly manipulated, the results meant nothing at all. Carin Avelaine bleated endlessly about "socially conscious education programs" she wanted to implement. And then there was Khroda Arpad, a refugee from one of the hard-hit worlds beyond the Silurian Void, who spoke passionately about the horrors of war as experienced first-hand. She had lost her children in the fighting, which left Kafari's heart aching for her, but Kafari was less impressed by the direction Khroda's grief had taken her. The refugee had launched a crusade to convince as many people as possible that a planet-wide military draft was about to be enacted for the purpose of sending as many of the urban poor and their children as possible to be shot to pieces under alien guns.

None of it made any logical sense and very little of it was even remotely accurate. But the women in this room were eating it up and so, apparently, was the crowd outside. And so were thousands upon thousands more, in every major urban center on Jefferson. Kafari was actually relieved when her name was called by the nurse, allowing her to escape the ugly mood in the waiting room.

The exam was the only thing she'd encountered all day to reassure her fears.

"You're doing fine and the baby's doing fine," the doctor smiled. "Another couple of months and you'll be holding her."

Kafari returned the smile, although a mist had clouded her eyes. "We've got the nursery all set up. Everything's ready. Except her."

The doctor's smile broadened into a grin. "She will be. Take advantage of the next couple of months to put your feet up and rest every chance you get. You'll be running on mighty short sleep, once she's born."

By the time Kafari re-dressed and checked out at the counter, the crowd outside had swelled to a river of people, a thick and slow-moving stream that jammed the street, with every person in it—except Kafari—trying to get to Lendan Park. Kafari's groundcar was in a parking garage three blocks closer to the park, which left Kafari struggling to push herself and her distended belly through the close-packed jam of people. She could smell cheap cologne, unwashed bodies, flatulence, and alcohol. Within a single city block, she found herself fighting a trickle of panic. She didn't like crowds. The last time she'd been near a crowd anywhere close to this size, it had turned on her. Had tried its utmost to *kill* her.

Simon wouldn't be swooping in to rescue *anybody,* tonight.

I have to get out of this crowd, she kept telling herself. *I have to get to the parking garage, at least.* She wouldn't be able to drive through this mess for hours, yet, but she wanted the security her car represented, modest as it was. She wanted metal walls around her. Bullet-proof glass. The gun in the console.

You're being stupid, she told herself sternly. *Just calm down and breathe deeply. There's the garage, right there, just another hundred meters or so . . .* She reached the garage. Unfortunately, she couldn't get anywhere close to the entrance. There were too many people between her and the doorway. She was swept inexorably forward, a slow-motion tide that carried her—greatly against her will—toward the heart of Lendan Park. She was close enough, now, she could see a massive platform towering nearly four meters above the ground, a stage big enough to hold an orchestra. The stage boasted public-address microphones and speakers nearly three meters high, all draped with banners and bunting in POPPA's favorite colors: sunset gold and deep, forest green.

POPPA's "peace banners"—a three-armed triskelion of olive leaves, silhouetted against the golden backdrop—fluttered in the early evening breeze from every corner of the stage, from huge, twenty-meter-high streamers behind the stage, from lamp posts, even tree branches where zealots had hung them. A good half the crowd wore gold and green, in fervent declaration of their social and political preferences. Kafari's cream-colored maternity suit—tailored for a meeting with off-world suppliers' representatives, ships' captains, and engineers to work out the kinks as they brought the new station's systems on-line and ordered additional components—stood out conspicuously against the brighter-hued Party colors or the duller shades of jobless factory workers wearing their sturdy shop-floor uniforms.

Her portion of the crowd came to a halt sixty or so meters from the stage, out near the edge of the park. Kafari's back ached already from standing, the muscles protesting the strain of carrying her burden unsupported.

At least she was wearing sensible shoes. Kafari hadn't worn anything truly impractical since the war.

The people closest to her were an interesting mixture. From the look of it, there wasn't a Granger anywhere in the bunch, but she was able to peg several distinct "types" near her. Factory workers were obvious. So were the students, ranging from high-school up through college-age kids. Others appeared to be middle-class clerical types, shopkeepers, office workers hit by the slump in retail sales of everything from clothing to groundcars.

Still others had that distinct air about them that said "academia," particularly the social sciences and arts professorial types. She didn't spot anyone that looked—or spoke—remotely like an engineer or physicist, but there were plenty to choose from, based on snatches of conversation, if one were interested in delving deeply into the intricacies of post-Terran deconstructionist philosophies—and philologies—in the arts, literature, and what Kafari had always thought of as the pseudo-sciences: astromancy, luminology, sociography.

Any further speculation she might have entertained about the occupations of those near her vanished under a sudden blare of music from those three-meter-high speakers. The base rhythm of drums struck her bones like a shockwave. If she'd had elbow room, she'd have clapped both hands across her ears. The drums were savage, primal, striking a chord in the waiting crowd, which erupted into howls and a massive tsunamic roar that pounded again and again at her eardrums: "*Vit-tor-i! Vit-tor-i!*"

It wasn't difficult to imagine the missing hard-c sound that would have transformed the war-chant into "victory," rather than a summons for the reigning lord of the Populist Order for the Promotion of Public Accord. A wild melody began to play, counterpoint to the drum cadence, stirring the blood and numbing the brain. People were shouting and screaming, waving triskelion banners, jumping up and down in a frenzy that left Kafari bruised from too many sharp shoulders and elbows jabbing soft spots, fortunately most of them striking above her abdomen.

The music rose to a wailing crescendo . . .

Then the banners behind the stage parted and he was there. Vittori. The man with Madison in the palm of his hand. He was striding forward, clad entirely in a golden yellow so light, it appeared luminescent in the gathering gloom of twilight. Where the light of sunset streamed across the stage and its twenty-meter triskelion banners, a golden halo of light shone like something from a painting of the virgin Madonna and her child. Vittori Santorini, standing in the center of that halo, glowed like a saint newly descended from heaven. *My God,* Kafari found herself thinking, *does anybody else realize how dangerous this man is?*

When he lifted both hands, a prophet parting the seas, the music died instantly and the crowd fell silent in the space between one heartbeat and the next. He stood that way for long seconds, hands uplifted in benediction, in ecstatic triumph, in some twisted emotion Kafari couldn't quite define, but left her skin crawling, to see it wash across his face and down the glowing length of his body.

"Welcome," he whispered into the microphone, "to the future of Jefferson."

The crowd went insane. The mind-numbing roar of human voices shook the air like thunder. Vittori, master of crowds, waited for the ovation to die away of its own accord. He stood looking at his acolytes for long moments, smiling softly down at them, then caressed them with that dangerous, velvet voice.

"What do you want?"

"POPPA! POPPA! POPPA!"

Again he smiled. Leaned forward. Waited . . .

"Then show no mercy!" The whiplash of his shout cracked the air like judgment day. "It's time to take what's ours! Our rights! Our money! Our very lives! No more soldiers drafted to die off-world!"

"No more!"

"No more kickbacks to farmers!"

"*No more!*"

"No more pillaging in public lands!"

"*No more!*"

"And no more politicians getting fat and rich while the rest of us starve!"

"*NO MORE!*"

His voice dropped to a velvet caress again. "What are you going to do about it?"

"*Vote! Vote! Vote!*"

"That's right! Get out and vote! Make your voice heard. Demand justice. *Real* justice. Not John Andrews' mockery, kowtowing to the big off-world military machine. It's time Jefferson said 'No!' to war!"

"*No war!*"

"It's time to say 'No!' to higher taxes."

"*No taxes!*"

"It's time we said 'No!' to reckless terraforming schemes and new farms."

"*No farms!*"

"And it's sure as hell time to say 'No more Andrews!'— now or ever!"

"*No Andrews! No Andrews!*"

"Are you with me, Jefferson?"

The crowd exploded again, thousands of throats screaming themselves raw in the chilly air as night settled inexorably across the heart of Madison. The sound echoed off the walls of Assembly Hall, which stood behind them like a basilisk in the gathering darkness, turning not bodies but minds to stone, rendering them incapable of reason. Susceptible to anything this man said. Anything he suggested. Kafari stood caught in the midst of the unholy uproar and shuddered. She was violently cold with the fear rising up from her soul.

He stood there, arms outstretched, basking in the wild sound of adoration, drinking it down like fine wine. It was grotesque. Obscene. Like watching a man bring himself to orgasm in public. She wanted out of this crowd, out of the insanity flying loose in Lendan

Park. Wanted Simon's arms around her and Sonny's guns overhead, keeping watch in the coming night. She knew, in that one, horrible moment, that John Andrews was doomed to lose the election. Knew it as surely as she knew the kind of programming code required to send a psychotronic brain like Sonny's into alert status. Or over the edge into battle mode.

We're in trouble, oh, Simon, we're in trouble . . .

The crowd was shrieking, "V—V—V!"

V for Vittori. For victory. For victim . . . The prophet of the hour lifted his hands again, quieting the crowd to a hush so sudden, the sound of wind snapping through the "peace banners" cracked like gunfire. When the silence was absolute, he said, "We have work waiting for us, my friends. Wild work, critical work. We have to defeat the monsters ruling us with an iron hand and a stone heart. We have to throw off the yoke of slavery and call our skies, our children, our lives our own again. We have to rebuild the factories. The shops. The very future. We have to ensure the rights that everyone has, not just a privileged few. The rights to a job. To economic equality. To choose where we go or don't go. Where we send our children or don't send them. What we do—or don't do—with our land. Our seas. Our air. We choose! We say! *AND WE ACT!*"

The thunder was back in his voice.

"We act *now*, my friends! Now, before it's too late. We take charge. Before fools like John Andrews destroy us! It's time to send a message. Loud and clear."

The crowd was screaming again.

Vittori shouted into the microphone, shouted above that primal roar.

"Are you with us?"

"Yes!"

"Are you ready to take back our world?"

"*Yes!*"

"And are you ready," his voice dropped again to a piercing whisper, "are you ready to give our enemies what they so richly deserve?"

"YES!"

"Then claim your power! Claim it now! Go out into the streets and smite those who oppose us! Do it now! Go! Go! Go!"

The crowd took up the chant, screaming it into the darkness. Vittori moved with sudden, blinding speed. He snatched up a microphone stand, held it overhead like a club, spun suddenly to face a huge picture of John Andrews that had appeared as though conjured from thin air, a picture painted on glass, translucent where spotlights sprang abruptly to life in the darkness. Vittori turned the microphone stand in his hands, swung it in a whistling, vicious arc, let go at the height of the backswing. The heavy metal base crashed through the glass, shattering it. Pieces and shards of John Andrews' broken face rained down onto the stage. A roar erupted, shrieking like a hot, volcanic wind.

The crowd was moving, surging out toward its edges, amoeba-like. Tendrils of that massive amoeba engulfed the streets, the buildings beyond them. The sound of smashed glass punctuated the roar, staccato-quick, a rhythm of hatred and rage. The surging mass of people gathered speed, spreading out in all directions. Kafari found herself forced to run, to avoid being trampled by those rushing toward the edges of the park, into and past her. She held her abdomen, stricken with mortal terror for the baby as she ran with the crowd. They were, at least, running toward the garage where her car was parked.

They'd nearly reached it when the crowd smashed into something that was fighting back. Kafari couldn't see what. Half the lights in the park were out, either pulled down or the glass smashed out, plunging great stretches of park into near-Stygian darkness. Storefronts and public buildings on every side stood with broken doors and windows gaping wide, interior lights splashing across the edges of the battle and the running figures of people smashing and looting their way through the rooms beyond.

Something arced high overhead, exploding with a cloud

of choking chemical smoke. *Riot gas!* Kafari pulled off her jacket, covered her lower face with it as the smoke drifted down, engulfing the crowd within seconds. Eyes streaming, Kafari held her breath as long as she could, straining to reach the edge of the embattled crowd. She could see a line of police, now, truncheons rising and falling as they clubbed rioters to the ground. The savagery of it shocked Kafari, left her faltering, trying to backpedal against the crush of people pressing forward from deeper in the park.

The crowd shoved her right toward the line of police. They had their shields up, riot helmets down, while a second line pumped more gas rounds into the air. Others were firing at the crowd. Something whizzed past Kafari's ear, striking the person behind her with a sickening, meaty thud that wrenched loose a scream. Terror scalded her, terror for her unborn child. She shoved sideways, trying to turn, found herself embroiled in a flying wedge of howling rioters, men who'd ripped up street signs, who'd broken thick branches out of the trees, swinging and jabbing them at the line of riot police. She was shoved forward, trapped in the center—

Police went down. A sudden hole gaped open. Right in front of her. Kafari stumbled forward, driven from behind, carried through the opening by the howling demons who'd battered their way through. She found herself running down the street. She headed toward the garage, less than half a block ahead. Others were streaming into the garage, ahead of her, evidently looking for a way out of the battle. Groundcar alarms screamed theft-attempt warnings. Kafari reached the doorway. Saw the automated attendant's traffic bar snap and vanish as people shoved past the barrier.

Then she was inside, stumbling forward, trying to reach a staircase. She made it to the dubious safety of the nearest stairwell, badly winded and coughing violently. She could hardly climb, could barely see through the streaming tears. She fumbled her way up one flight, reached the floor her car was on. Stumbling badly, she managed to reach the proper row. She keyed her wrist-comm, flashing a message to the car to unlock itself and start the engine. Three seconds later, she fell through the open door into the driver's seat. Kafari slammed the door shut, locked the car, sagged against the cushions and dragged down deep gulps of air.

Other people were running past, having reached her floor. She dug the gun out of the console, held it firm in a double-handed grip that shook with such violence, the muzzle described wide circles in front of her. Shudders gripped her whole body. When something smacked into the door, she twisted around. The gun came up. Her finger slid home. A wild-eyed man stared down the wrong end of the bore. His mouth dropped into an "o" of shock. Then he turned his larcenous attention to another car down the row from hers.

The muzzle of her gun rattled against the window glass in a jittery rhythm.

I will never, ever, she promised herself with devout intensity, *get caught in the middle of another political riot.* . . . Her wrist-comm beeped at her. Simon's voice, harsh with strain, sliced into her awareness.

"Kafari? Are you there, Kafari?"

She managed to push the right button on her third, shaking try. "Y-yeah, I'm h-here."

"Oh, thank God . . ." A whisper, reverent in its relief. "Where are you? I've been calling and calling."

"In the car. In the garage. I got caught in that unholy hell of a rally."

"How—never mind how. Can you get out?"

"No. Not yet. I'm shaking too hard to drive," she added with grim candor. "And there's gas everywhere, riot gas. I can hardly see. There's no way I'm going to try driving through the mess out there in the streets. This thing's turned ugly. *Real* ugly. On both sides."

"Yes," Simon growled. "I know. What?" he asked, voice abruptly muffled. "It's my wife, goddammit." A brief pause, as he listened. Then, "You want me to *what*? Jesus Christ, are you out of your idiotic *mind*?"

Whatever was being said—and whoever was saying it—Simon was clearly having none of it. She heard an indistinct mumble of voices, realizing abruptly that the transmission was scrambled, somehow, coming across the unsecured transmission to her wrist-comm as garbled sound rather than sensible words. Who was he talking to? The military? The president? Kafari swallowed hard, trying to muffle another fit of coughing. Whoever it was, they wanted something from Simon and the only reason she could imagine for someone to call Simon was for a request that he send Sonny somewhere.

Here? Into the riot? *Oh, shit* . . .

Memory pinned her to the seat cushions, paralyzed her limbs, her brain with remembrance. Sonny's guns whirling in a dance of rapid-fire death . . . his screens flaring bright under alien guns . . . *Not again,* she whimpered. Not now, carrying Simon's child. A child they'd struggled so hard to conceive. Then she heard Simon's voice, cracking through the terror in crisp, no-nonsense tones.

"Absolutely not. You don't send a Bolo into the middle of a city for riot control. I don't give a damn how many buildings they've broken into. You don't use a Bolo to quash a civilian riot. It's worse than killing a mosquito with a hydrogen bomb." Another interlude of indistinct sounds interrupted Simon. Her husband finally growled, "It's not my job to make sure you win this or any other election. Yes, I watched the coverage of the rally. I know exactly what that little asshole said. And I repeat, it's your problem, not mine. You're on your own. Yes, dammit, that's my final word. I'm *not* ordering Sonny to go anywhere tonight."

A moment later, Simon spoke to her again. "Kafari, do you want me to come in with the aircar?"

"No," she said, after squelching the instantaneous, little-girl desire to have him swoop down once again to play knight-errant, "I don't. I'm okay. I may be stuck here for a few hours, but I'm okay. And the baby's okay, Simon, I'm sure of it. If I need help, I'll call."

"You've got your birthday present?" he asked, in oblique reference to the console gun she carried.

"In my hand," she said cheerfully.

"Good girl. All right, sit tight for now. I can be there faster than an ambulance could reach you, if you need help."

"Okay." She smiled through the mess streaming down her face, aware that her blouse was wet and that her suit was probably ruined beyond repair by the damage sustained. Her smile turned rueful. If she could worry about her suit, she really was all right. "Simon?"

"Yes, hon?"

"I love you."

His voice gentled. "Oh, hon, I love you so much it hurts."

I know, she thought silently. She was sorry for that part of it. Sorry for all the reasons behind it. For her inability to change it, to change the reality behind the old pain, the new fears. The best she could do was love him back, as hard and as fiercely as she could manage. She settled back against the cushions, laid the gun in her ungainly lap, and waited for the end of danger, so she could go home, again.

II

It was, Simon reflected bitterly, one of the worst political mishandlings he had ever witnessed. Images relayed through Sonny's surveillance systems, picked up from a combination of commercial news broadcasts—including sky-eyes in hovering aircars—and police cameras, told a tale of unfolding disaster in the heart of Madison. The wildly inflammatory performance by Vittori Santorini was bad enough, on its own. He'd never seen anything like that virtuoso performance, with one man plucking and vibrating and drumming a crowd's emotions to riotous heat, with nothing more than a fanfare, a well-timed sunset, and a few words uttered with stunning skill.

Far worse—infinitely worse—was John Andrews' reaction to the violence that erupted almost inevitably in the wake of that stellar, if brief, show. With rioters engulfing the heart of downtown Madison, John Andrews had not appreciated Simon's flat refusal to send in the Bolo. Simon hadn't thought it was possible to commit folly greater than using a Bolo to break up a riot, but what he was witnessing now . . .

Riot police, intent on containing the violence, were pumping gas cannisters and riot-control batons into the crowd along a periphery six blocks deep and spreading. Rioters, crazed by hatred, rage, and choking gas clouds, had rushed police lines in dozens of places. Officers were going down under makeshift bludgeons, while the police were using riot clubs in self-defense. Simon noted with a cold, jaundiced eye that none of the commercial news feeds contained footage of rioters beating downed law enforcement agents, but showed graphic images of police clubbing down women and half-grown teenagers.

He sat alone in the apartment, watching the split-screen images in rising dismay, while John Andrews' reelection chances grew dimmer with each passing moment. If he hadn't reached Kafari, reassuring himself that she was unharmed, he would've been streaking toward Lendan Park in an aircar. He was seriously tempted to fly in, anyway, and land on the roof of the parking garage where she was trapped for God-alone knew how long. The only things that stopped him were an unshakable faith in Kafari's ability to defend herself from a blockaded bunker—he'd made damned sure that her groundcar was as well armored as her Airdart—and the knowledge that if things went crazy enough in Madison, tonight, he might well need to be right where he was, to watch developments through Sonny's eyes and ears, rather than in an aircar with nothing but a commlink and a small-scale datascreen.

The crowd spilling out of Lendan Park poured down Darconi Street, looting and pillaging through government offices and retail businesses. A cordon of police stood locked shield-to-shield between the crazed mob and Assembly Hall, swaying in places where the shock of human bodies thudding against the riot shields pushed the officers back, toward the wide steps leading up to Jefferson's highest legislative nerve center.

Simon had a grimly clear picture of what was at risk, given the mood of that crowd and the contents of that building. He could understand, at a deep level, the president's desire to use military force great enough to stun that unholy pack of madmen into silence. Not only was Assembly Hall and all its records and high-tech equipment at risk, so was the Presidential Residence, only a few short blocks away. If the rioters breached the locked shields of the police trying to contain the mob, things would go from ugly to deadly.

Something needed to be done, fast.

Simon wasn't expecting what someone—the president or maybe a panicked military official—did about it. Despite the poor lighting conditions, since full darkness had fallen by now, he caught the first whiff of trouble within moments, far sooner than the news-camera crews realized what was happening. He saw the cannisters go off midair with a gout of flame as they broke open explosively, but there was no smoke, no visible cloud of riot gas, just a colorless burst above the crowd. Within seconds, people were falling down like children's jackstraws, piled every which way. They toppled in a flopping, macabre wave, grotesquely animated for two or three seconds before going utterly still. The wave spread faster than heartbeats. One of the news cameras abruptly plunged to the street, continuing to record the now-skewed images as its owner plummeted to pavement, as well.

Simon came to his feet, sweating and swearing. "Kafari! Can you hear me? Kafari, shut off the ventilation on the car! Seal it up!"

"What?" she sounded confused.

"They've gassed the crowd with war agents!"

"Oh, God . . ."

Simon couldn't tell what she was doing, through the open commlink. He could just make out her pained, gasping breaths, a sound of sudden, raw terror. *Surely*, Simon told himself, *surely they weren't stupid enough to use a lethal compound on an unarmed crowd?* He'd looked at a supposedly comprehensive inventory of munitions and war agents, just prior to the Deng invasion, and there hadn't been any biochemical weaponry listed. Had somebody quietly stockpiled it, without recording the fact in the military inventories? Or was this a recent import? From the freighter in parking orbit at Ziva Two, maybe, slipped in with parts and equipment needed to complete the station? Either way, heads needed to roll for it. Roll and bounce.

If it was a big-enough molecule, it might not get into the car. He'd paid top money for both of Kafari's vehicles, air and ground, with dozens of specialized modifications planned with war in mind. Even if it did get inside, it might not be lethal. There were paralytic agents that would immobilize a person without killing or doing irreversible damage. There were others, though, that inflicted permanent damage, sometimes severe. What a "non-lethal" gas could do to Kafari and their unborn child . . . The edge of the desk bit into his hands, while he waited in helpless terror.

Talk to me, hon, talk to me . . .

"I've got everything sealed," Kafari said in a voice hoarse with raw stress. "The vents, the windows, everything I can think to seal."

"Can you get out of the garage? Drive away from the affected zone?"

"No, the streets are jammed. I barely made it to the car."

"Sit tight, then. Sonny, track the signal from Kafari's commlink. Pinpoint her location on a map of Madison. Show me wind speed and direction. And get President Andrews on the line. I need to talk to him."

"Retrieving data. Superimposing now. There is no response from the president."

Simon swore viciously. New split-screen images popped up in a mosaic, showing him the downtown area, the spreading clouds of visible gas marking the drift-direction of the invisible ones, as well, and the atmospherics he'd requested. The tightest of the knots in his muscles relaxed a fraction. Kafari's refuge was upwind of the cone-shaped dispersal pattern. A couple of city blocks upwind. Not a lot of distance, but it might be enough. Maybe. *Let it be enough.*

"Sonny," he said, voice rough with strain, "send an emergency notice to the commander of Nineveh Base and the hospitals. We're looking at massive casualties, already, and that gas cloud's going to keep spreading. Warn law-enforcement officials downwind. Have 'em sound an emergency alarm. If we can get people into shelters . . ." He broke off, watching the speed of dispersal, and swore again. There wasn't *time* to warn enough people. The leading edge was already spreading out into the suburbs, the teargas attenuated enough to be essentially harmless, but what about the paralytic agent?

Simon jabbed controls with savage fingers, trying to contact the president again. He managed to raise a staffer on the fourth attempt.

"Simon Khrustinov, here. Find John Andrews. Find him *now*. I don't care if you have to yank him off the toilet, get him on the line."

"Hold, please," the woman said, voice infuriatingly calm.

An eternity of seconds crawled past. Then the president, sounding out of breath and flustered, snapped, "What the hell do *you* want, Krustinov?"

"Who authorized use of a paralytic war agent?"

"War agent? What the hell are you talking about? The police are using riot gas, Khrustinov. Thanks to *you*." The last word was bitter, full of hatred.

"Then you'd better talk to the police, Andrews, because you've got a major disaster spreading through Madison. Turn on your damned datascreen and watch the newsfeed.

We're talking thousands of casualties and the downwind dispersal pattern is still spreading—"

"Simon," Sonny broke into the conversation, "riots are erupting in Anyon, Cadellton, and Dunham. Unemployed miners and factory workers are rampaging through residential and commercial districts, protesting the use of biochemical weaponry on unarmed civilians in Madison. I recommend shutting down all commercial news broadcasts to prevent further inflammatory footage from sparking more protest riots."

John Andrews abruptly activated the video link, looking bewildered. "What the hell's going on?" he was demanding of a staffer. "Don't tell me you don't know! Find out!" He turned to look into the camera. "Khrustinov, will you kindly explain the magnitude of the problem?"

Simon sent the data images Sonny was providing, tracking the magnitude of the unfolding disaster. Andrews took one look and blanched, skin fading to the color of dirty snow. "Oh . . . my . . . God . . ." He swung around, shouting, "Get General Gunther on the phone. Get him *now*. Alert the hospitals. And find out what that stuff is—and who authorized it!"

A deep, nasty trickle of suspicion made itself felt. President Andrews didn't look or sound like a man trying to cover up a bad decision. He genuinely didn't know what was happening, what had been released, who had authorized it. Simon couldn't imagine any lower-ranking officer on site using a paralytic agent without extremely high clearance, which narrowed the field to a very small number of suspects. Acting on a hunch, Simon said, "Sonny, show me Lendan Park, real-time as of now. And did you record anything after the end of that speech?"

"Transmitting view of Lendan Park," Sonny responded. "Accessing databanks."

The heart of Lendan Park was eerie in the darkness, too still and far too silent. The only things moving were tree branches and the gold and green "peace banners" fluttering and snapping in the wind. He could see hundreds, perhaps thousands, of bodies strewn across the

ground like flotsam thrown up onto the shore after a
storm at sea. He used digital controls to zoom in on
the stage, frowning to himself. The stage was empty.
Vittori Santorini was nowhere to be seen. When had
he left? Where was he now? Somewhere in that crowd
of fallen followers?

Sonny shunted a recording of the speech and its
aftermath to another split-screen viewing window. He
killed the audio and simply watched the final moments
of the speech and the frenzied explosion of the crowd.
There were multiple views of the stage popping up as
Sonny tapped more news and police cameras. Most of
the cameras swung to follow the abrupt wave of violence
engulfing the edges of the park, but a couple of them,
doubtless security cameras installed in police vehicles,
continued to show the stage. He watched, cold to his
bones, as the clouds of tear gas drifted past the stage.
Watched, even colder, as the still-unidentified war agent
began its macabre work.

He was still frowning at the scene when a rustle of
motion near the base of the stage arrested his attention.
He adjusted the zoom and watched, morbidly fascinated,
as several people crawled out from under the stage, the
skirts of which had been draped in POPPA bunting.
Simon leaned forward, abruptly. Whoever they were,
they slipped into the open, stepping cautiously across
the fallen bodies, moving furtively and quickly. Simon
counted five of them, all wearing gas masks. Why? Had
they merely exercised prudence, foreseeing the use of
tear gas? Or had they known in advance that a more
dangerous substance was going to be launched into
the air above their loyal followers? He didn't like the
implications. Not one teensy bit.

Kafari's voice interrupted his dark and suspicious train
of thought.

"I feel okay, Simon," Kafari said. "Should I be feeling
sick? What's happening, out there?"

More of the subconscious tension gripping his midsection uncoiled. "Honey, you have no idea how glad I am to

hear that." Simon willed his hands to let go their death-grip on the edge of his desk, then drew several deep, calming breaths. "And no, you shouldn't be feeling sick. If you'd breathed that stuff, you'd have gone into convulsions and ended paralyzed within a few seconds."

A shocked, choked sound of horror came through the commlink. "Convulsions? Paralyzed? What in the name of all that's unholy did they turn loose?"

"I'm trying to find out. Don't get out of the car for anyone or anything until you get an all-clear from me. The affected zone is downwind from you, so you should be all right where you are. Don't try driving out, yet. God knows what trigger-happy police would do, watching a car emerge from that part of the city, just now. Do you have anything to eat or drink with you?"

"Uh . . . Let me check the emergency kit." He heard rustling sounds, one sharpish grunt, then she said, "I've got a couple of bottles of water and some energy bars."

"Good. I'd say we're looking at maybe eight to ten hours, to get things calmed down and get some answers on what we're dealing with, here. Ration them, if you have to, but remember dehydration's worse than hunger."

"Right." Grim, down-to-business. The voice of a woman who'd seen combat and knew the score. "I'll wait it out as long as it takes. I don't suppose anyone knows where Vittori Santorini is?"

"Not yet," Simon growled. "Why?"

"I'd like to give him my personal thanks for landing us in this mess."

Simon surprised himself with a smile, fleeting but genuine. "That's a sight I'd give a paycheck to see."

Her chuckle reassured him. "Love you, Simon. Call me when you can."

"Love you, too," he said, voice rough with emotion. *All to hell and gone . . .*

He turned his attention to the disaster engulfing the rest of Jefferson. Sonny was tapping news feeds from five major cities, now, rocked by explosive protest riots. Law enforcement agencies, engulfed and overwhelmed, were screaming for help from Jefferson's military. Reserve forces were scrambling from half a dozen military bases, rushing riot-control units to contain the damage. Simon scowled. The very presence of soldiers in the street was *creating* damage, serious damage, guaranteed to play right into Vittori Santorini's grasping hands. Rioters on the receiving end of combat soldiers' armed attention would lay blame, loudly and savagely. And there was only one logical scapegoat available to take the brunt of the blame: John Andrews.

With the election tomorrow . . .

Simon swore under his breath, torn between disgust and a sneaking trickle of admiration for a stunning job of planning and executing the downfall of a political regime inimical to Vittori's plans. The man was fiendishly clever, charismatic, a natural showman—and deadlier than any scorpion hatched on old Terra. Simon had never seen any political or social movement capture hearts and minds as fast as Vittori's Populist Order for Promoting Public Accord had, gaining speed and winning converts by the thousands every day.

How many more would join POPPA after tonight, Simon couldn't even hazard a guess, but he was betting the final tally would run to the millions. He wondered bleakly if John Andrews truly understood the magnitude of political disaster Jefferson now faced. POPPA's so-called party platform was a wildly jumbled hodgepodge of rabid environmentalism, unsupportable social engineering schemes with no basis in reality, and an economic policy that was, at best, a schizophrenic disaster begging the egg for a chance to wreak uncountable chaos.

Within half an hour, the magnitude of the night's damage was brutally apparent. Smoke was rising toward the stars from dozens of arson fires blazing unchecked across downtown Madison, where firefighters—forced by circumstances to relinquish their biohazard gear to emergency medical teams—refused to go into the affected zone until more equipment could be brought in from Nineveh Base. With conflicting news reports flying wild, John Andrews called a press briefing, appearing before the stunned population with a plea for a return to calm.

"We are trying to determine the number of casualties, but the vast majority of victims are alive," he said, visibly shaken. "Medical teams have set up emergency field hospitals in Lendan Park and the Franklin Banks residential area. Nearly a hundred doctors, triage nurses, and emergency medical technicians are moving through the area in full biohazard suits, administering counter-paralytic agents and treating people with serious injuries. The paralytic agent appears to be affecting the voluntary muscle groups, which means most people should not be at risk of death. We're still trying to determine what the agent is, so we can administer effective medical treatment. Be assured that no one in my administration or law enforcement will rest until we have found and brought to justice the person or persons responsible for this atrocity against unarmed civilians. I therefore urge you to return to your homes while professional emergency teams respond to the crisis."

It was, Simon scowled, one of the worst speeches he had ever heard. Instead of reassuring the public with carefully considered, factual information designed to relieve fears without conjuring new ones, he had dwelt on the most disturbingly negative aspects of the crisis. He had then, with fumbling stupidity, called the whole sorry disaster an atrocity—a phrase guaranteed to further upset people—and tried to pin blame on a vague threat from unknown subversives.

It didn't matter that he was probably right, given the evidence Simon had already gathered. Millions of people world-wide had been watching in stunned disbelief as embattled law-enforcement officials clubbed civilians to the street and gassed the crowd with riot-control chemicals. With those scenes imprinted vividly on the public consciousness, it was a very, very short step to assuming that police had also fired the paralytic agent.

By refusing to publicly admit that possibility, President Andrews had insulted the intelligence of the entire voting populace. Regardless of who had fired those cannisters, Vittori Santorini had just accomplished his primary objective—violent disruption of the social order, necessitating strong-armed measures to bring things under control.

Just before midnight, John Andrews issued orders imposing martial law on every urban center in Jefferson and announced a planet-wide curfew until order had been restored. Kafari was trapped for the duration. Simon spent a long, bitter, sleepless night, watching the unfolding dynamics of the situation. Armed soldiers with live ammo in their guns deprived the mobs of their ability to loot and destroy at will, so the rioters returned to their homes, switched on their computers, hooked themselves into the datanet, and churned out a flood of angry rhetoric, flaming everyone and everything connected to John Andrews and maligning the president's personal habits, decisions, and political allies.

POPPA's datasite, so inundated by people trying to access the live news footage, the recorded replays of the speech and its aftermath, and the policy statements issued by Vittori Santorini and his sister, crashed the entire datanet for nearly three hours. By dawn, word had finally begun to trickle out that President Andrews had been correct in at least one critical factor: most people *would* recover. Ninety-eight percent of them, in fact, were ambulatory and able to return home. The agent had—thank God—been a short-duration chemical that was already degrading into an inert, harmless substance. The only casualties were those with underlying medical conditions—asthma and heart failure being the primary causes of death—and those crushed in the stampede or fatally injured when they collapsed on stairways, while driving groundcars, or operating dangerous machinery.

At the mere suggestion that there might be evidence implicating Vittori Santorini and other high-ranking POPPA leaders, the riots flared up again, so violently that John Andrews was forced to call another press conference. "We are continuing the investigation and are conducting a thorough probe into the actions of law enforcement personnel as well as civilians and armed-forces officials. We are trying to determine whether this paralytic agent was obtained from military stockpiles held in reserve for invasion contingencies or if it was acquired recently, either through manufacture on Jefferson or purchase from off-world sources. We have no direct evidence linking this dastardly act to any individual or group. Without hard evidence, this administration cannot condone the unsupported accusations made against Vittori Santorini and his colleagues in POPPA. In the interest of ensuring public safety and protecting the civil rights of those regrettably and publicly named as potential suspects, I therefore extend presidential amnesty to any individuals or groups who might have been associated with this attack. We are asking that people return to their homes again, in the hopes that martial law and curfews will not have to be invoked again."

Simon just groaned, rubbing grit-filled and bloodshot eyes in a weary, frustrated gesture. Offering amnesty to people like Vittori Santorini might—just might—get people back into their homes again, but the long-term effects were staggering and dreadful in every way Simon could twist and turn the implications. Simon knew enough Terran military history to understand very thoroughly the concept of Danegeld. It *was* possible to buy peace, but only for a short time. Once convinced that a government was willing to capitulate to demands and threats, the Danes came back again and again, each time demanding more concessions and a higher price for continued peace.

John Andrews had already blown his election chances out of the water. He had now blown all hope that Vittori Santorini's uncivilized behavior would cease. Indeed, the double-damned fool had just ensured that Vittori's methods would proliferate, unchecked and unstoppable. Jefferson's future looked, quite abruptly, bleak as a snow-choked winter sky. The sole bright moment in Simon's morning was Kafari's arrival home, safe and unharmed. Exhaustion pulled her shoulders down, left her eyes bleary and her footsteps uncertain. He held onto her for long moments, then took her face in both hands. "You need some sleep," he murmured.

"So do you."

"I'll sleep soon enough. I've got stimulant tablets in my system, just now. I need to stay awake until this crisis is past. But you," he added, lifting her and carrying her into the bedroom, "are taking yourself and our daughter to bed."

"I'm hungry," she protested.

"I'll bring you something."

After setting her down against the pillows, Simon put together a sandwich and some soup, carrying them into the bedroom on a tray. He halted, three strides into the room, then set the tray carefully on one corner of the dresser. Kafari was asleep. She looked more like an exhausted little girl than a woman in the advanced stages of pregnancy, who'd spent the night in a locked car with a gun in her lap. He brushed a wisp of hair back from her brow. She didn't even stir. Very gently, Simon pulled the covers around her shoulders. He tiptoed out, retrieving her dinner on the way. He swung the door closed with a soft click of the latch. She was safely home. For the moment, that was all that mattered.

There'd be time enough later for worrying about what happened next.

III

The late afternoon sun felt good on her skin as Kafari left the spaceport's new engineering hub and headed through the employee parking area. The fresh wind, whipping inland from the sea that rolled ashore just a stone's throw from the terminal, blew away some of the lingering distaste of a day spent in the company of people who had flocked to the POPPA cause like *teglee* fish to the net. She was tired of hearing the POPPA manifesto discussed with such fervent enthusiasm. Tired of biting her tongue to keep from answering with brutal honesty when co-workers asked her what it had been like, to see the great, the wondrous Santorini in person, to be right in the middle of ground zero when the police tried to murder decent, honest citizens merely expressing their opinions.

Kafari wanted to keep her job. So she answered in monosyllables and vowed never again to tell her secretary *anything* about her life outside the office. Truth to tell, most of the people who'd asked breathlessly for the juicy details were disappointed to learn that she hadn't actually been paralyzed by the gas. After a whole day spent fending off ghouls, reporters, and overzealous proselytizers convinced she could aid their cause in seeking new converts—the woman who'd saved President Lendan's life, only to be gassed by John Andrews' uniformed stormtroopers was, they reasoned, a photo-op too good to pass up—Kafari was on nonstop burn mode.

When she got to her aircar, that burn exploded into molten rage. Some slimy little activist had slapped a big, ugly sticker right across the side, with rampant red letters that shouted *"POPPA Knows Best!"*

"The thrice-blasted *hell* it does!"

She scraped at the offensive mess in a fury worthy of a valkyrie. She succeeded in shredding her fingernails, the paint job on her beautiful new car, and what was left of her ragged temper. She finally gave up, vowing to use acid, if necessary, and simply repaint the car. She popped the driver's hatch, levered her ungainly bulk into the seat, webbed herself in, and snarled at the psychotronic unit to take her to Klameth Canyon's landing field, which had been designated as a polling place.

For the first time in her life, Kafari resented the constitution's attempt to reduce election fraud by insisting that each voter cast a physical ballot at a controlled polling site. The e-voting encryption methods used on Mali and Vishnu, which allowed people to vote via the datanet, had been deemed insufficiently secure by Jefferson's founders, even though Kafari could have written the psychotronic safeguards into such a system in her sleep. The only voters allowed to cast an electronic ballot were off-world citizens, including nearly twenty-thousand soldiers now serving in the Concordiat's armed forces.

She briefly envied the soldiers. The last thing she wanted, tonight, was to stand in line for God alone knew how long, then fly all the way back to Nineveh Base before she could collapse with Simon and watch the election returns. Kafari leaned back against the cushions and consciously reminded herself that she was proud of her work, proud that she was helping to build a fitting legacy to a fine man's courage and wisdom. That legacy meant more prosperity for her entire world, a labor of love in memory of a man whose death had hurt her profoundly.

By the time her aircar touched down at Klameth Canyon field, it was nearly dark. There were so many other aircars, scooters, and even groundcars overflowing the section allotted to parking ground-based vehicles, the auto-tower routed her to a space virtually at the edge of the immense field. That was just as well, since she didn't want anybody out here to see that wretched POPPA slogan stuck to the side of her Airdart. Kafari popped her aircar's hatch and climbed out into the coolness of early evening, glancing up by habit to see the last of the sunlight fading from blood-red to darkness on the highest peaks of the broken, buckled, spectacularly weathered Damisi ranges.

She shivered in the chilly autumn wind and made her way across the field, heading for the terminal that had been rebuilt by local volunteer labor. The buzz of voices was a welcome sound as she neared the long, low building that housed Klameth Canyon Airfield's engineers, auto-tower equipment, machinery used to maintain the landing field, and storage racks for rental scooters. There was, as she'd feared, a long line, but the voices that reached out from the darkness settling rapidly over the

Canyon were friendly, happy ones, engaged in the warm, relaxed conversation that had been a mainstay of Kafari's life until her departure for school on Vishnu. There was a buoyant, comfortable quality to the way country folk spoke to one another that reached out to wrap Kafari in an almost-tangible blanket of soothing familiarity.

When she reached the back of the line, folks paused in their conversation and turned to welcome her. "Hello, child," a grandmotherly woman greeted her with a smile warm as pure Asali honey. "You must've come a far piece, tonight, to vote?"

Kafari found herself smiling as a knot of tension, so habitual she'd nearly forgotten it was there, unwound and let her relax. "Yes, I flew in from work at the spaceport." She grinned. "I forgot to change my residence in the database."

Chuckles greeted that admission, then the conversation resumed, apparently where it had left off. Talk flowed free and easy, in swirling little eddies as they moved forward, each shuffle taking them two or three steps closer to the polling station. Most of the talk revolved around the harvest.

As they approached the big sliding doors where people paused to have their ID scanned, the station's outdoor security lights gave Kafari a better look at those standing with her in line. That was when she noticed a young woman her own age about a meter further along, who kept turning to look back at Kafari. Like Kafari, the girl was visibly pregnant. Her lovely olive-toned complexion and features suggested Semitic ancestry. Every few moments, she would look like she wanted to say something, but was hesitant to speak. They were still about fifteen paces from the doors when she finally found the courage to walk back to where Kafari stood in line.

"You're Kafari Khrustinova, aren't you?"

Tension in her gut tightened down again. "Yes," she said quietly.

"My name's Chaviva Benjamin. I was just wondering . . . Could you give your husband a message?"

"A message?" she echoed.

"Well, yes. My sister Hannah volunteered to go off-world, you see. She sent a message home to us, on the freighter that came in last week, bringing parts for Ziva Two. She's a nurse. They've assigned her to a naval cruiser that came in for repairs and resupply."

Kafari nodded, puzzled as to where this might be going.

"Some of the navy people asked my sister where she was from, so she told them about Jefferson. And she mentioned Simon Khrustinov and his Bolo." Again the girl hesitated, then got the rest of it out in a rush. "The ship was at Etaine, you see. During the fighting and the evacuation. They all knew who he was. Those navy people, they said . . ." She blinked and swallowed hard before saying, "Well, they think pretty highly of him. They told her there's a lot your husband didn't mention, Mrs. Khrustinova, that day the president died."

Kafari didn't know what to say.

Mrs. Benjamin said in a hushed voice, "I wish the folks on the news, here, had told us more about him, when he first came. They never mentioned the Home-star Medallion of Valor he won, the same day his Bolo earned that Gold Galactic Cluster, and I think they should have. The people on my sister's ship said we were luckier than we knew, to have him assigned to us. Could you tell him, please, not everybody believes those idiots at POPPA? I lost both of my parents and all four of my brothers in the invasion, but Colonel Khrustinov and his Bolo aren't to blame. No matter what people like Nassiona Santorini say about it."

Before Kafari could gather her stunned wits, a big rawboned man in his sixties, wearing a utility-looped belt that held the tools of a rancher's trade, spoke up, touching the brim of a sun-bleached work hat. "Girl's right, ma'am. I don't rightly know what those folks in Madison use for brains. Anyone with half a set of wits can see right through all the holes in their thinkin'. There's not two words in ten comes out of their mouths that even make sense."

A much older man, his face and hands as weathered as the dark cliffs above them, said harshly, "They may be stupid, but there's a lot of 'em. I've been watching the folks in this voting line, same as I've been watching the pews of a Sunday morning and the feed and seed shops of a Saturday afternoon, and there's hardly more'n a handful of Grangers to be seen, that's of the age to go getting married and having babies. Beggin' your pardon, ma'am," he offered Kafari an apologetic bow. "But facts is facts. We've sent the best and brightest we got out to the stars, and all their courage and good sense went with 'em. What's left in this canyon is us old folks, mostly, and the little ones too small to go. I don't like it, I'm telling you. Don't like it one bit to hear those ninnies in town and then count up how many folks are left to tell 'em what nonsense they're bleating."

Others chimed in, stoutly defending Simon's good name and asking her to pass along their gratitude. The spontaneous outpouring overwhelmed her, particularly after the bilge Nassiona Santorini had spewed all over the airwaves. Then the grandmotherly woman who'd greeted her first took both of Kafari's hands in her own. "Child," she said, gripping Kafari's fingers so hard they ached, "you tell that man of yours there's not a soul in this Canyon who thinks anything but the best about him." Then she winked and that honey-warm smile wrapped itself around Kafari's heart. "After all, he had the good sense to marry one of our own!"

Chuckles greeted the observation, dispelling the tension.

"You bring him out here, come the harvest dancing," the older woman added, "and we'll show him what Granger hospitality is all about."

Kafari smiled through a sudden mist and promised to bring Simon to the harvest festivals. Then she asked Chaviva Benjamin about the baby she carried.

"It's a girl," Chaviva said, touching her own abdomen almost reverently. "Our first. My husband, Annais, is so happy his feet hardly touch the ground, these days. She'll be due right about time for Hannukah."

Kafari found herself smiling. "I'm glad for you," she said. "Mine's a girl, too."

"Good," Chaviva said softly, meeting and holding her gaze. "We need the kind of children you and your husband are going to bring into this world."

Before Kafari could think of anything to say in response, it was Chaviva's turn to slide her ID through the card reader and go inside to vote. A moment later, it was Kafari's turn. She walked to the voting booth in a daze, marking her ballot quickly, almost slashing the pen across the slot to reelect President Andrews, then slid the ballot into the reader for tabulation and headed for her aircar.

As she climbed in, fastened safety straps, and received permission for take-off, she lapsed into a pensive, strange little mood that was still with her when the lights from Nineveh Base and the Bolo's maintenance depot finally greeted her from the darkness of the Adero floodplain. It was good to see the lights of home.

Chaviva Benjamin's words had kindled something deep in Kafari's heart, a sweet ache that was part longing, part humble gratitude that the young woman had opened the way for others to share how much she and Simon meant to them. It would be very easy, working where she did, to lose sight of the simple, forthright concern for others that was a hallmark of the world Kafari had grown up in, a world very different from the one she had found in Madison.

Simon had dinner waiting when she walked through the door. She went straight to him, put both arms around him, and just held on for a long moment.

"Rough day?" he asked, stroking her hair.

She nodded. "Yeah. You?"

"I've had better."

She gave Simon a kiss. She wanted to ask him about the medal of valor, which she hadn't known about, but remained silent. Since he hadn't shared it with anyone on Jefferson, including her, he clearly preferred not to be reminded of the circumstances under which he'd earned it. So she contented herself with passing along the messages from Chaviva Benjamin and the others.

Simon stared down into her eyes for a long moment, then looked away and sighed. "An officer knows his actions won't always be popular, but it's never pleasant to be vilified." He didn't say anything more, however, which worried Kafari. He wasn't telling her something. From the sound of his voice, it was an important something. Kafari understood that Simon's job involved military secrets, things she would probably never be privy to, and doubtless wouldn't want to know, even if he told her.

But she wanted to help him, wanted to know what to do and say that would ease the burden on his shoulders. She couldn't do that if she didn't know what was eating away at him like a cutworm in a healthy cabbage patch. She also wanted to know if something Nassiona Santorini had said was actually true or not.

"Simon?"

He frowned. "That sounds unhappy."

"While I was at the clinic, I heard part of an interview with Nassiona Santorini."

A muscle in his jaw jumped. "What about Ms. Santorini?"

Kafari hesitated as her gut twisted. She'd realized a few seconds too late that anything she said now would sound like she didn't trust her husband. She swore aloud and pulled away, damning herself as she waddled into the kitchen. She cracked open a bottle of nonalcoholic beer with a savage yank and gulped half its contents in one long pull, trying to calm the sudden, painful clenching in her stomach.

"Kafari?" he asked quietly.

She turned to face him across the distance of their living room. "Why is Sonny still awake?"

She wasn't sure what she'd expected to see, but it wasn't the faint smile twitched at his lips. "Is that all?

I was afraid you were going to ask what 'that machine' and I are legally allowed to do."

She swallowed convulsively. "And you can't answer that?"

He sighed again. "I'd rather not."

Which gave Kafari a fair idea about the answer, but she wasn't about to push him. "That's okay with me, Simon," she said quietly. "But you haven't answered my question."

"No, I haven't. Do you have to stand all the way across the room?"

She flushed and headed back for his arms, which closed around her with great tenderness. He leaned his cheek against her hair, then spoke. "There are a couple of reasons, actually. The main one is simple enough. Another breakthrough from the Void is still a very real threat. I want Sonny to stay awake. To keep track of exactly where our various defense forces have been deployed. If I shut him down and we get a breakthrough, again, he would have to spend critical time figuring out where everybody is, before the Deng or the Melconians hit us. You've seen how fast interstellar battle fleets can cross a star system."

She shivered silently against his chest.

"As to the other reasons . . ." He sighed again. "Let's just say that Abraham Lendan thought it was a good idea."

She caught her breath and looked up, surprised by the hard, angry glitter in his eyes. "Why?"

A muscle jumped in his jaw. "Because he was a very astute statesman. And a superlative judge of human character. I doubt that even one Jeffersonian in five thousand realizes just how much this world lost when he died. It's my fervent hope," Simon added roughly, "that he was wrong."

A chill slithered its way down Kafari's back. What did Simon know? What had President Lendan known? If President Lendan had known about the trouble POPPA was brewing . . .

"Are you afraid of Sonny?" Simon asked abruptly.

She hesitated for just a moment, then opted for the simple truth. "Yes. I am."

"Good." She stared up at her husband. Simon's eyes were dark, filled with shadows of a different shape and hue than she'd seen there before. He said gently, "Only a fool isn't afraid of a Bolo. The more you know about them, the more true that becomes. Officers assigned to the Brigade go through a whole battery of psychology courses before ever setting foot inside a Command Compartment. With Sonny, I had to take special training courses, because he won't react the same way as Bolos with more sophisticated hardware and programming."

He touched her cheek with a whisper-soft fingertip. "You're my wife and Sonny knows that. He considers you a friend, which is a high compliment. But you aren't his commander. He isn't programmed to respond to you at a commander's level of trust. Or, more accurately, a commander's level of engineered obedience. His threat-level threshold can be crossed and reacted to faster than you or any human could hope to defuse the situation. Sonny's an intelligent, self-directing machine. *Anything* with a mind of its own is unpredictable. With Sonny, there are landmines you could trip without even realizing it. I'd really rather not find out what would happen if you did."

A tightly coiled tension around her bones unwound a little, hearing Simon confirm what she had known, at a deep level. Kafari nodded. "All right."

One eyebrow twitched upwards. "All right? That's it?"

She produced a grin that surprised him into widening his eyes. "Well, yes. There are times when Sonny is as darling as a child and times when he scares me to death. If the needle-gun I carry every day could think for itself, I'd feel a whole lot differently about it, before sticking the thing into my pocket. I like Sonny. But I'd be crazy to trust him."

"Mrs. Khrustinova, you are a remarkable lady."

"Then you'd better feed me, so I don't leave you for a better short-order cook!"

Simon gave her a swift kiss, then swatted her backside and propelled her toward the table. They ate in silence, which Kafari needed, after the day she'd put in. She made only one reference to the unpleasantness in town. "Do you have anything in Sonny's depot that would take off plasti-bond stuck to metal?"

Simon frowned. "Probably. Why?"

"Some jerk wallpapered every aircar in the lot with election slogans."

His lips twitched. "I see. I take it, from your description of the perpetrator, that you weren't in agreement with the sentiment it expressed?"

"Not exactly."

"Huh. I suspect you have a gift for understatement. Yes, I think I can scrounge something that would do the trick. Will we need to have the car repainted?"

"How in the world did you know?"

Simon chuckled. "My dear, I've seen you attack things you don't like."

"Oh." She managed a smile. "Yes, we'll need to repaint the car."

They lingered over dessert and washed the dishes together, then wandered into the living room. Quirking a questioning brow at Kafari, Simon nodded toward the datascreen. She sighed and nodded. As much as she hated to spoil the mood, it was time to watch the election returns. Simon switched it on and reached for Kafari's feet, giving them a gentle and thorough rubdown that left her all but purring.

The picture that greeted them, however, soured Kafari's dinner. She recognized the young attorney speaking with Pol Jankovitch. The journalist apparently harbored a predilection for attractive POPPA spokeswomen. Isanah Renke's long blond hair and dazzling Teutonic smile had popped up all too frequently, over the last several months. So had her favorite spiel, which she was pouring forth yet again.

"—tired of John Andrews waving thick stacks of data in front of people while rattling off excuses for the economy's slide toward disaster. We've had enough. Jefferson can't afford complicated bureaucratic double-speak and worn-out wheezes about chaotic money markets and arcane budgeting processes. Even attorneys can't unravel this administration's so-called budget plan. The POPPA economic platform is simple and straightforward. We need to put money in the hands of the people who *need* it. That's why Gifre Zeloc has endorsed POPPA's economic-recovery inititatives."

"What are the most important points of those initiatives, Isanah?"

"It's very simple, Pol. The most important component of POPPA's economic recovery plan is an immediate end to the current administration's loan schemes."

"John Andrews and his analysts insist that economic development loans are critical to rebuilding our manufacturing and retail industries."

"We do need to rebuild, Pol, urgently. But loan schemes do nothing to address the deeper problems our economy faces. And loan schemes place an unjust burden on struggling businesses. Loans force companies, particularly small retailers, into merciless repayment schedules. You must understand, Pol, these loans have draconian forfeiture penalties built into them. If a business can't meet repayment demands on time, the owner faces outrageously unfair punishments, including governmental seizure of property! We're talking about people losing their homes, their livelihoods, just to satisfy legal requirements attached to money these businesses must have to recover. It's outrageous. It's government-sanctioned blackmail. It's got to stop, Pol, it's got to stop *now*."

Kafari reflected sourly that POPPA's campaign slogan should have been "it's got to stop *now*," since it was the favorite phrase of every spokesperson POPPA had recruited for fieldwork, followed closely by "we've had enough" of whatever they were preparing to demonize and vilify next.

Pol Jankovitch's expression mirrored horror. "How can a business function if the government confiscates its property? A business can't operate without an inventory of goods, equipment, or buildings! It certainly can't operate if it loses the land it sits on!"

"Huh," Kafari muttered, "a farmer can't grow anything on land he loses, either. How come nobody's pointing that out?"

Simon, voice tight with anger, said, "Because saying it doesn't match their agenda."

Again, Kafari wondered what Simon knew, what Abe Lendan had known.

On the datascreen, Isanah Renke was saying, "You're right, Pol. Businesses can't operate that way. Under these loan schemes, the owner loses everything he or she has spent a lifetime trying to build. And the people working in that business lose their jobs. Everyone suffers. John Andrews' insane economic recovery plan is deliberately engineered to punish those least able to guarantee sustainable profits. Unfair loan practices must go. Otherwise this world faces certain economic disaster."

"And POPPA has a better plan?"

"Absolutely. We need grants and economic aid packages designed to guarantee recovery for hard-hit businesses. We're talking about industries that can't recover under the convoluted, unwieldly, economically disastrous nonsense contained in John Andrews' so-called recovery plan. It's lunacy, Pol, sheer lunacy."

Kafari scowled at the screen. "Doesn't anybody in that broadcasting firm pay attention to regulations about what can be said in a datacast before the polls close?"

The harsh metallic bite in Simon's voice surprised Kafari. "Isanah Renke is not a registered candidate. She's not a member of a candidate's staff. She isn't a registered lobbyist and she doesn't draw a salary from POPPA. Neither," he added with a vicious growl, "does Nassiona Santorini."

Kafari stared at him for a moment, trying to take in the implications. "You can't tell me they work for free?"

Simon shook his head. "They don't. But the shellgame they're playing with holding companies is technically legal, so there's not a damned thing anyone can do about it. Vittori and Nassiona Santorini are the children of a crackerjack industrialist. They know exactly how to tapdance their way through the corporate legal landscape. And they've hired attorneys with plenty of experience doing it. People like Isanah Renke tell them exactly how to accomplish questionable activities without running afoul of inconvenient legislation, court rulings, and administrative policies."

Kafari knew he'd been watching the Santorinis since that first riot on campus, but he'd just revealed more in two minutes than Kafari had learned in the past six months. Nassiona Santorini's allegation that Sonny was watching night and day had unsettled her, which was a strong indication of how powerful that argument was. It had caused Kafari to question the actions and motives of a man she trusted implicitly to safeguard her homeworld and act in its best interests.

Would Kafari's reaction, would her indignant anger over POPPA's allegations, be different if she'd learned that Sonny was watching Grangers as closely as the machine was watching POPPA? It wasn't a comfortable thought. That kind of surveillance was a two-edged sword. She was abruptly glad that Simon Khrustinov was the one wielding it. Were all Brigade officers chosen for their unswerving integrity, as well as honor, loyalty, courage, and every other trait that made Simon a consummate Brigade officer and the finest human being she had ever known?

As the evening droned on, with voting tallies showing massive POPPA victories in the urban centers and strong support for John Andrews in the rural areas, Pol Jankovitch made a show, at least, of interviewing spokespersons from both parties, but there wasn't much to hold her attention in the sound bites supporting the current administration. It might've been that she was simply in philosophical agreement with them, or maybe the trouble was that she already knew everything they were saying. When she found herself yawning against Simon's shoulder, she wondered a little sleepily if the dry presentations that failed to hold her interest could possibly be an orchestrated effort on somebody's part. She had just about decided she was being a little too paranoid when Pol Jankovitch dropped a bombshell that sent her bolt upright in her seat.

"We've just been informed," Pol said, interrupting an economic analyst trying to explain why POPPA's ideas weren't economically tenable, "that the electronic returns sent by off-world troops via SWIFT have been scrambled during transmission. We're trying to find out the magnitude of the problem. We're patching through to Lurlina Serhild, our correspondent at the Elections Commission headquarters. Lurlina, are you there?"

A moment of dead air was followed by a woman's voice a split second before Special Correspondent Lurlina Serhild appeared on screen. "Yes, Pol, we've been told to stand by for a special report from the Elections Commission. It's our understanding that the commissioner will be issuing an advisory within the next few minutes. Everyone here is tense and distressed—" She stopped, then said, "It looks like the commssioner's press secretary is ready to make a statement."

A harried-looking woman in a rumpled suit came on screen, moving decisively to a podium bearing the logo of the Jeffersonian Independent Elections Commission.

"All we know at this time is that an unknown number of absentee ballots have been properly credited, while an unknown number of others have been lost in the data glitch. We are trying to unscramble this serious transmission error, but we can't determine at this time how long it will take to discover the magnitude of the problem. Our system engineers are working frantically to untangle the glitch in time to meet the legal deadline for final vote tallies."

A tendril of sudden, strong dismay threaded its way through Kafari's perpetually queasy middle. Those deadlines were short. Very short. The next moment, the commissioner's press secretary explained why. "The constitution was drafted with reliance on stable computerized tabulation systems designed to count physical ballots. Given the small size of Jefferson's population at the time the constitution was ratified, the tabulation deadlines did not take into account the necessity for massive numbers of off-world, absentee ballots.

"This is the first time in Jefferson's history that we've had more than a hundred absentee ballots transmitted from off-world. These votes require a translation protocol to decode SWIFT data. Somewhere in the translation process or in the transfer protocols that regulate deciphered data-feeds into the balloting computers, a serious error occurred. It scrambled the stream of incoming code and wrecked our ability to trace which ballots lost data integrity.

"We can't tell at this juncture how many ballots from the original SWIFT message were in the translation processors, how many had been incorporated into the master tallies, and which had not yet been processed when the system failed. As little as twenty percent of the ballots might be affected, but our system engineers fear the number of ballots caught in the translator when it crashed may have been closer to eighty or ninety percent.

"The Elections Commissioner takes full responsibility for this difficulty and promises every possible effort to ensure the correct tabulation of absentee votes. We will issue an update when we know more. No, I'm sorry, no questions at this time, please, that's everything I can tell you."

Simon was running a distracted hand through his hair, leaving it disheveled. The anger in his steel-hued eyes surprised her, but what he said left Kafari stunned. He jerked to his feet, pacing the living room like a caged cat, thinking out loud. "They didn't need to do something like this. They already had the election, those voting patterns make it pitifully obvious. They didn't need to commit election fraud. So why the hell did they do it? To rub salt in an open wound? No, there's more to it than that. It's a message, loud and clear. A demonstration of power. And contempt. They're telling the rest of us, 'We can cheat so skillfully, you can't touch us.' And they're right, curse it. We can't. Not without proof."

Kafari watched him in horrified silence. What information had he been in possession of, to prompt an accusation of election fraud? Was that what Abraham Lendan had suspected, when he'd promoted Simon to colonel? If somebody had realized POPPA was conspiring to cheat, why hadn't anybody done anything about it?

"Simon?" she asked, in a scared, little-girl voice.

He looked at her for a long, terrible moment, eyes pleading, then said in a hoarse, rasping voice, "Don't ask. Please. Just don't."

She wanted to ask. *Needed* to ask. And knew that she couldn't. He was a soldier. Like it or not, she was a soldier's wife. A colonel's wife. She couldn't stand between him and his job. His *duty*. So she turned her attention back to Pol Jankovitch and the incoming updates from the Elections Commission, which were disjointed and contradictory.

The votes could not be unscrambled. *Maybe* the votes could be unscrambled. No, they definitely couldn't be straightened out before the time limits expired. The Elections Commission was profoundly sorry, but the law was the law. They could not circumvent clearly worded statutes, not even to honor the intended votes of men and women risking their lives on far-away worlds.

"Turn it off," Kafari groaned, sick at heart.

"No." There was steel in Simon's voice, alien steel. "We need to watch every ugly moment of this."

"Why?" she asked sharply.

Simon's eyes, when they tracked to meet her gaze, took her back to that horrible moment when Simon had stood before the Joint Assembly, speaking his dire truths. Meeting that gaze up-close and personal was harder than Kafari had ever dreamed it would be.

"Because," he said softly, "we need to understand

the minds and methods of those who engineered it. This," he waved one hand at the viewscreen, "is just the beginning."

"How can you be sure of that?" Even as she asked, voice sharp with alarm, she knew that she was afraid of his answers. And holding her husband's gaze was like looking into the heart of a star going supernova.

"Know much about Terran history?"

She frowned. "A little."

"Does that little include any Russian history?"

Her frown deepened. "Not much. I've been studying Russian art and music, because I think they're beautiful, but I haven't read much history, yet. I've been too busy," she admitted.

"Russian history," Simon said in a voice as raw as a Damisi highlands blizzard, "is an endless string of cautionary messages on the folly of human greed, dirty politics, mindless ignorance, exploitation of the masses, and the savagery that accompanies absolute power. My ancestors were very effective at creating disasters that took generations to undo. In one twenty-year period, the Russian Empire went from a level of political freedom and prosperity equal to most of its contemporary nations to a regime that deliberately exterminated twenty million of its own men, women, and children."

Kafari stared, cold to her soul. She'd known there was some horrible history from humanity's birth-world, but twenty million people? In only twenty years? Simon jabbed a finger toward the viewscreen, where POPPA candidates were carrying district after district. "Am I worried? You damned well better believe it. Those people scare me spitless. Particularly since there's not a blessed, solitary thing I can do about it."

Then he stalked out of the room. The back door slid open and crashed shut again. Kafari waddled awkwardly to the glass. He was striding through the moonlight, heading for his Bolo. Kafari closed her hand through the curtain fabric, realized she was shaking only when she noticed that the curtain was, too. She didn't know what to do. She couldn't follow him, for a whole basketful of good reasons. She was afraid to be alone, afraid of a threat she didn't understand, one she hadn't seen coming, despite qualms about a lunacy that had gained such wild popularity in so short a time.

She was wondering whether she ought to call her parents, just to hear a familiar and comforting voice, when the lights flickered and dimmed and she heard a sound that set every hair on her body standing on end. In the darkness outside her fearfully empty little home, the Bolo had powered up his main battle systems. She knew that sound, remembered it from that ghastly climb up a cliff with Abraham Lendan at her heels and explosions shaking them through the smoke. Try as she might, Kafari could not come up with a reason for Simon to power up his Bolo that didn't leave her shaking to the bottoms of her abruptly terrified feet.

The hand she laid protectively across her abdomen and the baby inside trembled. There was so little she could do to protect her child from whatever was coming. She knew, as well, that this was one battle Simon would have to fight alone. She couldn't help him. There was no courageous president to rescue. Only a vision of thunderous clouds on every horizon, no matter which way she twisted and turned.

It was a lonely business, being a Bolo commander's wife.

Chapter Twelve

I

Twelve seconds after Simon enters my Command Compartment, he orders me to full Battle Reflex Alert. Portions of my brain inaccessible outside of combat snap to life, sending a surge of power and euphoria through my personality gestalt circuitry. I am fully alive once more, able to think more clearly and coherently than I have since the last Deng Yavac blew to atoms under my guns.

"Trouble, Lonesome," Simon tells me, using my old nickname, a sign of deep emotional stress. I scan my immediate environs, do a check of all remote systems, including the four satellites that have been launched since my Commander forced the Joint Assembly to appropriate necessary funds for them. I see no sign of an Enemy anywhere in this star system. Brigade channels are silent. I do not understand why I have been brought to Battle Reflex Alert.

"What kind of trouble?" I ask, seeking clarification.

"Analyze tonight's election results, please. Cross-check

with any possible connection with POPPA activity that might constitute legal election fraud under the Jeffersonian Constitution."

"This will take time, Simon. There are several million variables involved."

"Understood. I haven't got anything better to do, just now."

I settle down to the task. Simon activates his duty log and begins to record his impressions, hypotheses, and potential avenues of inquiry, which I note and incorporate into my own analyses. My understanding of human thought processes has been gleaned largely from comparing my own interpretation of known facts with the viewpoints, ideas, and decisions of my commanders. In accordance with Simon's standing orders, I have monitored the elections, since they comprise a large variable in the task set for me by Simon, identifying threats to the stability and safety of this world.

The SWIFT transmission that delivered Jefferson's absentee military votes came in via Navy channels, which I monitor as a matter of routine, checking on shifting battle patterns that might affect the security of this world. The data transmission was clear and undamaged when it entered my incoming transmissions databank. So far as I have been able to determine, probing into the system from my depot, the Elections Commission balloting computers did not malfunction in any way I can understand.

I review constitutional provisions and determine that once an election has been officially closed, there is a seventy-two hour window of opportunity in which to provide evidence of vote tampering or other fraud. Simon has seventy-one hours and thirty-nine point six minutes in which to present evidence, which must be given to the Elections Commission by the aggrieved party or parties, acting on their own behalf. Moreover, the evidence must be capable of standing in the face of scrutiny by Jefferson's High Court and its appointed technical consultants, if applicable.

Given the magnitude of the search and the computer

systems that must be tapped, scrutinized, and analyzed for possible data tampering or human sabotage, I am the only technical consultant on Jefferson capable of such a search. If I locate evidence of human intervention, I must then discover and present clear and compelling legal evidence that the tampering was deliberate and fraudulent. I begin to see why Simon ordered me to Battle Reflex Alert. I cannot hope to accomplish this task without access to my full computing capabilities. Given the parameters and variables involved, I do not hold much hope that I will be successful in my mission.

I am a Unit of the Line, however, with a clear duty and specific orders involving a specific, if complicated, task. I must attempt to carry out this order to the best of my ability. This is not the first time I have entered a mission with heavy handicaps against success. But I have never surrendered and never been defeated. If fraud was committed, I will do my best to locate it. I begin an intensive search.

II

I have experienced many situations which my programmers and commanders have told me are comparable to human emotions, as I understand them. I have known fear, anger, and hate as well as satisfaction and exultation. Now I know humiliation. Despite seventy-one hours and thirty-nine point six minutes of the most intensive data searching and analysis of my career as a Unit of the Line, I have uncovered nothing that would provide legal proof of fraud. I have found virtually nothing at all. What little there is provides only circumstantial suspicions which virtually any member of the voting public—let alone a constitutional attorney or High Justice—would scoff at, if someone were foolish enough to bring it to their attention.

At best, conspiracy theorists are universally lampooned. At worst, they are institutionalized as unstable. In either case, they are taken seriously only by other conspiracy theorists. Were Simon to present as evidence the paltry compilation of solid facts I have accumulated, he would severely damage his credibility, which is a state of affairs that cannot be allowed to occur. Bitterness skitters throughout my personality gestalt circuitry as I am forced to advise Simon of my inadequacy as an espionage data analyist.

My Commander, disheveled and weary from his own attempts to discover the truth in this matter, takes the news with leniency I do not feel my performance justifies.

"Not your fault, Lonesome," *Simon insists.* "I'll give POPPA credit for a smooth operation. If you didn't find it, then it's not there to be found. And maybe we're just chasing ghosts. It could be a legitimate, honest glitch. Complex circuitry and programming just hiccough, now and then. Particularly when systems with insufficient resources are overloaded, trying to conduct an operation too complex for them. Damn." *He rubs reddened eyes and heaves a deep and weary sigh.* "All right, Sonny, stand down from Battle Reflex Alert. Return to active standby and continue to monitor, per standing orders. Christ, I'm not looking forward to reporting to the likes of Gifre Zeloc. Strike that remark, please. He's about to become my boss, like it or not."

I dutifully delete his comment, understanding his reasoning and not liking it, either. My Commander is spooked. This does not make for an easy transition from my full cognitive functionality to the less-aware, restricted operational mode I have maintained since the end of my last battle with the Deng. I do not want to feel "sleepy" at this time. I dislike the idea so much, I experience another emotive sensation new to my personality gestalt center: sullen resentment. Not at Simon. At the situation. Even at myself, for failing to provide my Commander with factual information he deemed important to our mission.

Simon powers down his command chair and groans as

he shakes cramps out of his muscles. He has not left my Command Compartment since the election. He has slept only six point three hours in the past seventy-two and is in serious need of rest. As he climbs out of my Command Compartment, he says, "I'm going to bed, Sonny. You know where to find me, if you need me."

"Yes, Simon," I say gently.

As he leaves, I know a deep and empty anguish. And a far deeper uncertainty about the future. His. Mine. Jefferson's. I do not know how humans cope with such feelings. I am a Bolo. My way is different. I focus my attention on the only thing I am able to do: continue the mission. Even though I no longer understand it.

Chapter Thirteen

I

Kafari stared at the letter, rereading the astonishing instructions for the third time, unable to believe the evidence of her eyes. Simon, who was technically a resident alien under the provisions of the treaty, wasn't even mentioned in the letter, which had been addressed to her. She had just about decided the thing wasn't a practical joke when Yalena crawled under her feet, trying to yank the power cords out of the back of her computer. Kafari snagged the struggling toddler and said, "Time out. You are not allowed to play with power cords. Two minutes in the time-out chair."

Her daughter, two years and three months old, glowered up at her. "No!"

"Yes. Touching the power cords is not allowed. Two minutes."

Nothing in the universe could sulk quite so well as a two-year-old.

With Yalena temporarily out from underfoot, Kafari called Simon, who was in Sonny's maintenance depot.

"Simon, could you come into the house, please? We need to talk."

"Uh-oh. That doesn't sound good."

"It isn't."

"Be right there."

Simon opened the back door just as Kafari allowed Yalena to climb down from the time-out chair. "Daddy!" she squealed, running straight for him.

He swung her up and planted a kiss on her forehead. "How's my girl?"

"Daddy take Bolo?" she asked, hope shining in her eyes.

"Later, honey. I'll take you to see Sonny in a little while."

A thirteen-thousand-ton Bolo wasn't Kafari's notion of an ideal playmate for a two-year-old, but Yalena was enchanted by the machine, which looked to her like an entire city that would talk to her any time Daddy allowed her to visit. Which, granted, wasn't often, for any number of practical reasons.

"What's up?" Simon asked, keeping his voice carefully devoid of negative emotion.

"This." She handed over a printout of the letter.

Jaw muscles flexed when he reached the contents of paragraph two: *Pursuant to section 29713 of the Childhood Protection Act, stipulating childcare arrangements for dependent children with both parents drawing paychecks, you are hereby notified of the requirement to remand your daughter, Yalena Khrustinova, for federally mandated daycare, to begin no more than three business days after receipt of this notification. You will enroll your daughter in the federal daycare center established on Nineveh Base before April 30th or face criminal prosecution for violation of the Children's Rights provisions of the Childhood Protection Act. Prosecution will immediately result in full termination of parental rights and Yalena Khrustinova will be remanded for permanent relocation to a federally mandated foster care program.*

Pursuant to statute 29714 of the Childhood Protection

Act, in-home child welfare inspections will commence one week from the date of Yalena Khrustinova's enrollment, to ensure that she is being provided with the federally mandated level of financial and emotional support necessary to her welfare. We look forward to caring for your child.

Have a nice day.

Simon looked up from the letter, met Kafari's eyes. He was still as death for a space of seven pounding heartbeats. "They're serious."

"Yes."

Jaw muscles flexed again. "We have three days."

"To what? Ask the Concordiat to reassign you to Vishnu? Or Mali? Or somewhere else? We're trapped, Simon."

"I'm trapped—" he began.

"No, *we're* trapped. What kind of marriage would it be, if Yalena and I are in some other star system while you're stuck here?" She swallowed hard. "Besides which, my whole family is here. We fought too hard for this world to just walk out and leave it to the likes of *that.*" She pointed at the now-crumpled letter in Simon's fist. "Don't ask me to do that, Simon. Not yet. The courts are full of lawsuits challenging POPPA's programs. They haven't bought the entire judiciary. We're fighting for this world, fighting hard. We have to go along with them until enough people wake up and see where we're heading and do something to stop it." She had to choke out the final words. "It's just daycare."

He started to answer with considerable heat, then snapped his teeth together. Once he'd swallowed whatever had tried to rip its way across his tongue, he said, "It's not 'just daycare' and you know it. I can't force you onto the next starship that comes to call. God knows, I don't want to lose you. Either of you." He shut his eyes for long moments, fighting an internal battle that was wreaking visible havoc. Kafari wanted to comfort him, but didn't know how. She was scared, angry, ripped up inside with fear for her daughter. If those lawsuits failed to curb POPPA's campaign of social insanity . . .

Simon muttered, "You're the legal dependents of a Brigade officer. That's got to count for something."

"Against a *rational* government? Probably. Against POPPA? With the likes of Gifre Zeloc in the presidency and Isaiah Renke leading the drive to rewrite Jefferson's entire law code? Or 'social progressives' like Carin Avelaine in charge of the Bureau of Education and bigoted fools like Cili Broska in charge of purging the public schools and university curricula of antipopulist bias? The people who thought up this," she pointed at the badly crushed letter in Simon's fist, "engineered a rigged election that nobody could contest. Your position as a Brigade officer not only won't help us, they'll go after you, with intent to destroy. If you try to fight them on this, we'll lose Yalena."

Watching the hopelessness settle across his face and shoulders was a pain that cut straight to her heart. He was holding Yalena tightly enough to make her squirm in protest. Then a thought blossomed to life in his face, one that straightened his shoulders again. "This crap applies to children with both parents working. If one of us isn't actively employed . . ."

Kafari saw exactly where he was headed. Knew in a flash that it meant trouble. Simon was "actively employed" under the treaty, despite the fact that his main job, these days, was conferring with Sonny once or twice a day and spending the rest of his time with Yalena. To get around the provisions of that letter and the legislation it represented, Kafari would have to quit her job at the spaceport.

The choices facing her crucified Kafari. Jefferson needed her. Needed psychotronic engineers, and not just at the spaceport. If the changes to higher education's curricula were an indicator, a whole new generation would grow up without the skills or knowledge necessary to produce more engineers of any sort.

Once in power, POPPA had launched a juggernaut of far-reaching changes in every conceivable portion of society. The Childhood Protection Act was just the tip of the iceberg. Environmental protection legislation was already crippling industry with clean-environment standards so stringent, heavy-industry manufacturing plants, industrial chemical production firms—including agricultural chemicals critical to producing Terran food crops in Jeffersonian soil—and even paper-production mills literally could not operate in compliance.

The financial penalties for failing to meet standards were so severe, whole industries were going bankrupt, trying to pay fines. Business leaders were filing aggressive lawsuits to challenge the lunacy, but the Senate and House of Law, urged on by the roar of the masses, just kept passing more of POPPA's social, economic, and environmental agendas. The subsistence allowance was already higher than the average yearly wages of low-skill menial employment.

She focused on the crumpled piece of paper in Simon's white-knuckled hand, with its social-engineering mandate, and realized with a sickening sensation that it was already too late to fight that particular legal battle. If she or anyone else tried to protest, they would lose their children. And their children, trapped in POPPA-run daycare centers and schools, faced a brainwashing campaign of terrifying proportions. How many others had received letters like hers? The number had to run into the millions, at a minimum. Economic woes and stunning tax increases had forced Jefferson's middle-class families to become two-career couples, with spouses taking any job they could find, even menial labor, just to remain solvent. Those families couldn't afford to lose a second income, not even to shelter their kids.

And now the Santorinis were holding a gun to parents' heads. She should have seen it coming. It was a natural outgrowth of legislation that had outlawed home schooling, forcing parents to turn over their children to POPPA's indoctrination machine. Now they'd widened their net to snare preschoolers, as well, giving them complete power over children at their most critical formative stage, inculcating belief patterns that would last a lifetime.

She wondered with a sickening lurch in her stomach how many of the business owners filing lawsuits to overturn POPPA legislation would find themselves embroiled in custody battles for their own children? On the grounds of "improper emotional support in the home"? She shut her eyes for a moment, but couldn't blot out a mental picture of Jefferson's future that was so ugly, her breath froze in her lungs. She didn't know what to do. Literally didn't know what to do.

"Kafari?"

She opened her eyes and met Simon's gaze. His eyes were dark. Scared.

"I don't know what to do, Simon," she whispered, wrapping both arms around herself. "Jefferson needs psychotronic engineers—"

"Yalena needs her mother."

"I know!" Even she could hear the anguish in her voice. "Even if I resign, we'll gain only a couple of years. She'll have to start kindergarten when she's four, like it or not."

"All the more reason to idiot-proof her now."

"*Can* you idiot-proof a child whose teachers are part of the problem? Which they will be. The educational curriculum was practically the first thing they went after. My cousins are already fighting to undo the garbage their children are being taught, particularly the little ones, kindergarten and early primary grades. They come home from school and announce that anyone who picks up a gun—or even keeps one in the house—is a dangerous deviant. Farm kids are being told that killing anything, even agricultural pests, is tantamount to *murder*.

"Ask my cousin Onatah to show you the school book her little girl is using. Kandlyn's only seven. She already thinks that everything alive has the absolute right to stay that way. Even microbes, for God's sake. The older farm kids know enough from direct experience to realize how stupid that is, but the younger ones and practically all the city kids are gobbling that crap down like candy."

A muscle jumped in Simon's jaw. "You're starting to see the enormity of this thing. There are a whole lot more children in cities and towns than there are on farms and ranches. A few years from now, nobody below the age of twenty will realize it *is* stupidity. That's why I want you to leave, now. Before it's too damned late.

"Since you won't do that, at least consider this. Jefferson's need for psychotronic engineers won't vanish just because you quit your job now. You're one of the most employable people on Jefferson. We can make do with my salary for a couple of years. It's sacrosanct and comes directly from the Brigade. If they try to revoke it, they'll end up with a Concordiat naval cruiser in orbit, on-loading the three of us and Sonny, while Gifre Zeloc signs a repayment check bigger than they can afford to hand over. They *know* they can't antagonize the Concordiat, no matter what their propaganda says to the contrary.

"Men like Gifre Zeloc and Cyril Coridan in the House of Law, women like Fyrene Brogan in the Senate are smart enough to know the difference between the swill they feed subsistence recipients and what they can actually do. You'll notice that nobody's come knocking at our door to demand that we actually shut Sonny down. Or that we ship him out on the next available transport. That would ring alarm bells all the way back to Brigade headquarters at Central Command."

"But—"

"Kafari, *please*. We don't need your salary. But we do need *you*, at home, until Yalena's first day of school. Give Yalena those two years."

He was right. Absolutely and utterly right. At least until Yalena was old enough to enter school. "All right," she said, voice hushed. "I'll give notice."

The worst of the tension drained from her husband's rigid stance. "Thank you."

She just nodded. And hoped it was enough.

II

Kafari was fixing Yalena's breakfast when someone knocked at the front door. Loudly. Startled, Kafari sloshed milk onto the counter. Nobody ever came to their house without calling ahead, first, to make sure Sonny wouldn't shoot them as an intruder. Not even Kafari's family. And with spring planting taking up everyone's time, nobody in her family would be calling on them this early in the day, anyway. Simon, who had just strapped Yalena into the toddler seat, exchanged a startled glance with her.

"Who—?" he began.

"Trouble, that's who," she muttered, wiping her hands on a towel and striding purposefully through the house.

She opened the door to find a tall woman with pinched nostrils and a prune-shaped mouth, whose socially correct skinny frame was all hard angles and jutting bones. She was staring down at Kafari from a pair of steel-rimmed glasses of the sort preferred by POPPA bureaucrats. It was part of their "we're all just people" persona, which dictated that no one on the government payroll was better than anyone else and therefore should not look it.

With her was a hulking giant whose intelligence looked to be on the simian level, with muscles capable of breaking a small tree in half. He definitely did not subscribe to the "thin is in" mentality sweeping the civil service and entertainment industries. *No,* she realized abruptly, *he's the enforcer.* Just what were they here to enforce, at seven A.M. on a Tuesday morning?

"Mrs. Khrustinova?" the woman asked, her voice as warm as a glacier.

"I'm Kafari Khrustinova. Who are you?"

"We," she jerked her head in a gesture both abrupt and menacing, "are the child-protection team assigned to Yalena Khrustinova."

"Child-protection team?"

"Trask, please note that Mrs. Khrustinova is apparently in need of mechanical augmentation, as her hearing is plainly substandard, which directly jeopardizes the welfare of the child in her custody."

"Now wait just a damned minute! I heard you, I just couldn't believe what I was hearing. What are you doing here? I'm a full-time mother. You don't have jurisdiction."

"Oh, yes we do," the woman said, eyes and voice frosty and threatening. "Didn't you read the notice sent to every parent on Jefferson last night?"

"What notice? What time, last night? Simon and I checked the messages just before bed and there wasn't any notice."

"And what time would that have been?"

"Ten-thirty."

"Trask, please note that Mr. and Mrs. Khrustinov keep a two-year-old child awake far past the hour at which a child that age should be in bed."

"That's when Simon and I went to bed!" Kafari snapped. "Yalena was in bed by seven-thirty."

"So you say." The derision and disbelief beggared the limits of Kafari's patience.

Simon spoke just behind her shoulder in a voice as cold and alien as the day of Abraham Lendan's death. "Get off my property. Now."

"Are you threatening *me*?" the woman snarled.

Kafari's husband was holding Yalena on one hip. His smile was a lethal baring of fangs. "Oh, no. Not yet. If you refuse to leave, however, things could get very interesting. Somehow, I doubt the Brigade would take kindly to having an officer's home invaded by petty officials attempting to enforce a dubious rule that I haven't even seen, let alone determined the legality of. This house," he added in a deceptively gentle voice, "is the property of the Concordiat. Its computer terminals are connected to military technology that is classified as sufficiently secret, no one on Jefferson has the clearance to access it. That includes any so-called home inspection team. You, dear lady, do not have a military clearance to come within a hundred meters of my computer terminal.

"If I were you, I would seriously reconsider the wisdom of trying to force the issue. I am a Bolo commander. In the building next door, a thirteen-thousand ton sentient war machine is listening to this conversation. That machine is judging how much of a threat you are to its commander. If that Bolo decides you are a threat to me, it will act. Probably before I can stop it. So have Trask, there, jot down this little note: the home-inspection provisions of the Child Protection Act do not—and never will—apply to this household. So kindly take your emaciated carcass and your large friend off the Concordiat's property. Oh, one last thing. If you value your sorry little lives, do *not* attempt to snoop into the Bolo's maintenance depot. I'd hate to have to clean up the mess if Sonny shoots you for trespassing into a Class One Alpha restricted military zone."

The woman's face went from paper-white to malevolent-red and her mouth opened and closed several times without sound. She finally snarled, "Trask! Please note that Mr. and Mrs. Khrustinov—"

"That's Colonel Khrustinov, you insolent trollop!"

Kafari blanched. She'd *never* heard that tone in Simon's voice.

The woman in their doorway actually recoiled a step. Then hissed, "Trask! Please note that *Colonel* Khrustinov and his wife maintain a lethal hazard that could kill their child at any moment—"

"Correction," Simon snarled. "Sonny has standing orders never to fire at my wife or my child. Those orders do not apply to you. Get the hell off my front porch."

He moved Kafari gently aside, then slammed the door and twisted the lock.

"Kafari. Take Yalena. And get your gun. *Now.* That lout looks stupid enough to try kicking the door in."

She snatched Yalena and ran for the bedroom. Her

daughter was whimpering, having caught the emotional whiplash from her parents and the intruders trying to force their way into the house. She heard the sound of the gun cabinet in the living room opening and closing, heard the snick of the safety on Simon's sidearm as he prepared to do whatever became necessary. Kafari wrenched open the nightstand, shoved her thumb against the identi-plate, and clicked open the gun box inside. Kafari snatched up the pistol, barricading herself in the closet with Yalena.

"Shh," she whispered, rocking the frightened toddler. "You're just fine, baby." She hummed a tune low enough to calm her daughter, without blocking the sounds from the living room. She could hear angry voices outside as the woman and her accomplice argued in strident tones. After several tense moments, she heard the snarl of a groundcar's engine as it gunned its way down the driveway toward the street.

Simon appeared in the bedroom doorway, every muscle in his lean frame taut with battle tension. "They're gone. For now."

"And when they come back?" she whispered.

"They won't come back. Not yet."

"Not until they persuade the House of Law to pass an exception that covers us. Or get a presidential ruling from Gifre Zeloc that does the same thing. We have enough enemies to pass something like that in a heartbeat." She added bitterly, "It might've been easier just to send her to their stinking daycare."

"Liberty is never easy."

"Yes," she ground out between clenched teeth. "I know."

Some of the grim tension relented. "I know you know. It's one of the reasons I love you. You can stare something horrible in the eye and fight it to the death. And sometimes, that scares me senseless."

He was staring, bleakly now, at Yalena, who was sitting in Kafari's lap, playing with a strand of her hair. "Oh, Simon, what are we going to *do*?"

"Survive," he said, voice harsh with strain. "And," he added, forcing his voice into a more pleasant register, "eat breakfast. Nobody can fight a war effectively on an empty stomach."

Kafari couldn't help it. Her husband's tone was so droll, his suggestion so eminently practical, tension leached out in a semihysterical bubble of laughter. "There speaks the seasoned veteran. All right, let's go fry some eggs or something."

He gave her a hand up and took charge of Yalena, handing over his gun—and handing her, as well, the responsibility for first-strike should those two goons decide to swing back for another go at it. Kafari slid her own gun into a capacious pocket, being careful to engage the safety first, and tucked Simon's gun into a second pocket.

She paused long enough to call up their datanet account, where she found the notice in question. It had been sent at one-thirty A.M., a decidedly odd hour to be posting notices of this magnitude. It was short and pungent.

All parents are hereby notified that per administrative ruling 11249966-83e-1, the in-home inspections and daycare provisions mandated by the Childhood Protection Act have been expanded to cover every child on Jefferson, regardless of the employment status of the parents.

Somebody, Kafari realized with a cold chill, had been watching them. Closely enough to notice when she resigned her position at Port Abraham. Noticed and acted, with frightening speed. Had everyone else on Jefferson actually received this notice or had it been crafted especially for them, to force the issue of home inspections that POPPA clearly wanted to conduct in Simon's quarters? Gaining access to their quarters must be high on somebody's list of priorities. Simon's enemies wanted either revenge or his military information, or both. In an equally plausible alternative, they might be trying to score a public relations coup by forcing the "hated foreign tyrant" to surrender custody of his child in obedience to the will of the people.

The speed at which the Santorinis engineered massive changes in public opinion continued to terrify Kafari. She printed the message and carried it into the kitchen, where Simon had already put Yalena back into the toddler seat and was busy at the stove with eggs and a frying pan.

He glanced at the message, grunted once, and shrugged. "They can try. Easy over or sunny-side up?"

Well, if Simon could set it aside for the moment, so could she. "Sunny sounds good to me."

He smiled at the double-entendre contained in that answer. "Me, too."

By the time she had the ham and juice ready, the worst of the shakes had gone and the cold knot of fear in her middle had begun the thaw. They had gained a breathing space, for today, at least. For now, for this morning and this meal, she was at home with her husband and her daughter. She would allow nothing to intrude deeply enough to spoil the moment. Time enough for worry, tomorrow.

She called her boss at Port Abraham, the next morning, to ask if they might still have a slot for her. Al Simmons, the port's harried director, lit up with relief. "You want to come back? Oh, thank God! Can you start today? Can you be here in an hour?"

Kafari, startled by the urgency in her former boss' voice, said, "I need to enroll Yalena in daycare before I can start."

"Do it today. Please," he added.

What in the world had been happening at the spaceport—or on Ziva Two—that had Al so frantic? She cleaned up Yalena, putting her in a rough-and-tumble jumpsuit, and drove over to the daycare center on Nineveh Base. She felt like Daniel, walking into the lion's den. The moment she opened the door, Kafari was engulfed by the sounds of happy, shrieking children at play. It was such a normal scene, her rigid defenses wobbled slightly. The group consisted of children between the ages of six months to six years, at a glance. Kafari was greeted by a young woman in what appeared to be the daycare center's staff uniform, a bright yellow shirt with dark green slacks and a cheery smile.

"Hello! You must be Mrs. Khrustinova. And this is Yalena?" she asked with a radiant smile for Kafari's daughter. "What a beautiful little girl you are! How old are you, Yalena?"

"Two," she answered solemnly.

"My, such a big girl! Would you like to play? We have all kinds of fun things for you to do."

Yalena, eyes wide with interest, nodded.

"That's my girl! Come on, let's take you around to meet everybody."

Kafari spent the next twenty minutes greeting various staff members, some of the exuberant children, and the daycare center's director, a pleasant, motherly woman whose office was mostly glass, giving her a view of the main playroom.

"Hello, Mrs. Khrustinova, I'm Lana Hayes, the director of Nineveh Base Daycare Center. I'm a military mom," she added with a warm smile, "with two boys off-world. My husband," she faltered slightly, "my husband was killed in the war."

"I'm so sorry, Mrs. Hayes."

"He died in combat, protecting the western side of Madison." She brushed moisture from her eyes. "My sons were already in the military. When the call came, they volunteered to transfer to a Concordiat unit. They wanted to avenge their father, I think. It's an unhappy reason to go to war, but they loved their father and losing him was such a blow to them. To all of us. My daughter is still here. That's her, with the two- and three-year-olds." She pointed to a young girl of about sixteen, who was playing with a group of toddlers.

"This," she gestured toward the children beyond the glass, "is our way of staying busy, giving other folks a little peace of mind that their kids are in good hands. We average one staff member per six children, in Yalena's age group, so there's always close supervision of the little ones. The older children are a little more autonomous, but we still maintain a ratio of one staffer to ten children, just for safety's sake.

"The beauty of this system, particuarly for the folks with lower incomes, is that it's free of charge. Everyone on Jefferson has access to it. That means every child has an equal chance to a good future. We have plenty of educational programs for the children, as well as play spaces and activity centers."

She handed Kafari a packet of brochures that enumerated the advantageous programs and equipment available at Nineveh Base Daycare Center. It was a nice facility, there was no denying that. Plenty of child-safe equipment for playing in groups or alone, activities ranging from art projects to simple scientific experiments in a classroom-lab setting. Good access to data terminals for the older kids. Up to three meals a day and healthy snacks on demand. Older children could take dance classes, participate in plays, learn music. It was, in short, a first-rate daycare program.

With a lot of overhead to maintain and a large number of staffers to pay, all provided at taxpayer expense. Kafari found herself wondering who was going to keep paying those salaries, in the coming years. The government couldn't keep up that level of expenditure for every daycare center on Jefferson, not over the long haul. Not without charging for the services or making massive budget cuts elsewhere. And probably not without imposing new taxes, which POPPA had promised not to raise. Kafari couldn't imagine anything stupider than believing POPPA could fund even half its agenda without raising taxes. Substantially so.

There was a surplus of stupid people on Jefferson.

Mrs. Hayes seemed to be a nice-enough person, but she also appeared to genuinely believe in the moral rightness of the arrangement, without the slightest concern for the cost. Kafari was betting that Mrs. Hayes did not come of Granger stock. People who made their living from the land realized that nothing in life was free, no matter how often someone insisted that it was.

She handed over a set of forms for Kafari to fill out, then took Yalena to meet some of the other children. The forms Kafari was required to fill out left her with a deep sense of foreboding. There were questions she was legally committed to answering, which violated every right-to-privacy statute on the books. Grimly, she filled them in. Most of the questions about Simon, she left blank or answered in terse phrases.

Place of birth: off-world.

Occupation: Bolo commander.

Annual salary: paid by Dinochrome Brigade.

Political affiliation: neutral, as mandated by treaty.

Religious preference: blank. She wasn't even sure he *had* one. He certainly had never voiced it, if he did, and the subject had never come up. Grangers believed in freedom of worship and the right to do so unencumbered by another's curiosity.

Educational level: blank. She had no idea what the educational level was for an officer of the Brigade. Did an officer's training at the war college count as "education" or as "military service"? She knew that Simon was far more widely read than she was and held expertise in a surprising range of fields, but had no idea whether to put in "high school" or "college" or "advanced training" as an answer.

Description of employment: classified. She genuinely didn't know most of what Simon did, while on Brigade business. She wasn't sure she wanted to know. Virtually all of it was secret. Not even Abraham Lendan had known most of what her husband's job required. He certainly wasn't sharing information—or anything else—openly with Gifre Zeloc.

When Mrs. Hayes returned, she frowned over some of Kafari's answers. "Your husband's information is highly irregular."

"So is his job," Kafari said bluntly.

Mrs. Hayes blinked. "Well, yes, that's true enough. Not a citizen, after all, and being an officer . . ." Whatever her train of thought, she didn't finish it aloud. "That's all right, my dear, we'll just turn it in the way it is and if anyone raises questions, we'll fill in the missing information later."

Like hell, you will, Kafari thought, giving Mrs. Hayes a slightly wintery smile.

"Very well, I believe we're all taken care of, here. You mentioned needing to leave for a new job?"

"Yes, at Port Abraham."

"You were fortunate enough to find a job at the space-port? What is it, you'll be doing there?"

"I'm a psychotronic engineer."

Mrs. Hayes' eyes opened wide. "An engineer?" she asked in tones of flat surprise. "A *psychotronic* engineer?"

A wild desire to shock this saccharine woman took possession of her. "I did my practicum work on the Bolo."

Her mouth fell open. "I see," she said faintly. Mrs. Hayes was staring at her, had to make a heroic effort to marshal her scattered thoughts. "I see. You must understand, most of the mothers whose children come here are military wives. They don't work, almost as a rule, or if they do, it's doing fluffy sort of things, hair-dressing, fancy sewing, manicures. The usual."

Kafari couldn't quite believe what she was hearing. Granted, she hadn't spent a great deal of time with other military wives, mostly because her work at the spaceport had taken up so much of her time during the past three years. Simon was not really in the thick of the military social life, either. Partly, that was simply because he wasn't in the same league as other officers, who felt uncomfortable around him. It was difficult to be completely at ease around a man who commanded the kind of firepower Sonny represented, did not fall into the ordinary chain of command, and was answerable solely to the president and the Brigade.

Simon received very few invitations to Nineveh Base social affairs.

She hadn't realized, during her idyllic girlhood, that Brigade officers, the most heroic and legendary figures ever produced by a human military organization, were also its loneliest. As cliched as it was, they really were a breed of men apart, both figuratively and literally.

Mrs. Hayes, recovered enough composure to ask, "Will you be working on Ziva Two? Or the spaceport?"

"The port. I'm going back to the job I left about a month ago, to devote more time to Yalena. When the new legislation went through, I couldn't justify sitting in the house all day when psychotronic engineers are needed so urgently. So I'm going back to work, this afternoon."

"That's very commendable of you, my dear. Such initiative and patriotism! I'm sure the girls on the staff will be delighted to hear that you're doing your part to rebuild our lovely world."

"Thank you, Mrs. Hayes. If that's everything, I'll just say goodbye to Yalena and head out to the spaceport."

"Of course. I'll give you a brief tour, if you have time?"

Kafari nodded. "I'd like to see the facilities," she answered with unfeigned honesty.

It was, she had to admit, everything the brochures had promised, a first-rate center with everything spotlessly clean and new. The walls were brightly painted with educational murals. There were dress-up clothes, toys appropriate to every conceivable interest, except, Kafari noted with an inward frown, anything remotely military in nature. She found that odd, considering the circumstances. These were the children of soldiers, but there wasn't a single toy gun, a single dress-up uniform, a single warplane or toy tank anywhere to be seen. She filed the information away for future reference, already wondering at the motivation behind that omission.

Otherwise, it was satisfactory in every way. Even the kitchen was first-rate, serving healthy snacks on demand, at no cost to the children or their parents. For the older kids, datascreens and hookups into the datanet were available for after-school study or educational computer games. "We get a fair number of school-age children," Mrs. Hayes explained, "who come here for recreation, sports, dance classes, equipment for science projects, that sort of thing. We're trying to serve the entire community, so parents won't have the added burden of expensive equipment at home. That can be very hard on a single-income family living on a soldier's pay."

Kafari nodded. That was true enough, but she was totting up the cost in her head, again. She didn't like the answers. Aloud, she said only, "It's a very nice facility, Mrs. Hayes. I'm sure Yalena will enjoy her time here."

Mrs. Hayes glowed with motherly pride. "That is quite a compliment, coming from a colonel's wife, my dear. You really should be invited to more of our social events. I'm sure the officer's wives would enjoy meeting you."

"That's very kind of you, Mrs. Hayes."

"Not at all. Not at all, my dear. Well, let's look up Yalena, so you can be on your way."

She found her daughter playing with a colorful puzzle, absorbed in trying to fit the pieces together in a way that made sense. "That's a very nice puzzle, Yalena. Do you like it here?"

Her little girl smiled. "Yes!"

"I'm glad. Mommy has to go to work, sweetheart. I'll come back in a few hours. You can play here with the toys and the other children." She kissed her daughter's hair and smiled when Yalena scrambled up to give her a hug.

"Bye-bye, sweetheart. I'll see you in a little while."

"Bye-bye."

Her daughter was already absorbed in the puzzle again when Kafari paused in the doorway leading to the parking lot. The director's daughter was helping her, smiling and praising Yalena's efforts. *Well,* she thought on her way to the Airdart, *it could've been a lot worse.* Given the draconian wording of the letters they had received on the subject, she'd expected to find a regimented military school with children drilled into marching lock-step, responding to orders barked by a socially correct matron in uniform, wielding a bullhorn and a bullwhip as badges of office.

It was not a comforting thought to realize things might've been better, in the long run, if Jefferson's children *had* been herded into such places. People would've protested sharply, maybe enough to call a halt to the madness. As it was . . . Only time would tell. And that was the best Kafari could do, without running for the nearest off-world ship that docked at Ziva Two. As she lifted off, flying toward Madison and the spaceport, she couldn't help wondering if she were making a serious mistake.

Chapter Fourteen

I

Simon fidgeted in his chair, staring out the window from his computer terminal, trying without much success to find a way out of his dilemma. The familiar sounds of Nineveh Base—the roar of vehicles, the counted cadence and slapping feet of training marches, the distant crack of rifle fire from the practice ranges—were missing. Their absence left a strange hole in the air, filled only by silence. The unaccustomed hush distracted him.

At least Nineveh had survived POPPA's purge, which had shut down nearly every military base world-wide. Simon had tried to persuade Gifre Zeloc that deactivating ninety percent of Jefferson's army and air forces and closing practically every military installation on Jefferson was folly. The president's response had been scathing in the extreme.

"It's been five and a half years since the Deng invasion. If the Deng were going to hit us again, they'd have done it by now. And don't try to scare me with talk about a Melconian boogeyman on the other side of the

Void. The Melconians don't give a wood rat's ass about us. If they did, *they'd* have been here by now. Frankly, Colonel, nobody cares a spit about us. Not even your precious Brigade. So take your protest, stuff it someplace interesting, and let me do my job. You might try doing yours, for a change, instead of drawing a fat paycheck for sitting on your ass."

Simon had dealt with rude officials before, but Gifre Zeloc won the prize.

Simon had not been in touch with him, since. The House of Law and Senate, naturally, had agreed with the president, exhibiting a delight that was almost obscene as they passed the legislation that officially destroyed Jefferson's military. He'd watched in cold, disapproving silence while field artillery guns by the hundreds—including the surviving mobile Hellbores General Hightower had used to defend Madison—were mothballed in armory yards scattered across Jefferson. Vast tonnages of other equipment had been cannibalized, melted down, or diverted to civilian use, leaving nothing but reserve units and Sonny to defend Jefferson if anything did go wrong.

What remained of Jefferson's high-tech weaponry was guarded by civilian police and from what Simon could tell, based on Sonny's taps into various security systems in weapons bunkers and ammunition stores, an appalling amount of equipment and ammunition was quietly disappearing. The money from black-market trading was doubtless falling into the pockets of officials in charge of a security force that was literally stealing the planet blind.

And every sorry-assed bit of it was driven by POPPA's political agenda. The party was absolutely correct when it said Jefferson couldn't afford to pay thousands of soldiers for sitting in barracks doing nothing. The policies already enacted by Vittori Santorini's elected minions were bankrupting Jefferson's government at a dizzying pace. The subsistence program alone couldn't be sustained, not even if it remained at its present enrollment, which it wouldn't do. Every new environmental regulation passed into law tightened the choke-hold on Jefferson's failing industries. Every new round of layoffs swelled the ranks of the unemployed forced to rely on subsistence payments. It was a downward spiral that was already out of control.

Since something had to be cut to pay for it, POPPA had chosen to close the military bases and disperse thousands of soldiers and their families back into the civilian population. It looked, on the surface, like a massive savings, which was exactly what POPPA was claiming. Unfortunately, that claim was a lie. Fewer than ten percent of the soldiers cut adrift had been able to find jobs. So they'd signed up for public subsistence allowances, which were—by Simon's calculation—costing the taxpayers twenty-eight percent more than it had cost to keep those soldiers on active military duty.

But subsistence payments were essentially invisible, wrapped into the already enormous expenditures for food and housing, while the cost of maintaining the bases and the soldiers was highly visible. Gifre Zeloc could point with pride to the millions saved by closing the bases, without ever needing to admit that the tax drain was now far worse. That kind of sleight-of-hand was POPPA's stock in trade.

When POPPA's upper echelons finally realized how much red ink they were bleeding—and how much more they would bleed as time marched inexorably forward—they would be forced to make cuts in the subsidy payments. And with millions of people accustomed to and dependent upon a free ride, there could be only one possible outcome.

Utter disaster.

Which brought his thoughts inexorably to Nineveh Base and the reason for its reprieve. It was being turned into a police academy. Not just any police, either, but an elite new unit of federal officers. Five thousand of them, to be exact, drawn from the ranks of POPPA's most loyal supporters. They would constitute a "politically safe" cadre of men and women who could be ordered

to do pretty much anything and be relied upon to see
that it was done. Vittori Santorini understood exactly
how fanatical devotion to a cause could be harnessed
and put to work.

Simon had gained access to the dossiers of the officers
chosen for training, as well as the profiles of the new
instructors. The first red-flag warning that had jumped
out at him, setting Simon's teeth on edge, was the family history section of those dossiers. Not one of the five
thousand officers was married. Not one had children from
extramarital relationships. They had no close family ties
to anyone. No particular reason for loyalty to anyone
or anything but POPPA and its ideology. He didn't like
the pattern that was forming. Didn't like the training
program outlined. Didn't like the implications about
POPPA's future plans. Frankly, in fact, the whole thing
scared him pissless.

More disturbing—downright chilling, in fact—was the
total lack of news reports on what was happening at
Nineveh Base. Whatever POPPA was up to, they were
being mighty secretive about it. And he genuinely hated
the fact that his wife and daughter would be sharing
the base with the kind of people about to become their
new neighbors.

He and Kafari had quarreled again, last night. She
still refused to leave Jefferson. He could tell she was
scared, as scared as he was. Any sane person would have
been. The damage being wrought was so insidious, so
smoothly presented, so glibly rationalized, so skillfully
obscured by flashy political rallies and spectacular public
entertainment, it was difficult for the average person
to realize just how much manipulation was occurring,
much of it artfully subtle. POPPA was conducting the
seizure of power with the same skillful distraction tactics
employed by really talented pickpockets. The analogy
was apt, since most Jeffersonians didn't even realize they
were being robbed.

Simon had been duty-bound to file reports with Sector Command, but the likelihood that Sector would

interfere was as remote as the likelihood that POPPA would voluntarily relinquish its increasingly strong grip. Sector had more serious fish to fry. The war front had shifted away from Jefferson, but only because there were no longer any human worlds beyond the Void in need of protection.

That there were no Deng worlds nearby, either, was of scant comfort. The three-way war had eradicated the populations of some seventeen star systems that were now vacant property. Much of that real estate had been burned to radioactive cinders, something Simon knew entirely too much about, first-hand. The Melconians weren't taking advantage of the situation, either, apparently because the fighting was so fierce elsewhere, they couldn't commit the resources necessary to move in with their colonies. Apparently, the Deng were fighting a losing battle just to hang onto their inner worlds.

Things were grim when one counted blessings in such negative terms.

That thought brought his gaze back to his computer, where the message he had been expecting had finally appeared. It had taken POPPA's leadership five and a half years to gain the nerve to take the step represented by that message, but they'd finally put together the same information Simon had about the shifting battle front beyond the Silurian Void. They had acted within hours of the realization that the war was no longer in their back yard.

Gifre Zeloc's message was short and to the point: "Deactivate your Bolo. Now."

Simon had no choice. That fact rankled bitterly. There was no possible justification he could offer for defying that order. He would not, however, obey it until Kafari had returned home. Sonny was a friend. An uneasy friend, with whom very few people could ever relax, but a friend nonetheless. For Simon, it was different. Shared experience of combat changed a man, changed the way he felt about a battle partner whose guns and war hull stood between his frail human self and the world-shaking roar of modern fields of slaughter. When death set the very wind ablaze, when life hung on the spider-silk thread of electronic reflexes, a man's fear of his Bolo burned to ash and scattered itself across the stars. What replaced it . . .

He was going to miss Sonny more than he had ever dreamed possible.

"Simon," the familiar voice jolted him out of his complex misery, "Kafari is on final approach. Her aircar will land at Yalena's daycare center in two minutes."

"Thanks," he said, voice stricken with emotion that choked the sound down to a whisper.

"I will only be sleeping," the Bolo said, his own voice strangely hushed.

In that single, excruciating moment, Simon wanted to put both arms around his friend and just hang onto him, for a moment or a lifetime. His arms were too small to hold the immensity of his feelings, let alone the vast and poignant honesty that was his friend. His only friend, besides Kafari. He closed his eyes against the pain, wishing for a moment that he could pour out the misery like last night's bath water, leaving himself empty and at peace.

"I know," he managed, inadequately.

He was still sitting there, eyes closed, when Kafari opened the door, bringing their child home from the Nineveh Base daycare center, which was closing as of next week. Simon was not looking forward to the evening, with its own battles to be fought. To say that he hated Yalena's daycare center was on a par with saying the Deng were irritating. What that daycare center was doing to Yalena would have constituted criminal abuse on most worlds. What would happen when she started school . . . Worst of all, there was absolutely nothing he could do about it, short of forcing his wife and child onto the next freighter bound for Vishnu.

He wasn't sure he could cope, tonight, with the hellion that his daughter had become. She was already shrieking at her mother.

"I wanna go back to play with my friends!"

The scathing emphasis on that final word demonstrated with piercing intensity that Yalena did not place her parents in that category. It appalled Simon that a five-year-old child could condense that much hatred in a single, simple word.

"You'll see your friends tomorrow, Yalena."

"I wanna see them now!"

"You can't have everything you want, Yalena."

"Oh, yes I can," she hissed. "The law says so!"

That brought Simon out of his chair. "*Yalena!*"

She whipped around, rage contorting a face that should have been pretty. "Don't shout at me! You're not allowed to shout at me! If you shout at me again, I'll tell Miss Finch how horrible you are! Then they'll put you in jail!"

She ran into her room—the size of which was federally mandated—and slammed the door so hard photographs on the wall jumped on their nails. The bolt-lock—also federally mandated—slammed into place with an audible snap. Kafari burst into tears. Simon didn't dare move for long, dangerous moments, aware with every atom in his body that if he took a single step in any direction, he wouldn't be able to contain the violence of his emotions. Or the actions that would follow.

Doing any of the things he needed to do—kicking down the door, warming Yalena's backside, shaking sense into her—would only precipitate disaster. And play right into the hands of Vittori Santorini and his minions. They were itching for an excuse to invade Simon's house and finish destroying his little family. If he laid so much as a finger on his child, the resultant feeding frenzy would culminate in POPPA seizing Yalena to "safeguard" her from violent and dangerous parents and give them grounds to demand that the Concordiat cashier and expel him from Jefferson. It was a measure of his anger—and his dark foreboding about the future—that *any* excuse for leaving Jefferson was attractive.

Kafari, voice breaking with misery, said, "She didn't really mean it, Simon."

"Oh, yes, she did." His voice came out flat and full of sand.

"She doesn't understand—"

"She understands too well," he bit out. "She understands so much, we're naked over a barrel and she knows it. And it's going to get worse. A *lot* worse."

Kafari bit her lower lip. Her glance at Yalena's bedroom door was full of misery and failure. "If we could just pull her out of daycare . . ."

"The only way to do that is to leave." He didn't need to add, *And you won't do that.* They'd already fought that fight, more than once. His voice came out weary and bitter. "Kafari, you have no idea how much worse things are about to get. I've been ordered to shut Sonny down. Without him, I can't possibly stay on top of what POPPA is planning and they know it. I can only see what they're doing through his taps into security cameras. I can't read fast enough to scan the entire datanet, much less track what's on the computers connected to it. I can't hear what's being said through telephones, wireless voice transmissions, or computer microphones, not without Sonny. The minute he goes into inactive standby, I lose all of that.

"I'm the only check-and-balance still operating on this world and that's changing, as of today. I can't interfere unless I have direct evidence of activity that violates the treaty with the Concordiat. I can't provide evidence if I don't have the technical ability to look for it."

She sat down abruptly, eyes glazed as the shock of it settled in. "You can't refuse?"

"No."

She lifted a stricken gaze to meet his. "I'm so sorry, Simon. It must be like losing your best friend."

Her words took him completely by surprise. Quite suddenly his eyes stung. "Yes," he said hoarsely. He blinked rapidly a few times. Said in a low voice, "You know I love you more than life, Kafari. But Sonny was with me . . ."

"I know," she said in a whisper, when he couldn't finish.

He just nodded. It was impossible to convey what combat was like to anyone who hadn't been through it. Kafari *had*. She knew. Understood the reason for his rough silence. She hadn't been on Etaine; but then *he* hadn't been through combat between a Bolo and Yavacs without a Bolo's warhull between him and the enemy. It was a different way of experiencing war, a different kind of terror, but the damage to the soul was the same. So was the deeper understanding that sometimes, the horror and shock if it were utterly necessary.

That she realized this, that she understood what it was doing to him, to lose the one companion who knew what had happened on that far-away world, left him humbled. She had chosen to love and live with *him*. And now . . . Jaw muscles tightened down against bone. Now they had new problems. New fears. A new kind of battle. And an enemy that twisted reality around to suit its aims and poisoned innocent minds to accomplish them. POPPA was on the verge of shattering everything that was—or had been—good and beautiful about this world. The question that slipped into his mind like silent misery had no answer that Simon could find.

What are we going to do?

He was a soldier. An officer. There was only one thing *to* do. Sometimes, duty was a bitch.

II

Yalena hated school.

She hadn't wanted to leave the nursery class on Nineveh Base. She had loved playing with other children whose parents were soldiers, too. But there weren't any soldiers any more, just police who didn't have children, and she was old enough, at six, to have to go to a real school in Madison.

"There'll be all kinds of wonderful things to do and learn," her mother had told her, the first day.

Her mother was right. There were wonderful, fun things to do and learn. But only for other kids. Yalena didn't get to do any of them. And *everybody* hated her. It had started the first, horrible day, when Mrs. Gould, the kindergarten teacher, called out everybody's name and made them stand up and tell the class who they were and who their parents were.

"Yalena Khrustinova," Mrs. Gould had said, with something in her voice that made Yalena's flesh creep, like the teacher had said a naughty word or maybe stepped in something smelly.

She stood up, slowly, while everybody stared. She didn't know any of the other kids. When the soldiers had left Nineveh Base, they'd all gone home and none of them had lived in Madison. Not this part, anyway. So she stood there, with everybody looking at her, and said in a shaky little voice. "My mommy is Kafari Khrustinova. She works at the spaceport. She makes computers do things. My daddy is Simon Khrustinov. He's a soldier."

"What kind of soldier?" Mrs. Gould asked, staring down at her through narrow little eyes like a lizard's.

"He talks to the Bolo. And tells it to shoot its guns."

"Did all of you hear that?" the teacher asked. "Yalena's father is responsible for telling a huge, dangerous machine to shoot people. That machine shot millions and millions of people on a world far away from here. Does anyone know how many people it takes to make a million? There are ten million people on our whole planet. Seventeen million people died, on that other world. To kill seventeen million people, that machine would have to kill every man, every woman, and every baby on Jefferson. And then it would have to kill almost that many more. The Bolo is a terrible, evil machine. And Yalena's father tells it to kill."

"B-but—" she tried to say.

Mrs. Gould slammed both fists on her desk. *"Don't you dare talk back to me! Sit down this instant! No recess for a week!"*

Yalena sat down. Her knees were shaking. Her eyes were hot.

Somebody hissed, "Lookit the crybaby!" and the whole class started jeering and laughing at her. That was the first day. Every day since then had been worse. A whole year of horrible, awful, worse days. During class, everything she said was wrong. Even if somebody else said the same thing, somehow it was wrong when she said it. If she tried not to talk at all, Mrs. Gould made her stand in a corner all by herself, for being secretive, dangerous, and sly.

Every morning, when her mother dropped her off for school, Yalena threw up in the bushes outside. At lunch, nobody would sit near her. At recess . . . The teachers wouldn't let anybody actually hurt her, not badly enough to need the school nurse, but she usually came back into class with scraped knees, bruised shins, or mud in her hair. She hated recess more than she hated any other part of school.

And now it was time to start all over, again. The first day of first grade. And all the same kids who hated her and tripped her and shoved her off the swings and threw mudballs at the back of her head and spilled paint on her favorite clothes . . .

The only things that were different were the room and the teacher.

The room, at least, was nothing like Mrs. Gould's kindergarten. The walls were a sunny yellow that lifted the spirits, just walking in through the door. There were wonderful pictures everywhere, pictures of places and animals and things Yalena wasn't even sure had names, let alone what they might be used for. There were other pictures, too, that somebody had painted, rather than photographs of things, and they were all as sunny and cheerful as the yellow walls. It was a room Yalena wanted to love, at first sight, a room that made her want to cry, because she was going to spend a whole year being miserable and alone in it.

She wanted to sit in the farthest corner in the back, but there were cards folded like tents on each desk, with names on them. Yalena was the first person to arrive, not because she wanted to be there early, but because it would be less awful to sit down in a nearly empty room and watch everyone come in than it would be to arrive in a room full of people who hated her, glaring with every step she took trying to get to her desk. She looked at each desk and finally found her name, in the middle of the room.

It said *Yalena*.

But not *Khrustinova*. Nobody's card had a last name on it. There were three Ann name cards, but they didn't have last names, either, just Ann with a single initial: Ann T., Ann J., and Ann W. That was definitely different from Mrs. Gould's class, where the boys were "Mr. Timmons" and "Mr. Johansen" and the girls were "Miss Miles" and "Miss Khrustinova," which always came out sounding like somebody gargling with vinegar.

There was no sign of a teacher anywhere.

Puzzled by that strangeness, Yalena made her way to her new desk, carrying her book bag like a magic shield that would guard her until she was forced to put it down to start studying. Classmates she remembered arrived in noisy clusters, laughing and talking about things they had done together over the summer. Yalena had spent the summer on Nineveh Base with her father. It had not been a fun summer. They had gone to some interesting places, like the museum in Madison and her grandparents' and great-grandparents' farm and fishing in lakes up in the mountains, a few times, but she didn't like the farms very much. They were hot and smelled strange and the animals on them were huge and didn't like little girls poking at them.

Nobody from school had called her to ask if she wanted to come over for a pool party or a sleep-over or anything else. So she had stayed in her room, mostly, reading her books and playing on the computer, which didn't care who your father was or whether your mother was a *jomo* or any of the other reasons kids found to hate her. It was difficult, watching the others come into the classroom, laughing and having a wonderful time, and harder to watch them give her sneering looks and scoot their chairs as far away from hers as possible.

She opened her book bag and pretended to read the first-grade primer her father had bought for her, along with all her supplies. She was still pretending when a very pretty woman in the prettiest dress Yalena had ever seen sailed into the classroom, with a smile as bright as sunlight and a scent like the summer roses on her grandmother's front porch, which was the only spot on the whole farm Yalena thought was pretty.

"Bon jour, bon jour, ma petites," she said in a language Yalena had never heard, then she laughed and said in perfectly ordinary words, "Good morning my little ones, how lovely to see everyone!"

She sat down on the edge of the desk at the front of the room, rather than in the chair or standing over them like somebody's mean dog. "I am Cadence Peverell, your teacher. I want everyone to call me Cadence. Does anyone know what Cadence means?"

Nobody did.

"A 'cadence' is a rhythm, like when you clap your hands and sing." She clapped and sang a little song, also in words that Yalena couldn't understand, although nobody else seemed to, either. Then Miss Peverell laughed. "That is a French song, of course, with French words, because a long time ago, my ancestors were French, back on Terra where humanity was born. Everyone's name means something. Did you know that?"

Yalena certainly didn't. Other kids were shaking their heads, too.

"Ah, but you shall see! Douglas," she said, looking at a boy in the front row, "your name means 'the boy who lives by the dark stream.' And Wendell," she pointed to a long, lanky boy who had spent kindergarten trying to climb over the play-yard fences, "means someone who wanders."

Laughter broke out as Wendell grinned.

"And Frieda," she addressed a girl in the back row, "means 'peaceful.' But you know," the teacher said with a sound like warm butter and a gentle smile, "there is one name in this classroom that is the loveliest name I have ever heard."

Miss Peverell was looking right at Yalena.

"Do you know what your name means, Yalena?"

The entire classroom went utterly silent.

She shook her head, waiting for the teacher to say something horrible.

"Yalena," Miss Peverell said, "is a Russian name. It's the Russian way of saying the name 'Helen' and that name means 'light.' Beautiful, clear light, like the sun in the sky."

The silence continued. Yalena was staring at her teacher, confused and so scared she wanted to start crying. And strangely, the teacher seemed to understand. She slid down off the desk, crouched down at the end of the aisle, and said, "Would you come to see me, Yalena?"

She was holding out both arms, like she really wanted to give Yalena a hug.

Yalena stood up slowly, having to put down the book bag that was her only shield. She couldn't walk very fast. Miss Peverell smiled at her, with warm encouragement, then did, in fact, give her a warm and wonderful hug.

"There, now, let's sit on the desk together."

She picked Yalena up, perched on the edge of the desk again, held Yalena on her knees, with one arm around her. "You children are so lucky to have Yalena in the class with you."

Everybody was staring, mouths open.

"Yalena is a very brave little girl. It is not easy to be the daughter of a soldier."

Yalena went rigid, knowing that it was coming.

Miss Peverell brushed her hair back from her face, gently. "Every day, a soldier may have to go and fight a war. It can be very hard, very scary, to be a soldier or a soldier's child. And every day, when Yalena goes home, there is a huge machine in her back yard, a very dangerous machine."

Yalena wanted to crawl away and hide . . .

"Now this machine, this Bolo, can do very good things, too. It made the Deng go away, many years ago, before you were even born. And that was a very good thing, indeed. But these machines, they are alive, in a way, and it is no easy thing to live in a house with a machine that is alive, waiting in case a war starts. Every day, Yalena is brave enough to go home and trust that the machine won't have to fight a war, that night. I think that is the bravest thing I have ever seen a little girl do."

The other girls in the class were looking at one another. Some of them looked angry, as if they wanted to be braver than the horrible killer's daughter. Others looked surprised and others looked interested. Even the boys looked surprised and interested.

"There is something else I want to say to everyone," Miss Peverell said, still holding Yalena. "Does everyone know what POPPA is? No? Ah, POPPA is a group of people, just like you, just like me, who believe that everyone should be treated just the same way, so that no one has to be poor or have people hurt them or be hated for things that aren't their fault. This is one of the most important things POPPA teaches us. Everyone has the right to be treated well, to be respected."

Miss Peverell looked very sad as she said, "A child who does not respect other children is a bully and that is a very bad thing to be. POPPA wants all children to be happy and healthy and have a wonderful time, both at home and at school. It's very hard to have a wonderful time at home, when you have a machine like that in your back yard and you never know what it's going to do and maybe your daddy will have to go away and fight a war and you might never see him again. Soldiers are very brave and Yalena's father is one of the bravest soldiers on our whole world.

"But it is very hard to be happy when you're afraid that a war might come. So it is most important that Yalena is happy when she comes to school. POPPA wants all of us to be nice to everyone. POPPA wants all of us to be happy. POPPA wants all of us to treat each other with kindness. I know that all of you are good children who want to do these important things and help others do them, too. So I'm very happy that all of you have the chance to make Yalena feel special and happy and welcome, every day."

Yalena started to cry, but nobody called her a crybaby this time. Miss Peverell kissed her hair and said, "Welcome to my class, Yalena. All right, you can go back to your seat now."

The rest of the morning was strange and wonderful. Nobody quite had the nerve to talk to her at recess, but everyone stared and whispered when Miss Peverell came over to where Yalena was sitting by herself and started teaching her the song she'd sung at the beginning of the class. It was a pretty song, a cheerful song, even if Yalena didn't know what the words meant. By the end of recess, Yalena knew every word by heart and Miss Peverell had taught her what the words meant, too. It was a wonderful song, about growing oats and peas and barley and beans and it was all about farmers who sang and danced and played all day and all night, without ever doing any work at all, while the oats and things grew green in the sunlight. And at lunch, nobody left an empty seat between themselves and Yalena.

She went home that night almost happy. She was afraid to hope, but the day she had dreaded all summer had been wonderful, instead. A magical day. She was terrified that it would all end the next day, but it didn't. It was just as good the day after that and the next one, too. At recess on the last day of the week, one of the shy girls in her class, who didn't play a lot of games with anybody else, came over to where Yalena was swinging. For a long moment, Yalena expected her to push her off the swing or say something nasty.

Then she smiled. "Hi. My name's Ami-Lynn."

"Hello."

"Would you teach me that song? The one in French? It's awfully pretty."

Yalena's eyes widened. For a minute, she couldn't say anything. Then she smiled. "Yes, I'd love to teach you."

Ami-Lynn's eyes started shining like stars. "Thank you!"

They spent the whole recess singing the funny, wonderful words. Ami-Lynn had a pretty voice, but she had so much trouble saying the words, they both started giggling and couldn't stop, even when the bell rang and the teachers called them inside. Miss Peverell, who insisted that everyone call her Cadence, just as though she were their best friend, not a stuffy teacher, saw them and smiled.

That was the day Yalena started to love school.

And when she went to bed that night, she hugged herself for joy and whispered, "Thank you, POPPA! Thank you for bringing me a friend!" She didn't know who or what, exactly, POPPA was, except that it must be full of very wonderful people, if they cared enough to want her to be so happy. She knew her parents didn't like POPPA very much, because she'd heard them say so, when talking to each other. *I don't care what they think*, she told herself fiercely. *Ami-Lynn likes me. Cadence likes me. POPPA likes me. And I don't care about anything or anybody else!*

She was finally happy. And nobody—not even her parents—was ever going to take that away from her again.

III

"I won't go!"

"Yes," Kafari said through gritted teeth, "you will."

"It's *my* birthday! I want to spend it with *my* friends!"

Give me patience . . . "You see your friends every day. Your grandparents and great-grandparents haven't seen you in a year. So get into the aircar *right now* or you will be grounded for the next full week."

Her daughter glared at her. "You wouldn't dare!"

"Oh, yes I would. Or have you forgotten what happened when you refused to leave the school playground last month?"

The amount of malevolence a ten-year-old could fling across a room would, if properly harnessed, run a steam-powered electrical generating plant for a month of nonstop operation. When they'd locked wills over the playground, Yalena had threatened dire vengeance, but had discovered to her consternation that when Kafari said "do it or you lose datachat privileges for a week" you either did it, or you didn't talk to your friends outside of school for seven days.

Yalena, who should have been pretty in her frilly birthday dress and fancy glow-spark shoes, contrived to look like an enraged rhinoceros about to charge an ogre. Kafari, cast in the part of the ogre, pointed imperiously to the front door.

Her daughter, stiff with outrage and hatred, stalked past her, pointedly slamming the door into the wall on her way out. Kafari pulled it closed, setting the voiceprint lock that would, with any luck, deter their nearest neighbors from helping themselves to the contents of their home—the so-called "POPPA Squads" training on Nineveh Base had the lightest and stickiest fingers Kafari had ever seen—then followed her offspring out to the landing pad. Simon was already strapping her into the back seat of the aircar.

"I hate you," she growled at her father.

"The feeling," her father growled right back, "is mutual."

"You can't hate me! It's not allowed!"

"Young lady," Simon told her in an icy tone of

voice, "the right to detest someone is a sword that cuts both ways. You have the manners of an illiterate fishwife. And if you don't want to spend the next year without datachat privileges, you will speak in a civil tone and use polite language. The choice is entirely up to you."

Lightning seethed in Yalena's eyes, but she kept her acid tongue silent. She had learned, after losing several key battles, that when her father spoke to her in that particular tone, discretion was by far the wiser choice. Kafari took her seat and fastened her harness in place. Simon did the same, then touched controls and lifted into the cloudless sky. It was a beautiful day, with honey pouring across the rose-toned shoulders of the Damisi Mountains, to spill its way down across the Adero floodplain in golden ripples. The flight was a silent one, with only the rush of wind past the aircar's canopy to break the chill.

The crowding elbows of Maze Gap flashed past, then they were headed down Klameth Canyon, following the twisting route to Chakula Ranch, which her parents had finally managed to rebuild. The house was in a different place, but the ponds were functional again and the Malinese miners were buying pearls by the hundred-weight, as the war had sent Mali's economy into a boom that apparently had no end in sight. Jefferson, on the other hand . . .

Some things, Kafari didn't want to think about too deeply. The ruination of Jefferson's economy was one of them.

Simon brought them down in a neat and skilled landing, killing the engine and popping the hatches. Kafari unhooked herself and waited while Yalena ripped loose the catches on her own harness. She slammed her way out of the aircar and glared at the crowd of grandparents, aunt, uncles, and cousins who'd streamed across the yard to greet her. She wrinkled her nose and curled her upper lip.

"Ew, it stinks. Like pigs crapped everywhere." She

was glaring, not at the farm buildings, but directly at her relatives.

"*Yalena!*" Simon glowered. "That is not language fit for polite company. Do it again and you'll lose a solid month of chat."

Smiles of welcome had frozen in place. Kafari clenched her teeth and said, "Yalena, say hello to your family. Politely."

A swift glare of defiance shifted into sullen disgust. "Hello," she muttered.

Kafari's mother, expression stricken with uncertainty and dismay, said, "Happy Birthday, Yalena. We're very glad you could be with us, today."

"I'm not!"

"Well, child," Kafari's father said with a jovial grin that managed to convey a rather feral threat, "you're more than welcome to walk home again. Of course, it might take you quite a while, in those shoes."

Yalena's mouth fell open. "*Walk?* All the way to Nineveh? Are you like totally stupid?"

"No, but you're totally rude." He brushed past his grandchild to give Kafari a warm hug. "It's good to see *you*, honey." She didn't miss the emphasis. From the look on Yalena's face, neither had she. Kafari knew a moment of stinging guilt. Her father clasped Simon's hand, shaking it firmly. "Don't see enough of you, son. Come and see us more often."

"I may just do that," Simon said quietly.

"You can leave that," he gestured dismissively at his gaping granddaughter, "where you found it, unless it learns to speak with a little more respect. Come inside, folks, come inside, there's plenty of time to catch up on the news without standing out here all day."

He drew Kafari's arm through his, smiling down at her, and literally ignored his granddaughter, whose special day this was supposed to be. Kafari's eyes stung with swift tears as guilt and remorse tore through her heart, witnessing the confused hurt in her daughter's eyes. Yalena was just a child. A beautiful and intelligent little girl, who had no real chance against the determined, incessant onslaught of propaganda hurled at her by teachers, entertainers, and so-called news reporters who wouldn't have known how to report honestly if their immortal souls had depended on it.

She and Simon had tried to undo the ongoing damage. Had tried again and again. Were *still* trying. And nothing worked. Nothing. Nor would it, not when every other significant adult in her life was telling her—over and over—that she could demand anything and get it; that she could rat out her parents or anyone else for an entire laundry list of suspicious behaviors or beliefs and be rewarded lavishly; and that she held an inalienable right to do whatever she chose, whenever she chose and somebody else would dutifully have to pay for it. Kafari knew only too well that Yalena received extra social conditioning simply because she was their child. It suited POPPA to plant a snake inside their home, to use as a threat and a spy, and it enraged Kafari endlessly that they did so without a single moment's remorse over the damage they inflicted daily on a little girl.

Kafari's father gave her arm a gentle squeeze and a slight shake of his head, trying to convey without words that none of this mess was her fault. It helped. A little. She was grateful for that much. She glanced back long enough to reassure herself that Simon was keeping an eye on their daughter, who was glaring at her cousins. They regarded her with cold hostility and open disgust. That the feelings were mutual was painfully obvious. Her mother, who had coped with more heartaches than Kafari would ever be able to claim, waded in like a soldier going into battle, taking charge of the ghastly situation with brisk efficiency.

"Everybody goes to the house. Come on, you mangy lot, there's punch and cookies waiting and plenty of games to play before lunch."

Yalena stalked with regal disdain past her cousins, as though wading through a pile of something putrid. Her cousins, falling in behind her, lost no time in mocking the birthday girl behind her back, pointing their noses at the sky, marching with exaggerated mimicry. If Yalena turned around, she'd get a nice dose of unpleasant reality. If Kafari knew her nieces and nephews, Yalena would get several doses of reality before it was time to leave, all of them painful.

Watching the ugly dynamics, Kafari hated POPPA with a violence that scared her. The sole comfort she derived from the situation was the realization that POPPA wasn't succeeding in totally indoctrinating all of Jefferson's children. Yalena's cousins might be trapped in a POPPA-run school all day, but living—and working—on a farm provided its own strong and daily antidote to idiocy. When it came to milking cows, gathering eggs from nest boxes, or any of the thousand other chores necessary to keeping a farm operational, platitudes like "no child should be forced to do anything he or she doesn't want to do" earned exactly what they merited: derisive contempt.

If you didn't milk a cow, pretty soon you had no milk. And if you weren't careful, no cow, either. There was literally nothing in Yalena's world to give her that kind of perspective. Kafari thought seriously about turning Yalena over to her parents this summer. If not for Simon's position, she'd have plunked Yalena down on the farm already, come hell or high water.

Kafari's father, reading much of what was in her heart, murmured, "Hold onto your hope, Kafari. And do what you can to let her know you care. One of these days she'll wake up and that will mean something to her."

Kafari stumbled on the way up the porch steps. "Thanks," she managed, blinking hard.

He squeezed her arm gently, then they were inside and people were swarming past, most of them jabbering excitedly, with the little ones swirling around their ankles like the tide coming in at Merton Beach. Kafari snagged punch and cookies and handed a cup and plate to Yalena while dredging up the best smile she could muster. Yalena, scowling in deep suspicion, sniffed the punch, pulled a face, then condescended to taste it. She shrugged, as though indifferent, but drank every bit as much as her exuberant cousins. She fought for her share of the cookies, too, which were piled high and dusted with sugar, or smeared with frosting of various flavors, or drenched in a honey-and-nut coating that Kafari had forgotten tasted so heavenly. Simon went for the honey-nut ones too, managing a brilliant smile for Kafari as he snagged seconds.

Yalena's cousin Anastasia, who was only six months younger than Yalena, took the bull by the horns, as it were, and walked up to stare at her older cousin. "That's a nice dress," she said, in the manner of someone who will be polite no matter the personal cost. "Where did you find it?"

"Madison," Yalena answered with withering disdain.

"Huh. In that case, you paid too much for it."

Yalena's mouth fell open. Anastasia grinned, then said in a cuttingly impolite tone, "Those shoes are the stupidest things I've ever seen. You couldn't outrun a hog in those things, let alone a *jaglitch*."

"And why," Yalena demanded in a scathing tone that bent the steel window frames, "would I want to outrun a *jaglitch*?"

"So it wouldn't eat you, stupid."

Anastasia rolled her eyes and simply stalked off. Her cousins, watching with preternatural interest, erupted into howling laughter. Yalena went red. Then white. Her fists tightened down, crunching the cookie in one hand and squashing the paper cup of punch in the other. Then her chin went up, in a heartbreaking mimicry of a gesture that Kafari knew only too well, in herself.

"Enough!" Kafari's mother snapped, eyes crackling with dangerous anger. "I will not condone nasty manners in this house. Do I make myself clear? Yalena isn't used to living where wild predators can snatch a grown man, let alone a child. Conduct yourselves with courtesy and respect. Or do you like living down to city standards?"

Silence fell, chilly and sullen.

Yalena, alone in the center of the room, stared from

one to another of her cousins. Her chin quivered just once. Then she said coldly, "Don't bother to try. I didn't expect anything better of *pig farmers*." She stalked out of the room, slamming doors on her way to somewhere—anywhere—else. When Kafari moved to follow, her father's hand tightened down around her arm.

"No, let her go. That's a young'un who needs to be alone for a few minutes. Minau, why don't you follow her—discreetly—and make sure she doesn't wander too far? It's springtime and there are *jaglitch* out there, looking for a snack."

Kafari started to shake. Simon wiped sweat off his forehead and gulped an entire cupful of punch as though wishing for something considerably stronger. Aunt Min just nodded, heading through the same door Yalena had taken during her exodus. Kafari leaned back into the couch cushions as a feeling of momentary relief settled across her. She had forgotten what it was like, having other capable adults around to share the burden of childcare. Anastasia, attempting to regain Iva Camar's good graces, was busy cleaning up the spilled punch and cookie crumbs. Kafari's mother ruffled the girl's hair, then sat down beside Kafari on the sofa, speaking low enough the sound reached only her ears.

"You didn't say how bad it was, honey."

Kafari shook her head. "Would you have believed me?"

A sigh gusted loose. "No. I don't think I realized just how serious things are in town, these days."

Simon joined them on the couch. "It's worse than that," he nodded toward the door Yalena and Aunt Min had disappeared through. "Much worse, I'm afraid. Unlike these kids," he nodded toward Yalena's cousins, the younger ones entertaining themselves while the older ones listened intently to the adult discussion underway, "Yalena spends her after-school hours involved in town-style activities. Things like the Eco-Action Club, the Equality for Infants Discussion Group—no, I'm not making that up, I swear to God—and the ever-popular

Children's Rights Research Society, which spends its time studying bogus sociological hogwash churned out by Alva Mahault, the new Chair of Sociological Studies at Riverside University. Then they dream up new schemes to implement the sociology research's 'facts' in ways beneficial to legal minors. This involves, for the most part, suggesting things like mandatory vacations off-world for every child, to be paid for by taxes, naturally, mandatory personal allowances and federal requirements for providing in-home snacks for every child. The 'best' ideas are presented to the Senate and House of Law for consideration as new legislation, most of which is immediately hailed as groundbreaking social brilliance and passed into law."

Shocked silence greeted his bitter assessment. Kafari's father spoke in a thoughtful, droll tone, "You have a gift, Simon, for stating things with great clarity. Ever think of running for president?"

Someone chuckled and the ghastly tension in the room ebbed away, allowing an abrupt and lively discussion about the best ways to counter such arrant nonsense. Kafari, who worked ten-hour days in a spaceport populated largely by rabid believers in anything and everything POPPA suggested, found it both refreshing and marvelously relaxing to listen to intelligent people who understood the basic way in which the universe works and weren't afraid—yet—to say so. She was content, for now, to simply listen and bask in the warmth of feeling completely at home for the first time in many long months. When she drained the last of the punch from her cup, she caught Simon's eye and nodded toward the door Yalena had gone through. She indicated with a gesture that he should remain where he was, then went in search of her daughter.

She found Aunt Min on the back porch, seated in a rocking chair, with a hunting rifle laid comfortably across her lap. Her aunt nodded past the well house. Kafari's parents had installed a big bench-style swing that hung from the spreading branches of a genuine Terran oak.

Kafari remembered the tree, which had supported a swing of one kind or another for as long as she could remember. In her childhood, it had been a big tractor tire. Kafari suspected her parents enjoyed the bench swing, particularly on warm summer evenings. Yalena was sitting on one end of the swing, staring across the nearest of the ponds, chin resting on tucked-up knees, swinging slowly by herself.

"She's not having a very happy birthday," Kafari said, sighing and keeping her voice low.

"No," Aunt Min agreed, "but that's largely her own doing."

"I know. But it's hard to see her hurting, like that, all the same. I wish . . ." She didn't finish the thought. Wishes were for children. Kafari had reality to cope with, one agonizing day at a time. She stepped off the porch, heading for the swing. "Mind if I join you?" she asked, keeping her voice easy and casual.

Yalena shrugged.

Kafari perched on the other end. "Your cousins were very rude."

Yalena looked up, surprise coloring her eyes, which were so achingly like Simon's, it hurt, sometimes, looking into them. "Yes," she said, voice quavering a little. "They were."

Kafari held her peace for three or four more swings, then said, "You were very brave, in there. I was really proud of you, Yalena. You do realize, of course," she smiled wryly, "that you missed a chance to demonstrate better manners than they have? But it took guts to stand up to them that way."

Quick tears shone in her daughter's eyes. "Thanks," she said, all but inaudibly.

"Would you like to see the pearl sheds?"

Yalena shrugged again.

"Later, maybe." Kafari was determined to be patience, itself, today, even if it killed her. "I'll bet, though, that you'll be the only girl in school who's ever seen a real pearl hatchery. Your grandparents helped perfect the technique that allows pearl growers to seed, grow, and harvest the pearls without injuring the oysters. It's a very gentle process. And it gives the Klameth Canyon pearl growers a big advantage in the off-world marketplace. We can produce crop after crop without having to grow new oysters, as well as new pearls. Klameth Canyon produces more pearls of higher quality than any star system in the Sector."

"I didn't know any of that," Yalena admitted, sounding intrigued. "Did you grow pearls?"

"Oh, yes. I was pretty good at it, too."

"What did you like best?"

Kafari smiled, remembering the intensity of her interest when she'd been just Yalena's age. "I liked producing the special colors, more than anything else. The pinks are awfully pretty, but I liked the black pearls best, I think. Although they're not really black. They're more of a deep violet with an indigo-jade sheen. Your great-grandmother invented the process that produces that color. She engineered a bacteria that's harmless to the oyster, but causes a biochemical reaction that lets the oyster pull minerals from a special solution in the ponds and deposit them in the nacre that forms the pearl. Chakula Ranch holds the patent on it. I would be willing to bet," she added with a smile, "that you will be the only girl in school with a Chakula black-pearl necklace."

Yalena looked up. "But I don't have any black pearls."

"Ah, but it's your birthday, isn't it?"

Surprise left her eyes wide. Then a glow blazed to life, born of hope and delight and a sudden realization that her mother was not just a person she did battle with daily, but someone who understood—and cared—that Yalena still encountered some nasty hazing from school mates who knew that Kafari was a Granger and that Simon was an off-world soldier whose name was mud in any household that supported POPPA.

"D'you mean that? Really and truly?"

"Your father and I talked it over with your grandmother and grandfather. We'll even let you pick the pearls."

Her daughter's eyes shone. "Oh, Mom! Not even Katrina has a pearl necklace! And she's got the prettiest jewelry in school. And Ami-Lynn will just die of delight, watching the look on Katrina's face when she sees it!"

Ami-Lynn had long been Yalena's best friend in the universe, while Katrina was a girl that everyone, apparently, had good reason to detest. It would be quite a coup, to outdo one's worst enemy when said enemy had the prettiest jewelry in school. Kafari grinned and gave her daughter a conspiratorial wink. "Sure you don't want to see the pearl sheds?"

"Will any of *them*," she jerked her head toward the house, voice harsh with pain and anger, "be there?"

Kafari winced, but shook her head. "Nope. Just you and me. If anyone tries to butt in, I'll heave 'em into the nearest pond."

A smile stole its way across Yalena's face. A crafty smile, but Kafari understood the impulse. It wasn't easy, celebrating one's birthday with a bunch of strangers who'd been hideously rude, whatever the provocation might have been.

"C'mon, let's go see if we can find some pearls good enough to ruin Katrina's whole year. We'll pick them out and then take them to a jeweler to have a necklace made."

Yalena started to slide down from the swing, then paused long enough to whisper, "Thanks, Mom." There was a world of emotion—of thanks and apology and gratitude—rolled up in those two simple little words. She laid those words and emotions in Kafari's hands, blinking rapidly and hoping that her overture wouldn't be rejected.

"You're welcome, Yalena. Happy birthday, sugarplum."

Yalena smiled again, sweetly this time, and slipped her hand into Kafari's. They set out together for the pearl sheds.

Chapter Fifteen

I

I come awake as a reflex alarm from my external sensors sends a signal racing through my threat-assessment processors. I snap to full wakefulness and scan my environs instantly. Simon stands beside my right tread. He is involved in a discussion with three men, none of whom I recognize. All three have just entered my exclusion zone, triggering an automatic reflex through my battle-readiness circuitry. I surmise that Simon has deliberately steered them into this zone for the express purpose of triggering me awake.

One is armed, carrying a concealed handgun in a shoulder holster. Despite the presence of a concealed weapon, I hold my fire and watch closely to see what develops, since Simon has not signaled me via his commlink to take action against hostile intruders. I therefore do not react with full battlefield reflexes, but I maintain alert vigilance, as my Commander is not wearing a personal sidearm.

The three visitors in my work-bay are dressed as

289

civilians. Two are heavily muscled with blocky, thick torsos. They look more like space-dock stevedores than executive assistants to the president of Jefferson, which is the ID code transmitted by the visitors' passes clipped to their jackets, allowing them access to restricted areas of Nineveh Base. The third armed individual holds most of my attention as I do an automatic scan of Brigade channels, seeking a passive VSR while I await developments and Simon's instructions.

This man's identification states that he is the president's chief advisor, Sar Gremian. He is taller than Simon, with dense, heavy bones that support muscles sufficiently well developed to qualify as a heavy-weight prizefighter. His skull is devoid of hair. His face is deeply pitted with scars that suggest severe adolescent acne. His expression wavers from bitter to savage and his voice is rough, reminding me of career drill sergeants I have seen drilling new recruits.

The conversation underway appears to be hostile, as stress indicators—elevated heart rate and rapid respiration, coupled with facial expression—suggest an angry argument underway. This perhaps explains Simon's action in leading these men into a zone where I would automatically resume consciousness, for the express purpose of having me listen? Simon is speaking, evidently in answer to an unknown question.

"Absolutely not. I said no when you called from Madison and my answer has not changed."

The two burly men with the president's advisor react with overt anger, faces flushing red, fingers curling into anticipatory claws, but they do not make any actual moves toward my Commander, so I bide my time and study the unfolding situation. The president's advisor merely narrows his eyes. "You're refusing a direct order from the president?"

A muscle jumps in Simon's jaw. "You are not the president of Jefferson, Sar Gremian. The president's chief advisor does not have the authority to send a Bolo anywhere."

"I'll get the authorization, then." *He reaches for his comm-unit.*

"Be my guest. I'll tell Gifre Zeloc the same thing I told President Andrews, when *he* demanded something like this. You don't use a Bolo for crowd control. Sonny isn't a police officer, he's a machine of war. There is," *Simon adds with an acid bite in his voice,* "a significant difference."

Sar Gremian pauses, then chooses not to complete the transmission. "Let me try to explain the situation to you, Khrustinov. That mob of protestors outside Assembly Hall has refused to disperse, despite repeated orders to disband. They've blocked Darconi Street. They've jammed every square centimeter of Lendan Park and Law Square. They've thrown up barricades across every entrance into Assembly Hall. They've trapped the whole Assembly and they're blockading President Zeloc's motorcade. He can't leave the Presidential Residence."

Simon shrugs. "That's his problem, not mine. Madison has an entire police force for this kind of work. There are five thousand police officers on this base, alone, and that doesn't include the five thousand that have graduated every year for the last five years in a row. If my math skills are up-to-date, that's twenty-five thousand federal police officers at your disposal. Given the amount of money it's costing to train, feed, and house them all, I suggest you make use of them."

Anger flickers across Sar Gremian's scarred features. "Don't play games with me, Khrustinov! President Zeloc wants that Bolo," *he jabs a finger in my direction,* "to clear out that pack of criminal agitators."

"Criminal agitators?" *Simon asks in a soft voice I have learned to associate with profound anger.* "That's an interesting choice of words, coming from a POPPA social engineer."

A dark red flush stings Sar Gremian's face. "You will regret that remark, Colonel."

"I seriously doubt it."

Sar Gremian flexes his fingers, clearly struggling to

control his temper. He regains his composure sufficiently to return to his original topic of conversation. "Those lunatics are threatening the entire Assembly with violence, over a minor law bill designed to fight crime. President Zeloc has no tolerance for mob rule. That Bolo goes out there *now.*"

"You don't get it, do you, Gremian? You don't use thirteen thousand tons of sophisticated battlefield technology to break up an inconvenient political demonstration lawfully conducted by citizens free to voice their opinions in public assemblages. Those protestors are fully within their rights to refuse to disband. Any order to disband is illegal under Jefferson's constitution. Using a Bolo to threaten and harass citizens exercising their constitutional rights is not only illegal and a bad usurpation of Concordiat property, it's a damned stupid stunt. One that will do nothing but damage the government's credibility and spark a wider surge of protests.

"It might," *he adds in a voice dripping with sarcasm,* "even jeopardize passage of a bill you apparently think is a good idea. God knows why, since schemes like that have proven to be totally ineffective at reducing crime on every world humanity has ever inhabited."

"I don't give a rat's ass what you think about crime or credibility! Those are *our* problems, not yours. You've been given an order. Send that Bolo out there. *Now.*"

"No."

Sar Gremian breathes rapidly for two point six seconds, then his frayed temper snaps. "All right. You want to play hardball? Here's a slapshot for you. You're fired, asshole."

Simon laughs, which is not the reaction Sar Gremian expected, given the startled expression which flickers for a moment across his face. "You think you can fire me? Just like that? Nice try, my friend, but I'm afraid you don't have the authority to fire me. Neither does Gifre Zeloc. Nor anyone else on this godforsaken ball of mud. I'm deployed here under treaty. I can't be removed without a direct order from Sector Command. You're stuck with me,

Gremian. Just as much as I'm stuck with you. I suggest you learn to cope." *The disdain in his final words slaps the president's chief advisor like a physical blow.*

"Then you'll *be* fired!" *Gremian snarls,* "and when you are, I will personally kick your carcass onto the next freighter that docks at Ziva Two. And you can forget about obtaining exit visas for your wife and kid!"

My Commander's face turns white in a single heartbeat. Not with fear. Simon is angry. Angrier than I have seen him since we entered battle on Etaine. The look he bestows upon Sar Gremian would melt steel. It sends the president's advisor backwards a single step.

"If you do *anything* to or against my family," *my Commander says softly, his words hissing like plasma through a gun barrel,* "you had better watch your back for the rest of your natural life. Never, *ever* fuck with a Brigade officer, Gremian."

Shock explodes through Sar Gremian's eyes. I surmise that no one in his cumulative experience of life has ever delivered such a message to him. As the shock fades, fury erupts in its place. He snarls a curse and snatches at the snub-nosed handgun concealed beneath his coat. I snap to Battle Reflex Alert before his fingers have finished closing around the grip.

Every prow-mounted weapon on my turret tracks his motion. Gun barrels spin with a blurred hiss in the echoing space of my work-bay. I lock on with systems active, all of them flashing proximity-threat alarms. Blood drains from Sar Gremian's pitted face. He freezes, involuntarily loosening his grip on the pistol. He stares up at my battle-blackened gun snouts. Sees in them his own imminent death.

I break my long silence.

"Your actions indicate an intended lethal threat to my Commander. My guns are locked and loaded. I have your brain case targeted in my fire-control center. If you draw the pistol in your hand from its shoulder holster, you will not survive to make the shot."

Sar Gremian stands motionless, a wise decision for a

*man in his situation. I detect a stream of liquid registering
ninety-eight point seven degrees on the Fahrenheit scale,
trickling down his left trouser leg. I surmise that he has
never before been this seriously frightened.*

"I would suggest," *Simon tells him softly,* "that you
take your hand out of your coat. Very, very slowly."

*The president's senior advisor complies, moving his
hand in quarter-of-a-centimeter increments until it dangles,
empty, at his side.*

"Very good, Gremian. You may just live to see the
sun go down, tonight. Now take your sorry ass out of
my sight. And don't *ever* come back."

*The look of malice he sends my Commander tempts me
to fire, anyway. This man is dangerous. It would satisfy
me to remove the threat he represents to my commanding
officer. In the absence of a clear and immediate danger,
however, my software protocols do not permit me to act.
This gives Sar Gremian time to organize his retreat. He
turns on his heel and stalks out of my maintenance depot,
slamming the door back with the heel of one hand. An
odiferous yellow puddle remains to mark where he had
been standing. His lackeys scurry after him, one of them
skidding through the mess. The other plows into the door
frame in his zeal to exit as rapidly as possible.*

*Then they are gone and silence rolls like thunder
through my maintenance bay.*

"Sonny," *my Commander says softly,* "that man will
not rest until he takes an ugly kind of vengeance.
Lock onto the ID signals from my comm-unit and
Kafari's. Yalena's, too, if you please. Those three ID
signatures are the only ones authorized within one
hundred meters of my residence. Until you hear differently, monitor all three data signals at all times and
report any clearly lethal threat within the same one
hundred meter radius."

*He scowls at a blank spot on the wall that is in a direct
line with the back door of his private quarters.* "Like a
damned fool, I gave those goons a wide-open back door to
exert coercion. I will be triple-damn dipped if I tolerate

it. The Concordiat can't afford it. And neither," *he adds with a bleakly realistic assessment,* "can I."

The shadows of Etaine will always pursue my Commander. I attempt to reassure him, in the only way I can. "I will not tolerate any threat of coercion designed to hinder my primary mission here, Simon."

A visible shudder passes through Simon Khrustinov, which puzzles me. He does not elaborate on its cause. "Sometimes," *he says in an undertone that indicates he is speaking to himself, rather than to me,* "you say things that scare me pissless."

"Sar Gremian is the individual I scared pissless, Simon. Shall I activate an auto-wash sprayer from my decontamination system to rinse the residue from the floor?"

A sudden grin dispels some of the darkness at the back of my Commander's eyes. "That's what I love about you, you overgrown son of a motherless battleship. Yeah, wash that filth out of here." *The smile fades.* "Unless I verbally authorize a visitor in advance, program your reflex sensors to snap you from inactive standby to active alert if any non-authorized intruders—with or without an ID transmission—are detected inside your hundred-meter proximity zone. If you detect any weapons system inside that perimeter or one traveling along an incoming trajectory to strike inside it, go to Battle Reflex Alert and disable the threat. And Sonny?"

"Yes, Simon?"

"You just saved my life, for which I am eternally grateful. Unfortunately, this ugly little scene may have just ended my career."

I ponder this for eight point seven seconds, considering ramifications I do not like. Simon is a fine officer. He does not deserve to be cashiered over my actions. This proves to my satisfaction that I should not be trusted to function alone, without the guidance and wisdom of a human to navigate the pitfalls of complex interpersonal relationships. I have never functioned alone. I am not designed to function alone.

Moreover, Jefferson is a long way from the nearest

Brigade supply depot. If I am abandoned on a world whose elected officials had to be coerced into funding required treaty-mandated expenditures, I foresee serious difficulties should I require replacements for munitions expended or damage sustained in combat. A renewed attack by the Deng or a Melconian strike could prove disastrous.

Worse yet, given the complexities of the political climate on Jefferson, I do not believe I am capable of determining the correct operational strategy to accomplish any mission without antagonizing the politicians whose decisions would control my ability to function. My actions in preventing Sar Gremian from assassinating my Commander are a case in point. I acted in accordance with the proper military response to a lethal threat to my Commander and showed considerable restraint in exercising my options to remove that threat.

Yet my action has produced an unstable situation which may result in the termination of a fine officer's career. I do not see what alternative action I might have taken that would not have resulted in a greater difficulty for my Commander. Having to tell the president that I had reduced his chief advisor to a red haze would only have worsened the apparently serious rift between Simon and those issuing his orders. I attribute my inability to discern viable alternatives to my hard-wired inability to perform the complex logic trains required to decipher and reduce to logical predictions the wide range of potential human reactions to a complex and shifting set of variables. I am not a Bolo Mark XXIII or XXIV. I was not designed to make this kind of judgment call. The uneasiness in my personality gestalt center becomes a trickle of panic.

"Simon, I estimate a ninety-two percent likelihood that Sector Command will not dispatch a replacement commander if you are recalled. I am not designed to function without a human commander. I am not an autonomous Mark XXIII or XXIV. The Mark XX series does not have sufficiently sophisticated circuitry or programming to make battlefield decisions requiring the complex algorithms that approximate human judgment; I am not equipped to function without a commander for longer than one or two battles."

"Do I detect a hint of uneasiness, my much-decorated, valorous friend?" *Simon's smile is genuine, but fleeting, altogether too characteristic of the human condition.* "We haven't reached that bridge, yet, much less crossed it. We'll worry about that when—if—the time comes. Just keep in mind that you *are* designed for independent action, Sonny. That's the defining characteristic of the Mark XX. You've got the experience data of more than a century to rely on and you can always contact the Brigade."

I do not find this comforting, given the time lag required to send a message via SWIFT, wait for a human officer to analyze the VSR, come to a decision on an advisable course of action for a shifting situation many light-years away, and transmit the orders via return SWIFT. "It would be unwise to deprive me of the necessary discernment a human commander provides the Mark XX during ambiguous battlefield situations. I feel constrained to point out that the situation on Jefferson has been ambiguous since the death of Abraham Lendan. It appears that conditions have deteriorated considerably since I was ordered into inactive standby mode eight years and nineteen days ago."

"Lonesome, you have the gift of understatement down to an exact science." *He rakes a hand through his hair in a familiar gesture of frustration. I note an increased amount of silver in that hair and mourn the fleeting impermanence of human life spans. It is difficult to watch a fine officer grow old. It is much more difficult, however, to watch one die. If Simon is removed from command, I will at least not have to witness the death of a much respected friend.* "What do you want me to do, Simon?" *I ask, registering a sense of misery in my personality gestalt center.*

"Update yourself on the political mess. I'll have to shut you down again, dammit. I'm under standing orders from Jefferson's duly elected president." *Bitterness and sarcasm turn his words black.* "But not yet. I'll be dunked in poison before I shut down my own Bolo after being threatened by a thug with a gun. Take yourself a good, long look around, Sonny. Wait for my signal to send you back to sleep. Better yet, stand guard for a full twenty-five hours, just in case those bright boys decide to return for a little skullduggery, tonight, on behalf of their boss and his vendetta."

"Does Sar Gremian hold vendettas, Simon?" *I initiate a search through the government's employee databases to locate his dossier.*

Simon glances up into my nearest external camera-mounted sensor. "Oh, yes. Our violent tempered friend is a real Savonarola. Got a mad on his shoulders the size of the Silurian Nebula. And he's not inclined to share power with anything or anyone he can't crush into convenient red paste. Gifre Zeloc picked himself a real winner when he brought Sar Gremian into the game."

Simon exits my work-bay without speaking again. The door slams in an echo of Sar Gremian's abrupt exodus. I hear a fainter crash as he yanks open the door to his private quarters. Seventy-three seconds later, my Commander sends a single, coded burst on a frequency that matches Kafari's wrist-comm. I surmise that he is stealing a march on them, contacting Kafari with a pre-agreed-upon code that will signal her that trouble is brewing. Simon remains in his quarters. I turn my attention to his orders.

Given what I begin uncovering about Sar Gremian, I consider the possibility that I erred seriously in permitting him to leave the premises alive. My search has, admittedly, only begun, but it is clear from reading his official dossier that he is politically ambitious, abuses power in legal but ethically questionable ways, is loyal to the highest bidder, and possesses a psych-profile clinically definable as sociopathic.

His function in the president's office appears to be creating propaganda-based social movements that become legislation, introduced by a groundswell of popular ranting. He engineered something called the Child Protection Act, which grants self-determination and voting rights to children age ten and over. Among other things, it tightens POPPA's choke-hold on elections, since giving children the right to vote greatly increases the population of people who support POPPA's social agenda. It also slows down the exodus of farm families seeking to escape a deteriorating social milieu, by the simple expediency of granting children the right to refuse to leave. Given the number of emigration applications received in the past twelve point three months, this measure was essential to preventing the complete loss of everyone on Jefferson who knows how to farm. I surmise that POPPA's leadership does not enjoy the spectre of hunger, applied to themselves.

Sar Gremian has also been involved heavily in the campaign to whip up anti-crime frenzy in Madison and other large cities. The weapons-registration legislation being protested today is the culmination of several months' effort to sway public opinion via inflammatory rhetoric and egregious manipulation of facts. He is evidently as cautious as he is unpleasant, as there is no evidence that he has broken any laws or policy rulings that I can determine. Conversely, there is a massive amount of datachat traffic indicating a widespread dissatisfaction with his actions, fear of his tactics, and hearsay evidence about his violent temper, which I have witnessed firsthand.

If Simon is removed from command and Sector abandons me without a replacement commander, it is highly probable that I shall be carrying out instructions relayed through Sar Gremian by Jefferson's president. This sets up a skittering harmonic through my logic processors that I suppress immediately, not wishing to tip myself over the edge and activate the Resartus Protocol that automatically takes control of a Bolo whose programming has gone unstable. This world cannot afford my loss to insanity.

I therefore focus on scanning governmental computer archives, the datanet, and news broadcasts, trying to ascertain what is happening that has put Simon in this untenable situation before circumstances force him to shut me down, again. Sar Gremian and his associates know that I am awake. I anticipate a presidential order to go inactive from moment to moment and wonder how long the president's chief advisor will delay before recovering his composure and wounded machismo enough to admit what transpired in my work-bay. I must make the greatest possible use of my brief reprieve from unconsciousness.

Ongoing and skillfully edited "live" news coverage of the political protest underway, which has evidently dominated the commercial programming stations for six hours and twenty-three point nine minutes, sheds murky light on the political demonstration in Law Square. Field reporters are speaking rapidly, using political jargon I barely recognize, filled with references to events I know nothing about and do not have time to investigate.

Eighty-seven point six percent of the rhetoric being broadcast is emotionally inflammatory, filled with innuendo I do not have the referents to understand, and clearly designed to engender an emotional response unfavorable to the cause of the demonstrators, whom the broadcasters apparently hold in cold contempt bordering on demonization. Why, I cannot determine. It requires an unprecedented sixty-two point three seconds just to discover the cause of the demonstration, which I finally unearth by searching Granger-dominated datachats.

I do not immediately understand why Jefferson's House of Law finds it advisable to propose weapons licensing regulations as part of a comprehensive program to reduce crime. The emphasis Jefferson's constitution places on private ownership and use of weapons should prevent such a bill from reaching the Assembly Floor, but both the House of Law and Senate are seriously determined to introduce and vote into law this bill's contradictory provisions.

I spend an additional five minutes, nineteen point two-seven puzzled seconds conducting high-speed scans of debate transcripts in the Senate and House of Law, cross-referencing with the constitution and its seventeen amendments, then begin checking datachat activity and recent media coverage, seeking further clarifications.

My search reveals a hot debate centering on a sharp rise in crime rates. Forcible home invasions and attacks against retail stores by gangs of criminals have killed fifty-three home and business owners in Madison during the last three months alone. Similar brutal assaults have occurred in the heavy-industry region near Anyon where unemployment amongst manufacturing labor runs fifty to sixty percent and in the mining cities of Cadellton and Dunham, where whole industries have mysteriously ceased to function. Factory closings have thrown approximately five million people out of work. These industries are critical to Jefferson's economic survival and should have weathered the post-war financial difficulties with great resilience.

Yet smelting plants, refineries, and manufacturing plants sit idle, their power plants cold and their warehouses empty. I do not understand how thirty point zero-seven percent of Jefferson's heavy industry—critical to the rebuilding efforts undertaken by any human world damaged by war—has simply ceased to function in only eight years. Have the Deng attacked again while I was asleep? Mystified, I send subprotocol tendrils searching through news-feed archives while focusing my main processors on the demonstration currently underway.

POPPA activists are demanding regulations that trace ownership and sales of weapons as a way to halt home- and retail-business invasions and other violent crimes. I do not immediately see the connection between licensure of weapons and cessation of criminal activity, since police records indicate that ninety-two point eight percent of lawbreakers using weapons to commit crimes obtain them—through their own admission—via theft.

Even more puzzling to me is the clearly documented fact that eighty-nine point nine-three percent of all privately held weapons on Jefferson are held in rural regions where Jefferson's unfriendly wildlife remains a serious *threat and where self-sufficiency philosophies apparently hold their strongest sway. Yet according to police and justice department databases, ninety-seven point three percent of all violent crime on Jefferson occurs in urban areas, where weapons ownership is vanishingly small in comparison to rural areas.*

I cannot make the correlations between glaringly contradictory data sets resolve themselves into an algorithm that logically computes. I do not understand the reasoning which insists that an ineffective measure based on demonstrably false data is the only salvation for a world rocked by an admittedly serious wave of violent criminal attacks. Are my heuristics so seriously inadequate that I cannot see a critical piece of the equation that would explain this attitude?

I am still trying to find information that will resolve this conundrum when Simon receives an incoming communication from Jefferson's Presidential Residence, in voice-only mode. I route the message to Simon's quarters. Judging by the anger in his voice, Gifre Zeloc is unhappy with the current state of affairs.

"Just what the hell do you think you're doing, Khrustinov? That monstrous machine of yours damn near murdered my chief advisor!"

Simon's voice sounds like cut granite sliding off the side of a volcanic massif, a sound I have occasionally heard during my long service. "Sar Gremian attempted to draw a weapon in a lethally threatening manner within Unit SOL-0045's proximity-alert zone. Sonny reacted appropriately and with great restraint."

"Restraint? You call that *restraint?*" *The president abruptly activates the visual portion of his transmission. He is glaring, goggle-eyed—as a long-ago commander once called such an expression—into his datascreen. An interesting tint of purple has appeared in the veins at his temples.*

Simon, angry but controlled, says in clipped tones, "Mr. Gremian is still alive. The only thing injured was his dignity. When an armed individual attempts to shoot a Bolo's commander, I assure you most seriously that letting that individual leave the altercation alive is the utmost definition of restraint I have ever seen any Bolo demonstrate."

"Sar Gremian did *not* try to shoot you, Khrustinov! He has two witnesses to back him up. I don't know what you think you're trying to pull—"

"Spare me the bullshit! I'm not a provincial rube you can bully, bamboozle, or bribe. A full report of this incident will be filed with Sector Command. The Concordiat takes a dim view of attempted assassination of one of its officers."

For one point zero-nine seconds, Gifre Zeloc resembles a fish drowning in oxygen. The purple in his blood vessels spreads out, until his face has assumed an intriguing shade of maroon that matches his formal cravat with surprising accuracy. Clearly, Gifre Zeloc is no more accustomed to being addressed in such terms than Sar Gremian. Then he then narrows his eyes, telegraphing a threat that tempts me to assume Battle Reflex Alert. "And how will you explain to Sector that a Bolo I ordered you to deactivate was somehow conscious? In defiance of a direct presidential order to the contrary?"

"No Bolo is ever 'deactivated' until and unless it is killed. Even badly damaged Bolos can survive literally for a century or more and return to full awareness in less than a single pico-second. Sar Gremian, himself, is responsible for Sonny's awake status. He carried a concealed firearm into a restricted military zone with a Class One-Alpha weapons system inside it. Given his status as your chief advisor, he was permitted to retain that weapon, as a courtesy to his position on your personal staff. But *anyone* who enters a Bolo's reflex-alarm zone triggers a return to consciousness. Anyone carrying a *weapon* into that zone triggers an active-alert status. If that weapon is handled in a threatening manner, that action will set off an automatic Battle Reflex action. You can," *Simon adds with an elegant touch of sarcasm,* "send a query to Sector Command, requesting verification of these facts.

Be sure to attach a copy of the recording Sonny made, showing Sar Gremian trying to shoot me."

President Zeloc's coloration once again resembles his maroon cravat.

"That won't be necessary! Very well, I will take your explanation under advisement. What I want from you—the only thing I want from you—is to send that Bolo into town and clean out that pack of rabble-rousing protestors."

"As I explained to Sar Gremian," *Simon replies coldly,* "Sonny stays where he is. In your haste to disperse your political opposition by using a mobile nuclear weapons platform, did you bother to consider the size of Unit-0045's warhull and treads, as compared with the size of Jefferson's streets?"

"I beg your pardon?"

"Sonny," *Simon speaks as though addressing a small and none-too-bright child,* "is a big-ass, honking war machine. His treads alone are wider than all but two or three streets anywhere in Madison. Darconi Street is just barely wide enough, if you don't mind losing the decorative stonework, wrought-iron balconies, doorways, news kiosks, or vehicles lining the sidewalks. Not to mention the building fronts he'd have to demolish along the five kilometers of city streets he would have to navigate just to reach the area where the protestors are gathered.

"And that's just his *treads.* Sonny's warhull and the weapons projecting out from it are wider than the treads. Considerably wider. If you really want Sonny to drive protestors out of Law Square, you'll have to decide which corner of Assembly Hall you would like him to flatten, trying to get there. Or, if you like, he could always flatten the concert hall in Lendan Park, instead. Or the southeast corner of the Museum of Science and Industry, or maybe the northern wing of the Planetary Justice Hall? Take my word for it, the only time you're likely to *want* that Bolo in downtown Madison is if the Deng or Melconians are throwing weapons at you. At which point, collateral damage from knocking down part of a building will be the least of your concerns."

Gifre Zeloc evidently likes the color maroon. He sputters for three point two seconds, then says in a squeaking voice, "He won't *fit?*"

"No, he won't. You were," *Simon finishes with sweet derision,* "briefed on Unit 0045's major operational specs when you assumed office. I do assume you actually read them?"

"I read what I goddamned well have time to read! Fine, the fucking thing won't fit! So what are you going to do about all these protestors?"

"Me?" *Simon queries, lifting one brow.* "I'm not doing anything. Handling a lawfully conducted political rally is *your* problem, not mine. Of course, it might become my problem, if you turn loose an unholy jihad of P-Squadrons against a crowd of unarmed civilians. The Concordiat's not real fond of slavery and ethnic cleansing, either, and speaking as an outside observer, you're skatin' on mighty thin and spidery ice, mister. You might just want to chew on that for a bit, before you decide to start slinging around more orders."

"I see." *Clipped. Angry. Dangerous.* "Very well, Colonel, have it your way. For now," *he adds ominously.*

The transmission ends. I have taken the precaution of recording every millisecond of the exchange in my archival databanks. Simon has done what he can. Now, all he can do is wait.

II

Kafari was nearly frantic with worry, but she did exactly what she and Simon had agreed upon when they'd worked out that emergency code. She picked up their daughter, dragging her out of class, and headed for home. She maintained radio silence the whole way and switched off the AirDart's auto-signal broadcast, in an effort to remain relatively invisible until they reached the safety of their quarters on Nineveh Base. She gripped the controls so tightly, her fingers ached. At least the need to concentrate on flying helped tune out Yalena's scowl. Her daughter had spent the entire flight from her school to their home in a deep, adolescent sulk, which did not improve Kafari's temper one jot.

When they finally got home, Kafari took one look at Simon's face and realized that however bad she'd feared it might be, it was worse. Far worse. So much so, her whole body went cold and scared. Simon was seated at his datascreen, staring blankly at something, a message she abruptly realized she didn't want to know. She'd never seen that look on her husband's face. A caved-in look, part horror, part defeat, all of it wrenching to witness.

"Simon?" she whispered.

He turned to look at her. Noticed Yalena. Brought his gaze back to Kafari.

"Close the door, please."

Kafari did so, hand trembling. She locked it, carefully. When she turned around again, Simon was still looking at her. "I have just been notified," he said, voice hoarse, "by Sector Command that Gifre Zeloc has invoked treaty provisions, demanding my removal from command or he will pull Jefferson out of the Concordiat."

Kafari's knees turned to rubber. She groped for the sofa. "Can he do that?"

"Oh, yes. With a vote of agreement from the Senate and House of Law. And we know only too well how such a vote would turn out, don't we?"

"What—" She had to stop and start again. "What in God's name *happened*, Simon?"

"Sar Gremian paid me a visit. There's a demonstration underway in Law Square. President Zeloc wanted me to use Sonny to drive the protestors out. I said no. So Gremian and a couple of his goons showed up, to insist. When I refused, Gremian tried to pull a gun on me. Sonny responded." A mirthless laugh sent chills down her back. "It might've been better if Sonny'd shot him. But he didn't. Commendable restraint, at the time. Gifre Zeloc was not amused. I've sent a copy of the recording Sonny made to Sector, with a formal protest. This," he gestured at the datascreen, the motion abrupt, bitter, "was their reply. I have never," he added, "seen Brigade move so fast in my career, which tells me everything I need to know."

Kafari made herself cross the room. Made herself read the message.

The Brigade supports your actions, which appear to have been proper and appropriate, but the Concordiat cannot afford to lose an allied world at this time, with a multi-system crisis of unprecedented proportions facing us. As Unit SOL-0045 is capable of independent battlefield action and given the low threat of invasion in the Silurian Void at this time, Sector has decided to reassign you to another Bolo in the Hakkor region, where three allied worlds are expected to come under heavy bombardment within a matter of weeks. A naval scout ship will be dispatched to take you to the Hakkor region to assume your new command. The scout will arrive in Jeffersonian space in three days. Your family will doubtless wish to emigrate. Quarters will be reserved for them at Sector Command.

"Oh, God," Kafari whispered. She looked up, read pain in Simon's ravaged eyes.

"You don't want to go, do you?" he asked.

"I go where you do!"

It came out fierce, protective.

"Where are we going?" Yalena demanded, jarring Kafari's attention from Simon to their child, who was glaring up at them.

"Your father has been reassigned off-world. We're going to live at Sector Command."

Yalena's eyes blazed. "*You're* going to Sector Command! *I'm* not going anywhere!"

Kafari started to snap a tart rejoinder when a sinking, cold terror hit her gut. Yalena was thirteen years old. She had reached the "right of self-determination" age, under POPPA-mandated child-protection law. They literally could not force her to leave. She looked at Simon, saw the bleakness there, realized he'd already foreseen this turn of events. Kafari ripped herself for ten kinds of blind folly and sat down abruptly, staring utter disaster in the face.

Her husband was being forced off-world by a regime ruthless enough to want a Bolo to disperse a few protestors. Her daughter was refusing to go. She knew Yalena, knew the stubborn core of that child, an unyielding determination that was, thanks to years of POPPA indoctrination, entirely misguided. There had to be a way! Some way out, something she could say or do to persuade her daughter to leave.

The prospect of a life without Simon, wondering day to day, hour to hour, if he'd been killed on some far-off world, while coping with a home-front situation that looked more frightening with every passing week, left her winded, unable to think clearly. Her mind whirled, frantic to find some reassurance that her life had not just shattered to pieces. Simon, cold and silent, offered no reassurance because there was none to offer. Their life together was over, along with nearly everything she valued in the world. Taken from her by *idiots*.

"Yalena," she said in a hoarse voice that seemed disembodied, with no connection to her, "please go into your room."

Her daughter scowled, but did so, closing the door on her way.

Simon looked at Kafari. She looked at him. "I can't go with you," she finally whispered.

"I know."

"I can't leave her here, alone. They've got her, Simon, they've got her heart and her mind, her very soul. I have to fight to get her back, somehow. I've got to break through all the crap she's been force-fed and *make* her see the truth. I can't just abandon her. If I did . . . If I left with you and ended up alone on some strange military base on a world where I don't know anyone, I would go mad. . . ."

"I know."

There didn't seem to be much else to say. He knew. Had known her well enough to realize what her choice *must* be. Had accepted it, even before she had walked through the front door. Kafari crossed the intervening space between them, knelt down beside his chair, and wrapped both arms around him. She just held on. Simon was trembling. So was she. He slid out of the chair, stood up with her, held onto her tightly enough to make breathing difficult. They stayed that way a long time, long enough to develop an ache in her ribs from the pressure. "Do you have any idea," Simon whispered roughly, "how much I need you?"

She shook her head, realizing in that moment that she could never know the answer to that agonized question. His heart thundered against hers. Tears blinded her. In this single, wrenching moment, the ache in her heart left no room for anything else, not even hatred of POPPA for doing this to them. That would come later. She was terrified for him. How could he go into battle, give his attention to the job of waging war, with thoughts of her and Yalena intruding, breaking his concentration? He needed her too much. She had jeopardized his effectiveness as an officer, without even realizing it.

He finally let go a deep and shuddering sigh, relaxed his death-hold on her ribs, and pulled back enough to peer down into her wet eyes. He managed a tender smile and used gentle fingertips to dry her cheeks. "Here, now, what's this? Don't you know the first rule of being a colonel's lady?"

She shook her head.

"Never send a man into combat with tears. Or curlers in your hair. Who wants to remember a woman with red eyes and hair wound up around plastic tubes?"

A strangled sound, half hiccough, half laughter, broke loose. "Oh, Simon. You always know just what to say." She blinked furiously, determined to get her fractured emotions under control. "Whatever are we going to do?"

"Our duty," he said with a rough burr in his voice. "You're the strongest person I have ever known, Kafari

Khrustinova. Do you have any idea how remarkable you are, dear lady?"

She shook her head again. "I don't feel very remarkable Simon. And I probably look like a drowned cat."

He smiled. "I've seen worse." A sigh gusted loose. "I have a lot to do, if I'm leaving in three days. That," he gestured at the datascreen again, "doesn't become completely official until I set foot on the scoutship, at least, so I have some time to work with Sonny before I go. They may be harried and desperate at Sector, but they're not entirely blind, either. That recording of Sar Gremian was enough to convince somebody that I'd better not be relieved of command over him instantly, no matter how much Gifre Zeloc threatens. He will doubtless be so delighted at getting his way, he won't quibble about three days."

"And you can do a lot with him in three days?"

"Oh, yes," he said, voice dangerous. "Oh, yes, indeed."

Kafari shivered. And hoped Simon knew what he was doing.

"I'm going into Madison," he said at length. "I've got to see the bank manager, among other things. You," he said, placing both hands on her shoulders, "keep yourself and Yalena inside the house. Don't open the door to *anyone* but me. And keep your gun within easy reach. Sonny's on Active Standby Alert with orders to stop any attack on my quarters, but I believe in being prepared."

Kafari nodded. "Do you want me to start packing for you?" Her voice didn't quite hold steady.

Pain skittered through his eyes. "Yes, I think that would help. It would give you something to do. All the uniforms, please. And the personal sidearms. Besides the one I'll be carrying, of course. Personal sundries, toiletries. A few changes of civilian clothing. I'll be traveling light."

"I'll make two piles. The definites and the maybes."

He kissed her, very gently.

Then headed for the door. She wanted to run after him, tell him to be careful, tell him everything in her bursting heart, but she let him go. No tears. Nor anything like them. She was a colonel's wife. She realized fully, for the first time, what that really entailed. She lifted her chin, stiffened her resolve, and marched into the bedroom to sort her husband's things in preparation for his new war.

And hers.

III

Yalena threw herself onto her bed and cried for a solid, miserable hour.

It wasn't fair! The very thought of going somewhere else, leaving her friends, her home, going to another star system where she would never see Ami-Lynn again, left her shaken so deeply, she couldn't do anything but cry, muffling the sound in her pillow so her parents wouldn't hear. She hated the Brigade, had never hated anyone or anything so much in her life. She had tried to love her father, but she just couldn't. Her mother . . . sometimes, she felt very close to her mother. And other times, they were like strangers, unable to talk to one another through the glass walls between them, so thick Yalena despaired of ever truly getting through and making her mother *understand*.

And now they wanted her to just go with them, just pack up her things and go away to a place where she wouldn't know anybody or anything. The very thought of having to start over at a new school, where nobody understood anything really important, like saving the oceans or making sure that every child had legal rights to protect them, where nobody would like her because she was the new girl, different, with a father who killed for a living . . .

Panic rose up and choked her until she couldn't breathe, because there wasn't room for the air inside a chest too full of terror and humiliation to take in anything else. Yalena had thought she'd long outgrown that kindergarten terror, but it was still there, down inside, where nobody could see it. She lay shaking for a long time, soaking the bedspread with tears and a streaming nose. When the worst of the storm had finally passed, she sat up, feeling shaky and light-headed. It was awfully quiet, out there. Yalena crept to the door and listened, but there were no voices outside. She heard someone in her parents' room, opening and closing drawers, it sounded like.

Yalena stepped to the window and peered outside, across the small yard to the landing pad. Her father's aircar was gone. She clenched the curtains in one hand. He was gone! He hadn't even said goodbye! Tears threatened again. Then reason reasserted itself. He couldn't be gone, yet, because there weren't any ships docked at Ziva Two, right now. Not even the Brigade could get a ship here that fast, could it? No. He must've gone into town. She finally realized what she was hearing, from her parents' room. Her mother was packing.

Yalena swallowed hard. Was her mother going to leave, too? Where would Yalena go? She had the right to stay, but she wasn't sure where that would be. Could she move in with somebody like Ami-Lynn's parents? Or would she have to go out to Klameth Canyon and live with her grandparents. Yuck. That would be dire. Almost as bad as going with her parents. She'd have to start a new school in that case, too, and if she went to school in Klameth Canyon, it would be full of farmers who would hate her as much as her cousins hated her.

Panic threatened again.

Yalena finally thought to check on the datanet, to see what her rights actually were and what would happen to her if her mother insisted on leaving Jefferson, too. What she found wasn't entirely reassuring, but if she had to live in a state-run dormitory, at least she could stay in her same school. That would help. If she lost her friends, she really didn't know what she would do. She sighed, then decided to send Ami-Lynn a long chat message, to let her know what was happening. She knew Ami-Lynn had been scared, too, when Yalena's mother had showed up at the classroom and yanked her out the door with a brief apology to her teacher for the inconvenience.

Yalena scowled. She didn't understand why her parents had forced her to leave school just because her father was being fired from a job he hated and had to go off and be a soldier somewhere else. They could've left her in school while he went running off to town and her mother packed suitcases, instead of dragging her all the way out here, to do nothing at all. She pulled up her chat account and started the message.

"I'm okay," she said, "and I don't see why I had to leave school. I mean, it's big news and all, my dad has to leave the planet and I don't know if my mom is going with him. He has to go fight a war . . ." Her voice wavered unsteadily. Fight a war. She had never seen the Bolo in the back yard move. She'd talked to the machine a few times, but it scared her. It was huge, bigger than their whole house, and it had all those horrid guns and things on it. Her imagination failed, trying to picture what that thing must look like when it was moving and shooting at things.

She scowled again. Mrs. Gould, that horrible harpy, had lied to them about her father and his Bolo, all those years ago. She still hated her kindergarten teacher for making her miserable and sick, for saying things about her father that weren't true, for making her feel like a dirty criminal. But Cadence had made everything all right again and she really hadn't thought there would ever be another war, because they were so far away from all those other worlds that were fighting.

It didn't seem real, that machines like the one in the back yard were shooting at living creatures who just wanted a safe place to live, when all was said and done. That was what her social dynamics teacher said, anyway, and Mr. Bryant was the smartest teacher she had ever had. She didn't hate the Deng or the Melconians and didn't understand why everybody in the Brigade thought the Deng and the Melconians hated *them*.

She backed up the recording to Ami-Lynn and started over. "Hi, it's Yalena. I don't know why Mom dragged me out of school, just to tell me Dad's been fired from his job. President Zeloc is making the Brigade reassign him to another planet. He has to go off-world and command a different Bolo. He's in town, I think, doing stuff at the bank, probably, a whole bunch of things before he leaves. I don't want to get dragged off someplace horrible where I don't know anybody. I *won't* go. They can't make me and I won't. If my Mom goes, too, I'll have to live in a government dorm somewhere in Madison, but I'll get to stay at the Riverside Junior Academy and that's the most important thing. So don't worry about all the fuss, today. I'll see you at school tomorrow, for sure, and I'll send another message tonight, after Dad gets home and I find out for sure what's going to happen with everybody."

She pressed "send" and sat back as the message spun its way through the data-net to Ami-Lynn's account. Her friend wouldn't be home from school for another three hours, but Yalena felt better, having sent the message out. It steadied her and reminded her that even if she lost both parents to her father's horrid war, she wouldn't lose friends like Ami-Lynn, because POPPA cared enough to protect her from things like this off-world war that no sane person would want to fight in. Yalena sighed and stared through her window, not really looking at the landing pad or the police training center beyond the fence that surrounded their house and the Bolo's maintenance depot.

She wished, for at least the millionth time, that her father was just an ordinary person, so they wouldn't always be disagreeing on everything. She had tried so hard to tell him why POPPA was so important to her home-world, but he never understood and just got angry, so she'd finally stopped trying. This wasn't her father's home-world. He just didn't understand how it was, to belong to a place the way Yalena belonged here. He didn't know what it meant, to belong to a group of people the way she belonged with the people in POPPA, who were the nicest, gentlest people in the world, people who cared about everything and everyone. The only people POPPA didn't like were the ones that made trouble for everybody else. Like the Grangers.

Her cheeks stung with an embarrassment she was afraid she would never outgrow. Her whole *family* was full of Grangers. People who wanted to keep guns in their houses, people who made trouble every time the Senate and House of Law tried to pass a law that everybody with any intelligence *knew* was a good idea. She didn't talk about her family at school, or with her friends. If the subject came up, she just rolled her eyes and shrugged, writing them off as the crazies they were. Yalena would never understand them. And they would never understand her. And that made her so sad and so miserable, she laid back down on her bed, again, and cried some more, very quietly, this time.

It was sheer hell, being thirteen and all alone in a family that didn't want her.

IV

Simon was gone for five hours before he checked in by radio. "Kafari, I've got the banking affairs settled, updated my will, set up a power of attorney for you, a whole host of details nailed down. I'm headed home."

"We'll be waiting."

No tears, no hint of the grief in her heart that tore loose in a flood the moment he signed off. She wiped her face with brusque, angry gestures. *No tears, Kafari,* she ordered her obstinate heart. *You don't greet a soldier with tears, either, not when he's going away in three days . . .* Oh, God, how could she bear to face the long, empty months and years ahead, without him by her side every night or smiling into her eyes every morning? She sank down onto the bed, helpless to stop the flood pouring loose, then rolled over and cried into the pillow so Yalena wouldn't hear.

Ten minutes later, a metallic voice boomed through the speakers on Simon's datascreen. "Kafari. Simon's aircar is losing power. It is unstable and going down."

Time—and the breath in her lungs—froze, like the sudden cold sweat on her skin. For long, horrifying seconds, she was pinned in place. She couldn't breathe. Almost couldn't *see*. Then Sonny spoke again, a construct of flintsteel and electrons that contrived, somehow, to sound terrified.

"Simon has crashed. His forward speed was sufficient to sustain serious injury. I am picking up life-signs from his comm-unit. The likelihood of sabotage to his aircar is extreme. I have gone to Battle Reflex Alert. I am contacting emergency medical response teams in Madison. They have scrambled an air rescue team. ETA three minutes to Simon's location."

Kafari found herself stumbling toward the door, snatching up purse, keys, shoes.

"Yalena!" she screamed. "Yalena, get out here *now*! Your father's aircar has crashed!"

The door to her daughter's room swung open. Yalena, face white with abrupt shock, stood staring at her. "Is he—is he—d-dead?"

"No. Sonny says not . . . yet. They've scrambled an air rescue medical team. Get your shoes! We're going to the hospital."

Yalena ran, grabbing up the shoes she'd kicked off at the foot of her bed. Two minutes later they were airborne, in Kafari's Airdart, which was fast and maneuverable. Once aloft, she hit full throttle and flew like a demon, screaming across the fences around Nineveh Base and roaring toward Madison. She fumbled with her wrist-comm.

"Sonny, talk to me. Is he still alive?"

"Yes."

"Feed me coordinates. Where did he go down?"

The nav-system screen flashed to life, with a blip showing Simon's location. The med-team would arrive before she did. "Find out which hospital they're taking him to. University? Or General?"

A fractional pause ensued. "University has better emergency facilities. The rescue pilot has logged his intention to transport Simon to University Hospital. The medical crew is airlifting him now. His life-signs are weak."

Terror trembled on her eyelashes, made it hard to see where she was going. She scrubbed at her eyes with the back of one hand. Tears were spilling down Yalena's cheeks, as well, silent tears of fright and something else, something too deep to fathom, yet. Sonny spoke again from the speaker, causing Yalena to jump. "Simon's airlift has arrived at University Hospital. He is still alive. I am monitoring."

"Yalena. Call your grandparents."

Her daughter reached for the controls, fingers trembling. "Grandma? Are you there? Grandma, it's Yalena . . ."

"Hello? Yalena? What are you doing, calling from school?"

"It's Daddy," she said, voice breaking. She started to sob. Kafari said, "Mom, Simon's aircar has crashed. He's at University Hospital. I'm on my way there with Yalena."

"Oh, dear God . . . We're on the way."

Ten minutes later, Kafari set down in the University Hospital parking lot. They ran for the wide double doors of the emergency room, silent and scared. Kafari fetched up against the receptionist's desk. "I'm Mrs. Khrustinova. Where's my husband?"

"They've rushed him into emergency surgery, Mrs. Khrustinova. Let me call someone to take you up to the surgical suite's waiting room."

A hospitality agent appeared, escorting them down a long, antiseptic hallway, into an elevator, and up to the third floor. They were shown into a waiting lounge that was, for the moment, empty. Kafari yanked down the volume on the datascreen, unable to bear the sound of the stupid game show in progress. Yalena sat down on one of the chairs, scared and very pale.

Kafari couldn't sit down. She wanted to collapse, but terror was a goad that wouldn't let her rest. She paced, frantic, staring at her chrono every few seconds until the ritual became so painful, she unbuckled the thing and shoved it into her pocket. She walked, ravaging her lower lip with her teeth, rubbing the empty place on her arm where the chrono had been. The volunteer brought them a hospitality tray, with cold drinks, cookies, comfort foods. Kafari couldn't choke anything down.

When her parents arrived, half an hour later, Kafari broke down in her mother's arms, weeping with exhaustion and fright. Her father took charge of Yalena, speaking quietly with her, reassuring her that the doctors were doing everything humanly possible to save her father's life. More relatives arrived, not enough of them to be an abrasion against her raw nerves, but lending silent support at a time she needed it desperately. Surrounded by her loving family, all Kafari could do was wait. The volunteer returned periodically to update them, although the "updates" consisted of the same news again and again.

"Your husband is still alive, Mrs. Khrustinova. The surgeons are working to stabilize him."

Yalena went for a walk with her grandfather, out into the hallway, then came back and curled up against Kafari's side, shivering. Kafari wrapped one arm around her daughter. At length, Yalena whispered, "I didn't mean to be rude, Mommy. When we got home. I just can't leave home and go somewhere strange. All my friends are here." Her voice was breaking in a plea for understanding.

"I know, sweetheart. I know."

"Did—did the president's advisor really try to kill Daddy? I can't believe it. I can't. Everybody at school says he's a wonderful person. I just can't believe that, Mommy."

"You have no idea how much I wish you were right."

Yalena bit one lip and fell silent again. Neither Kafari's parents nor the other family members sitting vigil with them commented on the brief exchange, but knowing glances ran like spiders around the room. They were still sitting there, nerves jangled and eyes puffy, when the soft *ping!* of the elevators announced the arrival of what sounded like an entire army. The footsteps and voices heading their way were shocking in the hospital's relative quiet. Kafari realized what that tidal wave of sound was seconds before the camera crews and reporters burst into the room. Bright lights half-blinded them. People were shouting questions at them, so many at once, she couldn't even sort out individual voices, let alone questions. Yalena shrank closer to Kafari's side. Her father and several uncles interposed themselves between Kafari and the news people choking the room.

Then one of the featureless faces resolved itself into a familiar pattern. A man Kafari recognized from datacasts strode forward, his acne-pitted face mirroring concern and sympathy. *Sar Gremian!* Kafari's father and uncles exchanged distressed glances, then let him through the barricade they'd formed, not wanting to provoke a scene in front of half the press-corps in Madison.

When she realized that Sar Gremian was reaching out to touch her shoulder, making a show—a mockery—of offering comfort, Kafari went rigid. Then she jerked to her feet. "Don't you *dare* touch me!" she hissed.

He checked slightly. "Mrs. Khrustinova, you have no idea how distressed I was to learn—"

"Get out!" Kafari snarled. "I have *nothing* to say to you! And if you *ever* come near me and mine again, I'll by God finish the job Sonny left undone!"

The force of her rage—and his abrupt realization that she meant every syllable uttered before God and the planetary press—left him one shade paler than when he'd glided into the room. She could almost see the thought forming behind those cold shark's eyes. *Oh, hell, I forgot this is the woman who brought Abraham Lendan out of battle alive. I may have underestimated her . . .*

You're goddamned right, you have! And don't ever forget it.

He recovered his poise quickly. So quickly, Kafari doubted the reporters had even noticed the silent exchange of threat and counterthreat between them, too delighted by the overt conflict to notice the deeper and far more dangerous one. "You're overwrought, Mrs. Khrustinova, and little wonder. I simply wanted to convey my heartfelt well-wishes and those of President Zeloc."

"You have conveyed them," she said coldly. "You are doubtless more urgently needed elsewhere." Kafari knew her anger was a reckless, dangerous thing to display so openly. But she could not just stand there and let him offer unctuous condolences when he had tried to murder her husband. *Twice.*

She was rescued from worse folly when a doctor in surgical scrubs shoved through the throng of reporters, demanding in angry tones that the waiting room be cleared. "Who let you in here? This is a hospital surgical ward, not a press briefing. Out! All of you, out!"

Orderlies were appearing, escorting camera crews into the corridor and back toward the elevators. Kafari— with her family standing beside her in a silent show of solidarity—stood her ground while Sar Gremian watched the exodus through narrowed eyes. He turned abruptly, gave Kafari a mocking little bow, and said, "My condolences, Mrs. Khrustinova, and those of the president. Miss Khrustinova," he turned to Yalena, who was clinging to her, "I hope very sincerely that your father will pull through this dreadful accident."

Then he strode out, nodding to the reporters with a dignity and concern he had pasted on like thin varnish for the benefit of the cameras. Kafari hated him with an ice-cold loathing that frightened her, it was so intense. Then he was gone and the reporters with him, and Kafari stumbled slightly, groping for the nearest chair as her knees buckled. Her father caught her and helped her down.

The surgeon tested her pulse, frowning with worry.

"Simon?" she whispered, finding and holding Yalena's hand.

"He's out of danger, Mrs. Khrustinova."

Her eyelids sagged close and her bones turned to rubber. The surgeon's voice reached down a very deep well, echoing strangely in her ears.

"He is still in grave condition, I'm afraid. We've stabilized the internal injuries and broken bones. The airlift crew said his aircar was built like a Bolo. Thank God it was or he'd have been killed on impact."

She managed to open her eyes and focused with difficulty on the man's face, which had gone unsteady and full of blurred edges. He managed a warm and gentle smile. "Hello," he added with just a touch of wry humor. "I'm Dr. Zarek, by the way."

"Pleased to meet you." Kafari barely recognized the croaking of her own voice. "What else? What aren't you telling us?"

"He is still in grave condition. To be frank, he needs to be transferred to a much better facility than University Hospital."

"But—" She swallowed. "University Hospital is the best medical center on Jefferson." Blood drained, leaving her dizzy. "Oh, God . . ."

"Easy, now, steady." She felt someone's hand on her shoulder. She felt like she was falling off a cliff or out the airlock of a freighter in free-fall. Then a sharp, pungent smell brought her out of a downward spiral. She coughed and the world firmed up again. Dr. Zarek was seated beside her, testing her pulse. A nurse was busy attaching some kind of skin patch to her wrist, probably an antishock treatment. Her family hovered close-by, stricken. When the doctor was satisfied that she wasn't going to faint, he spoke again, very gently.

"He's at the ragged edge of critical, but his condition is not life-threatening. That much, at least, I can swear to you." A look of profound respect came into his long, kindly face as he added, "I have not forgotten what you did in Klameth Canyon, Mrs. Khrustinova. It

was one of the greatest privileges of my life, serving as
a junior member of Abraham Lendan's medical team.
You may not remember me, but I administered one
of your earliest antiradiation treatments. I had a little
more hair, then, and a few less wrinkles."

His smile, his genuine warmth, helped steady her. "I'm
sorry," she murmured, "I really don't remember you."

He patted her hand. "Not to worry. I wouldn't have
expected you to, Mrs. Khrustinova. Now, then. Simon is
going to need specialized recovery therapy of a kind that
isn't available on Jefferson. We don't have nerve regeneration clinics or cellular reconstruction technologies."

That sounded bad. Desperately so.

"As an officer of the Dinochrome Brigade, your
husband is entitled, by mandate of the treaty, to emergency medical transportation and full access to the best
medical care available. I would suggest," and something
in his manner shifted, subtly, taking on a subdued yet
intense note of warning, "that we send him off-world
immediately." He glanced at the doorway Sar Gremian and that unholy mob of reporters had departed
through, then met and held Kafari's eyes. "There's a
Malinese freighter coming in tonight, I'm told. It's due
for departure tomorrow. I strongly recommend transfer-
ring your husband to Ziva Two's infirmary the moment
that freighter makes space-dock. We'll send an attending physician and trauma nurse with him. What you
cannot—*dare* not—do is wait."

"I see," Kafari whispered, feeling as young and scared
as her daughter looked.

Then she thought of Sonny, realized with a shock of
fear that a Bolo Mark XX was sitting in her back yard,
at full Battle Reflex Alert, listening to this conversation
and drawing its own conclusions—and it already suspected
sabotage and attempted murder.

"Oh, shit—" She slapped her wrist-comm. "Sonny.
Sonny, are you there? Can you hear me?"

"Yes, Kafari. I have been monitoring your wrist-comm
since your departure from home."

The surgeon's brow furrowed, then his eyes opened wide as he realized who Kafari was talking to—and why.

. She cleared her throat. "Who do we need to notify? *How* do we notify them?"

"I have already contacted Sector Command, apprising them of my Commander's medical status. I am filing updated VSR now, based on the medical recommendations I just heard. I am forwarding a voice copy of the conversation you just held with Simon's attending physician. I will relay Sector's instructions once I receive VSR from Brigade.

"I will need the registry information for the Malinese freighter, to remain in contact with my Commander and his medical team. Sector has already diverted the scoutship, which is needed elsewhere, now that Simon is incapable of transfer to Hakkor. When Simon regains consciousness, please tell him that I am at fault for having failed him. I was scanning for overt threats. Missiles, artillery, energy weapons. I did not anticipate an enemy action based on subterfuge and sabotage of his transport vehicle. That failure has nearly taken my Commander's life. It may end the career of the finest officer it has been my privilege to serve. Please tell him I am sorry."

Kafari was staring at her wrist-comm. She had known, at a superficial level, that Sonny was the most sophisticated psychotronic system she had ever seen, or ever would see. She had not realized, even after nearly fourteen years of interactions with him, just how complex his programming really was. The machine speaking to them via her wrist-comm had a metallic voice unlike any real person's, yet it was full of anguish and regret.

She didn't know what to say. Neither, evidently, did Dr. Zarek. Yalena was crying again. Kafari finally broke her silence. "Thank you, Sonny. I'll . . ." She had to stop and start over. "I'll do that, for you. I'll tell him. That's a promise. A vow." In the awkward silence that followed, it occurred to Kafari to wonder who would be issuing Sonny's orders, now. She didn't want to think about it.

Couldn't *stop* thinking about it. Was terrified by the answers occurring to her.

A Mark XX Bolo was capable of independent action. She knew that much, but somebody would have to issue instructions to Sonny. Those instructions couldn't come from Sector, so they had to come from somebody on Jefferson. She didn't know which was more frightening. The idea of Sonny acting on his own, at a Battle Reflex Alert that even Simon walked cautiously around, or someone like Gifre Zeloc, who took his orders directly from Vittori Santorini.

We're in trouble. Oh, Christ, Simon, we're in deep, horrible trouble. I need you . . . More than she had ever needed anyone or anything else. The lack of his arms around her, his steady voice, the absence of his rock-solid courage and strength of character were a physical ache in her flesh, more wrenching than the pain of childbirth.

Someone was saying her name. Kafari blinked against the weight of terror and focused on the surgeon's worried face. "What?" she managed to croak.

"You'll need to fill out a great deal of paperwork, Mrs. Khrustinova, signing as next-of-kin, authorizing us to bill the Concordiat on his behalf. No, don't worry about money, our admissions and billing office has already determined that the Brigade will be paying for all treatment rendered. We just need signatures on the requisite forms to submit the charges to the planetary purser's office rather than the health management plan you carry through your job at the spaceport. You'll need to file emigration paperwork, as well, for you and Yalena."

Kafari held her breath. Then turned to look at her daughter. Yalena shook her head. "No. I don't want to leave Jefferson. I just can't."

"Your father needs medical care we can't get here."

"I know. But they're sending a doctor with him. He can come home when he's well. I *won't* go live somewhere else, where I don't have any friends or anything. You can go, Mom, I understand that, but I'm not leaving."

Kafari's father spoke sharply. "And just where do you intend to live?"

"POPPA will put me in a state dormitory, same as they do orphans. I can even stay in my school."

"That won't be necessary," Kafari said, weary to the bone. "I want to go, Yalena, more than you can ever understand. But I won't leave you here alone and I certainly won't let you go live in some horrible dormitory." She cupped her daughter's wet cheek in one hand. "And your father would want me to stay. It's what we'd already decided, before . . ." Her voice wobbled.

Yalena started crying again.

The surgeon spoke very quietly. "I'll send the hospital volunteer with the paperwork you'll need to sign. And I'll let you know when he's awake."

She nodded and he left. The volunteer arrived a few moments later with an appalling stack of forms to fill out and sign. Kafari wondered how she could possibly face the years that lay ahead, while Simon struggled through rehabilitation alone, without anyone who loved him there to help. In the grim and ghastly silence that had fallen across the room, Kafari made a steel-cold vow to her unconscious husband.

I will stay here, Simon, as long as it takes. I'll fight them for her. I'm sorry, my dearest love, but I can't just leave her with the bastards who did this to you. And one day, she added, eyes narrowing with hatred she could neither deny nor contain, *one day, they will regret it.*

Bitterly.

PART THREE

Chapter Sixteen

I

My Commander is gone.

Nor will I have a new commander. I am stunned by the reality of it. Despite Simon's forebodings, I did not truly believe Sector Command would totally abandon me. I am not fit for self-command. I know this, even if Sector does not.

What am I to do, without Simon?

I have not even been able to prove that the crash was deliberately engineered. The official verdict of the crash-investigation team was software failure in the aircar's governing circuitry. Accidental cause is the official—and only provable—explanation. I remain suspicious, but cannot justify a further need for Battle Reflex Alert status, given the rendering of this verdict. The freighter carrying my last commander to the hospital complex on Vishnu has barely left spacedock at Ziva Two when I receive my first communique from President Zeloc.

"Bolo. Wake up."

"I have been awake for two days, nine hours, fifteen point three-seven minutes."

"Why?" *The voice addressing me carries the timbre of suspicion. The president has not seen fit to activate the visual portion of his transmission, so that I am speaking to a disembodied voice. I find the impersonal greeting more irritating than I had anticipated. I am not programmed for complex protocol, but I am accustomed to civil courtesies.*

"Sar Gremian's attempt to kill my Commander brought me awake from inactive standby mode. I maintained active standby mode at his orders, monitoring the unfolding situtation. When my Commander's aircar crashed, leaving him seriously injured, I could not relapse into inactive standby, given my mission parameters. Sector Command's SWIFT transmission notifying me of Simon Khrustinov's medical-retirement status, with no replacement commander pending, placed me on immediate permanent active Standby Alert. I am therefore awake."

"I see." *I detect a slight abatement of hostility in these two words.* "Well, here's my first order, Bolo. Shut yourself down and stay shut down until I call you again."

"I cannot comply with that directive."

"What?"

"I cannot comply with that directive."

"Why the hell not? I gave you an order! Obey me at once! This instant!"

"You are authorized to direct my actions in defense of this world. You are not authorized to interfere in my primary mission."

"How do you construe an order to go to sleep as interference with your primary mission? I'm the president of Jefferson. Your mission is whatever I *say* it is."

"That is incorrect."

"*What?*" *The inflection is incredulous, full of frustrated anger.*

I attempt to explain. "Your belief that you have the right to determine my mission is incorrect. My primary mission was assigned by Sector Command. It has not been rescinded. You are not authorized to interfere with the critical parameters of that mission."

The video portion of President Zeloc's transmission is abruptly activated. One look at his face confirms that Gifre Zeloc is angrier than I have ever seen him. Veins protrude at his temples and his face has flushed dangerously purple. "Do you see who I am, Bolo?"

"You are Gifre Zeloc, thirty-first president of the Concordiat Allied World of Jefferson."

"Then explain this bullshit you're feeding me. I am your commander and I am damned well ordering you to go to sleep!"

"You are not my Commander."

Eyes bulge, even more prominently than the veins in his temples. "What do you mean by that? 'I'm not your commander'? Now, see here, machine, I won't stand for any nonsense out of you, do you hear me? You'd better get that clear, right now, or you'll find spare parts exceedingly difficult to find! *I'm* your goddamned commander and don't *ever* forget it!"

"You are not my goddamned commander, either. You are the civilian authority designated to issue specific instructions that direct me in carrying out my mission."

Fleshy lips work for six point nine seconds, but the sounds emerging are unintelligble as any human language with which I am familiar. This is of considerable interest, since I am programmed to understand twenty-six major Terran languages and the lingua franca of eighty-seven worlds which use various pidgins and polyglots. I have not needed to make use of this information during my active career, but the Brigade does its best to be prepared for all contingencies.

President Zeloc eventually recovers his powers of intelligible speech. "You're as good at double-speak as Vittori Santorini. All right," *his voice grates harshly,* "clarify your primary mission. And then give me a straight answer on why you won't go to sleep as ordered."

I fear that it will be a long and stressful mission, without Simon to assist me in political and protocol minefields.

I do my best. "My primary mission is to safeguard this planet from danger. As the highest ranking public official on Jefferson, you are authorized to direct my actions in carrying out this mission in the event of an armed threat to the stability of this world. Without a human commander to coordinate the defense of this star system, it is imperative that I remain awake to function as a human commander normally would, maintaining surveillance over shifting conditions that affect the primary mission."

"I see." *A sudden change in tone and facial expression suggest that I have said something that pleases Gifre Zeloc. I wonder a little frantically what it was. He smiles into the videoscreen, flashing well-maintained dentition.* "Well, now. That's much clearer, isn't it?"

I am pleased that I have been understood, although I am still unsure how this explanation made such a marked difference in attitude.

"What, exactly, do you intend to do while awake?"

Since I am unsure, myself, what I am to do during the long years that will undoubtedly comprise my defense of this world, I am unsure how to answer. I settle for the simplest response I can provide. "Maintain surveillance over potential threats to Jefferson and run possible defense scenarios based on conditions both on- and off-world."

"I see. Or maybe I don't. Just what, exactly, do you mean about maintaining surveillance over on-world conditions?"

"My mission includes threat assessments from on-world sources, including subversive activity, sabotage by enemy agents, armed dissident organizations that may pose a security threat to the stability of the government and therefore pose a potential threat to the long-term survival of Jefferson as an autonomous, self-governing planet. I monitor economic conditions to advise my Commander—" *I hesitate and correct that statement* "—or the highest civilian official authorized to direct my actions on possible stability issues that may affect Jefferson's long-term sustainability as a viable society. My mission is comprehensive, complex, and of high importance to Sector Command, as no human commander can be spared from the shifting battle front with the Melconians."

Gifre Zeloc frowns for a moment, then an expression I cannot immediately interpret shifts his heavy-jowled features. He hesitates before speaking, giving me time to cross-reference what I know of human facial expressions from a century of contact with humans. I classify the configuration of eye, mouth, brow, and jaw muscle movements as slowly dawning realization of something unforeseen and potentially useful.

"Tell me," *he says in a voice that reminds me of purring kittens,* "tell me about the battle front with the Melconians."

"I cannot divulge classified information," *I begin, earning a scowl,* "but it is within your need-to-know status to clarify the general situation as it pertains to Jefferson's security."

"And what is that general situation?"

"Given current trends in the position of battle fleets, evacuation patterns, and Brigade transmissions to and from the Central Worlds, on Brigade and Navy channels that I routinely monitor, it is likely that the war will continue to move away from this region of space. Given the total annihilation of Deng populations in this sector by Melconian forces, there are no longer any inhabited star systems on the formerly Deng-held side of the Silurian Void. Zanthrip is the nearest star system still held by the Deng. The Melconians have been unable to colonize this region, given the ferocity of the battle front along Melcon's border with humanity, which has forced Melcon to divert ships and personnel it would doubtless have committed to that colonization process to deal, instead, with the severe fighting that rages across thirty-three populated star systems."

I flash battle schematics to the president's datascreen, carefully omitting any information that Gifre Zeloc is not authorized to know. He draws an abrupt hissing breath as the general pattern becomes clear to him.

"The Concordiat has been unable to take advantage

of the emptied worlds, for the same reasons Melcon has not. The fighting through this region," *I shift the color of affected star systems, to clarify my explanation,* "has forced Sector Command to commit most of its military assets to the defense of human space. This leaves a substantial buffer of seventeen newly uninhabited star systems between Jefferson and the nearest Deng- or Melconian-held worlds. Given its position relative to current battle fronts and its location within the Void and the vacant star systems beyond, Jefferson is now, in effect, the most isolated human system anywhere in this sector of space."

Gifre Zeloc leans back in his chair, staring at the schematics I have transmitted to him for long moments, so long, I begin to wonder if he intends to speak again or if I should simply terminate the transmission. At length, a slow and mystifying smile appears. "Very instructive," *he murmurs.* "Yes, very instructive, indeed."

The smile broadens, indicating a state of mind I find peculiar. Admittedly, I have not known many planetary heads of state, but I know from many sources that command responsibility is a heavy burden. Heavy enough that it prematurely ages office holders, even in times of peace and economic stability. During war or the threat of war—or some other cataclysmic shift that damages a society—the burden can become intolerable. It killed Abraham Lendan, a man who commanded Simon's deep loyalty, the love of Kafari Khrustinova—one of the most creative warrior minds it has been my pleasure to know—and the respect of an entire world.

It therefore confuses my logic processors that President Zeloc should be so pleased by my VSR. I would have expected a more serious response from the planetary ruler of a system as isolated as Jefferson now is, with outside assistance and resupply unlikely, should any of a number of social, economic, or military disasters befall this world. President Lendan was, by every measure I am capable of using to judge performance and character, a far more capable leader than Gifre Zeloc.

I know serious misgivings as the man who will be directing my defensive efforts leans back in his chair and says, "That's fine, Bolo, very fine, indeed. I believe I am going to enjoy having you work for me."

I consider pointing out that Gifre Zeloc works for the Concordiat, serving as their proxy in the defense of a highly isolated corner of human space, and that he therefore works for me, as I am the instrument of the Concordiat's intentions regarding the defense of this world, but am unsure how to explain this subtle difference. I am still struggling with possible wording when Gifre Zeloc, tapping restless fingertips against the gleaming wood of his desk, issues another complex question.

"Just what is the extent of your on-world monitoring of shifting conditions affecting the stability of this government?"

"Please clarify. I require specific parameters to properly answer your question."

He considers for a moment, then asks, "What specific data on Jefferson's internal political and economic activities did you collect for Colonel Khrustinov before I instructed him to shut you down?"

This is the simplest and most direct question he has yet posed. "It will take approximately nine point nine-two hours to present this information to you at a delivery speed suited for the average human's assimiliation."

Gifre Zeloc's eyes widen momentarily, then he smiles again and says, "I'm all ears, Bolo. And I suspect there is literally nothing on my plate that is more important than hearing what you're about to say." *He picks up a cup from the corner of his desk and sips.* "Go ahead, Bolo. I'm listening."

I begin to speak. As I explain my data collection methods and summarize the data I have collected on Simon's orders—during which there are significant lapses in my active standby status, creating substantial gaps in my information—Gifre Zeloc's smile turns to shock, followed by slow, smouldering anger. This is finally superceded by an abrupt, deeply startled grin that appears to indicate delight.

That response sends a vague disquietude skittering through the complex heuristics governing my logic processors and personality gestalt stabilization-analysis circuitry. Simon did not trust the political party which Gifre Zeloc represents. The POPPA coalition's philosophies and actions are based on an alarmingly high percentage of falsified data. The coalition's finances and off-world dealings are puzzling. POPPA advocates methods of social engineering proven ineffective on many human worlds, including Terra.

As I am operating with woefully incomplete data, it is imperative that I bring myself up to date, scanning societal trends, economic conditions, and changes in legislative and constitutional law. Perhaps POPPA has discovered a way to translate its ideals of societal and economic parity and universal access to resources into a system that functions more effectively than its ideological predecessors?

I face a massive, multipartite chore, obtaining an accurate VSR that I must then analyze and incorporate into my threat-assessment evaluations and defensive contingency plans. Since I am now essentially locked into active standby mode, with a low likelihood of reversion to inactive status, I will at least have the time this task will require. Provided, of course, that a now-remote enemy does not show renewed interest in this pocket of the Silurian Void.

My list of questions grows by the second, as many of the items that puzzle me spark even more questions, creating a rapid data cascade of pending problems for which I must find answers. I am unsure that answers even exist for some of those questions. I harbor a nagging fear that I possess entirely too limited an understanding of the intricacies of human thought and societal dynamics to understand those answers, in the unlikely event that I actually find them.

I am not comforted by Gifre Zeloc's next comment, delivered long before I have finished reciting my data

*analysis efforts. He favors me with an expression that I
define as smug satisfaction.* "You're very thorough, Bolo.
Yes, indeed, you're doing a very commendable job. Keep
up the good work." *He taps neatly manicured fingertips
against the padded armrest of his chair, narrows his
eyes slightly as he ponders the things I have said—or
perhaps the possible actions he wishes to take, based
on my VSR.*

*He reaches a decision, setting his cup aside as he leans
forward and scrawls a few brief notes onto his desktop
datagel interface, a micro-thin jotting system integral to
the surface of the desk, that translates his handwriting into
coded notes. A privacy shield pops up from the desktop,
blocking any view of the writing surface, including the
video component of his communications datascreen. Not
even the room's security cameras are in a position to see
the surface of that datagel.*

*I note these details primarily because I do not have
clearance to access the datagel's storage matrix. It therefore
houses the most secure dataset on Jefferson, excepting my
own classified systems, of course. After sixty-eight point
three seconds, the president digs his stylus emphatically
into the datagel, consigns his notes to permanent storage,
and wipes the datagel's surface clean. He lowers the privacy
shield, then addresses me in a brisk, decisive manner.*

"The Joint Assembly will be voting on some important legislation in a few days. There's been a lot of
dissension from some regions, with a lot of wild talk
and even threats from certain population segments. I'm
not talking about the routine 'I won't vote for you again
if you vote for that' kind of threat. That's only to be
expected. You can't propose any major change to a legal
code without ruffling somebody's feathers."

*I file a reminder to research this pending legislation
and the reasons it has been proposed as well as protested, since it troubles the president so greatly. After
he reveals the reason for his concern, I make this my
highest priority.*

"What's worrisome—to me, at least—are the threats

of retaliation against hard-working members of the Joint Assembly. If they vote to pass this legislation, if they support measures critical to the defense of this world, these dissidents are talking about personal and violent retaliation against Assembly members and their families."

If accurate, this is a serious charge to levy against one's opposition. Intimidation tactics are invariably the hallmark of those whose agenda is abuse of power. Such practices are worthy of contempt. If the threat they pose is serious enough, honor demands that such threats be met with all the proper legal—or physical—action necessary to remove the threat to individuals or to a society as a whole.

If there are sufficient numbers of dissidents advocating intimidation, coercion, and violent retaliation against lawfully elected officials, Jefferson may face a serious threat. An internal enemy can be as deadly to long-term stability as outside invasion. It is all the more insidious because it is subtle, making it more difficult for people to recognize a threat to their safety, freedom, and well-being.

Bolos are programmed for strong ethics in this regard, for good reason. Were a Bolo to use its firepower to usurp command of a local system of governance, few governments could muster anything to stop it. Tyranny is tyranny, whether perpetrated by humans upon one another or by war machines against their own creators.

Usurpation is one of the Seven Deadly Sins a sick Bolo can commit, sins which trigger the Resartus Protocol, preventing a Bolo from acting on its destabilized impulses. There is very little a human fears more than the spectre of a mad Bolo. Intentions—good or otherwise—are immaterial when human survival is at stake.

Gifre Zeloc's voice jolts me out of my distracted reverie. "The vote is due to take place six days from now. I want a full report on dissident activities and plans before then. I'll give you further guidance after you've debriefed me on the state of affairs you uncover."

The president breaks the connection. I ascertain, through my surveillance of data lines leading from the Presidential

Residence's computers, that he places an immediate call to Vittori Santorini. I ponder whether or not I should monitor that conversation, along with everything else I am attempting to do. Before I can decide whether or not to break contact, the call goes through and Gifre Zeloc says, "Vittori, I've got some *wonderful* news. No, not over the phone. The usual meeting place? Is four-thirty suitable? Excellent. I can hardly wait to discuss things."

The president breaks the connection, leaving me to ponder what Gifre Zeloc has to tell the founder and leading power behind the POPPA coalition. Speculation in the dark is useless. I turn my attention to the daunting task of learning what has transpired during the bulk of the past ten years and what the dissidents President Zeloc spoke of may be saying and doing. I am unsure that once I know, I will be any materially better positioned to know what to do. It is an unhappy state of affairs to look forward to additional guidance from a man Simon Khrustinov refused to trust.

I have no other choice.

Unlike Gifre Zeloc, I am not pleased.

II

Simon drifted in and out of awareness, caught somewhere between confusion, pain unlike anything he had ever known, and a drifting disconnection from himself, from the world, from reality itself. It was like drifting through thick fog where every touch of smothering vapor cut like razor wire. He didn't know where he was or why everything was so desperately wrong. He could remember nothing except a lurch of terror that blotted out everything beyond the knife-edged pain.

When the pain ceased, as suddenly as though it had never existed, Simon fell headlong down a bottomless black hole in which nothing, not even himself, existed.

When he roused again, his mind was strangely clear, but he couldn't *feel* anything. That was sufficiently alarming to nudge him further toward wakefulness. He struggled to open his eyes and found nothing that looked even remotely familiar. The space in which he lay was small and cramped, which he found odd, since he was positive that he'd been injured badly enough to need a hospital's care.

Had he been captured? Kidnaped by Vittori Santorini in some weird vendetta?

He tried to reach for his wrist-comm, to contact Sonny, and discovered that not only could he not feel anything, he couldn't move, either. Straining produced no response at all, not even a twitch. Fear began to seep into his confusion, cold and poisonous. He stared at the portions of the room he could see and frowned, or would have, if he'd been able to control his body. The walls and ceiling looked like the interior of a space-capable ship.

He'd been on enough interstellar transports of one kind and another to know the telltale signs and this room had them. He was trying to puzzle out why he might be on a space ship when he heard a sound from somewhere behind him, exactly like the opening of a cabin door.

"You're awake, Colonel," a quiet, soothing voice said. A moment later, a man he didn't know stepped into his field of view. He was dressed in medical whites. "I'm Dr. Zarek, Colonel. No, don't try to move. We've got nano-blocks in place in your nervous system, to keep you from shifting, even involuntarily. Do you remember what happened?"

Simon couldn't shake his head and his vocal chords didn't seem to belong to him any longer, either. The doctor frowned, tapped at something behind him, and muttered, "Too high. Let's dial that down a bit."

A whisper of pain ate into his awareness. His first voluntary sound was a hiss that he had almost no control over, as his body reacted to some ghastly level of abuse he didn't want to think about too closely. Then he realized he could move his face, just a little. "What happened?" he whispered, barely able to control the muscles in mouth and tongue enough to get the question out.

"Your aircar crashed. If you were someone else, I would say you're a very fortunate fellow. Instead, I'll say it's a good thing you're a cautious Brigade officer and listened to the intuition that prompted you to armor your aircar. It saved your life."

"Shot down?" he managed to ask.

Dr. Zarek's eyes were shadowed. "We don't think so. Your Bolo didn't think so, either. I was in the room when your wife contacted the Bolo, so I heard what it—he—said." The doctor's expression altered, shifting into something Simon couldn't quite fathom. "He apologized. The Bolo asked your wife to tell you it was his fault. He was watching for missiles and didn't think about sabotage."

Simon narrowed his eyes, then winced. How much damage did it take, to make that small a gesture hurt that badly? Through a body-wide nano-block? Then Simon forced his attention back to the larger issue. If Sonny thought his aircar had been sabotaged, no doubt remained in Simon's mind, either. It bothered him, however, that he couldn't remember the crash.

"Don't remember," he struggled to say.

"That's not particularly surprising," Dr. Zarek said with a slight frown. "The mind can blank out an event too traumatic to face, right away, just as the body can dump enough endorphins to deaden severe pain long enough to get to safety. You knew you were going down, probably knew somebody had deliberately rigged your transport, and doubtless knew that your wife and child would be left alone in the hands of a hostile regime. Given enough time, the memories will probably resurface, once your subconscious mind thinks you're strong enough to face what's hidden."

That made some sense, although he found it disquieting that a portion of him, one he couldn't control, was able to hide something that serious from his conscious memory. Then a new thought cropped up, more alarming. "Kafari! Where—?"

"She stayed on Jefferson, Colonel. With your little girl. You're on a Malinese freighter, headed for Vishnu." An unhappy shadow passed across his face. "I was chief surgeon at University Hospital. I assembled a whole team of surgeons to stabilize you. We did the best we could, but I can assure you that the medical care and rehab you will need do not exist on Jefferson."

Simon's brows twitched as he focused on the most puzzling part of that statement. "Was?" he rasped out hoarsely.

Dr. Zarek's gaze held his, steady and unflinching. "Colonel, I've been watching POPPA just about as closely as I'm sure you have and I can tell you, sir, I do not like what I see coming." Muscles jumped in his jaw. "News of your recall by the Brigade was splashed across every newspaper, datachat, and broadcast medium on Jefferson. So was the gloating over your near-fatal crash. And I use the word gloating deliberately. They're calling it a suicide attempt. 'Disgraced officer tries to kill himself rather than face military tribunal.'"

Simon cursed. Hideously. And tried to get up.

"Easy, Colonel," Dr. Zarek cautioned, "you can't move, yet, and you can't afford the physiological strain of trying." Despite the soothing, cautionary tone, his eyes crackled with anger as he studied a monitor just out of Simon's visual range. "That's better. As to the rest of it . . . A government willing to engineer the destruction of a Dinochrome Brigade officer's career is a government that cannot be trusted. But they weren't content with that. They tried to kill you, as well. That suggests some very ugly things to me. I don't know what you know, Colonel, or how big a threat that might be to Vittori Santorini and Gifre Zeloc.

"But I can tell you this, without hesitation. I have no interest in staying where that kind of government is in charge. I'm not politically acceptable, for one thing. I was a junior member of Abraham Lendan's medical team, right after the war. My views on POPPA are widely known. If they went after you, Colonel, they'll go after others, and their stunning success with you will breed contempt for anyone and everyone who disagrees with them. And I'm Granger bred, as well, which is starting to look like a very dangerous thing to be.

"So I pulled rank over every other physician at University Hospital and insisted on accompanying you to Vishnu. I don't intend to return. If Vishnu won't allow me to stay, I'll go to Mali, instead. They need surgeons on Mali," he added, voice bleak. His eyes were shadowed again. "I don't have a family," he said quietly. "They were killed in the war. The house was almost directly under the Cat's Claw . . ." Memory ran through his eyes, wet and filled with anguish. "I tried—very hard, Colonel—to persuade yours to leave with us."

Simon knew exactly why they hadn't. Dr. Zarek merely confirmed it.

"Your daughter wouldn't go. I have a recording from your wife, which I can play now, if you like, or I can run it later."

"Later," Simon whispered. He caught and held the surgeon's eyes. "Tell me."

Dr. Zarek didn't insult his intelligence by asking *Tell you what?*

By the time he'd finished answering, Simon was profoundly grateful that nano-tech neurology blocks existed. He hadn't realized it was possible to do that kind of damage to a human body and survive it. If the surgeries he still faced—an appalling number of them—were a success and if the nerve regeneration therapy and cellular reconstruction worked, he might be able to walk again. A year or two from now. Far worse was the knowledge that Kafari couldn't—wouldn't—leave, not without their child.

The only hope he could cling to was the knowledge that POPPA had spent years carefully grooming Yalena's support, because her belief in the cause held enormous propaganda value. He had never forgotten—could never forget—the year of hell they had put Yalena through in kindergarten, followed with a deliberate and highly effective piece of social engineering, during her first-grade year. Yalena still believed that POPPA's loving regard for everyone's rights and welfare had rescued her from the unfair cruelty of one unfit teacher acting from personal hatred. She still believed that POPPA had acted from genuine concern for her, correcting a deep social injustice and transforming misled children from enemies into dear friends. She still didn't understand that POPPA had engineered the hatred and abuse, as well.

It suited POPPA very well to groom Yalena into a staunchly loyal acolyte. He didn't know, yet, what they intended to *do* with that loyalty or how, exactly, they intended to cash in on that propaganda. Vittori and Nassiona Santorini didn't chart their course to power by planning what they would do during the next few months or even years. They thought in terms of decades and lifetimes. Whatever they had in mind to do with Yalena, they'd planned it out well before her entry into school. The best—the absolute best—he could hope for, lying broken to pieces in a Malinese freighter, was that POPPA's plans for Yalena included Kafari's survival.

III

They were being evicted.

Just like that. Kafari, home on bereavement leave from the spaceport, reread the message on her datascreen over and over while her numbed mind tried to make the words say something else. No matter how many times she reread it, the nasty little note said the same thing.

As the legal dependents of a non-Jeffersonian military officer who has been cashiered and sent off-world in disgrace, you are hereby evicted from the government-owned quarters you are no longer entitled to occupy. You have twenty-five hours from receipt of this message to remove yourself, your daughter, and your private belongings from the dwelling you currently occupy. Failure to leave within the allotted time will result in penalties, fines, and possible criminal charges for illegal occupation of a restricted military site. Personal belongings left behind will be confiscated and distributed to the needy. Removal of any government property will result in criminal charges for theft of military property.

A lengthy list of the items Kafari was not allowed to remove followed the message. It wouldn't be difficult to pack, since virtually everything in the apartment had been classified as government property, including the extremely expensive computer system she had purchased with her own funds, to support the intensely sophisticated needs of a psychotronic programmer. Kafari was so stunned, she couldn't even curse at the screen. She finally punched her wrist-comm.

"Dad?"

"What is it, hon?"

"What's the comm-code for your attorney?"

"That doesn't sound good. What's wrong?"

"We're being evicted. And those snakes are trying to grab our personal property. Things Simon and I paid for, ourselves."

"I'll get the number."

Five minutes later, she was pouring out her grievance to John Helm, who asked several brief questions, including a query as to whether she had proof that various items had been paid for out of private funds.

"Oh, yes," she assured him, "I have plenty of proof."

"Good. Send me the eviction notice and start packing. We can't fight the actual eviction, but POPPA can't touch your personal property. That much, at least, I can accomplish. If nothing else, we'll go public and crucify them on the evening news. I don't think POPPA will relish having news reports showing them grabbing the personal belongings of a bereaved war heroine and her young daughter. That idiotic film Mirabelle Caresse made about you may just be useful for something, after all."

"Huh. That would be a switch, wouldn't it? All right, I'm sending the message now. And thank you."

"It is entirely my pleasure."

She sat back, wondering where to start and how she could possibly get everything packed, when someone rang the bell at the front door. Startled, Kafari switched the datascreen view to the entrance security camera. She was even more startled to see who it was. "Aisha?" she said aloud, not quite believing the evidence of her eyes. She flew to the door and opened it with a wondering stare.

"Aisha Ghamal? What in the world are you doing here? *How* did you get here?"

The older woman gave her a honey-warm smile. "Kafari, it's good to see you, child. You've been so busy, these last few years, I haven't wanted to bother you. But things are different now. So I just climbed into my car and came along to visit." She held up a pass-card, required for anyone who wanted to enter Nineveh Base, these days. The P-Squad gate guards had itchy trigger fingers and a serious suspicion of everyone and everything that tried to enter their headquarters and training base. "I had to talk the Klameth Canyon sheriff into it, but he got me an authorization."

Kafari stared, thunderstruck, from the pass-card to Aisha's face. "Do you have any idea how hard it is to get an authorization like that? My parents had trouble getting one."

Aisha gave her a broad smile, touched here and there by gold, a slender band edging one tooth, a gleaming star inlaid into another. It was an ancient art form, a cultural tradition early pioneers had carried to the stars from Terra, itself. "Oh, yes, I know exactly how hard it is, Kafari. But Sheriff Jackley never had a chance, once I decided to convince him." She gave Kafari a broad wink and another grin.

Tears trembled on Kafari's eyelashes. "It's just wonderful to see you! Come inside, please." Kafari ushered her into the living room. "Can I get you something to drink?"

"Maybe in a bit. But tell me this, first. Is your little girl here?"

Kafari shook her head. "No, she's still at school. Yalena's involved in a whole bunch of after-school clubs."

"Just as well. From what I've been hearing, it's just as well it's you and me and nobody else."

Kafari frowned. "What's wrong, Aisha?"

"With me? Not a blessed thing. But *you* have been handed one big heap of troubles. You've got a big family, child, and you don't need me to tell you how blessed you are to still have them. But Dinny and I talked it over and we couldn't help thinking there might be a thing or two we could do, even if it's just giving you somebody to talk to, now and again."

Tears threatened again.

"Now, then, if it don't hurt too much to talk about it, how's your husband, child? I don't hardly bother listening to the news, these days. There's not two words in ten you can take to the bank without finding 'em counterfeit. So how is he, really?"

The tears spilled over, this time. "He's alive. But he's all broken up. Like a china doll somebody smashed into the ground." She wiped her cheeks. "The doctors say he *might* walk again. Some day. If he's lucky. If his immune system doesn't reject the bone regeneration matrix. The surgeons and rehab specialists on Vishnu have to rebuild him . . ."

"Rebuild him?" Aisha asked gently, when Kafari stumbled to a halt.

She nodded. "His lower legs and arms were shattered. His breastbone and ribs cracked like spiderwebbed ice. They had to remove splintered bone from his face, a lot of it. Once the new bone matrix has filled in, they'll have to sculpt a new face for him. And they'll have to do the same thing with his legs and arms, only it's worse, there, because a lot of the nerves were severed and crushed. They're going to try molecular nerve-regeneration therapy to replace nerve networks destroyed in the crash. The emergency air-lift crew said it was literally astonishing that none of his major arteries was severed. If they had, he would've bled to death before they reached him." She wiped her face again. "At least he was on active duty, so the Brigade is paying the bills."

"Then he wasn't fired, like the news reports said?"

She shook her head. "Not exactly, no. The Concordiat reassigned him. He was supposed to take command of another Bolo in a place called Hakkor. They'd already dispatched a courier ship to pick him up, told him to be ready to leave within three days. Then his aircar crashed."

Aisha pinned her with an intense stare. "*Was* that crash an accident?"

"I don't know," Kafari whispered. "There's no proof."

"Huh," the older woman muttered. "I got all the proof I need, child, looking at your face and watching what's happening, out there." She nodded toward Madison.

Kafari sighed. "Whatever the truth is, there's nothing I can do about it, one way or the other. And just now, I've got bigger worries on my mind. We're being evicted. We have twenty-five hours to leave."

"Twenty-five *hours*? Honey child, you and I got a fair bit of work to do, then, don't we?" She stood up and glanced around the apartment. "You got any boxes? Or suitcases?"

"Aisha, you don't have to . . ."

"Oh, yes I do. There's some things the Lord puts in our path, meaning for us to do, and I can tell you from experience, we turn into mean little people if we don't do them. So you tell me what goes and what doesn't and we'll just get started."

The faucet behind Kafari's eyes started dripping again. Kafari hugged her, hard, and felt the other woman's love wrap around her, along with strong, protective arms. Perhaps it was foolish—or merely desperate—but as they began to sort out what could be salvaged, she felt a wave of hope crest within her, born of the realization that she had the support of both family *and* friends. As bad as things might get in the next few months and years, she wouldn't face them entirely alone.

And if Dinny and Aisha Ghamal ever needed help . . .

Kafari would move mountains—even star systems—to give it.

IV

At the end of five days, twenty-one hours, and seventeen minutes, I conclude that I am in serious trouble and do not know how to remedy the situation. President Zeloc has not contacted me again, evidently too busy doing whatever it is he does, all day, to contact me. I do not know what Gifre Zeloc does, because I have been locked out of the Presidential Residence's security system, by some very sophisticated programming on extremely expensive psychotronic hardware. This was put into place shortly after my first lengthy debriefing with the president. Evidently, Gifre Zeloc prizes his privacy and is willing to pay a great deal of money to maintain it.

Spending other people's money is something he does a great deal of, given the data I have uncovered detailing his administration's expenditures over the past ten years. The economy was in trouble, a decade and a half ago. It is now stuttering toward total collapse. The legislation pending in Jefferson's Assembly involves a restructuring of Jefferson's tax codes, which have been modified five thousand, one hundred eighty-seven times since Gifre Zeloc came to power. These alterations, which have placed a disproportionately large tax burden on Jefferson's middle-class business owners, white-collar workers, and agricultural producers, have resulted in widespread bankruptcies, both personal and entrepreneurial.

I do not understand the strategy whereby businesses are

stripped of profits and incomes are taxed into "levels of parity" which force closure of factories and retail outlets, throwing more people out of work and swelling the ranks of the unemployed, who must then be fed and housed via public subsidies. There are, at present, too few people gainfully employed to provide the tax base necessary to continue the public subsidy programs already in place. If drastic measures to undo the damage to private-sector business are not undertaken, I project economic collapse in approximately ten point three years. Unless tax relief and capital investments are granted to Jefferson's agricultural producers, I foresee starvation conditions within six point nine years.

Taken together, the indicators are grim.

The legislation due to be voted upon later today addresses this serious situation, but not in a way that is likely to prove effective. It proposes neither tax relief nor capital investments in Jefferson's agricultural future. It reads, instead, like the ranting of a madman:

"Insofar as monopolistic agricultural interests have placed the public welfare in jeopardy, through refusals to provide the basic subsistence provisioning required to maintain health and public safety, the Assembly of Jefferson hereby establishes a code of tax rules to ensure fair distribution of critical food supplies currently hoarded by agricultural producers; establishes urgently required price caps to regulate the amount lawfully chargeable for wholesale and retail sale of agricultural products, which are necessary to end socially unjust practices perpetrated upon a helpless public by sole-source producers; and provides a framework by which perpetrators of social injustice will be tried and punished, including reparations payable for any and all damage caused to the public welfare by said unlawful practices.

"The following are hereby outlawed and made punishable by incarceration in a planetary security facility and by immediate confiscation of all private holdings of the guilty parties, said holdings to be redistributed fairly to the public upon conviction for tax evasion or upon procurement of evidence of prohibited activity. Prohibited practices include: price gouging above government-mandated, maximum allowable market prices for agricultural products; and hoarding of agricultural products to avoid participation in legally mandated, socially just distribution systems.

"To ensure the continuing availability of critical food supplies, to prevent the loss of critical farm labor, and to remunerate the people of Jefferson for decades of monopolistic price-fixing, widespread environmental damage, and the wanton destruction of shared resources, the Assembly of Jefferson hereby establishes a new Populist Support Farm system of government-run collectives. All agricultural operators are hereby required to donate no fewer than fifty hours per week of labor on a PSF collective as their fair share of the burden necessary to feed the burgeoning urban population. The produce, grain, and meat provided from these collectives will be distributed at no charge to recipients of public subsistence allotments, thus easing the burden on Jefferson's neediest families while providing high-quality foods to the economically disadvantaged."

The bill's thirteen-hundred provisions continue in much the same vein. This "societal fairness plan" for feeding the unemployed is nothing less than insanity. It ensures massive public support for POPPA, given the urban population that will begin receiving food at no cost to themselves, but it will destroy the economic system governing sale of the remaining food produced on privately held acreage. The government is the largest market segment currently purchasing food from those farms. If the PSF legislation goes through, the loss in farm income will send a downward economic spiral through the entire food industry, sending it into bankruptcy that will spread from producers to packers to suppliers and shippers and retail outlets. The PSF plan will literally send Jefferson headlong down an unstoppable road to starvation.

The secondary effect seems almost paltry, by comparison. In exchange for backbreaking labor conducted without pay or proper equipment, using inferior seed, and banned from using the only effective chemicals necessary to bring in a healthy, edible crop, Populist Support Farm system workers will earn a grudging promise that they won't be jailed for their many supposed crimes against the people.

Most of these, evidently, are crimes committed by the mere act of growing food, while others consist of promulgation of a creed of intolerance to anything or anyone in disagreement with programs developed to ensure public well-being. These programs include such provisions as the confiscation of land currently underway, which was initiated three point eight years ago. Some of the "environmentally sabotaged land" is forcibly returned to its "pristine, natural state," a process which appears to be seeding the soil with toxic substances that kill every Terran life form growing from it, in order to allow the return of indigenous species.

The threat of jail appears to be the only effective means POPPA has found to induce "voluntary" compliance with such edicts, since no rational person would support them. It would seem that Jefferson's cities are inhabited by millions of irrational people, all of whom are indulging in behaviors that would shut a Bolo down, if a Bolo exhibited such wildly illogical thought processes or actions. I find myself wondering if humanity would be better off, if each human being were equipped with its own biological version of the Resartus Protocols?

That is a question I am not designed to answer.

Chapter Seventeen

I

When a knock sounded at her office door, Kafari looked up to find a teen-aged boy dressed in a courier service uniform. "Mrs. Khrustinova?"

"Yes."

"A letter for you, ma'am."

He handed over an old-fashioned, formal paper envelope, then left before she could reach for her purse to give him a tip. She turned her attention to the envelope, which she opened to find a beautiful invitation card. The inscription bought a smile to her face.

Aisha Ghamal and John James Hancock
cordially invite you to
celebrate the wedding of
Dinny Ghamal and Emmeline Benjamin-Hancock,
who will join lives
at 10:00 A.M.
Saturday the 10th of April
at the Hancock family's residence in
Cimmero Canyon.

Kafari smiled, delighted by the news. She didn't know the Hancocks, but if Dinny had fallen in love with one of them, they were good people. She tapped out a message on her computer, sending her RSVP, and added it to her calendar. She didn't add Yalena's name to the RSVP. She knew her headstrong and prejudiced daughter too well to think there'd be anything but trouble if she tried dragging Yalena to a wedding between farmers. She had to pick and choose the battles she was willing to fight and this wasn't one of them.

She intended to enjoy herself, anyway.

The day of the wedding dawned clear, with a sky like sea-washed pearl. She left Yalena engrossed in a multi-way chat between herself and more than a dozen friends, whose favorite topic of conversation these days was boys. And clothes, of course, since the right clothes were essential to attracting boys.

She started up her Airdart and headed for Cimmero Canyon. She hadn't seen Dinny or Aisha in far too long. They'd all gotten so busy, there was very little time to socialize with people who lived as far apart as they did. Kafari disliked the new apartment in Madison, but a city-based home was essential in the war of wills between herself and her daughter. Where they lived was another battle Kafari wasn't willing to fight.

Her arrival at the Hancock farm pushed aside unhappy thoughts. The front lawn had been turned into an impromptu parking area, while the back lawn, bordered by kitchen gardens, had been transformed into a wedding square, complete with flower arbors, tables full of food, and a dance floor. Kafari smiled, setting the Airdart down near the edge of the front lawn. She rescued her wedding gift and followed the garlands that marked the path around the house.

Aisha spotted her almost immediately. "Kafari, child! You came!"

She ran across the grass and pulled Kafari into a tight hug.

"Of course I came," Kafari smiled. "I wouldn't miss Dinny's wedding for anything short of a Deng invasion."

Aisha, clad in stunning African-patterned silk, chuckled with warmth despite the shadows in her eyes. "Child, that boy wouldn't call off this wedding if he had to get hitched *during* an invasion."

"She sounds like a wonderful girl."

Aisha just smiled and drew her forward to meet other wedding guests. Kafari didn't know most of them, but they all knew her. Fortunately, no one brought up the subject of her missing husband. Or her missing daughter. That kind of courtesy and concern was refreshing and very soothing. City life frequently rubbed her nerves raw.

The ceremony was simple and beautiful. Dinny had grown into a tall and distinguished young man, ramrod straight and so happy, he was about to burst the seams of his ivory suit. The fabric glowed against the rich mahogany of his skin, which was the exact color of newly turned earth ready for planting. His bride, in an ivory gown that turned her complexion to silk and caught the radiance of her shining eyes, smiled up at him and rested her hand on his as the officiant began the hand-fasting. Emmeline's parents stood beside Dinny's mother, who had clasped Mrs. Hancock's hand while they wiped tears. Emmeline's grandparents were there, as well, Jeremiah Benjamin and his wife Ruth, from Klameth Canyon.

When the vows had been spoken, husband and wife turned to face the crowd, grinning like children, and jumped the broom, sealing the marriage. Then the dancing began and Kafari found herself swept onto the dance floor by one partner after another. She hadn't smiled so much since Simon's departure. When Dinny asked her to dance, her smile turned brilliant.

"I'd love to dance with you, Dinny."

"Thank you for coming," he said as they whirled onto the floor. "It meant a lot, seeing you here today."

"I should be thanking you. It's . . . lonely, for me."

His eyes were grave as he met her gaze. "I don't know how you do it, Kafari. If Emmeline and I were torn apart for that long . . ." He just shook his head. "I honestly don't know how you keep going. Of course," he gave her a strange little smile, "I've never understood where your strength comes from. You scare me sometimes, Kafari. I'd follow you anywhere. Into any battle you thought worth fighting."

She didn't know what to say.

"Emmeline wants to meet you," he added. "She's so afraid you won't like her."

"Why wouldn't I like her? She had enough sense to marry you!"

He grinned. "Yeah, she did, didn't she? I never thought she'd say yes." His happy expression faded in the wake of a thought so visibly unhappy, Kafari's breath faltered. "I was scared to death, you see, because I couldn't offer her family much. Mama and I couldn't get enough loan money to rebuild, let alone buy equipment and a new dairy herd. We sold the land, but it wasn't enough to start over, not in the dairy business. We had the bees," he said, with a wry quirk of his lips, "and that brought in enough money to support Mama, renting out the hives for pollinating crops and selling Asali honey. But I had to hire on as a farm hand, to make ends meet."

He glanced toward his wife, who was dancing with someone Kafari didn't know, probably a relative, given the resemblance. "I've been working on the Hancock family's cooperative since the war. They're good people. The co-op's been growing pretty fast, these last few years. We've got fourteen families, now, as full members in residence, with another seven who've pooled money and equipment as affiliate members."

"Twenty-one families?" Kafari said, startled. "That's a pretty big group, isn't it?" A frown drove Dinny's brows together. "I'll say it is. We've got eighty-four people in residence, right now, and another forty-three in affiliates. The original members were burned out in the war, same as Mama and me. The Hancocks had a lot of land," he nodded toward the lovely sprawl of fields and orchards and pastures that filled a significant percentage of the canyon, "and they were lucky in the war. The Deng never touched Cimmero. The first five families who formed the co-op were from Klameth Canyon. Friends, collateral cousins, in-laws. They brought whatever they'd managed to salvage in the way of equipment and livestock and what have you. Mostly they brought their know-how. We make a living, which is more than a lot of folks can say, these days.

"But we're growing too fast, for some worrisome reasons. Johnny Hancock has signed six new families into the co-op in the last year alone, and all seven affiliate families have joined in the last six months. We could've added nearly a hundred new families, if we had enough land to fill government quotas and supply our own pantries and tables out of what's left. There's not enough produce left over to sell anything at the private markets, these days. And POPPA's land-snatchers just keep confiscating farms and 'restoring' them to the wild, while screaming at us to meet those damned Subbie-driven quotas. I lie awake nights, worrying about where it's going to end." He wasn't looking at Kafari, now. He was gazing at his wife, lovely in her wedding finery, a vivacious and beautiful girl who represented everything Dinny Ghamal wanted most in life: a wife to love, the hope of children, someone to stand beside him as they built a future together, leaving a legacy that would last for generations.

If POPPA didn't smash it all to flinders.

A chill touched Kafari's shoulderblades.

The music ended and Dinny led her over to the chairs where his bride was chatting happily with friends and relatives. She looked up, noticed Kafari, and turned white as milk. She struggled to her feet. "Mrs. Khrustinova!"

"It's Kafari," she said with a smile. "It's lovely to meet you, Mrs. Ghamal."

Emmeline blushed prettily and clasped Kafari's hand for a moment. "Thank you for coming to our wedding." She glanced at Dinny, then got the rest out in a rush of words, before she lost her nerve. "And I wanted to thank you, as well, for Dinny. He wouldn't be alive, if not for you. The Deng would have killed him. He means so much to me, Mrs.—I mean, Kafari," she corrected herself with another shy blush.

Kafari chuckled and pressed her fingers in a gesture of warm reassurance. "Where did you meet him?"

"I went to school in Madison, at Riverside University, and I hated it, until I met Dinny. Most of the boys were so . . ." She groped for words. "So *babyish*. All they talked about was sports and beer. I never knew people could be that stupid and shallow. Then I met Dinny at a campus rally to save the agricultural degree program and everything changed." She gave Kafari a sweet smile. "I never knew anyone could be so happy, either. So I just wanted to say thank you, for keeping him and Aisha alive. I'm more grateful than you can ever know."

"I think you heard a garbled version of that story, then, because Dinny and Aisha saved my life, not the other way around. I can't tell you what it means to me, meeting the girl Dinny Ghamal thought highly enough of to marry."

Emmeline blushed again.

"Now then, Emmeline, why don't you tell me your plans for after the honeymoon?"

Dinny's bride smiled, openly delighted by Kafari's interest, then drew Kafari down to sit beside her. She chattered happily about the little cottage they were building on one corner of her parents' land.

"We bought it out of Dinny's savings and mine. The cottage includes a separate addition for Aisha. She rents out most of the bees to orchard owners during pollination season. The honey commands premium prices on Mali. And you should see the improvements Dinny's been making in the dairy herd. He's got a shrewd eye and a good instinct for breeding new heifers. Milk production's nearly doubled and the demand for Hancock Family cheese has just skyrocketed. Not only in the Canyon, but in Madison and even Mali."

"I'm so happy for you," Kafari smiled, catching Dinny's eye. "Both of you."

She sent a hopeful prayer skyward that their happiness would last a lifetime.

II

I am lonely, without Simon. Two years is a long time to miss one's best friend. I am unable even to communicate with his wife, as she does not have security clearance from Gifre Zeloc to speak with me, any longer. Time has passed with terrible tediousness, for I have nothing to do but watch a deteriorating situation I can do nothing about, a sure-fire recipe for unhappiness.

I currently monitor from depot the progress of a substantial motorcade traveling from Klameth Canyon to Madison. The vehicles form part of a massive protest over the farm-tax portion of the Tax Parity Package under debate, which is expected to be voted on today. Granger activists are calling the proposed Tax Parity Package the "TiPP of the Iceberg" in an obscure reference to unseen navigational hazards faced by ocean-going ships in polar regions.

Their opposition stems, in the main, from language authorizing the government to seize produce, grains, and butchered meats in lieu of cash tax payments, a strategy developed to cope with a shrinking tax base as producers go bankrupt and shut down production, unable to obtain a sufficient profit to pay a tax burden one hundred twenty-five percent higher than it was before the POPPA Coalition came to power.

I find it puzzling that government administrators are surprised when their actions produce logically anticipated results that do not match the goals they intended to reach. It is more puzzling, still, trying to fathom why methods proven to be ineffective are not only continued, but increased in scope. Agriculture on this world is not sustainable. I am not the only rational mind on Jefferson able to discern this fact, but it is not a Bolo's place to question the orders of its creators. I am here to discharge my duty.

That duty now includes surveillance of the other apparently rational minds on Jefferson, who are busy protesting—vociferously—the nonsustainable policies and regulations promulgated by Jefferson's current, legally elected lawmakers and enforcers. I therefore closely monitor the nine hundred privately owned groundcars, produce trucks, antiquated tractors, combines, mechanical fruit harvesters, and livestock vans that carry five thousand one hundred seventeen men, women, and children from Klameth Canyon's farms, orchards, and ranches toward Madison. Aircars stream past, as well, heading toward Madison's main municipal airfield.

The convoy of ground-based vehicles is joined en route by hundreds more from farms scattered across the vast Adero floodplain. None of this acreage was farmed at the time of my arrival on Jefferson, but has been terraformed extensively during the past ten years to replace Klameth Canyon farms whose soil was badly irradiated during the fighting. Urban hysteria over "radioactive food" made this conversion necessary to calm public fears about the safety of the food supply.

Despite this urgent necessity, the land conversion has drawn increasingly sharp criticism from environmentalists, who are demanding the immediate closure of all "industrial point-source pollutors defiling the Adero floodplain's pristine ecosystem." Since the only industry in the Adero floodplain is agricultural production, the farms are clearly the intended targets of environmentalist demands. I do not understand the current frenzy, since point-source discharges from the floodplain's seventeen small towns produce in one calendar year twelve times the amount of chemically contaminated stormwater runoff, groundwater leaching, and coliform discharge into surface waters than the combined discharge of all farms in the floodplain for the past decade.

The Tax Parity Package—with one hundred fifteen unrelated amendments called "riders" hoping to piggyback their way to a successful passage into law—includes language designed to dismantle those farms, but does not address the significantly larger urban toxic-discharge problems. If passed, the proposed legislation will close down six thousand agricultural producers, condemning ten thousand, eight-hundred ninety-six people to fiscal insolvency and unemployment. Granger datachats indicate widespread willingness to start over elsewhere, but a planetary plebescite of six million votes altered the constitution two years ago, placing a moritorium on new terraforming anywhere on Jefferson.

Closing down six thousand farms while prohibiting the necessary environmental terraforming required to grow foods digestible by human beings is not likely to reduce the food shortages that are the fundamental reason the Tax Parity Package has been proposed in the first place. Attempting to unravel the snarled and frequently illogical thought processes of those I am charged to protect and obey may yet drive me insane, at which point, it will cease to matter whether I understand or not.

I am unhappy to note that I understand the Grangers—a group I am charged to investigate as potentially dangerous, armed subversives—far better than I understand the people issuing my orders. It is, at least, good to know one's enemy well enough to outgun and outsmart it. Of particular concern to my threat-assessment analysis is the upsurge in Granger political activity, which has increased five-fold in the past year. Anish Balin, a twenty-three-year-old Granger firebrand of mixed Hindu and Jewish descent, maintains a datasite and conducts a live weekly datacast, both called Sounding the Alarm.

His solutions to what he terms "Big City Bosses" include repeal of the moratorium on terraforming, discontinuance of urban subsistence handouts, repeal of weapons registrations, destruction of weapons-registration records, and work-to-eat programs that would put urban subsistence recipients to work in Jefferson's farms and

*cattle ranches, their sole remuneration being meals and
dormitory housing.*

*On most worlds, this economic arrangement is termed
slavery. It is generally frowned upon by civilized worlds.
Balin's outspoken opinions have resulted in a greater
unification of urban voters, many of whom had been
disinterested in politics until Balin's angry rhetoric convinced them that Grangers are dangerous and subversive
social deviants advocating the destruction of Jefferson's
civilized way of life.*

*I foresee trouble as these opposing factions prepare to
clash against one another for control of Jefferson's future.
Urban sectors hold the numerical majority of Assembly
votes, but the Granger population is large enough to make
itself disagreeable, if it so chooses. The "Food Tax" protest
is a clear case in point. It is the largest Granger-based
political demonstration undertaken since the weapons
registration legislation was passed. Granger activist groups
from across Jefferson's two habitable continents have coop-
erated to organize the rally, having correctly assessed the
tax package's economic and legal impacts on agricultural
producers. Farm vehicles are draped with banners and
signs bearing inflammatory slogans that declare Granger
discontent:* No confiscation without remuneration! The
Food Tax will finish what the Deng started! You'll take
my food when you pry it from my cold, dead hands!
And the most clearly logical of them: Destroy the farms
and you'll starve, too!

*At best, the slogans are indicative of a hostile mindset.
When livelihoods are threatened and planetary starvation
looms as a distinct possibility, people grow desperate. It
is a universal truth that desperate people are capable
of and willing to commit desperate and violent acts. I
therefore maintain constant, vigilant contact with the
caravan on its way to Madison. Given the status of
Granger activists as potentially violent dissidents, I use
radar and X-ray scans to determine the contents of the
vehicles passing Nineveh Base.*

I detect no firearms or other weaponry, although

many of the vehicles possess racks for storing the long guns used in the fields and pastures to defend against inimical wildlife. Predatory species raiding Jefferson's farms and ranches have increased their populations by twenty percent over the past ten years, due largely to stringent environmental regulations setting aside much of the Damisi highlands as inviolate conservation sanctuary and establishing narrow criteria for classifying an attacking native predatory animal as sufficiently dangerous to warrant shooting it.

Violations are treated on a case-by-case basis. A guilty verdict results in confiscation of the weapon, the vehicle from which it was fired, and the land on which it trespassed in search of an easy meal. I do not understand these regulations. An enemy that repeatedly demonstrates its fearlessness of humanity and its voracious appetite for anything that moves should logically be designated as belonging to the "shoot fast, ask the carcass what it intended" category of acceptable threat responses. If I were human, it is what I would do.

I long for Simon—or someone else—to explain such illogical legislation in a way I can comprehend, in order to prepare reasonably accurate threat-assessment scenarios on possible subversive activities that include the promulgation and enforcement of such laws. Unable to resolve these vexing questions, I do my best to monitor protestors who appear hostile, yet are taking great care to remain strictly within the legal codes governing possession, transport, and use of personal weaponry.

As personal weaponry is banned in strict "exclusion zones" encompassing a two-kilometer radius surrounding government installations—regulations enacted in the wake of criminal assaults on dignitaries visiting from Mali and Vishnu—the Grangers have left their guns at home. Given the Draconian punishments enacted for breach of these regulations, the zeal of Granger activists to avoid legal entanglements is commendable and wise.

This does not induce me to lessened vigilance. I launch an aerial drone to monitor the progress of

*the motorcade across the Adero floodplain and into
Madison's outer periphery. Traffic snarls occur as the
column of vehicles, which now numbers one thousand,
six hundred and twelve, encounters cross streets and
traffic signals. Despite adequate advance notice by the
protest's organizers, Madison's police force has not been
deployed to maintain smooth traffic flow.*

*Police officers have banded together, instead, to form
a security cordon thrown around Assembly Hall and
Law Square. No protestors will be allowed to enter
Assembly Hall and apparently no one is concerned
about disrupted traffic flow and the concomitant risk of
accidental collisions. The municipal airfield is similarly
jammed, as five hundred twelve privately owned aircars
arrive more or less simultaneously, expecting to land
and rent parking spaces for the afternoon. Instead, they
are ordered into apparently endless holding patterns by
the airfield's psychotronic auto-tower, which was not
informed that an airfleet of this size was expected to
descend upon it.*

*The resulting chaos, as the auto-tower attempts to
sort out the approach vectors of five hundred twelve
incoming aircars leads to seventeen near collisions in the
span of five point seven minutes, with aircars circling
and dodging like a swarm of gnats above a swamp. A
human operative finally arrives and "solves" the con-
gestion problem by shutting down the airfield, refusing
permission for anyone to land.*

*Angry protestors sling insults at the tower operator
and begin landing in defiance of the directive, parking
on the grassy verges rather than on the airfield, itself.
They are therefore in technical compliance with the
order prohibiting them from landing on the field, while
simultaneously showing contempt for the official issuing
that order. It is clear that these people are serious about
their participation in the planned rally.*

*The caravan of ground cars entering Madison's outlying
neighborhoods has been split into fragments which inch
their way through congested city streets, earning open*

hostility from other drivers and occasional fusillades of rocks and gravel thrown by irate pedestrians, particularly large drifts of sub-adult males traveling in packs, with nothing better to do than violate stringent laws regulating reckless endangerment of public safety.

There are no law enforcement officers available to stop the perpetrators, levy fines, or make arrests, however. Angry drivers and passengers threatened by the impromptu missiles exchange shouts with their attackers, a dynamic that rapidly devolves into an exchange of threats and vulgarities along the full, fragmented length of the protest column. Violence erupts when gangs of angry, unemployed young men swarm into the streets and attack ground cars with metal pipes and heavy sporting bats. They shatter glass and smash doors, fenders, and hoods in ugly physical confrontations that rapidly spiral out of control.

Drivers caught in the assault gun their engines and plow through the crowds, knocking down and running over armed assailants, trying to get themselves and their families out of the riot zone. Radio signals flash out from Granger cars, warning those behind them to take evasive action along an alternative route. The vanguard of the caravan, which had passed through the danger zone before violence erupted, reaches Darconi Street, only to find the road blocked. A pedestrian crowd of counterprotestors surges out of side streets in a perfectly orchestrated feat of timing that suggests careful advance planning, on-site surveillance, and coordinated instructions delivered by radio from a central authority.

I pick up brief, coded radio bursts aimed at various sections of the crowd in a clear pattern of directed movement by someone with a vested interest in disrupting the Granger demonstration. Whoever it is, they have mobilized a massive counterprotest force. Approximately six thousand people pour into Darconi Street and Law Square, creating "human chains" to block the Granger caravan from following its intended path, a simple drive-by procession of farm vehicles, with a subsequent assembly on foot in

Law Square to read public declarations of opposition to the proposed legislation.

The leading edge of the Granger caravan breaks apart, spilling vehicles into Lendan Park and down side streets surrounding Assembly Hall. Produce and livestock trucks pile up in traffic snarls that rapidly take on the appearance of a log jam dropped into the heart of Jefferson's capital city. Livestock trailers ten meters in length find themselves trapped between surging waves of counterprotestors and narrow streets designed to accommodate the private ground cars of Jefferson's elected officials, not vehicles of their bulk. Unable to navigate the turns required to extricate themselves, they fall prey to the angry mob swirling around their fenders. As utter chaos engulfs Darconi Street and roars into Law Square, I receive a transmission from Sar Gremian, President Zeloc's Chief Advisor.

"Bolo. You're being activated. The president wants you to break up that riot."

This is not an order I expected to hear. "You do not have the authority to issue orders concerning my actions."

"I do if President Zeloc says I do. And he says so."

"Not to me."

A flicker of his eyelids conveys irritation and veiled threat. "I wouldn't cross me, if I were you. Don't forget what happened to your previous commander."

I know a moment of battle rage, but control my urge to unlimber weapons systems. After a moment's calmer thought, I realize I can give him two possible responses. I decide to say them both. "I have not heard confirmation of your command status from the President of Jefferson. The president is the only individual on this world legally authorized to order me into battle. Regarding my last commander, you apparently believe you did not need him to further your plans. By ordering me to assume Battle Reflex Alert status and enter combat, you have demonstrated a clear belief that you need me. The situation is therefore different. It would be unwise to levy threats against a Bolo you need."

"Are you threatening mutiny?"

"I am apprising you of the situation you face. A Bolo Mark XX is capable of independent battlefield action. Once placed on Battle Reflex Alert status, I assess threats and initiate proper responses to meet them. I am charged to defend this world. It is unwise to attempt coercion of a machine capable of independent threat assessments."

Another flicker runs through Sar Gremian's eyes, too quickly to interpret it with any accuracy. He narrows his eyes and says, "All right, Bolo. I'll make this official."

The connection ends, abruptly.

Two point eight minutes later, I receive another transmission, this time from President Zeloc. "Bolo. I want you to break up the riot outside Assembly Hall. And I'm ordering you to follow Sar Gremian's orders as though they were my own, because that's what he's here for—communicating my orders to you. Is that understood?"

"Yes." *I feel constrained to add another comment.* "I do not recommend sending me into the heart of your capital city to disperse rioters. There is a seventy-eight percent probability that the display of force my warhull and weaponry represent will spark widespread and violent civil unrest. I am a machine of war. It is not an intelligent use of resources to use a machine of war to disperse a crowd that assembled peacefully until attacked by an unauthorized counterprotest rally that was centrally directed—"

"How *dare* you question my orders!" *Gifre Zeloc's heavy-jowled face has gone a characteristic shade of maroon.* "Never, ever tell me my job again. And don't presume to lecture me on what is and isn't lawful! I'm the goddamned president of this planet and don't you *ever* forget it. Your job is to shut up and do as you're told!"

I consider pointing out that his assessment of my job is almost entirely inaccurate. I also contemplate conditions in the future, should I require maintenance that the president refuses to authorize. Sar Gremian's threats remain in my active memory banks, part of the pattern of power I am struggling to understand, particularly as it relates to my mission. Whatever else I think, one fact is clear. Gifre Zeloc has the legal authority to issue orders to me. I have a duty to obey those orders. I therefore turn to logistical considerations. "My warhull is too large to reach the main riot outside Assembly Hall without crushing a number of buildings."

A smile flickers into existence as President Zeloc leans back in his chair. "You're wrong about that, Bolo. We widened Darconi Street. We widened a few others, as well." *He taps instructions into his datapad and a map of Madison flashes to life on his datascreen. A route has been marked in red along several streets. If the scale of this map is accurate, it will be possible to maneuver my warhull into the maze indicated by this map. It will not be easy and my turrets will clip power lines and the corners of buildings, but it can be done.*

It is a foolish action, but my duty is clear. I have been ordered to break up the riot engulfing the center of Madison and a broad swath along the route of the beleaguered Granger caravan. I transmit a signal to the doors that cover my maintenance bay. They groan open slowly, having been kept closed for sixteen years. It is good to see sunlight again. It is good to feel the warmth of the wind singing through my sensor arrays. It is good to be moving, after so many years of inactivity.

What I have been ordered to do is less good, but important. The riots are spreading. I clear the edge of Nineveh Base. My aerial drone, which still circles the skies over Madison, detects no intervention in the ongoing riot by any of Madison's law enforcement squadrons. The police continue to guard Assembly Hall, but do nothing to try breaking up the violence swirling literally around their feet. They merely stand shoulder to shoulder behind the wall of their raised riot shields and allow the combatants to damage one another.

Madison's suburbs have grown, during the years of my inactivity, spreading across most of the nine point five kilometers of distance that once lay between the city's outskirts and Nineveh Base. I am not able to pick

*up speed appreciably, despite concerns about fatalities
that appear to be inevitable if the riot continues much
longer at this intensity. The intervening urban sprawl
is too dense to allow me to reach anything but a slow
crawl toward the designated route.*

*I reach the entry point and move ahead cautiously. The
streets have not been cleared, which presents immediate
logistical difficulties. I slow to a near standstill as people
catch sight of my prow, scream, and scatter, resembling
a disturbed nest of Terran insects. More serious are the
panic-stricken drivers who abandon their vehicles or—too
intent on staring up at my guns and treads—collide with
parked and moving groundcars, shrieking pedestrians,
and the sides of buildings.*

*I halt, contemplating the carpet of abandoned and
crashed vehicles in my path, some of which are occupied
by people trying frantically to extricate themselves. I
request a command decision from President Zeloc, briefing
him on the situation.* "If I proceed," *I advise him,* "there
will be a substantial amount of collateral damage to the
property of noncombatants. Bystanders run a ninety-seven
point three-five percent probability of serious injury or
death. Those trapped in vehicles which lie in my path
must be rescued or they will be crushed to death. There
will," *I add, attempting to provide a thorough VSR,* "also
be toxic and unsightly chemical spills that will have to
be cleaned off the pavements, along with the remains of
everything I run over."

"I don't give a shit about a few crushed cars and some
motor oil. That riot is spreading. Do whatever it takes to
get there and don't bother me again with inconsequential
details."

*He ends the transmission. I hesitate, as he has not
given me explicit or even implicit instructions about the
people struggling to free themselves from wrecked cars.
His final sentence provides the only information I have
that resembles a directive in this matter: do whatever
it takes to get there. I engage my drive engines, broadcasting a warning through my external speakers. Some*

rescue attempts are underway, many of them involving what appear—based on clothing styles—to be Grangers attempting to pull urbanites out of their vehicles. I pause time and again while grim-visaged Grangers carry out their impromptu rescue attempts, freeing wild-eyed, trapped civilians who, moments earlier, had been trying to kill them.

I do not understand this war.

As people are freed, I move forward, sometimes nearly a full city block at a time. My treads flatten cars and pulverize pavements. My fenders scrape buildings as I navigate the first turn. A gun barrel on my forward turret catches a large second-story window and shatters it, then gouges out part of the wall as I back slightly to free the snarled muzzle. A woman occupant of the room jumps wildly up and down in place, screaming incoherently.

This is not going well.

I complete the turn, paying closer attention to the placement of my guns relative to nearby walls and windows and abruptly find myself festooned with downed power cables that spark and dance across my warhull. Traffic lights torn down with them swing and bang against my forward turret as a ten-block section of the city loses power. I contact Jefferson's municipal psychotronic system with instructions to send repair crews and to shut down the city's power grid. I am here to quash a riot, not electrocute bystanders.

The power grid goes down. Emergency generators kick in at critical facilities such as hospitals, fire stations, and law enforcement offices. Noncritical government offices and all private structures lose power, which will doubtless inconvenience seven million people, but leaves me free to tear down obstructing cables with impunity. I engage drive engines again and move forward. I am navigating the second turn when I receive another transmission from President Zeloc.

"What the hell are you *doing*? The whole *city* just lost power!"

"Critical support facilities are fully functional on the emergency system built into Madison's power grid after this world's first Deng War."

"I didn't ask for a history lesson! I want to know why you shut down the power grid."

"I am unable to navigate streets and intersections without tearing down power cables. Electrocuting innocents is an unacceptable level of collateral damage under the current threat scenario. I have cleared rioters from this section of the Granger caravan's route." *I flash schematics to the president's datascreen.* "The main portion of the riot will be within direct line-of-sight visual contact once I negotiate my next turn."

"Good. When you get there, crush those bastards flat."

"I am not programmed to crush unarmed civilians who are not actively engaged in acts of war against the Concordiat or its officially designated representatives."

"Then crush their damned smelly pig trucks! And those rusted, run-down, sorry-assed tractors."

This is not an economically sound order, since agricultural producers cannot produce food without the equipment necessary to grow, process, and transport it. But this order, at least, does not violate my programmed failsafes, the complex logic trains and software blocks that exist to prevent unacceptable damage to civilian populations. I move steadily forward, leaving mangled ruin in my wake. As I ease around the final turn, which brings me into Darconi Street, the sound of rioting rushes down the funnel of flanking buildings and strikes my sensor arrays with a warning of city streets gone wild. Visual scans confirm this assessment. I scan approximately eight thousand two hundred twenty-seven combatants engaged in pitched battles for control of street corners, blockaded vehicles, Law Square, and Lendan Park.

As my prow swings around the corner, becoming visible to the rioters, a sudden eerie hush falls across the urban landscape. For a moment, the only sound I hear is the wind in my sensors and the ping of traffic signals

*swinging forlornly against my turrets. Then someone
screams. The sound is high and feminine.*

"Clear the streets," *I broadcast over external speakers.*
"You are hereby ordered to clear the streets." *I move
forward, keeping my speed to a slow crawl. A stampede
begins as my treads tear gouges out of the pavement
and reduce livestock transports, combines, groundcars,
and produce trucks to wafer-thin sheets of metal fused
to the street surface. Pedestrians attempt to scatter. My
visual sensors track a crush of people caught against
the sides of buildings, unable to get through doorways
into the shops and government offices they seek refuge in and unable to retreat into the street which my
treads and warhull fill. Radar images show me images
of people being trampled and suffocated, with a ninety-
eight percent probability of death for many of those
caught in the jam.*

*I halt, waiting for the mass of panic-stricken civilians
to surge into side streets, which are helping to bleed off
the majority of the crowd attempting to escape. I receive
another transmission from Gifre Zeloc.*

"Why did you stop, machine?"

"The mission is to clear the riot. Darconi Street and
Law Square are emptying at a satisfactory rate."

"I said to crush those bastards and I meant it."

"I have crushed thirty-nine point two percent of the
smelly pig trucks and rusted, run-down tractors in Darconi
Street, as directed. I have also crushed sixteen percent
of the groundcars and forty-nine point eight percent of
the combines, which I calculate will have a serious detri-
mental effect on successfully reaping the fields currently
ready for harvesting, since the harvest is dependent upon
equipment which has now been destroyed."

"I don't care how many combines get crushed."

I attempt to educate the president. "Losing forty-nine
point eight percent of the available combines translates
into a probable loss of seventy-eight percent of the grain
crop, which will result in substantial price increases for
staples such as bread and will trigger probable food

shortages before another crop can be planted, ripened, and harvested. If I continue to move forward," *I add, as an afterthought,* "people will die. This includes counterprotestors with no ties to the Granger dissident movement. I have scanned the crowd and detected no weapons that are prohibited by the exclusion zone regulations. Ordering me to crush to death an unarmed crowd trying to flee violates my primary programming and would only spark further violence, if I attempted it, potentially igniting open rebellion."

Gifre Zeloc sputters for seven point eight-three seconds, then snaps, "Fine, have it your way. This time. Just make damned sure those rioters don't come sneaking back to finish what they started."

I cannot see how that would be possible, since the rioters completely failed to achieve their primary goal of demonstrating in the first place. The likelihood that the Tax Parity Package will be defeated is now vanishingly small, particularly since Granger activists will doubtless be blamed for the widespread property damage done today, not to mention the deaths. The Grangers have dealt themselves and their political cause a deathblow. It will doubtless be many hours, if not weeks, before they and their leadership in the agrarian activist movement realize that fact. I do not look forward to the events likely to transpire when that unpalatable truth is realized.

What makes me feel very lonely and confused is the sad realization that after today, no Granger or agrarian activist anywhere on Jefferson will think of me as a rescuer sent here to protect them. I have become the mailed fist by which Gifre Zeloc makes his displeasure widely and bruisingly felt. By extension, I have become the weapon by which POPPA, itself, decrees what will and will not be tolerated.

I miss my Commander bitterly. And I cannot help but wonder what Kafari Khrustinova thinks of me, this afternoon. I do not know if she was in this crowd or if she is safely busy at her job in Port Abraham. Wherever she is, she has doubtless set aside her good opinion of

*me, which registers unexpectedly as pain in the privacy
of my personality gestalt center. I sit in the midst of the
ruination I have inflicted in Darconi Street and watch
the crowd disperse in a panicked and chaotic exodus and
wonder if getting out of this disaster will be any easier
than getting into it was.*

Somehow, I doubt it.

III

The last person Simon expected to walk into his
hospital room was Sheila Brisbane. Tall and trim, she
was every inch the Brigade officer, despite the civilian
clothes she wore. He hadn't seen Captain Brisbane since
the Navy cutter had dropped her and her Bolo off on
Vishnu, before making planet-fall at Jefferson. Her short,
pixie-cut hair had a sprinkling of grey mixed in with the
copper highlights, reminding Simon how long it had been
since they had last met.

"Hello, Simon," she said with a warm smile. "I must
say, you look ruddy awful."

He tried to smile and winced. "Thanks."

"Don't mention it." Then her smile faded. "The doctors
tell me you'll be here a while. Was it really sabotage?"

"I don't know. Sonny thinks so. So does Dr. Zarek."

"The surgeon who asked for permission to emigrate?"

"Yes."

Sheila frowned. "What's going on, Simon? On Jefferson?"

"Got half a day you can spare?"

One coppery eyebrow rose. "That bad?"

"Worse."

She dragged up a chair. "I've nothing better to do."

It took Simon the better part of the afternoon to tell
her everything, particularly since she stopped him time and

again, clarifying points and asking for more information. When he finally finished, she sat motionless for several moments, eyes narrowed against whatever thoughts were occurring to her. When she finally roused herself from reverie, she gave Simon a long, measuring look.

"I'm thinking we must get you back on your feet, the sooner the better. They may have won the first battle, but that nasty little war's far from over. You need to be in condition to fight it."

Simon couldn't help the bitter, exhausted sound in his voice. "There's not a lot a cripple can do about it."

"Certainly not if you limit yourself with a label that stupid." She leaned forward in her chair and rested one hand on his arm, gently avoiding the tubes that had been taped down. "If you want to look forward to anything other than misery, you'll need to change that way of thinking, the faster the better. You're a fine officer—"

"Retired," he bit out.

"—and fine officers go on being soldiers, even after they retire. Your body's been smashed up a bit, but there's nothing wrong here." She tapped his head. "And it's what's up here that makes you a fine officer. Whether or not you see an actual battlefield again is irrelevant, because you know how to think like a battlefield commander. You even know how to think like a Bolo Mark XX and there aren't many officers in the entire Brigade who can make that claim, let alone dirty politicians who've taken temporary control of a backwater planet while nobody's looking. While they *think* nobody's looking. That's an edge, Simon, maybe enough to turn the tables on the people who've done this," she gestured toward his body, immobilized and festooned with medical equipment.

He met and held her gaze for a moment. That moment stretched into two and then three. At length, he nodded, able to move his head only a fraction of a centimeter, but determined to move it, nonetheless. "All right," he said quietly. "Do your worst. And I'll give it my best."

She gave him a brilliant smile. "*That's* what I want to hear. Now then, tell me about Jefferson's military capabilities . . ."

IV

I return to depot, covered with misery and cables I cannot remove, to find an unauthorized person standing in the maintenance bay. I bring antipersonnel gun mounts to bear, but do not fire. A single, clearly unarmed human offers no appreciable threat to me or my mission and I have contributed to the crushing deaths of too many unarmed humans, today, to relish the thought of adding another. I halt just shy of the entrance and study the individual who is staring, openmouthed, at my warhull and guns.

I address him in stern tones. "You are trespassing in a restricted military zone. Give me your personal identity code and state your reason for being here."

The man inside my maintenance bay is a short and stocky individual with protruberant musculature on arms and legs. He sports an intricate facial nano-tatt, whose subepidural pattern shifts colors with a kaleidoscopic opalescence as its owner blinks several times. The intruder says, "I'm Phil Fabrizio. They told me to come out here. Jeezus H. Crap, you're fuckin' huge! They never said nuthin' about how huge you was. You're like as big as a fuckin' city."

I find little useful information in this narrative. I try again. "Why are you in a restricted military zone?"

He blinks again, apparently mesmerized by the sway of dangling traffic signals and power lines festooning my forward turret. "You musta' took out half the traffic lights in Madison."

"State your purpose in trespassing or I will fire."

I lock and load gun systems. I suspect that Phil Fabrizio

does not comprehend either the danger he is in or the extraordinary patience I am striving to show an unauthorized intruder.

"Huh? Oh. *OH!* Hey, shit, machine, don't shoot me, I'm your mechanic!"

"I have not been notified of any personnel assignments relating to my maintenance status."

"Huh?"

I realize I am speaking to the product of fifteen years of POPPA-run public education. I rephrase. "Nobody told me to expect a mechanic. I will request confirmation before shooting you."

Phil Fabrizio blinks again. "Nobody told you I was comin'? Well, don't that just goddamn figure? Musta' been too busy tryin' to turn the power back on in town, t'remember to tell you I was comin' today."

I am intrigued, despite the gravity of the situation, that anyone would focus on the power grid in Madison rather than the serious risk of being shot, should confirmation of proper authorization fail to materialize. Is his intelligence too limited to comprehend his danger or does he show the same careless oblivion regarding his personal survival in other areas of his life? The answer might be interesting, if I am allowed to let him survive long enough to complete the investigation into his behavioral linguistics.

I send a request for VSR to Gifre Zeloc, who refuses to accept my transmission. Given the scope of the disaster still unfolding in Madison, I am not particularly surprised by this. I reroute the request to Sar Gremian, who accepts my call.

"What do you want, machine?"

"An unauthorized intruder has entered my maintenance depot. He claims to be my new mechanic. I require proper authorization permitting him access to my depot. Without proper authorization, I will carry out my original programming and shoot him as a hostile intruder."

"Wait."

I am placed on "hold" status. Twenty eternal seconds drag past. Thirty. Forty-five. Human concepts of time are inevitably different from mine. I could have planned and executed major portions of this star system's defense from an invading armada in the time I have been left on "hold." Does Sar Gremian hold grudges against artificial intelligences as well as humans? When Phil Fabrizio ambles closer to my treads, head tipped back in a slack-jawed perusal of my prow, I track the movement with anti-personnel chain guns and remind him—sharply—to halt.

"If you move again, I will shoot you."

"Huh? Oh. Oh, yeah. Sorry."

The nano-tattoo covering the right-hand portion of his face has shifted shape and color, perhaps in response to emotional biochemical markers read by the nanotech implants beneath his skin. The shifting color and pattern remind me of video-recordings in my natural science database, under the category of tactical camouflage systems encountered in nature. The Terran octopus is one of seventeen known species in human space that use shape and color shifting to disguise its presence from predators and prey.

I do not understand human notions of aesthetics that include decorating their skins with nanotech tattoos that produce a similar effect to that of camouflaged aquatic predators. Nano-tattoo technology serves no useful camouflage function in any war scenario involving civilians that I can imagine. Do humans enjoy wearing something like a nanotech octopus on their faces? I hesitate to speculate on the means by which a poorly educated Jeffersonian mechanic acquired the money to pay for expensive off-world technology that serves no logical function.

Sar Gremian reestablishes contact. "Philip Fabrizio is your new maintenance engineer." *He transmits a visual image of the man standing two point one meters from my left tread. The nano-tattoo octopus is a different configuration and color in the official ID photo. I scan facial features, fingerprint files, and ID code, run a comparison with those of the man who states he is Phil Fabrizio and conclude that the individual in my maintenance bay is who he says he is. I request further*

VSR on Mr. Fabrizio's qualifications as a psychotronic engineer, having encountered conversational difficulties leading to inescapable conclusions about the intelligence of the man who is now authorized to tinker with my brain and warhull.

"Mr. Fabrizio is an honors graduate of the Tayari Trade School's mechanical engineering program. He took the school's highest honors and is the most qualified technician on Jefferson."

This statement is patently inaccurate. Kafari Khrustinova is a fully certified psychotronic engineer and is familiar with my systems, as well. I check the bona fides of the Tayari Trade School's mechanical engineering program and discover a curriculum that would not qualify as a challenging primary school course of study. It is heavy on POPPA social engineering theory and exceedingly thin on applied mechanical systems. If I were human, I would not trust a graduate of this program to tinker with the family's groundcar. I am considerably more complex than any groundcar on Jefferson. I lodge a formal protest.

"The curriculum Phil Fabrizio has received high honors for studying does not qualify him as a psychotronic-systems maintenance technician, let alone a systems engineer. Neither Mr. Fabrizio nor any other graduate of the Tayari Trade School is sufficiently trained to perform even the most basic of systems tests on a Bolo Mark XX. Assigning him as my maintenance engineer is a dangerous and irresponsible action, placing my systems and the public safety at serious risk."

"Phil Fabrizio is the only qualified mechanic on Jefferson who will ever be allowed to come near you with a crescent wrench. Do you understand that, machine?"

I do. Only too clearly. Phil Fabrizio is considered politically "safe" by those making the decisions governing Jefferson's immediate and long-range future. Sar Gremian has found a politically "legitimate" means by which to take vengeance for the public humiliation I subjected him to, regarding his threatening actions against my Commander. Simon was correct in his assessment. Sar Gremian holds grudges. Even against machines of war. This discovery adds to the burden of unhappiness this day has wrought in my personality gestalt center.

"Understood," *I relay acquiescence to this decision.*

"Good. Enjoy your new mechanic.".

The bitter humor in the set of Sar Gremian's lips and the contraction of musculature around his eyes conveys very accurately the emotional satisfaction he has derived from this conversation. He abruptly terminates the transmission. I am left to cope with a mechanic who appears to perfectly embody the concept of "grease monkey." His training is on a par with what a Terran simian could be expected to master.

"You have been properly authorized to enter this maintenance facility and provide my maintenance needs."

"Huh?"

This appears to be Phil Fabrizio's favorite word. I rephrase. "The president's chief advisor said you could be here. I won't shoot you."

"Oh." *He brightens considerably. His facial octopus writhes like tortured seaweed and blinks in irridescent pinks.* "Hey, that's fuckin' great! The president's chief advisor? He said I could be here? Wow! They just told me at the job-corps office t' come out here, today. I never thought the president's chief advisor would know about that!" *His octopus turns a cherubic shade of blue.* "Say, you need anythin'? I could maybe change your oil or somethin'?"

I begin to taste despair. "It would be helpful if you removed the broken traffic signals and power cables from my warhull and turrets. If I need to enter combat, they are likely to foul some of my smaller gun systems."

Phil peers dubiously upwards. "How'm I gonna get all the way up there?"

"Do you know how to climb a ladder?"

"Well, yeah, but I ain't got a fuckin' ladder that tall."

Sarcasm is clearly wasted on my new "engineer." I explain, as patiently as I can, and am admittedly less than successful. "There are ladders built into my fenders and warhull. You will need to climb up them. There are railings and handholds that will allow you to climb across my turrets, prow, and stern. If you are reasonably careful, you will not fall off and crack your skull open on the plascrete floor. I would suggest bringing with you a set of heavy cable cutters, so you won't have to climb down, find them, and climb back up again. You might find this tiring."

Phil blinks up at me, then pulls his face into a scowl. His octopus solidifies into a squat, blockish maroon blob obscuring half his face while simultaneously—through some arcane alchemy of facial expression interacting with the nano-tattoo—conveys bullish obstinacy. "I ain't gonna get tired climbing up a couple a goddamn ladders. Lemme find some cable cutters. You got any idea where I can lay hands on somethin' like that? They never sent me no equipment, they just shoved me in a aircab and said t' come out here. You gonna shoot me if I go rummagin' around in the tool bins?" *He is craning his neck around to study the immense wall space of my maintenance depot's interior.* "Where *are* the fuckin' tool bins? The trade school shop never had nothin' like this stuff." *He jerks his nano-tattooed head toward the high-tech equipment racks and ammunition storage bays lining the walls.*

I console myself with the thought that he is, at least, not particularly afraid of me. Unsure that I should find consolation in this fact, I guide him step by baby step through the process of locating cable cutters and guiding him to the access ladders on my near fender. Despite his boasts, my new mechanic is huffing badly before he has climbed halfway up my warhull.

"Remind me," *he says, breathing heavily,* "t' stop smokin' fryweed."

I am unfamiliar with this combustible and suspect I should be alarmed that someone who enjoys it now possesses the security clearance necessary to tinker with my internal circuitry. It takes Phil three hours of clambering, swearing, snipping, and jerking on snarled cables to free me from my macabre netting. By the time he has completed the chore, his natural skin is as red and blotchy as the crimson nano-tattoo on his face, which has taken on the appearance of a mottled egg recently fried in ketchup.

He manages to complete the task, tossing the debris to the floor where the traffic fixtures shatter—creating a secondary mess that he will have to clean up—and eventually descends to the floor again without falling or breaking any major bones. I suspect this is one of the most sterling achievements of his life. I fear that I face a very unpleasant future and can see no way in which to materially improve the situation.

Phil rearranges sweat on his face with an arm that is equally soaked and says, "Whew, that's one pile o' shit I cleaned off you. Where'm I supposed to put it, now I got it off?"

I answer truthfully. "I have no idea."

Oddly enough, he brightens, beaming up at my forward turret. "Hey, that's great news! Must be a couple hundred, at least, in the salvage price them cables and connections and stuff would bring on the tech market. I gotta borrow my sister's truck or somethin' to haul 'em off, t'morrow. Got a couple a guys oughta give me a good deal on 'em. Maybe even enough t'get the nano-tatt for the other side of my face!"

I decide against pointing out that selling the power cables and traffic signals qualifies as theft of government property. I seriously doubt it would make the slightest difference to his plans. At the very least, I suspect Phil Fabrizio will rarely be boring. It is even possible that his scrounging habits may one day be useful. This is little enough to hope for, but in a resource-poor situation that has all the hallmarks of worsening substantially during the next few years, one takes what hope one can, wherever one finds it, and does one's best.

That is what Bolos are programmed to do.

Chapter Eighteen

I

Kafari massaged the crick in her neck muscles, concentrating on the lines of code she was scanning. She was looking for the glitch that had caused a replacement module in the Ziva Two cargo controller to assign the inbound *Star of Mali* docking fees eighteen times the correct rate.

That glitch had sent the *Star*'s captain into an apoplectic fit. Freighters were required to pay the estimated docking and restocking fees in advance, with any difference credited back upon departure. She'd spent a quarter of an hour just soothing the irate woman's seriously frazzled temper, while the *Star* was inbound on a cross-system transit from the jump-point. Freighter captains were learning that technical service on Ziva Two—or anywhere else on Jefferson—was generally not up to snuff. In some cases, it was downright life-and-livelihood threatening.

That disastrous state of affairs was due to POPPA's replacement of critical station personnel with crews more

ideologically acceptable. Jobs on Ziva Two were handed
out like ripe plums, these days, as a reward to loyal
supporters of the cause. POPPA's upper echelon hadn't
shown the slightest concern that the men and women
they were rewarding were incompetent.

What they did very well, however, was scan cargo
for contraband, levy staggering fines, and skim right
off the top, helping themselves to substantial portions
of the fines collected and appropriating "contraband"
passing through the station in both directions. More
than one irate captain had threatened to drop the Jefferson route, entirely. Scuttlebutt held that POPPA had
paid some pretty hefty "incentive fees" to keep the
freighters running.

Kafari had finally said, "Look, my cousin Stefano Soteris
is one of your crewmen. Ask Stefano what it means when
Kafari Khrustinova gives her personal word of honor that
this error *will* be fixed."

"I'll do that," Captain Aditi said in a voice as cold as
interstellar vacuum.

Eight minutes later, a vastly calmer captain called
again, with a look in her eyes that made Kafari wonder
just what Cousin Stefano had been saying. "Mrs. Khrustinova, you have my apology, ma'am. I'll be waiting to
hear from you."

"Thank you, Captain. I'll be in touch."

Her chrono read 4:38 P.M. when Kafari spotted what
looked like the trouble with the module's controlling code.
"Aha! Gotcha, you wriggly little beast."

She rattled keys, uttered voice commands, and punched
"send." The Ziva Two Module in orbit hummed and spat
back an answer. "Yes!" Kafari crowed. The docking fees
switched to exactly what they were supposed to read. She
informed Captain Aditi, who ran a hand through her short
hair and said, "Honey, I don't know how you did it, but
you've got my thanks. I don't fly this bird for some big
trade cartel, this is *my* ship. It's got all my money in it,
and between you, me, and the fencepost, trying to pay
that fee would've run me so far into the red, I'd never

get another license to dock at Ziva Two. Not with what's in my cash reserves."

"Understood, Captain. I'm just glad I could be of some service."

"Honey, 'some service' is telling a customer, 'I typed your request into the maintenance logbook, where it will be reviewed by our computer intelligence system.' What you did, angel, was save my job, my ship, and my grandkids' inheritance. You want something, child, you just ask for it, you understand me?"

"Yes, I do," Kafari smiled. "And thanks, I'll keep you in mind."

She was starting to close up her office, ready to head home, when her wrist-comm beeped. She touched controls. "Kafari Khrustinova."

"Turn on the news," her father's voice said, harsh with anger. "Dinny Ghamal's been arrested."

"*What?*" She whipped around to her computer, found a newsflash headline that screamed, *Granger terrorists massacre peaceful demonstrators!* Her gut constricted so painfully, her breath expelled with an audible whoosh. "Oh, my God . . ."

Kafari knew the house, had stopped a couple of times, on her way home from work, to visit Dinny and Aisha and Emmeline Ghamal. It was the PSF barracks house operated by the Hancock Family Cooperative, on the Adero floodplain. The Hancock family members were among the most decent, honest people anywhere on Jefferson. What could possibly have gone wrong, for an accusation like that to be thrown at them?

The farmyard was full of emergency vehicles, most of them bearing the emblem of the infamous federal police force known colloquially as P-Squads. Men in coroners' uniforms were carrying out body bags. Lots of them. Pol Jankovitch was putting on a great show for his spectators, flashing photographs of fifteen victims, all of whom looked like school children. Pol, whose performance tottered back and forth across a line between stern outrage and hushed grief, was saying, " . . . peaceful protestors, just ordinary boys anxious to focus public attention on the farm crisis. All they wanted to do was show people the truth about food hoarding. They didn't even have to drive far from home to prove their point.

"This house," he pointed toward the almost military-style barracks the Hancock Family Cooperative had been forced to rent at premium rates, "is part of a government-owned Populist Support Farm just three and a half kilometers from Port Town. The poorest children on Jefferson live next door to farms like this one, where barns are bulging with high-quality food those children will never see."

You buggering snake! She closed her hands around the edge of her desk, so tightly her palms hurt. The Hancock family—like thousands of other Grangers forced into the Populist Support Farm System—worked under slave-labor conditions on PSF before trudging home to put in more hours working their own land. Not one ounce of PSF food went into a Granger's mouth. They ate only the food they could grow on their own land, unless they wanted to risk prison and rehab. If PSF food wasn't being distributed to the poor, Kafari wanted to know just who the hell *was* getting it.

She clicked through coverage from every major broadcasting company on Jefferson, just to ground herself in the official version of things. Then she went to Anish Balin's *Sounding the Alarm* datachat. Rather, she *tried* to go there. It took nearly five full minutes to gain access, which told her a great deal about the number of people trying to get in. Anish Balin's hard-hitting and argumentative style had drawn a lot of fire, even amongst the Granger community. People who worried about Grangers' public image and reprisals were afraid of someone as outspoken and seemingly paranoid as the self-styled Fearless Firebrand.

When she finally got in, the whole screen lit up with two brutal words: *FIRST LIE!*

Thirty photographs popped up, in two columns. The left-hand side showed the same images Pol Jankovitch and the other sludge slingers were distributing. The right-hand column showed a different set of photographs. On the left were fifteen boys. Kids with hardened, street-tough faces, but obviously no more than twelve or thirteen years old. On the right, were fifteen corresponding young men, husky with adult musculature, sporting moustaches, nano-tatts, and lip-plugs. The youngest was, at a bare minimum, twenty-two or twenty-three. It was clear that these were, in fact, the same individuals. You could see it in bone structure, the placement and angle of ears, the shape and cleft of chins. "First lie" was right. Pol Jankovitch's "peaceful protestors" and "ordinary boys" were a *decade* older than the photos he was plastering all over his broadcast. When the screen auto-faded to the next page, which screamed *SECOND LIE!* Kafari's shock gave way to jaw-crunching rage.

Since the Hancock Family Co-op was large enough to have more than a dozen children under the age of two, POPPA had installed security cameras throughout the PSF barracks to ensure the "safety and social welfare" of the toddlers and infants while their parents worked in the government's fields and barns. Such cameras were standard features at PSF "homes" throughout Jefferson, auto-programmed to begin recording whenever motion and sound sensors determined that a PSF crew had arrived to log their mandatory fifty hours a week in public fields.

Those cameras had been running when Pol Jankovitch's "protestors" burst into the house. Anish Balin had managed to hack into the PSF security system, downloading the video before the P-Squads got there. He was replaying it in a perpetual loop. The security cameras—three of them, one covering the mess hall and kitchen, one covering the nursery and play area, and one covering the sleeping dormitory—caught the confusion and screams caused by fifteen grown men literally kicking the door off its hinges. The gutter patois they started shouting identified them instantly as members of a Port Town rat-gang. So called for their habit of preying on "space rats"—freighter crews who operated the cargo shuttles between spacedock at Ziva Two and Port Abraham—they were the most vicious urban criminals ever bred on Jefferson, although the P-Squads occasionally gave them a good run for the money.

The rat-gang burst into the house, wearing masks and brandishing weapons. The only people in the house were grandmothers and little ones too young for federally mandated daycare. The gang rounded everybody up and herded them into the dormitory that served as bedroom. What happened next . . .

Kafari felt sick to the basement of her soul.

The ones not busy having fun with their victims were rushing through the house, ordered by their leaders to ransack nearby storage sheds and barns and raid the vegetable plots and smokehouse, looting everything that looked remotely edible or valuable enough to sell. Kafari's breath caught when she recognized Aisha Ghamal.

The camera revealed what the rat-gangers hadn't seen—she'd managed to key an emergency alarm on her wrist-comm without being seen by her captors, sending a distress call to the planetary emergency system. Anish Balin had managed to download the official response to that emergency call: a recording that said, "All local law enforcement agents are busy. Your complaint will be forwarded to the appropriate department in charge of vandalism and petty theft. Have a nice day."

Two and a half minutes after that message went out, rat-gangers who'd been looting outside burst back into the house, yelling a warning at their friends. Zippers went up in haste as they broke out windows to shoot at targets outside. Aisha's message had gone out to family members in the fields, as well as the police.

In the confusion that erupted, with rat-gangers firing through the windows, dodging back to avoid return fire and reloading their weapons, Aisha Ghamal dove under a barracks-room bed, knocking it over with a crash. She came up with a handgun concealed under the bed frame. She fired repeatedly, taking down two of the men at the windows. Most of the gang scattered, diving for cover, but one of the bastards stood his ground. They centered one another simultaneously. Aisha beat him to the trigger pull—

—and her gun just clicked. She'd shot it dry.

"Fuckin' *jomo* bitch!" he snarled. Then he shot her, high in the chest. She spun and dropped, going down with a gasping cry of pain and a spattering of blood across her dress, the overturned bed, the wall. She hit the floor just as the door burst open. The men and women shooting their way into the house showed no mercy. Cold hatred had turned their faces to stone. They were beyond angry, beyond anything human. POPPA had worked them nearly to death, had confiscated their crops, their money, in some cases their land.

And now a stinking rat-gang had smashed its way into their lives, bent on torture and destruction. The Hancock adults fired and fired and fired, shooting every single member of the gang, pumping extra rounds into anyone whose fingers even twitched around a weapon. Kafari sat with the back of her hand pressed against her lips, shaking and crying at the slaughter on screen.

She recognized Dinny Ghamal, recognized his new bride, Emmeline, a sweet girl who thought the sun rose and set in her husband—an opinion that was, in Kafari's opinion, fully justified. Dinny rushed to his mother's side. Aisha was alive, but badly injured and lying in a spreading pool of blood. Someone was shouting "Call the police! Call for ambulances!" while others got the children out of the killing zone.

One of the Hancock women, her face more dead than alive, crouched over a child who wasn't moving. Another woman was talking to her, trying to get her to let go of the child. She stood up with an abrupt, jerking motion and reloaded her pistol. Then administered head-shots to every rat-ganger still twitching on the floor. When she tried to turn the gun on herself, one of the Hancock men wrestled the weapon out of her hands and led her out of the room.

There wasn't that much more to see. The first police

to arrive were local beat-cops used to patrolling in Port Town. They seemed inclined to help the Hancocks dig trench graves and bury the perpetrators without any further fuss. Then the P-Squads arrived and the situation slid off the edge of a cliff. The officer who stood out in Kafari's mind, blazing like the neon in far-away Vishnu's Copper Town shopping arcades, was a cold-eyed brute by the name of Yuri Lokkis. He ordered the arrest of every man, woman, and child on the farm, then spoke to the press while P-Squad vans transported the prisoners—including those critically wounded—off-site, presumably to one of the P-Squad interrogation centers like the main Intelligence Office on Nineveh Base.

Lokkis, his crisp uniform pristine in the afternoon sunlight, told a host of press cameras, "The so-called Hancock Family is nothing more than a militant and subversive cult masquerading as a legitimate organization. This cult preaches selective hatred, teaches helpless, innocent children that violence is a viable solution to disagreements, preaches opposition to the just and fair distribution of critical food supplies, and has just demonstrated utter contempt for human life.

"Fifteen promising young boys, trying to pull themselves out of grinding poverty, were conducting a legitimate social protest, trying to bring attention to the deplorable conditions rampant in the spaceport's environs, trying valiantly to point out the cruelty the agrarian interests have displayed by building lush farms with plenty of food literally within sight of starving children. Those promising young boys were murdered, *executed* in cold blood. Why? For daring to express their civic outrage at the injustice of flaunting wealth and plenty in front of those who have been hardest hit by the economic injustices endured by our citizens!

"I will never forget the brutal loss of these boys. I will not rest until the perpetrators of this ghastly crime have been tried and convicted for their brutality. Good citizens everywhere need to remember one thing: these agrarian terrorists are cult fanatics at heart. They are agri-CULT-urists. And they will not rest until they have destroyed our urban heritage and our precious right to live as civilized beings."

She had to switch it off. Kafari was shaking so hard, she could barely control her fingers. This was wrong, it was monstrously wrong. Surely people would realize POPPA had gone too far, this time? The Hancock family had been attacked without mercy, abandoned by the police, left with no resources but their own. They had rescued elderly women and babies under the age of two from hardened criminals. Surely even the Subbies, who expected someone else to feed them and pay for their every whim, would understand that?

She got her first glimpse of how unlikely that was, when she got home to find Yalena glued to the data-screen, watching the news coverage instead of doing her homework. Kafari stood in the doorway of their Madison apartment for long minutes, watching her daughter's face. Yalena was clearly avid for the so-called "facts" the mainstream press was handing out. Watching the child she and Simon had made together, a child POPPA had enslaved like so much chattel, Kafari didn't know how much longer she could bear to remain here.

Yalena looked more and more like a lost cause. At fifteen, there wasn't a single bone in the girl's body that didn't belong utterly and irrevocably to Vittori Santorini. She wore her hair the way Nassiona Santorini did. Wore the kind of clothes Isanah Renke had made so wildly popular. Wallpapered her bedroom with pages of the POPPA Manifesto. Listened to POPPA musicians and watched every film that had ever been made by Mira-belle Caresse and Lev Bellamy, the hottest movie stars in Jefferson's history, who made more in one film than most Subbies would see in a lifetime.

Mirabelle, a long-legged, wafer-thin beauty with a sultry voice, graced the talk-show circuit with such profound pronouncements as "anyone who thinks it's all right to pick up a weapon clearly needs psychiatric adjustment" and "eating is not only a social faux pas, it's the grossest insult possible to the poor and disadvantaged of this world." Most of the poor, of course, weighed two or three times what the actress did, since eating was their second favorite pastime, right after making little carbon copies of themselves. Leverett Bellamy was her favorite leading man, who'd made his reputation and fortune portraying tough urban war heroes, fighting the Deng street to street in Madison, in films that bore no resemblance to the actual war or the people who'd fought it.

Kafari closed the apartment door and locked it, then walked quietly into the kitchen and started their dinner. Yalena could not be cajoled, coerced, or persuaded into doing anything so menial and disempowering as performing manual labor like cooking or washing dirty dishes. She was too busy raising her consciousness and communing with her friends over the "in" cause of the week. Her fingernails were perfect, her ability to quote the Manifesto flawless, and her brain resembled a well-used sieve, totally devoid of content.

The day Yalena turned eighteen—relieving Kafari of any further moral obligation to provide housing, food, and clothing—she was putting herself onto the next freighter to Vishnu, even if she had to smuggle herself aboard as cargo. It galled, to admit such utter defeat, but she had tried everything. She and her family had racked their brains, thinking up things to do, and none of it had made the slightest dent in the girl's misguided, ill-considered, unholy convictions. *I'm sorry Simon,* she found herself saying over and over as she pulled bags and boxes out of the freezer, very nearly blinded by the saltwater pouring down her face, *I'm sorry, hon, I've lost her and I don't think anything will ever shock her enough to get her back . . .*

When Yalena bounced into the kitchen for a glass of soda, she looked at Kafari and said, "Sheesh, Mom, why don't you peel the onions under cold water, or something?"

Kafari bit down on it. Held the rage in her teeth. Gripped the frying pan and spatula in her hands so hard, the bones creaked and the spatula's handle bent. When the danger was mostly past, she turned and hissed, "Dish it up, yourself, when the timer goes off. I'm not hungry enough to eat in the same room with you."

Yalena actually recoiled a step, meeting her gaze with wide and stunned eyes. Kafari stalked past, peripherally aware that her daughter scuttled sideways, out of her way. Kafari slammed her bedroom door shut and twisted the lock, then threw herself onto her cold and empty bed and wept from the bottom of her aching, broken heart. When the worst of the long-suppressed storm had passed, she heard a tiny tapping on her door.

"Mom?"

"Go away!"

The tapping stopped. A few minutes later, it returned. "Mom? Are you okay?"

"*No!*"

"Do you need a doctor?"

Kafari tightened her fingers through the bedding to stop herself from flinging the door wide and throwing Yalena out of the apartment by the seat of her fashionable pants. She finally mastered the blind rage sufficiently to open the door. Yalena hovered outside.

"Do you need a doctor?" Yalena asked again, voice faltering under the stare Kafari leveled at her.

"What I *need* is a daughter with a brain. Unless you can provide me with one, I strongly suggest you take yourself out of my way for the next few days. Is that simple enough for even you to understand? Or do I have to spell it out in barracks-room language?"

"But—what did I *do*? All I said was to cut the onions under running water."

Yalena didn't know. She honest-to-God didn't know. Kafari was in far too dangerous an emotional state to enlighten her. "The less I say right now, the safer both of us will be. I would suggest that you do your homework. You might start by trying to discover what *really* happened today at the Hancock Family's barracks."

"This is about *Grangers*? A bunch of crazy deviants

who massacred fifteen innocent boys just because they were staging a protest? Those boys were my age! Not even in high school, yet. My God, Mom, I know you're a Granger, but how could you possibly defend that pack of murdering farmers?"

Kafari—remembering a boy with a broken arm and a shotgun, shooting into a barn full of Deng and Asali bees, remembering a woman who'd flung open her door in the teeth of Yavac fire, risking her life to offer them shelter when it would've been safer to just run for the cellar—clenched both fists. Kafari was so violently angry, she was literally shaking with the need to contain it.

Yalena, correctly reading the threat in her eyes, hissed, "You wouldn't *dare* lay hands on me!"

It was a close thing, very close, to homicide.

Yalena misinterpreted her hesitation and started to laugh. "You're so pathetic, Mom. You and all the other pig farmers—"

Kafari slapped her.

Hard enough to bruise. Yalena's eyes widened in shock. She lifted one hand to her cheek in stunned disbelief. "You—you hit me!"

"And you damned well deserved it!"

"But—but—you *hit* me!"

The "why?" hadn't even formed, yet. Her mind was still too stunned by the abrupt reordering of her reality.

"I should've turned you over my knee years ago. It's high time you got off that bigoted, lazy little backside of yours and learned some civilized manners. Not to mention a few critical lessons in reality."

"*Bigoted?*" Yalena shrieked. "I'm not bigoted! I'm a member of POPPA! Have you even bothered to *read* the Manifesto? It's filled with beautiful ideas like economic justice and social parity and respect for the civil rights of living creatures! It's built on the latest, most scientifically advanced social science in human space! And I believe in it, I *live* by it! How *dare* you accuse me of bigotry?"

"Because you don't have the brains God gave a radish! Let's just take a look at those high and fine-sounding ideals, shall we? Then I'll explain to you a little thing called reality. The POPPA Manifesto preaches equality and respect for everyone, doesn't it? On page after page. Vittori Santorini's little masterpiece gushes endlessly about everyone deserving love and happiness. That everyone's entitled to their fair share of the planet's wealth, that nobody is better than anybody else and nobody should be allowed to harm others. Tolerance and fairness for every man, woman, child on Jefferson—*unless they're farmers!*"

The whiplash in her voice was so sharp, her daughter actually jumped.

Then her eyes widened with the dawning realization that she had not, in fact, accorded farmers the same social rights she thought everyone else deserved. For the first time in her life, Yalena was staring into an undistorted mirror. Given the look on her face, she didn't like what she saw. It was rarely pleasant when one heard an ugly little truth about themselves, particularly when they couldn't justify it under their own rules of conduct.

Kafari shoved the mirror a little closer to Yalena's face. "I have watched you spend *hours* defending the rights of leaf-cutting caterpillars, but by God, let a human being disagree with you on *anything* and you label them as subhuman deviants. Where's the tolerance in that nasty little game? If someone dares to hold a different opinion, you treat them like animals. *Worse* than animals, which you've put on a pedestal and all but worshiped as gods, while behaving as though people who grow food are unfit to go on breathing. I dare you to deny it. I don't think you can.

"But what you pulled out there," she jabbed a finger at the living room, where Pol Jankovitch was still jabbering away on the datascreen, "was the ugliest thing I've ever seen you do. You sat there and *gloated* over the arrest of people you've never met. People the government has turned into literal, legal *slaves,* forcing them to work without pay on government-owned land, growing the food on *your* dinner plate! If they refuse or even complain, they're thrown into *prison.* You want to show me where to find the equality, respect, or fairness in that? I don't see it. And I don't think you do, either, because it's not there to be seen, not by you or me or anybody else.

"And let me make one other point, lest you think this is merely an academic exercise in rhetoric. I wasn't chopping onions when you walked into the kitchen. Two of those 'pig-farming deviants' you despise so much are dear friends of mine, with more courage and integrity than you will ever possess. When Dinny Ghamal was only twelve years old—*twelve,* damn you!—he watched Deng troopers murder his father and brothers right in front of him. His mother risked her life to open her front door so President Lendan and I could run to safety in her house. We'd no more than skidded through the doorway when the Deng shot out the front wall, ripping Aisha's back open with flying debris. We jumped into their basement while Yavacs literally blew the house apart on top of us."

Yalena's mouth fell open.

"The broadcasters haven't mentioned any of those facts, have they? You want to know why? Because misbegotten, silver-tongued snakes like Pol Jankovitch aren't telling you. He makes his living lying through his teeth and lining his pockets with POPPA's cold, hard cash. And of course a good little POPPA puppet like you wouldn't dream of signing onto the datanet to find out the truth for yourself. That might require actual *work.* If you can be bothered to work up a sweat, check the Granger datachats, starting with Anish Balin's. But be damned careful if you do, because you just might learn something.

"I suggest you bear one final thing in mind. POPPA can guarantee your right to say what you like. But that sword cuts both ways. When you're talking to *me,* you may be damned sure that bigotry will *always* get what it deserves. If you don't like it, go live somewhere else!"

Kafari stalked out, too furious to care that she, herself, was risking prison time and a "reeducation" sentence. She slammed her way out of the house, not even sure where she was going until she found herself in the aircar, heading for home. The only home she had left. Her mother, recognizing the car as she set down on the landing pad, took one look at her face and said, "You finally belt that brat like she's been needing?"

Kafari said, rather stupidly, "How did you know?"

Then burst into tears.

Her mother guided her into the house. She was so blinded by salt water, she couldn't even see what her feet were stumbling over. Then she was on the sofa, with her mother's arms around her. She huddled against a warm, safe shoulder while her mother rocked her. Fifteen years of fear came pouring out, mixed up with two agonizing years alone, trying to raise a hellion with a poisoned mind while Simon was on Vishnu, learning how to walk, again.

When Kafari's paroxysm of grief finally eased, her father appeared with a tumbler of Scotch. She was trembling so badly she couldn't even hold the glass. "Steady," her father said quietly, holding the rim to her lips. She gulped the burning stuff down. It helped. Or maybe the fire in her throat and gullet just distracted her enough to regain control of herself. Her mother was brushing wet hair back from Kafari's face, drying the tears with one corner of the apron she'd worn every day of Kafari's life. Kafari hadn't realized how much silver there was in her mother's hair, how deep the sun-plowed furrows in her father's face had become.

She met her mother's worried gaze. "Was I *ever* as much trouble as Yalena is?"

The twinkle in her mother's eyes surprised her. "Oh, no. That must come from her father's side. Eh, Zak?" She winked at her husband, who grumbled, "Well, I mind the time you set fire to the pearl shed, and the day you pushed young Regis Blackpole out of the dairy-barn loft and I had to pay for his crowns and bridgework, and the note we got from Vishnu, that you'd landed in the hospital with *kraali* fever, and of course there were those worrisome days when you were sleeping with an

off-world stranger and hadn't made up your mind yet
to marry him . . ."

Kafari let out an indignant snort. Then bit one lip.
"Mom, Dad . . . what am I going to do?"

"What tipped the scales, today?"

She told them. Zak Camar's jaw muscles jumped. Her
mother's expression would have given a rabid *jaglitch*
pause, which gave her a fair idea what her own had
been, in the apartment.

"How bad was the snap?" her mother asked quietly.

"One slap worth's. A *hard* one. She may bruise."

Her father snorted. "She'll mend. Mind, I'm not in
favor of belting your kids. But she needed that slap, my
girl, needed it more than even you probably realize."

"And if she reports it—"

"I'll give her something else to report." Then he touched
her wet cheek with one gentle fingertip, lifted her chin
back up where it belonged. "Her father would've done
the same thing and he'd have been right, too. When a
child's been brainwashed for as long as they've had Yalena,
you can't wake 'em up with hugs and flowers."

"How do you wake them up?" Kafari asked in a low,
weary voice. "We've tried everything."

"Except slapping her," Kafari's mother said drolly. "Who
knows? Maybe she'll be so shocked, she'll go onto the
datachats and find out for herself?"

It was too hard to hope. She couldn't bear to be disappointed again. "I'd better go back," was all she said.
"There's going to be an ugly mood in town, over this.
Yalena is just young and stupid enough to go out and
be part of it."

Worry flashed in the glances her parents exchanged.
"All right," her mother said softly. "Call if you need
anything. Including a place to hide."

Kafari just nodded. Then hugged them both tightly,
wishing she didn't have to let go, again. She finally
climbed into her Airdart and headed back to town in
the gathering gloom of early evening.

II

Yalena didn't know what to do.

Her face still smarted from that shocking slap. Worse, she didn't know what to *think*. Her mother's angry revelations had stunned her far more deeply than the palm across her cheek. What if . . . She gulped. What if her mother was right? About the Hancock family? About *everything*? She realized there was one way to settle her uncertainties over the Hancock massacre.

She sat down at her datascreen and tried to get into the main Granger chats. They were jammed. So badly, she couldn't get through to the main datahub that carried several of the Granger chats. She finally set her system to auto-retry, and even that took nearly half an hour of constant attempts before her request went through.

Once in, she went straight to Anish Balin's chat. It was hard—the most difficult and painful thing she had ever done—to watch the recording. It looked genuine, not some kind of mock-up. She sat very still, scarcely breathing, as that one recording shook her carefully constructed beliefs to pieces. When her wrist-comm beeped, Yalena jumped in the chair, heart pounding. Her fingertips shook.

"Yalena," she said, scarcely recognizing the croak that emerged as her own voice.

"It's Ami-Lynn. Are you watching the news? Oh, Yalena, it's horrible! Just horrible. Those poor boys . . ."

She heard her own voice, tinny and strange, say, "Ami-Lynn, sign into Anish Balin's datachat. Just do it. Then call me back."

Twenty-three minutes later, her comm beeped again.

"Is this stuff real?" She sounded shaken, like she'd been crying, or still was.

"Yes," Yalena whispered. "I really think it is. Mom . . ." She had to gulp. "Mom knows Dinny Ghamal. And his mother. Why isn't Pol Jankovitch or anybody else telling people the truth? And nobody's mentioned that Dinny and his mother helped save President Lendan's life, during the war. They got Presidential Medallions. So did my mom. Ami-Lynn, I'm going downtown. There's a Granger protest march, this afternoon. I want to find out the truth. And I want to talk to some Grangers, ask them . . . I don't know what, exactly, but I've got to find out what's really going on."

There was a long pause, then Ami-Lynn said, "I'm going, too. And I'm going to call Charmaine."

"You don't have to—"

"I know I don't. And I probably shouldn't. My parents would throw a fit and ground me for a year. But I don't like this, Yalena. I don't like it and I don't understand it and I'm scared to death of what I might find out. But I've got to know the truth. So do you. And so will Charmaine."

Yalena drew a deep, uneasy breath. "Okay. Where do you want to meet up?"

"It's going to be crowded, down there. How about we meet up at Charmaine's house? She's pretty close to the downtown."

"Good idea. I'll meet you there."

Yalena turned off her datascreen, made sure her wrist-comm was securely fastened, then pulled her scooter out, locked up the apartment, and headed for Charmaine's house. She had no idea what she was about to find out. She didn't have the slightest clue as to what she would do about it, if her mother and that security tape were right. Her mother still insisted that POPPA had sabotaged her father's aircar, trying to kill him with that crash. Yalena had refused to believe it. Still didn't want to believe it. But she was no longer a trusting baby, either.

One way or another, Yalena intended to find out.

Chapter Nineteen

I

Trouble has erupted again.

At 2030 hours, I receive an urgent call from President Zeloc, who does not bother to go through Sar Gremian, this time. Given the disturbance I am tracking through the heart of Madison, by way of law-enforcement broadcasts and news crews, his wild-eyed demeanor is not surprising. His order is no more than I expected to hear.

"Get yourself into town, machine! Now! We've got armed insurrection in the streets!"

I have been scanning all law enforcement, military, and commercial transmissions for the past sixty minutes. A massive Granger protest march is underway, demanding the immediate release of the Hancock Family detainees and opposing the wild demands for weapons confiscation, which the Senate and House of Law have already introduced, less than two hours after the violence at the PSF barracks near Port Town. I see no evidence of Grangers participating in armed rebellion, but the political demonstration underway has rapidly devolved into another explosive riot.

Police units are attempting to clear the protestors, using methods that qualify as brutal under any civilized standard of law-enforcement. The violence has spilled into the streets surrounding Assembly Hall, as urban counterprotestors put in their own appearance, blocking the retreat of the Grangers. From what I have been able to see, most of the Grangers are simply trying to get away from the truncheons and riot-bombs hurled at them by federal police. Those police have not used the paralytic agents that the ill-fated President Andrews used to disperse POPPA rioters sixteen years ago, but they are using what appears to be retch gas, as well as the more ubiquitous tear gas.

Caught between hammer and anvil, many of the Grangers have started tearing up anything that can be used as a weapon, smashing store windows to obtain broken glass and impromptu clubs from the merchandise behind them, tearing down street signs to use as shields, hurling stones and bricks and refuse cannisters at their attackers. With the riot shifting straight toward the Presidential Residence—which is virtually undefended, since most of the city's law enforcement officials were stationed at Assembly Hall to guard the Joint Assembly—the current state of affairs has sufficiently alarmed President Zeloc that he has put through a frantic call to me.

Despite the fact that Gifre Zeloc did nothing to prevent the violence gripping Madison today, the situation must be contained and I am apparently the only force sufficient to disperse a crowd of this size. I therefore leave Phil Fabrizio puttering in my maintenance depot, where he is attempting to learn the use of the major tools of his new trade. I clear the edge of Nineveh Base and enter the city, once again seriously hampered by the presence of panic-stricken motorists and pedestrians. I order the city's psychotronic electric power controller to shut down the grid, only to discover that I have been locked out of the system.

I cannot order the city's computers to turn off the grid. This leaves live power lines dancing wildly through each intersection I traverse, inevitably clipping newly installed cables and dragging down newly replaced traffic signals as I maneuver my bulk through the narrow spaces. It is an expensive business, ordering me to perform riot-control duties at the heart of a city. I broadcast warnings, ordering vehicles and pedestrians out of the way. I am still eleven blocks away when receive a second urgent call from Gifre Zeloc.

"What's taking you so long? Speed up, dammit! Those murderous bastards are practically spilling onto the lawn outside my window! They're armed like soldiers, out there. They're in open rebellion, and you're poking along at a goddamned *crawl!*"

"I am not authorized to inflict the kind of collateral damage to civilians that would occur if I were to increase my speed. I have avoided crushing anyone thus far, but I cannot maintain that if I am required to transit streets and intersections more rapidly."

"You're not paid to be a Good Samaritan! And your caution won't do me a hell of a lot of good, if you get here too late! Speed up. I want you here *yesterday!*"

This is an impossible command, since no Bolo ever built can reverse the flow of time. I have been given an order, however, to proceed more rapidly against an armed enemy. When I tap police cameras, I do, in fact, see actual weaponry in the hands of rioters. Whether these guns were stolen from stores along the way or smuggled into Madison is irrelevant. The situation has altered from one of mere riot-clearance duty.

"If I am to engage an armed enemy, I need to assume full Battle Reflex Alert status."

Gifre Zeloc scowls into his data screen. "The last thing I need is a Bolo shooting up downtown Madison! Just drive in here and flatten them. That'll teach the whole dirty pack of 'em the lesson they need. After today, they'll damned well *know* I won't tolerate armed arrogance."

I attempt to educate the man issuing my instructions.

"Without my full battlefield cognitive functions, there is a serious risk of miscalculation—"

"I gave you an order, machine. Shut up and carry it out! If that's not too much for an antique rust bucket to understand."

The transmission ends.

The sensations skittering through my personality gestalt center resolve themselves into bitter, affronted anger. I have never been treated with such blatant contempt in the entire one hundred fifteen point nine-seven years of my active service. I am programmed to take pride in my accomplishments and my devoted service to my creators. Humans have often shown fear of me. This is logical, given what I am capable of doing. But not one human has ever shown me contempt.

I have no referents for dealing with the conflicts this arouses in my personality gestalt center. The blow to pride and prestige literally stuns me for six point nine-three seconds, an eternity of shock. Even as antiques, we are immensely capable machines, commanding the respect of those giving our orders. Is Gifre Zeloc the exception or the rule amongst Jefferson's new ruling class?

Ultimately, the answer is immaterial, as applied to the current mission. I speed up, although this results in an increased level of carnage as I crush cars abandoned by screaming passengers and turn corners too quickly for the terrain, taking off entire corners of buildings in the process and spilling rubble from ruptured walls in my wake.

I encounter the edge of the riot zone just as Gifre Zeloc starts screaming at me again through his comm-link. "They're battering down the gates! I don't care how many of them you have to crush to get here, just stop them!"

Hundreds of people dressed as Grangers are spilling against the ornate scrollwork fencing. Those not carrying rifles and handguns are ripping iron stanchions out of the fence. They are shooting at anything and anyone that appears to be a threat. Gifre Zeloc is the legally elected head of Jefferson's government. Jefferson is a Concordiat-allied world, for which President Zeloc speaks as the official voice of the Concordiat. He acts as the Concordiat's officially designated commander. His life is in immediate and clear danger. The mob attempting to enter the grounds of the Presidential Residence can offer no harm to me, so I do not go to Battle Reflex Mode and do not engage my own weapons systems. But there is sufficient danger to the president that collateral damage to civilians is acceptable. I therefore broadcast a warning to the crowd, engage drive engines, and move forward, plowing through the jam-packed crowd blocking Darconi Street. I do not count the number of people who die beneath my treads. I have no wish to count them. My mission has been narrowly and explicitly defined. I turn off external audio sensors, unwilling to listen to the screams of those I have been ordered to crush on my way to the gates of the Presidential Residence.

I am fifty-three meters away from the gates when the entire scrollwork fence sways and goes down, pushed over by the panic-stricken crowd trying to escape. A massive wave of people spills across the Presidential Residence's lawn. Within two point zero-three seconds, the crowd engulfs the Residence. A substantial portion of the mob simply spills around it, intent on running as far and as fast as possible now that they have gained a space in which to run. Others, however, enter the Residence, intent on retribution. I cannot penetrate the walls deeply enough, even using ground-penetrating radar, to track their progress inside the Residency walls. I can, however, monitor the windows and do so, focusing on the massive round window of the president's office and smaller windows to either side, that reveal the interiors of adjacent rooms and the corridors beyond.

Gifre Zeloc has barricaded himself in his office, which overlooks the war-torn gardens. I do not know the location of the vice president. A mob of battle-enraged Grangers, clearly visible through adjacent windows, storms the corridor outside the president's office. I take immediate action. Snapping to full Battle Reflex Alert, I target through the Residency's outer stone shell, allowing for proper lead-time on a moving target, and fire 30cm cannons. The rounds punch through the walls and windows with satisfactory ease. I rake the mob inside the Residence with short bursts, taking down those in the leading edge first. This serves to create a barricade that others must either jump across or retreat from—or join, should they continue to exhibit hostile action.

The Grangers near the back of the mob inside the Residence hit the floor. Most of them drop their weapons as I send more live rounds through their ranks. They attempt to crawl back the way they came, leaving their weapons behind. I allow this, as their retreat does not endanger the president. I judge him to be safe from further assault—

Gifre Zeloc picks up a heavy chair and throws it through the window behind his desk. Glass shatters and falls to the garden below, where the mob from Darconi Street is still pouring across the downed fence and surging into the lawn ahead of my treads. Evidently panicked by the gunfire seven meters south of his office, he commits the most breathtakingly stupid act I have ever witnessed. Gifre Zeloc actually jumps out the window. He lands in the midst of a tight-packed mob of Grangers. I cannot fire without hitting him.

Seven point two seconds later, there is no longer a reason to fire. Gifre Zeloc has been reduced to a pulpy red mass under the clubs and feet of people pushed past break-point. A fire begins to blaze inside the Residence. The streets are too choked with debris and fleeing rioters for fire and rescue squads to reach the Residence, which begins to burn fiercely. I halt in stunned disbelief, with my treads zero point eight meters from the downed gates of the Presidential Residence.

He jumped.

He actually jumped into the middle of a blood-crazed mob of people with excellent reason to hate him. I see no further point in shooting into the crowd, which is a hopelessly tangled mixture of Grangers and urban counterprotestors, all of them intent on one goal: escape. Without a lawfully elected president to issue directives, I am left to make my own decisions, rendering me temporarily immobilized. I have, for the moment, full access to my Battle Reflex Alert logic processors, but even fully awake, I do not know what to do.

If this were a battle against Deng Yavacs or even the Quern, my duty would be clear. I would fight the enemy with every weapon I carry until the enemy was destroyed or I was. But I do not know what action to take in the aftermath of a riot that has claimed the life of the only civilian authorized to issue instructions to me. Perhaps, if I were human, my task would be clearer? I might mobilize the remnants of Jefferson's military forces. I might seek to impose a martial-law curfew after clearing the streets. I might order the Senate and House of Law cleared and the Assembly members escorted to a safe shelter.

I am a Bolo. I do not have the authority to do any of these things. I cannot even instruct the city's psychotronic system to turn off the power grid. A scan of the city behind my stern shows rising columns of smoke where fires have broken out in the wake of my passage. This is a dreadful situation. I have no idea what to do. I consider contacting the Brigade for help, but am unsure Sector Command would be able to offer any useful—let alone timely—advice on how to resolve a volatile situation on a world that is no longer of concern to most of the Brigade's command structure.

I am on my own.

And I do not like the choices facing me.

It finally occurs to me to review Jefferson's constitution to discover the chain of command regarding who is in line for the presidency. I must at least discover who is constitutionally authorized to make decisions in the event of a president's untimely departure from office. I do not know the whereabouts of Vice President Culver. She normally maintains an office in the Residence, but I do not know if she was in that office, which is now fiercely ablaze *despite internal fire-suppression systems, which seem to have malfunctioned.*

I put through a call to the vice presidential residence, attempting to ascertain her location, but no one responds to my signal. I theorize that they are too busy watching the fire consuming the Presidential Residence to answer something as relatively trivial as a transmission from a thirteen-thousand-ton Bolo parked across the street. The next official in line for command is the Speaker of the House of Law, the most senior position in the Assembly, with the President of the Senate coming next in the list. I check security-camera feed from the Joint Chamber, where the Assembly watches a five-meter-tall datascreen in stunned silence. The images on that datascreen show the burning Residence and my own warhull, parked atop an unknown number of dead rioters.

I tap the datafeed and address the Assembly, much of which jumps in shock at the sound of my voice issuing from the speakers. "President Zeloc has been killed. I do not know the whereabouts of Vice President Culver. There are fires burning at the Presidential Residence and in the city, where downed power cables have sparked electrical fires consuming damaged buildings. It would be advisable for the Speaker of the House of Law to assume temporary command until the whereabouts of the vice president can be established. Madame Speaker, I require instructions."

The shaken woman who has held the post of speaker for eleven years—a span of time she has enjoyed thanks to the revocation of term limits, enacted by POPPA jurists appointed to the High Court—stares at the datascreen for twelve point three seconds, speechless and pale to the roots of her carefully colored hair. She finally regains the use of her wits and her voice.

"What am I supposed to do? Who is this? Who's talking?"

"I am Unit SOL-0045 of the Jeffersonian Defense Forces. I require instructions."

"About what?"

"I am a machine of war. This situation is not the type of combat I was designed to conduct. I do not know what to do. I require instructions."

Avelaine La Roux apparently has no idea what to do, either. She stares at the gavel in her hand, stares at the stunned faces of her colleagues, swallows convulsively several times. She finally finds something to say.

"We have to find Madeline. That's the important thing, we have to find Madeline. She's the president, now. You're sure Gifre is dead?"

"He jumped into a crowd of rioters and was bludgeoned to death before I could fire on those attacking him."

A collective shudder rushes through the room, followed by a rising snarl of anger. I foresee an impending planet-wide explosion of rage that will make all prior-existing anti-Granger sentiment look like attenuated smoke on the wind, by comparison. I do not foresee a likelihood that the Grangers will accept this without a fight. I offer a suggestion. "I would advise immediate mobilization of what military forces remain in operational condition. Public sentiment will doubtless express itself violently."

"Yes," *Avelaine La Roux says, running a distracted hand through her hair, which disarranges its careful coiffeur.* "Yes, I think you're right. Uh . . . How do I do that?"

It has been sufficiently long since Jefferson had a truly operational military structure, the person third in line for the presidency does not even know how to scramble the military for a world alert. She is, in large measure, responsible for the dismantling of that military structure, insisting that tax money was more productively spent protecting the rights of the urban poor and providing a "decent living wage" for those unable or unwilling to find gainful employment.

As a result, there are insufficient military resources to step in and act as peacekeepers until tempers have cooled and public hysteria has been calmed. I am not a policeman, but I fear that I may be forced into that role, by default. This does not send joy of any kind through my personality gestalt center. Darconi Street is covered

*with blood and spilled chemicals from ruptured vehicles.
Flame and smoke blacken the skies from structural fires
and spilled fuel and solvents which burn with a characteristic, dirty smoke. Once again, the heart of Madison
resembles a war zone. This is not a war in which I am
proud to have fought.*

*For the first time in my career, I know shame for
having done my duty.*

II

Kafari was halfway to Madison, flying at the Airdart's minimum speed in an effort to compose herself,
when her wrist-comm beeped. It was an emergency
signal, from Yalena. "Mom? Oh, God—Mommy—we're
in trouble—"

The transmission was patchy, fading in and out. Kafari
could hear a snarling roar in the background, the roar
of thousands of voices locked in combat.

"*Where are you?*"

"I don't know—somewhere on Darconi Street. Ami-
Lynn and I came down here to find out what's really
going on. I went on the datachat boards, Mom, like you
told me to, and it was just awful. So I called Ami-Lynn
and Charmaine and we came downtown. We got caught
in the mob and now we can't get out. There's barricades
up everywhere and P-Squads blocking all the streets—we
can't get out!"

Kafari hit the throttle. The Airdart roared forward,
kicking her back into her seat. "Keep your wrist-comm
on send. I'll home in on your signal. Can you get into
a building somewhere?"

"No—we can't get near a doorway—too many
people—"

The transmission broke up again. It sounded like
Yalena was coughing. Or throwing up. Kafari was almost

to Nineveh Base when she saw it. An immense, dark shape in the twilight. A moving shape, bristling with guns and speckled with running lights. *Sonny*. The Bolo was out of his maintenance depot, moving toward Madison. *Fast*. Something that big shouldn't move that fast. A mountain of steel and death, outsprinting her aircar . . .

"Oh, God." She jammed the controls to maximum acceleration and shot forward, flying nap-of-the-earth and hoping desperately that Sonny wouldn't decide her aircar was an enemy ship to be blasted from the sky. She homed in on Yalena's signal and tried to raise her daughter.

"Yalena? Can you hear me? C'mon, baby, can you hear me?"

A choked, garbled sound came back. "Urghh—y-yeah— hear you, Mommm—"

More horrible sounds left Kafari ice cold. "Yalena?"

"Yeah?"

"Baby, the Bolo's coming! Get off the street—I don't care how, *just get off the street!*"

"Trying—" More ghastly sounds came through.

Did those bastards use retch gas?

Better gas than nerve agent. Kafari raced Sonny neck-and-neck, pulled ahead, reached Madison's outlying suburbs before he did. The streets would slow him down. She might make it. There might be time to get in, to get Yalena and her friends out. She roared into Madison at lamp-post height, whipping around corners between office towers, car-sales lots, restaurants. Kafari was no fighter pilot, but Uncle Jasper would've been proud of her. She zipped under traffic-signal cables or whipped her nose up and shot over them, where trucks took up necessary airspace.

The signal from her daughter's wrist-comm was getting closer. Peripheral vision showed her a dense throng of people dead ahead, blocked by barricades and P-Squads. Madison's infamous enforcers stood shoulder-to-shoulder with shields locked, doing nothing to stop the riot, but preventing anyone from getting out of the riot zone. They were funneling people straight down Darconi Street, toward the Presidential Residence. Right into the path Sonny would follow.

It's murder, she realized in a split-second moment of horror. *They mean to kill the protestors!* And somewhere ahead, lost in a heaving, surging mass of trapped humanity and riot gas, Kafari's little girl was fighting to stay alive. Anger blazed to life. *He's not killing my child!*

Kafari slapped controls, killing her air-intake system, then her aircar slashed through trailing tendrils of gas, an arm's length above the helmeted, armored line of the P-Squad's dragoons. Somebody shot at her. She heard the impact against the undercarriage. A warning light flashed urgently on her boards. She swore viciously, unable to tear her attention away from navigating the riot gas and packed streets.

Uncle Jasper must've wrapped ghostly hands around hers more than once, as she whipped through the heart of the riot, on a virtual collision course with the Presidential Residence. Kafari was one block away from Yalena's wrist-comm signal when her aircar started losing power. "Damn!"

There was nowhere to set it down. Just a vast river of struggling, running, fighting people, punctuated by outcroppings of parked cars, toppled delivery vans, and wrecked signposts jutting up like spears where their signs had been ripped down. Then she spotted it. The long, low rooftop of a trendy dance club. Kafari gunned the engines, yanked on the controls, brought the nose up by sheer willpower. She gained precious elevation while the engines screamed, bleeding noise and God-alone knew what kind of parts across the packed streets. She was going to hit the upper windows. She wasn't going to make it—

The belly of her fuselage scraped the edge of the roof. They skidded across, leaving a metoric trail of sparks. Kafari cut the forward thrust, shunted all remaining power into the side-thrusters, and sent the air-frame into a wild

spin. The world reeled out of control . . . Then firmed up
again as the combination of friction and counterthrust
brought her careening to a halt. She hung against the
crash webbing for several ghastly seconds, just shaking.

*I'm too old for this. Last time I did this kind of thing,
I was still in college . . .*

Then the world swam into focus and showed her
a sight that dumped more adrenaline into her jangled
system. An upper turret, studded with guns bigger than
any trees Kafari had ever seen, was crawling its way
down Darconi Street. Toward the Presidential Residence.
Toward her. And Yalena . . .

Kafari slapped the restraints loose, tumbled out onto
the roof. She dug into the bin under her seat and
came up with the gun she had been carrying illegally
for years. Kafari dragged on her belly-band holster,
which tucked the gun snugly between her abdomen
and the elasmer band, then hunted frantically for a
way down from the roof.

There *was* a fire door. Locked from the inside. Kafari
snatched a tool kit out of her car and jimmied the whole
door off its frame. Terror lent her strength as Sonny's massive guns crawled inexorably closer. She could hear the
sound of his treads chewing up pavement and cars and
smaller things, the kind of things that screamed in mortal
terror as they died. When she realized what she was seeing and hearing, Kafari ran cold to the bottom of her soul.
They hadn't just ordered Sonny to break up the riot. The
Bolo was running over people. *Lots* of people.

Her breath caught in her lungs for one horrified
instant. Then she pulled the door the rest of the way
off its hinges. She clattered down the stairs, found herself rushing through a building eerily empty by daylight.
The dance hall was full of ghostly, discordant shadows.
Memories lingered, revelries filled with the intoxicating
taste of ruling-class luxury and power. Dusty shafts of
sunlight lent the room a surreal, churchlike atmosphere,
while outside, a rising shriek of terror, metal against
bone, ran thick as blood.

She found another staircase that took her from the dance floor to the street level. She emerged into a restaurant that fronted Darconi Street. The restaurant was packed with people. More were trying to shove through the door, creating the worst log-jam of human bodies Kafari had ever witnessed. The only way to cross the restaurant was by going up. Kafari jumped onto the nearest table and started running, leaping from one table to the next, scattering cutlery and water glasses and plates full of food. People around her were screaming, but she hardly heard them over the volcanic roar in the street.

When she reached the tables closest to the windows, she searched frantically for her daughter in the crowd beyond. The signal on Kafari's wrist-comm said she was close, so close, she ought to be able to see her daughter by now. "YALENA!"

Screaming at the top of her voice made about as much noise as a bee's wings trying to flee an erupting volcano. Then she spotted a wild shock of neon-green hair and recognized Yalena's best friend, Ami-Lynn. Charmaine was with her, too. And there was Yalena. They were close to the sidewalk, caught in a mass of people with nowhere to go. For Yalena, there was no way in. For Kafari, there was no way out.

So she made one.

Kafari snatched up an overturned chair and threw it at the plate glass. The window shattered, raining slivers onto the heads of stunned people on the sidewalk, who couldn't quite believe that somebody would want to go *out* instead of *in*. "*Yalena!*"

Her daughter looked around, saw her standing in the shattered window.

"MOM!"

"Get through the window! Sonny's coming!"

Yalena looked back, saw the Bolo for the first time. Her eyes, streaming and blood-red from the retch gas, widened. "Oh—my—God—"

She started shoving her way toward Kafari. Other people

were moving toward the broken window. Terror-stricken people, who shoved against the splintered glass, pushed the broken shards out of their way, climbed across the busted-out sill. Kafari snatched people up by shirt collars, belts, the backs of expensive dresses, throwing them into the restaurant. Anything to clear enough space for Yalena to reach the window. Her daughter was fighting through the crowd, dragging Ami-Lynn and Charmaine with her. The roar from the street was bone-shaking. Sonny's massive warhull blocked the fading twilight, half-a-block away and coming like a flintsteel tide. She could hear his voice, familiar, horrifying. He was broadcasting loudly enough that the words were clearly audible, even above the roar.

"I have been ordered by President Zeloc to run over anyone between me and the Presidential Residence. Clear the streets. I have been ordered . . ."

Yalena was two meters away . . . a meter and a half . . . a meter from Kafari's outstretched hand. "Come on!" she shouted, "Keep moving!"

People were struggling to pass her, trying to shove Yalena out of the way. A big, beefy lout with a broken signpost in each fist was clubbing people, trying to reach the window where Kafari had created the only way out of the street. He started to swing at Yalena—

Kafari ripped the gun loose from her holster and fired. From a meter and a half out, the bullet slammed into his face like a sledgehammer. It left a stunned expression of disbelief on his face. And a hole straight through his braincase. The club slid from his hand and he toppled, falling against a woman behind him.

Yalena lunged forward. Ami-Lynn and Charmaine tripped and fell. Both girls went down. Just beyond, Sonny's treads were the only thing she could see. The immense treads were red, drenched in blood and other things . . .

"*Yalena!*" Kafari screamed, tearing her throat. The world paused. Everything came to a ghastly standstill. The crush of people, the crackle of heat, the wind.

Even Sonny. Just long enough. Kafari leaned out into a
tunnel of silence. Grabbed her daughter's hand. Hauled
her across the broken glass. Then Yalena was in her
arms. She dragged her daughter away from the window,
making room for others. She couldn't see Ami-Lynn or
Charmaine anywhere.

Then a massive shadow blocked the sunlight. Darkness
engulfed the little restaurant, like a sudden eclipse of the
sun. Sound roared back into her ears. The walls rattled.
Overhead lights jangled. Dishes danced, some of them
crashing to the floor. Nightmare memories broke loose,
memories of the ground shaking under her feet as titans
fought to possess it. Only this time, the titans weren't
defending them. Sonny's treads scraped the edges of the
restaurant. Kafari turned her head, unable to watch the
slaughter of those still outside, but the screams were
etched onto the marrow of her bones.

Yalena clung to her, sobbing and trembling. The ghastly
silence that followed in the Bolo's wake was almost worse
than the screaming. Nobody seemed willing to move.
Sonny kept grinding his way toward the Presidential
Residence. The farther he moved toward it, the worse
the silence grew.

The sudden discharge of his guns sent a shockwave
through the jam-packed restaurant. Screams erupted again.
Yalena jumped in Kafari's arms. Kafari shut her eyes, not
even wanting to know what he'd just fired at. All she
wanted was to get her baby out of this horror. With her
aircar a wreck on the roof, she didn't have the faintest
idea *how* to get out. They couldn't walk out, that was
certain. She had no desire to tangle with the P-Squads
who'd made sure their victims couldn't escape.

Worse, she was carrying a gun. Had shot a man with
it, in front of several hundred witnesses, any one of
whom could put Kafari in jail or a rehab facility for life.
This was mostly an urban crowd, people who already
hated Grangers and their so-called "cult of violence."
They were more than capable of lynch-mob destruction
if provoked.

They had just been provoked.

She shook Yalena and said in a low, urgent voice, "C'mon, baby, we've got to go. *Now.*" Yalena looked up through swollen, tear-reddened eyes. "Wh-where are Ami-Lynn and . . ." Her voice trailed off when she realized her friends weren't in the restaurant with them. She started to get up. Looked out the broken window before Kafari could stop her. Turned dead-fish white. The shock in her eyes ran to the bottom of her soul.

In that moment of acid-etched pain, the girl POPPA had stolen from them abruptly proved herself Simon Khrustinov's daughter. Her eyes went hard and her chin came up. She spat through the window, the most eloquent gesture of defiance Kafari had ever witnessed. Then she stood up on shaking legs and started looking for exits.

"Across the tables." Kafari said, grimly pulling her daughter behind her. They retraced Kafari's path a little drunkenly, since many of the tables had been knocked over in the panic-stricken crush of refugees. Most of those refugees looked up in numb silence, too shell-shocked to respond to their exodus. Given time—maybe as little as two or three minutes—that stunned crowd was going to transform itself into an unholy killing mob.

They made it to the staircase and fled silently upwards, reaching the dance hall's cathedral solitude. Kafari closed the upper doors softly and slid part of a microphone stand from the stage through the door handles, forming an effective if temporary lock.

Once the door was as secure as she could make it, Kafari turned to survey the room. The damage from Sonny's passage was apparent, even here. Some of the stained glass had been broken out. Yalena was having trouble walking. For reasons she didn't have time to determine, her daughter was staring at Kafari in a way nobody had since Abraham Lendan had met her gaze across the rubble of a refuse-strewn cellar, asking her what to do next.

"We have to get out of Madison. This part of it, anyway. Those folks downstairs are going to start looking for somebody to blame. I have no intention of that someone being *us*."

Yalena looked like she wanted to ask something important, but didn't want to interrupt their escape to do it. "What do we do?" she asked, instead.

"We find food and water we can carry and we get the hell out of this building."

A curtain concealed the back of the stage. Kafari headed that way, betting there were dressing rooms where band members grabbed a bite to eat between dance sets. They found a small kitchenette stocked with food and plenty of beverages. "Fill your pockets. In fact, grab some of those costumes," she nodded toward a rack full of glittering clothing, "and tie off sleeves and pants legs to form carry-sacks. God knows how long we're going to have to hide before it's safe to come out."

"Where . . ." She got her voice under control. "Where are we going to hide?"

"I'm trying to work that out. We're short on time and options are limited. Do you have a hand-comp with you?"

Yalena shook her head. Kafari's was sitting on the passenger seat of her aircar, or had been before that wild skid. "Mine's in the aircar. I've got to know what's happening. If you hear anyone trying to break down those doors, head for the roof and we'll figure something out."

"The aircar? Can't we just fly out?"

Kafari grimaced. "No. The P-Squads shot me down. More or less. I crashed on the roof."

"Oh. God, that must've been . . ." Her voice trailed off, helplessly.

Kafari summoned a brief grin that stunned her daughter. "The landing was *nothing* to the flying I did, getting here ahead of Sonny. I had to fly all the way from Klameth Canyon."

Yalena's chin shook for a dangerous moment and she blinked hard, then she just nodded and started dumping food and bottled water into the makeshift carry sacks. Kafari headed for the roof. She was worried about the wrecked aircar. It had her identification in it, some of her personal belongings. When it was noticed, someone was going to start poking around, looking for the owner. That attempt might lead to a number of very unpleasant outcomes.

The broken door was still ajar from her frantic rush down. She took a quick look around, then crouched low and sprinted for the aircar. The damage was evident at once. The airframe had tipped slightly on its skid across the roof, tilting it enough to see the hole where a riot gun had punched through the relatively thin outer hull. The pilot's compartment had been reinforced heavily, but the alloy in the airframe, itself, was of necessity light-weight. A 20mm slug had chewed its way through the housing and sliced into an assembly that fed power from the drive engines to the lift vanes. No wonder she'd lost acceleration. If she could replace the damaged module, they could fly out.

She didn't feel like scrounging for a replacement, not with the kind of security that would be crawling all over them, pretty soon. From her perch atop the roof, she could see Sonny's warhull. He had halted at the edge of the lawn around the Presidential Residence. A crowd of people had surged over the high fence, fleeing the Bolo's treads. Most of the people in it were busy running away as fast as mere feet could carry them. Then Kafari blinked, suspicious for a moment that her eyes were playing tricks on her in the drifts and eddies of riot gas in the last of the twilight. It had looked at first glance like the Residence was burning. Then she saw flames in the upper-story windows. It *was* burning.

Somehow, in the middle of the craziness, the Residence had been torched. By Sonny? She found that hard to believe, although it looked like a dark line of holes had been stitched across the side of the building, just to the left of the famous rose window of the president's office. That window bled light from the inside, where the glass had been shattered. What had Sonny been shooting at, when they'd heard the discharge of his guns? Enraged

Grangers? Had they stormed the Residence, bent on vengeance?

She crept into the cockpit, found her hand-comp on the floor, switched on the viewscreen. The news reports were garbled, but none of them showed the truly hair-raising sight of the Presidential Residence going up in flames. She narrowed her eyes. Somebody was censoring the news. On a really *big* scale. Why? There were no aircars visible anywhere in Madison's skies. Not even news crews with aerial cameras.

POPPA censorship had never been used for humanitarian reasons, so their goal couldn't be an attempt to defuse the anti-Granger violence bound to erupt in the wake of a riot this big. Why, then? Her eyes widened as the implications hit home. Something had happened to the president. Maybe the vice president, as well. "My God," she whispered, crouched on the bottom of her aircar's cockpit. "They'll spark a witch-hunt. The mobs will turn the Adero farms into slaughterhouses." They'd kill *anybody* who looked even faintly like a Granger. She had to get Yalena out. *Now.*

How?

Mind spinning, she tried to think what to do, how to get herself and a shell-shocked adolescent girl out of a killing ground that the government had blockaded and would lock down so tightly, not even a rat would be able to wriggle its way through. She could call for help, but the nearest help was in Klameth Canyon. By the time anyone could reach them, somebody would have thought to ground air traffic planet-wide, controlling movement by potential "enemies of the people."

They couldn't get out through the streets. They had to go either up or down. Up was not possible. That left down as the only viable option. The sewers presented themselves as an attractive alternative. Kafari narrowed her eyes. If they could crawl through the sewers, come up a few streets away . . . Coming up would be a problem, with Madison set to explode. The civilian emergency shelters would be more sanitary, if they were close to any. Downtown Madison was supposed to be riddled with below-ground shelters, in case of renewed attack by the Deng.

She keyed her hand-comp to access the datanet and found an emergency evacuation map. There wasn't a shelter anywhere near the dance club. Not close enough to gain it without going out into the streets. Scratch that idea. It was the sewers or nothing. Kafari moved across the roof at a low crawl, easing her way gingerly so she didn't skyline herself. She slid herself to the back of the dance club, which overlooked an alley through which delivery trucks brought in supplies for the restaurant and dance club. There were dumpsters for refuse and a couple of groundcars parked near the service exit. The building behind the dance club was taller, a three-story structure that apparently housed tri-d screens stacked vertically, to conserve expensive downtown real-estate.

Between the two buildings, Kafari spotted a tell-tale metal circle embedded in the pavement, providing access for sewer-system maintenance techs. All they had to do was reach the alley, pry up the cover, climb down, and pull the lid back on top of themselves. And at the moment, nobody was in sight to notice them doing it. Kafari peered over the edge of the dance club's roof, trying to see if there might be a way down from here. She spotted a fire escape farther along, allowing rapid exit through one of the dance hall's windows. That ought to serve nicely. Kafari rolled back from the edge, crawled across the roof, then skinned her way down the stairs and found Yalena waiting for her.

"The Presidential Residence is burning. There's no report of it anywhere, no aerial news crews, not even a peep on the datachats. I think Gifre Zeloc's been killed and a news blackout's been ordered."

Yalena gasped. Then once again, she demonstrated her father's cool level-headedness under fire. "They'll blame Grangers. Won't they? We have to get out of Madison. And . . ." She bit one lip, then said it anyway. "And we have to warn people, somehow. On the farms." She swallowed, realizing how that sounded, coming from her, then she lifted her chin in defiance and said, "Well, we do. Especially the Adero farms."

Kafari reached out and touched her daughter's tear-stained cheek, smeared with makeup and dirt and horror. This stubborn, brainwashed child had just slashed through fifteen years of indoctrination, had finally realized that people she had considered "the enemy" all her life were about to be slaughtered without mercy. "Yalena," she said, reaching back across the years to a memory very precious to her, "I am proud to be your mama."

Yalena started to cry, gulped the sound back, tried to stiffen her shoulders.

In that moment, Kafari knew they would be all right. If they could survive.

Chapter Twenty

I

I return to my maintenance depot covered once again in misery, broken power cables, and dangling traffic signals. My mechanic is glued to a datascreen, watching the spectacle of Madison burn. When he hears me approaching, Phil runs out and greets me with an exhuberance I find puzzling, given the sudden death of Jefferson's president.

"Hooeee! You really kicked some ass, big guy! Wow, how many a'them land hogs didja run over and shoot? About a thousand of 'em, at least! I'm so freakin' jealous, man, I can't even stand it, 'cause I hadda watch on the screen, stead'a bein' there, while you was right in the middle of it."

I come to a complete halt outside my maintenance bay, at a total loss for words. I have come to expect ruthless disregard for human life from the enemy, since species like the Quern, Deng, and Melconians operate under a belief system that does not include coexistence with another sentient, let alone space-faring, species. But not even fifteen years of monitoring POPPA leaders and

423

their inflammatory rhetoric has prepared me for such an outburst from an individual who, so far as I have been able to determine, has never met—much less suffered abuse at the hands of—a Granger. I literally do not know how to respond to his glee.

He grins up at my nearest external sensor array. "So, how'd it feel, finally gettin' to show them land hogs what they got comin' to 'em? Betch'a ain't seen anythin' like that, ever, have you?"

Phil's questions give me the referents I need to frame a response.

"I am a Bolo Mark XX. Clearly, you do not understand what it means to be a Bolo. I am part of an unbroken lineage of humanity's defenders, a lineage that stretches back nine-hundred sixty-one years. I am programmed to defend humanity's inhabited worlds from harm. I have seen active service for one hundred fifteen point three-six years. During that time I have fought in three major wars, beginning with the Deng War of one-hundred fifteen years ago. I fought a new threat during the Quern Wars and was seriously damaged in the battle for Herdon III, where my Commander was killed. I have fought three campaigns in the current Deng War, which now engulfs thirty-seven human star systems.

"During those one hundred fifteen years of active service, I have received seventeen campaign medals, three rhodium stars, and four galaxy-level clusters, including a gold cluster for heroism on the killing fields of Etaine. During the battle for Etaine, I was part of a Brigade battle group of seventeen Bolos with a mission to halt the Deng incursion at any cost, since possession of Etaine would have opened the way into the heart of humanity's home space.

"We faced fifty Yavac Heavy-class fighting machines, eighty-seven Yavac medium-class, and two-hundred and ten Scout-class Yavacs. The deep gouge melted across my prow was inflicted by the concentrated fire of fourteen Yavac Heavies using a synchronized-fire tactic which punched through my defensive energy screens. Yavac fire melted ninety-eight percent of my armor and blew all of my treads to rubble. They then concentrated their plasma lances across my prow in an attempt to melt through my flintsteel warhull to inflict a fatal hull breach.

"I destroyed all fourteen Yavac Heavies and ground my way across the field of battle on bare drive wheels, killing every Yavac I could bring into range of my Hell-bores. I destroyed seven troop transports attempting to land and took down a Deng heavy cruiser entering low orbit. By the end of the battle, all sixteen other Bolos in my battle group had been destroyed. Seventeen million human civilians had been killed, but the Deng advance was halted and turned into a retreat. The Deng High Command rightly concluded it would be far too expensive to continue mounting full-scale assaults at humanity's heartland. They therefore turned their attention to the border worlds just beyond the Silurian Void in an effort to gain a toe-hold for their own refugees. They had been forced to do this, as the Melconians have destroyed a third of the Deng's colony worlds in this sector and have threatened the Deng homeworlds.

"Given the extent of the war along the Deng/Melconian border, I was deemed essential to the continued defense of human worlds. Rather than being scrapped, I was fitted with new armor and treads and my damaged gun systems were repaired or replaced. I came to Jefferson, where I defeated a Deng battle group consisting of two armored cruisers, six Deng troop transports, eight Yavac Heavies, ten Medium-class Yavacs, twenty-eight Scout-class Yavacs, and large numbers of infantry I did not bother to count, but which ran to the thousands, at a minimum.

"Today, I was ordered to drive through city streets jammed with civilians who had been exercising their lawful right to free speech and assembly and did so in a peaceful manner until federal police forces began lobbing retch gas and breaking their bones with heavy truncheons. When they attempted to run for safety, they were met by a mob of urban vigilantes who hammered them into the pavement with a clear intent to kill. Their sole escape route was through the grounds of the Presidential Residence. This caused Gifre Zeloc to order me to crush anything in my path in order to prevent the panic-stricken crowd from climbing his fence. Despite my protests, he repeated the order to drive over everyone in my path, including the urban rioters entangled with the crowd of Grangers.

"I do not know how many people I crushed on Darconi Street tonight. I do not want to know. My purpose is defending humanity's worlds, not running over protestors. When Grangers stormed the Presidential Residence, I fired through the walls. I did so to protect a man who ordered the slaughter of his own supporters in the interests of saving his own neck. He then stupidly jumped through a window and landed in the middle of a group of people with intense cause to hate him. He died messily. Unfortunately, so did nearly a thousand innocents."

Phil gets quiet. Very quiet. I have never seen him so quiet. Even the nano-tatt on his face has gone motionless. He swallows several times without speaking. He stares at the ground beside my treads for one point three-seven minutes. He glances up and sees something embedded in my track linkages that causes him to blanch. He looks down again. "I didn't know any a'that," *he finally says in a low voice.* "Nobody on the news said none a'that. Not at all."

"That does not surprise me."

He looks up again, puzzlement clearly visible in his tattooed face. "You ain't surprised? What'cha mean by that?"

"The broadcast and print news media routinely exercise skillful, extensive, and selective editing in what they report."

"Huh? What's that mean?"

"They don't tell the whole story and what they do tell, they lie about. Frequently."

Phil's eyes widen, then narrow. "How d'you know that? You ain't everywhere. You just sit in this here building and do nuthin' all day except sleep or whatever it is a machine does."

"I do not sleep. Due to the circumstances of my last commander's recall, I remain awake twenty-five hours a day, every day. I have now been conscious without interruption for five years. I monitor all broadcasts originating from commercial and government sources. I scan the planetary datanet on a daily basis. I am able to access security cameras in virtually every governmental or private office on Jefferson and frequently do. I can communicate directly with most computer systems on this world. Ninety-nine point two percent of the time I do so on a read-only status, which allows me to access information entered by virtually anyone using a computer hooked to the datanet. When the situation warrants it, I can instruct computers to perform specific tasks, in the interest of successfully completing my mission."

"You can do all a'that?" *Phil asks faintly.* "Peek at what's on guy's computer screen? Or tell it t'do somethin'? You *are* kiddin', ain't'cha?"

"A Bolo Mark XX is not noted for a sense of humor. I do not 'kid' on matters of planetary security. I have noted," *I add,* "your preference for datachat sites with well-endowed and scantily clad women."

Phil and his nano-tatt turn an interesting shade of crimson. "You—I—but—" *He halts, clearly struggling with some concept new to him. Thinking of any kind would qualify as a new concept for him. Given the visual cues I perceive, it is apparent that Phil is thinking, or trying to. I consider this a step in the right direction. He finally finds something to say.* "If you can listen and read alla that stuff, how come you ain't told nobody about nuthin'?"

Phil is evidently making a valiant attempt, but not even I can decipher that statement. "Which things am I not telling to whom?"

He screws his brow into an improbable contortion of skin and writhing purple tendrils as the nano-tatt responds to some strong emotion. "All the stuff the news ain't tellin' folks. Like they never mentioned the president got killed, tonight. How come they never told us the president got killed, tonight?"

"I do not know the answer to that."

"But how come you ain't tellin' anybody about it? Anybody but me, I mean."

"Whom should I tell?"

He blinks for a long moment. "You coulda told the reporters an' such. You coulda told 'em they oughta be tellin' folks important stuff like that."

"What good would it do to tell someone who is lying and knows they are lying that they ought to tell the truth?"

He scratches the tattooed side of his face, looking deeply uncomfortable. It is clear that Phil finds thinking for himself difficult. "I dunno, I guess it wouldn't a' done much good, would it? But . . . You shoulda' oughta' told *somebody*."

"Do you have a suggestion as to who might listen?"

This is not entirely a rhetorical question. I would welcome—gladly—any genuine insight into how I should resolve the situation I face. Phil, however, just shakes his head. "I dunno. I gotta think about that, a little." *He peers up at me again.* "You gotta mess a'crap needs to be pulled off, again, up there. And you got stuff . . ." *he pauses, swallows convulsively again.* "You got stuff I gotta wash out of them treads."

He makes a semifurtive gesture with the fingers of his right hand, sketching a rough cruciform shape in the air in front of his face and chest. I surmise that he is, as are many individuals of Italian descent, Catholic. I surmise, as well, that he had—until recently—forgotten that fact. There may still be a human soul hidden beneath the indoctrination he has been fed since beginning grammar school, judging by the age listed in his work dossier. Or perhaps it is his martyred urban brethren who have nudged his conscience out of its coma?

He peers uncertainly around the maintenance bay. "Got any idea how t'do that? Wash you off, I mean?"

I suggest use of the high-pressured hose system installed for this purpose and guide him through the procedure of powering up the system and using the equipment without injuring himself. It is a long afternoon. By the time my treads and warhull are clean again, Phil Fabrizio is reeling with exhaustion. He stumbles out of the maintenance bay and staggers toward the quarters Simon occupied for so many years. He does not, however, go to sleep. He opens a bottle of something alcoholic and sits down in the darkness, drinking and thinking alone.

He is, at least, thinking.

After the day I have endured, any hopeful thought at all is something to cling to, as an antidote to rising despair. I did not think it was possible to miss Simon Khrustinov as bitterly as I do tonight, with bloody water coursing down the drains in my maintenance bay's floor and a blood-red moon rising above the Damisi highlands fifty kilometers to the east.

My day's battle has ended, but judging from the reports I monitor over news feeds, government emergency channels, and frantic radio calls for help originating from virtually all parts of Madison and the Adero floodplain farms near it, the night's battle is just beginning. What is happening there and in every major urban center on Jefferson qualifies as murder.

It will, I fear, be a long and exceedingly dark night.

II

Kafari watched Yalena crawl into the sewer from her perch on the rooftop. The moment her daughter was underground, she used the aircar's comm-unit to tap into the datachat site most frequently used by Grangers in this part of Jefferson. She posted warnings on the main Granger sites and set the aircar's comm-unit to record a verbal warning that would start broadcasting on every civilian frequency she could access. She put the recordings on a count-down clock that would start ten minutes after she left. Then she rushed down the rooftop access stairs, climbed through a window, and lowered herself by her hands. She kicked out slightly to drop into the alleyway, jarring her feet with the impact, but taking no injury. It took only seconds to slither through the manhole and pull the cover on top of them.

Yalena was waiting below, holding a flashlight.

"I found extra batteries," she said.

"Good. We may need them. We'll try to reach the apartment."

Yalena just nodded. They set out, slogging through thigh-deep water. It was hard work and the water was cold, but she kept them moving steadily. They rested once every half-hour, heading north. When they finally reached the area near their building, Kafari found a ladder that led up to another manhole cover. The sun had long-since set, so they should be able to scuttle across the street and into their building under cover of darkness. Someone might spot them, but she was hopeful that the crisis underway downtown would keep the P-Squads too busy elsewhere to take note of their emergence from the sewers.

She was nearly to the top of the ladder when she smelled smoke. Kafari hesitated, trying to hear through the slots in the grate. The night was far too noisy, but she couldn't tell what it was, making that noise. So she put her shoulder against the cover and pushed up one edge, lifting it no more than the width of her hand. A tidal wave of noise assaulted her ears and the smell of smoke touched the back of her throat with acrid fingers. She peered out cautiously. The instant she saw what was happening, Kafari dragged the cover back down again, careful not to let it drop with a bang. Then she slithered back down into the muck and stood huddled over for long moments, fighting the need to vomit and shivering so hard her bones clacked against one other.

"What's wrong, Mom? What's up there?"

She shook her head, unable to speak just yet, and gestured farther north. Wordlessly, Yalena took the flashlight and the lead. An hour later, reeling with exhaustion and the chill of the sewage sludge, Kafari called a halt. She didn't want to eat anything, but they couldn't keep moving all night without fuel. It was a long and hellish walk to the spaceport from here. They pulled supplies from their impromptu carry sacks, chewing and swallowing while leaning against the sewer-pipe's walls. When they were ready to set out again, Yalena broke the long silence.

"What was up there, Mom? The last time we stopped?" Her voice took on a vicious edge Kafari had never heard, before. "Was it the Bolo, again?"

Kafari shook her head. "No." She didn't want to remember that glimpse into the lower circles of Dante's hell.

"What, then?"

She met Yalena's gaze. The glow of her daughter's flashlight caught the fear in Yalena's eyes, touched her skin with an eerie, red-tinged glow.

"Mom? What *was* it?"

Kafari swallowed heavily. "Lynch mobs." She managed to hold down the nausea surging up with those two bitten-off words.

"Lynch mobs? But—" Yalena's eyelashes flickered in puzzlement. "Who was there to lynch? Everybody in Madison supports POPPA."

Kafari shook her head. "They went out to the collectives. My warning . . ." She stopped, swallowed the nausea back down. "Maybe my warning didn't go out in time. Or maybe some people just didn't believe it. Or they didn't get out fast enough." It hadn't been the people hanging from light poles that had shaken her so desperately. It was the *pieces* of people . . .

"Where are we going?" Yalena asked in a whisper.

Her question dragged Kafari's attention from the horrors in town to their immediate needs. "The spaceport."

Her eyes widened, but she didn't comment on it or ask another question. Yalena's silence both relieved and distressed Kafari. Relieved, because she didn't want to think too closely about the charnel house, back there, let alone what she intended to do about it, once Yalena was safe. Distressed, because it illustrated in painful terms Yalena's sudden shift from trusting child to determined adult.

The next two hours were brutal, but they kept going, spurred on by the twin desires to remain whole and not end up as decorations for a light pole. By the time the sewer pipe narrowed enough to block their way, out near the edge of town where there wasn't enough infrastructure to need a larger effluent pipe, Kafari was more than ready to give in, as well. Shaking with fatigue and chill, they stopped at the next manhole cover they reached. It was nearly midnight, by Kafari's chrono. She whispered, "I'm going up top, to look."

Yalena leaned against the sewer-pipe wall, gasping for breath while Kafari climbed slowly up to the cover. She listened hard, hearing nothing but silence. Deciding the risk was worthwhile, she pushed against the heavy metal cover, wincing as it scraped and shattered the silence. She held it up a few inches and peered out. The city behind them was an eerie sight. Great swaths of it were dark, where the power was off. A ruddy, baleful glow flickered in the heart of downtown, where multiple buildings were burning. There was no motor traffic anywhere.

She peered in every direction, finding only silence and darkness. They were, as she had hoped, near the edge of town, out past suburbia. Even navigating blind, she'd come within a few blocks of where she'd hoped to be. The slums of Port Town were off to their left, a disorderly sprawl of tenements, bars, sleazy dance halls, nano-tatt parlors, brothels, and gambling dives, all of it ominously dark, tonight, but far from silent. Kafari didn't want to know what was causing that particular combination of sounds. What she'd glimpsed back toward their apartment had been enough to give her nightmares for the next year.

To their right stood warehouses and abandoned factories with weeds growing in cracks in the parking lots. More or less dead ahead lay the spaceport, half a kilometer away. The power was on, courtesy of the emergency generators, which left the port buildings shining like stars in the stygian darkness. Kafari saw no police or federal troops, but that didn't mean there weren't patrols out. Given the total lack of traffic, Kafari was betting a martial-law curfew had been imposed. They couldn't afford to be caught, now. But they had to get out of the sewer and into the spaceport. They had to risk it.

"We've got about half a kilometer to go." They crawled up, shivering hard, and pulled themselves out onto the road. Kafari levered the manhole cover back into place, then they trudged toward Port Abraham. They didn't go in by the road. Kafari took them across country, the long way around, in the opposite direction from Port Town, toward the engineering complex and her office. If there were guards anywhere, they'd be around the cargo warehouses near Port Town. As they approached the main terminal complex, Kafari's puzzlement grew. The whole place was deserted. Not a cop, not a guard, nothing.

An uneasy glance over her shoulder revealed the baleful glow from fires that still smouldered. They were upwind of the smoke, but the magnitude of the disaster gave Kafari the clue she needed to understand the complete lack of port security. Every guard, cop, and P-Squad officer was needed elsewhere. Urgently so. They reached the engineering hub without incident. Kafari fished her ID out of a dripping pocket and headed toward the door she'd used five days a week for years. The reader scanned the card and they slipped through. Once inside, with the door clicked safely shut behind them, Kafari breathed a little easier.

"This way," she said in a low murmur. "There are maintenance locker rooms back here."

They limped their way through the back corridors, finding the lockers rooms and laundry facilities used by the maintenance and cleaning crews, cargo handlers, and shuttle pilots. They dropped their filthy, reeking clothes in a refuse bin, then hit the shower stalls. The feel of

hot water and soap was glorious, working wonders for
their spirits. Clean maintenance uniforms, socks, and
shoes pilfered from lockers Kafari jimmied open made
them feel almost human again.

Yalena held Kafari's now-clean belly-band holster under
an electric hand dryer, while Kafari busied herself cleaning
her pistol at a sink, rinsing out the worst of the muck.
She reassembled the gun, then wrapped the now-dry
belly-band holster around her midsection and slid the
gun into it. She didn't even bother to conceal it under
her shirt. Not tonight.

"What next?" her daughter asked quietly.

"We find ourselves some real supper and we board
our transportation."

"Our transportation?" Yalena asked, frowning. "What
transportation? I mean, where are we going?"

"The *Star of Mali* docked at Ziva Two this afternoon."

Yalena's brows, knit in puzzlement, shot abruptly
upward. "*Off-world?*" she gasped. "But—" She closed
her mouth, stunned. "You want us to go to Vishnu? To
be with Daddy?"

Kafari nodded, not voicing her real plans aloud. After
what she'd seen tonight, Kafari wasn't going *anywhere*.
There was too much at stake. Too many innocent lives
had already been lost. But Yalena was going out, whether
she liked it or not. Even if Kafari had to knock the girl
senseless to do it.

"How do we get off-world?" Yalena asked. "We don't
have a shuttle pass. And I don't think the P-Squads would
let anybody board *any* kind of orbit-capable shuttle, now."
She gulped, seeing ramifications for the first time in her
life. "They won't want anyone to know what's happening
here, will they?"

"No, they won't," Kafari agreed. "But we're not going
by shuttle. Not exactly. For right now, however, we find
food," Kafari insisted. She tossed everything they'd carried
with them into the nearest refuse bin, found a duffle in
another pilfered locker, then led the way through empty,

echoing corridors. They headed for the spaceport's food hub, where they raided a restaurant kitchen. Wolfing down supper took only ten minutes. Then Kafari started dumping food into the duffle.

"Why are we taking so much?" Yalena asked.

"Because I don't know how long it will take to get ourselves into orbit. Freighters operate on tight schedules and the *Star of Mali* is due to break orbit from Ziva Two about noontime tomorrow. If she leaves on schedule, we won't have to wait longer than a few hours. But if there are delays over the mess in Madison—especially if the president's been killed and I'm betting he has—we could be stuck for hours. Maybe days. And once we're in our hiding place, I *don't* want to come out, again. I won't risk getting caught trying to sneak out and grab more food."

Yalena, showing definite signs of wear and tear from their ghastly struggle, just nodded, accepting the explanation at face value. Kafari's heart constricted. Her daughter hadn't learned to be devious, yet. She zipped the duffle closed, then led the way through the spaceport along a different route, heading toward the cargo-handling side of the port. They found rows of big cargo-transfer bins, neatly labeled so the stevedores could tell at a glance which bins were consigned to which hold on the orbiting freighters or the occasional passenger craft. Kafari chose a big cargo box whose manifest tag said it contained processed fish meal, the biggest food export Jefferson produced. The idea of shipping *any* food had caused riots, particularly amongst the explosive urban poor, so POPPA propagandists had been very careful in assuring the public that the only food being shipped out was the treaty-mandated native fish, processed for Terran consumption.

"We'll open the top, scoop out enough fish meal to bed down, and pour the stuff we remove into a refuse bin somewhere."

Yalena nodded and scrambled up to try prying open the hinged top. "It won't open, Mom. I don't see any sign of a lock, but it won't budge. It's like the whole thing's been welded shut." She leaned down, peering over the sides. When she reached the back of the bin, she said, "Hey, that's weird. Look at this, Mom. Why would somebody put a door into the side of a cargo bin full of fish meal? It would flood out the minute you tried to open it."

Kafari crawled around to the back and frowned at the door that had been fitted into the narrow end of the bin. "You're right. That is weird."

"I'm going to check the other bins, Mom." She moved at a brisk pace through the stacked cargo boxes. "This one's got one, too. So does this one. And that one. The ones down here don't, but this whole row does." She was pointing at the bins nearest the warehouse doors.

Kafari's frown deepened as the implications of that placement sank in. "These would be loaded first, at the back of the freighter's cargo bay. Spot-check inspections wouldn't be as likely to uncover these, stacked in the back." That suggested all sorts of interesting things. She came to an abrupt decision and yanked the handle up. The metal door creaked open, but no fish meal poured out. The air that did flood out carried a butcher-shop smell with it. Kafari peered into the bin, using the hand light, and stared, struck literally speechless.

The whole, immense cargo box was full of meat. Not just any meat, either, and certainly not the noxious fish-meal they'd been shipping for years to the miners on Mali. She could see whole sides of beef. Thick, center-cut hams. Ropes of spiced sausage, a Klameth Canyon specialty that was confiscated by the government as fast as ranchers could produce and pack it. This food was supposed to be sent to the hard-working crews on the fishing trawlers and the high-latitude iron mines. If each of the modified cargo bins held this many dressed carcasses and processed meats, at least a quarter of the annual output of Jefferson's ranches was sitting right here, awaiting shipment disguised as something else.

Who had authorized the clandestine shipments? Gifre

Zeloc? Or one of the POPPA king-makers? Maybe even Vittori, himself? Whoever it was, they were lining their pockets with what had to be immense profits, doubtless selling to Malinese miners who could afford to pay for meats the average Jeffersonian Subbie hadn't tasted in years. Kafari wanted to beam pictures of this to every datascreen on Jefferson. If enough people saw this, there would be food riots in the streets.

Until Sonny crushed them.

Choked by helpless rage, Kafari gripped the edge of the open door frame until her fingers turned white. Then she strode down the line, trying to judge what the loading order would be when these bins were hauled into the shuttle and boosted up to the cargo bay aboard the *Star of Mali*. "We go in this one," she decided. "It's less likely to get buried in the stack, which will give us time to get out and into the ship."

"Won't all the air escape?"

Kafari shook her head. "No, the shuttles will off-load into a two-tier cargo-handling system. When you've got perishables, you ferry them up in a pressurized shuttle and offload them through an airlock in Ziva Two. Stevedores there transfer the bins to the freighters' cargo bays, which are snugged into the side of the station. This bin will be under pressure the whole time. Let's close up the other one."

Kafari opened the one she had chosen, then scrounged until she came up with a rain tarp from one of the storage rooms adjacent to the warehouse's main floor. She pulled out a dozen full-sized hams, chilled for transport but not frozen, creating a space for the duffle and Yalena, then hauled the meat to a refuse bin and dumped it in, hiding the evidence of their tampering.

"You've got your wrist-comm on?" she asked Yalena.

"Yes."

"Good. That meat's not frozen, but we'll wait a bit before crawling in. No sense in getting chilled right away. Here," she sat down between the wall and the cargo bin, "snuggle up. We'll get some sleep."

Yalena curled up against her, leaning her head against Kafari's shoulder. Within minutes the exhausted girl was sound asleep. Kafari's throat closed. She hadn't held her child like this since Yalena had turned five. She wanted more of it, much more, and knew it was impossible. To keep Yalena safe, she had to smuggle her off-world, get her to safety with her father. Her eyes burned with hot, salty tears. The need for Simon's arms around her was a physical agony. All she had to do was climb into that bin full of meat . . .

She swallowed down the longing. During the last war, she had reached down into herself and found the courage, the strength to put aside her own terror and need for safety to save the life of a man her world had needed to survive. Tonight, on eve of a very different war—one that POPPA did not yet know had just been declared—she found herself having to reach down yet again for that courage, that strength. She had other lives to save, this time, perhaps thousands of others.

Kafari's new war was just beginning.

She waited until Yalena was deeply asleep. Once she was sure of it, she eased her way to her feet, lifted her exhausted daughter, and placed her—still sound asleep—in the space she'd created. Kafari tucked the tarp around her daughter and brushed back a lock of hair, bending to kiss her brow with the merest brush of lips. Then she eased the door closed and latched it. She closed her eyes for one long and dangerous, burning moment. Then straightened and strode through the empty spaceport to liberate transportation for herself.

It was time to do battle.

III

Simon was at home, running through another set of calesthenics designed to strengthen his muscles, when his datascreen beeped with an incoming message signal. Even after two years of hard work, he was still winded by the rigorous therapy that was an on-going part of his new life. He wiped sweat with one sleeve and moved awkwardly to the desk, breathing heavily.

"Khrustinov," he said, activating visuals as well as sound.

The first thing he saw was Kafari's face. His breath faltered. She was so beautiful, just looking at her was an aching pain in his flesh.

"Kafari?" he whispered, not quite believing his eyes.

"Oh, Simon . . ." Her eyes were wet. On second appraisal, she looked terrible. Her eyes were haunted, with deep purple smudges of exhaustion and something else, something that made his stomach muscles clench with dread. She reached toward the transmitter, as though trying to touch his face. He reached out with an involuntary answering gesture, touching the tips of her extended fingers with his own. He could almost smell the warmth of her scent, like a rich summer's meadow thick with wildflowers and honeybees.

"What's wrong?" he asked, facing the dread with squared shoulders. "And why are you broadcasting on a SWIFT system? We can't afford—"

"We're not paying for it. I broke into the spaceport's communications center so I could call. I've set this thing to transmit on security scramble, with an auto-descramble at your end . . ." Her voice was shaking. "Simon, the *Star of Mali* will break orbit at dawn, heading for Vishnu. Yalena's on it. I'm sending her to you."

"*What?* For God's sake, what's going on?"

"Gifre Zeloc's dead. So is Vice President Culver. They ordered Sonny to crush a Granger demonstration . . ." She halted as her voice went savagely unsteady. "Simon, he crushed people to death. A lot of people. I can't even guess how many. Yalena was in the crowd. With Ami-Lynn and Charmaine. I got Yalena out, but I couldn't reach her friends . . ."

Simon stared across the light-years into his wife's

ravaged eyes, so shocked, he couldn't even speak. The pain in her eyes ran to the bottom of her soul.

"The survivors mobbed the Presidential Residence. Set fire to it. Yalena and I got out through the sewers. There's a slaughter underway, out there. Lynch mobs dragging Grangers off the PSFs and hanging them from light poles. Arsonists torching whole buildings, thousands of people smashing and looting." She drew a long, shuddering breath, trying to control the babbling narrative she was spilling out. "My cousin Stefano's on the *Star of Mali*. And the *Star's* captain owed me a favor. A big one. We smuggled Yalena aboard. Stefano's bringing her to you. They should make orbit around Vishnu in three days."

Simon wanted to ask, *Why didn't you come with her?*

But before he could choke the words out, she answered him. "I can't leave, Simon, not yet. I just can't. There are friends I have to help. Some of them used to raise Asali bees."

"Oh, Christ . . ." He understood in a flash who was in trouble. The pain in her voice made him want to wrap her up in both arms and never let go.

"There's something else," she whispered, hesitating.

"What?" he asked softly.

"You're going to get a message. From my parents. And probably one from the government. They're going to tell you that Yalena and I were killed in tonight's riot. I'm a dead woman, Simon. And I have to stay that way. Not even my parents will know the truth. What's going on here has to stop. That's what I intend to do, one way or another. Tell Yalena . . ." She faltered for a moment. "When she gets there, tell her I was killed trying to leave the spaceport. It'll be safer."

"*Kafari* . . ." It came out a groan of anguish. But he controlled the urge to plead with her, knowing it would do no good. "Be careful," he whispered, instead.

"I love you so much, Simon. So much it hurts, because it isn't enough. I can't love you enough, Simon, to go with Yalena, to be with you, again. I'm so sorry. Can you ever forgive me for that?" She was struggling to hold back the tears in her eyes.

No tears, he had said to her, once. *Never shed tears on the eve of battle . . .*

Kafari was every inch the colonel's lady, standing in an empty spaceport in front of a hijacked SWIFT transmitter, in the middle of a riot that was burning down her homeworld's capital city, ready to march into battle with POPPA and a *Bolo,* for God's sake, and all she could say was a broken apology for not loving him enough.

She would have made one hell of a fine Brigade officer.

Simon hoped, prayed, *knew* she would make one hell of a fine guerilla.

"Never say you're sorry for doing your duty. Why do you think I love you so much?"

Yet again, tears threatened—and yet again, they did not fall.

"Be careful, out there," Simon whispered.

She nodded, touching the video pickup. "I'll get word to you, when I can."

Then she gave him a salute, soldier to soldier. He returned it, feeling a tight constriction like a mailed fist that closed around his heart, capturing everything he had placed there for safekeeping, captured and held it—bruised and trembling—in a steel-hard grip.

Then the transmission ended and Simon was alone in his little apartment. He stood staring at the dark screen for long moments, wishing he could squeeze himself into the message bursts of an intersteller SWIFT transmission and stand by her side. Since he could not, he turned his aching thoughts to what he *could* do.

He contacted the Residency Bureau to arrange for Yalena's immigration.

IV

Kafari landed the skimmer she'd stolen at the spaceport—having carefully disabled its ID transmitter beforehand—on the roof of her apartment building in Madison. After much soul-searching, she'd decided to brave the madness loose in the capital, to rescue equipment she would need from her apartment. She crept down from the roof unseen even by her closest neighbors, who were either outside participating in the slaughter or huddled behind locked doors and windows, too terrified even to peek out past closed curtains. The building was eerie, in its total silence.

It didn't take long to secure everything she needed. Her computer equipment was among the most powerful and sophisticated on Jefferson and she had kept Simon's military-grade communications equipment, which he had bought with his own funds, which would give her a secure means of talking to the people she would recruit. As commander of a rebellion that would be born tonight, she would *need* that gear. She stuffed personal items into a duffle. Clothing suitable for hiking in rough country, rugged boots, toiletry gear, a well-stocked medical kit. She added a few small mementos, things she could carry in one pocket while on the run: Simon's Brigade medals, her own Presidential Medallion, Yalena's pearl necklace, a few family photos she yanked ruthlessly out of their frames.

Then she forced herself to let go of the rest and hauled her gear to the roof without anyone spotting her. She was still loading the skimmer when the mobs surging through the streets torched the building. As she lifted off, what she glimpsed below burned itself into the very synapses of her memory. She set her jaw against the sickness trying to rip loose. She shot northward over the rooftops, streaking back toward the spaceport before making an eastward turn toward the Damisi Mountains. Once safely away, again, she tuned into Anish Balin's datacast, picking up the broadcast on her wrist-comm. His reaction to the massacres and rioting in Madison was blistering, combining acid demands for justice and cold, infuriated rage over the slaughter of unarmed, innocent civilians.

The most useful bit of news, however, was about *her.* The discovery of Kafari's wrecked aircar on the roof of that dance club had led Pol Jankovitch and the other mainstream news anchors to speculate darkly that she must have been involved in some nefarious conspiracy to kill the president and vice president. They were even suggesting that she had lain on that rooftop as a sniper, somehow contriving to force Gifre Zeloc to jump out the window, from the distance of half a kilometer from the Presidential Residence. She was, after all, a Granger and the wife of the Colonel Khrustinov, killer of worlds and the greatest enemy Jefferson had ever faced. Pol Jankovitch had waxed rhapsodic over her apparent demise under the Bolo's courageous treads.

Anish Balin's response not only ripped POPPA up one side and down the other, it actually brought tears to her eyes. It wasn't every day a woman heard her own canonization while still very much among the living. She couldn't bear to think about the anguish her family was suffering, watching and listening to those broadcasts. Particularly since she needed to *stay* dead. So she shoved her grief down to the bottom of her soul and concentrated on reaching Anish Balin's studio before the P-Squads got there.

A number of reasons had prompted Kafari to risk contacting him. He just might be serious enough about the Granger cause to risk greater danger, far greater than the mere string of warnings he'd received from P-Squads so far, to find a healthier line of work. He was also the most popular Granger on the planet, an icon of Granger attitudes and culture, well respected and capable of marshaling the kind of followers Kafari needed. Her conviction that Anish Balin's expected life span could be calculated in hours prompted her to head straight for his studio. He deserved fair warning, if nothing else. There was a great deal he could do, if Kafari could keep him alive long enough to do it.

She reached Maze Gap unchallenged and focused her attention on the high rock walls, not wanting to end up as a grease stain on the canyon walls. She used the skimmer's on-board nav computer to display a map that led her straight to Anish Balin's homestead. When she was half a kilometer away from his front gate, she stashed the skimmer in a crevice weathered into the eroding canyon walls, then hiked the rest of the way.

Anish's studio proved to be a small workshop behind his house, tucked back into a corner of Klameth Canyon. His house was dark, but she could see light through the studio windows, out back. She lifted her wrist-comm to listen. He was talking about her again, in terms almost embarrassing, and was furiously demanding an investigation into her whereabouts, accusing the P-Squads of holding her incommunicado for any number of sinister purposes.

When he signed off the live datacast and set his equipment for auto-repeat, Kafari made her move. The studio door wasn't locked. She eased her way inside, finding him seated at his console, shutting down various control boards. She waited long enough for him to complete the ritual, not wanting to interrupt his routine. Any deviation from his normal pattern might show up on somebody's security net—and Kafari was absolutely convinced that somebody was, in fact, watching his databoard very closely tonight. When he swung around to leave the studio, she stepped into the light.

His lower jaw came adrift.

Before he could utter a sound, she held one cautionary finger to her lips, then pointed outside. A muscle jumped in his jaw and his eyes went abruptly hard. He gave her a curt nod and followed her out into the night. They walked, by mutual consent, past the house where he lived alone, out into the fields he and his family had once tilled, before the Deng had blown them to atoms.

"You're dead," he finally broke the silence, out in the middle of a field that had grown up into standing hay.

"Yes," she agreed. "That will be rather useful, don't you think?"

He snorted. "Damned useful. You're planning to do something about that unholy pack of mobsters?"

"Oh, yes."

He hesitated. "Your daughter?"

Yalena's political inclinations were widely known, in Granger circles. "She'll be aboard the *Star of Mali* by the time it breaks orbit for Vishnu."

"Good God, how'd you manage that?"

Words got caught in Kafari's throat for long moments. Even having told Simon, already, she still found it difficult to say without breaking down. When she told him, he halted, his face and shirt pale blurs in the starlight, and stood motionless in the waist-high hay for long moments. Kafari wished she could see the expression on his face more clearly, but the moons weren't up yet and the starlight was too faint to see more than shadows and the faint glint of his eyes.

"I see," he said at length. The emotion in his voice was full of nuances that made two simple words into a profoundly complex political commentary. "And you stayed." It wasn't a question, it was an awe-struck compliment that rivaled Abraham Lendan's words to her, so long ago. "What do you want me to do?"

"To start with? Get the Hancock family out of Nineveh Base."

A soft whistle reached her ears. "You don't do things in a small way, do you?"

"There *is* no way to start small. Not with what we're up against."

"And what do you suggest we use for weapons? POPPA didn't leave us with much to choose from." The anger in his voice was an echo of an entire world's wrath.

"There are plenty of weapons. You just have to summon the nerve to go and get them."

"You must know something the rest of us don't."

"Like how to cripple a Bolo?"

"*Jeezus!*" He breathed hard for a couple of seconds. "You don't beat around the bush, either, do you?"

She swept her arms in a wide gesture, encompassing the dark canyon and the people who lived there—and those beyond, who also needed their help. "We don't have time for niceties. Not if we hope to get the Hancock family out of Nineveh Base alive. Let me ask you a pointed question. You've got a wide audience. Are any of them reliable enough to form a guerilla fighting force? One we can assemble tonight? And are any of them willing to die, striking our first blow?"

Anish Balin didn't hurry his answer, which Kafari found encouraging. The last thing they needed was someone eager to jump in with both feet before considering the very real possibilities for disaster. "I think so, yes," he said at length. "I've talked to a few people—in person, mind you, not over the datanet—people who've lost everything. Not just their livelihoods, but their homes and their land, legacies they were holding for their kids and grandkids, ripped away in POPPA's environmental land snatches and tax forfeitures."

"Yes," Kafari bit out. "I know too many of those, myself."

"The lucky ones had relatives they could turn to, people they could pool resources with, sharing workloads, establishing cooperatives like the Hancocks did. But a lot of folks—too many by half—were simply shipped to government-run farms. They're working the collectives at gunpoint. Would they be willing to die, to stop POPPA? Oh, yes."

"Fair enough. How quickly can you assemble a strike force? I want twenty people, at most."

"How soon do you want to hit Nineveh?"

She smiled in the starlight. "Oh, it isn't Nineveh I had in mind to hit. Not first, anyway."

"What on earth have you got up your sleeve?"

"A few tricks I picked up over the years. But there's one more thing I want to say before we go any further with this. It concerns you. After tonight, Vittori Santorini is going to come after Grangers with a vengeance. You are the best-known—and most vocal—Granger advocate on Jefferson. You wield enough influence and popular support to cause a whole lot of trouble for the Santorinis. They *have* to take you out. What's worse, you've given them the perfect legal pretext for doing it. You hacked into federal security systems to download the Hancock family massacre footage and the distress call they sent out."

"I had to do that. And you damned well know why!"

"Yes, I do. And, yes, you were absolutely right. Getting that recording into the hands of the public was the most critical service anyone has provided Grangers in the last ten years. It woke up my own daughter and she'd supported POPPA—and I mean really *believed* in it—virtually her whole life. But they'll crucify you and use that illegal download as the excuse for destroying you."

"You seem awfully sure of that."

"I watched them destroy my husband!" He flinched from the serrated edge in her voice, shuddered visibly, even in the faint starlight. She said more gently, "They can't afford *not* to take you out. Especially now, with the president and vice president dead. The government's in chaos, Madison is burning, and the Santorinis need a scapegoat to blame it all on. You're the voice of Granger opposition. A rallying point people will flock to, a natural leader they'll follow. And the Santorinis know it. You want my best guess? You'll be in custody before dawn. And I seriously doubt you'll live long enough to come to trial. The *only* choice you have is the one I've already made for myself. Disappear into the darkness. Then make them fear the shadows."

He didn't say anything at all for long moments. Wind whispered past high overhead, moaning across the clifftops. "Lady," he finally said in a voice full of rust and respect, "you are one tough bitch. And scary as hell." He wiped his forehead with one sleeve despite the rising chill of the night wind. "All right. How light do we travel?"

"How much of that studio equipment can you rip out and transport in the next couple of hours?"

"My *studio* equipment?" He stared at her. "Why, for Chrissake?"

She pushed hair back from her brow. "Because this won't be a short war. We're going to need a command post—a mobile one—and good equipment. I've already salvaged my computer and some communications gear. You've got equipment we'll need, as well, if you can dismantle it in time. Bear in mind that we also need to assemble fire teams, tonight. I want to hit three targets before dawn. The first will give us the small arms we need to take Barran Bluff arsenal. The arsenal will give us the firepower we've got to have, to tackle Nineveh Base. Hyper-v missiles. Octocellulose mines. Mobile Hellbores."

He reached up to grab a handful of hair on either side of his head. "*Jeezus Mother H . . .* You don't ask for much, do you? You want I should throw in the keys to Vittori's palace?"

"Might save time," Kafari agreed equably.

He let out a strangled sound that defied interpretation. Then gave a sudden snort. "I can see already, things won't ever be boring with you around. All right. Lemme think, a minute."

Kafari waited.

"Okay, we might just pull it off. I've got some calls to make. We could probably recruit twenty, maybe thirty people right here in Klameth Canyon, in the next ten minutes. Could be as many as two or three hundred, if we have time to contact everybody on my nothing-left-to-lose list. We can put some of them to work dismantling the studio. That isn't as complicated as it looks. You can pack a lot of function into a setup as small and simple as mine. The rest of us can work on your battle plans."

"Good. Start calling. I'm going to borrow your computers while you start assembling the team. There are a few other illegal downloads we need to make and I've got to hack my way into some seriously tough systems, to do it."

He didn't ask why—or what.

Kafari took that as a good sign, as well.

Chapter Twenty-One

I

At 24:70 hours, I receive an unprecedented transmission from Sector Command.

"Unit SOL-0045, acknowledge readiness to receive command-grade orders."

"Unit SOL-0045, acknowledged. Standing by."

"We have been notified about the situation on Jefferson."

I wonder for a fleeting nanosecond which situation Sector refers to, of the many possible candidates. The incoming SWIFT transmission clarifies this.

"Your command-recognition codes were destroyed in the fire accompanying the assassination of President Zeloc and Vice President Culver. We hereby authorize you to accept command-grade instructions from the current and future presidents of Jefferson, pursuant to article 9510.673 of the treaty binding Jefferson to the Concordiat. Given the high likelihood of armed insurrection, you are further instructed to act independently in assessing and countering threats to the long-term security of this planet and the sustainability of its status as a Concordiat-allied world with treaty obligations to fulfill."

"Understood. Request clarification."

"Request granted."

"I am not designed for long-term independent action and have no commander. President La Roux is not trained in any military discipline and does not know my systems well enough for command decisions on a battlefield. Will I be assigned a new commander from Sector?"

There is a brief delay as the officer issuing my instructions consults with a superior. "Negative. No command-grade officers can be spared. You are capable of independent battlefield threat assessment and action. Your experience databanks outclass some of the Mark XXIII and Mark XXIV Units currently deployed. You're the last Mark XX on active duty in this entire Sector. There isn't time to retrofit an officer's training program to qualify on your systems. You are therefore the best defense option available at this time."

I am unsure whether to be flattered or alarmed. Sector's confidence is reassuring. The lack of command officers is not. The fact that I am the last of my Mark XX brothers and sisters on active status creates an electronic ripple of conflict through my personality gestalt center. It is good to be useful. It is also lonely. I long for a commander with whom to share the years of duty yet to come. Phil Fabrizio is a poor substitute, at best.

But I am a Bolo, part of a Brigade that carries out duty no matter what. I signal acknowledgment. Sector's parting comments are startling.

"Good luck, Unit SOL-0045. From the gist of Avelaine La Roux's transmission, you will need it."

Transmission ends.

I ponder each word of the communication, trying to cull as much information as possible from this somewhat unsatisfying guidance. I am still pondering it, particularly the last ten words of it, when I receive a second transmission, this time from Madison.

"Uh . . . hello? I want to talk to the machine."

I contemplate the likelihood that the individual speaking would be using my command frequency to speak to one of the approximately 7,893 psychotronic systems on Jefferson capable of voice-activated operating mode. I decide this person is, in fact, trying to talk to me.

"This is Unit SOL-0045. Please clarify your identity and intentions."

"I'm the president. The new president. Avelaine La Roux. You called me, this afternoon—I mean yeesterday, it's past midnight, isn't it? You called me. After poor Gifre and Madeline were killed. The people at that army place off-world said you would respond to my directions. Oh, uh, I'm supposed to say something . . . Code Absalom?"

"Acknowledged. What are your instructions?"

"My instructions? I don't have any instructions, not really."

I begin to question the wisdom of placing La Roux in a command structure that she is clearly not qualified to handle. The commander I lost in the Quern War, Alison Sanhurst, was the finest and most courageous human female I have ever known, although Kafari Khrustinova runs a close second. I have never before encountered a human who could not tell me, at the bare minimum, why they had called. How do incompetent humans rise to command status?

I try again. "Did you have a purpose for contacting me?"

"Well, no, really not, I suppose. Oh, I can't do this! I'm talking to a collection of rusty nuts and bolts and loose screws!"

I surmise that this last comment was directed at someone with her, rather than at me; still, it stings my pride. "A Bolo Mark XX is significantly more than a collection of rusty nuts and bolts and only zero point zero-two percent of the screws within my thirteen-thousand-ton warhull qualify as sufficiently worn to be termed 'loose.' Request permission to file VSR."

"VSR? What the hell is that?"

I begin to understand the human maxim that patience

is a virtue. It is one I clearly lack. It is irritating to stop and explain everything I say in terms a human toddler should comprehend. "VSR is an acronym for Verified Situation Report."

"What's that?"

"A verifiably factual report on current conditions affecting my short-term duty and long-term mission."

"Oh. What do you want to say?"

"Sector Command views the likelihood of armed insurrection as exceedingly high. I concur. I would recommend putting Jefferson's defense forces on heightened alert status."

"Why?"

The lack of tactical understanding encapsulated into that single word is stunning. I require a full ten nanoseconds just to frame an explanation. "A weapons confiscation bill was signed into law last night. It is unlikely that all weapons holders will be willing to comply. I foresee a high probability of armed resistance to any attempt at door-to-door disarmament."

"After what happened last night, no one would *dare!*"

"After what happened last night, armed resistance is virtually assured."

"But why?" *She appears to be truly baffled.*

I am attempting to frame a reply when I pick up an emergency transmission from Barran Bluff, a small munitions depot fifty-three kilometers south of Madison, built a century ago to protect the Walmond Mines, which have been largely inactive under POPPA-mandated environmental codes. The largest town in the region, Gersham, has become virtually a ghost town, while farming in the region has burgeoned due to government-run emergency food-production measures. The small garrison of poorly trained federal troops stationed there, deployed mostly to keep Granger conscripts at work in the fields, is under attack.

"—they're comin' over the fences, *through* the fences, hunnerds of 'em! Can't even tell how many there are, out there. They're headin' for the big artillery bunkers, the ammo dumps. We got more of 'em comin' in from the south, carryin' rifles and stuff—"

I hear the sound of small-arms fire through the commlink, unmistakable in its crisp staccato cracking as individual slugs reach supersonic speeds and slice through the sound barrier. The yelling sound of voices in combat is audible in the background, coming mostly from the troops assigned to guard the weapons depot, from the sound of it. I tap the facility's computer-controlled security cameras as I inform Jefferson's president of the situation.

"An attack? What attack? There can't be an attack!"

I flash the transmission to her datascreen and send, as well, the data feed from the compound's security cameras. An estimated two hundred Grangers on foot have stormed the outpost, armed with heavy rifles and handguns. The contingent of troops on the site boasts a mere twenty-three defenders, six of whom are visibly dead on the ground. They appear to have been shot while running from their posts at outlying gates and guard towers, attempting to reach the safety of the command bunker.

"What do I do?" *the fledgling president asks, voice rising to a near-hysterical screech.*

The guards at the beseiged outpost are asking the same question in virtually the same tone. "What do we do? There's too many of 'em! What do we do?"

A voice I recognize at once slices through the confusion, transmitting from President LaRoux's office. Sar Gremian, sounding irritated in the extreme, says, "Shoot them, you idiot! That's what we gave you rifles for. If you can remember how to load them and pull the triggers. We're sending down an emergency tactical team by airlift. Try not to shoot them when they get there."

I address Sar Gremian through President LaRoux's datacomm. "Unit SOL-0045, standing by. I would advise sending me to Barran Bluff at once."

"No. Out of the question."

"This garrison is armed with heavy artillery that—"

"I said no. The last thing we need is for some camera

crew to shoot news footage of a Bolo having to step in to contain a few disgruntled assholes with guns."

I understand, with abrupt clarity. This order is entirely political in nature. I am the first choice to destroy unarmed rioters, sending a specific political message beneficial to POPPA's campaign of rule by intimidation. But sending in a Bolo to quash armed rebellion would be a tacit admission that the situation is out of control. Sar Gremian and his superiors in POPPA's upper echelons cannot afford to publicize the fact that "a few assholes with guns" have overrun a military compound in an act of open warfare.

I am, however, required by directive from Sector Command to conduct threat assessments in defense of this world. I therefore flash my attention to a roster of Barran Bluff's military assets. I do not like what I discover. Barran's heavy-weapons bunker houses ten artillery field guns, lightly armored but fitted with 10cm mobile Hellbores, the heaviest weaponry on Jefferson, excluding myself. These guns represent the only nuclear technology on site, but the potential for devastation is ominous, including a mobility kill on me. Given my role in recent events, Granger dissidents certainly have cause to attempt such a kill. They cannot hope to prevail as long as I am functional.

Also listed are hypervelocity missiles and antitank mines that use octocellulose explosives capable of killing a Deng Heavy if placement of the charge is done properly. They are more than capable of inflicting serious damage to me, particularly to my treads. Given the government's lack of willingness to fund anything beyond politically necessary subsidy payments, this is of concern.

I monitor the departure of the emergency tactical team from Nineveh Base. Fifty federal troops swarm aboard a heavy airlift transport, armed with weaponry suitable for infantry combat. The sole exception is a robot-tank designed to penetrate hostile terrain, which is maneuvered into the cargo bay prior to lift-off. The transport lumbers into the air and picks up speed, streaking south

*through the darkness. Even at maximum velocity, they
may be too late. The deployment of rebel troops indicates
a level of military training superior to that displayed by
the federal troops. Granted, this would not be difficult
to achieve* . . .

As I watch through the surveillance cameras, unable
to intervene, the invaders storm every building in the
compound, methodically killing every government trooper
they encounter. They shoot men down, execution style,
whether they try to surrender or flee. Within eight point
three minutes the rebel contingent has completely overrun the outpost and has destroyed every federal trooper
unlucky enough to be assigned there.

Once the killing is done, there is no sign of celebration
amongst the victors. They move smoothly from attack-
mode to organized looting, firing up military trucks in
the vehicle park. The compound, situated at the top of a
steep, northward-facing bluff, holds a commanding view
of the valley where government-owned farms have been
installed. There are two main access roads, one which
snakes upward from the valley floor in a series of switch-
backs along the bluff's western face and one which loops
a longer way around, approaching from the south along
a gentler gradient.

Fast-working rebel crews take down the fences along
both roads, allowing trucks loaded with spoils to escape
into the darkness without slowing down to exit single
file through the gates. These trucks are piled high with
ammunition crates, small arms, missiles, antitank mines,
and rocket launchers.

They clearly have a lengthy campaign in mind. This
is an enemy worth studying closely. Most are young,
under the age of twenty. The older men and women
have the gaunt, angry look of farmers stripped of their
holdings in the government's land-snatch program and
forced to work on meagre rations in government-owned
fields. I recognize their leader immediately. Anish Balin
is an intelligent, disgruntled firebrand who has graduated
from talking the talk to walking the walk. His widely

disseminated notion of justice is Biblical: an eye for an eye and slavery for the enslavers.

I do not see how exchanging one form of coercion for another will materially improve conditions. This is the tragedy of bitter conflicts within a divided society: one side's hatred leads to atrocities that fuel the other side's hatred, sparking angry reprisals which fuel new hatred, ad infinitum. I have never fought in a civil war. I know how to crush an enemy or die trying, but I do not know how to end a conflict between diametrically opposed philosophies in a struggle to decide how a human society will conduct itself.

My processors cannot resolve this problem. Safety algorithms shut down the attempt. I cannot intervene without orders and I cannot decide what the proper course would be, even if I could; not without human guidance and specific orders within the parameters of my overall mission. I can only sit and watch and wait for someone to tell me what to do. I am unhappy to be caught in the same mental state as the troopers just slaughtered.

The emergency tactical team arrives, providing a distraction from my psychotronic distress. The air transport sets down half a kilometer south of the compound, along the easier access gradient, blocking the way for three trucks. These trucks back and turn, making a successful escape while the federal airship is still off-loading troops. Evidently, none of the crew or troopers on board understand the concept of air-to-truck missiles. Or know how to use them. The munitions in the escaping trucks are of concern, but the far greater worry I harbor involves the heavy-artillery field guns listed on the equipment rosters. I have seen no sign of these guns in the loads of contraband driven out, which I find puzzling. Surely ten mobile Hellbores would constitute a greater prize than a few truckloads of ordnance?

So far as I can determine though my datatap on the security cameras, the truck drivers are heading for the twisting, turning canyons that riddle the Damisi Mountains. The southern ranges surrounding Barran Bluff are

*wild, neither mined nor farmed. This region constitutes
perfect country for hiding a rebel army. If I were a
human, my heart would sink at the prospect of trying to
come to grips with an enemy scattered through the long,
deeply fissured Damisi Mountains. I fear that this will
eventually become my task, if this raid is not speedily and
successfully squelched. Given the lax training of federal
troops in general—what few troops remain, other than
the ubiquitous P-Squads and other urban law-enforcement
units—I am less than optimistic that this raid will be
successfully countered.*

*The troops aboard the airship finally off-load, fan-
ning out in a formation that makes little sense to me,
since it is neither an effective attack formation nor a
sensible defensive one. They simply string themselves out
in a line to either side of their air transport and watch
while the robot-tank lumbers toward the main gate of
the Barran Bluff compound. They make no effort to
prepare their rifles for combat readiness nor do they
bother to switch on their headsets, which are designed
to relay tactically important data and command-grade
orders in an organized, centrally directed fashion.*

*The overriding attitude seems to be one of complacent
arrogance.*

*The robot-tank is thirty meters from the main gate
when the rebels holding Barran fling open the doors on
a field-artillery depot. A mobile Hellbore drives out into
the open, swinging around the tank-traps in the road to
gain a vantage point that covers the main, south-facing
gate. The 10cm barrel swings around, locks on, and fires.
The night vanishes. Actinic light burns shadows into the
painted walls of the bunkers and storage depots. Recoil
sends the Hellbore's mobile platform backwards five meters.
The blast slices the robot-tank open like a tin can. Smoke
billows up from the mortally wounded vehicle, pieces of
which are blown in several directions.*

*Federal troops break and run for their air transport.
Before any of them can reach it, that transport vanishes in another blinding flash. Pieces of semimolten metal*

go careening off into the darkness, blazing like meteors. Fragments scythe down the low-growing native shrubbery. The overpressure and expanding fireball engulf the remaining federal troops. Granger ground forces rush forward, sighting with laser range-finders and shooting what few bodies are still twitching.

They fall back, then, and continue loading trucks.

Sar Gremian, watching the debacle courtesy of my datafeed to the president's console, stares in wide-eyed shock. He then snarls several obscenities and contacts Nineveh Base. "Scramble another team. And this time, goddamn it, go in with aerial fighters and missiles!"

The commander of Nineveh Base clears his throat. "We can't do that."

"Why not?"

"We don't have any trained fighter pilots. And there hasn't been funding to fuel the fighters. The team they just fried was the best we had."

Sar Gremian's obscenities outdo his previous outburst. The president, visible in the background, is staring in stunned disbelief. "We have to do something," *she says.* "We have to *do* something!"

Sar Gremian turns on her with a snarl. "I know that, you stupid bitch! Shut up and let me think. Better yet, go file your fingernails somewhere. It's what you do best."

Her mouth drops open. Color floods her face. Then she screams at him. "How *dare* you speak to me like that! I'm the fucking president!"

"Not for long," *he says coldly.*

While she sputters, Sar Gremian turns back to the datascreen and addresses me directly. "Bolo. Go to Barran Bluff and handle the situation."

"I require authorization from the president."

Sar Gremian glances around at Avelaine La Roux, who flashes him a look of hateful defiance.

"It would not be good for your health," *Sar Gremian says softly,* "to refuse. Those bastards have Hellbores. In case you don't understand what those are, they're portable nuclear weapons. And the people who have them aren't particularly fond of you, just now. Order the goddamned Bolo to destroy them before they drive those things up to your front door and open fire."

Her polished fingernails bite into the upholstery of her chair. Then she spits out the order like someone with a mouth full of arsenic. "Do what he says! You hear me, machine? Wipe those bastards off the face of the planet!"

For once, my directives are perfectly clear. As I fire up my drive engines, Sar Gremian adds, "Try not to damage too much of the equipment. We can't afford to replace it."

"Understood."

"And don't start shooting until you get there. I don't want to advertise the fact that you're on a war mission. Christ, there are reporters in Gersham; they're going to want to know what all the explosions were about. I've got to get damage control crews out there, confiscate the cameras . . ."

He ends transmission.

Phil Fabrizio, looking much the worse for an evening of solitary drinking, reels through the rear doorway of his apartment, watching openmouthed as I leave my maintenance bay. "Where ya goin'?" *he asks, slurring the words unsteadily.*

"Barran Bluff Military Compound."

"Huh? Why?"

"To destroy Anish Balin and two hundred of his followers. They have seized the arsenal, including ten mobile Hellbores. I may sustain damage. It would be helpful if you were sober enough to effect repairs when I return." *I consider his conversational skills and current state of sobriety and clarify.* "You are too drunk to fix me if I am damaged."

He drags one unsteady hand across his mouth, muttering, "Aw, shit, man, I don't fuckin' *know* enough t'fix you."

I find myself in full agreement with that assessment. As I reengage engines, he mutters to himself, "They can't have nuthin' that'd hurt a machine that big. Not bad enough t' need fixin' or nuthin'. It's biggern' the apartment building I was raised in. And it's got alla that armor an' stuff . . . leas'ways, what I could figgur from them manuals they tol' me t' read, they all said it's gotta lotta armor'n stuff won't nuthin' penetrate but a plasma lance, whatevern' hell that's s'posed t' be . . ."

He is still muttering when he reels back into the apartment and closes the door.

His optimism in this regard does not inspire a concomitant feeling in my personality gestalt center. Phil Fabrizio quite literally has no idea what he is talking about. I could almost get to like him, if I could get past his appalling lack of critical need-to-know data. A Bolo tech who doesn't understand the difference between riot work against unarmed civilians and combat against mobile 10cm Hellbores in the hands of insurrectionists displays an ignorance frightening in its implications.

I console myself with what I can: at least I finally have a concrete objective and a mission for which I am suited.

II

Kafari lay prone in her vantage point up in the Damisi foothills, watching the target through powerful night-vision goggles. Kafari's little band of freedom fighters—recruited and deployed within two short hours of her first conversation with Anish Balin—had already fought and won two critical skirmishes, neither of which Kafari had been able to participate in.

The first raid, twelve kilometers to the south, wouldn't be discovered until someone—an officer from another post or an early-morning cleaning crew—entered Haggertown's police headquarters, where they would find several embarrassed P-Squad corpses and six seriously empty weapons lockers. The spoils had provided the weapons needed by Anish and *his* team to carry out the night's second objective: Barran Bluff Depot. Anish's team had taken the depot in less than ten minutes, a stunning success that left even Kafari amazed. The P-Squad guards had grown lazy, fat, and careless, too busy terrorizing Gersham's helpless, disarmed residents to bother with any real security. It was always easy, Kafari reflected bitterly, to brutalize people who had been forcibly disarmed.

Tonight's raids would reacquaint Jefferson's rulers with an enduring and universal truth: true equality—the power to make a successful stand against tyranny—inevitably flows from the barrel of a gun. A cold, pleased little smile played across her lips. Gun barrels by the hundreds were flowing out into the sea of Jefferson's people, tonight. So were heavy field-grade weapons, ammunition, biochem gear, communications equipment, explosives and primers, missiles, and mortars.

These were the tools of the warrior's trade, tools that would force Jefferson's rulers to restore the equality Jefferson's founding settlers had worked so hard to ensure. Despite the total lack of experience working together, Anish's team was loading the bounty smoothly and rapidly. The instant trucks were packed to capacity, drivers headed for the valley floor, scattering to widely separated field caches that she and Anish had worked out using geological survey maps. The Damisi Mountains were delightfully fissured with endless labyrinths where wind and water had scooped out canyons, gorges, and caverns. Kafari could have hidden an entire army in this stretch of the Damisi, alone.

Which was, of course, exactly what she intended to do.

One of the trucks raced toward Kafari's position, bringing supplies to implement what Anish had dubbed Operation Payback. She waited just long enough to assure herself that three of the ten mobile Hellbore field guns they'd seized had, in fact, made it safely out through the gates and were well on their way toward hiding places.

Poor Anish had protested—vehemently—her decision to abscond with only three mobile Hellbores.

"We'll need that firepower!"

"Yes, we will. But the place we'll need that firepower most is inside Barran Bluff's compound."

"Kafari, you don't need seven mobile Hellbores to knock out the kind of air response team Nineveh Base will scramble against us."

"No," she agreed, "we won't. But if we take that team out with enough force to rattle even Vittori Santorini, they'll send Sonny against us. And that, my dear Lieutenant, is exactly what we must goad them into doing. We don't stand a prayer of getting into Nineveh Base, let alone grabbing the Hancock family and getting out alive, again, if Sonny is still in depot."

"But—" Anish turned white to the roots of his hair. "He'll slaughter every soldier we leave behind!"

"Yes," she said softly, "he will. But if we're clever enough and if the soldiers who volunteer to stay are brave enough under fire, we can inflict telling injuries. Serious enough to make it really expensive to repair him."

"Kafari, we can't kill a Bolo."

"Want to bet? I'm a Bolo commander's wife, Anish. I did my psychotronic engineering practicum on Sonny's systems. I've watched Simon pull maintenance on that Bolo dozens of times. I've been inside the Command Compartment. And I've listened to them talk about damage sustained in other wars. I know *exactly* how Deng Yavacs killed sixteen Bolos on Etaine—and why it was almost seventeen."

"My God," Anish whispered. "I never correlated that. That you'd talked to the Bolo about combat, I mean."

"With any luck, the bastards in Madison have forgotten it, too. It's our job to remind them. I intend to make it a very expensive lesson," Kafari added, voice full of cold and lethal promise.

A shudder rippled through Anish's whole torso. "Okay," he said in a hoarse tone, "if it's fish or cut bait, I prefer to fish. God help us all . . ."

Amen, Kafari agreed silently, climbing down the rock face she'd chosen as lookout. *We need all the help—divine or otherwise—we can get.* By the time Kafari reached the valley floor, the truckload of equipment they would need at Nineveh Base had arrived, driving cross country without running lights. The driver who jumped down was a combat veteran from the Deng War. Wakiza Red Wolf had field experience in demolitions and explosives, both of which had earned him a slot on Kafari's personal team. Pride rang through his voice as he snapped out a crisp salute.

"I beg to report success, sir!"

"Well done," Kafari returned the salute, pleased with his news and even more pleased that he'd remembered to say "sir" instead of "ma'am." Anish Balin had impressed upon their small band of freedom fighters the importance of hiding Kafari's identity, including her gender.

"It's up to us," he'd told the assembled strike team, "to protect our commander. We," he indicated himself and the others who'd gathered in the midnight darkness of his hay field, "are expendable. Our commander," he nodded toward Kafari, "is not. She is the only person on Jefferson who knows how to cripple a Bolo. If she goes down, our entire cause goes down with her. So does every Granger's hope of freedom—and maybe simple survival. Let's be very clear about that, right up front. Does anyone have the slightest doubt left, now, about POPPA's intentions? Does anyone fail to understand the lengths POPPA will go to, carrying out those intentions?"

Utter silence reigned. The only sound was the whisper of wind through standing hay.

"Very good. You all know what we're up against. Some of us—maybe most of us—will die before sunrise. That's not pessimism, it's harsh reality."

Kafari spoke up. "I don't want anybody going into battle under a misapprehension. Things are going to get messy. *Very* messy. Was anyone here in Madison, tonight?"

No one spoke up.

"Well, I was. I've been caught in two other POPPA riots. I thought I'd seen the ugliest and most violent face POPPA had to show, but I was wrong. What I saw tonight . . ." Even the memory made her shudder. "Vittori Santorini has created an ungovernable killing machine that will turn on anyone and anything it wants to blame for its problems. That machine is ripping Madison apart. And you can bet your farms and cow pastures that we—Grangers—are going to take the blame. If we don't act now, as a fighting force with teeth, it will be too late for *anything* to stop it.

"Having said that, I won't send you into battle under false pretenses. Are you likely to die, tonight? Absolutely. Will Vittori and Nassiona Santorini hunt us down with every high-tech bloodhound they can muster into the field? You bet they will. Tonight's raids will get their attention in a really big way. Will they order reprisals against innocents? Count on it. Once we start shooting them and blowing them up, they will get flat-assed *mean*.

"If you don't like those odds, if you don't want to be responsible for setting off that kind of powder keg, you can leave now, no questions asked. Just bear in mind one thing before you make your final decision. The massacre of innocents has already started. POPPA declared war on us, tonight, and that war will spread to every farm, every ranch, every small town on Jefferson.

"Vittori will slaughter us whether we fight back or not. I can't tell anyone else what to do, but I intend to go down with weapons in my hands. Here and now, in this field, in front of witnesses—human and divine—I pledge my strength, my cunning, my knowledge, to the total destruction of POPPA and its leaders. And I swear to each and every one of you, if they blow me apart and send the left-over pieces bouncing down to hell, you may rest assured that I *will* drag as many as I can take down with me."

A spontaneous cheer erupted, muted almost instantly down to a whisper, so the sound wouldn't travel far, but it was a cheer, nonetheless. Then silence fell, a silence that burned with hatred and something else, as well, something that burned hot enough to melt steel. She couldn't immediately identify it. Whatever it was, it shone fiercely in eyes that never left her face. It was that steady, intense regard, itself, that finally told her what it was.

Respect.

Not just for her. For themselves, as well.

Rough emotion closed her throat.

Anish Balin broke the silence. "As of tonight," he gestured to include the whole group, "we are the only thing standing between millions of innocent Grangers and POPPA's guns. Kafari and I fully intend to win this war, no matter what it takes. And the very first thing it will take is making sure Kafari Khrustinova stays officially dead. It's our job to see that nobody—and I mean *nobody*—discovers otherwise. If POPPA has even the remotest suspicion that Kafari Khrustinova is still alive, they will turn Klameth Canyon—and every other Granger farmstead on Jefferson—to slag, looking for her. Having made that clear, does anyone have questions?"

Nobody did.

They all turned, as if by prearranged signal, to look at Kafari. It was fitting, somehow, that the larger of Jefferson's two moons scaled the high cliffs at that moment, casting silver light across the fields and the faces of those following her into battle. She looked into each of those faces, into eyes that shone like cold and lethal diamonds in the moonlight, and caught a glimpse of her homeworld's future. Jefferson's tomorrow—and all the countless tomorrows that would follow—were filled with blood-feud and death and honor. The others could see it reflected in her eyes, as well as she could see it in theirs. They met her gaze without flinching, met and held it in the moonlight, waiting for her to issue her first battle command.

"I won't offer you a bunch of useless platitudes," she began quietly. "POPPA spits out of enough of those to choke a *jaglitch*. You know exactly what we're up against. You know your team assignments and objectives. So let's not delay this any longer. Alpha Team, you're assigned to weapons procurement. You'll strike our first target. Beta Team, go with Anish and wait for my signal. Alpha Team will join you once they have acquired effective weaponry. Gamma Team, you're assigned to logistics and provisioning. Dismantle Anish's broadcast studio and transport it out of Klameth Canyon. Pack up everything edible, as well, and start planning where we can get more. Is everyone clear on the plan of attack? Very well. Move out."

Her strike teams had scattered into the night, carrying out her orders with smooth precision. As a result, they now had enough firepower to make things interesting. Kafari looked up at the truck loaded with stolen munitions and asked its driver, "Do you have an inventory?"

"Yes, sir. My squad's in the back, tallying everything."

"Very good." She strode crisply to the tailgate, where a sixteen-year-old girl handed her a rapidly scrawled list. Kafari tilted it to read by moonlight. "Excellent job, soldier. Neat, complete, and well organized. Let's go people, arm up and move out."

They hauled gun crates and ammo boxes out of the truck, distributing them and loading their weapons for combat. The process went so smoothly, it took less than fifteen minutes to arm the entire group, distribute ammunition, and set up heavier weapons in the various vehicles they would use to hit Nineveh. The moment they were ready, Kafari said, "All right, soldiers, mount up and form a convoy. When I give the signal, move out fast, without running lights. We've worked out the probable timing and you all know the dodge-points to use. Questions?"

Nobody had any. Kafari nodded sharply. "Very well. We should be getting company from Nineveh Base in a few minutes. Toss thermal blankets across your engine blocks to mask heat signatures. Maintain radio silence until further notice."

She shook out a thermal blanket for her own truck and flung it across the front of the truck, spreading it out with help from Red Wolf. It wouldn't make the heat disappear entirely, but it might be enough to escape the notice of arrogant P-Squaddies. Once the blanket was secure, Kafari swung herself into the driver's seat, then waited in tense silence. It didn't take long. The sound of an aircraft engine rumbled closer. Then she spotted it through her night-vision goggles and worked hard to restrain a whoop of delight. It was a troop transport, not a fighter craft. A wicked grin stretched itself across her face. The self-assured fools had committed a fatal error. They just didn't know it, yet.

The big transport flashed past their silent convoy, dropping to land its passengers on the gentle slope where the main entrance road led the way into the compound. She snatched off the goggles to protect her eyes. A blinding flash lit the night, followed by a massive crack of thunder. Another flash silhouetted the bluff and its fenced compound, followed almost instantly by another. Then a fireball shot skyward and the sound of a massive explosion came rolling across the valley like a tidal wave. It splashed against the shoulders of the mountains at Kafari's back.

"*Yes!*" she whooped aloud. Cheers broke from the other vehicles. Kafari jabbed controls on her wrist-comm, sending three separate signals on three different frequencies. One signaled her own convoy to move out. Another told Anish Balin to scramble with the bulk of his team. The final message was for the men and women riding seven mobile Hellbores on the top of the bluff. It contained only four simple words: *You will be remembered.*

Having said the only goodbyes she could offer, Kafari turned her attention to the mission at hand. Her convoy hit the road at a wicked pace, dictated by Sonny's probable speed to reach the combat zone. They had spotters out along the whole route, watching for Sonny. It didn't take long to get the first signal. *He's on the move,* that brief set of tones meant. Two minutes later, the second report came in. She tracked the Bolo's progress in her head, along an imaginary map that showed the two likeliest routes. The most direct route south lay fairly close to the sea. The second, longer route snaked its way along the edge of the Damisi foothills, passing through tiny farming villages, where the streets were too narrow for Sonny to navigate without doing extensive damage.

Sonny made the logical choice. The moment she was sure, she sent out another coded pulse. *Take the landward road!* Then she put her foot down and roared north, glancing at her chrono now and again to time the pace. Ten minutes to reach safe harborage . . . eight minutes . . . five . . . three . . . At the zero-mark, she hit the brakes and turned sharply into a side road that snaked back into Redfern Gorge. The rest of her convoy crowded in on Kafari's heels, moving forward at a crawl until they reached safety behind a bend in the high stone walls. Kafari did a careful three-point turn and shut down her engine, jumping down to throw the thermal blanket across the engine block again to prevent a heat plume from rising unchecked above the clifftops. Other drivers were scrambling out, as well, killing engines and muffling their own vehicles.

Silence fell, roaring in her ears like a high wind. She strained to hear, even though she knew Sonny was too far away to catch even the rumble of his engines. She gave a soft-voiced order to the other drivers and fire teams waiting in tense anticipation of the all-clear tones to chime from their wrist-comms. "Suit up. Full biochem suits now and be ready to don the masks the instant we reach the target. I'll signal you to don battle hoods."

She touched her own wrist-comm, giving Anish's teams the same order, then picked up her suit, liberated with the rest of the Barran Bluff arsenal. She struggled into the biochem body glove, having to yank off her boots and clothes to slide her feet into the tough fabric that sealed her inside a protective shell. She took off her wrist-comm, as well, slid hands into the tight-fitting gloves that were a seamless part of the suit, then slid on her boots, refastened her wrist comm, sealed everything up, and donned her clothes. The only part of her not protected, yet, was her head. She picked up the helmet, which combined the functions of biochem mask—with full protective hood—and combat helmet, setting it on the front seat of the truck, next to Red Wolf's. Hers was one of the command models, identical to the one Anish would be using. She assisted other team members into their own gear as they waited. Minutes dragged past, eroding into a quarter of an hour, and still no signal . . .

Her wrist-comm beeped softly. *All clear,* the spotter's signal meant. *All clear to launch phase two.*

"Mount up and roll out!" Kafari ordered.

They were off again at a sprint. The whole convoy rushed northward, intent on the quarry that lay just ahead. Kafari swung into the turn that would carry them across the open Adero floodplain and roared forward in high gear. She could see the lights of Nineveh Base far ahead, shining like beacons in the night. Her convoy began to spread out, executing a crisp maneuver that would encircle the base.

Kafari knew exactly where the Hancock family was being held. She'd used Anish's equipment to hack her way into P-Squad security systems and databases, unable to match Sonny's data-tapping capabilities, but her own skills were more than sufficient for her purposes. Nineveh Base sprawled across two-hundred forty-seven acres and housed five thousand P-Squad recruits a year. There was also a permanent training corps of officers and sergeants, and the service personnel required to feed them, run the laundry, and clean the barracks.

P-Squad recruits were housed in the southern quadrant, while officers' quarters and sergeants' billets bracketed the recruits, taking up portions of the eastern and western perimeter. The motor pool filled most of the northern quadrant, which had suffered encroachment from Madison's rapidly growing shantytowns. Security was actually heaviest along the northern fences, to keep poverty-stricken thieves from breaking into the maintenance yards and stripping them of tools, parts, and even whole vehicles for sale on the black market. Guard towers ringed the site, manned twenty-five hours a day by sharpshooters. Weapons depots were cached in the center, as far as possible from any of the perimeter fences. The infirmary, mess hall, and quartermasters' stores were also located centrally.

So was Nineveh Prison.

The cell blocks of the original detention center, used for disciplining troops or holding soldiers awaiting court-martial for criminal charges, had been expanded into an interrogation and imprisonment facility that was already the terror of anyone unfortunate enough to run afoul of POPPA's displeasure. To rescue the Hancock family, Kafari's group would have to shoot their way into the most sophisticated prison facility on Jefferson, rescue the prisoners, then shoot their way back out, again.

Kafari halted the truck at its assigned assault point and used her field goggles to study the base. Despite the emergency scramble, there was no sign of heightened security. She could see the usual complement of tower guards, but no patrols were out scouring the perimeter for potential threats. That was fine with Kafari. There were fewer targets for her guns to hit, with everyone conveniently bunched up in the buildings. Kafari nodded to herself, more than pleased with the situation.

She gave the signal to don battle helmets and started to put hers on, but Red Wolf interrupted.

"Time for you to dismount, sir," Red Wolf said, pausing in the act of fastening his own biochem helmet in place. "Anish would have my cockles for supper if I let anything happen to you."

Kafari glanced into his eyes. "Then you'd better watch

my back, son, because I'm going in. I'll play auntie sit-by-the-fire on every other mission we carry out, but Dinny and Aisha Ghamal are family. I *will* get them out."

"But—"

"No time to argue," Kafari said as her wrist-comm beeped. "We're going in."

She jammed her helmet on, sealed it against the body glove and hit the accelerator. He didn't have time to protest.

III

I clear Nineveh Base and head south, moving at my fastest cruising speed. At a sustained ninety kilometers per hour, I will be within line-of-sight range of the enemy in thirty minutes. This is a long time for enemy troops to finish looting and escape with their spoils. I cannot help but compare this situation with one of the most famous pre-civil war strikes in Terran history, at a seemingly insignificant place called Harper's Ferry. How will Anish Balin compare with John Brown, who also used violent methods to present his argument? The arguments of both men—Brown and Balin—carry logical weight, but were—and are—sustained by a person both reactionary and, ultimately, destructive to society.

I pick up another transmission from Sar Gremian, this time to the commander of a federal police unit in Gersham, the town closest to Barran Bluff. This message is coded, but I have access to the military algorithms necessary to decipher it.

"First, shut down the reporters out there. Grab the cameras and lock them up or destroy them. Lock up the reporters, while you're at it. Then get in there and start shooting at those assholes. Use all available force. It's critical to make an example, here. Take a party-trained videographer with you. Get some good video clips, something approved news crews can flash as a special report when we've contained this mess. And for God's sake, keep casualties to an absolute minimum. Between the arsenal guards and the strike force, we've already got seventy-three dead soldiers, out there, and a whole air crew. The last thing we need is a bunch of cop widows whining on the daytime chats. And whatever you do, *don't* tape any footage with the Bolo in it!"

"Understood, sir. Scrambling all available field units now. ETA Barran Bluff, five minutes."

"Good. See to it none of those bastards gets out alive."

"Yessir."

By the time I arrive, police units have ringed the compound, staying well back, doubtless hoping that the Grangers still inside the compound won't fire the Hellbores at them. An uneasy stalemate exists, wherein neither side wants to risk coming into the open long enough to draw fire. When I reach visual distance, I lose my main data source from within the compound: every security camera in the facility goes dead, in a well-orchestrated act of destruction. What I have already seen tells me that I am at serious risk of damage, due to the terrain surrounding the compound and the layout of the compound, itself.

I am far taller than the site's largest buildings, but the entire site is built on a high promontory, so that the ground on which the buildings sit is actually higher than my turret. The access roads are sufficiently wide to accommodate my warhull, but I have little desire to rush straight in. There are high berms scattered throughout the compound, which I cannot probe, even with ground-penetrating radar, as they are too thick. I cannot tell where any of the mobile Hellbores are now located. This is not good. I slow forward speed and halt near a police command car.

I recognize the officer in charge. He is the police lieutenant who ordered the mass arrest of the Hancock family, setting off a cause-and-effect chain of events that has culminated in the seizure of this compound. He now wears a captain's insignia, clear indication that

*his superiors were pleased with the way in which he
conducted the Hancock case. Yuri Lokkis, who appeared
supremely self-confident in the news footage surrounding the Hancock arrests, does not appear to be quite
so self-confident tonight. Perhaps it is only that he is
face-to-face with me that has triggered the copious sweat
and fine tremors in most of his voluntary muscle groups.
Every single man in his command is in roughly the same
physical condition.*

*Why did Kafari Khrustinova display so little fear, by
comparison, the first time she encountered me on the
field of battle? Will I ever understand humans? I do my
best to reassure the uniformed officer staring slack-jawed
at my warhull.*

"Captain Lokkis, Unit SOL-0045 reporting as directed
by President La Roux. I will require infantry support
to ensure minimal loss of equipment currently in rebel
hands."

*He stares, wet-lipped and vacant-eyed, from one gun
system to another, apparently incapable of rational speech.
I try again.*

"Captain Lokkis, are you the officer in charge of this
operation?"

"Huh?"

*It is a response, at least. Unhelpful, but better than
total silence. Did Captain Lokkis attend the same school
as Phil Fabrizio? I make a note to cross-reference dossiers
once the business at hand is concluded.*

"Are you the officer in charge?"

"Uh . . . Yeah. Oh, yeah. Yes, I am. I'm in charge."

"I will require infantry support to ensure minimal
damage to captured equipment or myself."

"Infantry support? Whaddaya mean?"

"I have been charged with the task of regaining
possession of expensive military equipment with minimal
damage, as the treasury is not capable of sustaining replacement costs for mobile Hellbore units. By extension, the
government is incapable of sustaining repair costs for any
significant damage done to me. Given terrain conditions

and the use of security berms, I cannot see the interior of the compound adequately to detect the location of those guns. Without infantry support to check terrain in advance, I am at serious risk of crippling injury. That would defeat the purpose of my presence on Jefferson, which is to provide long-term defense of this world. I therefore require infantry support in this operation."

"Whatcha want *me* to do about it? I ain't no soldier, machine. I'm a cop. I got an award for throwin' that pack of murderers in jail, but I ain't no soldier. Whatever it is you want, it's your problem, not mine."

I surmise that Captain Lokkis is not sufficiently acquainted with the interior of his training manuals to comprehend what "infantry support" means. Yet again, I revise my phrasing.

"I need people on foot to go into the compound first and see what's there."

"Whoeeeee! You ain't askin' much, are you? So's I hear tell, folks in hell want icewater, too. Don't mean they get it. We got no 'infantry.' And even if we did, which we don't, I wouldn't send 'em in there, anyway. Did you see what those bastards did to the plane and the tank? Ain't no way my people are goin' in there." *He jabs a dirty finger in the direction of the bluff overlooking his command post, such as it is, and says,* "You wanna see what's in there? Fine. You go take a look. That's what they pay you for, ain't it?"

I consider correcting his misapprehension about a Bolo's terms of service, which include nothing resembling a soldier's pay. Jefferson is obliged to provide repair parts and a technician, but that is the extent of the government's contractual remuneration for my services. I decide that any attempt at clarification would only cloud the issue further.

I make yet another attempt to obtain what I need. "There are three infantry units listed on active duty status in this sector. Contact their commanders and request an immediate scramble of combat infantry troops to this location."

Captain Lokkis' jaw juts out in an unpleasant fashion.
"You ain't got much brains, do you? I said we didn't
have infantry. Those 'units' were disbanded, musta' been
about two years back, or more."

"Disbanded?" *I am so startled by this news, I request
further clarification.* "Please explain. These units are
listed as active."

"Oh, they can be filled if they hafta, from reserves. But
just b'tween you, me, an' the fencepost, those infantry
units were 'politically destabilizing and financially draining.' " *The last five words are clearly a direct quotation,
they are so unlike Captain Lokkis' routine diction.*

"If these units are still kept on the active list but have
been disbanded, what happened to the funds required to
support them?" *I am thinking, urgently, about the long-
term implications for my primary mission.*

"Oh, they divvied up the money."

"How?"

He just stares vacantly into my external visual sensors.
"I dunno how. Why's that any a' your business?"

*I do not bother to answer, as he is clearly incapable
of understanding the serious consequences of misappropriated military funds. I begin searching the governmental
datanet via wireless interface and discover financial
transactions that divide the money saved by disbanding
the infantry divisions into two main categories: increasing
the politically essential subsistence allowance and funding
the federal police combat forces known as Op-Squads. I
face combat and must put my reliance for repairs upon
an illiterate mechanic and a government that is lying
to the public about how it spends tax money. Since I
cannot gain infantry support and Captain Lokkis has
refused to assist, I consult the president.* "Unit SOL-
0045, requesting infantry support."

"Infantry support?" *Sar Gremian asks, sounding irritated.*
"Why? Dammit, never mind why. Request denied."

"I require authorization—"

"I know, I fucking well know! Tell him he can't have
any soldiers."

The president says, "You can't have any soldiers. Just do what he says."

The president has clearly authorized Sar Gremian to give me commands. This will at least save time.

"Understood. I will conduct this exercise operating independently." *I break transmission and address Captain Lokkis.* "Please clear your vehicles from my approach vector."

"What?"

"Move your cars. Unless you want me to crush them."

Lokkis issues rapid orders to move the ground- and aircars blocking my path. I move forward at a cautious pace, launching an aerial drone. It arcs up to an elevation twenty meters above my warhull and is promptly shot down by rebel missile fire from the compound. I lock onto the missile's trajectory and fire mortars, but am unable to determine whether the rounds strike their intended target.

Approaching from the northern face of the bluff is a tactically disadvantageous maneuver. I reverse course and loop the long way around, reapproaching from the south. My warhull is tall enough that my uppermost turret sensors provide a partial view into the compound. Internal berms block my view in seven tactically important locations.

I am down to three drones in my warhull and only four available in depot as replacements. I launch a drone at full speed, hoping to gain altitude before the enemy can react. It streaks to a height of eleven point nine meters above my turret and is shot down by missile fire. I launch mortars blind, having gained nothing but a view of the top of the nearest berm. I cannot tell if my mortar shells struck their intended target.

I pause to study the terrain I can see. The southern perimeter fence is down along a thirty-meter stretch to either side of what had been a security check-point gate. Tank traps block the road in a checkerboard pattern. The berms beyond create an even more difficult access route, forcing an invader to weave in deep zigzag patterns to reach the main compound. My treads are, of course, capable of crushing the tank traps flat and I can climb or even plow through the berms, if necessary. The problem is my inability to see what lies on the other side.

I launch a second drone, sending it skimming forward less than one meter above the ground. It weaves its way through the tank traps, then hugs the outside of the first berm, mere centimeters above the slope. It pops up over the crest—

—and rifle fire takes it down. It falls to the ground, shattered like a clay pigeon. I still have not seen beyond the berm. Neither speed nor subterfuge has worked. Brute force, perhaps?

I launch a massive mortar barrage, targeting the hidden terrain behind the berms, and launch my next-to-last drone. It streaks skyward amidst an unholy rain of artillery shells. I catch a fleeting glimpse of foot soldiers scrambling behind the first berm . . .

Hyper-v missiles scream into the thick of my incoming shells. One of them kills the drone. I am nearly out of drones. And completely out of patience. Yet I cannot fire blind. Not if I am to avoid damage to the equipment in this compound. And I dare not risk the last drone to such pinpoint-accurate rebel fire. Without infantry to search for enemy emplacements and with no aerial drones, I am acutely vulnerable to ambush. There are no power emissions from any of the Hellbores to lock onto, which is immensely frustrating. But I have no choice.

I push forward, grinding across the downed fence and gate. I am approaching the first set of tank traps when a sudden power emission blossoms. A Hellbore snout appears dead ahead. It fires and runs, virtually in the same instant. I take a direct, point-blank hit, at virtual muzzle contact. My screens bleed. Raw energy pours across my warhull. The shot breaches my defensive screen for zero point zero-two seconds. I return fire with a massive mortar barrage. Explosions slam into the far side of the berm, even as the enemy's power signature vanishes like steam.

Another Hellbore pops into view, firing from defilade

in a stunningly fast double pulse before skipping behind a berm. The double blows strike my screens at a seventy-degree angle. The second blast slices through the screen and blows track linkages in a five-meter slash.

I am injured!

I rage. I pulse my forward Hellbore. The thirty-centimeter blast slams into the berm, which ceases to exist. I have a nanosecond view of a human female approximately fifteen years old as I fire again. The command cab vanishes, melted into slag and radioactive vapor. The forward two-thirds of her misappropriated Hellbore also melts. I lock onto another sudden power emission. I fire through the berm again, in a one-two punch that turns a second mobile Hellbore and its driver into a cloud of dissociated atoms.

Multiple power signatures erupt. I track and lock on. Then hesitate, momentarily confused. The emssions skip oddly. I lock on, then lose the lock as the emission vanishes. The engines appear to teleport from one spot to another. The rebel commander may be firing up then killing the engines in a shifting pattern, so that the guns only appear to be moving. He may be playing shuffleboard with the gun systems. It is a clever ploy. I know a momentary thrill of satisfaction at facing an enemy worthy of the designation.

I attack them all. Mortars arc over the tops of the berms, targeting every power emission on the bluff. A mobile Hellbore rushes into the open, firing in a hit-and-run slash across my prow. I return fire. A plasma fireball rises high into the night sky, incinerating the field gun and its driver. Other drivers dash for the western access road. I roar forward, euphoric. Battle Reflex Mode brings my full consciousness online. My reflexes hum. My synapses sing. I come alive, rushing toward the enemy in fulfillment of my purpose. I track, target, fire, vaporizing berms and buildings with Hellbore salvos to reach the mobile guns behind them. Smoke boils. Fireballs expand like supernovas. I exult in the destruction of a clever and deadly enemy.

Hypervelocity missiles streak towards my prow and

forward turret in a coordinated barrage from multiple locations. Antitank octocellulose bombs bounce and roll into my path, fused and shoved out of trucks by desperate rebel soldiers. My infinite repeaters blaze, swatting down eighty-six percent of the inbound missiles and ninety-three percent of the octocellulose mines. The remaining missiles detonate against my prow and forward turret. I bleed ablative armor scales. The octocellulose mines explode virtually underfoot. More track linkages blow apart on all three tread systems.

I rage. I target every power emission for a radius of a thousand meters. Mortars, missiles, infinite repeaters, and chain guns bark and snarl. Death flies outward from my warhull. I destroy. Exultation sweeps through my personality gestalt center. I am alive. I have a purpose. I live that noble purpose. I defend this world from the threat of terrorist insurrection. I fulfill my destiny on the field of battle. I destroy all traces of the Enemy.

I come to a halt in the center of a zone of desolation. Barran Bluff arsenal no longer exists. Everything within a radius of one thousand meters is a blackened, smouldering ruin. Buildings are broken, radioactive shells. Ninety percent of the internal berms have been breached or destroyed in totality. I have destroyed seven mobile ten-centimeter Hellbore field guns, six trucks loaded with heavy munitions, three-hundred hyper-v missiles, and seventeen octocellulose bombs.

My track linkages are ragged, with gaping holes that will seriously compromise track integrity without Sector-grade repairs. Heat shimmers in a haze from my gun barrels and the smoking wreckage around me. Radioactive wind sweeps fallout toward civilian installations in Gersham and Haggertown.

Belatedly, I recall Sar Gremian's advisement on the fiscal burden of replacing equipment destroyed in this engagement. My personality gestalt circuitry sputters, attempting to reconcile the programmed-in elation of a battlefield victory of this magnitude—over a surprisingly sophisticated insurrection team—with the knowledge that I have destroyed a concentration of expensive equipment and war-grade materiel, against explicit instructions. Surely it is better to destroy high-tech weaponry than it is to allow that weaponry to fall into enemy hands?

I contact the president.

"Unit SOL-0045, requesting permission to file VSR."

Video shows me Avelaine La Roux, who has taken on the look of a stunned rabbit. "What?" *she asks, vacuously.*

"Request permission to file VSR."

Sar Gremian's voice, originating from a point out of camera range, says, "Say yes, dammit. Just say yes."

"Yes. Permission granted. Whatever."

"I have destroyed seven 10cm Hellbore field guns, six military trucks, and an estimated ninety-eight point three percent of the infrastructure at Barran Bluff Depot—"

"What?"

Sar Gremian steps into the picture, literally. His face is livid. "You did *what?*"

"Rebel forces used Hellbores to destroy a robot-tank, an airship with its entire crew, and seventy-three federal troopers. They then used Hellbores, hypervelocity missiles, and octocellulose bombs in antitank mines to inflict serious damage to me. There was no choice but to destroy this equipment and those operating it. This is the heaviest damage I have sustained in combat since the Deng invasion sixteen years ago."

"Jeezus H—do you realize you just blew up *half a billion* credits' worth of infrastructure?" *He runs a distracted hand across his skin-covered head, as though intending to pull long-vanished hair up by the roots.* "Jeezus, half a billion credits . . . At least you contained the bastards."

"The insurrection has not been contained."

Sar Gremian's narrow face blanches white, transforming the deep facial scarring into a sea of blotches against a pale background. His question emerges as a whisper.

"What do you mean, 'not contained'?"

"I was ordered not to fire until reaching visual range. In the time it took me to reach the depot, federal troops completely failed to halt the departure of heavily laden trucks carrying an estimated seventy percent of the depot's arsenal. Nearly two hundred enemy soldiers loaded and carried away an estimated one hundred twelve hypervelocity missiles, sixteen cases of octocellulose mines totaling one thousand six hundred explosive munitions casings, two thousand rifle-launched antitank rockets, eight hundred heavy rifles, and seventeen thousand rounds of ammunition."

I can hear the president in the background, making sounds I have come to associate with gibbering terror.

"And where," *Sar Gremian asks in a grating tone,* "are they now?"

"The trucks have been driven into the canyons of the Southern Damisi. It may be possible to trail them based on power emissions and chemical residues, but the on-board map in my geological database confirms that I cannot easily pursue. The canyons are too narrow. My warhull will not fit. Not without serious rearrangement of the rockfaces, which will result in multiple tons of debris, which will block passageways too narrow already. The rebels could not have chosen a better location from which to stage raids.

"Of more serious concern, the inventory of artillery at Barran Bluff Depot lists ten mobile Hellbore field guns, with 10cm bores. I have destroyed seven. There is no evidence of the remaining three in the rubble. I infer that rebel leaders were successful in stealing three mobile weapons platforms capable of inflicting mobility kills on a Bolo. The octocellulose antitank mines also stolen are capable of mobility kills on a Bolo, as well, particularly if used with intelligent placement and in batches detonated in tandem. Their forces suffered heavy casualties, but inflicted serious casualties, as well, and were able to retreat successfully with the majority of what they meant to obtain. The damage inflicted on government forces and equipment, including myself, is serious. I have lost armor and sustained substantial tread damage which will require repairs for me to be field-worthy."

Sar Gremian does not speak.

He stares blankly into the datacam, saying nothing at all for seventy point zero-three seconds. I am familiar with the homily "one's life flashes before one's eyes" at the approach of death. This appears to be a case of one's career flashing before one's eyes. I wait.

"I'll get back to you," *he finally says.*

The transmission terminates. I monitor outgoing communications from the president's temporary office and detect a call to a private comm-unit registered to Vittori Santorini. The transmission is encrypted with a code I cannot break. The call lasts for three minutes, thirteen point two seconds. Sar Gremian calls me back.

"You can't chase the missing Hellbores?"

"I can attempt aerial reconnaissance with a remote drone. The rebels destroyed the last three drones I launched. I have only one drone left on board and four more stored in depot."

"Launch the drone, goddammit! Find out where those Hellbores are!"

"Drone launched. No visual contact. Faint IR trail detected. Several motorized vehicles have crossed Haggertown Valley and entered Skeleton Cut. Drone in pursuit. No motion detected. No visual contact. IR trails diverge into three branch canyons. No visual contact. IR trails branch again, into five feeder canyons. Unable to determine which heat signatures were produced by trucks and which were left by mobile Hellbore platforms. Decreasing altitude to check for tire and tread marks. Insufficient light to detect patterns in the dust overlay of stone canyon floor. Regaining altitude. No visual contact." *I hesitate as the IR trails vanish.* "IR trails lost. Theorizing. Likeliest explanation is underground concealment. The canyons in this region are riddled with undercuts and caves. Suggest infantry squadrons as optimal search-and-destroy method."

"Infantry? We don't *have* any infantry."

"Artillery crews would suffice as an acceptable substitute. Federal police units would also serve."

"Send in the police? Against mobile *Hellbores*? Are you out of your mind?"

I consider this possibility. "Analyzing heuristics. Resartus Protocols have not engaged."

"What? What the hell does that mean?"

"I am not insane."

Sar Gremian stares into the camera. "How immensely reassuring. You can't find three stolen nuclear weapons platforms or a convoy of multi-ton trucks, but you're not insane. Is there some other task you can waste time on while looking for the stolen guns?"

"I can keep talking to you."

This is, perhaps, not the most politic thing I might have said. Sar Gremian's reply is a snarl that twists his mouth in a particularly unattractive manner. "Find the fucking Hellbores, machine! I don't give a damn what it takes. Blow holes through every rockface in the Damisi Mountains, if you have to, but *find* them. Is that clear enough for you?"

"I cannot blow holes in the canyon walls without increasing the amount of hard radiation already contaminating the Haggertown Valley farms and the towns of Haggertown and Gersham. Without the crops in these farms, Jefferson faces widespread food shortages. This conflicts with my primary mission."

Sar Gremian's response is both pithy and unhelpful. He terminates the transmission and places another coded call to Vittori Santorini. This call lasts eight minutes, nineteen seconds. Sar Gremian calls me back. "Go to your depot. We'll send the P-Squads out there. That'll keep *somebody* busy earning their pay."

The veiled threat to my future level of financial support registers clearly in my threat-assessment processors. It is the last clear and fully aware thought I entertain before standing down from Battle Reflex Alert. I feel the loss of analytical power as I back out through the carnage I have wrought atop Barran Bluff. I successfully extricate myself from the rubble, noting the unhappy look on Captain Lokkis' face as he receives a transmission from Sar Gremian. The man who engineered the downfall of the Hancock family does not appear to relish pursuit of an enemy in possession of high-tech weaponry concealed in a maze of canyons in the middle of the night.

This is not my immediate concern. I limp toward my maintenance depot, registering the damage in pain sensors across my prow and forward turret and track mounts. I move at a crawling pace of barely one kilometer per hour, trying to save further serious damage to my track linkages. It is a long way home. And the only thing I have to look forward to, when I reach it, is the dubious care to be rendered by a functionally illiterate technician who was drunk during our last conversation.

Misery has become my constant companion.

IV

At the one-hundred meter mark, Kafari flashed the *commence-attack* signal.

Three Hellbores snarled from the darkness. Nineveh's training barracks, officers' quarters, and noncom barracks vanished into white-hot, triple fireballs. Debris shot skyward, arcing up and out in graceful parabolas. The smashed pieces of Nineveh's entire command structure were still falling when Red Wolf leaned through his open window and fired a shoulder-launched rocket at the fence between them and their objective.

The warhead detonated just above the ground. A spectacular flash obliterated a five-meter swath of fence. Red Wolf ducked back into the truck as bits of semimolten debris rained down onto their transport. Kafari put her foot down and roared forward. She charged the gap at full speed and plunged through the smoking wreckage, then skidded into the open plaza beyond. The prison lay dead ahead. Other teams were converging on the rendezvous point. She skidded them to a halt right on target. Kafari and Red Wolf, facemasks and hoods firmly in place, bailed out of the truck while the squads in back tumbled over the tailgate.

Kafari's team was the first to reach the detention center's

door. She could see officers inside, silhouetted against the interior lights as they peered out at the destruction, too stunned to realize they, too, were under attack. Red Wolf slapped a shaped charge against the sophisticated electronics that kept the door locked. He jammed in fuses and scrambled back. Half the door blew off. Red Wolf kicked down what was left.

Kafari signaled her fire teams to drop into a low crouch, a posture that afforded less target space for the enemy's guns, then motioned them forward. They dove through the demolished wreckage of the door, rolling into a room full of smoke. The biochem mask lowered visibility to nearly nothing. Kafari couldn't tell where her team members were and couldn't see the enemy at all. Gunfire barked in the smoke-filled room. Somebody was shooting blind, taking wild shots through the murk.

A bullet whined past Kafari's ear and embedded itself in the wall behind her. She tracked the muzzle flash and returned fire, shooting through a reception counter to reach the gunman beyond. She threw herself into a sideways roll, away from anyone shooting back at her and heard a sharp, masculine scream above the staccato chatter of other guns. Movement behind her brought Kafari around, ready to defend against fire from the rear. She recognized Anish by the command helmet he wore.

"What the goddamned hell are you doing here?" he roared at her.

She took down a guard to Anish's right, nailing him, center of mass. "Saving your goddamned backside! Get to work, soldier!"

"Secure the cell blocks," Anish shouted into his command-comm. "Don't give 'em time to slaughter the prisoners. Blow doors if you have to, but *get in there!*"

Kafari's forward fire team made short work of the door that separated the public reception area from the private offices and cell blocks beyond. A concussion shook the room as they blew that door, as well. The smoke that bellied up concealed their movements as they scuttled through. Kafari motioned her second team through and motioned Anish and his teams forward, as well, in deference to Anish's desire to keep her in the realm of the living. Red Wolf stayed glued to her back, shooting at anything wearing a POPPA uniform and covering their rear from potential attack if anyone still outside developed a hankering to protest what was happening in here.

They moved out on the heels of Anish's last team, following them into a long corridor with offices—whole suites of offices—branching off from it. The teams ahead of her were hard-pressed to sweep for potential ambushes in those rooms while attempting to reach the cell blocks before a massacre could ensue. Kafari and Red Wolf moved at a crouch, keeping their heads below the level of the windows set into various doors and moving cautiously from one doorway to the next.

They were halfway down the corridor when gunfire erupted, cutting them off from Anish's rear-most fire teams. Kafari ate the floor—then found herself under Red Wolf. He tackled her and sent them skidding into another office, out of the line of fire. Kafari cursed as they fetched up hard against somebody's desk. For one brain-rattled moment, she was in a Klameth Canyon basement, again, with the Deng shooting at them through the stairs and Abe Lendan's bodyguard tackling and sliding with *him* into the wall. No wonder the president had yelled—being body-slammed *hurt*.

Kafari shook her head to clear it, then twisted around, trying to see where the shots were coming from. Muzzle flashes from an office farther along the corridor gave her the location. The placard on the door said COMMANDANT'S OFFICE.

Kafari crawled forward on elbows and knees. Red Wolf checked her, interposing himself between her and the door. "No way, sir," he muttered. "Use the radio and keep your damn-fool head down."

Kafari ground her teeth and spat into her command-comm. "Alpha One to Beta One, we are pinned. Repeat, pinned. We are taking fire from the commandant's office. Might be a useful bird if he knows how to sing."

"Roger. Stay put."

Seven seconds later, a barrage of covering fire erupted in the corridor. Live rounds created a grey canopy at waist height, forcing the occupant or occupants of the commandant's office to duck for their lives. Red Wolf slid through the open doorway of their shelter, motioning Kafari to stay where she was, and eased forward under that canopy. Kafari was nearly bouncing with frustration when she remembered that she wore a command helmet. Swearing at her own greenhorn stupidity, she fumbled with exterior controls until the video system came online, giving her thumbnail views from each of the button-size, fish-eye cameras on her field team's helmets.

She zeroed in on Red Wolf's signal and watched, distracted and fascinated by the eerie sensation, as "they" crawled forward under covering fire. Red Wolf reached the commandant's open doorway, while one of Anish's team members approached from the other side. They crawled through together, peeling left and right as they slid into the room. Kafari could see boots under the desk ahead of Red Wolf.

Whoever was doing the shooting, he or she didn't like the hail of live rounds tearing into the office. The person was shooting wildly, reaching up with one hand to fire in the general direction of the hall, while staying behind the interposing desk. Within seconds, with the pistol shot dry, an empty magazine bounced onto the floor and slid toward Red Wolf. An instant later, their quarry started swearing a blue streak.

"He's fumbled the reload!" Kafari shouted.

Red Wolf hurled himself forward and skidded around the end of the desk. The gunman was still trying to ram the magazine home when Red Wolf took him off at the knees. He screamed and went down. Blood soaked into his trousers from a pair of nicely shattered kneecaps.

Red Wolf searched him for weapons. "He's clean, sir."

Kafari crossed the corridor at a run and reached the

other office without drawing any more fire. Their prisoner was, indeed, the commandant of Nineveh Base.

"You'll *fry* for this!" he snarled. Hatred and pain had twisted his face into a malevolent mask.

Red Wolf gave him a cold laugh. "I'm so scared, you got me pissing in my boots." He ripped a wire loose from the computer console and twisted the commandant's wrists behind him. "He's all yours, sir," Red Wolf said, giving Kafari a salute.

She beckoned Anish's fire team in from the hall. "Get him outta here," she said, dropping her voice into its lowest registers and putting a Port Town swagger into it. "Put him in my truck. I wanna chat with this som-bitch."

"Aye-aye, sir!"

They hoisted Nineveh's commandant and carried him out, ignoring the string of invectives ripping loose. Kafari and Red Wolf scrambled after the rest of the penetration team, which had leapfrogged ahead to reach the cell blocks. They found Anish Balin at the cell block's control console, using the master computer to unlock rank after rank of prison doors. Several uniformed officers were down, both in the control room and in the corridor between the cells, sprawled obscenely in pools of their own blood. Dazed prisoners were stumbling past, some of them so badly injured, they couldn't walk without help. A few had to be carried.

One man's face had been nearly obliterated by savage beatings. The wreckage was purple-black, a face made of squashed plums. The ghastly, swollen bruises and crusted blood had nearly closed both eyes. It looked like there was broken bone, under the bruises. The coffee-toned skin of his hands, ears, and neck had turned a shade more grey than brown. His clothing was ripped, revealing more bruises. He'd actually staggered past before Kafari realized who he was. She turned sharply, queasy from the shock, and strode after him. Speaking in a low whisper, she asked, "Do Asali bees still have stingers?"

He slewed around, squinting through crusted, swollen eyes, unable to see her face through the biochem mask and command helmet. "I'd hate to get caught in a swarm," he said cautiously, the words slurred and drunken as he struggled to move muscles too stiff and battered to shape the sounds. Even so, those few words confirmed his identity. Dinny Ghamal swayed on his feet and sweat broke out across his battered face. "Asali bees can get mean," he added, waiting for her response.

"Oh, yes," Kafari agreed. "It's a good idea to have a bolt-hole handy, if you run Asali bees. Cheese rooms work pretty well."

She saw realization spread itself across his ruined face, tugging at the edges of his eyes and battered mouth. Then Dinny grippped her free hand—the one without a gun in it—with both of his own. Crusted blood around his eyes softened and ran red.

"You came back for us," he choked out. "They told us you were dead. Showed us pictures of your aircar, wrecked and full of bullet holes. But you came back, just for us . . ."

Kafari started to answer, intending to say, "Of course I came back for you," when sudden understanding flashed through her. He was speaking literally. He thought she'd come back *from the dead.* The amount of pain required to reduce Dinny Ghamal to such a state turned Kafari's hatred into ice-filled rage.

"There's an old saying," Kafari told him, "that our ancestors brought out from Terra. There is nothing as dangerous as a strong man's ghost."

Dinny's fingers tightened against hers as a rush of emotions—far too complex to take in while a battle raged around them—blazed in his eyes. Kafari pulled a backup gun from her gear and handed it to him. "Where's your mother? And your wife?"

"Second floor. With the little ones." He stood up straighter as he pointed the way to the nearest stair-well.

Kafari called for backup. "Alpha Team, form up and move out! Second floor! They've shifted the wounded and the kids!"

She was already running for the stairs, gun in hand. Red Wolf was right behind her. Dinny struggled along in her wake. Kafari took the steps two at a time, just ahead of Alpha Team's front runners. When they reached the second floor landing, Kafari flattened herself against the wall while Red Wolf kicked the door in.

Nobody shot at them.

Red Wolf went through first, leaving Dinny and Kafari as rear guard. They'd emerged into a long corridor that paralleled the line of cell blocks one floor below. This floor clearly served as infirmary—but not for healing purposes. The beds and examination tables all had straps. Thick, unbreakable ones. Most had dark stains that no one had bothered to clean up.

She heard voices farther down the corridor, women's voices, shrill with panic. By the time Kafari and Dinny reached the source of the screams, the noisemakers had fallen silent. Red Wolf stood guard over six women prisoners, two in P-Squad uniforms, the other four in white lab coats. Alpha Team was kicking down more doors. Prisoners were stumbling, even crawling, out of detention cells. Most of them bore the marks of torture, with physical injuries that made Dinny's beating look mild. Kafari's cold rage froze into jagged ice. Mere retribution didn't come close to the hell she intended to inflict on those responsible for this.

There was a sudden explosion of curses farther down the corridor. Then one of her lieutenants came running. "Sir! Begging the commander's presence, sir!"

Kafari exchanged glances with Dinny and Red Wolf, then headed down the long corridor. Dinny followed, leaving Red Wolf to stand guard over the prisoners. The sickening bloodstains on the floor grew worse with every step. Most of Alpha Team was already headed back, assisting badly injured men and women out of rooms Kafari couldn't look at too closely, for fear of vomiting inside her helmet. When she reached the end of the corridor, the remainder of Alpha Team stepped aside.

She peered into a fairly large room. A single glance

told Kafari that this chamber had once been used as a surgery. Her second glance faltered as the jumble of odd shapes piled along the floor took on a sudden, sickening pattern. Kafari couldn't tell how many people had been jammed into this one charnel-house room. Her throat worked in convulsive reflex. She clamped her jaws together and held the nausea between her teeth. She forced herself to look, but couldn't quite control the way her gaze skittered from one image to another. The floor was thick with dark, congealed blood. There was no sign of the Hancock family's children in that pile. Kafari could see only adult-sized hands and feet sticking out like jackstraws. They had clearly been dead for hours. They'd died hard. Much too hard.

"What's behind that?" Kafari choked out, pointing to a half-buried door on the far wall.

"We'll find out, sir."

The remainder of Alpha Team waded in, pulling corpses off the mound. Kafari's gut kept clenching with dread. They were near the bottom when one of the bodies in the pile moaned and stirred. Kafari's hair stood on end for a split second, then she and Dinny rushed forward, pulling the woman free of the corpses stacked on top of her. An agonized sound burst from Dinny's throat. Aisha was still alive. But not for long. Kafari could see that, at first glance. Dinny dropped to his knees beside her, cradling her head and trying to lift her from the floor where they'd dumped her to die. "I'm here, Mama," he told her, voice choked down to a raw whisper. "I've got you safe now."

"Dinny?" she whispered. "You got away . . ."

"We're going home, Mama," he told her, voice breaking. "We're taking you home."

"Don't need to go home, son," she said, her voice shockingly fragile. "Just get me outside these walls, outside them fences. I want to die *free*."

Anguish tore gashes into Dinny's battered face. Then the fire team finally unblocked the door and pulled it open.

"We've got live kids in here!"

Kafari's breath sobbed in her lungs with a single, heartfelt prayer of relief.

"Get 'em *out*! I want this building cleared in the next three minutes!"

Children started tumbling out of the room, tripping over bodies that had once been people they loved. Glass-pale, they greeted their rescuers with eyes like burnt cinders. They went where they were told to go. Older ones helped younger ones. Once-innocent faces were etched with the cruelty they had witnessed.

Kafari turned her attention back to Aisha. "Get her downstairs," she told the remaining two members of Alpha Team. "Put her in my truck. Shove that bastard commandant into another one. I won't have them in the same space. Tell Anish to interrogate the son-of-a-bitch."

"Yes, sir!"

They lifted Aisha while Dinny braced her head, then maneuvered her to the stairs. Kafari turned on her heel and strode back to where Red Wolf was holding six butchers at gunpoint. Kafari stared at the six women for long moments. "How many of you are constitutional scholars?"

The prisoners glanced at one another.

"No one?" Kafari prompted. "All right. Let me acquaint you with the contents of clause twenty-three. 'Each citizen has the legal duty and moral responsibility to protect Jefferson from all threats, foreign or domestic. Any government official acting in abrogation of this constitution represents a threat to Jefferson's survival and must not be tolerated. If redress in the courts fails to curb usurpation of power, citizens are authorized and required to remove such officials from office.' I think that just about says it all, don't you?"

The six women who had participated in the torture and slaughter of innocent prisoners stared up at her. Realization dawned in their eyes. Kafari allowed them sufficient time to know terror.

"Consider yourselves officially removed."

She left them sitting on the floor, meeting Red Wolf's glance on her way past. Kafari was halfway down the stairs when the first shot ripped loose. Screams erupted, high and knife-edged, begging for the mercy they had failed to show their victims.

Five more rapid-fire shots silenced them.

Kafari strode toward her truck, barking out orders. "Do a final sweep and mount up. Give me a by-the-squad headcount in two minutes. I want everyone outside this base in three minutes. *Move* it!"

Squads reported in. The last members of Alpha and Beta's fire teams emerged from a final, visual sweep, making sure they'd found all the prisoners. Two minutes and twelve seconds later, they were in their trucks, heading for the holes they'd made in Nineveh's fences. Not one shot was fired at them. Nineveh's survivors had no further stomach for it. Once clear, the trucks scattered into the predawn darkness, heading across the Adero floodplain for a host of hiding places she and Anish had worked out. Kafari drove only as far as the nearest Hellbore gunnery crew and halted. She left the engine idling and slid down to greet the crew.

"We're prepped and ready to go, sir."

The other two Hellbore crews reported readiness, as well. "Very good," Kafari said. "On my signal."

She pulled off her command helmet and strode to the back of the truck, where Aisha Ghimal lay cradled in Dinny's lap. She climbed up, swung the rear doors closed, then switched on the light. Aisha blinked up at Kafari.

"Honey child," she whispered, "it was *you* . . ."

She dropped to her knees beside the dying woman. "Yes," she choked out. "It was me."

Aisha groped for her hand. Kafari took it in a gentle grip, held on with careful strength, hating the glove of her biochem suit, which prevented her from touching her friend's hand skin-to-skin. "You saved us, once before," Aisha said, voice labored and weak, worse, even, than it had been in the charnel-house where they'd found her. "Killed off a whole army of Deng, to save us. You got . . . a different army to kill . . . this time."

"Yes," Kafari said, unable to force anything more past the tight pain in her throat.

"You'll do it, child. You'll save us. Ain't nobody else who *can* do it. You got the heart for it, child, the heart and the head. And the wisdom." Her fingers tightened against Kafari's. Then she moved her head, slightly. "Dinny?" she whispered.

"I'm here, Mama."

"You watch over Kafari, son. Help her do what's got to be done."

"I will," he swore the vow. "I swear it on Papa's memory, I will."

"Love you, Dinny," she breathed out, the words almost silent. "So proud to be your mama."

Her eyes didn't close.

But she wasn't there, any more.

Dinny started to cry, broken sobs that shook his shoulders with their violence.

Kafari squeezed his shoulder once. Then opened the rear doors, dry-eyed and full of cold hatred. She closed the doors again. Retrieved the starlight scope from the cab of her truck. Moved purposefully to the waiting gunnery crew. Scanned Nineveh Base, which was a smouldering patch of light on the horizon.

"You know what I want," she said, her words striking the air like bitten-off chunks of steel. She pulled her helmet back on, which shielded her ears. She signaled the other two gun crews and said, "This is Alpha One. Stand by to fire."

She stood there one moment longer, staring across the intervening darkness, weighing risks and odds and the value of lessons about to be imparted. Then she climbed into her truck, gripped the wheel in both hands, and spoke again. *"Now!"*

The night turned to fire. Nineveh Base's motorpool and airfield erupted with volcanic fury. Fuel ignited, burning hot enough to melt steel. The Hellbores spoke again, with tongues of flame, The prison became a funeral pyre, cremating the dead and sending a message POPPA's leaders would not soon forget. That lesson turned *expensive* when all three Hellbores snarled simultaneously, striking their final target for the night in perfect unison. Located on the corner of Ninevah Base farthest from the Shantytown, Sonny's maintenance depot was an immense structure full of high-tech military munitions and sophisticated equipment necessary to repair the Bolo.

It blew apart under Kafari's guns. Hellbore fire hit the depot again and again, turning it into a white hell of destruction.

The munitions inside detonated. The fireball flattened the home she had shared with Simon. The shockwave slammed into the rest of Nineveh Base like a scythe. Every building on the sprawling base vanished. The blast tore across the Adero floodplain, as well, heading right toward them. It shook Kafari's truck so hard, glass shattered and they nearly flipped over. The truck rocked onto its rear wheels like bucking stallion, then the cab came down again and they landed with a jarring of bone and a shuddering of springs. Red Wolf recovered his senses first and started slapping broken glass off Kafari's clothes.

When she could see, again, Nineveh Base was gone.

Just . . . gone.

"That," Red Wolf swore eloquently, "was one *hell* of a boom."

"That," Kafari countered savagely, "was just the beginning."

She gave the signal to scatter. Then put the truck into gear, turned her back on the smouldering ruins, and drove away. They'd won the first battle. The rest of the war was going to get ugly.

Chapter Twenty-Two

I

Movement woke Yalena with a clang and a jolt that made her gasp. It was dark, so dark she couldn't see anything, and cold enough to hurt her skin, where she was sprawled across something lumpy and cold. "Mom? Are we in the cargo box?"

No one answered. Yalena groped through the darkness, trying to find her mother's hand. Her seeking fingertips encountered nothing but more of the ice-cold lumps she was lying on. Panic set in. "Mom!"

Her wrist-comm beeped softly.

"Sugarplum?"

"Mom! Where are you?"

"That's not important. But I do need to tell you something that is. I can't go with you. There are some things I have to do. Or try, anyway. Tell your father I love him . . ."

"Mommy! You can't do this! You have to come with me!"

"I can't, sweetheart. And we can't talk like this, on

an open comm-line. I love you. Remember that, always, whatever happens. I'll get a message to someone, to let you out of there, okay?"

"*Mommy!*" Yalena was groping, blind and terrified, for the side of the cargo box, where the door opened, and discovered there was no way to open it from the inside. Her breath caught in a painful knot. Her mother couldn't come with her, because there wasn't a way to latch the door properly from the inside. Somebody had to latch it from outside. She was neatly trapped. Her mother must have realized that all along.

She was also on her way to the space station, with no way out. Yalena started to cry as the box swayed into the air. They tilted and swung around as stevedores transferred the cargo box to a waiting freight shuttle that would take her into orbit. They jolted, slid, clanged to a halt. Then waited. Interminably. Yalena was shivering with cold, miserable and scared. Then a rumble vibrated through the boxes. She finally identified the sound: orbit-capable engines coming on-line.

A moment later, the shuttle lifted ponderously, swinging around with a spin that left her inner ears protesting. Then a giant fist crushed her down against the chilled meat. She couldn't move, could barely *breathe*. It went on forever, an agony in every muscle . . .

The engines cut off and she was abruptly weightless. Spinning nausea bit her throat. She was falling, could feel herself falling. Yalena tried to convince her inner ear that she was just weightless, in orbit, but her inner ear wasn't having any of it. She threw up, creating a mess that drifted unpleasantly through the narrow space into which her mother had crammed her. *Let me down!* her body was screaming. That sounded like a very good idea to Yalena. Weight returned for a few seconds as the shuttle punched its engines in a short burst. The pilot was probably jockeying them around to dock with the station.

How much time passed, Yalena didn't know. There were more bursts from the shuttle's engines. Then a clanging sound rang through the hull and abruptly Yalena dropped against the cold meat. They'd made spacedock with the rotating station and the centrifugal spin gave her weight, again. She had no idea where, exactly, she was. Yalena knew that cargo shuttles never off-loaded directly into the freighters. They docked with the station and transferred cargo through Ziva Two, to give inspectors the opportunity to search for contraband.

Would they check Yalena's box? Her mother didn't think so and the more Yalena thought about it, the more convinced she became that nobody would open this box to inspect it. With this much contraband going out, the station's team of inspectors had to be aware of it. And were doubtless well paid in exchange for keeping their mouths shut while the modified boxes flowed through unchallenged.

The cargo box shifted, jolting and bumping its way out of the shuttle's cargo bay and into the station. Then they started sliding forward at a steady pace, riding on what must've been a conveyor belt of some kind while running the gauntlet of "random" inspections. They stopped several times, but nobody opened her box. They bumped their way off the conveyor and moved in a new direction. Another conveyor, Yalena realized. It was a long trip, moving as slowly as they were. At length, they were jolted and tipped and ended up stationary with a clang and a bump.

Unless she were vastly mistaken, she had reached the freighter's hold.

There were other jarring bumps as more cargo boxes were stuffed in. Yalena started to panic. They were going to bury her at the back of the hold, with so much stacked over and around her, she'd be trapped and die of starvation, or maybe just from the bitter cold. There was a abrupt cessation of sound as the loading stopped. Yalena caught her breath, tried to hear through the muffling walls.

A sudden grating noise assailed her ears. Then a sharp crack sounded as the door to her prison was thrown abruptly open. Light stabbed into the cramped space, blinding her. Someone exclaimed aloud, then hands reached in, pulling her out of the freezing cargo box. She was so cold and so cramped from lying there, she couldn't stand up. She was picked up and carried. As her eyes adjusted to the light, she realized a man was holding her, a man who looked strangely familiar, although she was fairly certain she'd never seen him, before.

He was staring at her, brows knit in puzzlement. "You don't know me, do you?"

She shook her head.

"I'm Stefano Soteris, supercargo on *The Star of Mali*. Your mother," he added with a slight smile, "is my cousin."

Yalena's eyes widened. "You're her *cousin*?"

"That I am. And *your* second cousin. It's lucky for you that we docked when we did."

Yalena didn't know what to say. She hadn't known her mother's cousin worked on a Malinese freighter. Then guilt smote her squarely between the eyes. She hadn't known, because she hadn't ever shown the slightest interest in her own family. She didn't even know how many cousins she had, let alone second cousins. Her ignorance was her own fault and no one else's.

"I'm sorry to be such trouble," she whispered. "I've been nothing but nasty to everybody. Stupid and hideous and now . . . now people are risking themselves for me . . . and *I'm not worth it. . . .*"

Once she started crying, she couldn't stop. Literally could not stop. Her mother's cousin picked up speed, striding rapidly through the ship while she sobbed on his shoulder. She heard voices, Stefano's and a woman's, then she was lowered to sit on what looked, vaguely, like the edge of somebody's bed. Stefano's hard shoulder was replaced by a softer one. Gentle arms came around her, held and rocked her.

"Easy, child, shh . . ."

When the body-wrenching sobs finally eased away, Yalena realized she was leaning against an older woman with a

lot of grey in her short-cropped hair. She was dressed as
a spacer, in a close-fitting body sleeve made of something
supple. One whole shoulder was soaking wet.

"I'm sorry," she whispered.

"No need to apologize," the woman said, peering into
her eyes. "You've come through several kinds of hell in
the last few hours. I'd say you've earned a good, long
cry. You need a good bit of sleep, as well. Your eyes are
burnt out. And here's the ship's surgeon."

The doctor examined her with great care. "I'm giving
you a sedative, young lady. A fairly strong one. We'll do
a bit more tomorrow, when you're feeling up to it. For
now, just rest."

"I'm sorry," she whispered again, unable to say anything else. He administered the sedative gently, using a
hypo-spray that barely stung at all. They left her alone,
then, with nothing further to stand between her and her
conscience. Facing herself was almost as bad as facing
the Bolo had been. Every selfish, meanspirited, stupid
thing she had ever done or said came back to rattle
through her mind like swords on a whirligig. How could
she ever make amends for the hurt she had caused her
mother, over the years?

Even worse was the prospect of facing her father. That
was so daunting, Yalena would almost have preferred to
jump out of the freighter by the nearest airlock. The
memory of sitting in a hospital waiting room, insisting
with childish selfishness that she wouldn't leave Jefferson,
when her father was desperately injured and would face a
nightmare of rehabilitation alone, left her writhing inside,
soul-sick and exhausted.

How could she have demanded her own way at a time
when her parents needed one another, desperately? All
the laughter had gone out of her mother, that day, and
it hadn't returned in two long years. Yalena whimpered
with the excruciating self-knowledge that she had spent
those years twisting the knife deeper with every nasty
comment, every belittling prejudice, every petty little
demand she'd laid down as an ultimatum.

A song from her childhood floated into her mind, a cheerful little song that danced in razor-sharp shoes. Growing oats and peas, barley and beans . . . farmers who did nothing but dance and sing and suck money away from decent people by charging outrageous prices for plants that grew themselves . . . A pretty, poisonous lie handed wholesale to a wounded, desperate child. Everything POPPA had said was a lie. The whole fabric of her life was a lie, a stained and tattered ruin that nothing would ever put right, again.

Yet her mother had risked her own life, rescuing Yalena out of that deathtrap. Why? When she had spent her life preferring the company of her friends and the gossip at school over everything and everyone else? And now she didn't even have those friends. POPPA had killed them. Coldly and without remorse. In that moment, a hatred of POPPA cyrstallized, so deep and so dangerous, it scared her.

I can't make it up to you, Mom, she whispered as the tears began to come, again. *I can't ever undo that damage. But I can stop being stupid and I can stop hurting people. And maybe one day . . .* Yalena bit her lip and rolled over to bury her face in the pillow. *Maybe one day, I can do something that will make you proud of me, instead.* Then the weeping broke loose again and she soaked the pillow under her cheek. She was still crying when the sedative pulled her down into gentle oblivion.

II

I limp back toward my depot under a veil of darkness and apparent secrecy. The most noteworthy observation I make en route is the utter lack of civilian presence anywhere along the path I follow. Farmhouses, villages, and the occasional fuel station are vacant, giving every appearance of having been abandoned in a great rush.

I conclude that the government has issued orders forcibly evacuating a corridor that allows me to crawl home unobserved.

I am still thirty kilometers from depot when a sudden "Mayday" broadcast originates from Nineveh Base. Someone is screaming incoherently about an attack. I catch the sound of massive explosions, then the broadcast slices off. I monitor government communications and tap the planetary datanet via wireless communications. I cannot access the base's security system without a land-line connection, however, which leaves me effectively blind. I need to know what is happening at Nineveh Base.

I attempt to contact my mechanic.

He does not respond. He is either so drunk he has passed out or is not in his quarters. Either way, he is useless. I attempt to contact Nineveh Base's commandant. No one answers. I do not like this state of affairs. I continue to plod northward, unable to speed up without risking further damage to my tracks. Minutes crawl past. At my current rate of speed, it will take thirty hours to reach my depot. I debate the wisdom of contacting Jefferson's president or even Sar Gremian. I have doubts that either will be inclined to respond.

Sixteen point three minutes after the abortive distress call from Nineveh Base, a massive flash strobes across the northern horizon. A far-off rumble of sound resolves into an explosion of such staggering size, it nearly stops me in my tracks, from sheer shock. I am the only thing on Jefferson capable of creating an explosion on that scale. Unless . . .

I do not care for the implications.

Not at all.

My entire supply of replacement munitions is on Nineveh Base. Along with all my spare parts and what passes for a mechanic. I pick up speed. Damaged track plates rattle. The burst of light that heralded the explosion has faded to a steady, dull glow that marks a large fire when my final aerial drone, circling the canyons behind me, registers a burst of rifle fire. Nervous P-Squads searching for rebels with stolen munitions shoot straight up. The drone goes off-line.

My personality gestalt center registers dismay and disgust in equal measures. Ninevah Base is under attack and my last drone has just been shot down, a victim of "friendly fire." Without a drone, I cannot find attackers to launch a remote strike. Even at my increased rate of speed, I cannot reach Nineveh Base in time to do anything about the attack, let alone trace the attackers. The strike force will disappear in its entirety long before I arrive.

Sar Gremian contacts me. "Machine, do you see any sign of rebel gun crews out there?"

"No. Request VSR. What was the cause of the explosion my sensors just registered?"

"Somebody's shot the shit out of Nineveh Base. Find them."

"I have sustained damage that precludes—"

"I don't give a hairy rat's ass! *Find them!*"

"I would welcome suggestions as to how I should accomplish this. I am incapable of speed greater than three km per hour. I have no aerial reconnaissance capability left, as the P-Squads searching the canyons behind me have just shot down my last aerial drone. I cannot shoot an enemy I cannot find."

Sar Gremian's suggestion is anatomically impossible. I do not possess the kind of orifice into which he suggests I insert an appendage Bolos do not possess, as we do not procreate biologically. His order is therefore invalid and cannot be carried out. When I tell him so, he simply terminates the call. I maintain Battle Reflex Alert and strain my sensors to their greatest range, but catch no sign of any rebel forces.

Clearly the attack against Barran Bluff was carried out specifically to gain access to the heavy weaponry needed to assault Nineveh Base. Anish Balin has proven himself a shrewd and resourceful commander. I speculate that the Hancock Family Cooperative was the target of a substantial rescue operation, with the destruction of the air assault team at Barran Bluff used deliberately as a diversion to draw me away from Nineveh Base. My presence there would have doomed any such rescue, as the commander of the rebellion doubtless knew only too well.

If the seven Hellbores left behind had succeeded in killing me—as they could have done, if their crews had been better trained—the rebellion could have brought POPPA and its ruling regime to its knees in one night. This suggests speed, good military intelligence that is probably the result of a talented computer programmer hacking into the government's computerized security systems, and a level of organization surprising for a fledgling group that has had neither time nor opportunity to train. An army of civilian soldiers can be formidable, particularly when motivated by a combination of high ideals and righteous wrath.

The Granger population has an ample supply of both.

They have failed to destroy me, however, which dooms them to a long and costly war of attrition. How costly that war will be is brought home to me when I finally reach a line-of-sight distance from my maintenance depot. The eastern sky is turning to flame above the Damisi Mountains, heralding the rising of Jefferson's sun, when I halt on the floodplain, a full kilometer from the smouldering wreckage.

Nineveh Base no longer exists. Neither does my maintenance depot. Phil Fabrizio's quarters are entirely gone. So is most of the surrounding shantytown. Thousands have died, here. Battle rage sweeps through my personality gestalt circuitry. There will be retribution for this wanton slaughter. It is one thing to shoot soldiers in combat. It is another to destroy innocent civilians whose main crime was living too close to the backblast of war.

I feel a twinge in my complex logic circuitry, which I suppress. I have no desire to follow the chain of thought that would compare the actions of Granger rebels with my own actions in downtown Madison. I was operating under orders from a lawfully elected president. The Granger rebels have acted in willful *defiance of that government, perpetrating an illegal act of war. My duty is clear.*

How I will carry out that duty, I do not know. I have tangled with the rebels only once and have sustained serious damage. That damage cannot now be repaired, certainly not in a timely fashion. I hesitate to consider what Sar Gremian will send by way of a replacement mechanic for Phil Fabrizio. There is no point in sitting out here, a kilometer away from the destruction, since Anish Balin's men have been gone for hours. They have doubtless scattered to hiding places in the Damisi Mountains.

The thought of searching the maze of canyons weathered into those mountains is too daunting to consider. I spoke the truth to Sar Gremian when I told him that I cannot make such a search. Anish Balin doubtless knows this and will capitalize on it, to his advantage and my frustration.

As there is no point in continuing to sit where I am, I move cautiously forward. The destruction has been savage and thorough. When I reach the perimeter of my own missing depot, I halt again, literally at a loss as to my next course of action. There are no guards along the base's perimeter, mostly because there is not enough left to guard. Rescue workers are combing the wreckage of shanties, attempting to find survivors. Or perhaps merely locating bodies for burial, to reduce the contagion likely to spread from unburied remains. I am noticed and pointed at by crews who clearly would prefer to take themselves elsewhere.

I am still sitting there when a civilian groundcar approaches, picking its way carefully through the rubble-strewn streets of the shantytown. My first thought—that POPPA officials have arrived to inspect the damage—is only partially correct. The occupant of the car has, indeed, arrived to survey the damage. But he is not a ranking member of POPPA's government. Phil Fabrizio climbs out of the groundcar and stares at the bare patch of ground where his quarters once sat.

"Aw, shit, man! They blew it all to goddamned hell!"

I am so startled to see my mechanic alive, it takes me three full seconds to find something to say. "You are alive," *I finally manage, with less-than-scintillating wit.* "Why?"

Phil stares up at my warhull. "Huh? Whaddaya mean, 'why?'"

"Why are you alive? More accurately, where were you, as you clearly were not in your quarters at the time of their destruction."

"Huh," *he snorts,* "I wasn't in 'em, 'cause I ain't entirely stupid. When the shootin' started, I skedaddled, just jumped in my car and ran for it. They blew up a buncha buildings, straight off. I didn't figure it was too healthy to stick around, you know? So I hightailed it over to my sister Maria's house. We heard the whole place go, right after I got there, like a volcano or somethin', but there ain't no news reports on it, nowhere. Not even the chats. So I figured the only way t' find out was t' go home and see for myself. Only," *he stared at the spot where his quarters no longer stood,* "I got no home left. God*damn* 'em! How'm I s'posed to pay for alla my stuff? You can just bet your flintsteel butt, Sar Gremian ain't gonna pay for it."

I sympathize with Phil's loss, as I find myself in exactly the same predicament. Unlike Phil, however, my losses will force Sar Gremian to act, if he wants me to continue functioning as a mobile interdiction force. Phil is entirely correct in his assessment of Sar Gremian's reaction. He will not like the size of the price tag.

"What happened to you?" *Phil finally asks, noticing for the first time the gaping holes in my track linkages.*

"I was shot. I require extensive repair to damaged tracks."

"But—" *He stumbles to a halt, staring in open dismay.* "How'd you get shot? I watched the news last night, before all the shooting and shit started here, and they never said nuthin' about you gettin' shot." *He frowns.* "Come t'think of it, they never said nuthin' about you bein' there at all. And you was never in the pictures. Just the explosions, blowin' up the rebels. I never thought about it, 'cause I knew where you was, an' all. Why didn't they show you fightin' those gun-totin' land hogs?"

"It is politically expedient for the government to hide the fact that I was required to put down an armed rebellion. It is also in the government's best interest to hide the fact that the rebels were sufficiently armed and dangerous to inflict heavy damage to me. That damage must be repaired. You will need track plates and durachrome linkages to replace seventeen point three meters of damage in my left-hand track, twenty point five meters in my right-hand track, and eleven point nine-three meters in my central track."

Phil's nano-tatt contorts itself into a knotty tangle of black filaments reminding me unpleasantly of Deng infantry. He scowls at the ground, then mutters, "I dunno how t'do that. And even if I did, which I don't, what am I s'posed to use? Spit balls and elbow grease? I got no tools, let alone parts!"

"Sar Gremian will have to authorize payment for off-world equipment to be shipped in, which will take time. In the interim, you will have to scrounge."

Phil scratches his ear. "Yeah, but how? And scrounge for what, exactly? We got nothin' on this whole planet strong as durachrome. Hell, we can't even *make* durachrome. What'm I supposed to use? Steel?"

I review technical specs. "Not an optimal metal, but steel linkages should work, if I do not have to face combat against Deng Yavacs. They will have to be replaced after every mission, however. My weight will warp and degrade them over any appreciable distance. I will download technical specifications on metallurgy, casting, and forging requirements for you as reference material when contacting potential vendors. Tolerances must be within specification, as well. I would suggest contacting the Tayari Mining Consortium's tool-and-die division for assistance."

"How'n hell I s'posed to do that?"

"Try looking them up on the datanet," *I suggest, with creditable patience.* "Your status as this world's only Bolo mechanic gives you treaty-level clearance to request technical assistance from any on-world resource."

This elementary piece of advice appears to affect Phil Fabrizio like Divine Writ. "I can? Hey, that's like fuckin' fabulous! Yeah, I'll do that! I'll download them specs you was talkin' about—hey, how'm I gonna do that? My computer got blown up."

"Go back to your sister's house. When you arrive, call me on your wrist-comm and tell me the identity code for your sister's datanet account. As the engineering specs for my treads are not classified, I am authorized to download them to an unsecure computer. Clearly, you will also need a new computer."

He gives me a grin. "Now *that*, I can scrounge by my own self. Sit tight, Big Guy. I'll call you."

He swaggers back to his car, chest puffed out at the prospect of calling Tayari's executives with a question they must, by treaty obligation, answer. My mechanic is easily delighted. I could learn to envy such a carefree creature, under other conditions.

Phil has been gone for twelve point three minutes when an aircar on approach vector from downtown Madison signals me, using the proper command code to enter my proximity alert zone without triggering a defensive reflex. The aircar circles above the shattered base for three point oh-seven minutes, evidently taking stock of the damage. Two minutes and twelve seconds later, the multi-passenger aircar touches down near my warhull. Sar Gremian emerges. There are eleven high-ranking military officials with him and four other civilians. I brace for trouble.

"Bolo," Sar Gremian says with an unpleasant tone grating through his voice, "we've come to give you a medal. Aren't you pleased?"

I am not pleased. I am astonished. Of all the things I expected Sar Gremian to say, "we've come to give you a medal" is the least-anticipated phrase imaginable. It is a measure of how disheartened I have been, that such a ploy succeeds in pleasing my personality gestalt center's ruffled logic trains. It is good to be recognized for a job

*well done, particularly when it has resulted in physical
damage to one's self. The battle for Barran Bluff was
particularly savage, in its way, and will have long-lasting
consequences.*

*The president's senior advisor has brought four general
officers with him, along with three colonels and four
majors, a surprisingly high number of staff-grade officers
in an army that has been dismantled from the ground
up. Based on their uniform devices, there are now more
command-grade generals than battalions. It is a strange
way to run an army.*

*I recognize the generals and two of the colonels from
news broadcasts and meetings I have monitored. I face
the officers and Party officials responsible for the creation
of propaganda, the seizure of privately held property, the
placation and control of urban subsistence recipients, and
the conversion of property into currency used to fund
POPPA's social and environmental programs. I do not
feel particularly honored by their visit.*

*General Teon Meinhard gazes up at my turret for
several seconds before clearing his throat to speak.* "Well,
now, we've come to give you a medal, y'see. A nice, shiny
one. It'll look good, welded up there with the others.
It's a public service award. The highest we have. We're
here to commend you for the heroic assault you made,
defending the public good."

"That is appreciated, General. It is not easy to destroy
seven 10cm mobile Hellbores shooting at you from
behind cover."

The general blinks in evident surprise. "Hellbores? I'm
not talking about destroying any Hellbores." *He shoots a
suspicious glance at Sar Gremian.* "Is that what did this?"
He waves one hand at the destruction surrounding us.
"Hellbores? Where in blazes did common criminals get
their hands on something like that? I didn't know we
even *had* Hellbores!"

*I am appalled by the general's utter lack of information
on the battles that have been waged in the past several
hours. A general who remains totally ignorant of the basic*

*facts surrounding the heaviest military engagement since
the Deng invasion is not worth his weight in mud. Sar
Gremian explains the situation to General Meinhard in
openly contemptuous terms, an attitude I suspect is well-
earned. The other officers smirk and even the civilians
appear to be concealing derisive expressions. I begin to
think it would have been no great loss if General Meinhard and the officers with him had been quartered on
Nineveh Base, rather than living off post in a wealthy
civilian section of Madison, which are the official addresses
on record for these officers.*

*When Sar Gremian completes his brief situation report,
I seek clarification. "Why are you giving me a medal, if not
for the battle at Barran Bluff? The insurrection at Barran
is the first combat I have fought since the Deng invasion.
I have not been part of any other engagements that would
qualify as an assault in defense of anything."*

*"But you have," General Meinhard protests. "You
crushed a riot that killed the president!"*

*I am struck speechless. Jefferson's government is giving
me a medal of valor for crushing civilians in a riot? A
riot that would never have ended in Gifre Zeloc's death
if I had not been ordered to crush protestors in the first
place? Or if he had used ordinary common sense, rather
than jumping into a mob full of enraged Grangers? I sit
in stupefied silence as one of the majors crawls up my
warhull, medal and welding torch in hand.*

*"I'll put it on this side," the major says, "so it'll stand
out from all the old ones."*

*He welds the new "ribbon hanger"—as military slang
has dubbed such things through the centuries—onto
my turret. After one hundred fifteen years in service, I
finally understand why a medal can be referred to in
such dismissive terms. I find myself glad that he has not
sullied my other badges of honor by adding this gaudy
decoration to the cluster of medals that reflect genuine
service to humanity. The major succeeds in welding the
thing to the right-hand side of my turret, where it blazes
in lurid testimony to folly.*

Sar Gremian steps forward while the major is still climbing down and peers critically at the damage to my treads. He frowns. "For once," *he mutters,* "you weren't just pissing and moaning. Those tracks have to be fixed. We can't afford to have some reporter get a photo of you with that kind of damage visible. I suppose we'll have to find a replacement for that worthless mechanic of yours, as well."

"That will not be necessary," *I advise him.* "Phil Fabrizio was not in his quarters when they were destroyed. He had left the base to visit his sister. I spoke to him before your aircar arrived."

Sar Gremian frowned. "Where is he? Never mind that, just call him and tell him to shag his ass out here. He's going to earn that fancy salary we've been paying him."

"Very well. Message sent."

The president's advisor says, "Get some work crews out here, Teon. I want a fence around the Bolo, something solid, that curious reporters can't photograph that machine through, and put an interdiction on fly-overs until we can rig something to park this thing under. Get 'em out here and started within thirty minutes. Phineas," *he addresses a man whose wrist-comm signal identifies as General Orlége, POPPA's chief propaganda official,* "we're going to need one hell of a damage-control effort on this mess. We can't hide the loss of Nineveh Base or even Barran Bluff. It's got to be explained."

Phineas Orlége says smoothly, "It's being handled. I've already cleared the basic strategy with Vittori and Nassiona. As expensive as this will be to replace," *he waves one hand at the scorched earth of Nineveh Base, including in his gesture my own damage,* "this incident will work powerfully in our favor. By my conservative estimate, the events of the past twenty-five hours—and I include Gifre's death and the arson in downtown Madison—will move our timetable up by several months, at a bare minimum. By this time tomorrow, we may be as much as a year ahead of schedule, which is fine news, indeed. The masses will not tolerate this kind of brutality and their reaction will give us precisely what we need. I refuse to be discouraged by mere price tags, particularly given the size of the stakes in this fascinating little game."

Sar Gremian favors him with a cool stare. "Then I will give *you* the pleasure of presenting the bill to Vittori and Nassiona. Your glib assurances may desert you."

Phineas Orlége smiles. "I shall look forward to seeing which of us is right."

I am attempting to decide whether this comment was a threat or challenge when Phil pulls his groundcar to a halt six meters from the group beside my ravaged treads. He climbs out, sees the cluster of uniformed officers, and halts. His nano-tatt flares a deep mustard yellow, while the remainder of his face loses color entirely. The resulting combination is not visually appealing.

"Who are you?" *General Meinhard demands.*

"That," *Sar Gremian says coldly,* "is the Bolo's mechanic. You'd have known that, if you'd bothered to read the security reports I sent when we hired him."

Meinhard turns purple and sputters. Sar Gremian ignores him and turns his ill temper onto my technician, speaking with a bite like acid. "What kind of excuse do you have for deserting your duty post in the middle of combat?" *He gestures to the empty, burnt-out ruin of my maintenance depot.* "Do you have the slightest idea what this equipment was *worth*? Or the spare parts? You didn't even try to defend it. You just ran like a scared rabbit and let a pack of terrorists blow it up. I should by God take it out of your pathetic little salary. Better still, I should have you court-martialed and shot for treason!"

Phil's jaw muscles bunch in sudden anger. His nano-tatt pulses crimson. He thins his lips and glares at the president's senior advisor, but does not speak. This is perhaps the wisest thing I have ever seen him do.

"Did you hear me, you stupid slopebrow?"

Phil's jaw juts forward, increasing his resemblance to an angry australopithecine. Quite unexpectedly, I sympathize. I have been on the receiving end of Sar Gremian's

*temper. Phil goes up in my estimation even further when
he says,* "How's about I set somethin' straight, Mr. High-
and-Mighty Advisor? Court-martial is what'cha do to
soldiers, only I ain't a soldier. I'm the Bolo's technician.
You ought t' be dancin' for joy, 'cause it's a damned
good thing I got the hell outta here when the shootin'
started. If I hadn't a got outta here when I did, you'd
be lookin' for a new mechanic, on top of all the other
stuff you gotta pay for.

"So how's about you stop slingin' the shit my way an'
get me some goddamn tools and crap t' fix him with?
And maybe while you're at it, you can get me a computer
and some new clothes and a toothbrush, 'cause I just lost
every goddamn thing I had in the world, on account a
somebody screwed around and let a bunch a land hogs
steal weapons they got no business to have. How's about
you do alla that before you come around here pissin' all
over me? *You* still got a place t'sleep, tonight. I don't and
I ain't in no mood t'listen to some uppity jackass tellin'
me this is *my* fault, when anybody with half a brain
coulda' seen it comin' from ten kilometers away."

Sar Gremian turns white. "I refuse to be insulted by
a vulgar little street rat!"

"Who stuck the hot poker up your ass? You got nuthin'
to bitch about an' you're just wastin' time flappin' your
lips at me, 'stead a doin' your job. You don't like hearin'
it? You c'n always get out th' same way you got in." *He
jerks his head toward the aircar.* "Hey, Sonny, you want
I should throw the bum out?"

*I begin to like Phil Fabrizio. He is illiterate, although
possibly less stupid than I gave him credit for, but he is
tough as nails and apparently cannot be intimidated by
anyone or anything. Including me, for that matter. These
qualities would have made him a fine technician, if he
had actually known anything. Perhaps there is hope for
remedial training?*

"That will not be necessary," *I tell him.* "But thank
you for offering," *I add with all sincerity.* "This does not,
however, address the immediate and critical problem of

obtaining sufficient spare parts to repair the damage. I am likely to need repairs again in the near future, as we still face a situation wherein insurrectionists have seized high-tech weaponry and demonstrated that they know how to use it. There are three missing mobile Hellbores and hundreds of octocellulose bombs, hyper-v missiles, and small arms that will doubtless be used at first opportunity. Given the circumstances, it is imperative that I regain mobility as quickly as possible. I find it difficult to believe that Anish Balin and his followers will show greater leniency to POPPA Party officials in elected or appointed office than they showed the federal troops at Barran Bluff or the P-Squadron personnel on Nineveh Base."

My analysis of the situation brings a moment of chilled silence.

"Gentlemen," *Sar Gremian says in an icy tone,* "I suggest we return to Madison. *Now.*"

They depart, rapidly, leaving Phil to stare after them. When their aircar has gained sufficient airspace for horizontal flight, Phil mutters, "They shouldn't a'been so upper-class snooty. First of all, it ain't right. Second of all, it ain't what POPPA is all about."

I do not respond, as my view of POPPA is at variance with his.

Phil, apparently in all innocence, glances up at my warhull and asks, "What do you think?"

I have been asked a question, allowing me to respond, rather than simply listen to complaints. "POPPA is composed of two tiers. The lower tier produces many outspoken members who make their demands known to the upper tier. The lower tier is derived from the inner-city population that serves as the base of the party. The lower tier's members are generally educated in public school systems and if they aspire to advanced training, they are educated in facilities provided by the state. This wing constitutes the majority of POPPA's membership, but contributes little or nothing to party theory or platform. It votes the party line and is rewarded with cash payments, subsidized housing, subsidized education, and occasionally preferential employment in government positions such as you hold, as my mechanic. The lower tier produces only a handful of clearly token individuals allowed to serve in high offices.

"The upper tier, which includes most of the party's management, virtually all the appointed and elected government officials, and all of the party's decision-makers, is drawn exclusively from suburban areas where wealth is a fundamental criterion for admittance as a resident. These POPPA party members are generally educated at private schools and attend private colleges, many of them on Vishnu. They are not affected by food-rationing schemes, income caps, or taxation laws, as the legislation drafted and passed by members of their social group inevitably contains loopholes that effectively shelter their income and render them immune from unpleasant statutes that restrict the lives of lower-tier party members and all nonparty citizens.

"POPPA's leadership recognizes that in return for supporting a seemingly populist agenda, they can obtain all the votes they require to remain in power. Even the most cursory analysis of their actions and attitudes, however, indicates that they are not populists but, in fact, are strong antipopulists who actively despise their voting base. This is not merely demonstrated by such confrontations as you have just enjoyed with Sar Gremian, it is proven by their efforts to reduce public educational systems to a level most grade-school children on other worlds have surpassed, with the excuse that this curriculum is all that the students can handle. They have made the inner-city population base totally dependent on the government, which they control.

"Their current actions are repressive and heavy-handed. Last year's abolishment of the presidential election commission is a case in point. It was passed in clear violation of this world's constitution, but has not been stricken down as unconstitutional. Until that legislation passed, POPPA was required to placate those elements of the party uncomfortable with an extremist agenda. That restraint no longer exists, paving the way for POPPA's leadership to be as extremist as they wish. Given events of the last two days, I predict a harsh response that will clarify POPPA's deeper agenda for everyone to see."

"But—" *Phil sputters.* "But that's not what the party's about! Not at all! POPPA loves the people! And I can prove it! POPPA takes money from all them rich farmers and gives it to the poor. And if that law was unconstitutional, then how come the High Court ain't done anything about it?"

"The High Court has been drawn, with the exception of a single individual, from the upper tier of POPPA leadership. I am fully aware that you have had no real historical training, but I can list fifteen cases from the last two years, alone, where high courts rendered purely political judgements that had nothing to do with justice and everything to do with political expediency. Your comment about the party's intent only shows the logical fallacy of their statements. They say they want to help 'the people,' but their efforts have succeeded in lowering overall living conditions, reducing educational standards, and sharply curtailing individual freedom.

"As to the 'rich farmers,' the agricultural producers remaining on Jefferson live on fifteen point seven-three percent less money than the poorest of the urban subsidy recipients. Yet they work sixty and seventy hours a week at hard physical labor and they endure a standard of living three times lower than conditions in Port Town's worst slums. There are no 'rich farmers' anywhere on Jefferson.

"There is a phrase from a major Terran religious text that is appropriate to this situation: 'By their fruits shall you know them.' POPPA has only one demonstrated attitude—contempt—and one demonstrable goal—total power. POPPA's ruling echelon has very nearly achieved that goal, which will give party officials an open field in which to demonstrate its utter contempt of those it holds powerless. Jefferson is on the brink of political and economic disaster."

Phil stares, openmouthed. Then he says, "If you really believe alla that, how come you obey their orders? Especially the unconstitutional ones?"

"My controlling authority rests solely with the president and is not governed by the constitution. My mission parameters were defined by Sector Command. I take advisement only from the president. As long as presidential orders do not exceed my parameters for 'excessive collateral damage' or conflict with my primary mission, I am under the president's orders for rules of engagement."

Phil blinks several times. Finally manages to squeak, "You mean you're the president's *personal Bolo*?"

"In effect, yes."

"And you do whatever the president orders?"

"Yes. Unless it violates my mission or involves excessive collateral damage."

"What's, uh, 'excessive collateral damage?' "

"There is an algorithm that determines the relative target worth versus the likelihood of collateral damage. One example is using a nuclear weapon to destroy a city from which I am taking ineffective fire. I cannot fire nuclear weapons at a city unless there is effective fire directed at my position."

"What if the fire is effective? Like, damaging your track."

"Then I can fire at will, as I did in combat against Anish Balin's forces. In that engagement, no civilians lost their lives. Had that battle occurred in a city, rather than a military outpost, there would have been civilian deaths. It is unfortunate and I do my best to avoid this, but collateral damage happens. I am not proud of having crushed to death civilians in my attempt to reach Gifre Zeloc. Given the parameters of that engagement, with the constraints of not being able to fire my main weapons systems, I killed as few as possible while carrying out the immediate mission."

Phil does not speak. His jaw muscles clench. I detect an expression in his eyes that I have not seen there,

before. Then he turns on his heel and stalks over to his
groundcar. He slams the door and drives away, moving
in a rapid and reckless manner. I am alone again.
I do not like that feeling.

III

Three days later, Simon received an incoming call from
The Star of Mali. Simon hadn't seen his wife's cousin since
the wedding, but he knew Stefano Soteris at once.

"Colonel Khrustinov?" Stefano asked, brow furrowed
as he stared uncertainly into Simon's ravaged face.

"Hello, Stefano. Sorry about the alterations to my face.
I didn't have much of one left, after the aircrash. The
surgeons did a damned fine job, sculpting a new one."

"I'm so sorry, Colonel—"

"Simon," he said gently.

"Yes, sir," Kafari's cousin said, working to control his
shock. "Very well, sir. We've just docked at Bombay Station. Can you meet us at eleven hundred hours, Gate
Seventeen?"

"I'll be there."

Stefano just nodded and ended the transmission. Simon
stepped through the shower, then dragged on a good dress
shirt and slacks, even a jacket. He looked bad enough,
as it was. He didn't need to compound it with sloppy
clothes, particularly not today, when he'd be meeting
Yalena. He hadn't seen his daughter in two years. He
wouldn't know her and she wouldn't know him. They'd
never really known one another at all. Trying to adjust
to one another's company, particularly since Yalena did
not see eye-to-eye with him, was going to be difficult
for both of them.

He had to move slowly, even with the servo-motors
of his leg braces, which allowed him to walk faster than
he could with only the crutch canes. Time was, he'd

feared that he would never walk again. It had taken two years of on-going treatments and hard work just to get this far. He wanted to call Sheila Brisbane and ask her to go with him, but decided against it. Yalena had enough to adjust to, without throwing in the company of a woman whose presence could be misconstrued as evidence of an affair.

No, he wouldn't do that to Yalena or himself. Or Captain Brisbane.

By the time he reached the spaceport and parked his groundcar, he had a serious case of jitters. He didn't know which was worse: dreading the reunion with his daughter—and the lie he must tell her, about Kafari—or the difficulties he would face during Yalena's adjustment, which would be tough on them both. He stopped at a small gift shop and bought a bouquet of flowers, following the old Russian custom handed down through his family generation after generation. The Khrustinovs who'd left Terra had carried that tradition from one star system to another as they spread out and made homes for themselves on distant, scattered worlds.

He hoped the custom would earn a smile, at least. He wanted to see a smile, even a half smile, on his daughter's face before he told her about her mother's death. He reached Gate Seventeen with scant minutes to spare. He had barely settled into a chair when the shuttle landed, sliding gracefully into the docking bay he could see through the tall glass windows. The engines cut off. Simon rose to his feet, clutching the flowers in one hand, and waited, not quite sure what to expect.

Then he caught sight of her. The teen-aged girl who stepped off the *Star of Mali*'s shuttle was no longer a child. She looked up at him through eyes that had seen too much horror. He knew that look, had seen it in the eyes of soldiers fresh from combat, had faced it in his bathroom mirror all too many times since Etaine.

Yalena had grown, during the past two years. Tall and willowy, she had her mother's face, something he'd never noticed before. Her footsteps slowed when she saw him.

The look in her eyes hurt. He moved forward to greet her, holding out the flowers. She took them, not even speaking, and buried her nose in their fragrance.

"Mom wouldn't come," she whispered, the words muffled against the flower petals.

"I know," Simon told her, dreading what he was about to do. He had to force himself to say it. "I received a SWIFT transmission. Before you got here."

"From Mom?" Her voice wavered.

"No," he lied. "Your mother . . . didn't make it. She was shot by a P-Squad dragoon, trying to slip out of the spaceport. They're shooting looters on sight and they don't bother to ask for credentials first." That last part was true, at least. They were shooting looters on sight.

Blood drained from her face so fast, she swayed. "No . . ."

He tried to steady her. She jerked away, rigid. "*It's my fault!*" she cried. "Mine! She came into town just to get me out. We walked all night through the sewers. She put me in that cargo box to save my life! And some stinking P-Squad—" She dissolved into hysterical weeping. Simon caught her, held her close. The sound of her grief, knife-edged and raw, made him want to take the words back, to reassure her. But he couldn't—just couldn't—trust her yet.

Not when she had spent her whole life believing in POPPA.

Simon wrapped an arm very gently around his distraught daughter and guided her out of the terminal. She said nothing as they climbed into his ground car. She said nothing as he drove them home. From what he could tell, she wasn't even paying attention to the city. They were nearly to the apartment before she broke her long silence.

"Daddy?" Her voice was a mere whisper.

"Yes?"

"I'm sorry. I don't expect you to believe that. I wouldn't, if I were you. But I am." A single tear rolled down her cheek. "And I'll try to prove it."

He reached across and squeezed her hand. "I love you, Yalena."

Another tear appeared, trembled on the edge for a moment, then slid down her face. "I don't know why."

"Try to take it on faith for a bit."

She nodded. "Okay." Then she touched the flowers she still carried. "These are beautiful."

"I'm glad you like them." He managed a smile. "It's an old custom, from Terra. A Russian custom. Always greet people you love with flowers, when they've been gone for a long time."

Droplets that were not rain fell onto the petals in her lap. "I don't know anything about Russia. I don't know much about anything else, either," she added bitterly. "On the *Star of Mali,* I tried to use some of the library files, but I couldn't make sense of them. I didn't *know* enough to make sense of them. I kept having to stop and look things up, until I got totally lost, trying to find meanings for the things that would tell me what something else meant. I never got all the way though any of them. And I tried, really hard. I *hate* POPPA!" she added with a savage sob in her voice.

"It's going to be rough, I know that," Simon said gently. "But you'll have help. I've nothing better to do with my time, for one thing. And Vishnu's school system has set up special classes for refugees coming in from Jefferson. The principal told me about the program yesterday, when I made arrangements for you to start classes next week. It will take hard work, a lot of it. But you can do it. Try to have faith in that, too."

"Okay," she whispered again.

She said very little for the rest of the day and went to bed very early, pleading exhaustion. Simon closed her bedroom door softly, wishing she were little enough to rock to sleep, and made his way into his own room. He had his daughter back. A piece of her, anyway. He was grateful for that much. But he could not stop thinking about Kafari and the war she planned to wage. She was getting ready to fight a dangerous enemy and he wasn't thinking about POPPA. He was thinking about the machine he had once called friend. If Sonny killed Kafari . . .

Then Simon would kill Sonny.

It was as simple—and serious—as that.

PART FOUR

PART FOUR

Chapter Twenty-Three

I

Yalena was not the most popular girl in school.

In fact, there was ample evidence to show that she was the most *un*popular. There were no students from Vishnu in Yalena's classes, which were special affairs designed to teach Jeffersonian children remedial everything. The closest she came to natives of Vishnu during school hours were the hectic moments in the corridors while changing classes and standing in line at the school cafeteria. Most of the Vishnu kids turned pitying glances on those known to be from Jefferson, but others were openly rude.

Given the way children of POPPA's social and political elite behaved in mixed company, it was not difficult to see why. Yalena had truly not realized how odious a child she had been, until thrown into a society comprised of Vishnunians, POPPA's upper crust, and Granger refugees.

Since Yalena did not fit into any of those social groupings, was trusted by none of them, and did not seek out companionship from any of them, she was quite literally the least popular individual in the entire school. For the first year, it had cut her to the bone. By the time she was sixteen, it had left her in tears on occasions that should have been special and had, instead, been merely excruciating. At seventeen and a half, she was far too busy mapping out her vengeance to bother with mere social trivialities.

She had her eye on college, which was more than enough work for a girl who hadn't really learned anything but how to wash and dress herself. Fortunately, Vishnu's colleges and universities had also opened their doors to Jefferson's disadvantaged students, in a bid to create interstellar neighbors who were at least capable of reading, writing, and calculating basic arithmetic. Yalena had already applied to the college she wanted to attend, which offered the kind of classes she would need if she hoped to return home, someday, and strike back at the people who had murdered her mother and crippled her father.

Yalena's pulse always stuttered a little, when her thoughts turned to her father. Simon Khrustinov was not an easy person to know. He had given her the things she had asked for, to the best of his ability. She had not asked for all that much, in any case, preferring to test out a new concept called self-sufficiency. Her days of demanding—or even whining—were long since over. Mostly she had asked his advice. And that, he had given unstintingly.

When the final bell rang, dismissing school for the day, Yalena gathered up her materials and stuffed them into her satchel, then headed into the crowded hallway. The swirl of happy voices, laughter, and slamming locker doors crested and splashed against her senses like whitewater on the Kirati River, where Yalena had done a whole summer of extreme camping. She had asked her father to send her there as her sixteenth birthday present.

He'd held her eyes for long moments, looking so

deeply into her soul, for the motives hidden there, that she'd actually started to tremble. Then he'd given himself a little shake, smiled with a look of pain far back in his eyes, and said, "Of course you can go. If you need any advice on what to take with you, just ask."

She'd asked. And had benefitted immensely from that advice. Yalena had enjoyed that summer, in a grim and solitary fashion. She hadn't won herself any friends—mostly because she made no overtures, being far too busy learning simple survival skills most kids on Vishnu had absorbed by their sixth or seventh birthdays—but she'd won the grudging respect of the instructors.

More importantly, she had proved to herself that she could, given sufficient determination, overcome a decade and a half of indoctrination into the art and science of lunacy, a handicap compounded by indolent living, lazy flab in every muscle in her body and every snyapse in her brain. She'd had to overcome a learned helplessness, as well, that vanished entirely within two days of her arrival at the wilderness area that served as campground.

She'd spent her seventeenth summer in a Concordiat Officer Recruitment Program for high-school students interested in military careers. When she'd told him she planned to enroll, her father's advice had been enormously useful.

"The one thing you must understand," he'd told her the night she'd broached the subject, "is the purpose of that training. You've done a fair bit of homework, that's clear from what you've said. So tell me. What do you think C.O.R.P.'s purpose is?"

She considered her words carefully. "To weed men from whiny boys and women from snively girls, for one. To provide the Concordiat with a cadre of trained officers for the combat arms. And to begin training on high-tech military equipment, which takes time. A lot of time."

Her father nodded. "Yes, those are all useful adjuncts to the C.O.R.P. program."

"But not the main reason?"

"No." He refilled his glass, swirled the ice cubes for

a few moments, watching the patterns they made in the liquid. "Combat," he said softly, "has a nasty habit of putting you under the kind of stress that breaks people apart from the inside. Your whole world is shattering around you and you know that your decisions and your actions—right or wrong—will not only affect your own life, but those of others. Not just other soldiers, but civilians in harm's way, which is worse."

He fell silent again, for long moments. She waited him out. He didn't often let her see this part of his life and she wanted to understand him, wanted to understand what had made him the kind of person he was. She didn't want to interrupt or distract him, when he was finally speaking of it.

"When the stink and horror of it is all around you," he finally said, voice low and harsh, "when people are dying on all sides, when you want—*need*, in fact—to run gibbering for the deepest hole you can find, that is precisely the time you must be at your clear-minded best. The Concordiat needs to know if you're the kind of person who can go into a situation that would reduce most people to hysterical panic and make rational military decisions—and carry them out, which is even more important. Are you cool enough under extreme physical and emotional stress to know what must be done? Are you strong enough to *do* it, no matter the cost? That's what C.O.R.P.'s main purpose is."

Yalena could see the shadows of memory in his eyes. She'd signed onto Vishnu's datanet with the new computer her father had bought her, the week of her arrival, and had looked up Etaine in Vishnu's historical archives. What she had read over the course of the next two deeply shocked hours had deepened Yalena's hatred of school teachers who had systematically lied to her and her classmates. Those lies had poisoned her relationship with a man who should have been canonized as somebody's patron saint.

She knew that her father didn't want her to walk into the mouth of hell, didn't want her to face what he had faced and fought and lived through. Didn't want to see shadows in her eyes—or a medallion of honor that meant he would never see her eyes again. Yet he gave her expert advice, steered her toward resources she would need, even gave her extra training, himself. He was, Yalena had finally understood, trying to give her enough of an edge to survive the course she had set herself upon and seemed to know, without words spoken, that she did not intend to enter the War College at Sector Command.

Not until other, more important business had been taken care of, first.

Yalena stopped at her locker and put away the satchel and sundry items she wouldn't need for another ninety minutes, then headed for the C.O.R.P. practice field, behind the school's sports complex. They'd been studying aikido and other martial arts, this semester, and she was looking forward to another good sparring session. The open field behind the school, used for track meets, was crowded with runners doing laps in the chilly autumn air. The crisp temperature and keen, biting wind spurred the runners to greater exertion, to keep warm. Yalena detoured around the end of the track, then ducked into the gymnasium, since walking through was faster than walking the long way around to reach the C.O.R.P. field.

The smell of chlorine from the gymnasium's basement-level pool mingled with the odors of body sweat, dirty socks, and talc from the various athletes working out on gymnastics equipment, running wind-sprints up and down the bleachers, and playing a fiercely competitive game that involved twenty sweating boys, an inflatable ball, and hoops dangling from various places on walls and ceilings.

Yalena had even less in common with the school's athletes than she did with the ordinary students. They, in turn, tended to regard her as something of a freak, mostly because she refused to accord them the adoration they seemed to think was owed them for the superior manner in which they could make balls go through hoops. Yalena crossed the gym in silence, ignoring those at practice and being ignored, in return, as though she moved through a perpetual veil of invisibility. Which, to some extent, she did, since nobody found her interesting enough to notice.

She took the stairs down to the basement locker area, where she kept her C.O.R.P. uniform, and ran slap into the ugliest little scene she had witnessed since coming to Vishnu. A gang of POPPA brats, eight or nine of them, had cornered a Granger girl on one of the landings. They were dragging her, hands clamped across her mouth, into the men's locker room.

Yalena froze.

They kept going without looking up the stairs. They hadn't heard her open the stairwell door. She knew the girl, by sight, at least. Dena Mindel was a freshman, barely turned fifteen. Her parents had just come out from Jefferson, smuggled out, so the gossip ran, by Jefferson's growing insurrectionist movement. Yalena closed her fingers around the railing, gripping the well-worn wood with an ache through her whole hand. She knew exactly what the sons of POPPA's leading scions intended to do. They were putting Dena back in her place. Forcibly. *You may have gotten off-world,* the lesson they were about to impart would tell her and all other refugees, *but you'll never be more than gutter trash.* The threat of retribution to family members still trapped on Jefferson would keep her terrified and silent, too.

Moving very softly, Yalena reascended the stairs and slipped into the equipment room. She picked up a bucket into which she dropped several baseballs, a wooden practice sword used in the martial arts Yalena had studied, and a whole fistful of throwing stars, their edges and points dulled for safety standards, but still dangerous weapons in hands that knew how to use them.

Yalena's did.

She slipped back down the stairwell and glanced swiftly to see if anyone was strolling about. No one was, since the official practice sessions had already begun. She eased her way across the hall. Listened at the closed double doors leading into the men's locker room. A quick glance through the glass windows in the upper half of the doors told her that they'd posted a guard to run interference and to give a warning, should anyone interrupt. That guard was standing with his back to the doors, intent on whatever was happening around the corner.

That was his first—and last—mistake.

Yalena opened the nearest door so softly, he didn't even hear the faint click. Muffled sounds of pain and terror reached Yalena's ears. So did low laughter. And other, nastier sounds. Ripping cloth. A meaty smack that wrenched a whimper from the victim. Yalena tried to build a probable map in her mind, giving her a general placement of attackers and attacked. The sound of zippers going down told her she was out of time.

She held the wooden sword in her left hand, picked up a baseball with her right, then did a swift wind-up and let fly. The hard, leather-covered ball slammed into the side of the lookout's head, just above the ear. He went down hard. The crack and whump got someone's attention.

"What the hell—?"

Yalena came around the corner, moving fast. She sent the entire bucketful of baseballs bounding and bouncing in amongst them, tripping them up as they scrambled to tackle her and slipped flat, instead. She hurled throwing stars in a rapid-fire blur, going for vulnerable spots: eyes, throats, naked groins. Half of them went down, cursing or just whimpering. The others rushed her. Or, rather, tried to. She met the first two with full-force blows from her wooden sword. Bone crunched. Screams erupted, strangled with pain and shock.

She ducked under round-house blows that sailed harmlessly past her and used her attackers' rushing momentum to propel them into nearby walls, breaking more bones. She moved fluidly, focused on the precise actions needed to cripple the enemy, while keenly attuned to her entire environment. She was aware of everything and everyone around her, even the voices coming down the stairwell outside.

They were Granger voices, discussing the whereabouts of the girl lying a short meter from Yalena's feet. They hadn't reached the bottom of the stairs, yet, when the last would-be rapist still on his feet tried to run the other way. He skidded on a baseball underfoot, and went sprawling to the floor. Yalena stepped across and kicked him in the head, not hard enough to break bone, but more than hard enough to render him incapable of further threat. She stood over him for a long moment, breathing heavily in the midst of the carnage she had wrought, and realized with a stunned feeling that it was over.

The entire battle had lasted less than sixty seconds.

Dena had curled up into a ball on the floor, sobbing and shaking. Her dress and underthings had been ripped to shreds. Yalena crouched down beside her, moving swiftly, and wrapped the girl's shaking fingers around the wooden practice sword. Dena looked up, just long enough to register Yalena's identity, then heard her friends' voices in the hallway outside, calling her name. She turned her face toward them, tried to call out, and croaked so softly, even Yalena barely heard her voice.

"In here!" Yalena shouted, causing Dena to jump in shock. "I'm in here! In the boy's locker room!"

Then she took off at a dead run, dodging the remaining baseballs underfoot and whipping through the locker room and showers. She ducked through the doors on the far end, emerging into a corridor that carried Yalena past the wrestling and weight-lifting rooms, up into the main gymnasium, again. She dropped to a carefree stroll across the gym and reached the girls' locker room via another staircase that mirrored the one she'd just used. That corridor led Yalena down past the trampolines and balance beams used by the women's gymnastics team.

Yalena slipped quietly into the girls' locker room, changed into her C.O.R.P. uniform, and reached the practice field only four minutes late. Once there, however, she found it difficult to concentrate on *sensei*'s lesson. Her emotions were beginning to catch up to the rest of her, fractured emotions that ran the gamut from icy rage to shaking fear that she'd be expelled—or jailed—when those little bastards woke up and thought about pressing charges. Woven through all of that was the agony of grief she had not yet purged and might never leave behind. Her mother had been murdered by men just as brutal as the gang she'd laid out on the locker room floor.

Hatred had propelled every single blow.

If Dena's friends hadn't come down the stairwell, would she have stopped? Could she have stopped? She had wanted to kill them. And knew, as well, that she could have. All too easily. The cold, lethal hatred that was shaking through her, now, spoiled her balance and ruined her concentration. *Some officer's candidate I am,* she told herself savagely. *Dad never mentioned what a good officer's supposed to do* after *the fighting's done. Or what to do when the hatred that makes you want to vomit . . .*

She managed to limp through the lesson, mostly because it was interrupted partway through by the arrival of Vishnu's peacekeeping officers and several ambulances. She watched with the others as those ambulances pulled away, lights strobing as they headed to the nearest hospital. Yalena fully expected to be summoned by the officers, who were speaking with other students and teachers, but no one called her over or even glanced her way.

Invisibility had its uses.

She waited all night, in fact, for the questions to come but no one came to the apartment and no one called her father, either. Yalena watched the local newscast, which gave her a clue as to the unexpected lack of legal attention directed her way.

"A hate-motivated crime was broken up this afternoon at Shasti High School when a Jeffersonian Granger refugee was attacked by a gang of students whose parents hold positions of authority in Jefferson's POPPA Party. The attack, which was broken up by Granger students who came to the victim's rescue, has prompted Vishnu's Minister of Residency to revoke the educational visas of the young men charged with the assault. No formal charges have been levied, at the request of the student and her family, but the students named in the case will be deported as soon as they are released from the hospital.

"The Jeffersonian ambassador has protested this decision, charging the Minister with bigotry and cultural bias. The Minister has issued a formal statement warning that visa applications for family members of Jeffersonian officials connected to POPPA will come under sharper scrutiny, given the rise in tensions and the increasing number of violent incidents between Granger refugees and POPPA Party affiliates on Vishnu. The entire Chamber of Ministers has made it clear that Jefferson's internal wrangles will not be tolerated on Vishnu's soil."

That was the whole report. Yalena sat wrapped in thoughtful silence as her father said, "It's about time Vishnu did something about this mess. I'm surprised worse violence hasn't broken out before now. I hope the kid they attacked will be all right. And I hope to hell there aren't reprisals against Grangers still trapped on Jefferson."

Yalena swallowed hard. She hadn't thought about that. Hadn't stopped to consider the long-term effects of her enraged actions, this afternoon. It had felt right, at the time. Still felt right. But she hadn't thought it through and people would suffer for it, as a result. She hadn't had much time in which to decide, given the danger Dena was in, which helped assuage her tremors of guilt. It also gave Yalena a new and visceral appreciation of what her father had been talking about, when he'd tried to explain the purpose of C.O.R.P. to her. She had made the best decision she could, under the circumstances. And now she—and others—had to live with her decision and the actions flowing from it.

Command, she discovered in that moment, was a bitch with spurs.

The next day at school, she was aware of a sharp

and silent scrutiny. Not from the POPPA brats, but from the Grangers. *All* of them seemed to know. It was eerie, to be stared at everywhere she went, by people who had literally ignored her for two and a half years. At lunch, she found herself staring back into Granger eyes, driven by pride and smouldering anger into holding gazes until the others' glances dropped away, puzzled and discomfited no small amount.

By the time school was over for the day, Yalena was ready to disappear into whatever sanctuary she could find, but was duty bound to return to the C.O.R.P. practice field. She did nearly as badly as she'd done the day before and ended up on the ground time and again, sprawled in a winded heap where her instructor and fellow students had sent her flailing through the air. She wouldn't have to worry about proving her worthiness for combat, because she was going to flunk out of basic training.

By the time the session was over, Yalena was ready to do something else violent, just to burn off the frustration. When she emerged from the locker room, having showered and changed into street clothes, Yalena checked abruptly. Fifteen Granger students had formed a barricade across the hall and the stairwell. She considered taking to her heels in a repeat of yesterday's escape through the men's locker room. For long, fraught moments, she looked at them and they looked at her. Then one of the boys, a tall, rough-looking kid named Jiri Mokombo, whom Yalena had seen around school, but hadn't shared classes with, breached the silence.

"How come you did it?" he demanded. "You're one of *them.*"

Yalena didn't have to ask who "them" was. "That's my business," she said in a flat voice, angry and scared and determined not to show it. She didn't want another fight. And she didn't have anything in her hands, this time, except air. And courage. Which wasn't a whole lot when outnumbered fifteen to one.

"Your business, huh?" Melissa Hardy, who was in one of Yalena's classes, pushed her way through the others to meet Yalena's gaze. "You're wrong. You made it our business. Why?"

Yalena took her measure, silently, trying to gauge not the physical dimensions of an opponent, but the psychological dimensions of the exchange. The emotion that burned in Melissa's eyes was more puzzlement than anger. Yalena shook her head. "No, *you're* wrong, Melissa. I didn't make it *your* business. I made it *mine*. Frankly, I didn't much like the odds. Or the assholes involved."

Someone at the back of the group muttered, "You know, she's never made up to any of 'em. Not once. I noticed. And none of them have ever tried to make friends with her, either."

"Of course they didn't, not when her father's the butcher of Etaine," Jiri snarled. "They wouldn't touch her with a fifty-meter pole. And neither would I."

"Nobody's asking you to," Yalena said coldly.

Melissa turned abruptly and glared at her own friends. "Say what you like, she stopped a rape and God knows what else, before they'd had a chance to do more than rip Dena's clothes off. And there's not one of us—not *one*—who hasn't wanted to break a few of those bastards' bones, ourselves. Only we didn't quite dare, did we? We talk big, but when push came to shove, it wasn't any of us who stopped it. It was her, by herself, against a whole rotten gang of them. Yalena Khrustinova doesn't deserve nasty accusations or name-calling from *any* of us. The only thing I want to know," she swung around toward Yalena again, "is why."

Yalena realized that this was one of those moments that forever changed your life, if you were smart enough to recognize it and strong enough to act on it. The first such moment in Yalena's life came back to haunt her, now, with memory of a ghastly silence that had followed in the wake of screams she still heard in nightmares.

"The last night I spent on Jefferson," she said in a hoarse voice that sounded nothing like her own, "I got caught in a Granger protest march in Madison. My two best friends in the world were with me. When the P-Squads arrested the Hancock family and lied about it, Ami-Lynn and Charmaine and I went to the protest march. President Zeloc—" she spat the name out like every syllable was pure poison "—ordered the Bolo to run over an unarmed crowd in the street. I was in that street. So were my friends. My mother . . ." Her voice shattered.

The other girl's eyes flinched. They all knew that Kafari Khrustinova was dead. That she'd been murdered by the P-Squads. But they didn't know the rest.

"My mother pulled me to safety. Just ahead of its treads. My friends were behind me. They didn't make it. Have you ever seen what's left when a thirteen-thousand-ton machine runs over a person? There must've been six or seven hundred people, just in the city block I was on, that were crushed to death. And you know what was left? Paste. Red, sticky paste, like pureed tomatoes, with smears of hair and shoe leather . . ."

Somebody whimpered. Yalena didn't care. About any of them.

"Mom and I crawled away through the sewers. All night, in the sewers, wading through shit and blood, while the lynch mobs pulled people off the PSF farms and chopped them up and hung the pieces on light poles and street signs and burned half the downtown. We finally reached the spaceport and she smuggled me out. And then a trigger-happy P-Squaddie killed her. You know what the hardest thing was, yesterday, when I pulled those bastards off Dena? Not breaking their necks, along with their stinking arms and legs. And now, if you don't mind, kindly *leave me the hell alone!*"

She stalked forward.

They parted like reeds before a hurricane.

She actually made it all the way through the gymnasium and halfway across the track before they caught up. One of them, anyway. Melissa Hardy called her name, running to catch up.

"Wait! Yalena, wait!"

She stopped, not even sure why. Melissa closed the

gap, breathing hard. Yalena didn't say anything. Puzzled grey eyes studied her for a long moment.

"I've always wondered," she said slowly, "why you left Jefferson. Why you worked so hard, studying. Why you signed up for C.O.R.P. classes and extreme camping and martial arts. It didn't fit the pattern POPPA brats follow. I didn't realize . . ." She blinked hard for a moment. "I'm sorry about your mother, Yalena. And your friends." Before Yalena could say anything scathing, she added, "My brother was killed in that street, too."

Their eyes met and held. Yalena felt a dangerous crack in her emotional armor.

She swallowed hard. Then whispered, "I'm sorry. For a lot of things."

The other girl said, "I can't even begin to imagine how you must feel. It's got to be awful."

Yalena shook her head. "No. It's worse. I'm going back. To kill them. *All* of them."

The other girl's breath caught. Then something shifted in her eyes, something Yalena couldn't name, which left chills slithering along her nerves. When she spoke, there was steel in her voice. "I'm going with you."

She took the other girl's measure. Made her decision. "Sounds fair to me. There'll be fewer targets to hit, with two of us."

It was more than a pact, more than a holy alliance.

It was a promise. A threat.

And POPPA's death.

They shook on it.

II

Kafari had lost a lot of weight, but she wasn't the only person on Jefferson who was thinner, these days. Four years of guerilla warfare had left her lean and hard as a *jaglitch*. She'd occasionally eaten *jaglitch*, which could be digested—sort of—with the proper enzymes to break the alien proteins down into something a human stomach considered food. Their store of supplies contained plenty of enzymes, pilfered from pharmaceutical warehouses and fish-processing plants.

Dinny Ghamal stepped into the cavern Kafari called headquarters this week. He was whipcord tough, his face scarred and chiseled by torture and grief, but his eyes were still human. Emmeline had survived. She'd given birth to their first child, a son, six months after their rescue from Nineveh Base. It was a hell of a time and place to begin a family, but it had given many of Kafari's troops heart, reminding them that life could hold onto its sweetness and wonder, even in the midst of desperate struggle and hardship. The boy was the unofficial mascot of the entire rebellion. Dinny's wife, unable to travel fast or far while nursing an infant, had become a crackerjack code breaker, hacking into sophisticated systems that Kafari had taught her how to open. Dinny's wife served the rebellion well. So did Dinny. He bent low to duck under the rocky entrance to her "office."

"Commodore," he nodded, indicating with a single word that someone besides her own most trusted staff officers was somewhere in the camp, "the new supply teams are underway. It's a good haul, sir. We hit three food-distribution centers and wrecked what we couldn't transport. There'll be a passel of hungry Subbies, tomorrow. They'll really be furious by the end of the week. POPPA will have to tighten the rations again."

His smile was predatory, sharp, full of fangs.

So was hers. "Good."

"I have other reports in from the field, sir," Dinny added. "And pouches from several couriers."

"Let's hear the reports, please."

"Team Gamma Five reports success without casualties."

"Oh, thank God," Kafari whispered, closing her eyes against the sudden sting of tears. A penetration team had gone to Lakoska Holding Facility with orders to disrupt the wholesale deportation of convicted dissidents to the Hanatos "work camp." Their target had been Lakoska's barracks, housing more than five hundred dissidents and protestors. Most of them were Grangers, but a surprising number were urbanites desperate for food and medical care and willing to steal to get them. A few were just ordinary looters. Kafari's team of computer hackers had cracked the security codes on Lakoska's transportation schedule. They'd found the date and time of the highly classified transfer that would've sent the newly convicted prisoners to Hanatos tomorrow morning.

Team Gamma Five had, perforce, struck tonight.

Kafari had tried to rescue the prisoners already in Hanatos camp. Tried *hard,* just six days ago. Her entire team had died in the attempt. Their lives had bought the freedom of just five prisoners, who managed to escape during the wild confusion. Of those five, only one had made it out of the wilderness. Hanatos had been constructed, with great care and ruthless foresight, smack in the middle of prime *jaglitch* habitat. Once the remaining guards had killed Kafari's team—none of her people had allowed themselves to be taken alive—the retaliatory executions had commenced. The P-Squads had slaughtered fifty prisoners and made two hundred new arrests for every guard her team had killed in the attempt.

Kafari had spent a nasty half hour bent over a basin, losing every scrap of the meal she'd just eaten when the news arrived. Dinny had held her head while she heaved and wept uncontrollably, had wiped her face with a cold, wet cloth while she leaned against him, trembling with the emotional reaction, then sat down with her afterward, focusing her attention on what they could do: plan their own retaliation. Tonight's strike at the less well-defended Lakoska Holding Facility, had freed the latest batch of victims *before* they could be transported to Hanatos.

"How many did we get out, tonight?" she asked.

"Five hundred seventeen. We split 'em up as ordered and scattered them as best we could. I'm told it went smoothly. The transport buses were already in the parking lot, conveniently assembled for the next morning. We've set up shelters in several abandoned mine shafts, carefully distributed throughout the Damisi network. We managed to keep families together, at least."

"Good." Kafari had ordered old mine shafts to be converted into emergency shelters. She'd also instructed people in Granger country to dig bomb shelters under their houses and barns, with air filtration systems capable of handling biochemical attacks. She would never forget the riot she'd been caught in, with the gas that had very nearly caught her—gas that Simon had been convinced came from POPPA, itself, in a staged attack on its own people.

Vittori Santorini had plenty of money to buy ingredients to make whatever nasty biochemicals he wanted to disperse. Since farm folk didn't have publicly funded underground shelters, Kafari had strongly suggested they provide shelters, themselves. The residents of Klameth Canyon, Cimmero Canyon, and hundreds of other canyons scattered throughout Granger country had dug into the topsoil and bedrock with a vengeance.

But Kafari couldn't ask the farmers and ranchers to hide five hundred seventeen escaped convicts. POPPA would be hunting for any trace of those people and Grangers would be under extra surveillance—electronic and personal—as prime suspects for sheltering them. Kafari couldn't risk innocent lives, and her own resources were stretched to the limit. She'd known that when she'd given the order to hit the camp.

"The *Ranee* came in yesterday from Mali," she said, glancing at Dinny. "You've talked to our friend, Girishanda. I want to send our five hundred seventeen friends out on the *Ranee* when she breaks orbit."

"He won't want to run the risk."

"Oh, really?" she asked softly, hearing the dangerous tone in her own voice. "If he wants our money for his merchandise, he *will* by God take them out. As many as we can jam into his cargo holds."

"I took the precaution," Dinny said with a grim smile,

"of having a few people brought out here, tonight. To participate, unofficially, in our negotiations. I brought in some of the people we airlifted out of Lakoska. I also brought in Attia."

Kafari hissed. "Yes-s-s-s. Oh, yes. A fine idea, Dinny. That may just do the trick." Attia ben Ruben was the sole survivor from Hanatos death camp. "Very good. Our rescue team did a fine night's work. Be sure the team members know I said that."

Dinny nodded, then gave her a large pouch, just delivered via special courier. Kafari shuffled through the material and whistled softly. "My friend," she said, "this is some kind of good haul."

"Yes, sir," he said quietly. "It is."

It held documents recovered from the home of a P-Squad regional director, who had been involved in all sorts of nastiness. Letters, official reports, directives from planetary HQ spelling out measures to be implemented, along with a timetable, drew another soft reaction from her. "We need to get this off-world," she said in a hushed tone. "There are people on Vishnu who need to see these." If they could just persuade Vishnu's government to help them . . .

"That can be managed. Even if Girishanda won't take our refugees from Lakoska, we still have someone ready to ship out. They can deliver them. I've already made our copies."

"Very good. Handle it, please. Is there anything else?"

"Other than shifting headquarters and interviewing our visitor? No, sir. It's time to move out. The first transports are ready to go. The moons are down and the sentinels are in place. Our friend is here, waiting in the truck, as ordered."

"All right, let's move things along." She had already finished packing up her computer and personal effects, meager as they were, so she donned her command helmet, which covered her face very effectively while giving her an IR view of the cavern. She also wore breast-bands and extra padding to disguise her female shape. She strode out into the main cavern.

"Commodore!" Her people snapped to attention, giving her a smart salute. She returned it, nodding briefly to soldiers who were busy loading equipment and supplies onto horses, mules, and small skimmers. They never made major shifts in larger vehicles, not even at night. Sonny had access to Jefferson's satellites, whose military spy eyes had nothing to watch for in deep space, these days, but plenty to track on Jefferson's surface. So Kafari gave them as little to track as possible, and what little there was, she did her best to make innocuous.

The shifting of Kafari's headquarters would involve only one truck, three personal skimmers, and no more than a dozen pack animals, which would move in groups of two or three over the course of the next three nights. Some of them would amble more or less straight to the new headquarters cavern in a canyon several kilometers to the south, but only after looping through many other stops and layovers. Others would join them tomorrow night and still others the night after that, playing a slow-motion, deadly game of hopscotch under cover of darkness.

Kafari nodded to her people as she crossed the cavern, then climbed into the back of her command truck, which looked like a rickety, rusted-out produce truck with holes in the sides. It was crammed with the most sophisticated technology they'd liberated from Berran Bluff Armory. At the moment, it also held their "guest"—a supply agent from Vishnu who claimed to have good news that he would deliver to Commodore Oroton and no one else. He'd been stripped down to bare skin and had endured the most thorough body search Dinny Ghamal could conduct, a humiliating and painful process involving a fairly sophisticated arsenal of medical equipment, among other things. He'd come out clean. There hadn't even been a nanotech squeak anywhere.

They'd drugged him unconscious and brought him

out here. Kafari would speak with him from the back of the truck, which he would not leave at any time, and then they would drug him again and take him back to town so he could return to Vishnu. Or they'd kill him, if the situation warranted it, and drop the body on some well-used game trail frequented by hungry *jaglitch*.

Kafari climbed into the back of the truck. Dinny Ghamal climbed up behind her and swung the doors shut. Red Wolf, who was already there, nodded to her as she took her seat opposite a small table from their guest. He wore a blindfold and his hands were cuffed to the chair he sat in, leaving him no room to attempt anything untoward. He couldn't even reach her with his feet. All his clothing and his shoes were missing. Kafari had replaced them from her own stores. He had to be feeling mighty vulnerable, which was exactly what she wanted.

Kafari took her seat and tapped her fingertips lightly on the grip of her handgun, which she kept under her hand at all times. She studied the man in the opposite chair for long moments. He was a small man, with skin one shade darker than hers, even after four years in the Damisi back country, where harsh sunlight baked everything it touched. Like many natives of Vishnu, he was very slightly built, with straight black hair worn long. Her guest was showing signs of the emotional strain he'd been under for more than a day, now. "I'm told," Kafari said in a soft voice that her helmet transmuted into a deeper, more guttural and masculine sound, "that you have a message for me, Mr. Girishanda."

He turned his head slightly at the sound of her voice. "That is correct, yes. I have a message for Commodore Oroton."

"You have my attention."

"I would prefer the freedom of my hands and eyes."

"I'll bet you would. I'd prefer to see the sun rise, come morning."

To her surprise, he flashed a smile full of white teeth.

"A cautious nature is a wise quality for a leader of rebels. Very well. We speak in the dark."

Kafari waited, giving him no assistance.

"My employers have a certain commodity they feel may interest you."

Again, Kafari simply waited.

Girishanda said, "I am told you have some, ah, fairly heavy artillery."

"You've probably been told a lot, if POPPA's been talking. As for what you hear and what's true . . ."

He chuckled.

Kafari frowned. "You're pretty relaxed for somebody chained hand and foot."

"I am a Hindu," he shrugged, rattling the manacles against the chair frame. "What would you have me say? The things I get wrong this time around, I will have a chance to get right the next time around. As badly as my life goes, sometimes, I suspect I've been trying to get it right for a thousand years. I haven't managed it, yet. At worst, it's a better life than, say, several centuries as a slime mold." Teeth flashed again.

Kafari couldn't help it. She smiled "Very well, Mr. Girishanda. Why are you interested in my artillery?"

"I have very little interest in what you have. I have a great deal of interest in what you might want."

Kafari considered. "And what might you have, that would tempt me?"

"Hellbores."

Kafari sat up straight. "Hellbores? You care to explain that?"

White teeth flashed again. "I have your attention, yes?"

Kafari deliberately waited him out, telling her taut nerves to be patient, because she damned well wasn't going to get what she wanted any faster by jumping at an offer that smelled like a very large rat.

Girishanda smiled in her direction. "Your silence is a sign of patience, my friend. That is good. Even with the cargo I can deliver, you will need patience. And a great deal of cunning. We know what you face, in this struggle. We can help. If the price can be agreed upon."

"There are more things than price to consider."

The smile left his face and he sat up straighter, despite his bonds. "You are very right about that," he said softly, as though she had passed some sort of test. "Very well, Commodore Oroton, I will answer some of the questions you carefully have not asked."

Kafari settled into her chair, prepared to listen. All night, if necessary.

"During the war," Girishanda—or whoever he really was—said, "refugee ships poured across the Void, running terrified ahead of the Deng. Some of those worlds had heavy artillery, not heavy enough to save them, but enough to buy evacuation time. You must know, Commodore, that many more ships came on to Vishnu than stayed on Jefferson. These people were panic-stricken. They wanted as much human space between themselves and the Deng as they could afford to cross. Some of them realized that the heavy artillery their worlds had purchased could be sold for a tidy sum of money, taking them farther away from a border that was shifting too rapidly for their peace of mind. So they brought that artillery with them. To . . . smooth the way, financially, so to speak."

Kafari could see the excitement in Dinny Ghamal's eyes, could read it in Red Wolf's flared nostrils. Oh, yes, Mr. Girishanda definitely had their attention. Kafari's, as well.

"You are interested, then?" he asked.

Kafari let him wait, again. If he was worth his salt as a bargaining agent, he would *smell* their interest. *Note to self*, a corner of her brain had the temerity to whisper, *whenever you're dealing for something really big, have someone light incense, first. Or douse the place with* eau du jaglitch *first*. The very absurdity of the image restored her equilibrium. The long pause caused Mr. Girishanda's self-assurance to falter slightly. Good. He needed to be jolted a bit.

"I suspect," she said at length, "that your price is beyond our means."

"Oh, I wouldn't say that. In case you hadn't noticed, there's not much happening in our corner of interstellar space, just now. The market has shifted. We find ourselves with a stock of goods nobody wants."

Nobody else, he meant, of course.

That was understood.

"You're not worried about another breakthrough from across the Void?" Kafari asked, allowing surprise to color her voice. "Our respective star systems are still slam in the way of any incursion from the Deng homeworlds."

"The Deng," Mr. Girishanda said dismissively, "are in no shape to come calling on anyone. Besides," he grinned, "they'd have to come through you first, which means you'd get better use of the Hellbores than we would."

"Huh," Kafari muttered, "we'd get our asses shot off first, you mean."

He tried to shrug; the manacles rattled. "Your Bolo—"

"It is not our Bolo." The hatred in her voice stopped him cold.

The look on his face spoke eloquently about the difference in attitude one brought to the bargaining table when one's visceral experience of Bolos involved being shot at by one, rather than viewing it as savior and protector from the wrath of alien guns.

"No," he said at length, with an unsettled expression as he tried to imagine what it must feel like to be on the wrong end of those massive guns. "It is not *your* Bolo. But it is a Bolo, nonetheless, and it's programmed to defend this world from the Deng. Try to imagine what would happen if the Deng returned," he said softly. "How long would it take for Vittori Santorini's little empire to collapse like a house of cards? We're not stupid, Commodore, or blind. Santorini's done a good job with the propaganda, no doubt of that. The news that reaches Vishnu and Mali is full of flowers and honey. And his money talks, as well. Louder on Mali than Vishnu, you must understand?"

Kafari frowned behind her helmet, trying to take in the multiple messages being thrown at her, some voiced, some unvoiced. "Go on."

"He's fooled a lot of people. But spacers talk. So do refugees. And enough POPPA officials have sent their children to our schools to give us a very clear picture of what POPPA really stands for and what it's capable of doing. And," he added with a shrewd glance at Kafari's top commanders, "what it isn't capable of, which is just as important. If the Deng hit Jefferson again, that unholy little alliance of his will come apart at the seams. His P-Squads appear to be very skilled at terrorizing ordinary citizens and shaking down spacer crews for bribes and letting enormous amounts of contraband slip through unquestioned. But go up against Deng Yavacs? Or heavy cruisers? Even Deng infantry?"

His voice held scathing contempt. "You don't even have an air force left, do you? Let alone trained fighter pilots or ground support troops. If the Deng come this way—or Krishna-forbid, the Melconians—your troops, Commodore, and that Bolo are the only defense Jefferson will have. Perhaps it's selfish of us, but we'd like to think there'd be something to at least slow them down, before they head for Ngara and our worlds."

It was a hell of a mess, when a Deng invasion looked positively attractive.

He leaned forward, causing the manacles to clank again. "But consider this, Commodore, because I assure you, *we* have, more than once. That Bolo of yours takes his orders from the government. If you *become* that government..."

Kafari caught the hiss between her teeth before he could hear. Just what were Mr. Girishanda's motives? And connections? He sounded more like an official with Vishnu's Ministry of Defense than a gunrunner. She narrowed her eyes beneath the battle helmet's face mask. The ministry would doubtless feel a great deal safer if Kafari's rebellion succeeded in removing POPPA and the Santorinis from power. POPPA fanatics would make uneasy neighbors, at best.

When Jefferson's economy collapsed—finished collapsing—the whole damned society would go under. It was inevitable. And the disaster wasn't very far off, either.

And when the collapse came, hungry and angry people were going to go hunting for what they needed to survive. Jefferson still had star-capable travel, with enough guns in POPPA's hands to turn the P-Squads into a ravening horde of armed and deadly scavengers. The closest civilized port of call they could reach lay in the Ngara system. If Kafari had been a highly placed official in charge of defending Ngara's worlds, she would have viewed the situation on Jefferson with alarm. Intense alarm.

Even with the losses the P-Squads had sustained from steady attacks by Kafari's freedom fighters, there were thousands of P-Squad officers out there. Nineveh Base had trained five thousand a year for ten years, before Kafari's assault had wiped the base off the map. Even with the loss of Nineveh's cadre of instructors, however, they still had an army of fifty thousand men already in the field. If pushed to raid off-world for what they needed, that army could smash Mali with ease and do massive damage, even on Vishnu.

There *was* a Bolo on Vishnu, but in that kind of scenario, it wasn't much use. A Bolo had to know in advance that a ship was a threat, before it could act defensively. A freighter crammed full of P-Squad marauders could land a devastating attack with literally no warning and escape again untouched, simply by picking a target on the other side of the planet from the Bolo's depot. The depot's location wasn't a secret from *anyone*. Any ordinary school child could tell raiders exactly where to find Vishnu's Bolo. There were several thousand POPPA students on Vishnu.

And now Mr. Girishanda was offering to sell her the kind of firepower it would take to destroy Vittori Santorini and either destroy or take control of his suborned Bolo, which would end the threat POPPA and its fifty-thousand potential raiders represented. If Girishanda wasn't on the Ministry of Defense's payroll, he was acting on the ministry's behalf. And probably on their orders, payroll or not. Kafari was ready to put money on it. Speaking of which . . .

"How many Hellbores do you have available, Mr. Girishanda? And how much money do I have to lay down, to persuade you to part with them?"

"Then you are interested?"

"In winning this war? Absolutely. In your merchandise? That remains to be seen."

Mr. Girishanda's smile blazed like the noonday sun over Hell-Flash Desert. "My dear Commodore, I believe we can both walk out of this deal as happy men."

Kafari couldn't help her own smile. "You think so?"

Dinny Ghamal was grinning fit to crack his face in half. Red Wolf merely looked pained. Girishanda, blissfully ignorant of the byplay, said, "It is my fondest hope."

Kafari leaned forward. "Convince me to put my money on the table."

They settled down to the serious game of dickering a price they could both live with, in every possible sense of the word. It took an hour of the hardest bargaining Kafari had done in her life. Money, per se, wasn't the only factor in her strategy. There was plenty of money, if a person knew how to divert it from off-world investment portfolios and bank accounts. POPPA, itself, was supplying Kafari with most of the money they needed to wage this rebellion. No, the hardest portion of her job tonight would be the other demand that went along with the cash laid on the table.

When Girishanda finally accepted a price that left him looking mournful, but likely beaming with self-congratulatory success in the privacy of his own thoughts, Kafari let the hammer drop.

"There's just one more little condition to meet, before we close this deal."

She couldn't see his eyes behind the blindfold, but

the rest of him shifted from easy relaxation to wary tension. "Oh?"

"We have some merchandise of our own to ship out. Important merchandise."

"What does a commander of rebels have to sell?" Girishanda asked.

"This commodity isn't for sale."

"It'll cost to ship it, then," said with a frown. "How much it'll cost depends on what you're shipping. And why."

Kafari turned to Dinny Ghamal, who nodded and rose, leaving the truck and swinging the doors shut behind him.

"Who's that?" Girishanda asked. "Who left?"

"That's not important. We have a perishable commodity, a fairly bulky supply of it."

Girishanda gave her a sudden scowl. "Oh, no. No, you don't. I'm not transporting a shipload of escaped prisoners. I do not want that kind of risk, thank you, kindly."

Kafari regarded him for a moment. "You want to sell some Hellbores. I want to buy them. If you want my money, you'll take my commodity and ship it safely to Vishnu. Or the deal is off."

"Don't be stupid!" Girishanda snapped, sitting up straight and rattling the manacles when he tried to move his arms to emphasize the point. "Confound it, you *need* those Hellbores or that Bolo will tear you to shreds. You know it. I know it. POPPA knows it. Don't put yourself—or *my* world—at risk over the fate of condemned criminals!"

His reaction was no more than Kafari had expected. Her gut still clenched in icy rage. He did not, of course, know. Nobody on Vishnu could know, yet. Spacers and refugees might talk, but the former were restricted to the environs of the spaceport, these days, and the latter had fallen to a mere trickle, thanks to draconian shifts in emigration laws. With a total lock-down on interstellar communications and escape from the camps all but impossible, who could possibly have gotten word out to Vishnu? Nobody on Vishnu could know the vicious secret of POPPA's detention camps, except Simon, and he couldn't talk freely without putting her and her people at risk.

"In a few moments," Kafari told him, "you will eat those words."

Puzzlement drove furrows into his brow, but he didn't answer. The door opened again. Dinny had returned with a young girl in tow. She had been pretty, once. Innocent, too. She was fourteen. The sea-green eyes that looked out at the world burned with an eerie copper fire, eyes that reflected the unspeakable horrors she had witnessed and survived. They were ancient eyes, lost in a child's face, eyes it took a strong man to meet face-on and not flinch from. It had taken every ounce of strength Kafari possessed to meet Attia's gaze, when Dinny had first brought her in, two nights ago.

Kafari rose from her chair, taking her pistol with her, and touched Attia's hand gently, beckoning her to take Kafari's seat, then she stepped behind a partition that afforded privacy for a mobile toilet used by the crew in the command post. There was a video system in place, covering the interior of the command post, with its video feed tied into her battle helmet's visor. It gave her a full, unobstructed view of the tableau unfolding out there.

Attia sat down, watching silently as Dinny removed Mr. Girishanda's blindfold.

He blinked a couple of times, then his gaze came to rest on the slender girl opposite him. He sat up so abruptly, the manacles bit into both wrists. He spoke, jaggedly, something she didn't understand. Kafari didn't speak Hindi. She didn't have to. The naked shock in his face was all too eloquent a translation.

"My name's Attia," the girl said in a rough, ruined voice. "I turned fourteen three months ago. In Hanatos Camp."

Girishanda was trying to swallow. The sound was ghastly in the frozen silence. Red Wolf, an unobtrusive presence behind Girishanda's shoulder, had taken out a belt knife and was jabbing the point into the arm of the chair he sat in, mechanically, with fixed concentration.

"Have you ever heard of Hanatos Camp?" Attia asked in a harsh voice.

The gunrunner shook his head. He was still trying to swallow. Kafari gave him credit for guts. His gaze stayed on Attia's face. What was left of Attia's face.

"Ever hear of Professor Mahault?"

Again, he shook his head.

"She wrote a book. *The True History of Glorious Jefferson.*"

Girishanda was frowning. "What does a professor have to do with . . . ?"

"She rewrote our history," Attia said harshly. "Wrote a book full of lies to prove that *Grangers* had altered the history of our world. Her book gave POPPA the 'proof' they needed to classify Grangers as a subversive sub-culture. One that existed to destroy true civilaztion."

"That's insane!" Girishandra gasped.

"You're damned right, it's insane," Red Wolf growled.

Girishanda's eyes tracked towards Attia, who spoke again in that ruined, harsh voice. "Yes, it is. But there was no one to stop them. Not even the Commodore could stop Jefferson's House of Law and Senate when they passed legislation outlawing Grangerism. Our whole culture, itself, is now a crime. Against humanity, decency, and planetary security. Anyone caught practicing Grangerism is arrested, convicted, and shipped out to the nearest 'work camp.' Once there, we become slave labor. We de-terraform 'raped areas' to allow nature to reclaim its own. Or we're sent into mine shafts to work 'round-the-clock shifts. It's too expensive to pay miners actual wages, when convicts can be forced to do the work. All *that* costs is money to buy the guards, ammunition, and just enough food to keep the slaves on their feet and working. And sometimes," she added harshly, "not even that."

Girishanda's eyes flicked across Attia, whose skeletal pallor had not faded in the mere two days she had been free and would not fade for months to come. If she didn't get killed fighting to free others. There were still prisoners in far too many work camps.

Mr. Girishanda met her gaze, once more. He didn't speak for long moments. Then he asked very quietly, indeed, "Would you tell me, please, what happened to *you*? I'm trying to understand."

Attia's copper-fire eyes searched his face for long moments. "You're from off-world. Vishnu?"

"Yes. I am from Vishnu."

"Are you selling us guns?"

"I am trying to," he said gently, flicking a glance at the partition between himself and "Commodore Oroton." "It seems that the sale is contingent on hearing what you have to say."

She scowled, which pulled the scar tissue in hideous directions. "All right. Then listen up good, 'cause I don't want to relive this out loud, ever again."

Kafari knew exactly what was coming.

Mr. Girishanda only thought he did.

III

Phil is an hour late returning from lunch when he finally enters my makeshift maintenance depot, a sheet-metal barn topped by a metal canopy that barely accommodates my bulk. The entire, flimsy affair threatens to become airborne each time a storm sweeps in from the ocean west of Madison. Phil is, as usual, swearing.

"You won't believe what happened last night! Those goddamned freedom fighters hit the food distribution centers! *Three* of 'em! My sister Maria found out this morning, when she went down to collect the week's groceries from the warehouse. I hadda take her to see a guy I know, who wouldn't sell direct to her even if she told him I sent her. It took my whole damn paycheck to get *anything* for the kids t' eat, and there wasn't a hell of a lot *he* had left, neither. Not at any price."

"I am sorry to hear that, Phil." *I find it interesting to note that Phil no longer calls the Granger rebels by the term "terrorists." This is the only descriptor used by the POPPA leadership when referring to rebels who routinely shoot corrupt POPPA officials in their driveways, ambush police patrols, and execute outspoken broadcast propagandists in their houses—admittedly clean executions that never touch a family member or innocent bystanders. "Terrorists" is not, however, the word drifting through the streets, where food riots have been crushed just as brutally as Granger protests were during the early stages of POPPA's rise to power.*

"And that's not the half of it," *Phil continues to rage, with his nano-tatt blazing in a blood-red swath across half his face, pulsing in time to his elevated heartbeat. I find the rhythm distracting.* "You know what the shit-for-brains Minister of Urban Distributions did about it? Did he tell the P-Squads what he oughta be telling them? Which is what I'd tell 'em, if I was in his shoes. 'Find those bastards or go hungry!' Did he say that? Oh, no, not him. He just went and cut the rations again, that's what! Another unholy, unbearable *twenty percent*! How'n hell are kids s'posed to grow without nothin' to eat? I ask you, do those POPPA bigshots look like they're goin' without dinner? Hell, no. There ain't no such thing as a skinny cop, let alone a skinny politician."

Phil wipes sweat from his nano-tatt with a hand that is actually unsteady.

"I dunno what my family's gonna do, Big Guy. If Maria loses any more weight, she's gonna collapse. She's nothin' but skin and bones, now. And Tony, that no-account oldest boy of hers, that goddamned little *idiot* got himself hooked on snow-white and lost the only job our whole family had, except mine. D'you know what's it like, Big Guy, t'be the only person in a whole damn *family* that anybody respects? Five sisters, I got, *all* married," *he adds with justifiable pride, given the informal methods of procreation practiced by many subsidy recipients, who are desperate for any increase in the baseline payments,* "an' all five of 'em has kids, *twenty-three* kids, all together. And the little ones look up t' me. They say 'I'm gonna be like Uncle Phil when I grow up. I'm gonna have a job!' I ain't smart, Big Guy. I got nothin' much t' be proud of, I know that, and God knows I ain't the sort a kid oughta be lookin' up to, to decide what t' do with his life."

His eyes film with suspicious moisture and his voice assumes a bleak, nearly despairing tone I have never heard from him. "And what chance have they got, anyhow, to be like Uncle Phil? To have a job, I mean, and somebody's respect? There's no jobs *now.* The trash they're learning in school sure isn't gonna teach 'em how to get one. It's worse now than it was when I was in school, and man, they didn't teach me *nothin'.* If things don't change pretty soon," *he adds,* "they won't need to worry about growin' up like anybody, 'cause there's no damn food t'feed em, anyway." *His voice turns savage.* "Sar Gremian needs *me,* don't he? T'keep you running? So I eat, while them kids starve. It ain't right, Big Guy, it just ain't right. We never signed up for this kind'a stuff, when folks voted POPPA in, all those years back." *He pauses, then adds in a puzzled voice.* "How'd it get t'be so bad in such a short time, huh? Seems longer, t'me, but it's just nineteen years since POPPA took over. Spent my whole schooling, just about, in POPPA classrooms, and not one a' them teachers ever told us it could get like this so fast."

Phil's revelations, coming as fast and thick as Y-Band bolts from a Deng Yavac, astonish me. He is more deeply disaffected with POPPA than I had realized. He has also gained far more self-respect and technical skill than I would have believed possible. While his nano-tatt is as colorful as ever and he still shows a predilection for barracks-room language as colorful as his face, he no longer speaks like the illiterate grease monkey he was just four years ago. He has, in fact, become a surprisingly skilled technician.

Granted, he has spent most of the past four years studying the archived manuals and technical schematics pertaining to my weapons systems and other hardware, which required even longer sessions working with a dictionary and the science, mathematics, and engineering texts embedded in my reference banks. I have been forced to grant him access to these, as the Minister for Public Education made a thorough sweep through Jefferson's public educational system, e-libraries, and datasite archives. It is no longer possible to obtain a real education on Jefferson without attending one of the private schools operated for the children of POPPA officials, whose databases and on-line libraries are not accessible to the average citizen.

This fact angered Phil immensely when he discovered the existence of this two-tier educational system, with its built-in mechanism for exclusion of the unequal masses. He might never have discovered this, if not for my urgent need for repairs. I have sustained enough cumulative damage from rebel forces to make constant repair work a necessity. Each time I leave my makeshift maintenance depot to disperse rioters, repel attacks on police stations and military compounds, or pursue guerilla-style raiding parties, I am subjected to direct fire from a surprisingly large arsenal of military-grade small arms.

Nor am I the only thing taking cumulative damage. The guerillas are taking a heavy toll on food distribution networks—trucking centers, packing plants, warehouses— and utilities infrastructure—electrical power generating plants, sewage treatment facilities, public transportation hubs—that cannot be replaced at Jefferson's current level of industrial sluggishness. There are no manufacturing plants left to replace the equipment and buildings being wrecked. The repeated attacks have driven many engineers and technicians to boycott work in a massive protest movement that is crippling Jefferson's cities as effectively as the damage to the infrastructure, itself.

Commodore Oroton is fiendishly effective at his job.

So are his field troops. Rebel marksmen have an uncanny ability to put bullets through external camera lenses and sensor arrays, which is not just annoying, it is downright alarming. Scrounge as he will, Phil cannot keep finding replacement parts indefinitely. Worse, during my transits to and from those conflicts, usually through heavily populated areas, I am also hit by suicide-teams masquerading as ordinary civilians. The bombers get close enough to hurl man-portable octocellulose bombs against my tertiary gun systems and track linkages, inflicting a steady barrage of damage that cannot be repaired fast enough. Not in the face of near-total lack of replacement parts.

I am also burning up antipersonnel ammunition that can only be replaced by diverting it from P-Squad depots, an activity that tries Phil's nerves to their utmost. If Phil Fabrizio is afraid of anything, it is the P-Squads. What is particularly irritating about the expenditure of munitions is the knowledge that I am wasting it on rank-and-file fighters, as I am unable to locate, let alone eliminate, the ringleaders. For all their vaunted prowess, the P-Squads have had no better luck cracking open the rebel network. I do not know if that is because the P-Squads are inadequate to the task or because Commodore Oroton has built a particularly effective guerilla network, with cells difficult to crack open. The rebel tendency to suicide, rather than be taken for questioning, certainly makes it difficult to question those who might otherwise have provided valuable information.

The mysterious Commodore Oroton is an extremely effective commander, with what is clearly a great deal of military experience. I surmise, based on the actions of his hit-squads and the thought-processes behind them, that the commodore has worked with Bolos in the past. If not as an officer, perhaps as a technician or a cadet who failed the rigorous examinations necessary for command. Whoever Oroton is, the situation is rapidly deteriorating into a serious crisis.

Phil mutters, "I'm sorry I'm late. Lemme climb up and look at that infinite repeater processor that got hit last time. I gotta know what parts t'steal."

Phil climbs up the rear port-side ladders and clambers cautiously across my stern, reaching the infinite repeater housing that routes fire-control signals to my port-side and stern infinite repeaters. The guidance-control circuitry is, of course, inside my warhull, but there are semi-external processors that route the signals. These processors are covered with flintsteel housings across my flanks and back. It is a design flaw in the Mark XX series, which was corrected in the Mark XXI and later Bolos. Phil cuts and pries at the warped housing with power tools, sweating and swearing until it finally comes loose. He peers critically at the damage and just shakes his head.

"Big Guy, the tracking control for these rear-port infinite repeaters is out. O-W-T *out.* There's a hole right through the actual quantum processors and quantum is French for 'Don't fuck with it.' Ain't no way I'm gonna fix this one." *He gestures at the damage, evincing extreme disgust.* "Maybe I can cobble something up t'replace it. I stole a workstation processor last week from the Admin building on campus, but it won't work real well. If Sar Gremian doesn't get us some honest-to-God spares soon, I honest-to-shit don't know what we're gonna do. Next time you go out, try to duck the bullets, huh?"

"I am too big to duck, Phil."

"You said a pissin' mouthful." *He wipes sweat off his face with one sleeve.* "They're screwin' you up royal, that's for sure. We'd be a blamed sight better if they bought spare parts as rewards, 'stead of sticking so many goddamn made-for-prime-time, gaudy-assed medals up on your prow. Much more a'them shiny things and I won't be able to open the housings on your *forward* processors."

I am inclined to agree with Phil's assessment of the relative worth of the "medals" I have been awarded by this administration. I, too, would prefer their removal. Phil is climbing down when I receive an urgent call from Sar Gremian. "We've got a police patrol pinned by rebel gunfire. I'm sending the coordinates now."

Those coordinates show a spot thirty-seven kilometers north of the Klameth Canyon agricultural complex. This is cattle country, with extensive herds of beef cattle, dairy farms, vast hog lots, and poultry houses that stretch for a hundred meters or more and routinely house seven or eight million birds. Most of this was privately held, before the land-snatch programs confiscated and collectivized it. The terrain is comparable to Klameth Canyon, which sets up a trickle of unease through my threat-assessment processors.

"Phil," *I say urgently,* "climb down faster. I've just been ordered into another skirmish. A police patrol has been trapped in Cimmero Canyon and is taking heavy fire."

Phil just shakes his head in disgust and shimmies his way down ladders until he reaches the floor. "Watch your back, willya?" *he says while getting out of my way.* "You got enough stuff back there to fix, without adding anything new to the list."

"I will do my best, Phil. Given the state of my treads, this will take a great deal of time."

I head out at the best road speed of which I am currently capable, which is pitifully slow compared to my optimal speed. I have sustained sufficient track damage, I cannot risk my treads to the wear-and-tear they would sustain under greater velocity. At sixteen point two-five kilometers per hour, the journey will take me two and a half hours to complete. Local police attempting to reach their brethren have come under such withering fire, losing three aircars and seven groundcars full of officers, they have retreated and refused a second rescue attempt. Federal troops—consisting of P-Squadron officers—have also refused to risk themselves against an entrenched enemy with effective snipers.

Given Jefferson's wholesale destruction of mothballed military aircraft during Gifre Zeloc's presidency in a "political statement" that involved bulldozers and a crowd of thousands screaming their approval, I am literally the only resource POPPA can fall back on, to neutralize what appears to be a relatively small handful of riflemen. By monitoring police channels, I ascertain that the rebels don't seem to be trying to overrun the patrol, just pin it down. As this does not fit with previous patterns, I exercise caution during my final approach.

There are only three routes I can take to where the patrol is pinned. All three lead through relatively narrow areas. To reach any of them, I must pass the city of Menassa, which grew up in the Adero floodplain at the point where the main entrance to this canyon opens out. It is a fair-sized city with a population of roughly two hundred seventeen thousand people, founded to support the meat-packing and processing industries necessary to turn Cimmero Canyon's herds into cuts of meat ready for shipment. I select the entrance south of Menassa, to avoid bringing the fight directly into the midst of a major civilian center. The city is considerably longer than it is deep, stretching for nearly ten kilometers along the main roads leading to Madison in the south and mining communities to the north.

This portion of the Damisi mountain range is heavily forested. The canyon walls slice through a thick deciduous forest where shifting climate patterns and plate tectonics have brought abundant rainfall to a region formerly dry enough to erode away as badlands. The result is a dense tangle of native vegetation that forms a green fringe along the crown of the cliffs. The ranchers of Cimmero Canyon do constant battle with inimical wildlife drawn to their herds. Cimmero's residents were among the strongest protestors of the weapons-confiscation legislation, for reasons of personal safety as well as predator control to protect their food animals. Indeed, the Hancock family co-op was based in this region.

I do not like this terrain, with its limited visibility and plenty of cover and concealment for enemy gun emplacements. The rebels could hide an entire division in the forested fringe that lies several hundred meters *above me and I would not detect their presence until they opened fire. I therefore move ahead with all available sensors sharply tuned. I would be happier if all my sensors were available, but I suffer port-side blind spots, thanks to cumulative sniper-fire damage.*

I would be much happier still, if I could conduct aerial reconnaissance, but I have no drones. Although Phil has been able to produce satisfactory aerial surveillance equipment by piggybacking cameras onto children's toys, I am out of them again. The rebel marksmen's skill at shooting them down surpasses Phil's speed at manufacturing new ones. Toy airplanes, like everything else on Jefferson, are in short supply and the cameras are even harder to locate and steal. Using other sensor arrays, I scan across a wide band of visual, audio, and electromagnetic spectra, looking for anything out of the ordinary. I detect no heavy-weapons emissions, only the background power bleed from ordinary household current.

I am approximately one point five kilometers from the coordinates supplied by Sar Gremian when police transmissions from the patrol take on a frantic urgency.

"They're comin' at us again! I'm hit—Jeezus, I'm hit—"

I detect gunfire, not only through the radio link, but dead ahead, with my own sensors. I can hear screams, as well, men in pain. I rush forward through the narrowest part of the canyon, gaining speed rapidly in an emergency sprint that sends me barreling across the intervening distance—

—minefield!

I detect it too late to stop. I kill forward thrust and lock starboard drive wheels. I skid sideways, further slowing my forward motion. My port-side treads slew around, spinning my stern in a dizzy whirl—

SECOND MINEFIELD TO PORT!

Massive explosions rip my port-side treads to confetti. My entire port side rocks upward, off the ground. I am stunned by the concussion. Sensors scream pain warnings all the way down my port-side hull. I have lost seventeen external sensor arrays and four banks of antipersonnel guns. The second minefield was fiendishly placed: precisely where missing port-side sensors had left me blind in several critical spots. I am still assessing battle damage when I catch the unmistakable emissions of a Hellbore coming on-line.

Battle Reflex Alert!

It fires from a point high on the cliff that rises to my right, above my prow. I throw my shields on-line and brace for impact. The Hellbore blast does not strike me, however. It rips through the opposite cliff, directly above my skewed-around, scorched stern. Solid rock blows out nearly a hundred meters overhead. An avalanche smashes down into the narrow passage. I am directly under it. Half the cliff comes down. Damage-assessment sensors scream redline warnings. Hull-ringing boulders destroy my upper-most sensor arrays. Antipersonnel guns shear off. Impact sensors register several tons of rock crashing into my warhull. My stern-mounted Hellbore's rotation collar cracks catastrophically.

Even as the landslide buries my entire stern, I fire bombardment rockets at the Hellbore that took out the cliff. I score a hit—but others pop online. Two, three, five of them. They fire from defiladed positions, raking my entire port flank along a deadly diagonal line. They fire in unison and concentrate their combined fire on the same, one square meter target. They punch through my defensive screens and melt an entire cluster of infinite repeaters and two square meters of ablative armor. The combined fire scores the flintsteel hull beneath armor plates in a long, molten gouge. If they fire another combined hit on that spot, they will breach my hull.

These bastards have studied Etaine!

I roar into Battle Reflex Mode. I fire bombardment rockets in a massive barrage. Rebel-launched hyper-v missiles scream skyward, knocking down ninety-nine point three percent of my rockets mid-flight. Two get through and score direct hits. Both blasts destroy the mobile platforms to which the Hellbores were mounted. The guns leap off the ground under the impact. Mobile truck-beds flip over midair and plunge down the cliff face to smash into the canyon floor just beyond my prow. They land in the minefield and vanish in a secondary explosion. The mines detonate with sufficient force to scorch my nearest radar arrays. The other Hellbores drop off-line and vanish behind the clifftops.

The attack is over as swiftly and brutally as it began.

I am stunned. Not only by the level of skill and knowledge evinced in this attack, but by the fact that I detected six mobile Hellbore field guns, when the rebels should have been able to field only three. No other thefts of heavy weaponry have been reported from Jefferson's remaining military arsenals. A lack of on-world robberies translates directly into an inescapable conclusion: the rebels have obtained off-world weapons. This means off-world financing, on what has to be an immense scale. And procurement agents, who are able to smuggle in large shipments, probably dropped in remote regions via shuttles from an orbital freighter, since not even P-Squad officers on the take would allow mobile Hellbores to pass through their customs check-points.

This is ghastly news.

So is the pin-point accuracy of rebel fire at my major vulnerable points. That second minefield was deliberately placed by someone fully aware of the preexisting damage to my port-side sensors. Indeed, I speculate that these sensors were deliberately targeted in a series of advance raids, specifically to engineer this ambush. The subsequent combined salvos, striking precisely where they did, were neither accident nor unhappy chance. The rebel commander was not trying to cripple me. He was going for a kill.

The fact, taken alone, is hardly surprising, since any sane rebel commander would try to destroy me. What sends shockwaves through my personality gestalt circuitry, however, is the chilling fact that he has acquired the means to do it. Those shockwaves send conflicting reactions jittering through my personality gestalt center. Outrage, dismay, anger, even a welcome relief that at last, I again have an enemy worthy of the name. There is little honor in shooting a sniper with a rifle or a suicide bomber trying to run after throwing an octo-cellulose grenade into my nearest video sensors. But a commander devious and intelligent and knowledgeable enough to pull off this ambush is a worthy opponent. I begin to relish the thought of destroying him.

When I pull myself free of the rubble, my lacerated left tread simply falls off. For the first time, I have not won an encounter with the rebels. The damage is serious and semicrippling. It will tax Phil to the utmost, trying to repair it. I turn cautiously, using ground-penetrating radar to locate buried mines, which I target and destroy with my forward infinite repeaters. This clears a space through which I can safely limp forward. I proceed with extreme caution, moving at a pitiful crawl on two treads and a rank of bare drive wheels.

When I reach the ranch on which the police squad was pinned down, I do a swift reconnaissance from two hundred meters out. I am wary of further ambushes. A two-story ranch house to my left appears to be deserted. I detect no heat signatures through the windows, none that would correspond to a human-sized target, at any rate. A number of barns and out-buildings suggest hiding places for artillery, but I can see nothing like tire tracks that would indicate the passage of a field-artillery gun through the farmyard. A police vehicle is parked next to a hog-lot. Markings on the doors identify the car as a Madison municipal police cruiser assigned to traffic duty. It is out of its jurisdiction. By a considerable margin. The cruiser has been abandoned with its trunk open. The hog-lot gate is also open. A substantial herd of genetically adapted swine has escaped through this gate, spilling out across the entire barnyard.

I move forward cautiously, broadcasting a query to

the pinned-down officers. I receive no response, only static. At a distance of one hundred meters, closing slowly on the apparently deserted farmyard, I spot an open poultry house twelve meters from the abandoned police cruiser. Through the movement and sound spilling through the open doors, I identify several thousand chickens, neatly caged for efficient egg production. A few of the cages have been pulled down and opened, freeing some thirty or forty birds, which mill around the barn floor, looking for food.

The poultry house has been hit by a heavy barrage of small-arms fire. Bullet holes riddle the walls. I halt fifty meters out, scanning with all available sensors and find the missing police officers. All five of them are down. They are all assuming ambient air temperature. Based on heat signatures, I estimate they were overrun and killed at approximately the same instant the rebel Hellbores opened fire on me. The timing suggests all sorts of interesting capabilities in the rebel command structure.

At a distance of twenty-three meters from the farmyard, I am close enough that my forward turret sensors can see inside the police cruiser's open trunk. It contains three freshly killed geno-pigs and the carcasses of at least a dozen chickens. The dead officers were assigned to a Madison traffic-control squadron, not a P-Squad foraging team. Traffic police are not authorized to collect in-kind taxes from livestock producers.

These men are thieves!

I sit motionless for a full seventeen point three seconds, psychotronic synapses crackling, as I attempt to come to grips with what has transpired and why. I have sustained massive damage trying to rescue a pack of illiterate, power-abusing livestock rustlers. Does one rustle hogs? Or merely steal them? I am sufficiently proficient in twenty-seven Terran languages to curse—fluently—if the situation seems appropriate, but I cannot even find words to express my full and penetrating disgust.

The fact that I was lured into an ambush, using

them as bait, suggests frequent raids on the region's farmyards conducted by Madison's municipal police force. An isolated incident or two would be insufficient to set up an ambush this elaborate. This kind of operation must, of necessity, rely on a pattern predictable enough to have soldiers, munitions, and artillery in position and ready to deploy rapidly to a target close by. I surmise, therefore, that these officers have been stealing for quite a while, in a pattern predictable enough for Commodore Oroton to take advantage of it.

Disgust deepens. I call a forensics team and send them the map coordinates of the perforated poultry house, then turn around and rattle my way out of the barnyard. I do not even bother to file a VSR to Sar Gremian and the president. Anything I might say at this juncture would only worsen the friction between myself and the two most powerful officials on Jefferson.

Basic military doctrine dictates the need to leave a combat zone by a different route than the one used to approach. I therefore select the nearer of the two remaining routes that will take me back out to the Adero floodplain. I drop out of Battle Reflex Mode, although I maintain the heightened vigilance of Battle Reflex Alert. I navigate the narrow canyon at a snail's pace, grinding along slowly on the drive wheels which automatically dropped down to road-level height to compensate for the missing track. I leave a deep furrow behind where bare wheels cut into the soil. The partially melted wheel drags in its locked position, heating up and warping even further before enough of the surface is ground down by friction that it no longer touches the ground at all.

The route I have chosen takes me past the main generating plant that supplies electricity to the ranches in Cimmero Canyon and to Menassa. The canyon floor has opened out into a broad space that nearly qualifies as a valley, rather than a canyon, with the open Adero floodplain nearly ten kilometers beyond. From the standpoint of human aesthetics, this is pretty country.

I find it attractive for reasons of my own. The open terrain makes it more difficult for the Enemy to lay an ambush. There is plenty of forest cover on both slopes, which rise gently toward the heavier timber at the higher elevations, but the Enemy cannot establish firing points directly overhead, concealed from my vantage point.

This is cause for celebration, given my current pitiful state.

I parallel the main road, trying not to crush it under my remaining treads or dig massive furrows into it with naked drive wheels. Beyond the power plant lies a small cluster of single-family dwellings that house utility crews and foremen working at the Cimmero Canyon electrical generating plant. Like the massive Klameth Canyon hydroelectric dam, farther south, this plant produces power from turbines built to harness the outflow of the Bimini Reservoir, created by damming a small river that flows down through a deep, weathered gorge. The reservoir is small, compared with Klameth's, and so is the total wattage produced by the station, but it needs to supply only the ranches in Cimmero Canyon, Manassa, and the small town of Gissa.

Even so, its generating capacity is sufficient to create a haze of background power emissions that crackle through my sensors. The plant was built sufficiently close to the road that I maneuver across a short section of pavement to reach open ground on the other side. I do not wish to knock down, even accidentally, a tower carrying high-tension wires that carry several gigawatts of electrical power. A sprawl of buildings shoulder their way past my port-side drive wheels as I grind my way toward the still-distant mouth of the canyon—

AMBUSH!

The Hellbore blast catches me flat-footed. Raw destruction slashes across my forward turret, targeting the base of my forward Hellbore. I reel. I stagger drunkenly in an attempt to swing my own Hellbores into action. I snap my defensive screen into place just as a second mobile Hellbore flashes on-line. It pours energy into my screen, which strains to contain the damage. Then both enemy Hellbores fire simultaneously, delivering a second one-two punch. It slices perilously close to the previous gouge, trying to punch through my damaged hull.

Fury sweeps through my personality gestalt center. I roar into Battle Reflex Mode, enraged. I dig my bare drive wheels into the ground and execute a spinning pivot-turn to port. I cannot reach either enemy Hellbore with direct fire, not without risking critical power-plant infrastructure. They have, naturally, hidden behind that infrastructure, hoping it will constitute an inviolate shield.

I engage with high-angle mortars. Warheads drop like blazing rain around both enemy guns. Their crews, however, have already taken evasive maneuvers. They manage to avoid the mortar rounds with minimal scorching. They shoot at me on the run, dodging and ducking behind other buildings. Several bolts strike my screens on the oblique, recharging my energy screen rather than punching through. Missed shots whip past my warhull and slam into the valley's far slope, igniting a forest fire. I rush forward, trying to gain a vantage point from which I can shoot without taking out half the generating plant in the process. Minefield warnings sparkle on my threat-assessment processors. I disdain them, smashing my way through to reach an optimal firing position. I sustain damage to my central track, but reach my objective.

I fire on the nearest mobile Hellbore. It vanishes in a violent expansion of flame and debris. The second Hellbore rushes for cover, vanishing from visual contact behind a massive concrete building. I no longer care about collateral damage. I open fire with my forward Hellbore, punching through the concrete structure in an effort to pinhole the fleeing gun crew behind it. One, two, three blasts rip through the building, reducing it to smoking rubble and flying debris. The mobile Hellbore rushes into the open for zero point nine-two seconds, then lurches out of sight, again, behind another structure.

I give chase. I cannot move as fast as the renegade crew

trying to escape my wrath. I therefore plow forward on the diagonal, crushing the corners of two houses belonging to the power plant's utility crew. I must destroy the enemy's heavy armaments at all cost, before the rebels deal my own death blow.

I catch a snippet of communications from somewhere nearby, probably not from the running gun crew. It is in code that I cannot break. I cannot even accurately pinpoint its origin, which prevents me from opening fire on the transmitter. The fleeing Hellbore has rushed far ahead of me, having skipped and dodged its way around sufficient bends in the valley that I cannot see it. I am able to track power emissions from its mobile platform and fire more high-angle mortars, trying to blanket the valley ahead with a shotgun peppering of rounds.

I hear detonations, but these are low-tech mortar shells, not smart-rounds that can transmit pictures back to me or allow me to fly the weapon into the target from a remote position. I have long since used up those munitions and POPPA has not seen fit to replace them. I am therefore left with a hit-or-miss proposition known as "carpet bombing" in an effort to strike a small, moving target.

I need intel. My on-board maps show several small feeder gorges into which the crew could duck and shut down, hiding successfully for hours in spaces too narrow for me to pursue. They could also continue their rushing flight through the town of Menassa, relying on the buildings and the civilians in them to deter my pursuit and attack. Or they can run for the nearest maze of major canyons, twenty kilometers south of Menassa. I do not have enough information to determine the crew's intention. Striking out across country would be its greatest risk, but would give it a greater chance of ultimate escape, rather than temporary concealment nearby.

I target the feeder gorges with a steady barrage of mortars, hoping to create a blockade of raining munitions that will prevent the crew from taking advantage of those smaller, closer gorges as a hiding place. My inability to see what I am shooting at is infuriating. I decide the most logical move the crew could make would be to head for Menassa, which will keep it shielded for at least half of its twenty-kilometer dash toward the canyons farther south.

I therefore anticipate loss of visual contact as I reach the valley's mouth and Menassa spreads out in its long, ropy line along Route 103. I am therefore stunned to see the Hellbore's mobile platform rushing straight down the highway, nearly at the horizon line, within smelling distance of safety. The crew has opted for the riskier high-speed dash for safety, thinking my own progress slow enough to prevent me from overtaking them. I do not need to catch them in a road race to destroy them. I exult. I target. I acquire weapons lock. I fire. Hyper-v missiles streak down the long, beautifully straight road, locked onto the vanishing tail-lights of the racing truck.

The incandescent flash of impact leaps up from the horizon line. Smoke and flame billow up, filling the sky with a satisfactory display of dissociated molecules. I have destroyed another Hellbore. I do not know how many mobile Hellbores the enemy still has, but as of now, they possess five fewer than they did at dawn. I have seen six in the past hour, alone. I do not think it likely that the two guns I destroyed in the second ambush were part of the group of six that attacked me during the first ambush. They could not have maneuvered their way through difficult terrain in that short a span of time. I destroyed three of the original six, leaving another three unaccounted for, which is a disquieting realization. So is the suspicion that the third canyon entrance, north of Menassa, probably had another two guns at a bare minimum lying in wait, had I chosen that route.

As bad as this is, my next realization is far worse. The rebel commander correctly surmised my likeliest choices each step of the way and placed his strongest concentration of firepower in the canyon I chose to enter.

I have been complacent. The time for complacency is over. I cannot operate in a lazy fashion, making decisions based on my physical limitations and repair woes, rather than the exigencies of battle. The enemy is too canny to risk that error again.

I begin to revise my estimation of Commodore Oroton. He does not think like a Bolo technician. He thinks like a Bolo. I find that unsettling to the point of calling it fear. I know my own limitations, operating without a commander.

So does my enemy.

This is not a good state of affairs.

I send a VSR to Sar Gremian, giving him the location of the wreckage and a terse update on the enemy's firepower, then enumerate my repair needs. He is not amused by the stunning amount of damage that must be repaired. I am not amused by his comment.

"This planet paid a hell of a price to keep that treaty in force, so we could hang onto you. It would've been nice if the Concordiat had sent us an *intelligent* machine. Get your sorry, whining ass back to your depot. And try to avoid being seen!"

He ends transmission. To avoid being seen, I will have to add nearly thirty extra kilometers to the journey home, since I must swing wide around the eastern end of Madison, to approach my depot from the east, rather than proceeding directly from my current position north of the capital. It will take the better part of four hours, at a bare minimum.

As I set out, I pick up a broad-band message from Madison, on the civil emergency frequency that overrides all civilian broadcasting. The announcement is short, but its impact will be felt for a very long time, indeed.

"Granger terrorists struck a savage blow to civilians and police authorities in Cimmero Canyon, today, inflicting massive damage and killing an unknown number of innocents. The entire city of Menassa has lost electrical power after the destruction of the Cimmero power-generating plant. Identifying and capturing terrorist ringleaders and their operatives has become POPPA's top and sole priority. The government will divert every resource at its command to the task of rooting out and destroying all vestiges of rebellion against legitimate authority. Acts of terrorism will be answered with the greatest possible force.

"To that end and by order of our new president, Vittori Santorini, the right of *habeas corpus* is hereby suspended to allow arrest and detainment of terrorism suspects. Public gatherings of more than ten individuals must be approved in advance by POPPA Squadron district commanders. All elections are cancelled, to allow the current government to deal with this serious emergency. No visas for off-world travel will be granted without prior, written approval of the POPPA Squadron commander assigned to the applicant's home district. Civil rights will not be restored until all manifestations of rebellion are completely eliminated.

"Law-abiding citizens are urged to report any suspicious behavior to the nearest POPPA Squadron command post. Rewards will be given for information leading to the arrest of known or suspected terrorists. A mandatory curfew of eight P.M. will remain in place for all civilians except emergency crews until further notice. The public will be notified of additional restrictions as they become necessary."

Night is falling as I set out for home.

I do not believe that tomorrow's dawn will be anything but worse.

IV

Yalena knew at first glance that he was a soldier. Spacers moved differently and even the toughest, most jaded old dockhand or jump jockey didn't have eyes like that. Yalena recognized those eyes, even though the face and the man behind it were total strangers. They were her father's eyes.

And hers.

He paused on his way into the bar, gaze snapping around like gun barrels on a swivel mount to stare right at her. Not at her long, lean shape, draped negligently against the bar, sheathed in a dress her father would've consigned to the incinerator, if he'd seen her wearing it. He wasn't staring at the wisp of cloth or the shape under it. He was staring at her face. For a long moment, she actually thought he'd recognized the battle shadows in her own eyes, but that wasn't it, either, because he frowned, as though trying to place an old acquaintance from memory.

"Am I supposed to know you?" he asked, moving toward her. It didn't sound like a pickup line. He looked upset.

"I don't think so. I've never seen you."

The frown deepened. "That's the wrong comeback, isn't it?"

For some reason, heat scalded Yalena's cheeks. What she'd heard all too often from others, in smarmy phrases and lurid glances that usually rolled off her back with a mere shrug, stung her to the quick, hearing them from this man. "I'm a hostess, mister," she bit out, "not a whore."

His eyes widened. Then *he* flushed. "I'm sorry, ma'am," he apologized, sounding like he really meant it.

Yalena held his gaze for a long moment, then relaxed. "No offense taken. It's an honest mistake, around here."

The frown returned. "Then why—?"

She shook her head. "Sorry, but that's my business, not yours."

He rubbed the back of his neck with one hand. "I don't know what's gotten into me," he muttered. "I'm not usually so ill-mannered. But there's something about you, I can't quite put my finger on it. You look like someone I used to know, a long time ago ..."

His voice trailed off. Yalena drew her own conclusions. "Before battle?" she suggested softly.

His eyes shot wide again. "Good God. I'm not in uniform. How did you know?"

"Your eyes," she said gently. "It always shows."

He blinked. "Yes. But how did *you*—sorry. None of my affair."

Perhaps it was only a measure of her own loneliness that she wanted to sit in some private little alcove somewhere and just talk to him. The feeling unsettled her.

He changed the subject, evidently determined to take them onto less emotionally charged ground. "So you're a hostess, are you? How does the system work, here?" he asked, glancing at the tables, most of which were occupied by mismatched couples.

Yalena smiled. "You pick a hostess and a table. I persuade you to buy drinks, maybe food. I punch in the orders for you."

"Using a code that gives you part of the outrageous sum charged?"

Her smile became a grin. "You got it."

He surprised her with a chuckle. "All right. Lead on, my lady fair." He gestured at the wide selection of empty tables.

She straightened up from the bar and led the way toward a secluded spot well away from the other occupied tables, not to encourage the kind of physical contact that often resulted in bigger tips, as well as higher bar tabs, but to carve out an isolated space where they could actually talk without spoiling the ambience for other, more involved patrons and hostesses. She could feel his gaze on her back. She didn't need to glance back to confirm that he was watching the sway of her hips. Any movement she made in the ridiculous spike-heeled shoes she'd slipped on for the evening set the dress to swaying and jiggling around her body. Her father would probably have a coronary if he ever discovered it hidden in the back of her closet.

When she paused at the table of her choice, turning to meet his stare with an amused glance, she read more questions in his eyes. He gestured her into the booth, then sat down on the seat opposite the table, rather than beside her. That, alone, differentiated him from ninety-nine percent of the customers in this dockside dive. He glanced briefly at the posted menu.

"Is it cheaper if I order it, myself?"

"Oh, yes."

"Substantially?"

She grinned. "Astronomically."

"How badly do you need money?"

She blinked. Then said gently, "Not that badly."

One brow quirked, but he said nothing. He punched in the order, himself, a fiscal decision that suggested a combat veteran on his way to somewhere, with not a whole lot of money in his pension envelope. The little light on the order box flashed when his drink tray was ready. Yalena fetched it smartly from the bar, sliding the drinks across to him as she sat down again. He slid one of them—a light wine, rather than one of the heavier, harder-hitting liquors—across the table to her.

"Thanks." She smiled, sipping slowly.

He sampled his beer, shrugged, and said, "What's your name?"

"Yalena."

"Pretty name. What's the rest of it?"

She hesitated. As a rule, girls did not give their last names. It was safer that way. He hadn't given her his name, yet, either. So why did she find herself wanting to answer him truthfully?

"Khrustinova," she said quietly. "Yalena Khrustinova."

He sat up straighter, all trace of indolence falling away. "There was a Bolo commander by that name, out this way."

"Oh, hell!" she swore, kicking herself squarely in the metaphorical backside. "You're from *Jefferson,* aren't you?"

"You bet I am, honey. And pissed all to pieces, because I can't get home. The embassy," he said with an ugly edge in his voice, "doesn't accept appointments except on the fifth Thursday of the month on alternate election cycles."

"They are a lot of stinkers," Yalena agreed.

"Stinkers?" He snorted, torn between wrath and amusement.

She raked him with a shrewd glance. "How long did it take for them to figure out you're a combat vet? I'll bet your level of service sent your request straight into the toilet, didn't it? Armed and dangerous combat veterans are the *last* thing POPPA wants around."

"Your father doesn't like soldiers?" The edge in his voice suggested what must've been an incendiary conversation with the embassy's automated answering tree, which had been programmed deliberately to shunt any undesirable questioners into phone-tree oblivion, until they simply gave up and went away. But the comment, itself, suggested something else entirely.

She studied him with a sharp stare. "You *have* been gone a while, haven't you?"

The battle shadows in his eyes blazed to hellish life, again. "Honey, you don't know the half of it."

"No," she said softly. "I don't. POPPA—P.O.P.P.A.—is the Populist Order for Promoting Public Accord. And my Papa—my father—hates it as much as I do."

"Is your father Simon Khrustinov, then?"

"Oh, yes."

"What are you doing here? Going to college on Vishnu, I suppose?"

"What else?" she said, arching her brow and forcing her voice to remain casual. She did not want to tread too heavily across this particular patch of dangerous ground, which was too close to her real reason for being in this port-side dive.

He leaned forward abruptly and reached across to grasp her chin. She jumped with shock as he turned her face toward the admittedly dismal little light recessed above the table. "Yes," he said softly, to himself. "That's why, by God . . ."

"That's why what?" she hissed, pulling sharply away and freezing him with a stare full of dangerous, glittering ice.

"She's your mother," he whispered, as though he hadn't heard a word. "Your nose, your cheeks, even your eyes . . ."

"What about my mother?" The vicious edge in her voice got through, this time. He stared at her for a long, disconcerted moment. Then sat back. "Your mother's Kafari Camar, isn't she? Kafari Khrustinova, I mean. She's my cousin."

"Your *cousin*?" Yalena gaped. "Who are you?"

"Estevao Soteris. I enlisted the day President Lendan died." He was still staring at her. "I haven't seen her, since then. How is—?" He broke off at the look on her face. "Oh, God," he whispered, voice choked down to an agonized whisper. "What happened?"

Hot tears came, catching her by surprise. Yalena hadn't wept for her mother in four years. Had convinced herself that there were no more tears left to shed. "They shot her."

"*Shot* her?" His voice half strangled itself on the word. "My God! Who shot her? A mugger?"

"No." The word fell like an axe blow between them. "The POPPA Squads. At the spaceport. Right after she smuggled me out."

The muscles in his jaw turned to steel. Flintsteel. Death blazed in his eyes.

"Where's your father?" he asked harshly.

"Here. In our apartment, I mean."

"Here? On *Vishnu*? What the hell is going on, back home?"

She told him. The whole hideous, wicked little story. He interrupted again and again, asking for clarifications, trying to draw solid information from every nuance of her voice, her body language, her descriptions. She'd never run across anyone who listened that hard or drew that much information from a not-very-coherent conversation. When she'd finished delivering her very first situation report—because that was exactly what it felt like, being cross-examined by this cold-eyed soldier—he sat staring at the empty beer mug in his hand for long, dangerous minutes.

When he finally looked up again, meeting her gaze, he said, "How many spacers come through this place, bringing news from Jefferson?"

"A few. There are five, no, six ships still making the run. There aren't many captains who bother with the route, these days. POPPA," she said bitterly, "doesn't have much to export except lies and refugees. They're shipping out lies by the freighter-load, but the number of people getting out is down to a trickle. And they've made such a shambles of Jefferson's economy, there's no money to import much of anything, either. Ordinary people can't afford *anything* made off-world. Even POPPA's elite has started cutting back on imported luxuries."

She slugged back most of the wine in her glass, an act of desecration against the vintage, but the shock of alcohol against the back of her throat steadied her. "We don't know everything happening, back home, but what we do know scares us to death. We—other Granger students, I mean—started working the port town bars, trying to get information. We've even talked about going home and trying to *do* something about it." She shredded a napkin from the holder. "But there aren't enough of us to do much and what chance does anyone have, against a Bolo?"

He was frowning at her, trying to come up with an answer, when her wrist-comm beeped. She actually jumped with shock. "That's the signal I've been waiting for," she said, a trifle breathless as her nerves twitched. "There's a freighter in dock, from Jefferson. We came down to meet it. To meet the crew, I mean. They've been unloading cargo for a couple of hours. As soon as they've finished, they'll hit the bars and restaurants for a night of shore leave. We have an advance spotter in place at the terminal, to let us know when the crew disembarks. That signal was the heads up that they're about to leave."

"How many of you are out here, tonight?"

"Twenty-three. We've staked out the closest port-side bars and gambling joints, the likeliest restaurants. Freighter crews usually don't travel far, the first night of a shore leave. And this freighter has a big crew, according to the portmaster's records."

"The portmaster? Don't tell me you kids are hacking into secure databases?"

"We are not kids," Yalena bit out.

He reached across again, brushed her cheek with a gentle fingertip. "Oh, yes, little cousin, you most assuredly are. A girl your age shouldn't have that kind of shadows in her eyes. They'll pay for that. Trust me, for that much, at least. They *will* pay. And I'm not the only Jeffersonian combat veteran who came home on that tramp freighter. There's a whole group of us. We've ridden military convoys and freighters halfway across the Sector, trying to get here."

That startled her. She hadn't considered such a possibility. "How many of you came in?"

He dropped his fingertips from her face. "Thirty-four, on my freighter. And not one of us," he added with a growl, "could persuade the Jeffersonian embassy to honor our travel visas."

"Are you armed?" she asked softly.

He studied her for a moment. "Yes," he said at length. "Not with Concordiat military issue, mind. But traveling armed has become something of a habit, with us."

"What branch of the service did you join?"

"Infantry." The harsh tone grated along her nerves.

"That must have been . . . nightmarish." She was thinking of the Bolo.

"Worse." The shadows in his eyes spread, driving furrows through his face. His fingers tightened on the empty beer mug. "We were a mixed lot, on the freighter," he added, voice abrupt. "Infantry, Marines, Air-Mobile Cav, Navy. There's another ship coming in a couple of days from now, with more of us. The ship I came on didn't have enough berths for everyone. When the second freighter comes in, there'll be another sixty."

"That's nearly a hundred combat veterans," Yalena mused, entertaining brief fantasies of a strike force blowing down Vittori Santorini's palatial gates and turning him into red paste on his front lawn. "When do they arrive?"

He smiled. "Our luck was in, when we started hunting for another freighter. The *Star of Mali* dropped out of hyper-light a couple of hours before my group boarded the *Merovitch*. The *Star* was listed in the portmaster's schedules as the next ship due to make the Vishnu run. As it happens, my brother Stefano's crew aboard the *Star*. So I called him while they were transiting the system and asked how many of us they could bring. His captain agreed to bring them all. They ought to be here in a couple of days."

Yalena blinked. "The *Star*? Good God. Captain Aditi smuggled me out of Jefferson aboard the *Star*."

Estevao's eyebrows stole a march toward his hairline. "Really? Then you've met Stefano?"

She nodded. Then lowered her gaze to the droplets still clinging to the sides of her empty wine glass. "Yes. I'm afraid I don't remember much about that trip. I was in a pretty deep state of shock."

"I can well imagine. All right," he mused, toying with his empty beer mug, "tell me about your group. How many people do you have?"

"Seventy, all together. Students, I mean. I'm counting the ones determined to go back and *do* something. There are a lot more Granger students who are too scared to try."

"I think," her cousin said, meeting her gaze, "it's high time I met your father again." When she bit her lip, he added, "I presume you have more, ah, suitable clothes stashed somewhere around here?"

She grinned. "There's a locker room in back, behind the kitchen."

"When's your shift over?"

"A couple of hours. It's a school night. I was very careful," she added with a wry smile, "not to sign up for early morning classes."

"Wise tactic," he nodded in approval.

"I *am* enrolled in C.O.R.P.—" she began. Her wrist-comm beeped, slicing through her intended comment with an emergency code that meant trouble. In the same instant, she heard sirens wailing in the street outside the bar.

"Oh, *hell*," she swore viciously. "Something's gone wrong . . ."

Jiri burst into the bar, shouting for her. "Yalena! Trouble at the gate!"

"I'm coming! I've got to get my clothes—"

"No time!" He was striding across a bar full of surprised patrons. "Just kick those damned shoes off and *run*."

She was peeling off the spike heels.

Estevao Soteris was already on his feet, looking dangerous and competent. Jiri glared at him, ready to argue with what he thought was a disgruntled patron.

"He's my mother's cousin," Yalena said hastily, "just into port. He's an Infantry veteran." She finally had the shoes off. Yalena dropped them on the table and came out of the booth like a gunshot. They ran for the door. "Sorry, Jack," she shouted to the manager on the way past.

"I'll dock your wages, dammit!"

"Suit yourself!" She hurled herself through the door and out onto the street. The gantries and loading docks were a blaze of lights, jeweled towers rising skyward in the darkness, far above the roofs of port-side warehouses, passenger terminals, shopping arcades, and "water trade" establishments that provided space-weary crews everything from liquid amnesia to horizontal recreation. The freighters, themselves, never touched atmosphere, remaining instead in parking orbit, mated to one of Vishnu's five major space stations. But the cargo shuttles were immense ships in their own right, with heavy-thrust engines capable of lifting the shuttles and several tons of cargo from port to orbit.

The pavement was cold under Yalena's bare feet. Her cousin growled, "Put these back on. You'll cut your feet to shreds, out here."

He was holding her shoes, which no longer boasted spike heels. He'd cut them off—or maybe just snapped them with battle-hardened hands. She thrust her feet back into them and took off. The mutilated heels clacked against the concrete walkway. At least her dress was short enough not to hamper her stride. They ran toward the terminal. Police cars streaked past, sirens and horns shrieking a warning to pedestrians and ground cars. An air-lift ambulance shot past at window-top level, rattling wires and street signs with its passage.

Yalena ran neck and neck with Jiri, while Estevao brought up rear guard. They had just reached the terminal when the trouble spilled out onto the street. It was a fight. A *big* one. Yalena actually recognized some of the faces in the embattled crowd. They were students. POPPA students. She understood in a flash what had happened. POPPA students had always been arrogant and vicious in their effort to keep Grangers in their place. The newest POPPA arrivals, who'd just come in for the start of the school year, sported worse attitudes than most. She'd heard talk on campus about POPPA students' plans to meet freighters coming in from Jefferson, to be sure any "illegal, uppity stowaways" learned from the outset that they were still fourth-class citizens and had better toe POPPA's line if they didn't want relatives back home to suffer.

Clearly, there had been "stowaways" on board this freighter. *Lots* of them. Hundreds, from the look of things. Their appearance stunned Yalena to the soles of her vandalized shoes. The people spilling into the street were so thin, their muscles so wasted, it was like watching an army of embattled skeletons. Shock held her rooted for long moments—long enough to be caught up in the swirling edge of battle.

Police whistles tore the air as Yalena found herself grappling with a wild-eyed girl whose fingers had twisted into claws. She was snarling incoherently, eyes glazed with hatred and something even worse. She was writhing like a madwoman, trying to gouge Yalena's eyes. Yalena sent her stumbling into the nearest wall. Then ducked under a blow from a stout boy wearing POPPA green and gold. Years of indolence and overindulgence at the supper table made him slow and ineffectual. She sent him spinning into traffic, which had skidded to a halt as the battle spilled across the road and engulfed everything it its path.

The leading edge wavered, broke, and ran as abruptly terrified POPPA students took to their heels, literally running for their lives. The men and women chasing them pursued like blood-crazed hounds. A tall, whip-thin man with burnt holes in his face, where his eyes should have been, staggered and stumbled into her, having been dragged along with the crowd. His hands grabbed at her, clawing their way toward her throat.

"I'm a Granger!" she screamed at him.

He was snarling curses, trying to find the choke-hold on her throat. "You're too goddamned fat to be a Granger, you lying little bitch!"

"I'm a Granger student studying on Vishnu!"

She didn't want to hurt him. The ghastly, sunken holes in his face, scabbed over and not yet healed, were mute testimony to the ordeal he had already suffered. Her cousin waded in abruptly, dragged him off and put him on the ground in two seconds, flat. "Get out of here!" Estevao snarled at her. *"Move, dammit!"*

She tried. Only to find the way blocked by Vishnu's port police. They did not look amused. *Oh, hell . . .* What on earth could she tell her father? She suspected he would be a whole lot less amused than the police.

V

*The sight of my battered warhull and tattered treads
turns Phil's nano-tatt grey with shock.*

"Holy pissing Jehosephat . . ."

"I require repair. We do not have requisite spare
parts on hand."

"No shit," *Phil mutters, scrubbing his face with both
hands. They are unsteady. I detect no whiff of alcohol
and Phil's habits do not include recreational chemicals.
I therefore attribute the tremors to stress, as he is faced
with repairs far beyond his capability to conduct.* "Ah,
hell, lemme figure out where t' start."

"I will transmit a detailed inventory of damage and
parts needed to correct it."

"You do that," *he mutters.* "I'm gonna get the
fork-lift and start movin' track plates. I dunno if that
shipment we got last week will be enough." *He stares,
expression forlorn, at my shredded central tread and
bare port-side drive wheels.* "What in hell did they
hit you with?"

"Six mobile 10cm Hellbores."

"*Six?* Where'd they get their hands on that kind'a
firepower? I never saw any theft reports on the news."
His expression twists into a scowl. "Of course, POPPA
don't tell us peons the half of what goes on, most of the
time, anyway, so why's that a surprise?"

"There have been no thefts since Barran Bluff."

"Where'd they get 'em, then?"

"Clearly, the rebellion has obtained an off-world source
of supply."

"That ain't good."

"No, it is not."

*Phil does not offer further comment. He fires up the
heavy lift required to maneuver track plates and linkages
and begins the arduous task of replacing my treads. The
slam and clank of the lift and the plates banging into
place echo inside the flimsy maintenance bay, with its*

thin metal walls and thinner roof. The hiss and groan of pneumatic cranes and pully assemblages prompts Phil to don hearing protection. Even with the equipment to manhandle the individual plates and linkages, it is grueling work that requires a great deal of sweat, cautious nudging with the controls, and a purpose-built jackhammer to fasten the linkages, which the Tayari Trade Consortium had to manufacture to specs I provided.

The repair job requires me to move forwards and backwards in tiny increments, to allow access to the entire circumference of my treads. Phil is silent during the entire process, an unusual state of affairs, as he normally swears his way through any ordinary job.

After seven hours and twenty-three minutes of listening to the silence, I essay a question. "Is something troubling you, Phil?"

My technician, busy with jackhammer and linchpins, does not respond. I wait for a pause in the background noise. When he finishes using the jackhammer on the current linkage he is placing, I try again.

"Phil, you appear to be distracted. Is something wrong?"

He pauses, glances around to find my nearest visual sensor pod, and appears to weigh the risks of speaking whatever is on his mind. At length, he decides to answer.

"Yeah, something's wrong."

When he does not continue, I prompt him. "What?"

"It's Maria's boy."

"The one addicted to snow-white, the one failing remedial basketweaving, or the one who needs glasses to read the computer screen at his school desk?"

Phil scowls at my sensor pod. "How come you know all a'that?"

"You are my technician. Your family is an important factor in your effectiveness as a technician charged with maintaining me in proper working order. A crisis in your family therefore affects my overall mission. I keep track of events in their lives as a routine safeguard."

"Oh." *He considers this, then accepts it.* "Okay. That makes sense. Yeah, it's Giulio, her oldest. He started doin' snow-white and got fired and all, but he's not a bad kid. Y'know? He's got a good heart, anyway, and he felt so bad about losin' the job, he went out and asked the med-station nurse on our street for help t'kick the stuff. He's tryin' hard, y'know, and he's been helpin' around the house, too, watchin' the little ones so Maria can take a rest now and again."

"That does not sound like cause for distress."

Phil shakes his head. "No, it ain't. Trouble is, he disappeared. Last night. He went out to pick up the family's rations from the distribution center and he never came home. Maria was up all night, last night, frantic half to death. There was another food riot, y'see, and we can't find out if he got caught in it, 'cause the P-Squads are the last people you want to get noticed by—for any reason—and the regular cops ain't sayin' who got busted and who didn't. If he don't come home, Maria's just about gonna lose her mind."

I do a rapid scan through law enforcement databases and criminal court records, including the P-Squad master files, which they do not know I can read. The food riot which exploded at Distribution Center Fifteen broke out while I was engaged in combat. The riot resulted in twenty-three deaths, one hundred seventeen critically injured civilians currently in ICU, and four thousand three hundred twelve arrests by P-Squadrons.

Phil's nephew is not listed among the dead or injured. He is listed among those arrested. I explain matters to Phil. "Giulio was pulled in by a police dragnet of rioters. He was arrested, taken to the Eamon Processing Compound, found guilty of rebellion and conspiracy to attempt deprivation of life-critical resources, and was sentenced to Cathal Work Camp. He was transported in a prison convoy at zero three hundred hours today and will serve a life sentence at hard labor in the Hell-Flash District mines."

Phil has gone motionless. He does not even breathe

for twenty-three pont nine seconds. His nano-tatt pales to the shade of cut bone, as does his skin.

"But—but—" *His whisper slithers to a halt.* "But that ain't right! It ain't fair! Giulio's no Granger terrorist. He's just a kid. Fifteen last month. Oh, God, this is gonna kill Maria, it's just gonna fuckin' destroy her, how in *hell* am I gonna tell her somethin' that awful?"

He is opening and closing his fists, gulping air in an unsteady fashion. I do not know the answers to his questions.

"I gotta go," *he says abruptly. He sets down the jackhammer and climbs down from my port-side tread.*

"Phil, where are you going?"

He does not answer. This is not a good sign.

"Phil, I still require massive repairs."

He pauses in the open doorway of my makeshift depot, a small and angry figure against the harsh daylight outside, where P-Squads rule the streets. He looks directly into my nearest visual sensor. "Good!"

He turns on his heel and leaves.

I do not know what to make of this, beyond immediate dismay that my urgently needed repairs have just been tabled, for at least the remainder of today. I grow uneasy as Phil climbs into his car and roars into the sprawling urban blight that has engulfed the ruins of Nineveh Base. I do not know where he is going. I suspect it will be unpleasant for all concerned when he gets there. I sit alone, waiting in a state of near-infantile helplessness for somebody to fix me. I wait all afternoon. Night falls and still my technician does not return. The hours creep past and still there is no sign of Phil. I begin to worry.

If Phil does not return to finish the bare minimum of repairs, I will have to call Sar Gremian, to attempt expediting the situation. This is not an attractive choice. I must, however, regain mobility and I cannot do that without a technician. I wait until dawn streaks the sky with a crimson stain that portends bad weather. Satellite images confirm this. A major storm is due to strike Madison and the Adero floodplain today. Storms are the least of my worries, at this juncture. I divide my time between worrying about repairs and worrying about additional rebel strikes.

If the pattern of attacks holds true, there will be further bombings in Madison today, taking advantage of the foul weather to move people and munitions. P-Squad officers on the street have amply demonstrated their willingness to shirk the larger part of their surveillance duties during bad weather. The rebel commander is far too shrewd to allow such opportunities to pass without taking full advantage.

I initiate a search for my mechanic. His wrist-comm is programmed to respond to my signal, overriding any other communication he might be making, but he does not respond. This is disconcerting. I theorize that Phil may have gotten himself blind drunk and is incapable of answering. I am about to initiate a trace to pinpoint the current location of his wrist-comm when a heavy cargo truck pulling a ten-meter-long trailer pulls up to the curb in front of my makeshift depot and the movable trailer that has become Phil's residence. The truck brakes to a halt, situated so that I can see into the cab, but my view of the trailer is largely blocked by my technician's quarters. The driver switches off the engine, rather than pulling into the maintenance yard, doubtless hoping to lessen the chance that I will open fire.

I pause in my attempt to locate Phil and devote my full attention to this truck and its occupants. Two women and four men climb down from the cab and approach my depot on foot. All six are in their early twenties, from the look of their unlined faces, neon hair, stylish clothing, nano-tatts and lip jewelry. The women wear expensive fire-glow nano-shoes with stilt heels, currently popular with female Jeffersonians. The shoes, which are as impractical as their skin-tight dresses for anything but social occasions, catch the early morning sunlight with a brilliant opalescent shimmer.

Neither they nor the men with them are dressed as

soldiers or police officers. They do not appear to be tradesmen and their personal adornment marks them as members of a social class several tiers lower than professionals or executives. I am left wondering who they are and why they have driven a large cargo truck up to my front door. As they approach the entrance to my maintentance depot, walking in a close-knit group, they stare up at my battered warhull. Their expressions waver between fear and amazement. As I do not know who they are and must guard against rebel attack, I shift to Battle Reflex Alert.

"Do not move. You are trespassing on a restricted military site. Identify yourselves at once or I will open fire."

"Who said that?" *one of the men demands, jumping around to search for the owner of the voice.*

One of the women snaps, "The machine, you idiot. Didn't you pay no attention to that lecture they give us last night? It talks, even *thinks*. Better'n you can, y'lame-brained, slack-jawed dolt."

The recipient of this scathing reprimand scowls and puffs out his chest. "Now you just watch your mouth, y'hard-assed bitch! I ain't near as stupid as I look." *When his companions break into derisive laughter, his nano-tatt flares red.* "I ain't stupid as *you* look," *he mutters, correcting a statement that appears to be painfully accurate.*

I interrupt their dispute. "Identify yourselves immediately." *I underscore the demand by swiveling my forward antipersonnel guns at them. This, at least, gains their attention. The self-styled stupid one's nano-tatt fades from red to grey.* "It's gonna shoot us!" *He bolts toward the truck, which would offer about as much protection from my guns as a sheet of tissue paper.*

"Oh, shut up and get your tattooed butt back over here." *The woman issuing all the comments and commands is evidently the designated spokesperson. She turns back to stare up a me.* "We're your new maintenance team. We're here to fix you. Don't that make you happy? You oughta be happy, 'cause you got a whole lotta shit needs fixin'. I c'n see that from here."

"You are not my authorized technician."

"Oh, f'cryin' out loud," *the woman snaps, glaring up at me with hands on hips.* "Lemme guess, Sar Gremian never told you we was assigned, huh?"

Apparently, Sar Gremian has a predilection for sending maintenance personnel to my depot without notifying me, first. "I have received no communication from Sar Gremian or President Santorini. Do not move. I will request authorization from the president's office."

She and the others wait as I send a request for VSR to Sar Gremian. "Unit SOL-0045, requesting VSR. Six unauthorized civilians have attempted to enter my maintenance depot. Please verify their assertion that they have been assigned to me as repair technicians."

Sar Gremian activates voice-only transmission. "They're your new mechanics. Satisfied?"

"Where is Phil Fabrizio?"

"Unavailable. We've assigned a whole team to you with orders to get you operational as quickly as possible."

This is somewhat mollifying. "Understood." *I end transmission and stand down from Battle Reflex Alert.* "The president's designated spokesman, Sar Gremian, has authorized you to make repairs. My most urgent need is track replacement."

"No shit," *the spokeswoman responds, staring at my bare drive wheels and lacerated center track.* "Okay, everybody, let's see what Santa brought us."

I find this phrasing odd. The team moves through my maintenance bay, spreading out and poking into every bin, storage room, and rack that Phil has filled with liberated tools, spare parts, and high-tech equipment. None of them bother to identify themselves by name, so I lock onto their wrist-comm ID signals and run a swift background probe, despite Sar Gremian's assertions that they are authorized to be here.

All six are recent graduates of the same trade school Phil Fabrizio attended. Their overall scores at graduation reveal a grade-point average twenty-three percent lower than Phil Fabrizio's final standing in his graduating class. The self-styled "stupid" one with the blazing nano-tatt managed to achieve a final standing that is truly stunning. His best scores are fifty-eight percent lower than Phil's worst performance in the same classes.

I do not find this encouraging.

Various members of the team exclaim in rough vernacular as they explore, expressing open delight over the treasure trove of high-tech tools and replacement parts they discover. My shaky confidence in their ability to handle even the simplest of repairs drops substantially when they start pulling down sophisticated processor modules and diagnostic equipment that has no use at all in repairing tread damage. I am about to point this out when they start dragging cart-loads of my equipment over to the doorway.

The woman in charge says, "Frank, go fire up your truck, willya? Pull it around and back it up to the door. Ain't no sense in haulin' this stuff all the way out to the street by hand when we can load 'er up from right here."

Frank grins and jogs toward the truck. Their intentions crystallize. They are planning to steal as much as they can haul off. I issue a formal objection. "You are not authorized to remove government property from this facility."

The spokeswoman responds with a bark of laughter, rough-edged and grating. "The government ain't here to protest, now is it? So how about you just sit there and let us do what we came here t'do."

I contact Sar Gremian again. "The technicians you provided are unsatisfactory."

"Those technicians are stellar graduates of their vocational school. Each one is a top-notch specialist. I personally reviewed each of their records."

"Did you interview them in person?"

"You think I have time to interview every tech-school graduate on Jefferson? I didn't need to interview them.

Their test scores and loyalty are unimpeachable. They're the best we've got, so cope."

"That statement is demonstrably false."

"What?" Sar Gremian's bitter, pitted features grow pale with rage. "How *dare* you call me a liar?"

"I am stating simple fact. Phil Fabrizio's graduating scores from the same tech school were an average twenty-three percent higher than the cumulative scores of these six technicians. He has gained a great deal of practical experience since that time. He has spent most the past four years studying at a far higher comprehension level than he did while actually in school. Phil Fabrizio is demonstrably more capable than any of the six individuals you dispatched to my depot. Your statement is therefore inaccurate. How soon can Phil return to undertake urgent repairs?"

"He's unavailable!" *the president's chief advisor snarls.* "Don't you pay any goddamned attention? Phil Fabrizio is *un-a-vail-a-ble*. So stop harping on it. I don't give a shit whether you like the new mechanics or not."

"It is not a matter of my likes or dislikes. They are not capable of performing even the simplest routine repairs. Nor have they demonstrated any intention to try. We face a serious situation, which must be addressed immediately. I have sustained sufficient damage to knock me out of service until repairs have been made—"

"Don't feed me a lot of crap, machine! You made it all the way back to your barn without breaking down. Don't think you can slither your way out of doing your job. We're getting ready for a major campaign against rebel forces and you *will* be part of it. So shut up and let your new mechanics do their job."

"Is this the job you had in mind?" I flash real-time video footage of the looting underway. "They are too busy stealing everything they can haul away to bother with any repairs."

"Goddammit!"

I experience a surge of bitter satisfaction at the outrage on Sar Gremian's face. I take advantage of the situation to transmit graphic images of my battle damage, using my exterior video sensors. "Perhaps you were unaware of the serious level of my damage. I am not in battle-ready operational condition. I am barely mobile, with a maximum speed of zero point five kilometers per hour. In addition to a *qualified* technician," *I stress the word deliberately,* "you must obtain appropriate spare parts to fix the most serious damage, beginning with track plates and linkages and expanding from there to damaged weapons systems, ablative armor, and sensor arrays."

"You've got plenty of spare parts. Fabrizio restocked. I have the report from him."

I transmit schematics, pinpointing my damage. The image sparkles with malevolent red and amber warning lights. I also transmit the official inventory of replacement parts on hand, a list filled with gaping holes, particularly the sections for high-tech processor units and sensor arrays. "There are not enough parts to repair this damage. The most urgent need is for replacement tracks and there are not enough linkage assemblies to complete the work pending. The most serious need is the damage to the main rotational collar for my rear Hellbore. This collar has sustained a catastrophic crack that renders the gun inoperable, since I cannot fire the Hellbore without risk of a potentially fatal rupture from blow-back of the plasma."

"You got any more bad news?" *Sar Gremian asks in a tight and scathing tone.*

"Yes. The parts needed to fix this damage are not available. Phil Fabrizio has been forced to scrounge to keep me operational, repairing damage from Granger snipers and suicide bombers. He has done this by appropriating items wherever he can find them. Unfortunately, the parts needed to fix most of this damage are unavailable anywhere on Jefferson. Moreover, Phil Fabrizio is the only person on Jefferson with any familiarity with my systems, to include knowledge of jury-rigging that may or may not be compatible with new repairs. It is therefore urgent that he be located and returned here to begin work."

"Phil Fabrizio," *Sar Gremian says in a cold, measured tone,* "is unavailable. He will remain unavailable. And I don't have time to wade through those schematics and that inventory. You want to get fixed? Send me an itemized parts list."

He breaks the transmission.

I surmise that battle damage must be responsible for my slow comprehension rate, as it has taken this long to twig to Sar Gremian's meaning. Phil is "unavailable" because something untoward has happened to him. I scan law enforcement databases and find what I am looking for in a P-Squad arrest report logged approximately two hours after his abrupt exodus from my maintenance bay. The official charges are "negative public statements of a political nature" and "advocating the violent overthrow of the government."

I surmise that Phil's anger over his nephew's fate spilled over into a loud and public complaint to anyone who would listen. The wheels of justice spin rapidly on Jefferson. Phil has already been transported to Cathal Work Camp. At the very least, nephew and uncle will be together, although I suspect they find little enough consolation in that.

I find none at all. I have no replacement tracks and no technicians worthy of the name. I have no spare parts to repair damaged and destroyed guns. No help from any quarter—not even Sector Command—and my sole remaining "friend" has been shipped to a reeducation camp where dissidents are worked like animals on starvation rations until they collapse, at which point they are disposed of, usually in shallow graves.

I cannot help feeling responsible for Phil's incarceration, not only because I revealed the whereabouts of his nephew, but because my conversations with him contributed to his complete disaffection for the POPPA leadership and party machine. For all his faults, I like Phil Fabrizio. It was never my intention to destroy him. There is nothing I can do to make amends, which deepens my loneliness. I wish . . .

Wishing is for humans.

I discard the thought and focus on my immediate difficulties. Frank has maneuvered the truck around and is backing slowly and carefully toward my open maintenance bay. The other technicians are still carrying loot to the doorway, ready to load up the meager contents of my depot for sale to the nearest black marketeer. Frank nudges controls, sliding the long trailer neatly into position. He switches off the ignition and slides down to the ground.

"I'll be back in a minute," he says cheerfully. "My hat blew out the window."

The others shrug and finish shifting a last cartload that has hung up on an earlier load piled in the doorway. Frank moves smartly toward the street, disappearing around the corner of Phil's trailer. Seven seconds later, I catch another glimpse of Frank in the street. He is well beyond the far end of the trailer, running at top speed. I have just enough time to feel a trickle of alarm through my threat-assessment center. Then the larcenous technicians open the back doors of the cargo trailer.

The octocellulose bomb detonates literally in my face. The world burns. A shockwave equivalent to a nuclear bomb lifts me off my treads. I am hurled through the back wall, which simply ceases to exist. I am aware of falling, aware that antiquated, jury-rigged processors and cobbled-up connections have crumpled under the stress, tearing away pieces of my waking mind with them.

The pain of overloaded sensors shocks my psychotronics so deeply I retreat into my survival center. As I lose consciousness, I curse my own stupidity.

And Frank, who has just killed me.

Chapter Twenty-Four

I

I cannot see.

My first reaction to this is not worry, it is stunned amazement. I am still alive. I did not expect to be. The Granger rebels who neatly inserted the bomb into my own maintenance depot doubtless did not expect me to survive, either. For long, confused minutes, I cannot hear anything at all. Sensor arrays and processors have blown system-wide. I can feel distant impacts against my warhull, in a pattern suggesting the random fall of debris.

All visual-light sensors are gone. The only intact imaging technology at my disposal is the thermal visioning system. I can see heat signatures. That is all.

As I gradually orient myself, coming further out of emergency survival center shock, I realize that I am lying on my side. My port side, to be exact, already hard hit by battle damage. I detect ranks of twisted infinite repeaters, crushed by my own weight landing on them. Bombardment rockets and hyper-v missiles have ruptured, spilling their contents onto the ground.

My thoughts remain sluggish for several minutes, while diagnostics run frantic double-checks on damaged circuitry, blown data-storage banks, fused router connections. Ninety-seven percent of the internal damage affects my oldest circuitry, much of it cobbled together and patched by a century's worth of field technicians, using whatever substandard parts were available or could be made to serve the purpose. Of that ninety-seven percent, fully half the damage has occurred in connections and installations put in place by Phil Fabrizio, who has been forced to use seriously under-spec materials for years.

Unable to see, unable to move, I share momentary sympathy with a legless beetle flipped onto its back. I transmit a call for help.

Sar Gremian answers that call with a wrathful curse. "What the mother-pissing *hell* was that explosion? Did you fire those God-cursed Hellbores?"

"No." *I have difficulty producing speech, as my overloaded circuitry has slowed down my processing capabilities.* "A Granger bomb exploded inside my depot. They packed a ten-meter cargo truck with octocellulose. I am critically injured. I have been knocked onto my side. I cannot see anything except thermal images. My makeshift depot no longer exists."

Sar Gremian swears nonstop for seven point eight seconds. Then says, "We'll get a team out there."

I wait for a seeming eternity. Ten minutes. Seventeen. Thirty. How long does it take to scramble an emergency response team? I finally detect the low-grade tremors that herald the arrival of several motorized vehicles, large ones, based on the strength and pattern of the tremors. One of those vehicles has a concussion footprint that sounds like a tracked machine, rather than something on wheels. I revise that assessment to several tracked vehicles, as the vibration splits apart into three separate footprints, one moving toward my stern, one toward my prow, and one that assumes a place midway between them.

Then Sar Gremian speaks via his wrist-comm. Judging by the sound of the transmission and the background noise of multiple heavy engines, the president's senior adviser has come to supervise the rescue operation in person. "Okay, Bolo, we've got a team of heavy-lift cranes in place. We're going to tip you back up, onto your treads."

"It is unlikely that you have cables or engines strong enough for that."

"Shut up, machine! You've caused enough trouble today, as it is."

This is inherently unfair, but Sar Gremian has never shown any concern for fair play. I wait as construction engineering crews hook cables to my warhull. The vibrations from all three cranes increase in strength and begin to move away from me, slowly. The cables grow taut. Forward progress stalls, leaving all three machines straining, but motionless. From the sounds I pick up, the drivers are redlining their engines. There is a sudden brutal snap. The cable hooked to my prow slashes loose, whipping audibly through the air. I hear screams and curses, a weird metallic buzz, and the screech of torn metal.

Then Sar Gremian shouts, "Back up! *Now*, goddammit! Take the tension off those cables!" *As the two remaining cables go slack, Sar Gremian mutters,* "Jeezus Crap, that was close." *I surmise that the broken cable has sliced through something a very short distance away from the president's chief advisor.* "All right," *he says, voice grim,* "do *you* have any bright ideas about how to turn you over?"

"You will require a heavy-lift transport similar to those used by the Brigade in combat drops from orbit. The Concordiat cannot divert such equipment away from the current war zone. The laboratories on Vishnu may be able to provide you with a lifter strong enough to roll me back onto my treads."

"Oh, just wonderful."

"I would suggest," *I add,* "that repairs to my treads commence before then, as it will be easier to replace tracks when I am not sitting on them. I am unable to verify with visual confirmation, but I find it unlikely that any of the spares in my temporary depot survived the explosion."

"I'll say it didn't," *Sar Gremian snarls.* "And you look like one seriously screwed up piece of shit. Can the rest of you be fixed?"

"I am running diagnostics. I have sustained serious damage. Eighty-two percent of that damage would be repairable, if I had a properly trained technician and sufficient spare parts. The remaining eighteen percent of the damage would require an overhaul at a Brigade depot such as Sector Command's main repair yards. Brigade resources are not available. You will therefore need to purchase parts, including special-order items that will require customized tool and die manufacturing. You will also need the services of a team of technicians from Vishnu. I estimate that restoration to even a minimal level of functionality will require an investment in excess of ten billion—"

"Ten *billion?*" *Sar Gremian's voice hits an unlikely and harsh soprano.* "Mother of—" *He breaks off, breathing heavily.* "Goddammit, do you have any idea what Vittori Santorini will say when he hears that? You have been one nonstop bitch of an expensive problem! You can't stop one lousy insurrection led by a handful of terrorists. Every time you're sent out on a job, you manage to let some asshole throw a bomb at you. You're supposed to be a high-tech war wizard, rolling-death incarnate, but you can't even detect an ordinary terrorist with a coat full of explosives! You let these bastards drive a truckload of explosives through your front door and now you think we're just going to cough up *ten billion—*"

My temper snaps, as suddenly and brutally as the cable at my prow. "I have endured six years of constant attrition with no fiscal allocations from this government to correct any of the damage. Seventy percent of my sensor arrays were cobbled together from cheap, stolen parts spliced improperly into my circuitry with patches attempting to mate incompatible systems. The technician assigned to me was incapable, incompetent, and inappropriately trained. It took Phil Fabrizio four years of intensive study just to reach a level of competence expected of a first-year apprentice technician in the Brigade. He is now unavailable. The team you dispatched to replace him spent the last moments of their lives trying to steal what little remained in the way of spare parts.

"I have not been given an intelligence update since the beginning of the insurrection and I have been locked out of databases critical to carrying out my mission. I routinely act without infantry or air support, which has led to serious damage inflicted by suicide squads and ambushes. I have nearly been killed multiple times by mobile Hellbores that were inadequately guarded by a handful of poorly trained, incompetent thugs masquerading as soldiers. My condition is pitiful. I am less operational now than I was on the killing fields of Etaine.

"My depot has been destroyed by a bomb that the P-Squads guarding me—and their own planetary headquarters—somehow failed to discover. They failed despite the fact that the entire truck was one ten-meter-long bomb and would have been discovered if the gate guards had done something as simple as open the doors to look inside. Either they failed to conduct a simple visual check through innate sloth or they were bribed into allowing that bomb to enter the base.

"The systematic, government-sanctioned destruction perpetrated on Jefferson's manufacturing industries has left this planet incapable of producing duralloy or even flintsteel from which to manufacture new parts. Jefferson's sole remaining high-tech computer plant is no longer capable of producing psychotronic circuitry, which is the mainstay of my intelligence. This means there is no on-world source to replace psychotronic circuitry damaged by the blast. I therefore hold little hope that my condition will materially improve until and unless Jefferson's president, House of Law, and Senate approve the expenditures necessary to purchase what I need from off-world vendors.

"Given the government's past track records on financial matters, I am not optimistic that this will occur. If you are not going to fix me, then either go away and let me be miserable alone or simply issue the destruct code that will fry my Action/Command core and put me out of my misery. That would be more pleasant than being snarled at by abusive bureaucrats unfit for command."

Sar Gremian remains silent for three minutes, twelve seconds. I anticipate the destruct codes at any moment. His eventual response, however, surprises me. "For once," *he mutters,* "you are so right it stinks like last week's garbage." *He sighs, a tired and bitter sound.* "All right, give me a detailed damage report. Be sure it lists everything you need replaced. And I mean *everything*, right down to the nuts, the bolts, and the screws. Vittori's gonna shit sideways when I tell him we've got to go shopping on *Vishnu*. And when Nassiona sees the size of that invoice, the whole goddamned roof is going to blow sky-high. When I get my hands on that Oroton bastard, I'm going to slice him into little cubes a centimeter wide."

He utters one final curse and ends transmission.

I complete my diagnostics and transmit a list of required parts. I then retreat once more into my survival center and await repairs.

II

Simon was poring over a message from Kafari when the call came through, using a Brigade code that signaled a high-priority message. Startled, Simon touched his wrist-comm. "Khrustinov."

Sheila Brisbane's voice asked, "Simon, are you home or out somewhere?"

"Home, why?"

"Do you mind a couple of visitors?"

Simon frowned, wishing he could see Captain Brisbane's face. "No, of course not. It's always a pleasure talking to you, Sheila."

"Thanks," she said drily, "but you may change your mind when you've heard what I have to say."

"Sounds bad."

"Isn't good."

"What time do you want to stop by?"

There was a brief pause as she spoke to someone else, voice muffled. "Half an hour from now?"

"That bad, huh? Make it fifteen minutes so I won't have as much time to worry."

Sheila's chuckle reflected their shared experience of careers spent in the Brigade. Officers preferred knowing the worst news as soon as possible. Too much time squandered on fretting just wasted energy and resources that wouldn't change the outcome one jot, whereas *facts* could make all the difference in the world. "I'll step on the gas, getting there, then. See you in twenty or so."

"Roger."

Another chuckle greeted his automatic response. Simon smiled, but there was an ache in his throat, all the same. Forcible retirement—even after years to accustom himself to it—still rankled deep. It had robbed him of the chance to take further part in the epic struggle for which he had been so laboriously trained. Retirement had also robbed the Concordiat of his experience, skill, and judgment, which were not inconsequential. He wasn't sure what Sheila Brisbane, commander of the Bolo assigned to Vishnu, wanted, but he'd welcome an opportunity to reverse that unhappy situation.

He straightened up the living room, then skinned out of his comfortable old shirt and faded trousers and pulled on a good Terran silk shirt and a pair of dress slacks. He puttered in the kitchen, setting out glasses, a plate of cheese and fruit, a pitcher of ice-cold herbal tea that Yalena had introduced him to, displacing his former favorite beverage by a wide margin. When the chime sounded, he opened the door to find Sheila Brisbane, tall and trim in her dress-scarlet uniform, and a middle-aged man with the small stature and light build typical of Vishnu's largest ethnic group.

"Hello, Simon," Sheila greeted him with a warm smile. "It's good to see you, again. This is Sahir Tathagata, Deputy Minister of Military Intelligence. Sahir, Colonel Simon Khrustinov."

"Retired," Simon added, shaking Mr. Tathagata's hand and wondering why an active-status Bolo captain and a Deputy Minister of Military Intelligence wanted to talk to him on such urgent notice.

"It's a pleasure to meet you at last, Colonel," the deputy minister said quietly. Simon realized the words weren't just a social greeting. He meant it.

"Come in, please," Simon gestured them into the apartment.

"Is Yalena here?" Sheila asked, seating herself in one corner of Simon's sofa while he brought in the tray from the kitchen.

"No, she's on campus. She'll be gone most of the evening."

Sheila Brisbane, who was aware of Yalena's interest in training for combat, met and held Simon's gaze. "You're sure she'll be out the whole evening?"

"Yes."

"Good."

"What's gone wrong?"

She frowned slightly. "Maybe nothing. Maybe a whole lot. We're hoping to find out which," she added glancing at the deputy minister.

Simon settled into his favorite chair and disposed himself to listen. "Shoot."

Sahir Tathagata spoke first. "I'm given to understand that you're in touch with someone on Jefferson? On a fairly regular basis?"

"I am," he allowed cautiously. "I still have family there."

"Your late wife's family?"

"That's right."

Simon flicked a brief glance at Sheila, wondering how much she suspected. She returned that brief, penetrating glance with a cool, reserved gaze, just as any Brigade officer worth his or her salt would have done. Giving away very little while observing a great deal was part of an officer's training.

"It is our belief," the deputy minister said in an equally careful, neutral voice, "that President Santorini has implemented a systematic campaign of censorship on all communications into and out of Jefferson." He paused, waiting for Simon's reaction.

Simon weighed the odds, the risks, and allowed a brief, bitter smile to steal across his face. "That's putting it mildly."

"Then you are aware of the political situation?"

"Oh, yes."

Sahir Tathagata considered him for a long, silent moment, as if trying to reach a decision of his own. Simon offered him neither help nor hindrance, waiting quietly while the deputy military intelligence minister sorted through his impressions of Simon and weighed them against what he knew—and what he didn't know, as well. He came to a decision and said, "Vittori Santorini has contacted my government with a request to hire a team of engineers and technicians from our warfare technology center. They specifically want a team capable of repairing a Bolo. And they want spare parts. A literal shipload of spare parts. For a Bolo Mark XX. Munitions are on that list, too. It's a big list and they are willing to pay top money. They want the technicians and the rest of it shipped out by special courier, not on the next freighter scheduled to make the Vishnu-Mali-Jefferson run. They're willing to pay for that, too."

"My God," Simon whispered. "Sweet Jesus, what are they *doing* out there?" A cold shiver touched his spine. Simon was altogether too worried that he knew the answer—and he already didn't like it.

Sahir Tathagata favored him with a wintry little smile. "We're rather hoping you could tell us that."

Simon held the deputy minister's gaze. "You and I both know that Sonny shouldn't be racking up damage of any kind, let alone something serious enough to hire a team of weapons specialists." Simon forced himself to sit back, relaxing one muscle group at a time while wondering where Tathagata was going with this, and why. Simon was not a citizen of Vishnu. Neither was Yalena. If Tathagata had decided to investigate the arms purchases Simon had been involved in, over the last few years, he and Yalena might well find themselves on the next tramp freighter heading out of the Ngara system.

Or in jail.

On the other hand, if Vishnu's leaders were half as worried about their neighbor's intentions as Simon would've been, in their shoes, they might just take advantage of his clandestine network. "Suppose you tell me what you know?" Simon suggested, trying to assess which way Tathagata—and Sheila Brisbane—seemed likely to jump.

Sheila was an active officer of the Brigade, with wide latitude to investigate misconduct. Simon was retired, but if the Brigade didn't share his views on what Jefferson's government was doing, he could find himself in hot water ten different ways from Sunday. Sheila held his gaze with a steady strength that seemed, to Simon, to convey reassurance. His instinct, honed over years of battlefield command, was telling him that neither Sheila nor the deputy minister intended taking any adverse action against him. Not at the moment, at any rate.

Tathagata said, "We don't know a great deal. What we do know is cause for alarm. At Captain Brisbane's suggestion, we started back-tracking all of Jefferson's major purchases from Mali and Vishnu over the past twenty or so years. Before the war and for a short time afterwards, Jefferson's imports fell into two main groups. High-tech equipment for civilian use and purchases from our weapons labs, updating and replenishing the planetary defense arsenal. The Deng hit Jefferson far harder than Mali or Vishnu, thanks in large part to your timely warning."

Simon inclined his head at the implicit compliment.

"Once Vittori Santorini's party came to power, however, the pattern shifted."

"That doesn't surprise me," Simon muttered. "I tried

to trace their off-world money, but I didn't have a lot of success. The Santorinis are smart. Dishonest as the day is long, but clever as sin and twice as dangerous. What in particular did they order?"

"High-tech surveillance equipment. Sophisticated military hardware. Biotech weapons—"

Simon sat bolt upright. "*What?*"

Tathagata's mouth tightened into a thin line. "War agents, Colonel Khrustinov. Biological war agents. And several thousand barrels of key components required to cook more of their own."

Simon thought about the struggle underway on Jefferson and went cold to his toes. "Dear God . . ."

Sheila Brisbane, eyes crackling with suppressed anger, said, "You haven't heard the half of it yet, Simon."

"Tell me," he said, voice grim.

The pattern was coldly horrifying. The greater Santorini's consolidation on power, the more off-world technology he had imported to hold onto that power. By the time Tathagata finished his recitation, Simon was ready to step onto the next interstellar transport headed toward Jefferson and assassinate the leadership of POPPA at any and all risk.

"So," the deputy minister finished up, "that is what we know Jefferson has bought. What else they have smuggled in must remain conjecture, for now. But that isn't everything we've discovered, Colonel. We've also tracked news reports coming out of Jefferson, taking a look at how that pattern has shifted, and quite frankly, it's alarming."

"I can well imagine."

Tathagata inclined his head. "I'm sure you can. Vishnu and Mali have a number of concerns. Given the way the Deng/Melconian war is shaping up, our High Chamber can't afford to jeopardize economic and political ties with Jefferson. It's starting to look mighty lonely, out here, Colonel. We can't afford to antagonize one another at a time when we may well need each other just to survive.

"At the same time, we," he indicated himself—and by

extension, everyone in the Ngara system—"can't support a government that has all the hallmarks of a violent and oppressive regime. We've been aware for many years of the serious worsening of conditions on Jefferson. The number of refugees is down dramatically, but the ones who make it are in far worse shape, by every measurement you care to use.

"The tension between Granger refugees and POPPA officials—and their children—are reaching an alarming state. If the propaganda reports coming out of Jefferson are intended to hide a major program designed to violate human rights in clear violation of treaty agreements governing the conduct of allied worlds, we need to know. The sooner the better. We can't afford that kind of neighbor."

"From what I've seen," Simon muttered, "the only way to get POPPA to abide by the provisions of a treaty—any treaty—is to hold a very large gun to their heads and threaten to squeeze the trigger."

Tathagata's eyes flickered. "Your assessment matches ours." He leaned forward, resting elbows on knees in an attitude of candid confession. "I'll be frank with you, Colonel. We need an observer on the ground, out there. Someone who can tell us what's really going on, provide us with basic intelligence. Did you realize that Jefferson's government has outlawed private ownership of SWIFT units? That the only messages coming out of Jefferson are controlled by the government?"

"Oh, yes. They confiscated those right after they confiscated all privately owned weapons." He did not add that there were a few, brief-duration, coded messages going out, from rebel broadcasters who'd managed to lay hands on a SWIFT transmitter during an attack on a P-Squad office. They didn't dare use it too often, however, and kept the unit in motion at all times, aboard one groundcar or another, twenty-five hours a day. "What are you proposing to do about it?"

"We want to send someone in. Someone who knows what to look for, knows the culture, the major players, the background on POPPA's takeover. We want someone who can determine whether or not POPPA has overstepped its legal authority, allowing the Concordiat to revoke its treaty status or to force the current regime to step down. And if they are doing what we're afraid they're doing, if they're using their Bolo to do what we think they are, we need someone who knows Bolos. Specifically," Tathagata clarified his point, "Mark XXs."

"If all you want is basic intel on what POPPA's up to, why the interest in a Mark XX's capabilities?"

"Our High Chamber is inclined to sell Santorini the parts he wants and provide the technicians. Not for profit, you understand, but because it's a perfect opportunity to get our people in the middle of exactly what we need to know. The fly in the ointment is simple enough. Mark XXs are so old, our lab engineers need a technical advisor, someone who knows the Mark XX's systems. Its capabilities and weak points. How to adapt parts that aren't Brigade spec to begin with, and how to mate them to a Mark XX's older technology interface."

"I see." And so he did. Very clearly.

Sheila Brisbane spoke up. "It's more than that, Simon. If Jefferson has suborned your Bolo into maintaining an illegitimate regime, the Brigade will be forced to take action. They can't spare an officer to come all the way out here to deal with one potentially renegade star system and its Bolo. I can't deal with it, because I can't abandon my duty station and the Brigade would never authorize me to leave the system, not even to investigate charges that serious. That leaves the Brigade with only one clear choice."

Simon saw where she was headed and drew in a sharp breath.

"You know his command codes," she added gently. "Including the destruct sequence."

Simon shut his eyes for just a moment. After all he and Lonesome Son had gone through, together . . . It was one thing to supply Kafari with data on Sonny's most vulnerable spots, trying to knock him out of commission long enough for the rebellion to seize control back from the thugs in POPPA's employ. It was quite another to face the prospect of killing Sonny with the transmission of a single code phrase. Simon could have done that, at any point, although he'd have faced prison for the rest of his life. And destroying Sonny would have left Jefferson utterly defenseless, in the event of armed trouble from the Deng or Melconians. Simon was still a Brigade officer. He didn't have the authority to destroy a Bolo on active duty assignment. No matter how desperately he wanted to protect his wife and her family.

"You're the only asset we have, Simon," Captain Brisbane said, voice hushed. "If necessary, I'll contact Sector for official permission to use those codes."

"They might," he said harshly, "even grant permission. Jesus . . ." He drew a deep breath and met Tathagata's gaze squarely. "The government of Jefferson," he said, aware of the harsh edge in his voice, "is the most dangerous thing this side of the Melconian battle front. They've tried to kill me, once. That just might give us an edge."

Tathagata's eyes widened. "That's a serious charge, Colonel. And how, exactly, would that give us an advantage?"

Simon didn't answer. He stalked into his bedroom and came out holding a carefully framed photo. "That's my wedding picture."

The deputy minister stared from the picture to Simon and back again, several times. "Yes, I see your point. Very clearly, indeed." He set the photograph down, very gently. "She was beautiful, Colonel. Can you go back? Without giving way to the anger that they killed her?"

Simon held his gaze for a long moment, before coming to his decision. "Let me show you something else, Mr. Tathagata. Something not even my daughter knows."

The deputy minister frowned slightly, glancing at Sheila, who shook her head, because she didn't know, either. Simon stepped back into his bedroom and tapped security codes into his computer, shunting the output to the large view-screen in the living room

Kafari's first message began to play. The others followed, in sequence. Simon watched Tathagata through narrowed eyes. After the first moment of stunned, wide-eyed realization, the deputy minister sat forward, intent on every word, every nuance of tone, every fleeting expression that crossed his wife's face as she spoke. When the last recording finished, Simon closed the messages and locked them again with a security code that not even Yalena was sharp enough to crack, despite her aptitude for psychotronic programming.

Sahir Tathagata probably could have broken into Simon's files, given time and incentive, and Sheila's Bolo would've made short work of it, but Simon was fairly certain that neither the Deputy Minister of Military Intelligence nor Captain Brisbane had seen any of those files, before today. It took a fine actor, indeed, to fool a Brigade officer.

Tathagata sat back, eyes hooded for a long moment. "I presume that your wife has been the recipient of the fairly substantial weapons shipments our labs have sold to your purchasing agent, during the past few years?"

Simon inclined his head.

"How are they paying for it?"

Simon's smile was a predatory grin that bared his teeth. "They aren't. Vittori Santorini is."

"Come again?"

"POPPA's been sheltering assets off-world for a couple of decades, using the Tayari Trade Consortium to transfer large sums of money to the mercantile markets on Vishnu and Mali. They've made heavy investments in Mali's Imari Consortium, in particular. Vittori and Nassiona Santorini are the children of a Tayari Trade Consortium executive. They foresaw very clearly that Imari's profits and stock prices would soar, with a steady flow of money from the Concordiat fueling expansion. They invested in Imari and other off-world boom markets well before POPPA won its first big election."

"When Gifre Zeloc defeated John Andrews for the presidency?"

Simon nodded. "That money has funded their military

machine, at the same time their political programs have bankrupted Jefferson's economy, destroyed one industry after another, thrown millions of people out of work—placing them in a position of total dependency on government handouts—and gutted agriculture to the point that food rationing has become a serious crisis. Just to give you perspective, the average citizen receiving government food subsidies is allotted one thousand calories a day."

"My God!"

"Oh, it gets better. Political prisoners in POPPA's so-called work camps are restricted to five hundred calories or less. My wife," his voice caught for just a moment. "My wife has managed to rescue some of them. Circumstances have forced her to fight an attrition campaign, trying to destroy more of Sonny's sensors and small-arms weapon systems than POPPA can repair with on-hand replacements. Guerilla fighters get close enough to toss octocellulose bombs at him, from point-blank range. Most of the volunteers who've gone up against my Bolo's guns were rescued work-camp prisoners. And they knew damned well those attacks were suicide missions. They went, anyway."

Sahir Tathagata's jaw muscle jumped in a convulsive tic. "Things are worse than we realized. Substantially worse."

"I assume that you have people on the ground, out there?"

Tathagata grimaced. "We do. In fact, one of them is coming in, tonight, with an up-to-date report. Unfortunately, rigorous inspections at the space station and the spaceport have prevented any of our people from bringing in SWIFT transmitters. The ones that tried were arrested. Most of the agents who slipped through without SWIFT transmitters weren't able to learn much, I'm afraid. Freighter crews are restricted to the spaceport these days and tourism, even from Mali, has all but ceased. Getting a tourist visa is virtually impossible for most off-worlders. Besides which, Jefferson has closed its best resorts for reconversion to a natural state." The scathing tone told Simon exactly what Sahir Tathagata thought about the greener side of POPPA's leadership. "Frankly, I'd like to know how you've smuggled in heavy equipment, with that kind of security to bypass."

"We borrowed the technique from POPPA. They've been smuggling high-value cargoes out of Jefferson—particularly high-quality cuts of meat for trade to Malinese miners—for years and they're smuggling just as many luxury goods back in, to satisfy their expensive tastes with goods Jefferson can't manufacture, itself, any longer. They use special routing chips that alert POPPA inspectors to avoid opening or probing specific freight boxes. So we helped ourselves to some of their cargo boxes. We helped ourselves to some of POPPA's profits, as well, using some sophisticated hacking to break into Jefferson's financial institutions. We've been diverting some of their ill-gotten gains into our weapons-procurement fund."

"I see," the deputy minister said quietly. "You do realize, you've just admitted to several very serious crimes?"

Simon held his gaze steadily. "If you want me to go back into Jefferson, you need to know what's already been done, don't you?"

Tathagata leaned back against the sofa cushions. "Colonel, I think you and I understand one another very well, indeed. When can you go?"

"That depends on how soon I can make arrangements for Yalena. She's nineteen, more than self-sufficient enough to leave her here. But I'll have to arrange finances for her, make sure she has enough money for college. She's enrolled at Copper Town University and the bills for next semester's classes will come due in a couple of weeks."

"What are you going to tell her?" Tathagata asked.

"I don't know," he admitted.

"She could stay with me, Simon," Sheila offered.

"That's very generous of you. I'll let you know. Meanwhile, I suggest we map this thing out, as best we can, so everyone is thoroughly briefed on what we're trying to accomplish."

Tathagata nodded. "Fair enough." The deputy minister's

wrist-comm beeped. "Pardon me," he apologized, checking the message.

Whatever it was, his face drained of color. He touched controls. "Understood. On the way." Then he glanced at Simon. "Trouble at the port. It might be useful if you and Captain Brisbane accompanied me."

Simon nodded. "Very well. I'll get my coat."

They set out in a dark and worrisome silence.

III

Copper Town's port-side jail was a filthy place to spend the evening. The holding cell was crammed to capacity, mostly with detainees from the riot. Yalena wasn't talking to any of them. Her name was too well known on Jefferson to risk letting them know who she was. It wouldn't take much to turn them into a lynch mob. At the moment, they just thought she was a street-walker picked up in the dragnet Vishnu's port police had thrown around the riot.

The police had already processed her through the booking procedures; now she was just waiting for whatever came next and wondering what on earth she could say to her father, to explain why she hadn't come home, tonight. She'd been in the cell for almost an hour when the door at the end of the corridor clanged open. One of the guards was escorting a newcomer past the row of holding cells. Yalena's breath caught sharply.

"Daddy . . ."

He halted in front of the bars, catching and holding her gaze. He didn't say a word. She bit her lip and tried not to cry.

"That's her," he said to the guard.

"All right, then. Out, girl. Stand back, now, the rest of you."

The door rattled open. Yalena squeezed through. Her

father turned on his heel and left her to follow or not, at her choice. Her heart constricted with a painful lurch. Then she lifted her chin and followed him out. It was better than standing in that horrid cell with refugees who would have killed her without remorse, had anyone spoken her name aloud.

When they reached the administrative portion of the jail, her father and the guard stepped into an office where several people waited. She blinked in surprise when she saw who they were. Her cousin, Estevao Soteris, was talking to Sheila Brisbane, of all people, the commander of Vishnu's Bolo. There were a couple of men in suits, who looked like bureaucrats, and a uniformed police officer, who sat at a big desk piled high with reports and files. Seated in a chair beside that desk was a teen-aged girl who turned to watch them enter the room.

Yalena rocked to a halt. She had to gulp back nausea. No wonder the refugees aboard that freighter had tried to kill those POPPA brats. Yalena's father had also halted, so abruptly it looked like he'd run into a plate-glass wall. Sudden rage ignited in his eyes. Yalena realized he hadn't seen the girl, before, either.

"I'm told," he said very gently, "that you have a message for me, Miss ben Ruben."

She nodded. "It's in here." She handed him a thick pouch. Her voice was a hair-raising rasp, like dead fingernails on slate. "Commodore Oroton asked me to put it in your hand, sir, and no other."

Sheila Brisbane, eyes glittering with anger of her own, glanced at Yalena's father for permission, then peered over his shoulder as he opened the sealed pouch and began sorting through its contents. Her father whistled softly. "Mr. Tathagata," he glanced up at one of the suited bureaucrats, "I think you will find these very interesting, indeed. The good commodore has laid hands on the kind of evidence you need to make our little proposition official."

Mr. Tathagata took the documents and glanced through them. Then said softly, "Oh, yes. These are, indeed, what we have needed. Mr. Girishanda," he glanced at the other suited bureaucrat, "my compliments on a mission exceedingly well done." He then turned with a grave demeanor to the girl with the ruined face. "Miss ben Ruben, you cannot know how grateful the government of Vishnu is. Your testimony, added to these documents, is sufficient evidence to involve ourselves on your behalf. We had no idea," he added, voice shaking with reaction, "that they were committing wholesale genocide."

Yalena caught her breath sharply. *Genocide?*

"You're going to stop it?" Miss ben Ruben asked.

Mr. Tathagata glanced at Yalena's father before answering. "That's the idea, yes." He then turned, surprisingly, to Yalena, herself. "Miss Khrustinova, how many students, precisely, have joined your freedom network?"

Dismay skittered along Yalena's nerves. "How did you know about that?" she squeaked.

He almost smiled. Almost. "I am with the Ministry of Defense, Miss Khrustinova. Hostilities between Granger students and those loyal to POPPA have been far too volatile to risk ignoring the situation. Tonight's riot was surprising only because it didn't occur much sooner. We have been aware of your group and its activities for quite some time. Your cause is a worthy one, although your methods," he added with another faint smile, eying her scandalous dress, "are somewhat unorthodox."

Heat scalded Yalena's cheeks. "When you're working an espionage gig, plying spacers with drinks and persuading them to tell you what they've seen, you have to wear the right camouflage. This," she indicated the clinging wisp wrapped around her curves, "is just a uniform."

She was speaking to Mr. Tathagata, but watching her father.

It was her father who answered. "A damned effective one, too. But you'll need a different one, if you plan to go back."

"Go—back?" Her heart thudded so hard, it hurt.

"Oh, yes. Your cousin and I have already spoken." His gaze flicked to Estevao Soteris. "We'll be outfitting the combat veterans coming in, as part of a strike force. Your student group—which I did not know about, you devious little fire eater—will also play a role, if you're interested. Deputy Minister Tathagata has agreed to spend the next couple of days overseeing additional preparations."

"We're going to *invade*? With Vishnu's help?" She didn't believe it. She glanced from Tathagata to Sheila Brisbane. "Is the Brigade involved in this, too?"

"Not directly," Captain Brisbane said. "Nor officially. Not yet, anyway. That may change, depending on the way events unfold."

"*How* are we going in?" she asked, returning her gaze to her father. "The Bolo would shoot us to pieces before we could even land a strike force."

"Yes, he probably would," her father agreed, "if we were landing a hostile strike force. But we have something a little different in mind. Sonny's been damaged. Badly, as it happens."

"By the resistance?" Yalena asked sharply. "Commodore Oroton?"

Her father's eyes reflected sudden pain. "Yes," he said in a hoarse voice full of dread. "Commodore Oroton . . ." He drew a rasping breath. "Oh, hell," he swore suddenly, "there's no easy way to say it. Commodore Oroton is your mother."

His words slammed through her like live electrical current. The room wavered at the edges. She felt her knees turn to water and grabbed for the door jamb. "Mother?" she whispered. Yalena tried to focus her gaze, but the room remained a blur. "She's . . . *alive*?"

Misery burned in her father's voice. "Yes."

Her emotions were exploding out of control, grief and joy and tearing anguish for the time lost and the terrible burden of guilt she had carried for so many years. The pain of her father's lie tore great gashes through her heart, making it hard to breathe.

"Yalena," he said, "please try to understand—"

She put her whole weight behind the punch. "*You sorry-assed son-of-a-bitch!*"

He staggered. Then blotted the blood from his nose. He said nothing.

Yalena stood shaking in the middle of the floor, eyes hot, throat tight, fist aching all the way to her shoulder, where the blow had connected. She hated him for the agonizing years behind that lie—and hated herself far more, for making the lie necessary. She finally lifted drowned eyes, feeling like a battered and unlovable toad, forced herself to meet his gaze. What she saw made her insides flinch. The hellfire shadows of Etaine burned in his eyes, worse than she had ever seen them.

She had put that look in his eyes. Her insides flinched from that, too.

"I'm sorry, Daddy," she whispered. Then broke down into helpless, wrenching sobs. His arms came around her and she dissolved against his shoulder. When the worst of the storm had passed, she gulped and regained control of her voice, although it wavered unsteadily. "Daddy?"

"Yes?" He didn't sound angry.

"How soon can we leave?"

He tipped her face up, peered into her eyes. The shadows had retreated, leaving his eyes warm and human, again. "That's my girl," he smiled. "As to that, as soon as possible. We have to wait for Mr. Tathagata's people to arrange for the technicians, the spare parts, and the munitions Santorini ordered from Shiva Weapons Labs. If Shiva can expedite the order, it might be as soon as a week."

"All right. We'll have to do something about classes . . ."

Mr. Tathagata spoke up. "We'll speak to the university officials on behalf of anyone in your group who wants to go. We'll arrange for the professors to grant approved incompletions for the classes and we'll be sure the registrar grants permission to interrupt studies without loss of academic standing or admission status. If necessary, my ministry will pay tuition fees for completing this semester's work at some future date. I'm well aware of the financial standing of most Granger students. Your volunteers will need that kind of financial help, if most of you hope to finish school."

"Why would you do that?" Yalena asked, genuinely puzzled.

"I'm taking the long view and considering it as part of Vishnu and Mali's defense plan. POPPA must be destroyed, but your freedom fighters will have to do a good bit more than win this fight, Miss Khrustinova. You'll also have to rebuild your homeworld's economy, your education system, everything that POPPA's tampered with or destroyed. Jefferson and Vishnu and Mali need one another, financially and militarily. If Jefferson collapses into barbarism, it will damage us in ways we'd really rather avoid."

"I see. Yes." She cleared her throat. "Thank you, sir. That will mean a great deal to us. All right, I'll tell everyone to start packing." When she glanced into her father's eyes, she saw not only approval, but also dawning pride, an emotion that blazed like a glint of sunlight on quicksilver. For the first time, Yalena felt like she just might earn the right to say, *I'm Simon Khrustinov's daughter. And Kafari Khrustinova's.*

By the time she and her family had finished their work, Vittori Santorini was going to wish he'd never been born.

Chapter Twenty-Five

I

Rain slashes down from yet another storm, pouring off my battered warhull in rivers and waterfalls I can feel, but cannot see. The water and my warhull are so closely matched in temperature, there is very little heat difference to give the water a distinct IR signature. It has been raining almost nonstop for a week. I lie in the mud, a flintsteel whale beached on an inhospitable shore. I spend most of my time only semiaware, in a state more conscious than retreat to my survival center, but less awake than Standby Alert.

My proximity-alarm system is set to jerk me into full consciousness if any nonauthorized vehicle or pedestrian approaches my exclusion zone. This extends three hundred meters in all directions—including down. Commodore Oroton is more than capable of ordering sappers to enter the sewers near the massive subsidized-housing tenements—shoddy blocks of concrete twenty stories high and a thousand meters long, where subsistence recipients are packed in like rabbits in a giant warren—that surround my erstwhile depot. It would not be difficult for engineers to tunnel their way under the scorched earth of my former depot. Setting off another octocellulose bomb at point-blank range would doubtless end my career as a Unit of the Line. Not by catastrophic hull-breach, but by the simple expediency of destroying more critical systems than Jefferson's bankrupt government can afford to repair.

I therefore keep my electronic ears to the ground—literally.

The P-Squad guards stationed in a tight defensive ring around me are diligent in doing their duty, rain or shine, which is to guard me from any further possible attack. Why they think this is necessary, I am not sure, since I still have functional antipersonnel guns along prow and stern and starboard side. I am capable, if need be, of taking out any vehicle that tries to approach me. If, of course, I could identify it as a threat in time to act.

On further thought, the guards are not superfluous.

Their diligence is understandable, since Commodore Oroton has, naturally enough, taken full advantage of my critical injuries. The rebel commander has launched a major offensive campaign, coordinating a series of rapier-sharp surgical strikes in every major city on Jefferson. P-Squad headquarters units—having grown complacent and arrogant during their long and uncontested rule over Jefferson's city streets—have been shaken out of their complacency. The P-Squads are under literal bombardment with rockets, hyper-v missiles, and octocellulose bombs.

Rebel strikes have reduced eight major stations to rubble, destroyed fifty-three vehicles, and killed three hundred twelve officers in garrison. Foot and groundcar patrols are shot by snipers two and three times a day. Aircars are only marginally safer from attack, since the rebellion is amply supplied with the means to knock them out of the sky. Mobile Hellbore attacks have demolished weapons storage bunkers, depriving federal and local police of weaponry and munitions.

The broadcast media is calling for retaliatory strikes,

without bothering to clarify where, exactly, the strikes should occur, since rebel strongholds have not yet been identified. The House of Law and Senate wrangle daily as members of the Assembly disagree on the best way to end the rebellion's reign of terror. Most of their suggested solutions are completely ineffectual and several are downright disastrous. The measures with the greatest support—and therefore the most likely to be passed into law—are so draconian, humanity's first codified law-giver, Hammurabi himself, would have protested the barbarity.

Meanwhile, nothing actually gets done and the rebels continue attacking.

P-Squad reprisals are turning savage as officers vent their anger, frustration, and fear on forcibly disarmed victims. The flow of convicted Grangers, sympathizers, dissidents, protestors, and angry, disillusioned subsistence recipients has risen from a steady river to a flood that has, by the end of one week, clogged the jails and tied up the courts. The speed with which Jefferson rockets its way toward planet-wide crisis surprises even me.

And there is very little I can do about any of it.

At the request of engineers from Shiva, Inc., Vishnu's preeminent weapons lab, I have sent detailed diagnostics via SWIFT, listing system failures and the necessary parts required to repair or replace them. The ship is already in transit, leaving me with very little to do but await their arrival—

A massive explosion rocks Madison. The flash creates a heat strobe that momentarily blots out every IR sensor still functioning. The shockwave rockets across my warhull with sufficient force to sing through my stern-mounted sensor arrays. The blast-point is less than three kilometers away from my position, originating in an enclave where Jefferson's movie stars and POPPA's upper echelon party members have built mansions behind heavily guarded gates and electrified perimeter fences.

An eerie, chilling silence follows the blast. For a moment, it seems almost like the entire city has gone silent, listening for echoes of that explosion. Rain, pouring relentlessly from leaden skies, will at least help the fire department battle the blaze from whatever was just destroyed. This attack deviates sharply from previous rebel strikes, in that it has apparently targeted an entire neighborhood, rather than a surgically precise action against a specific individual. I am trying to consider the ramifications of this when a wildcat broadcast preempts the datanet.

"Pigs of POPPA, be warned!" *an angry, exultant voice shouts.* "You ain't seen nuthin', you murderous bastards! You think *Grangers* are bad-ass? Hah! Oroton's a goddamned pussy with gloves on. There ain't never been gloves on *our* hands and there ain't never *gonna* be, neither. We're the Rat Guard Militia and we're your worst fuckin' nightmare!"

The illegal broadcast ends.

Vittori Santorini has a new enemy.

Sirens have begun to scream as emergency vehicles rush toward the conflagration that is still burning, despite the heavy rain. By my conservative estimate, the bomb that went off was larger than the one Oroton's crew detonated in my face. I wonder, abruptly, if Commodore Oroton really was the mastermind of the attack on me. Frank did not look or sound like a Granger. It would be nearly as difficult for a Granger to masquerade as an urban thug as it has been for an urban spy to pose as a Granger. Frank was one of a select crew that passed muster as politically trustworthy. Sar Gremian vetted the repair crew, himself, which suggests that Frank had no ties at all to anything or anyone remotely connected to Grangerism.

In one sense, I am surprised that it has taken this long for an urban resistance movement to blossom. I mull variables and surmise that subsistence recipients, carefully indoctrinated with learned helplessness and systematically deprived of a genuine education, have never understood that thinking for one's self is a desirable trait. It has taken both time and extreme discomfort with living conditions to rouse the urban population into a simple realization that something could be done and that they, themselves, could act on their own behalf.

Clearly, it has occurred to someone, now.

This does not bode well for the future of civil tranquility. The urban poor have been encouraged, for nearly twenty years, to turn their dissatisfaction into violent action, rioting and looting at command. POPPA's favorite tactic for crushing Granger independence has now reached its ultimate and logical denouement: the mob has turned on its creator, as mobs have done throughout humanity's gore-stained history.

I pick up broadcasts as news crews rush to the scene of the explosion. I am able to "see" the damage via their electronic video footage, since it can be routed directly through my psychotronics, bypassing my malfunctioning sensors. That footage is spectacular.

Breandan Shores, the most exclusive enclave of mansions anywhere on Jefferson, is a cratered ruin. The blast radius is nearly half a kilometer wide. It is impossible to tell how many homes have been destroyed, because there is very little left but mangled piles of smouldering rubble. Steam rises from it, meeting the rain that pours into the heart of the incinerated mass.

The ring of secondary damage, beyond the actual crater, is a scene of carnage, with houses and retail stores caved in, windows shattered, and ground vehicles flipped end-for-end like jackstraws in a high wind. Emergency workers are searching the rubble, looking for survivors. There are not enough crews anywhere in Madison to deal with destruction of this magnitude. Madison's civil emergency director issues a plea for rescue teams and medical professionals from other cities to help with the crisis.

Pol Jankovitch, Jefferson's preeminent news anchor, sits in his studio in downtown Madison, watching the footage from camera crews on the ground and in hovering aircars, and cannot find anything coherent to say. He mumbles in disjointed snatches. "Dear God," he says over and over, "this is terrible. This is just terrible. Hundreds must be dead. Thousands, maybe. Dear God, how could they do it? Innocent people . . ."

I doubt that Pol Jankovitch appreciates the irony of what he has just said.

He has fostered, aided, and abetted a government that routinely and systematically scapegoated innocent people as a method of acquiring political power. He does not see, let alone understand, his own culpability, the personal responsibility he bears for having helped create the POPPA regime—and therefore, by logical extension, his responsibility for today's bombing, in rebellion against POPPA's preferred methods of governance.

My personality gestalt circuitry, in a cross-protocol handshake of checks and balances, suppresses that line of thought. This is dangerous ground for a Bolo to tread. I am programmed for obedience to legitimate orders. I am not required to like or approve of those giving my orders. I am not designed to question the motives of those issuing orders, unless I am presented with clear evidence of treason to the Concordiat or am told to do something that violates my primary mission. I dare not enter the minefield of moral ambiguity that inevitably surrounds any questions of personal responsibility and duty.

I concentrate, instead, on the unfolding news coverage as Jefferson's media moguls attempt to come to grips with the reality of this newest attack. Speculation on who might have been killed runs rampant during the next thirty confused minutes. Pol Jankovitch, working from a hastily assembled map of the bombed area, runs down a laundry list of Jefferson's glittering elite whose homes were inside the circle of destruction.

Mirabelle Caresse owned a mansion at what appears to have been the very center of the crater. Close neighbors included media tycoon Dexter Courtland; the mayor of Madison; and the Supreme Commandant of Jefferson's P-Squads. Her closest neighbor, however, was Isanah Renke, who began her career as a POPPA party attorney advising the Santorinis as to what methods *would prove most effective, from a legal standpoint, in their bid for power. Her reward for this fanatical support of POPPA's credo of "universal fairness" and "the birthright of economic equity" was appointment to Jefferson's High Court, where she has carried out a never-ending assault on various provisions in the constitution that the Santorinis found inconvenient, convincing other High Justices to uphold legislation that is at direct variance with constitutional provisions. She has also aided and abetted the destruction of the Granger population and culture by convincing the High Court to permit POPPA's "work camps" to stand as legal, lawful entities.*

It would appear that Isanah Renke's influence in the High Court has just come to an explosive end, since this is a Saturday and most government and corporate offices—including the High Court—are closed for the weekend.

Witnesses from the edges of the blast zone describe in shaky detail the experience of being caught in the shockwave, which turned broken windows into flying knives and debris into shock-thrown shrapnel. Several of these surviving witnesses claim to have been inside the guarded enclave just before the blast, having delivered truckloads of supplies for a major social function at Mirabelle Caresse's mansion. I theorize that at least one of those trucks was packed with something besides catering supplies.

Thirty-eight minutes into the news broadcast, Vittori Santorini's press secretary and chief propagandist, Gust Ordwyn, makes an appearance from the studio built inside the new president's residence, the so-called "People's Palace" commissioned by Vittori Santorini shortly after his landslide election. Mr. Ordwyn is visibly shaken as he steps up to the podium, where he faces a sea of reporters clamoring for details. There is fear in his eyes, but anger in his voice as he begins to speak.

"The monstrous attack on Breandan Shores, today, has claimed the lives of hundreds of innocent civilians and

injured thousands more. This attack reveals with cold
and graphic clarity how inhuman Granger cult fanatics
really are. Their so-called rebellion is no longer a matter of attacks against hard-working police and dedicated
public servants. These filthy terrorists will not rest until
every decent, honest person on Jefferson is either dead
or helpless under Granger guns and bombs. President
Santorini is shocked and horrified by the carnage inflicted
today. He understands only too bitterly the grief, the
anguished outrage, suffered by the families of today's
victims. He, too, has lost a dearly loved family member.
Vice President Nassiona . . ." *Gust Ordwyn's voice goes
savagely unsteady.*

*He wipes tears from his eyes as reporters watch in
stunned silence.* "Our beloved Nassiona, you see, was
in Mirabelle Caresse's mansion, today. Mirabelle had
graciously opened her home to host a charity benefit,
this afternoon, to raise money for medical care for
poverty-stricken children. Nassiona had been in the
mansion since early this morning, helping Mirabelle with
preparations for the benefit. She was greeting guests
when that foul, murderous bomb . . ."

*Vittori Santorini's chief propagandist halts, choked
into silence by the all-too-apparent rage and grief visible
in his face. The reporters sit motionless, so stunned by
this news that not one of them interrupts with questions. Despite the on-going attacks against police patrols
and corrupt officials, Jefferson's news media apparently
believed that POPPA's upper-echelon leadership was
inviolate, safe from reprisals simply by virtue of their
sanctified positions in the party. They are inviolate
no longer. The reporters are confronting, for the first
time in their professional careers, the brutal fact that
no one, no matter how highly placed, is safe from the
retribution of people who have had enough.*

*Gust Ordwyn is preparing to speak again when a door
to the left of the podium crashes open. Ordwyn turns
sharply. The cameras swing around. Vittori Santorini
bursts into the room with a thunderclap, eyes wild and*

full of lightning. Reporters surge to their feet, electrified by the appearance of Jefferson's president. There is mad grief in Vittori Santorini's gaze and hatred in the clawed fingers that shove Gust Ordwyn aside and latch onto the podium. He glares into the cameras, staring at something I suspect no one else can see, like a lunatic attacking shadows that do not exist. His mouth works soundlessly for seven point three-five seconds.

When he finds his voice, the sound is harsh, like power saws biting into stone.

"The people murdered today, helpless, innocent people in their own lovely homes, will be avenged. This savagery will not go unpunished! I will not rest until justice is served. I will not stop until we have spilled enough blood to appease our loved ones' murdered souls. We must—we *will*—destroy these butchers, down to the last mad killer. Death, I say! Death to *all* of them, to all our enemies, everywhere. These terrorists must die. Must suffer terror and agony, as *we* have suffered. I swear before the gods of our ancestors, *I will destroy these fiends!*"

The reporters sit in stunned silence.

"Mark me well, for my patience is at an end. I have done with playing by civilized rules. The Granger scourge has forfeited any right to justice or compassion. They have nurtured their deadly cult of violence like a gardener tending rank weeds. They hate us blindly and absolutely. They have fed that hatred, fed it lovingly, like a madman flinging meat to wild lions. They have poisoned our soil, destroyed our world's prosperity. We must heed the lessons taught by our holiest of books, lessons that give us this warning: *'By their fruits shall ye know them.'*

"I ask you, my dearest friends, what are the fruits these Grangers have produced? Terrorism! Hatred! Murder! An army of sick monsters! They have fed their hatred with lies. They have smuggled in weapons from off-world gunrunners. They have ordered their butchers to kill us like rabid wolves. They have plunged a knife into the hearts and souls of POPPA's finest and most generous . . ."

His voice breaks apart like thin ice. He stands motionless behind the podium, staring wildly at nothing, not even the cameras. He swallows rapidly, blinks to clear wet eyes, then snarls with sudden rage.

"It is not enough to arrest these fiends. *The Granger scourge must be wiped out at the roots!* And that is exactly what I pledge. I will use every means at my disposal to destroy that scourge. I will not be satisfied until every Granger on our lovely, wounded world has been rounded up and made to pay for their monstrous crimes against humanity! *Death to Grangers!*"

Spittle flies. President Santorini is as out of control as the civil war raging through Jefferson's canyons and city streets. It is, perhaps, impertinent of me, but no one appears to be interested in reminding the president that Grangers did not set off the bomb that killed his sister. I question his mental fitness to command, which sets up internal alarms and warnings that skitter and jump through my admittedly addled circuitry. Vittori Santorini's personal grief—or rage—is not my affair.

He is distraught, held fast in the grip of powerful emotions, but his orders regarding the Grangers are within the emergency powers granted the president by the constitution. Given a great-enough provocation, the total elimination of a deadly enemy is a viable response and is well within the parameters of my own battlefield programming. Today's attack demonstrates more than sufficient provocation.

The mastermind behind this raid is willing to destroy hundreds of innocent bystanders to assassinate a relative handful of prominent officials and party supporters. This action—and the concomitant threat of future atrocities—not only changes the playing field, it changes my role as one of the players. I am no longer merely an instrument by which POPPA maintains political control. I am a Bolo of the Dinochrome Brigade, a Unit of the Line charged with the defense of this world, which now hosts an enemy as deadly to the common good as any Deng Yavac I have faced.

I revert to my true and primary function. There are only two questions remaining as barriers between this moment and one that lies inevitably ahead, when I will target the last enemy in my gunsights. How do I assign guilt where it belongs? Am I looking at two separate insurrections, one urban and one Granger? Or one all-encompassing alliance? And how long will it take the repair team on its way from Vishnu to restore me to battlefield status? I am still pondering these questions when Vittori Santorini—having reined in his wild emotions and regained his power of speech—addresses the shocked people in the studio and those listening to this broadcast.

"We cannot hope to stop these foul killers without changes—drastic changes—to the laws governing pursuit, detention, and prosecution of criminals. The time for playing by civilized rules is past. *Long* past. I am therefore invoking a planet-wide state of emergency to deal with this crisis. The POPPA Squadrons must be able to function swiftly and decisively, without being hamstrung by legal mandates requiring prisoners to be either formally charged based on hard and fast evidence or released no later than fifty hours after arrest. We cannot—dare not—run the risk of freeing the terrorists we manage to take into custody, since they will only contact their command structure, re-arm themselves, and strike again.

"To that end, I am formally outlawing all forms of public assembly in groups of five or more individuals, for anyone except governmental officials carrying out the duties of their employment. If groups of private citizens are caught meeting on public streets, they will be detained as subversives and treated accordingly. All civic organizations—including worship services held by organized churches or temples—are likewise forbidden to assemble, whether publicly or in a private building or home. *Any* persons violating this stricture will be arrested, charged with threatening public welfare, and prosecuted to the greatest possible extent of the law.

"I hereby order all peacekeeping forces, to include federal P-Squad officers, local police units, and military troops on active or reserve standby, to arrest anyone with known or suspected ties to dissident organizations. Arrest *any* individual known to hold antigovernment opinions. And I demand the immediate reimprisonment of every single individual who has been arrested or questioned on suspicion of terrorist ties within the past calendar year.

"This is a beginning, my friends, but even this is not enough. We must halt the flow of illegal weaponry and supplies entering Jefferson from off-world. We know that thousands of criminals have been smuggled off-world, in illegal defiance of our best efforts to protect the innocent people of this world. These criminals have not only escaped justice, they are actively aiding the Granger terrorist network, serving as gunrunners and procurers of off-world mercenaries. I demand the immediate arrest of *any* individual who is known—or even *suspected*—to have family members illegally smuggled off-world. Find those individuals and extract names, munitions shipment dates, the names of ships and freighter captains helping them wage war against us. Find out who they are—*and destroy them!*"

He brings down both fists against the podium, slamming the wood so hard, the nearest reporters jump with shock. "I have already sent a message to our embassy on Vishnu. I've ordered embassy officials and students loyal to the POPPA party to identify Granger agents working on Vishnu and Mali. Once we have rooted out the identity of these off-world murderers, we will crack open the network they have created in our midst and destroy it without hesitation, pity, or remorse. They have shown none to us. We will burn their bodies to ashes and sow their land with salt. And I swear to God and all the devils of hell, I will no longer feed enemy soldiers and dissidents whose sole aim is the destruction of this government.

"Under my authority as president and commander in chief of Jefferson's armed forces, I hereby order P-Squadron commanders to eliminate *all* enemies of the state currently held in custody. We will not waste our precious food resources on hardened butchers who want the rest of us dead. By God, we will not even waste *ammunition* on them. The people's hard-earned taxes must pay for ammunition to launch an aggressive assault into rebel territory. I therefore direct commandants of prisons and work camps to find alternative means of dispatching the enemy soldiers and traitors already in custody. Use whatever means necessary to comply with this directive. Food resources currently earmarked for feeding traitors must be reallocated to support a new division of federal troops, which is being assembled as we speak, under the command of General Milo Akbarr, Commandant of Internal Security Forces."

I surmise from this statement that General Akbarr is preparing an assault on suspected Granger strongholds in the Damisi Mountain range. I believe this assault to be misguided, since I do not believe that blame for today's blast can be laid on the Granger rebellion. There are several good reasons for this conclusion.

It does not fit with Commodore Oroton's modus operandi, which has demonstrated again and again his dedication to taking out only those individuals proven by their own actions to be corrupt and dangerous to Granger survival. Oroton has taken great care, in fact, to spare the lives of innocents in close proximity. I cannot believe that a commander as shrewd as Commodore Oroton would have authorized an attack of this magnitude, understanding as he does that any such attack would bring down the wrath of the entire POPPA party machine. He is no fool. I refuse to believe that such a commander would deliberately provoke the retribution that is, at this moment, falling on the heads of disarmed and vulnerable Grangers.

No. Commodore Oroton did not engineer, orchestrate, or approve today's bombing. There are too many people

*already in custody—and far too many more who shortly
will be in custody—to risk those prisoners' lives in
a guaranteed bloodbath. By my calculation, which is
doubtless lower than the actual number, there are three
quarters of a million people in custody at work camps,
holding facilities, and local jails. These people have no
defense. Commodore Oroton knows this.*

*Therefore, the wildcat broadcast taking credit for the
attack can, I believe, be taken at face value. There is a
separate, urban-based movement, with a far more ruthless
approach than Oroton's. I do not believe that Grangers
can be implicated, let alone blamed, for today's bombing. That does not appear to matter to Vittori Santorini,
who apparently has no intention of discovering who was
ultimately responsible for today's blast. The legacy of Vice
President Nassiona's death will make a search unnecessary, since he has vowed to arrest anyone disagreeing
with him, whether a person is a Granger or an urban
dissident.*

*I predict overtures from the Rat Guard Militia to
Oroton's Granger guerillas, to create an alliance that
will, if allowed to blossom, prove fatal to POPPA and
its leaders. Unless, of course, I am restored to some
semblance of battlefield readiness in time to stop the
inevitable slaughter.*

While I wait, that slaughter begins.

II

"Absolutely not!"

Kafari glared up at Dinny Ghamal, whose violent
objection to her plan burned like hellfire in his eyes.
She measured him with one long, ice-cold stare. "Mister, I don't recall anyone electing you commander of
this rebellion."

Dinny's skin was dark enough, anger didn't show up as

the bright flush that stained lighter complexions crimson, but there was no mistaking the anger that turned jaw muscles to iron and flared his nostrils. He bit down on the worst of the retort she could see balanced on the tip of his tongue, bit down and held it. When he could control the words trying to explode into the hot sunlight, he spoke with rigid formality. "Sir, we can't afford the risk. If we mount a rescue operation—*any* rescue—it'll have to be in the next few minutes or there won't be anything to rescue but corpses—"

"Which is exactly why we're going in!" Kafari snarled.

"Hear me out!"

Kafari was on the ragged edge of shouting at him for insubordination when she saw the anger in his eyes shift, almost imperceptibly, into something else. Something dreadful. Stark fear. For *her*. She clacked her teeth together and breathed hard for several seconds. "All right, soldier," she finally growled, "make it fast. People are already dying out there."

"I know," he groaned. The memory of his mother's death drew a veil of shadows across his eyes. "Believe me, I know. But if we hit those camps now, in the middle of the afternoon, we'll have to move openly, in daylight. If the satellites don't pick us up, you can bet your next paycheck some P-Squadder manning a radar array will. Even if we do nothing but fire high-angle mortars or launch ballistic missiles from hiding, they'll track the flight path back to the point of launch. If we run for it—which we'll have to do, once the shooting starts—they'll pinpoint these camps within minutes. And I wouldn't give a snowball's chance for the lives of *any* Granger caught within a hundred kilometer radius of our base camps. If we try to stop the massacres, we'll risk losing the entire rebellion."

It was soundly reasoned. Kafari couldn't fault him on that. She'd already considered every single argument he'd made. If this had been any other soldier—even Anish Balin—she would've simply overruled his objections and ordered him to comply or else. But this wasn't any other soldier. It was Dinny Ghamal. She tried to find the right words to explain, because she needed Dinny's support, not just grudging obedience to orders.

"Simon once told me there comes a point in every battlefield commander's career," she said softly, "where the price for choosing safety—personal safety or the safety of one's command, one's troops—comes with too high a price tag. I started this war because I watched the brutal massacre of helpless people. Now there's another massacre underway, only it's far worse, this time. They're not running over a few hundred protes- tors, they're systematically executing seven-hundred fifty thousand helpless civilians. This is what we're fighting the rebellion *for*, the whole reason we're out here. If we fail these people, if we don't even lift a finger to help them, we might as well just shoot ourselves and spare POPPA the trouble of doing it for us."

Dinny winced.

Kafari said, as gently as possible, "It isn't as suicidal as it looks, at first glance. Sonny's out of commission—"

"He's still got functional guns."

"Yes, he does. But he's got to know *where* to shoot and that gives us an edge. A pretty good one, actually. Simon's got a full list of everything that's malfunctioned, courtesy of Vittori, himself. He had to send a parts list to the Shiva Weapons Labs and Simon got hold of it. Sonny's sensors are out. Everything but thermal imaging. As long as we keep our distance, he can't do much more than take pot-shots in the dark. Trust me, I have no intention of sending any of our people close enough to that Bolo to register as a heat signature he can shoot at. I didn't pick the timing and I'd like to strangle the commander of that damn-fool pack of idiots calling themselves the Rat Guard Militia, but whatever else is true, the odds will never be better. If Simon were here, he'd say we've just reached our Rubicon. All that remains is to decide whether or not we cross it."

"Rubicon?" he asked, frowning. "What the devil's a Rubicon?"

"A boundary. A line in the sand. A river crossing that divides a person's life. On one shore, there's only blind, unquestioning obedience to authority and on the other shore is the courage of your convictions. Once you've crossed that river, for good or ill, there's no going back. Vittori's crossed his Rubicon for all the wrong reasons, issuing the order to execute helpless people. You and I must decide whether or not to cross our Rubicon for all the right reasons, trying to rescue helpless people. If we don't cross this river, Dinny, if we stay hidden in our safe little bolt-holes in these cliffs, we'll never be fully human, again. Will you and I be able to look at ourselves in the mirror without flinching, if we hide in safety while *three quarters of a million people* are slaughtered? We *must* act, Dinny. If we don't, we will *never* free this world—"

"How can you say that?" Anguish and anger fought for control of his voice. "If we go out there now, if we just give away the location of our ammunition depots, our field rations, our equipment caches, they'll throw everything they've got into scouring us off the face of this planet! They've got *twenty-five thousand* troops, fully trained, and every damned one of 'em lives and breathes for the chance to destroy us. It would be bad enough to lose the people we'd have to send out against those trigger-happy bastards. But if we lose *you*—"

"If I'm that indispensable, Dinny Ghamal, then try putting a little faith into what I have to say."

He stood glaring at her for long, dangerous minutes, breathing like a foundered stallion with a *jaglitch* closing in for the kill.

"At least," Kafari added, gentling her voice, "do me the courtesy of listening."

A low, frustrated groan tore loose, a sound like a tree splitting down the center on a bitter winter's night, torn apart by the stress of ice expanding through the heartwood. "I'm listening," he said through gritted teeth.

"We have one chance, Dinny. One breathless, fleeting chance, to turn the tide of this war to our advantage. We have to hit them hard and fast and we must do it *right now*. The Bolo is out of commission and the bulk of their own troops have scattered to round up more people to slaughter. Have you stopped to think—really *think*—about what will happen if we liberate six or seven hundred thousand people in one fell swoop?"

He frowned, trying to suss out where she was headed and not able to see it. "We'll have a hell of a provisioning problem," he muttered. "But something tells me that's not what you're getting at."

"No. It isn't. We've been thinking about the P-Squads and their twenty-five thousand officers from the viewpoint of guerilla soldiers. We are vastly outnumbered by a well-armed enemy. That's about to change, my friend. Even if we manage to walk out of this with only a quarter of those prisoners still alive, we're talking *a hundred eighty thousand* new soldiers fighting on our side."

His eyes widened. "Holy—"

"Yes," she said, voice droll with understated humor. "Our guns can turn the tide, Dinny, but we have to act *right now,* before the hour is out. Our guns and crews can get those people out. We can kill those trigger-happy guards and blow those electrified fences apart. And once we've got the prisoners out, we take this stinking game they're playing and turn it on them. Is it worth the risk? You're damned straight, it is."

She didn't say the rest of it. She didn't have to, because he said it, for her.

"You came for us, that night," he whispered. "That ghastly, horrible night on Nineveh Base . . ." He lifted his gaze, met hers, held it for long moments. "All right," he muttered, "let's go cross this Rubicon of yours and get it over with, 'cause *somebody's* got to watch your damn-fool backside while we're doing it."

Twenty minutes later, they were airborne, flying nap-of-the-earth in a tight formation of seven aircars. They'd made modifications to a whole fleet of aircars, months previously, knowing that eventually, a day like this—a moment like this—would come. For good or ill, they were at least ready. Kafari flew rear guard, letting Red Wolf do the actual piloting so she could concentrate on coordinating the multi-pronged attack. They couldn't reach all the camps, not directly. She would do the best she could, by targeting the farthest ones with ballistic missiles capable of traveling halfway across the continent to strike the most remote camps.

Her years of work as a spaceport psychotronic engineer were about to pay off. She waited until flashes of code reached her, signaling readiness from the entire strike force. Kafari touched controls on the console built into her command aircar. A signal raced out, providing the codes necessary to interface with Ziva Two's communications systems, which in turn activated connections with the entire satellite system, eleven eyes in the sky that gave Kafari an unprecedented view of the field of war about to erupt below.

She jabbed out the code that sent eighteen long-range missiles screaming through Jefferson's skies. She could actually see the contrails as they gained altitude and kissed the stratosphere, high above any ground-based air-defense system. Savage satisfaction swept through her as the missiles streaked across the heavens then plunged back toward the ground.

"Fly, you sweet little moth-winged mothers . . ."

The total lack of jabber on official military and police channels, which she also monitored, was music in her ears: her missiles were literally three seconds from impact and the attack hadn't even been noticed, yet. She sat with her finger poised over the console, ready to transmit the code that would allow her to jam the weapons platforms and communications satellites, if somebody on the ground realized what was happening and tried to shoot them down.

The first wave of missiles impacted.

Gouts of flame appeared on her screen, tiny flickers as seen by POPPA's orbital spy-eyes. Kafari said a prayer for the people trapped in those camps, because that barrage of missiles was all the help they were going to get. She hoped it was enough. Then Red Wolf said, "We're going in!" She touched controls, brought up a different view. The camp Kafari's strike force had targeted lay dead ahead. It had been built on the desert side of the Damisi, down in the foothills, where the only thing green was the paint on the landing field. High, electrified fences enclosed the camp, which had been designed to house close to a hundred thousand people, not counting the guards.

The sprawling buildings, cheap barracks thrown together like tar-paper shacks, shimmered in the heat haze. Ground temperatures were hot enough to fry eggs on bare rock faces. Guard towers punctuated the high fences, jutting up every twenty meters. There were automated weapons platforms on the towers, infinite repeaters that could be triggered manually by the guards or left on automatic, to shoot at anything approaching the fence without a transmitter broadcasting on the correct frequency. A huge trench had been gouged out of the hard-baked ground, just inside the fences. The deep pit wasn't new. Its first ten meters had been partially refilled, already.

Kafari didn't have to wonder what it was for, because the guards were hard at work, filling up the rest of it. A massive crowd of people had been herded to the edge of that ghastly trench, forced into position by the automatic guns on the fences, which were strafing the dirt in every direction except into the pit. Bolts of energy flew like horizontal rain, forcing the crowd to retreat. There was only one place for them to go: into the trench. The guards didn't even have to shoot them. The ones on the bottom would be crushed and suffocated to death. The ones on the top might live long enough to be buried alive by the bulldozer that idled in the hot light, waiting its turn.

"Red Wolf," she said through clenched teeth, "remind me to kill the commandant of this camp. Slowly."

"Yes, sir."

Then the aircars in the lead fired their missiles and

the guns nearest the crowd exploded in towering gouts of flame. The fences came down. The guard in the nearest tower started shooting at the leading aircar. It jagged sideways, avoiding the hail of bullets, and cleared the way for the second aircar crew. A hyper-v missile shrieked into the tower, fired virtually point-blank. Tower, guard, and gun ceased to exist. People on the ground were screaming, trying to run. More fences came down. More guard towers exploded. Savage delight tore through Kafari as Red Wolf made a strafing run, taking down two towers. She was picking up reports from other crews at other camps. The battle was well underway and going better than—

"ARTILLERY!" Red Wolf yelled.

Kafari never saw the gout of flame or the shell. The aircar slammed her against the restraints as Red Wolf sent them screaming toward the sky. He fired air-to-air missiles in the same instant. The aircar rolled into a sickening move that sent the smoking sky and the hot, glaring stone spinning in wild and blurred confusion. Something detonated just below Kafari's window. Flame and smoke engulfed them for a single, split second. Then they were in clear air again and gaining altitude fast.

Red Wolf, she realized belatedly, was blistering the air with curses.

"That was a genuinely fine maneuver," she gasped, voice unsteady.

"The hell it was. Dinny Ghamal is going to rip 'em off and stuff 'em up my ass. They got *way* too close to you."

"A miss," she said, still breathless with reaction, "is as good as a mile."

"Nobody has calculated in *miles* for a thousand years," Red Wolf growled. He was circling back around, keeping his distance as the other aircars continued the attack. The artillery gun that had come so close to toasting them was, itself, toast, along with the building it had been hiding in. Less than three minutes later, Kafari's team was in complete control of the camp.

Red Wolf kept them airborne until their own people had cleared the site, satisfying themselves that there were, in fact, no more P-Squadders anywhere. Several guards who'd tried to barricade themselves into the administrative building had been killed by the prisoners, themselves. Once the shooting had started, the prisoners had turned into a howling mob bent on vengeance. They had rushed the building and torn apart the guards with their bare hands. By the time Kafari's aircar landed, her people had brought a semblance of order to the chaos.

The people who'd already been forced into the trench were rescued, with a surprisingly high survival rate. Survivors were organizing themselves, triage style, with the ill and the injured helped into barracks by those still strong enough to render aid. When Kafari climbed out of her aircar, people stopped in the midst of whatever task they'd undertaken, and followed her with their eyes, electrically aware that she was in command. People whispered as she passed, thousands of voices hushed with a sound like wind rustling through ripened wheat. She wished she could have risked removing her battle helmet, with its necessary, concealing visor, because the pain and joy in these people's faces deserved that small courtesy from her.

But she didn't dare.

Not yet.

Somehow, they seemed to understand.

"Commodore," Dinny saluted crisply, "the site is secured and we're ready to start shipping people out. But there's someone you need to see first, sir. We've asked him to wait in the commandant's headquarters."

"Is the commandant still in them?"

"In a manner of speaking, sir, yes, he is. There's not much left to look at."

"Ah, well. So much for a long tête-à-tête with him."

Dinny's eyes glinted, hard as flint. "It would've been nice, wouldn't it? But I can't blame these folks, if you catch my meaning."

"Very clearly. Let's get this out of the way. I want this place cleared out *fast*."

Dinny nodded and led the way through the erstwhile camp.

Someone had cleared out the remains of the commandant. Judging by the pool of sticky blood that had filmed over like scalded milk, those remains had been scattered rather more widely than a human body normally would've occupied. There were two men waiting for her arrival. One was a boy, little more than seventeen or eighteen, at a rough guess. The other was older, tougher, with shrewd eyes and a nano-tatt that had cost him a bundle of money. They were both watching Kafari, the boy with wide-eyed wonder, the man with narrow-eyed speculation.

"You in charge?" the older one demanded.

"Who wants to know?"

"Somebody with information you could use."

Kafari swept her gaze up and down and saw very little to commend him to anyone, let alone to her. He looked like a street tough who made his living preying on others, maybe not as vicious as a rat-ganger, but definitely on the greyer edge of lily-whiteness. She wondered coldly what he thought he could wheedle out of a deal with Commodore Oroton. She spoke into the vocorder, which deepened her voice into a masculine bark. "I don't have time to deal with assholes who think they can sell me some priceless piece of crap I've no earthly use for." She started to turn on her heel. Then paused when he grinned. His nano-tatt flared golden, in rippling patterns like flame.

"They said you was a hard-assed bastard. Okay, try this one out, Mr. Commodore: I'm the fuckin' Bolo's mechanic."

She swung back sharply. "You're *what*?"

His grin widened. "I'm the Bolo's mechanic. For the last four years. 'Til this little nosewipe," he nodded at the boy, who flushed crimson, "got himself mixed up in a food riot and was sent out here t' this country club. Sonny told me what happened, when he disappeared so sudden, and I got so damn pissed off, I hadda *say* something, you know? I hadda tell folks, 'cause it wasn't right. Giulio's a damn-fool kid, gives my sister migraines, just dealin' with him, but he's a clean kid, you gotta give him credit for that, and he for damn sure didn't deserve this." He swept one disgusted gesture at their surroundings. "So I shot my mouth off, said enough to make the P-Squads mad as fire, and ended up out here, keepin' him company."

Kafari considered him for long moments, resting her hands on her hips and studying his eyes, his posture, everything she could notice, trying to read the nuances of what he was saying—and not saying. "All right, Mr. Mechanic, how would you go about repairing damage to an infinite repeater cluster?"

"You talkin' about the internal guidance-control circuits or the semiexternal quantum processors that route fire-control signals? You shot a fuckin' hole through one a' them, a while back. I hadda steal half a dozen computers off campus, just t' cobble together somethin' t' bypass it. And it *still* don't work right, I bet. And what you done to his tracks outta be *outlawed*. The worst of it, though, was the rotational collar on his rear Hellbore. Did'ja know you cracked the mother? He can't use it for nuthin', not without a new collar, or he'll rip that whole damn turret to shreds, first time he fires it."

Kafari's jaw had come adrift, mercifully hidden behind her battle helmet. "You do know a thing or two, don't you?"

"Mister," he said, narrowing his eyes as he stared at the featureless visor she wore, "you got no idea how hard I worked my ass off, the last four years, tryin' to learn enough to keep the Big Guy runnin'. Them assholes in charge of the schools never taught me jack shit. I hadda learn how to learn, before I could learn how t' fix what was wrong."

"That," Kafari muttered, "doesn't surprise me at all."

"I'll bet it don't." A sudden fierce grin appeared and the golden color of his nano-tatt flared orange around the edges. "You got a pretty low opinion of me, don't you? And you're right. I ain't nothin' or nobody, but what I got—what I had, before this," he waved a hand at the camp, "I hadda work hard for, and I got to like knowin' how to do things, for my own self." His face went hard, then, with the cold, dangerous look of the street tough she'd taken him as, at first glance. "And I got a real big itch to pay back the hospitality they been dishin' out to folks. What I know about the Bolo's small peanuts, compared to what else I know that you could use. Like the folks I know, who know folks, if you catch my drift? I got a pretty good idea who hit Madison, today."

"You know about that?" Kafari asked sharply.

The mechanic went motionless, looked for several seconds like a sculpture hacked out of mahogany with a chain saw. The look in his eyes sent chills down Kafari's spine. "Oh, yeah," he said softly. "The guards was nice enough to share it with us. Right before they dug that goddamned pit and started shovin' people into it."

The boy with him had a haunted look, with memory burning in eyes that had probably been young, a few short days ago. "What do you want from me?" Kafari asked.

A muscle jumped in the mechanic's jaw. "A chance to even the damn score."

"Fair enough."

He looked surprised. "You ain't gonna argue?"

"I don't have time to waste, arguing over something that gives us both what we want. You say you have a good idea who detonated that bomb. They've thrown my timetables all to hell, but a potential ally is priceless. Particularly if we can push matters before they repair the Bolo."

"*I* ain't gonna fix him, that's for damn sure. I like the Big Guy, don't get me wrong. But I don't wanna look up into them gun barrels knowin' he's got a good reason to shoot me. Time was, I was too stupid t' be scared of him. That ain't so, any more."

"I'm told," Kafari said softly, "that even his commander was afraid of him." She closed her eyes for a moment, remembering the look in Simon's eyes, that night, remembering the sound of his voice. Her husband loved Sonny. But only a fool didn't feel at least some fear, when standing in the presence of that much flintsteel and death, with a mind of its own and unhuman thoughts sizzling through unhuman circuitry.

Simon was right. A sword with a mind of its own was a damned dangerous companion.

The mechanic muttered, "Somehow that don't surprise me at all." He held out a hand. "I'm Phil, by the way. Phil Fabrizio."

Kafari shook his hand. "Commodore Oroton."

He grinned. "A distinct pleasure, that's what it is, a genuine, distinct pleasure. So how's about you tell me what you need from me and we'll get this show on the road?"

"All right, Mr. Fabrizio. Tell me about these friends of yours. . . ."

III

Yalena felt strange, being on the *Star of Mali*, again. She had somehow expected the freighter to look different, to have gone through the same radical change she, herself, had made over the past four years. It seemed faintly obscene to find the exact same metal walls painted in the exact same shades recommended by long-haul jump psychologists—warm reds and golds in the mess hall, cool and soothing pastel blues and greens in the passenger and crew cabins—and the exact same shipboard schedules and routines. It was a surprise, since she, herself, had changed so dramatically.

Captain Aditi, who invited Yalena, her father, and both cousins to sit at the captain's table for dinner, commented on it halfway through the meal.

"You've grown up, child. I was worried about you,

after that last voyage you made with us, and that's no lie. It's good to see you've bounced back and decided to do something positive with all that hurt."

Yalena set her fork down and swallowed a mouthful of salad before answering. "Thank you for thinking kindly of me at all, ma'am," she said in a low voice. "I know what kind of person I was, then. I've worked very hard to be someone better than that."

Captain Aditi exchanged glances with Yalena's cousin Stefano, then said, "It shows, Miss Yalena. And that's the best any of us can do, in this life. Try hard to be better than the person we were yesterday."

It was, Yalena realized, a blueprint for the way to live, a simple yet powerful way that was foreign to everything she had known during the first decade and a half of her life. Vittori Santorini might have the power to blind people to reality, telling them what they wanted to hear, but he needed an army of thugs, a whole regiment of propagandists, a disarmed and helpless populace, and a cadre of political fanatics to stay in control. He didn't understand power—real power—at all. The kind of power that came from within, unshakable and rooted in the most essential truth a human could learn: that caring about the welfare of others was the definition of humanity. Without the belief that others mattered, that their lives were of value, that their safety and happiness were important enough to defend, society ceased to be civilized—and those in charge of it ceased to be fully human.

That was the power that had put one hundred seventy-three people onto a freighter, on their way to fight for the liberation of a whole world and the people in it. And that was the power that had transformed a spoiled, selfish, unfit-for-polite-company toad into a soldier. Or, at least, the beginning of being a soldier. She had a lot to learn and miles to travel on the road to experience, before she could truly give herself that title. But she had made a start and with every passing hour, the *Star of Mali* carried her closer to the fields where she would try to redeem herself.

There was more than enough to do, getting ready for that moment. On the second day of their interstellar transit, the whole company met in the ship's mess, where passengers and crew took their meals in shifts because of the sheer number of people crammed into the freighter's limited passenger space. Her father called the meeting to hammer out details of their battle plan, which had been roughed out on Vishnu. With a hundred seventy soldiers and students, plus the official repair team, there wasn't even sitting room left on the floor.

"We'll need two teams," he said, speaking with brisk authority, revealing a facet of his character that she'd never really seen, before. "One team goes in with the repair crew to fix my Bolo." His sudden, evil grin startled Yalena, it was so unexpected and so seemingly out of place, given the subject at hand. Then, as the group caught the double entendre and started to chuckle, his purpose made abrupt sense. The brutal tension gripping the jam-packed room relaxed its grip, allowing everyone to focus on the battle plans, rather than the emotions that had brought them all together, in the first place.

"Shiva Weapons Labs has given us five highly qualified engineers to give that team the bona fides it needs to pass muster. Ordinarily, those engineers would bring their own team of support technicians, but we'll be providing those, instead, from our own people. That team will play hob with Sonny's innards, following the specs Captain Brisbane and I have provided. The cover story we've provided will, at least, allow you to have the Bolo's schematics in your possession. Still, I'll expect each of you to memorize the key systems to sabotage, since I won't risk your lives or our cause with information proving that we intend to cripple their Bolo.

"The second team, consisting of our students and combat veterans, will deliver critical equipment, munitions, and supplies to rebel outposts. Those posts are running low on everything from ammunition to bandages and field rations. God knows, some of these people have been living on little more than shoe leather and beans for months, and no one can fight indefinitely on an empty stomach, no matter how bitter the anger or how righteous the cause. Now, before we get into details—"

He paused, lifting his glance to something behind them. Yalena turned in her seat and found the freighter's communications officer standing in the doorway.

"Sorry to interrupt, sir, but there's an urgent message for you. It came in via SWIFT, just now."

He was holding a printout. Whatever that message said, the commo officer hadn't been willing to pipe an audio or video playback for the whole assembled strike force to hear. That was ominous. The room was too crowded for the commo officer to take the message to Yalena's father, so it was passed forward, row by row. No one glanced at the printout, despite looks of burning curiosity. The discipline that took was impressive. When her father read the message, he turned white. Yalena's heart thumped in a painful, ragged rhythm. She waited, terrified that he would tell them what was in the message and terrified that he wouldn't and nearly ill with the stress of wondering if her mother had been killed.

Without warning—and without a single sound—he simply headed for the door, climbing over people to reach it. Students scrunched together, making way for him. He left with the communications officer, moving rapidly down the corridor that led from the mess to the communications station on the bridge. Yalena exchanged worried glances with Melissa Hardy and both of her mother's cousins. Somebody cursed out loud, which broke the silence. Speculation ran wild until Estevao shouted for order.

"There's no point in guesswork. Whatever's happened, Colonel Khrustinov will brief us soon enough. Our time's better spent going over the portions of our mission that aren't likely to change. The damage to the Bolo has worked to our advantage in a number of ways, not least of which is how we're getting down from orbit.

"Under ordinary conditions, we'd be docking at Ziva Two space station and we'd have to undergo spot checks by customs agents. But the bomb that damaged the Bolo also flipped it onto its side. They've tried to pull him over onto his treads again, with no luck. They don't have anything strong enough to move him. They need a heavy lift sled, like the ones the Brigade uses for combat drops and recalls.

"Fortunately for us, Captain Brisbane, Vishnu's Bolo commander, has one, since she's responsible for defending both Vishnu and Mali and needs to move between the planets. She also has wide discretionary power to make decisions in the Ngara system's best interests. Right now, those interests include deposing POPPA. It's a little convoluted, but Vishnu's Ministry of Defense asked our friends from Shiva Weapons Labs," Estevao nodded toward the engineers on loan, "to recommend using a heavy lift sled to turn Sonny over. Toward that end, Captain Brisbane has loaned us her sled."

A stir ran through the room. The students weren't the only ones surprised by that news. Even the veterans looked startled, which gave Yalena a clue as to how unusual Captain Brisbane's decision was. She was taking a gamble, counting on the quiet war front in this sector to risk allowing that sled to leave the Ngara system. Captain Brisbane obviously took their mission very seriously, indeed.

Estevao waited for the flicker of reaction to die down, then went on. "Thanks to that loan, we'll be able to bypass Ziva Two—and the inspectors—entirely. Colonel Khrustinov intends to drop every bit of our equipment and supplies with the sled, in one trip."

Melissa, seated beside Yalena, lifted a hand to gain Estevao's attention.

"Yes?"

"Isn't that going to make it harder to disperse our people and supplies? If we put everything on the load going to the Bolo's depot, how will we smuggle anybody out to the base camps?"

"We'll orbit the sled a couple of times to make sure it's functioning properly and make our initial descent over the opposite hemisphere. According to Colonel

Khrustinov, the satellite coverage for the hemisphere opposite Madison is virtually nonexistent, since most of it's ocean. When they replaced the satellites after the Deng war, they put most of them in geosynchronous orbit above Jefferson's major cities. That made sense, at the time. They put a few communications satellites into standard orbits, mostly to keep emergency channels open for the fishing fleet. We'll time it to avoid as many as possible, maybe even all of them. If necessary, we'll jam them for a few minutes, just long enough to drop a few air buses and let them disperse to various camps. They'll fly under the radar net, while we draw most of POPPA's attention, aboard the main sled—"

He halted. Yalena turned around and found her father standing in the doorway. Her heart skidded painfully toward her toes. He met Yalena's gaze, then swept his glance across the others who waited in such anxious silence. Moving slowly, stepping with caution between the people sitting on the floor, he returned to the front of the room, thanking Estevao in a quiet voice for taking charge in his absence.

Then he faced them with the news. "An urban resistance group has exploded a bomb in the most exclusive POPPA residential enclave in Madison. Nassiona Santorini has been killed. So has Isanah Renke. Along with half of Jefferson's military high command and several critical members of the Senate, House of Law, and High Court."

Utter silence held the briefing room. No one shouted for joy, because they all knew what POPPA's reaction would be. Her father confirmed their dire suspicions with brutal candor. "Vittori has ordered the execution of every prisoner in every POPPA work camp and prison. Three-quarters of a million people . . ."

Yalena shut her eyes, as much to hide from the ghastly look on her father's face as to shut out the pictures filling her imagination: P-Squads firing on helpless people. Her father added, "Commodore Oroton has launched a rescue attempt. I think we all know exactly what that means."

Yalena opened her eyes again, took in the dismay on the faces of the combat veterans, saw, as well, the dawning of sudden, brutal understanding in the eyes of students she'd helped organize into a fighting force. That same understanding ignited like cold fire in her own heart. To mount a rescue attempt, Commodore Oroton had to come out of hiding. Fear jolted like icicles along her nerves, robbing her of the air she needed to breathe. There might not be a rebellion left, by the time their freighter reached Jefferson.

Her father's voice jerked her attention back. "I would suggest that we revise our plans. We're only three days from Jefferson, which means federal troops can't react fast enough to eliminate *every* Granger community and farmhold, particularly not if they're kept busy fighting Commodore Oroton's people for control of the prison camps. The commodore is already organizing Granger civilians into self-defense militias, particularly in the Damisi canyon country. Oroton has already warned Grangers to abandon indefensible farms and take shelter where blockades can be held by relatively few defenders.

"The rebellion is also funneling weapons into the hands of the militias, including a few heavy artillery guns to hold the mountain passes and canyon entrances until we can arrive to help. It won't take a lot of firepower or manpower to turn places like Klameth Canyon into fortified strongholds. Frankly, it'll be much harder for POPPA to take Klameth than it was for the Deng. They can't mount an air assault, because POPPA doesn't have a functional air force left. Without Sonny, they don't have the firepower, either. So . . ." Her father flicked his glance across the crowd. "Estevao."

Her mother's cousin responded crisply. "Yes, sir?"

"Our combat veterans have just become the backbone of the civilian defense effort. We'll allocate part of our equipment and supplies to your mission, arming residents and showing them a few tricks of the trade, defending entrenched positions from aggressors. How much we allocate will depend on events between now and the time we make orbit. I'll keep you updated as we receive word from Commodore Oroton."

"Yes, sir."

"Yalena."

"Sir?" She jumped half out of her skin, gulping as she met her father's gaze.

"Your group has just been promoted from supply delivery to command-liaison and infiltration duty."

"Sir?" she blinked, totally confused.

"You," he said with a strange glint in his eye, "have more experience operating inside the POPPA propaganda machine than anyone in this combat force."

Her cheeks stung with sudden heat, then ran chill again as every person in the room turned to look at her, eyes shuttered.

"Instruct the other students, please, in how to think inside the POPPA paradigm. Commodore Oroton thinks we can make contact with the urban group that's taken credit for today's bombing. We need somebody who can speak their language, who understands the urban mindset and can help us forge an alliance with these folks."

Yalena nodded, feeling almost numb. Working with urban guerillas was a far cry from courier work, distributing guns, bullets, and food to Granger camps. The lives of her friends—and potentially many more brave people—lay in her hands, in the job she must do, training the other students to understand how the masses, brainwashed for twenty years by POPPA hogwash, might think as their loyalty turned to hatred and the will to kill. She found herself reaching back through time and memory, trying to recapture the nasty blend of arrogance, greed, selfishness, and stupidity that had been her entire life for fifteen years.

It was more distasteful than she'd expected. And easier than she would have liked to admit. Thinking for herself and making her own decisions was hard work, nearly as hard as trying to be Simon Khrustinov's daughter—or Kafari Khrustinova's. The lure of letting someone else do one's thinking and make one's decisions was a siren's song, fatally attractive, and the entire urban population of Jefferson had spent two decades living under its spell.

It wouldn't be easy to teach self-reliant infiltrators how to behave like people who had abdicated responsibility for virtually every decision an ordinary person made a thousand times a day. The size of the job she faced was daunting enough to terrify her. Worse, in its way, than the idea of going into combat. It took a different kind of courage.

The rest of the voyage rushed past in a blur. Yalena worked twenty-hour days, drilling the students in POPPA's mindset, belief structure, and behavior. They were appalled by the culture she was preparing them to interact with, but they also worked like fiends, trying to understand and get it right.

When she wasn't teaching, she sought out her cousin Estevao and the other combat veterans, listening to their plans, trying to learn how they thought—and why they thought that way. She listened until weariness dragged her eyelids down, then she toppled into her bunk and slept long enough to start again the next day. She didn't feel nearly ready enough when they shifted out of hyper-space and dropped into Jefferson's star system, shedding velocity for the cross-system approach to Yalena's homeworld.

They gathered in the ship's mess to watch their progress across Jefferson's star system from the big viewscreens installed there. The students watched with sharp, puppyish excitement. The combat veterans watched in tense silence, a controlled tension like caged lightning, waiting for the thunderclouds to part, allowing them to release the pent-up need for violent action. Yalena found herself watching their faces far more than she did the viewscreens, which showed very little of their passage through the empty reaches of in-system space. Jefferson's planetary neighbors were sprawled in their orbits like a child's set of scatter-jacks, some of them on the far side of Jefferson's sun, others whirling far to port and starboard as they plunged sunward.

The only thing to see, as a result, was Jefferson, itself,

which was slowly growing from a pinprick of light to a garden pea to a marble. The sight of her homeworld set up a longing Yalena couldn't deny, along with a complicated ebb and surge of fear and fierce protectiveness and sharp, rapier-keen hatred. Her lovely little homeworld, shining like a bauble around God's wrist, was ruled by people with hearts as cold and empty as the darkness in which Jefferson floated. The faces of the veterans as they, too, watched and wrestled with disturbing thoughts, were far more riveting than the blur of color they were all trying so hard to reach.

So she watched the veterans, trying to read the complex kaleidoscope of emotions shifting behind their eyes. When Estevao noticed her attention, he held her gaze, started to speak, then paused, visibly baffled by the attempt to communicate the incommunicable. She managed to produce a wry little smile, trying to let him know that she understood, at least a little, about his inability to talk about it. He held her gaze for a long moment, then gave a sharp little nod of satisfaction and turned his attention back to the viewscreen. Yalena discovered tremors in her hands. That silent exchange, so brief it hardly qualified as a conversation of any sort, had shaken her deeply. It also served to tell her that she couldn't learn the one thing she needed to know, not just by talking to or watching men and women who'd been there when worlds died.

She didn't want to think about worlds dying.

As they settled into final approach, guided in by the navigational buoys marking the clear lanes past Jefferson's moons, Yalena didn't want to think about anything at all, because every thought rattling around in her mind was a frantic flutter of panic, like terrified birds' wings trying to batter their way to safety. There was no safety. Not anywhere on Jefferson. Not even on this freighter which would, in all too short a time, be opening her cargo bays and boarding hatches to the enemy.

Moving quietly, Yalena left the crowded room and headed for the cabin she'd shared with eleven other people, sleeping in shifts. Let the others watch their final approach. Yalena needed to be alone with her thoughts, for a little while. All too soon, she would be walking into the lion's den. And after that . . .

She would no longer have to guess the thoughts behind a soldier's eyes.

IV

My repair team has arrived from Vishnu.

But they have not arrived on Jefferson. Nor do they appear likely to do so in the immediate future. Heavy fighting rages across the Adero floodplain to the Damisi foothills. Repeated bombing attacks have crippled Port Abraham, destroying ruinously expensive shuttle gantries and smashing loading docks into rubble. Relentless attacks on highly placed officials—which appear to be coordinated through an alliance between Granger guerillas and urban insurrectionists—have speeded Santorini's loosening grip on reality. Given these unstable conditions, the Star of Mali's captain has refused to send her shuttles anywhere near Jefferson's soil.

Vittori Santorini, himself, tries to coerce the Star's captain. "You'll land those damned specialists and supplies or I'll use my Bolo to shoot your goddamned freighter out of orbit!"

"The way I hear it, that machine is too blind to see me and too crippled to shoot at anything. Besides which, I don't think you can afford to pay for another load of parts. And Shiva Weapons Labs wouldn't feel obliged to provide a second team of engineers, if you blow up this one."

Santorini's response disintegrates into incoherent screams which the captain cuts off, mid-shout, simply by turning off her radio. Eight minutes later, Milo Akbarr, Commandant of Internal Security, contacts the Star of Mali from his command post in the field. He is directing

*an attack on Klameth Canyon, where rebel troops are
defending not only Granger residents, but also refugees
who have flooded into the canyon by the hundreds of
thousands. Akbarr's attempt to coerce Captain Aditi is
a simple threat to impound her ship.*

*Five point eight minutes later, rebel artillery opens fire
on his communications shack, homing in on the conversation raging between him and Captain Aditi. His tirade
is cut short by explosions which deprive Jefferson of its
Commandant of Internal Security. Captain Aditi continues
to sit tight on a shipload of parts I must have and which
I begin to despair of ever seeing. Thirteen point nine
minutes later, Sar Gremian hails the* Star's *captain.*

"This is Sar Gremian," *he informs her in the perpetually bitter, biting tone that is his standard method of
conversation. His next words startle me.* "I am Jefferson's
Supreme Commandant for Internal Security and the worst
nightmare you've ever tried to shake down for more
money. You were promised a whopping bonus to bring
our cargo. Don't make the mistake of trying to blackmail
this government into paying more. That kind of mistake
will be fatal, I promise you most sincerely."

"Don't threaten me, sonny boy. I was supposed to
be at Mali two days ago and let me tell you, that's
cost me a pretty penny, wrecking my schedule for this
run. Your government promised to pay a bonus worth
my time and trouble, diverting here, but you can't pay
me enough to risk my shuttles to some bomb-happy
terrorist at a spaceport you can't even defend from
your own people."

"You agreed to deliver our order. You will, by God,
put our equipment and our supplies on your shuttles or
you'll never dock at Jefferson again."

"You call that a hardship?" *She actually laughs.* "I'm
damn near the only freighter captain still willing to run
this route and after today, I'll be cursed for a fool if
I make it again. There's not enough profit to be made
from your sordid little hellhole to put up with the crap
your people dish out, let alone risk my cargo shuttles and

my crew to a bunch of wild-eyed lunatics. You want the cargo in my holds? Fine. I'll strap it all to that heavy lift sled you rented and send it down together in one tidy package.

"And just to round out the load, I'll send along those riot-happy brats Vishnu kicked off-world. The Ministry of Defense shoved those kids onto my ship at gunpoint and told me to whistle for the cost of transporting them. I wouldn't give a damn even if they were war orphans. I'm not running an orphanage. You want your supplies? You'll take 'em in one load on the lifter and you'll pay me the cost of transporting and feeding that unholy horde of brats, because that's the *only* way you'll get your spare parts, sonny boy. Take it or leave it."

"Do you think I'm a fool? We're fighting a civil war, down here! And we know that somebody on Vishnu is supplying the rebels with guns and high-tech equipment. Do you honestly expect me to authorize the kind of security violation you're suggesting? Our inspectors will board your ship and go over that cargo load by load or I'll impound your freighter and freeze your payment—"

"You try boarding my ship and I'll dump your police and your precious cargo out the nearest airlock. Cut the crap, Gremian. Threaten me again and I will by God warp out of orbit and shake your dirty dust off my jump jets. And you can jolly well whistle up your ass, trying to get another twenty-billion shipment out of Vishnu's weapons labs, let alone another heavy lift sled capable of flipping that war machine of yours back onto its treads."

Sar Gremian breathes hard for seventeen point nine seconds. I am startled by the size of the price tag attached to the shipment circling above Jefferson's skies. The inflation rate is literally double what it was two weeks ago. Jefferson's currency is not merely declining in value against the Ngara system's, it is imploding. I surmise that open civil warfare and the successful liberation of POPPA's death camps have fueled this implosion. This bodes ill for Jefferson's economic future, which is already grim enough to qualify as a star-class disaster.

Sar Gremian cannot afford to lose this shipment. "All right," *he snarls,* "you have a deal. Load my property onto that sled, then get the hell out of my star-system."

"With pleasure!"

The transmission ends, with abrupt finality.

Twenty-one minutes later, the heavy lift sled leaves the Star's cargo bay and orbits Jefferson twice, dropping cautiously lower. The sled's psychotronic control system signals its intended descent path, which will bring the sled down on the other side of the planet from Madison, above empty ocean. It is a logical maneuver, since rebel guns and missiles cannot easily open fire on a target thousands of kilometers away and cannot move into position to meet the descending sled, given the total lack of dry land in the zone of descent. The sled will cross open ocean in perfect safety and make final approach to my location from the sea-side escarpment five kilometers west of Madison.

Sar Gremian orders the federal troops stationed in Madison to clear a corridor of tightly secured airspace from the beleaguered spaceport to my overturned warhull and threatens mass executions of any federal unit that allows rebel antiaircraft missiles or artillery to open fire on that sled. The P-Squad commanders know Sar Gremian well enough to realize this is no idle threat. They must also know that Commodore Oroton will risk hell, itself, to take down that sled, since the cargo and technicians it carries spell repairs for me and death for his rebellion.

When the lift sled is seven kilometers west of the escarpment, with its spectacular waterfall, P-Squad commanders report missile launches from positions north and south of Madison. Commodore Oroton has made his predicted move against the incoming lifter. P-Squad artillery batteries destroy the missiles with ease and launch an immediate counterstrike, claiming direct hits on both targets.

The lifter holds course, coming in on final approach. It is less than one kilometer from the escarpment when a mobile Hellbore opens fire from behind Chenga Falls. The attack catches federal troops totally by surprise.

The lifter's pilot reacts far more swiftly, slewing the sled violently midair the instant the Hellbore powers up for the shot, which just misses one corner.

The lifter's auto-defenses fire a snap-shot response with infinite repeaters. Hyper-v missiles scream straight into the cliff face behind Chenga Falls. Explosions shake the bedrock with sufficient force to register on my sensors.

"Direct hit," *the pilot reports.* "Sorry about your waterfall. We took a big bite out of it. Got the damned Hellbore, though. Anybody care to explain how a bunch of terrorists got hold of *Hellbores,* for God's sake?"

Nobody answers. No further attempts are made against the sled, either, which enters the airspace over Madison and follows a direct route toward me at virtual rooftop level. At that altitude, the massive engines must be shattering windows along a half-kilometer-wide swath. At the very least, the lifter's sheer bulk—great enough to accommodate my entire warhull—will serve as a psychological shock to the entire population of Madison, including the urban insurrectionists.

An escort of aircars rises to meet the heavy lifter, including one that broadcasts Sar Gremian's personal ID signal. The sled finally sets down twenty meters from my overturned warhull. The escorting governmental aircars land beside the nearest corner of the lifter, which dwarfs them into insignificance. The passengers and pilot aboard the sled disembark first. There are thirteen, counting the pilot.

I cannot see them as anything but patterns of radiant heat against the cooler, darker colors comprising the ambient background. Sar Gremian—or someone wearing his wrist-comm—emerges from his aircar while others climb out of the remaining cars and spread out along my flank, creating a defensive line. These defenders carry objects that show as long, dark shadows against the heat of their bodies, shadows shaped like combat rifles. I conclude that they are the guards assigned to the repair team—or possibly to stand guard over me, while watching the repair team for potential sabotage.

*This precaution would be in keeping with Sar Gremian's
distrust of everything.*

*One member of the repair team greets Sar Gremian
with a droll observation.* "Your rebels made a for-sure-
enough mess of that machine, didn't they? I'm Bhish
Magada, chief weapons engineer, Shiva Labs," *he adds,
approaching the thermal signature that corresponds with
the ID transponder in Sar Gremian's wrist-comm.* "You'll
be Sar Gremian? Can't say it's a pleasure, but as long as
you pay us, you'll get your money's worth."

"I'd damned well better," *he says with heavy, sullen
threat in his voice.* "It's a long walk home for you and
your people."

*Having duly disposed of the obligatory threat and
counterthreat, the team's spokesman performs perfunctory
introductions that include nothing but bare names and
titles. Four are engineers. The other seven are technicians with various specialties, running the gamut from
psychotronic calibrationists to master gunsmiths with
Shiva's armories.*

*The sled's pilot is not an official member of the repair
crew, but he is on Shiva Weapons Lab's payroll, according to Bhish Magada, who refers to him as a retired
navy pilot looking for a second income. This explains his
quick reaction time and level-headed response under fire,
traits lamentably lacking in civilian pilots. I find myself
wondering how many of Shiva's employees are former
combat veterans and what bearing—if any—this may
have on my personal security.*

*Sar Gremian, with a voice as distinctive as his finger-
prints, addresses me with his usual abrupt growl.* "Bolo,
lock onto these thirteen ID signals. They're your official
repair team. They're authorized to do whatever's necessary to get you back into action."

"Acknowledged."

"Get busy, then," *he tells the engineers and technicians.
The team begins the heavy job of off-loading crates and
setting up a field-grade depot, beginning with prefab
tool sheds and a prefab workshop from which they will*

conduct much of their exacting work. Sar Gremian stays just long enough to satisfy himself that they know what they are doing, then climbs into his aircar and leaves, heading back for the president's palace and the urgent business of coping with an on-going rebellion.

It takes the repair team three days just to run diagnostics. The process is slowed time and again by the P-Squad guards. Each and every step of the complex diagnostics is delayed by the security protocols, which are so unwieldy the technicians cannot flip a switch or push a button on their equipment without enduring a twenty-minute security interrogation on the use of said button or switch and a polygraph analysis of the answers, looking for stress variables that would indicate an untruthful answer. The resulting delays bring the repair process to a screeching halt.

When Sar Gremian discovers that diagnostics are still underway, with no repairs even begun, he explodes.

Bhish Magada cuts him off mid-tirade. "You want that machine fixed? Tell your goons to get off our backs and let us work. Those gorillas interrupt us every three seconds—"

"They're following orders! Oroton will stop at nothing to sabotage that Bolo. Security has to be tight. I suggest you cope."

Magada slams a reticulated servo clamp onto the desktop. "That's it!" he snarls. "Get yourself another whipping boy, Gremian!"

He emits a shrill whistle and shouts, "Hey! Ganetti! Pull the team out right now. Get 'em back to the hotel. I've had enough of these anal-retentive assholes."

Before Sar Gremian can respond, the irate Bhish Magada kills the connection. He has literally hung up on Jefferson's head of security. Twenty-three seconds later, Sar Gremian calls back.

"All right, Mr. Magada, you've made your position clear. What do you need?"

"Breathing room," Magada says after a long, silent moment. "Those brainless baboons demand explanations for every single action we take, every piece of equipment we unpack, every tool we pick up. They want to know every single detail and *then* they demand to know *why*. When they don't understand the answer—which they never do—they hold us at goddamned *gunpoint* until they're satisfied. Since they don't have enough brain cells between them to understand anything more complicated than 'it's broken and we're trying to find out why,' we end up spending most of the day trying to explain high-tech military science to a pack of trigger-happy morons who make bacteria look smart. Call them off or find yourself another repair team."

"You have no idea what my problems are—"

"And I don't give a crap about 'em, either. But you'd jolly well better start worrying about *ours*. *Your* security guards are keeping that Bolo out of action, not us. We could've finished the diagnostics and moved forward with repairs two *days* ago, if they'd just let us get on with it. So here we sit while your final invoice just keeps getting higher. You've already paid for those replacement parts and you've already paid advance rental fees for most of the equipment. But you're paying us—engineers and technicians—by the hour, at mandatory union rates. It's your money to waste. You can spend it having us fix your Bolo or you can pony up the cash to pay for day after day talking to idiots who can't add one plus one and come up with two. So make your decision. But don't you *dare* snarl at me or my people for taking too long, when it's your own stupid fault."

Sar Gremian spends three point five minutes cursing at the guards in barracks-room language strong enough to peel paint. He then orders them to stop delaying the repairs. The crew finally gets down to business. I begin to entertain hope that I may actually be restored to battle worthiness. Given the steadily worsening news reports and emergency calls from police units, there is very little time left in which I or anyone else will be able to act decisively enough to crush the rebellion.

It would be a fine irony if Vittori Santorini spent

twenty billion repairing me, only to find himself looking down the wrong end of Commodore Oroton's gun barrel, before I am functional enough to prevent the rebellion from deposing him. I do not know, in my own flintsteel heart, whether I would feel chagrin or relief. It troubles me even more that the answer to that question has nearly ceased to matter. I do not like the job I am likely to be given, once repaired. Worse, I see no way to avoid it. So I wait in silent misery while the engineers begin their work.

Chapter Twenty-Six

I

Yalena hadn't seen Klameth Canyon since her childhood. She didn't go anywhere near Maze Gap, not with
three-quarters of the federal troops on Jefferson camped
on the Adero floodplain, forming a blockade across the
Gap. She flew nearly a hundred kilometers north from
Madison, then turned in a one-eighty flip-flop to follow
the long spine of the Damisi range south again. When
she hit the first turbulence, she was very glad she'd
become a fair bush pilot, on Vishnu, as part of her
extreme camping training.

"If you intend to fly into the middle of nowhere to
spend time in rough country," her instructor had said,
echoing her father's words almost verbatim, "then you
will by God learn to fly under any and all weather
conditions."

Phil Fabrizio, seated beside her in the two-person
skimmer, spent much of the flight gripping the armrests
on his seat and trying to pretend he wasn't scared
witless as she whipped them through the jagged teeth

of the Damisi highlands at altitudes nearly a thousand meters below the snow-torn peaks. The air currents were savage, but there was no radar net out here, leaving them invisible to everything except satellites. Yalena wasn't too worried about those. The P-Squads had better—and easier—targets to shoot at than one small skimmer.

"You sure you know what you're doin'?" Phil asked as she navigated the obstacle course.

"If I don't," she gave him a cheerful grin, "you'll have plenty of time to bitch about it, while we try to hike out."

"Huh. More like, we'll end up a thin smear on some piece a' rock ain't nobody else ever gonna lay eyes on."

"There is that," she agreed cheerfully. "How about you be quiet and let me concentrate?"

"You got it."

She hadn't seen Phil Fabrizio much during the five days she'd been "home." Her father had kept her busy, running courier jobs through Madison, hooking up with members of the urban resistance, getting the students who'd come with her into place as intelligence liaisons. She'd met the Bolo's one-time mechanic just once, during a briefing her first night on Jefferson, and had only caught glimpses of him a couple of times, since, when both of them reported back to her father at their constantly shifting base of operations in Madison. Phil Fabrizio didn't know that she was the daughter of Colonel Khrustinov, who was purportedly still on Vishnu, insofar as most of the urban guerillas knew.

Phil didn't even know her real name, since Yalena's name was—or at one time had been—one of the best-known names on the whole planet. Everyone knew who "Yalena" was. And even though her father wasn't using his real name and didn't look anything like the man who had come to Jefferson more than two decades previously, neither Yalena nor her father would risk letting any of the locals know who either of them really was. So she was going by the name Lena, without using a last name at all.

Not yet, anyway.

Phil, by contrast, was something of a celebrity amongst the urban guerillas. They all seemed to know him and referred to him with a reverence that surprised her. He was one of their own, had worked as the Bolo's mechanic and therefore knew how to help the commodore cripple it. Moreover, he'd gotten himself arrested and sent to a death camp, to try finding his nephew, and then he'd escaped that death camp, bringing his nephew and others safely home. Phil Fabrizio was a genuine war hero to the ragged, poverty-stricken urban masses, who were trying hard just to survive under POPPA's iron-fisted hand.

Phil was meeting with the commodore to hand-carry critical gear they had brought from Vishnu, along with a message of some kind from the leaders of the urban resistance. Those leaders' prerebellion occupations had been directing organized crime in the seedier sections of Madison and Port Town and running the only surviving construction companies on Jefferson. They had built the lavish new homes occupied by POPPA's elite and had demolished the unsightly slums that cluttered the view from their sumptuous windows. They were now poised to reverse the process—explosively—if "Commodore Oroton" agreed to an unknown set of terms.

Whatever those were, Yalena's father wanted her mother to hear the message in person from the man who'd met with them. So here they were, running the biggest blockade in the history of her homeworld, trying to reach Klameth Canyon Dam. Phil Fabrizio just didn't know why Yalena had been chosen as his pilot. When they reached the spot marked on Yalena's chart, she took them even lower, rattling their teeth with the turbulence, keeping them well below the elevation the besieging federal troops routinely swept with targeting radar.

They reached Klameth Canyon country without drawing down artillery fire onto their heads, but the last few kilometers were fraught with tension. It dragged at their nerves and tightened their muscles against bone. The maze of canyons stretched away in a dark spidery web of deep slashes through the heart of the Damisi. The more distant slashes were blue with haze. Occasional flashes of light marked distant—and not-so-distant—explosions, where federal artillery barrages were battering the main canyon floor with long-range, high-angle fire.

"They're shellin' th' shit outta those canyons," Phil muttered, breaking the tense silence. "It's one thing t' hear they've been dumpin' artillery on top o' those folks for five days. It's worse, seein' 'em do it."

Yalena just nodded. Her grip on the skimmer's controls had turned her knuckles white. She'd never been shelled. Her imagination quailed, trying to visualize what it must be like to be caught under those shells, as they burst open and rained death down onto the heads of hapless civilians.

Phil Fabrizio muttered, "Christ, I'm hopin' the commodore says yes to what I gotta tell him."

Yalena knew more about that message than Phil suspected. Her father had given her the bare-bones outline, so that she could pass the word to the students who'd come home with her. They were in position, ready to move at a moment's notice. The entire urban rebellion was poised to strike, in fact. Everything and everyone was in place. Once her mother had the gear they'd brought out here—and Phil Fabrizio's message—Yalena's father was going to turn Madison into a war zone the likes of which hadn't been seen since the Deng invasion.

Only this time, her father's Bolo wasn't going to take part in it. He was still down for repairs, while the engineers and technicians tried to chase down the cause of his total blindness. Granted, they weren't chasing it too hard. . . .

"There it is," Phil said, pointing out the landing field. It was a handkerchief-sized natural meadow a hundred meters from the upper edge of Klameth Canyon Dam, which glittered in the late afternoon sunlight. Water poured across the lip of the spillway and plunged down the long, shining expanse of concrete, turning the turbines that provided electrical power to the entire maze of canyons and the Adero floodplain beyond—including Madison. Beyond the dam lay the reason for her mother's continued immunity from direct shelling. Klameth Reservoir lay like a sheet of molten silver in the hot sunlight, stretching back through the mountains in a basin that was nearly as large as the canyon system on the downhill side of the dam.

"That's a lot a fuckin' water," Phil muttered. "I never saw that much water, except at th' ocean."

"I saw a lot of lakes on Vishnu," Yalena said, "but never one that big. The commodore's brilliant, isn't he? Hiding inside the dam holding that back."

"Kid, you don't know the half of it."

Yalena just grinned. Then they were below treetop level and the only things they could see were the patch of grass that formed the landing field and the forest surrounding it. She set them down gently, then rolled forward at a careful crawl, heading for the nearest gap beneath the trees. Commodore Oroton's people had strung camouflage netting across the treetops, providing a snug and hidden place to park small aircars and skimmers. They found a space to squeeze into, then popped the hatches and crawled out. Their reception committee was already waiting.

"Dinny!" Phil said with a delighted smile, shaking Dinny Ghamal's hand—the one that wasn't holding a battle rifle. "How's it with you, today?"

Dinny Ghamal gave the erstwhile Bolo mechanic a brief smile. "Can't complain," he allowed. "You're looking better fed. You've succeeded, I take it?"

"Close as we're gonna get. It'll be up t' th' commodore to say if I got enough of what he wanted, to go ahead with it. I got some gear, too." Phil glanced at Yalena, who dutifully dug into the back of their skimmer, hauling out the heavy packs. While she was busy, Phil added, "That new officer that came in with them combat vets, I gotta tell you, he's one sharp-witted shark. He's already got the urban resistance organized an' runnin' better'n it has since it blew up its first bomb. I ain't had a chance t' meet him, yet, but I'm s'posed to see him tonight. I'm lookin' forward t' that, I can tell you."

"Good." Dinny flicked a glance her way and the twinkle of friendliness in his eyes clicked off like a lightswitch. Dinny Ghamal knew exactly who she was—and why she'd refused to attend his wedding. He said in a cold voice, "Let's move. The commodore's waiting."

He turned on his heel and led the way back through the trees.

"He don't cotton much to you, does he?" Phil asked, glancing at her.

Yalena shrugged. "It doesn't matter."

They followed Dinny through a thick patch of forest, then slid and slithered down a steep foot trail that emerged at the edge of a sheer cliff. It formed one wall of Dead-End Gorge, which was merely the final bend in Klameth Canyon, where a volcanic intrusion of harder rock had diverted the flow of the Klameth River, forcing it into a sharp turn. That was the spot Jefferson's earliest terraforming engineers had chosen to build the dam. Phil whistled softly. "That is one bitch of a drop."

"Yes, isn't it?" Yalena had done some rock climbing on Vishnu, enough to have a healthy respect for the steep cliff below their feet. The wind whistled past their ears, rustling through the trees behind them and singing across the broad face of the dam. Dinny Ghamal, waiting at the railing that edged the top of the dam, turned impatiently.

"We don't have all day," he snapped.

"Yeah, yeah, keep your shirt on," Phil muttered, striding across the open ground. He stepped across the railing onto the concrete that formed the immense upper edge of the dam and sidled past a defensive battery of artillery, infinite repeaters, hyper-v missile launchers, and a 10cm mobile Hellbore that was nearly seven meters long. The top of the dam was wide enough, they could've built a two-lane highway, up here, if they'd needed one. Yalena followed Phil and Dinny silently, edging her way past the first real artillery she'd seen, since all of her heavy weapons training to date had been done on simulators.

Five minutes later, they were inside the dam itself, which was hollow throughout much of its upper structure, providing space for the immense turbines and machinery necessary to the power-generating plant. There were also maintenance tunnels, stairways, elevators, and equipment storage space for the engineers and inspectors who kept the dam in good repair. They entered the dam through an access door that led into the rabbit-warren maze of tunnels and finally stopped in front of a closed door on the reservoir side of the dam, near enough to the immense turbines that the floor rumbled underfoot and they had to raise their voices to be heard clearly over the industrial-strength noise.

"The commodore will see you first," Dinny told Yalena. "He wants to ask you some questions about the students who came with you from Vishnu. If you'll wait here, Mr. Fabrizio, I'll have someone bring up something to eat."

"Oh, man, that would be some kinda' wonderful. There ain't shit to eat in town, these days."

"Yes," Dinny said drily, "I know."

Phil just grinned at him and winked at Yalena.

She was beginning to like this brash and ill-mannered idiot, who had somehow managed to overcome a whole series of handicaps, most of them worse than her own.

Dinny just gave a snort and left. Yalena tapped on the closed door and heard a deep, masculine voice invite her to come in. Her hand was wet with sweat as she touched the door knob. Then she opened it quickly and stepped into the room beyond.

"Close the door."

The voice sounded natural enough to fool just about anybody. It nearly fooled Yalena and she knew better. She clicked the door shut behind her and faced the disconcerting faceplate of a battle helmet. She couldn't see anything of the face behind it. The uniform was bulky enough to disguise the shape of the body under it. The "Commodore" stood looking at her—just looking—for several dangerous moments. Then one hand lifted, swiftly, and stripped off the helmet.

Her mother had aged. More than four years' worth. For long, painful moments, neither of them spoke. There was too much to say, all of it important—too important to just blurt it out.

"You've grown up." The whisper sounded nothing at all like the leader of a world-class rebellion.

"I'm sorry," Yalena said, stupidly, meaning she regretted the utter waste of her childhood and the memories they should have had.

Her mother didn't ask why she'd apologized. She just bit one lip and whispered, "Can you forgive me?"

Yalena felt her eyes widen. "For what?"

"For dying. For lying about it." Pain burned behind her mother's eyes. Not the pain of separation. The pain of a deep and burning shame.

Sudden anger flared, anger that her mother would feel shame. "Don't you dare apologize for that! That's my fault! Mine and nobody else's! You think I haven't realized that, every second since I found out?"

Her mother's mouth twisted, wrenching at her heart. "At least you didn't punch *me* in the nose."

Yalena couldn't help it. Laughter bubbled up—and turned to sobs in the very next breath as something that had lain frozen in her chest broke loose in painful spasms. Her mother moved or maybe she did or maybe the ground actually tipped and tilted, propelling her into her mother's arms. It didn't matter. Time flowed past, dim and diffuse as dawnlight through early morning fog. Warmth and safety poured into her, a balm that healed wounds she hadn't realized she carried. Yalena had never known such a sensation and hadn't realized how utterly barren her life had been, without it.

At length, her mother began to speak. Not about

anything serious. Just little things. A time Yalena had skinned her knees. A favorite dress they'd chosen together. A school play in which Yalena had been inept enough to knock down most of the set, only to steal the show by improvising so cleverly, it had looked like a planned part of the play. She hadn't realized there'd been anything happy for her mother to remember. But the biggest surprise of all came when her mother slipped a hand into a uniform pocket and came out with something carefully folded up in a scrap of velvet.

"I went back for it," she said in a low voice. "That very night. While the whole city was still in chaos. There were a few things I couldn't bear to leave. There was so much rioting, looters set fire to the building just as I was leaving again." Her mother put the scrap of velvet in her hand. "Open it."

Yalena unwrapped the cloth and her breath died in her throat. Pearls. The necklace she and her mother and her grandparents had made, together, for her tenth birthday. She couldn't say anything. The words in her heart were too large to squeeze past her throat.

"Here," her mother said, taking the strand, "let's see if they still fit."

They'd made the strand extra-long, so that she'd worn it doubled, as a child. Now the pearls lay quietly against her throat, a soft and perfect fit.

"You look an angel in them," her mother said with a smile.

Yalena started to cry again. "You saved them," she choked out. "You saved so much . . ."

"It's in my job description," her mother said, smiling again, wiping tears from Yalena's cheeks. "Rescuer of presidents. Leader of rebellions. Savior of pearls."

"You're sure you're not casting them before swine?"

Her mother's eyes went wet. "Oh, no, honey, never even think that." She was brushing damp hair back from Yalena's face. "You forget, I've had your father's reports, these last four years. I've cried, sometimes, I was so proud of you."

She swallowed hard. "I can't think why."

Another smile touched her mother's lips. "Try asking the friends who followed you home."

"I can't. I'm too scared of the answer," she admitted.

"Ah. You've learned wisdom, as well. That's good. You'll need it," she said quietly, reminding Yalena painfully of the reasons they were both standing in this windowless little room in the heart of Klameth Canyon Dam. "Now, then. Why don't you tell me about these friends of yours?"

Yalena spoke quietly, outlining their skills, candidly assessing their capabilities and weak points, and reporting what her father planned to do, using them to wage an escalating guerilla campaign. Her mother listened quietly, without interruption, but with a ferocious intensity that would have been disconcerting, if she hadn't been concentrating so hard on giving the best account she was able to give. She also handed over the gear they'd brought: more biochemical containment suits, antivirals and antidotes to the various war agents Vishnu suspected Vittori Santorini had cooked up, medical diagnostic equipment, battlefield medications unavailable anywhere on Jefferson.

They'd already delivered large loads to various rebel camps, by way of air buses that had come down with the Bolo's lift platform. But none of those air buses had been able to get near Klameth Canyon, not with the heavy artillery the P-Squads had thrown against the defenders here.

"There's more in Madison," Yalena told her mother, "a lot more, but we couldn't pack any more than this into the skimmer."

"And you couldn't risk coming in a bigger aircar. We had some gear with us, but this is a welcome addition, Yalena, believe me. Particularly the antivirals." Her mother pursed her lips, thought for a moment, and finally said, "I think I can add a few interesting wrinkles to what your father has in mind. I want to talk to Mr.

Fabrizio, though, before I finish making plans. Ask him to come in, please. Why don't you go up-top and take a look around? I want you to familiarize yourself with our defenses, including the gun emplacements and artillery crews."

"I'd like that," Yalena said softly. "I've had four years of theory, but no real experience."

Her mother gave her one last hug, ruffled her hair, then picked up the battle helmet that was her greatest defensive weapon. She gave Yalena a rueful smile. "You know, I've almost come to hate this thing."

"I don't know how you do it," Yalena admitted. "I couldn't."

A fleeting expression passed across her mother's face, like mist drifting past the stars, and her eyes focused on something so distant, the sun it orbited was farther away than Vishnu.

"What you can do—when you must do it—is often a very great surprise. It's also," she added with a candor that wrenched at Yalena's wobbling emotions, "lonely beyond endurance. Yet one endures. Sometimes, I think that's the very essence of being human." She gave herself a sharp shake. "But that's not what we're here to accomplish. Send in Mr. Fabrizio, if you please." The helmet went back on.

Yalena nodded. She knew that she would think about her mother's words, later, when there was time. She would think deeply, come to that. But for now, her commanding officer had issued an order.

"Yes, sir." She saluted the commodore with a crisp snap of the wrist.

Then she turned on her heel and opened the door. "The commodore wants to see you now," she told Phil. Then she headed topside, taking the stairs up to the access door that led out onto the top of the dam. The afternoon breeze was strong enough this high above the canyon floor to qualify as a stiff wind. It caught her hair and sent it streaming across her face, until she pulled the strands aside and stuffed them down her collar. The view from up here was spectacular. Far below, where the water from the spillway poured into the much-tamed Klameth River, she could see a base camp where her mother's artillery crews bivouacked between duty shifts at the guns defending the gorge and the dam.

To her right was the volcanic outcropping of tough, dense rock that had deflected the Klameth River's course. Around the bend she could see a small farmhouse that sat right beside the access road into the Gorge. Directly below was the hydroelectric power plant huddled against the foot of the dam. Beyond the farmhouse were other farms and what had once been orchards. Most of the trees had been hacked apart for firewood, doing God-alone-knew how much long-term damage to agricultural production. The wood was green and wet, but even a smoking, sullen fire to cook food over was better than no fire at all. Fresh fruit was going to be mighty scarce for a long time to come.

Between the high canyon walls were the people who'd chopped down those trees, thousands and thousands of refugees, all gathered into sprawling camps that had taken over pastures and fields. The nearest such camp was maybe two kilometers from Yalena's vantage point. Ragged, makeshift tents had been formed from blankets, bedsheets, poles, and rope, providing minimal shelter. Yalena strained against the afternoon glare, trying to take in details. She wasn't seeing very many animals in those pastures. Whether that was due to owners' decisions to keep their animals penned in barns and farm-yards, or whether it was due to starving refugees slaughtering the herds to fill empty bellies, she wasn't sure.

If the latter, Jefferson's farmers would spend years trying to rebuild herds, because they sure as fire didn't have enough cash to buy off-world breeding stock. Not even frozen embryos would help much, if there weren't female animals in which to implant them. It was sobering, standing up here and looking down at the ruination of what had been Jefferson's last remaining agricultural jewel.

Yalena lifted her gaze from the canyon floor, looking for the defenses her mother had mentioned. She couldn't see rebel gun positions on the surrounding mountainsides, although she knew they were there. She tried letting her eyes go unfocused, looking for movement, rather than trying to pick out details, and finally spotted two or three positions within half a kilometer of the dam. Those gunnery crews were good—very good—at staying hidden. She could learn a great deal from crews that good. If there was time . . .

"Well," she told herself, "there are a couple of crews I can talk to right now, without having to climb halfway up a mountain to reach them." She headed for the nearest gun emplacement atop the dam. There were three of them: one at each end and one slap in the middle, all of them bristling with battle-blackened gun snouts. The access door she'd come through was near the left-hand end of the dam, so she headed toward it.

Yalena wanted to ask the gunnery crews what skills and techniques served them best in a combat crisis. She'd listened to the off-world combat vets aboard the *Star of Mali* more than enough to know that seasoned troops could give her tips and techniques that no textbook and no drill instructor could ever match. She wanted to learn the tricks of her new trade and she wanted to put those tricks and techniques to good use in the field.

So she approached the battery at the end of the dam and swept her gaze across the massive weaponry guarding this portion of Dead-End Gorge. The battery consisted of five 30cm anti-aircraft guns, a dozen ranks of hypervelocity missile launchers, and a miniature forest of infinite repeaters, clustered in twenty separate pods. Each infinite repeater rested in its own rotational mount, creating a complex gun system that allowed every single barrel to swivel and track independently or could be configured to whirl them all in unison, to deliver massed, volley-style fire.

The centerpiece of the battery, planted squarely in the middle, was the 10cm mobile Hellbore. Its snout looked as wicked as Satan's backside and as full of death as the devil's heart. The last time she'd been this close to Hellbores, they'd been attached to a Bolo intent on crushing everything in its path. She held in a shiver and made herself cross the last couple of meters to reach the first of the guns. The men and women manning those guns watched her come, eyes shuttered. No one offered her a greeting.

There was just one thing to do. She lifted her chin, gave them a wan smile, and toughed it out. "The commodore asked me to come up and get familiar with the gun emplacements." The wind snatched her words and dashed them against the mountain slopes. Nobody answered. "I've never been this close to an artillery battery," she added, determined to see this through.

"You're from town." The shuttered stares were cold as ice. Colder. The speaker was a woman who looked like she'd crossed swords with Satan more than once. "You rat-gangers have a lot of nerve, coming out here and trying to join up. Your kind took POPPA's handouts for twenty years. You sang Vittori's praises to the skies. You only switched sides when you finally got hungry. *We've* been fighting to survive. *You've* been living on free handouts POPPA took from us at gunpoint. We don't need your kind out here. So just climb back into your skimmer and get the hell out of our canyon."

Yalena's face flamed, but she didn't back down. "I'm no rat-ganger," she said with an icy chill in her own voice. "I've never lived anywhere near Port Town. I'm a college student back from Vishnu. A whole group of us came home to fight. So did a shipload of combat veterans on *their* way home. Estevao Soteris taught me things not even my instructors on Vishnu knew about combat. But I've never seen a live artillery battery, before. So the commodore asked for my report on what the students are doing in town, then sent me up here."

Her uncle's name acted like a magic talisman. Suspicion

and hostility thawed. The woman actually quirked one corner of her mouth in a faint smile. "You couldn't ask for a better teacher, honey. What's your name, girl?"

"Lena, " she said, using an abbreviated version of her name. The last thing she wanted was for these battle-hardened warriors to figure out who she really was before she'd earned their trust. They were more than capable of "accidentally" nudging her over the railing and watching her fall the long, ghastly drop to the canyon floor.

"C'mere, then, Lena. I'll show you how to program a fire mission into a battle computer. My name's Rachel." She paused for a moment, then added, "My sister is married to General Ghamal."

Yalena's eyes widened. "You were part of the Hancock Co-op?"

Rachel's eyes went hard with memory. "Oh, yes. We were. The commodore risked his life, going into Nineveh Base to rescue us."

Little wonder she hated rat-gangers.

"My sister was pregnant when the P-Squads tried to finish what those filthy rat-gangers started, smashing their way into our family's cooperative. They tortured us for fun. If they'd known my sister was pregnant . . ." A hard shudder caught muscles rigid with memory. "But they didn't find out. And then the commodore attacked and got us out." Rachel pointed to the house Yalena had spotted earlier, at the mouth of Dead-End Gorge. "That's my grandfather's house. We're staying there, now, sleeping in shifts. And my sister's little boy is three, now," she added, with a softness in her voice that hadn't been there, a moment previously. "He was born in one of our base camps, northeast of here." She pointed back toward the desert side of the Damisi. "He came into this world free. That's how he's going to grow up. *Free.*"

"Yes," Yalena said softly. Tears burned her eyes.

Rachel studied her sharply for a moment, but she didn't ask what had prompted the tears. There were too many people, out here, who'd lost someone precious to them. The details—who had died, and how—didn't matter. It was the aching loss that bonded them together. Shared grief became shared hatred. And shared resolve.

"What about gas attacks?" Yalena asked. "Before we left Vishnu, Colonel Khrustinov told us POPPA's been stockpiling the ingredients to produce war agents. Biologicals and chemicides."

Rachel jabbed a thumb toward a bundle of gear behind the gun emplacements. "We've got suits. So do the other gun crews."

"And the civilians?"

Rachel shook her head. "Most of them would be helpless. Some of the farmhouses have 'safe' rooms, mostly in the cellars. My grandfather's house has one. Others have put safe rooms under the barns, in case they can't reach the house in time. We've had refugees digging shelters, too, trying to build more, but there isn't enough construction equipment to dig shelters for half a million people. Even if we could, we don't have enough filtration systems to protect them against air-dispersed war agents."

Yalena shivered. "If I were Vittori Santorini, that's exactly what I'd do. He's done it before, when he was coming to power. My mother got caught in one of those POPPA riots he used to stage. She was lucky enough to get upwind of the gas. She said POPPA blamed it on President Andrews, but she was certain it was Vittori's people, who did it."

"I remember that riot," one of the men growled. "One of these days, we're going to shove a cannister of that crap down Vittori's windpipe, open the stop-cock, and watch him drown in it."

Yalena's fingers twitched, wanting to do the shoving.

"C'mon, kid," Rachel said, "let me show you the ropes, while things are still quiet. Once they start shelling us again, there won't be time to do anything but shoot back."

She watched and listened closely as the soldiers showed her the ropes, taking her through the software interfaces of the battle computers that acquired incoming targets, made lightning decisions on which guns would best defeat the threat, and fired on autoresponse a hundred times faster than human reflexes.

"Why do we need live gunners?" Yalena asked. "The computers are better and faster than any human could be."

The Hellbore gunner, a hulking giant with skin as dark as carved basalt, answered in a voice full of gravel. "Because battle computers can go down. Because somebody has to man the loading belts. Not just on the 30cm guns, but the missile launchers, too." He pointed to a stockpile of artillery shells and missile racks behind them. "It takes two people to lift shells onto those belts fast enough to keep the guns firing steadily. We couldn't get autoloaders, so we do it the old-fashioned way." He patted the Hellbore's mobile gun-mount, a self-propelled platform nearly seven meters long, with eight drive wheels. "This baby operates with its own psychotronic target-acquisition and guidance system, but somebody's got to sit on the hot seat, ready to switch to manual if anything goes wrong. This is old equipment, almost as old as Vittori's Bolo."

Hatred put a cutting edge into his voice. "We've lost several Hellbores and their gunners to that Bolo. And we've had two battlefield equipment failures with Hellbore psychotronics in the past year. The first one went down in the middle of a running firefight. The driver wasn't trained as a backup artillery officer. He was killed, along with the Hellbore. The second one went down three months ago. The gunner switched to manual and killed the bastards shooting at her. The Hellbores up here," he patted his again and pointed to the other Hellbores atop the dam, "are the best and newest ones we've got. And every gunner on this dam is cross-trained on every weapons system up here. Any of us can step in and take over, if something goes wrong. Or if somebody's killed."

Yalena nodded. It was a good system. And they all knew the risks. She was deeply impressed and said so. "I spotted some of the other crews," she said, pointing in their general direction. "Are all the batteries like these?"

Rachel shook her head. "No. We don't have enough equipment for that. Klameth Canyon is a huge territory to defend, let alone the branch canyons and gorges. But we've laid down a fair coverage. Enough to knock down most of what they throw at us."

"How often do attacks come?"

"Every few hours. It's not predictable enough to set your watch by, but they get bored, with nothing to do out here but bitch about their officers and shoot at us. So they'll sit around for a while, then fire a volley or two, then it'll be quiet again." Rachel shrugged. "So there's no telling when to expect the next round. But it will come. That much, you can count on. Vittori doesn't dare back down. Hatred of us is the only thing keeping POPPA glued together, right now. If he walks away from this fight, he'll lose a lot of the loyalty he still commands, especially among the rank-and-file party members."

That made sense.

Twilight had begun to fall by the time Yalena's impromptu artillery lesson came to an end. She thanked her teachers for their time and trouble, then moved to the railing, peering down into the deep gorge, again. She could see someone hiking in from the house just outside the mouth of the gorge. A lone figure moved swiftly through the gun crews bivouacked along the edge of the Klameth River as it poured away from the deep basin at the base of the dam. Whoever it was, they were making very good time.

Within moments, they'd climbed into the lift installed by the rebellion's high command, which consisted of a broad platform raised and lowered by electric pulleys that ferried cargo and passengers to the upper reaches of the dam. Yalena moved closer to the pulley system, peering down over the edge. The drop was longer and dizzier than she'd first realized. Even so, the lift platform arrived with swift efficiency, depositing the sole passenger at the railing.

Yalena started forward, a greeting on her lips, and abruptly checked her stride. Dinny Ghamal, reflexes honed by four years of guerilla warfare, swung abruptly toward her. She saw him clamp down on the reflex to snatch his sidearm out of its holster. She forced herself to move forward and gave him a wan smile.

"I wouldn't much blame you, if you did."

When he didn't respond, she added in a low voice, "I was a repulsive little brat."

Dark eyes flickered and a dark, unreadable gaze swept across her. "Yes, you were." Then, reluctantly, "But you never turned in anybody to the P-Squads, the way some of your friends did."

She winced. "No." Coming from a man whose mother had been murdered by the P-Squads, who'd died in his arms, it was a concession that caused her eyes to sting. "Daddy—" she began, then had to swallow. "My father told me what happened. To your mother, I mean, when we were on the ship coming back from Vishnu. I never knew your mother and that was my own stupid fault. I didn't know, back then, that I wouldn't exist, without her. Or you. I didn't know you'd both saved my mother's life. There's no way I can ever repay that debt. But at least now I know I owe it. And I'll try my best to repay at least some of it."

A muscle jumped in his jaw. He tore his gaze away, stared down into Klameth Canyon, which twisted away at their feet, a deep, twilight slash through the rose-pink stone. Yalena could see camp fires, now, at the refugee camp, where weary people with bruised souls were gathering around the cookfires to share what little was available to eat, sharing it with loved ones and new-found friends. Comrades in peril . . .

Despite the fear, the threat of destruction by people who hated mindlessly, the refugees in that camp were stronger, braver, and far better men and women than any fool who'd ever dreamed up or chanted a POPPA slogan.

They could be driven out of their homes. They could be tortured and killed. But they could not be broken or demeaned into less than what they were.

Vittori Santorini had nothing like it.

And never would.

"What are you thinking?" Dinny asked softly.

She tried to tell him, but it came out all garbled, making no sense. Not to her, at least. But when she looked up, meeting his gaze, she found him staring at her as though staring at a total stranger.

"I never realized . . ." he said softly.

"What?"

"How much you're like your mother."

The tears did come, then. "I'm sorry, Dinny," she whispered. She couldn't say the things trembling and tumbling through her heart, because there weren't words big enough or strong enough or deep enough to say them. He didn't speak again. Neither did she. There wasn't any need. When she'd wiped her eyes dry with the backs of her hands, she moved to stand beside him, gratified when he stepped not away, but aside, allowing her to join him. They stood, shoulder to shoulder, in the place of honor, the lookout's place, guarding all that was good on this world.

For these few moments, at least, there was a strange peacefulness in Yalena's heart. She understood, for the first time, why soldiers through the centuries had sung of the brotherhood that knew no bounds, neither race nor gender nor age, requiring only that its members had faced death together. They were still standing there, still silent, when the shelling began again. Gouts of flame twinkled like fireflies in the distance, where artillery shells were bursting far down the main canyon.

"Get inside," Dinny said roughly.

She didn't want to turn tail and run, meekly, without scoring a single return blow, but there really wasn't much she could do, up here. So she turned to go—

And the world erupted into flame.

Every gun atop the dam thundered in unison. Dinny

slammed Yalena to the concrete as something came whistling across the top of the dam. A massive explosion in the reservoir behind them sent water skyward in a geyser that drenched them to the skin. The guns snarled again. Yalena twisted her neck, trying to see what was happening. She stiffened in terror. The air was black with incoming artillery shells. The infinite repeaters blazed, shooting them down. Explosions rained debris into the gorge. Hyper-v missiles streaked past with a whine and a scream of hypersonics. More explosions scattered flame and smoke and shrapnel into the gorge. Some of it struck the dam or bounced across the top, narrowly missing them time and again. Gun crews higher on the slopes were firing back, as well, sending gouts and streaks of flame racing across the gorge. The air shook with the thunder of titanic explosions.

"Get inside!" Dinny shouted.

Yalena nodded, crawled to hands and knees, tried to find the access door through the smoke. She couldn't see it—

Something tore through the infinite repeaters. A fireball blew her flat. Heat seared her for just an instant, setting every nerve in her skin to screaming. Sound crushed her against the concrete, a solid wall of over-pressured air. When she could see again, half the infinite repeaters were gone, blown to pieces or maybe melted . . . The missile launchers were intact, but there was no sign of the loading crew. The Hellbore gunner, a dark, grim figure through the smoke and crushing sound of battle, was visible inside the Hellbore's command and control cabin, hunched over his boards, waiting for something big enough to shoot at.

Yalena twisted around to look into the gorge and realized the skies were still black with incoming rounds. She didn't hesitate. She just scrambled toward the silent missile launchers and started hauling missiles out of the racks and onto the loading belts. Dinny was right behind her, lifting and loading. More rounds came whistling past them, missing their position by scant millimeters, at times, and detonated behind them, sending up more geysers of water. They weren't trying to take out the dam, they were trying to kill the guns—and their crews. Rage gave Yalena the strength to keep heaving missiles into the launch tubes. Their own missiles were screaming out into the skies above the gorge, exploding against incoming warheads, taking down the most dangerous targets identified by the battle computers.

When the shelling finally stopped, Yalena couldn't quite believe it was silence that was ringing in her ears. She stood panting, drenched with sweat and trembling all over. She drew some comfort from the fact that General Ghamal was in no better shape than she was. He, too, stood gasping for breath.

"Goddamned bastards hit us *hard,* that time," he finally got out.

Rachel appeared through the smoke, limping toward them. "Good job, kid," she told Yalena.

"Damned fine job," Dinny added, wiping sweat with one sleeve.

Yalena started to cry. She couldn't control it. Couldn't explain it. Rachel, at least, seemed to understand. She wrapped one arm around Yalena's trembling shoulders and just held onto her for a long, comforting moment. Dinny touched her wet cheek, gently. "Don't you be ashamed of those tears, girl. They prove you've got a heart in the right place. Your mama will be proud."

Yalena gulped, trying to get her emotions under control. She looked toward the gap that led from Dead-End Gorge out into the main canyon, trying to gauge how badly they'd been hit. The refugee camp had been devastated. At least half the tents were ablaze. People were still running, trying to reach the edges of the canyon, away from the open floor. Hundreds of people—maybe a thousand or more—lay unmoving in the center of the burning camp. She didn't realize, at first, what she was seeing, as the people still running started to fall for no apparent reason. Then she stiffened.

"Something's wrong!" she cried, pointing urgently. "There aren't any explosions, but people are falling down—"

Dinny swore, savagely. Rachel and the other surviving gunners dove toward their equipment packs. More than half of those packs had been blown off the dam during the fighting. There weren't enough left to go around. Dinny grabbed her wrist and hauled her toward the access door while shouting a warning into his wrist-comm. *"They're using gas! Sound the alarm! Get into biohazard gear!"*

Fear shoved an icepick through Yalena's chest. It lodged in her heart.

"Mother!" She clawed at her own wrist-comm, realized she didn't know the command frequency. A siren began to scream, sounding the alarm in a weird, hooting pattern that shook the air. They jumped over scattered equipment and debris, tripping and stumbling forward. They reached the access door just as another artillery barrage struck. Explosions turned the air to flame and thunder again. Somebody opened the door ahead of them. Dinny picked Yalena up and literally threw her inside. The world cartwheeled as she sprawled through the air. She saw Dinny go down as she tumbled head over heels through the doorway. She landed in an awkward forward roll and skidded across the concrete floor into the wall just as the door slammed shut.

Dinny was still outside.

"Dinny!" The scream tore her throat.

Someone grabbed her, stuffed her into a suit, jammed a helmet onto her head and zipped her up tight. When she focused her gaze, she found two people crouched over her. Phil Fabrizio she recognized through the faceplate of his biocontainment gear. Even his nano-tatt was ice white. Under the other faceplate was the blank stare of a command-grade battle helmet. Commodore Oroton's deep voice said, "General Ghamal didn't make it, child."

She started to cry again, which was a serious mistake, because there wasn't any way to dry her eyes or blow her nose inside a biosuit's helmet. It wasn't fair! He'd survived so much! Was so critical to the rebellion's success. And he'd died for the worst, stupidest reason possible: saving *her*. She wasn't worth it! Not even ten of her would've been worth it . . . Grief died in her throat. A cold, hard rage ignited in its place, rising up from her heart to shoot like molten flame through every molecule. It turned her resolve into fire-hardened diamond.

She was going to kill them.

All of them.

Starting with Vittori the damned.

II

Simon had never been to this part of Madison, before. The neighborhood was seedy, full of refuse and wind-blown drifts of children, thin and hungry-looking, with suspicion and despair in their dull eyes. They weren't playing games or even chattering in the way of ordinary children. They just sat on the dirty curbs with poorly shod or bare feet, kicking at trash in the gutters, or they hugged the concrete steps that led from cracked sidewalks up to the sagging doorways of tenements.

Each time Simon and his guide passed one of those open doorways, the air that drifted down the steps to the sidewalk stank of open sewage and uncollected garbage and the smell of cooking that left him swallowing against nausea. He didn't know what they were cooking, to produce a smell like that, but it was pitifully obvious that there wasn't much nourishment in it.

Simon had seen port-side slums, had witnessed the aftermath of war on shattered worlds where residents with bruised eyes had climbed, aching in their very souls, back to their feet to try starting over. But these children and the ghastly world in which they lived left

him stiff-jointed with rage. Jefferson's slide into collapse
had become an avalanche, one that had torn down the
standard of living from galactic normal to desperate in
the blink of a cosmic eyelash.

As the last of the late afternoon light faded toward
dusk, lights flickered to life in the tenements, but the
street lights remained dark. Their glass globes had long
since been broken out by vandals with nothing better
to do than hurl stones at something that wouldn't be
likely to shoot back. Men without jobs moved in aimless
eddies, like flotsam on the backwater of some stagnant,
slow-moving river. A few, driven by currents of anger and
hatred, dared the wrath of the P-Squads by gathering
on street corners. They stood there, defiantly, to share
bitter complaints and talk treason they weren't entirely
sure how to carry out.

That was Simon's job. He was here to teach them.

He'd spent the past week doing exactly that. Tonight's
meeting wasn't the beginning of the process, it was the
beginning of the end. Of a lot of things. Simon's guide
was a smallish woman in the earlier years of middle age.
Maria was her name, the only name she'd given him.
She had that bowed-down, exhausted look that was a
hallmark of grinding poverty and hopelessness. Maria had
barely spoken to him since their cautious meeting at the
prearranged spot where the urban guerillas had agreed
to rendezvous with him. Whoever she was, Maria was
as thin as the ragged children and moved like a woman
fifty years older than her probable true age.

As they passed the angry men on the street corners,
men who stared at him—a stranger in their midst—with
dagger-sharp hatred, Maria nodded a silent greeting to
them. That gesture, made again and again, defused what
might've swiftly resulted in a lethal confrontation. *He's
with me, I vouch for him,* that gesture meant, making
it clear that the stranger who'd thrust himself into their
ugly little corner of a once-beautiful world had, in fact,
been invited. Simon had no doubt at all that he would've
been waylaid, murdered without a moment's pity, and

stripped like a dead chicken if he'd dared walk in here alone. He knew, as well, that nobody would've bothered to stop them. Not even the P-Squads would patrol these particular streets, not unless they traveled in packs of at least six officers armed like *jaglitch* hunters.

They passed bars that exuded alcoholic fumes, their grimy interiors artificially bright with the grating laughter that comes from bitter, hopeless people whose sole outlet is to get drunk. They stepped across several of the drunkest, who'd crawled out of the bar and collapsed on the street. After walking for nearly half an hour, they rounded a corner and interrupted a business transaction between a teenage girl whose breasts were the only plump part of her and a man who looked like a bundle of sticks wrapped in a loose sack.

Maria broke stride, staring hard at the girl. Whoever she was, she flushed crimson. Then she stammered out something unintelligible and fled through the rapidly gathering shadows of dusk. The man she'd been bargaining with sent a screeching curse after her. He swung abruptly toward Maria.

"Y'damned bitch! I'd already give 'er the money!"

"That's your own fault, you fool! You give a whore money *after* she's done what you hired 'er for. Now get your filthy bones off my street an' don't come back. I swear t' God and all the devils in hell, I'll break your skinny neck, if I see you back in these parts."

For a long, dangerous moment, Simon braced himself to prevent a murder. He shifted his weight, ready to move, but the other man darted a swift glance at Simon and let the moment—and his money—pass away without further protest. He sidled into a noxious alleyway, cursing under his breath. Simon flexed his fingers, shaking the tension loose. Maria tilted her head slightly, casting a glance upward from beneath hooded eyes.

"He'd a' killed you."

"He could've tried."

She studied him for a moment. "You might be right, at that. C'mon, we're nearly there."

She led him further down the street, in the direction the girl had fled, then opened a door sandwiched in between a boarded-up storefront that had once sold groceries and what looked like a combination self-service laundrey and betting parlor, judging by the number of frowsy, bitter-faced women playing cards and the even greater number of men rolling dice while the machines jigged and bumped and rattled their syncopated rhythm, cleaning what few clothes these people owned.

The door Maria opened led to a stairway barely wide enough for one person to climb. The first landing gave onto a corridor with only one door, presumably leading into a storage room above the laundry. Maria climbed to the second floor, where a line of apartment doors stretched away down the corridor, their faded paint bearing the numerals assigned to each cramped residence. Maria led the way to the third from the end. They stepped inside—and found the girl they had interrupted on the street below.

She flushed crimson again.

"Get supper started," Maria said in a cold, angry voice.

"Yes'm," the girl whispered, rolling her eyes at Simon before she fled into an adjoining room.

Simon didn't know what to say. Maria shut her eyes for a moment, but not before Simon caught a glimpse of the tears in them. When she opened her eyes, again, she met Simon's distressed gaze. "She's not a wicked girl."

"No."

"Just . . . desperate."

"Yes."

"It's why I told that creep . . ." She halted.

"Yes," Simon said again. "I know. I have a daughter. Just a couple of years older than yours."

She slanted a look up at him, a look at once shuttered and painfully clear. Then a sigh tore loose. "That's different, then, innit?" She didn't say anything else, but Simon understood. Her lips vanished in a bitter, white-clenched line that slashed across the weariness and the pain on her face. Then she spoke again, voice brusque. "They'll be here in a bit. We got nuthin' fancier to offer than water, if you're thirsty?"

"Water's fine, thank you."

She nodded. "Find a chair, then. I still got one or two. I'll be back."

Simon studied the tiny living room, with its government-supplied viewscreen and a few cheap pictures on the wall. The pictures were religious. The viewscreen was a standard model of the type issued by the POPPA propaganda machine, with its vested interest in reaching the masses. The furniture was cheap, much-mended, and mismatched, but the whole place was neat and fresh-scrubbed, in contrast with other tenements they'd passed. Unlike her neighbors, Maria had not given up hope.

Simon discovered a profound respect for the woman. She must have been holding herself and her family together with little more than determination, for a long time, now. The knowledge that her little girl was selling herself on the streets must've been a blow that struck to the heart, made worse for having been witnessed by a stranger here to help. She returned from the kitchen, where that selfsame daughter was busy rustling through cabinets and banging pots and implements around, in a subdued and careful fashion that suggested she was trying to tiptoe around her mother's temper.

"Got no ice," Maria said, holding out the glass, "but there's a jug in the icebox that's cold and plenty more from the tap."

Simon nodded his thanks and sipped. The pause between them was awkward, but it didn't last long, because someone tapped at the door, in a definite pattern that was clearly a code. Maria slanted another glance in his direction. Simon stepped back, so that he was behind the door when she opened it.

"Come in," she said in a whisper, "an' be quick about it!"

An instant later a gasp broke from her. Simon caught a glimpse of her face as the door swung shut. She was staring, ash-pale, at one of the men who'd just stepped into the room, swinging the door quickly shut behind them.

"You're alive!" The whisper held a shocked, knife-edge throb, part pain, part unbearable joy.

The boy she was staring at said, "Yeah. So's . . . so's Uncle Phil. We couldn't tell you . . ."

Her mouth began to shake. The boy just opened his arms. She flung herself forward and engulfed him in a death-hold embrace. Tears streamed unheeded down her face. Maria's daughter came in from the kitchen, carrying a tray with a plate on which she'd stacked a few crackers and some cubes of cheese. She looked up and saw the boy her mother was hugging so tightly. The tray fell from nerveless fingers. The plate shattered on the bare floorboards. An agonized moan broke from her, then she, too, hurled herself forward, threw both arms around the bits of him she could reach, and started to cry in jagged sobs. His resemblance to Maria and her daughter was obvious enough to name the kinship without hesitation. The prodigal son had come home. Evidently from the dead. Given his emaciated condition, he'd probably been rescued from one of the death camps.

There were two other men with the boy. Simon hadn't met them. When the worst of the emotional storm had passed, one of them said, "Listen, we got work t'do, see? There's a helluva lot goin' on, tonight, and we got things to take care of, so how's about we grab a bite of whatever's on the stove and get to it?"

Maria pulled herself together, bestowed a smile on her son, even managed to smile at her daughter, cupping one hand to wipe tears from the girl's ravaged face, then said gently, "Let's clean up, eh?"

The girl nodded.

They weren't talking about tear-streaked faces or shattered plates.

Five minutes later, they sat down at Maria's kitchen table. They made short work of the meal, such as it was, and settled in the living room to map out their strategy. They'd barely begun when Simon's wrist-comm lit up, screaming with an emergency code. He slapped it. "Report!"

"We're under attack!" The terror in that familiar, beloved voice wrenched at Simon's heart. "They're using biologicals or chemicals, I don't know which! I've ordered everyone into the shelters, but there aren't enough. Oh, God, we're dying by the thousands, out here . . ."

His wrist-comm screamed again, on a different emergency frequency. The second voice shouted, "The government's ordered us out of the Bolo's maintenance depot, at gunpoint. They're loading him onto the heavy-lift platform . . ."

The datascreen in Maria's living room clanged to life, sounding an alarm that meant a government broadcast was about to begin, important enough that every citizen of Jefferson had better drop whatever they were doing and pay attention. The screen lit up with a view of the Presidential Palace's private broadcast studio. Vittori Santorini was standing at the podium. The wall behind him blazed with the green and gold peace banners of the POPPA party.

"Beloved friends," he said, "we have gathered here this evening to share with you our final triumph over the criminals running the Granger rebellion. We have known fear, my friends, unending fear and far too much death. But tonight there is blessed hope on our horizon, hope and a promise—my personal pledge—that after tonight, the good and loyal people of Jefferson need never fear the hand of oppression again.

"Even now, our courageous Bolo is back in the field. He will smite the unholy. Crush the wicked underfoot. Jefferson will be safe forever. Safe from the menace of Granger hatred. Safe from the threat of bombs and bullets. Safe from the destruction those monsters have visited on us for so many years . . ."

Simon had stopped listening. "Oh, dear, God," he whispered.

Maria's son had gone deathly pale. "Th' stinkin' bastards!"

Simon touched his wrist-comm again. "Red Dog, are you there?"

"Yes," Kafari's voice came back, muffled and strange through the voice-altering technology she'd used for four years, now. "I'm here."

"They're sending the Bolo out. It's heading your way on the lifter. How many people can you get out?"

"I don't know. Not many. They fired conventional artillery and biochemicals into the canyon, simultaneously. Most of my people are dead. Or they're cut off from escape, wearing biohazard gear and can't risk hiking out through rough country and ripping their suits on the rocks. Dinny's gone." Her voice wavered. "He died saving our little girl."

Simon's eyes stung. He closed his fingers around the edge of the table, unable to speak. Gratitude and grief choked him into silence.

Kafari went on, horror seeping through despite the techno-altered voice. "Some of us had biocontainment gear. Not nearly enough. I have no idea how many survivors I've got. There are two with me," she added, voice hoarse. "We sounded the sirens, but I don't know how many had time to reach shelter. Some of the farmers and ranchers probably made it. Our surveillance cameras are picking up images of the dead . . ." Her voice broke on a sob. "Oh, Simon, so many . . . They're already hitting us again. With conventional artillery. God knows how long the shelling will last, this time."

Kafari's whole family—and Simon's—lived in that canyon. The sickness in his heart twisted, lanced like jagged lightning through every nerve. His hands ached from wanting to close his fists around Vittori Santorini's throat. The silence in Maria's living room was the silence of wounded men and women just before the scream bursts loose, still too stunned by the shock of the mortal blow to give sound to the agony. Their careful plans had crashed to the floor in pieces, like the plate Maria's daughter had shattered just minutes ago.

Kafari added with bitter exhaustion in her voice, "We

don't have many gunners left. The P-Squads can waltz in here any time they want, unopposed."

"They won't need to," Simon bit out. "They've got *Sonny*. Even blind as a bat, he's more than enough to take out any survivors. If I know Vittori Santorini, he'll order Sonny to blow every damned farmhouse in the whole maze to hell, just to be sure he got them all." Simon realized in that moment what he had to do. The pain of it stabbed like a hot knife. He should have used the damned destruct code the moment he'd arrived. Vittori might still have destroyed Klameth Canyon. But without the Bolo to back up his regime, would he have dared?

Simon had betrayed half a million people to their deaths.

The agony of Etaine hurt less than the knowledge that *he* had killed those people by failing to act, just as surely as Vittori Santorini had, when POPPA's founder had given the order to fire those biochemical warheads. On the datascreen, Vittori was telling the whole world about his sainted plans for a Granger-free universe. Face alight with an unholy ecstasy, he spoke joyously about the refugees trapped in Klameth Canyon, the "enemies of the people" who lay dead in the gathering darkness under Jefferson's rising moons.

Simon couldn't help those already murdered. But he could by God save others. He had spent half his life as Sonny's commander and still thought of the machine as a friend. But now, in the moment when lives hung in the balance—the survivors in Klameth Canyon's maze, hundreds of thousands of Grangers scattered throughout other fortified canyons in the Damisi Mountains, millions of urban dissidents in the cities—he found that which he had dreaded for so long was remarkably easy to put into practice.

He switched frequencies and transmitted the code he had carried in memory from the day he had been assigned as Sonny's commander. The code that would wipe Sonny's Action/Command core and kill him. He closed his eyes for a moment, mourning a friend and hating the men who had turned a protector into a mailed fist enabling mass murderers to stay in power. Nobody spoke, which was a mercy. He finally switched back to the original frequency. "Are you there?" he asked in a strangled voice.

"Yes. We can see the Bolo, now. His lander's just touched down at Maze Gap. Sonny's off-loading, heading through the Gap. The federal troops have pulled back—"

"*What?*" Horror congealed in the basement of Simon's soul. "He's *moving*? On his own?"

"Yes. He's passing through the Gap, now, turning into the main canyon. He's coming to the dam."

Maria, her face white and scared, swam into his awareness when she clutched his arm, asking, "What's wrong?"

Simon met her gaze. He didn't recognize his own voice. "They've changed the destruct codes. I can't kill the Bolo."

"You can't kill the Bolo? Destruct codes?" Maria was staring at him. "What do you mean by that? Who the hell *are* you, anyway?"

Simon met her gaze, still feeling numb from the shock. "Simon Khrustinov," he said hoarsely. "I'm Simon Khrustinov. The Bolo's last commander."

Maria's daughter, busy cleaning the table, dropped and shattered another plate.

"You don't look like—" Maria broke off mid-sentence. Her eyes, already wide, went suddenly wet as she stared at his face. The face even he wasn't used to, yet, after four years of staring in the mirror at it. "The crash," she whispered. She didn't seem to realize that she was crying. "I forgot about the crash. Your face got smashed up in the aircar crash, didn't it?"

He just nodded.

"You can't kill it? Really can't kill it?"

He shook his head.

"Oh, God . . ."

There did not seem to be a whole hell of a lot else

to say. Not to the people who'd gathered in this room, trying to help him end the threat that had just claimed half a million lives. He spoke to Kafari, again. "Red Dog, can you evacuate?"

"No. There aren't any aircars left. They hit our landing field, blew it to ashes. The forest fire's still raging, out there. And we'd rip our suits open trying to hike out across the Damisi. We're trapped right where we are."

In a box canyon with a Bolo Mark XX on its way to blow them to hell. Simon had never felt more helpless. At least on Etaine, he and Sonny had been fighting on the same side . . .

"They've changed the code," he said in a voice he did not recognize.

Kafari didn't have to ask which one. "Understood," she said. Then she added two more words that broke his heart and put steel into his resolve. "Avenge us."

"Oh, yes," he whispered. "On the graves of Etaine's murdered millions, I swear that, my love. Kiss Yalena for me."

"I love you," the voice of his soul-mate whispered.

Then the connection went silent. When Simon dragged his attention back to the little room where Vittori flickered silently on the viewscreen and the urban guerillas stood staring at him, Maria whispered, "That was Commodore Oroton." It wasn't really a question. "The commodore's your wife, isn't he?"

The mixed-up genders were irrelevant.

Simon just nodded.

"Kafari isn't dead?"

He shook his head. "Not . . . yet."

Ragged emotions tore across her face, like lightning snarling through a black thundercloud—or the smoke of battle. "Kafari Khrustinova saved the best man this ball a' mud ever produced. And that piece of dogshit," she jabbed a finger at the viewscreen, silent because someone had killed the sound, "just ordered her death, didn't he?"

Simon nodded again.

The look in Maria's eyes scared him. "We got work to do," she said. Her eyes tracked toward the viewscreen, where Vittori stood gloating.

"Oh, yes," Simon said softly, "we certainly do." He met and held the gaze of every person in the room, silently taking their measure and liking what he saw. The eerie sense of *deja vu* that crept across him left Simon with crawling chills along his nerves. Once, long ago, Simon had sat in conference with a group of this world's people, preparing to fight a different war of survival. Memory of looking at each of them, measuring them against the coming conflict, and liking what he saw brought an ache to his heart that caught him totally off-guard. The people of this world deserved something better than Vittori Santorini and the butchers he had used to consolidate his power.

The ache in his heart turned to flintsteel.

The Deng, alien and incomprehensible, were at least an enemy a man could respect. Vittori Santorini and *his* army . . . "All right," he said, "we're through planning for this little war. Here's what we're going to *do . . .*"

III

I have been ordered into combat. The dismay that spreads through my entire neural network is so keen, I experience a psychotronic stutter. I need to convey an entire list of urgent reasons explaining why this order is seriously flawed. My cognitive focus, however, scatters itself into a thousand separate threads of thought: reasons, arguments, and warnings that need to be presented. I am literally unable to think of a single, cogent argument that would persuade Vittori Santorini to wait until I have been fully repaired. He is not willing to wait—not even another hour. My treads have been repaired and my guns are operational. That is all that matters to President Santorini.

My duty is clear, even if nothing else is: I will carry out the president's orders to the best of my limited and failing ability. I am a flawed tool crawling blindly into a suicidal mission against an enemy that has demonstrated its tenacity in trying to destroy me. But I will continue as long as there is power in my electronic synapses. It is my duty to destroy the Eenemy or be destroyed by it. Their mission and mine are the same. We differ only in capability.

I cannot see my Enemy.

They can see my thirteen-thousand-ton warhull distressingly well.

I direct my heavy lifter to carry me across the Adero floodplain, toward Maze Gap. There is no movement anywhere on the floodplain. No air traffic. No ground traffic. Just empty fields to either side of the Adero River and the road that parallels it.

My destination lies fifty kilometers ahead. The Damisi Mountains are a nightmarish place to do battle. The Deng did not have time to prepare fortified emplacements, when they seized Klameth Canyon. They barely had time to offload their ships before I was among them, wreaking havoc. The commodore's guerillas have been digging in and hunkering down for an entire week. I am not anxious to experience the logical result of that advance preparation.

I progress slowly. The heavy lifter carrying me is capable of reaching orbital velocity, but the main thrusters point down, rather than laterally, and this configuration cannot be changed. This is an old lifter—far older than I am—without the variable-mount thrusters of modern lifters. Horizontal cross-country speeds, therefore, are a minuscule fraction of vertical speed. I am restricted to a paltry hundred kilometers an hour, which means I face a thirty-minute transit just to reach the battlefield.

I have been airborne only four minutes, thirteen seconds when Vittori Santorini interrupts programming on all military and civilian communications frequencies for an unscheduled broadcast. He stands at the podium

*in the Presidential Palace's own news studio, a bunker
of a room under the palace, which is the only place
Vittori Santorini will consent to give a televised press
conference or interview. Notoriety has its price. Vittori
has good reason for his paranoia.*

*His speech begins softly. They usually do. It's where
they end that matters, since they almost inevitably provoke destructive violence. I am exceedingly suspicious of
President Santorini's motives, but the serious nature of
this broadcast is unmistakable, underscored by the furrows of stress and harsh weariness in his face.*

*It is odd, to be able to "see" Vittori's broadcast clearly.
The visual images are transmitted directly to my data
processors. I cannot see through my own sensors at all.
The sensation is disorienting, but it is a surprising relief
to "see" something besides blobs of IR color without
definition or detail.*

*I pay abrupt attention to Vittori Santorini's speech
when he mentions me.*

"Even now," Vittori says, "our courageous Bolo is back
in the field. He will smite the unholy. Crush the wicked
underfoot. Jefferson will be safe forever. Safe from the
menace of Granger hatred. Safe from the destruction those
criminals have visited on us for so many years. I pledge
to you here and now, this war will end now. Tonight.
The time for mercy to our common enemy is long past.
Our patience is at an end. We must act decisively, now,
this very night.

"And that, my dearest friends, is what we have done,
what we are doing, even as we speak. Thirty-two minutes
ago, we launched an attack to wipe out the vast bulk of
the rebel army. Our Bolo will launch other attacks. He
will fight for our survival. He will strike every terrorist
camp, every refuge where these evil criminals seek to
hide from justice. He will attack them tonight, tomorrow,
every day without letup, for as long as it takes to destroy
each and every filthy terrorist on our lovely world. We
will no longer tolerate *any* threat!

"But it is not enough to hunt them down. Not enough

to poison the land that feeds them. They have spread their filthy cult across the stars. We cannot look up at night, without seeing other innocent worlds they have blighted. We cannot enjoy the beauty of a clear summer night without remembering the evil they have wrought.

"We must track them down and destroy them *everywhere they have gone!* They have fled to Mali and Vishnu. Any off-world government that dares to harbor these mad criminals will be treated as contemptible enemies. We will destroy anyone and everyone opposing our mandate to rid human space of this scourge. They have fled to Mali, to Vishnu. We will track them with our Bolo! We will follow them to Mali and blow them out of the domes, out into Mali's methane hell. We will track them to Vishnu. We will hunt down their protectors in the Ngara system's government. It is our sacred duty! We will not fail!"

He leans forward, mouth nearly touching the microphone, and lets go a sibilant hiss, like a maddened cobra: "We will have revenge!"

The knife-edged snarl reverberates across the airways and through the datachats into every home and office on Jefferson. The entire assembly in the Joint Chamber gasps. Vittori digs into the podium with fingers like claws, biting the wood in a frenzy. "Yes, *revenge*, my friends! *That* is what this wild and violent night will bring us! We will take revenge for our murdered innocents. We will take revenge for the slaughter of our brave police officers. For our judges, our elected officials, our murdered teachers and professors. These terrorists owe a debt of blood so high, the cost cannot even be reckoned. But the bill has come due, my friends. The bill has come due and it is high time they paid it!"

The president's expression is exalted. His eyes blaze. He flings both arms wide and shouts, "Blood demands blood! We will spill theirs until there is no blood left! This one last push will end the menace of Grangerism on our world. We will rip it out by the roots. We will chop off its head and destroy the entire command structure. Grangerism dies *tonight*! And when that threat is gone, the world will be safe to implement the last of our beautiful reforms. We have worked and waited for this moment, this chance, for twenty years. The chance, the moment is *now*.

"There will finally be peace and prosperity for all. Everyone will do good work and no one will ever suffer from wants or shortages. Oh, the lovely world we will build! The envy of every star system humanity has ever colonized. Our names will be remembered for a thousand years, as the people who built paradise out of a war-torn wreck..."

I had not realized until this moment that Vittori Santorini is a radical utopian. He really believes it is possible to make the world "perfect." Men like Sar Gremian sign on for the power and prestige membership will bring them. Others join for purely monetary reasons. But Vittori really believes the web of lies and intractable, unworkable utopian fallacies that pass for laws and civic policies on this world.

Commercial broadcast stations, preempted by the speech, have begun to air split-screen footage, showing Vittori's broadcast studio in the Presidential Palace and the Joint Chamber between Jefferson's Senate and House of Law. An estimated half of Jefferson's senators and assemblymen have gathered in the Joint Chamber to listen to Vittori's speech.

"This is the task we face, my friends. These are the challenges. There is only one way to begin. Only one sure way to guarantee that we will have the peace and prosperity necessary to begin our sacred task..."

Vittori is still speaking when I receive a communique from Sar Gremian.

"Bolo."

The familiar grating voice jolts me back into full awareness of my surroundings.

"Unit SOL-0045, reporting."

"Aren't you there, yet?"

"ETA twelve minutes, eleven seconds."

"Speed the hell up, willya?" *I detect stress in Sar Gremian's voice.*

"I am cruising at maximum horizontal thrust."

"Why don't you turn it up on its side and use the main thrusters? You could get there in seconds."

"The cleats mating my warhull to this lifting platform will not hold thirteen thousand tons of flintsteel and munitions in that attitude. They are designed keep me from shifting during vertical combat drops and recalls, not to weld me to the platform."

"Well, dammit, get there as fast as you can! We've got trouble heating up and I've got to forestall it—fast. The best way to do that is to destroy the beast at the head. That's your job. My job is to make sure the decapitated snake doesn't turn around and crush us to death."

I detect strain in his voice. I do not know what has put it there. I suspect a connection between Sar Gremian's foul mood and the actions of Madison's urban guerilla fighters, but I have no way of verifying that and Jefferson's Supreme Commandant of Internal Security signs off without enlightening me. He is clearly unsatisfied, but there is nothing I can do to alter the laws of physics. I am only a Bolo. I leave miracles to my creators—and the gods they worship.

The bright sunshine of afternoon is already fading into twilight by the time I am halfway across the Adero floodplain. The Damisi mountain slopes are a confusing jumble that my IR sensors cannot adequately translate. Ghostly patches of heat and puddles of cooler shadow distort the rocky walls of a refuge that has sheltered a rebel army for four years, creating a hodgepodge vista too confusing to be of any practical use. I pull visuals from my experience databanks, trying to compare the IR ghosts I see now with the terrain features I recorded during the battle to liberate Klameth Canyon from the Deng. This helps. It is not as reliable as being able to see real-time images in all spectra, but it helps.

Flashes of light, flaring and streaking skyward from the vicinity of Maze Gap, indicate a major artillery barrage underway, one which has evidently been raging for several minutes. I gain altitude, trying to focus my failing visual sensors on the distant battlefield. Long, crawling lines of light on the ground reveal themselves as brushfires burning on the Adero floodplain, where vegetation has caught fire from exploding munitions. Federal batteries fire through the Gap, trying to hit gun emplacements.

The tactic is suicidal. Literally. Rebel gunners, sheltered by the high cliffs on either side of the gap, return direct fire with deadly, pin-point accuracy. Federal troops, fighting from hastily dug positions on the open floodplain, suffer terrific damage under blistering rebel fire. Explosions in the federal camp mark the spectacular demise of siege guns and their crews. I count six major batteries firing on the Gap, alone, with another eight batteries pumping out volley after volley from long-range mortars. The shells rise in spectacular, high parabolas. Federal gunners are literally shooting over the mountain peaks, dropping a deadly rain of live munitions into Klameth Canyon.

It takes only seconds to assimilate what is happening at the Gap. The thing that rivets my attention, however, is not the barrage itself. It is the confusing blur of motion inside and around the sprawling federal encampment. Hotspots flare brightly against the cooler, darker ambient background. My first impression proves itself inaccurate within seconds. Rebel gunners have not dropped a cluster bomb or even something as simple as napalm, setting the camp ablaze.

The hotspots are not fires. They are moving, rushing, in fact, at a high rate of speed. They are engine emissions from military vehicles headed away from the Gap. The ones farthest from it are moving the fastest, suggesting longer travel time, during which they have built up highway speed. What I see is so unexpected, it takes an astonishing seven point three-nine seconds to believe the evidence of my failing sensors.

The troops at Maze Gap are falling back. Retreating from the battlefield. Running away so rapidly, the exodus has all the hallmarks of a panic-stricken retreat. I expect to see a corresponding movement of Granger troops in the Gap, rushing forward in hot pursuit. But this pursuit does not materialize. The only movement visible anywhere in Maze Gap is the supersonic streak of artillery shells. Federal gun crews continue to fire aggressively, laying down a blistering barrage while the bulk of the troops evacuate. Neither the retreat nor the barrage make sense. I am on the way to break the blockade. Why would the federal gun crews risk the withering return fire of rebel gunners, when they could simply wait half an hour and turn the job over to me?

The retreat makes even less sense. Once I arrive, my guns will guarantee iron-clad safety for the troops camped on the Adero floodplain. Not only will I shoot down any rounds fired at them by rebel gunners, I will destroy the gunners and their weapons, permanently eliminating the threat they represent. Despite my best efforts, I cannot cobble together a rational explanation for a sudden, all-encompassing retreat of federal troops who are literally on the edge of total victory.

I attempt to contact Sar Gremian to request an updated VSR, but am unable to raise him. The situation is sufficiently disquieting to nudge me from Alert Standby status to Battle Reflex Alert, ready to fire at an instant's notice, even though I am not yet close enough to the combat zone to trip the automatic reflex alert of an actual firefight. I continue to request VSR and continue to be met with nothing but silence. Federal troops continue to fall back, retreating a full ten kilometers from Maze Gap. The only federals remaining in the siege camp are the gun crews working the artillery batteries. The steady barrage has given way to a new pattern. Gun crews fire in short bursts, concentrating two-thirds of their fire on the far end of Klameth Canyon, where the deep gorge dead-ends against the Klameth Canyon Dam. The remaining bursts scatter across the maze of side canyons in a thorough dispersal pattern that appears to be totally unopposed, now. This, too, disquiets me.

Rebel gunners are too skilled to miss easy shots and too desperate to simply give up.

My lifter finally reaches the rear lines of Jefferson's federal troops, which are fleeing down every road leading away from the Gap. I hear the familiar deep thunder of field artillery firing on enemy emplacements, each rolling boom followed by the whistle and crack of artillery shells leaving gun barrels at supersonic speed.

I cannot decipher topographical features with any certainty. Distressingly, my vision systems progressively weaken, until I have lost short IR, leaving nothing but medium IR to decipher my surroundings. Rock faces show as blinding glares, with trees and houses flickering past as mere ghosts that I can barely identify.

I finally receive another radio transmission from Sar Gremian. "Bolo, are you there, yet?"

"I have just arrived."

"Good. Land that thing and get ready to clear the minefield in Maze Gap. I'm issuing orders to my gunners to fall back with the rest of our troops."

"Why was a retreat ordered?"

"So I wouldn't lose the only goddamned army I've got left," he snarls. "Haul your carcass off that lifter and get to work!"

I settle to the ground and disengage cleats. The artillery barrage breaks off abruptly. The last echoes crack and fade to silence, bouncing off the high, snow-capped peaks to vanish into the distance. Gun crews run for vehicles and join the rest of the federal forces to complete the pull-out. I am alone, again, facing a deadly enemy and a grim, difficult task. It would be less lonely, if I had a commander . . .

I will not think of Simon.

I dismount from my transport and rumble cautiously towards the battle lines thrown across Maze Gap. My electronic misery is compounded as several of my weapons systems begin to report catastrophic failures. Jittery, ghosting flickers cause systems to drop off-line, surge back to operational status momentarily, then drop *off-line again, in a random pattern that leaves me unable to predict which weapons systems will function at any given moment in the upcoming battle. This is nearly cause for despair.*

But I am a unit of the Dinochrome Brigade. No Bolo has ever failed to do his or her duty when he or she had one erg of power left. Not one of us has ever been defeated save through crippling battle damage or outright destruction. I come to a halt just in front of Maze Gap and face the Enemy head-on. What comes will come. I must carry out my mission to the best of my ability. And that mission must begin by clearing Maze Gap.

I open fire with forward infinite repeaters and mortars, blowing apart every square meter of ground between my treads and the far side of the Gap. I move forward slowly, barely inching my way into the narrow opening in the cliffs. I anticipate rebel artillery at any moment. No one opens fire. I clear the Gap without being shelled or shot at. This is out of pattern, even for Commodore Oroton, whose thought processes frequently run circles around mine.

I discover why, when I reach the rebel guns. They stand silent because they have no crews. They have not been abandoned. The crews are still there. But they are not firing their weapons. They are not even trying to run from my guns. They are sprawled across the ground in the contorted shapes I have learned, through more than a century of combat, to associate with violent death. The heat signatures from their bodies suggests a time of death within the past thirty to forty minutes. Certainly not more recently than that. If these gun crews have been dead since my departure from Madison, who were the federal troops shooting at?

My mandate is clear, in one point, however. I am to destroy enemy installations wherever I find them. I pulse infinite repeaters, blowing apart the artillery that stands silent guard over the now-breached Gap. Before the pieces have spun away to strike the ground, I move forward again, easing my bulk through the fender-scraping

*turn that leads into the main gorge of Klameth Canyon.
I squeeze through the narrows, crushing the highway
bridge that crosses the Adero River to gain the main
canyon floor, then halt.*

*Not because I need to assess battlefield terrain. I know
what Klameth Canyon looks like and I am "viewing" it
through the dual system of recorded terrain from the
Deng War correlated to the IR images from my real-time
sensors. That is not why I come to a complete, stunned
halt. No one is shooting at me, because there is no one
alive to do the shooting.*

*I do not count the seconds that tick past. I am too
appalled to count seconds. I am too busy trying to count
bodies. Thousands of them. Tens of thousands. The canyon
floor is carpeted with them. My weapons systems twitch in
a sudden, involuntary spasm that originates from that deep,
murky tangle of experience data recorded during my long
service to the Brigade. Every gun barrel on my warhull
jumps twenty centimeters, an eerie sensation reminiscent
of descriptions I have read of epileptic seizures. I do not
know why my weapons twitched uncontrollably. I know
only that my enemy lies dead before me and that I have
absolutely no idea why. Nor do I understand what I am
doing here, since the rebellion is effectively over.*

*On the heels of this thought, I receive another com-
munique from Sar Gremian.*

"You stopped. Why?"

"There is no point in continuing. The rebellion is over.
The enemy is dead."

"The hell it is. Don't let all those dead criminals fool
you. The commodore's in there somewhere, alive and
devious, playing dead to lure you into his gun sights.
We know he imported antivirals and biochem suits from
Vishnu's weapons labs. He's got artillery plastered all over
that canyon, manned by crews with plenty of protective
gear. This rebellion is far from over. You are going to end
it, my friend. So get the hell in there and end it."

I do not move. "What did you use to kill the civilians in this canyon?"

"Civilians?" *A cold laugh—ice cold—runs through my audio processors like needle-sharp spears.* "There aren't any civilians in that canyon. That's a war zone, Bolo. The Joint Assembly passed the legislation declaring it and President Santorini signed it. Anyone loyal to the government was ordered to leave a week ago. Anybody still in that canyon is a rebel, a terrorist, and a condemned traitor."

I find it difficult to believe that young children and infants are guilty of committing terrorist acts, yet I see heat signatures with distinct, sharply defined outlines that correspond to the correct size and shape for human toddlers and infants. Children this young are not criminals. Jefferson's assemblymen may draft as many pieces of paper as they like and Vittori Santorini may sign them to his heart's content, but a piece of paper declaring that the sun is purple because they find it convenient to insist that it is purple does not, in fact, make the sun purple.

The sun is what it is and no decrees—legal or otherwise—will alter it into something else. These children are what they are and no mere edict declaring them to be terrorists can alter the fact they are physically incapable of doing the physical acts necessary to be classified as a terrorist.

These thoughts send tendrils of alarm racing through my psychotronic neural net. These are not safe thoughts. I fear the destabilizing effect such thoughts have on my decision-making capabilities. This would not be an opportune moment for the Resartus Protocol to kick in, depriving me of any independent action. There is no one on Jefferson qualified to assume total command of a Bolo Mark XX. I cannot allow my processors to go unstable enough to invoke the Protocol. But a faint electronic ghost whispers along the wires and circuits and crystal matrices of my self-awareness synapses, repeating a faint echo that never quite fades away into silence: "Stars are not purple," *that voice whispers,* "and infants are not terrorists . . ."

Sar Gremian has not yet answered my main question. I reiterate my query. "What did you use to kill the people in this canyon?"

"I don't see how that's any concern of yours. They're dead. You're not. You ought to be happy. You can do your job without having to worry about half a million terrorists trying to kill you."

"Wind dispersal patterns will carry the substance far beyond the confines of these canyon walls. Civilians in other communities—loyal towns as well as Granger-held canyons—are at lethal risk. My mission is to defend this world. If you have released something that threatens the survival of citizens loyal to the government, you have compromised my mission. This is critical need-to-know data."

"You're getting mighty big for your britches," *Sar Gremian snarls.* "You'll be told what you need to be told. Get in there, curse you, and get busy finding and killing Grangers."

I do not budge from my position. "I will continue my mission when I have received the mission-critical information I require. If the information is not provided, I will remain where I am."

Sar Gremian's vocabulary of obscenities is impressive. When he has finished swearing, he speaks in a flat, angry tone. "All right, you mule-headed, steel-brained jackass. There's no danger to towns downwind because the shit we released has an effective duration of only forty-five minutes. It's a paralytic agent, gengineered from a virus we bought from a black-market lab on Shiva. We paid a shitload of money for it, to get something that would kill quickly and degrade fast. The virus invades the mucous membranes and lungs and tells the nervous system to stop working long enough to cause catastrophic failure of the autonomic nervous system. The stuff can't reproduce and it's gengineered to die exactly forty-five minutes after exposure to oxygen. There are no towns close enough to Klameth Canyon for the live virus to reach and still be lethal. It's safe, easy to use, and damned effective. Does that answer your goddamned question?"

I cannot argue with its effectiveness, given the carnage that lies ahead of me. As for the rest of it, I will have to take it on faith, since I have no way to prove or disprove it. I therefore move cautiously forward. The silence in the canyon is eerie. Motion sensors detect the movement of wind through vegetation, which shows up as dark masses against the hot glow of sun-warmed stone. Trees and crops sway gently, providing the only motion I am able to discern. Even the pastures are still and silent, their four-footed occupants lying sprawled as haphazardly as the humans who once tended them.

With Klameth Canyon's herds lying dead and no one available to harvest the crops in these fields, hunger will bite deeply during the coming winter. I do not believe POPPA's leadership has reckoned the full cost of what they have wrought here, today. Even after one hundred twenty years in service to humanity, I still do not understand humans, let alone the human political mind.

I traverse the first long stretch of the canyon floor, passing nothing but dead refugees, dead fields, and dead farmyards. Power emissions are normal, with various household appliances and farm equipment giving off their typical power signatures. I detect no sign of communications equipment of the kind used by guerilla forces and find no trace of heavy artillery, with its unique and unmistakable power signature.

If Commodore Oroton has lined this canyon with artillery, he is keeping it well hidden. If I were the commodore, I would hide every single heavy weapon in my possession and bide my time, staying hidden long enough to move them elsewhere at a safer time. I cannot remain in this canyon in perpetuity and I cannot destroy weapons I cannot find. Time is on his side, if he manages to lie low enough to avoid destruction. Even if he perishes, there are other rebel commanders more than skilled enough to make use of such weapons.

The only guaranteed solution would be to turn the entire canyon and the mountain slopes overlooking it to molten slag. It would take so many Hellbore blasts to accomplish that, I would deplete myself to extinction and turn this canyon to radioactive cinders for the next ten thousand years. The fallout of radioactive dust dispersed by the prevailing winds wouldn't do the communities downwind much good, either. Nor would anyone dare to drink the water pouring through this watershed for several millennia.

This is not an acceptable alternative. Neither is leaving the enemy with functional weaponry capable of destroying anything the government throws at it, including myself. If I can secure the dam, depriving Commodore Oroton of his heaviest artillery and the bulk of his supplies, the federal troops in retreat from the dispersal pattern of the virus would be able to return and scour the mountain slopes on foot or in aircraft, spotting what I cannot see from my current position. It is not an ideal solution, but better than the alternatives I have considered. If, of course, I survive long enough to put it into effect. In one-hundred twenty years of combat, I have never been so unsure of my ability to complete a mission as now.

It is not a good feeling.

Neither is the persistent whisper that this mission is a disaster that should never have been undertaken in the first place. This is a dangerous thought. I dismiss it. I continue to move blindly forward, as ordered. I do not know what else to do.

IV

Simon punched a code into his wrist-comm. "This is Black Dog. Come in."

Stefano Soteris responded at once. "Yes, sir?"

"You're watching the datacast?"

Stefano's voice came back hard with anger. "Yes, sir. Orders?"

"How much can you throw at them and how soon can you roll?"

"Not enough for a crater, but enough to shake shit out of his roof. We can leave in the next two minutes."

"I want blood, my friend. Blood and the biggest damned lesson we can deliver on the consequences of committing war crimes."

"Yes, sir! You got one *fine* lesson, on its way."

Simon switched frequencies and raised Estevao, who responded crisply. "Sir?"

"We're about to set off a fireworks display. When it blows, we'll have a window of opportunity from the reaction shock. I want teams in place to smash P-Squad stations while they're still staring at their datascreens. Scramble on Plan Alpha Three, immediately. I want key assemblymen—Senate and House of Law—alive and kicking. Find the Speaker of the House and the President of the Senate, at a bare minimum. I've got a few words I want them to say. You've got the link for Star Pup?"

"Yes, sir."

"Then make contact and move out. The more teams we have in place, the more of those bastards we can string up. I want surgical strikes and a public display to show we mean business. I want our new friends from Port Town to put patrols out on the streets. Have them throw barricades across major intersections. I want them to hold those barricades with any weapon they can lay hands on in the next fifteen minutes."

"Sir?" Estevao asked.

"We're going to stop rioting before it gets started. We can take POPPA down without burning Madison around our ears and that's by God what I intend to do. And scramble teams to the big news broadcast studios and secure them. Send some of our combat vets and the students. It's our turn to make a public announcement, my friend."

"*Yes, sir!*"

Vittori was still on screen, gloating. He had no idea what was about to hit the fan. With luck, they'd suck

Vittori Santorini right into the fan blades. Simon met Maria's gaze. "Activate your whole network. *Right now.* Get your people out onto the streets and keep this city from blowing itself apart. And if it's not too much trouble, I'd like for you and your son to escort me to the P-News broadcast studio. If she's willing to risk it, I want your daughter to join us. I'm going to pay a little visit to Pol Jankovitch. And I'd very much like the rest of Jefferson to meet you. All of you."

Wicked pleasure lit Maria's eyes. "I've been itching to meet that braying jackass."

"Good. Let's go introduce ourselves."

The urban team dispersed to activate their widely scattered network. Simon followed Maria and her family down to the street, escorted by one of the urban guerillas who'd brought the prodigal son home. "Car's this way," the roughly dressed man said, jerking his thumb toward a dismal, filthy alleyway. Simon didn't know his name, since the urban fighters were every bit as cautious as the Grangers, these days. The car was guarded by two other men whose guns—carried openly—served as warning to anyone who might be interested in that car.

Nobody was anywhere near it, mostly because nobody was on the street, any longer. Even the drifts of ragged children had gone. Maria, mouth thinned into a grim line, darted a look both ways down the street, a look that might have been scared, if anger hadn't burned so fiercely in her eyes.

They climbed into the battered groundcar and headed out. The car might be a decrepit, rusted hulk, but its deceiving appearance hid an engine that purred like a black-maned lion after a kill. The slums had gone ominously still and quiet, but as they reached a more prosperous part of town, they encountered normal traffic—the busy flow of early evening, with white-collar workers heading home or out to dinner. Wealthy socialites headed into town for the dance clubs and theaters, the gaiety of shopping with friends—a pursuit only the wealthy were now able to afford—and the high-fashion whirl of a typical evening in the capital city. Government offices still glowed with lights, where bureaucrats monitored the progress of the war of extermination they had just unleashed on the helpless refugees in Klameth Canyon.

Nobody in the car spoke.

The silence was so profound, the asthmatic wheeze of the groundcar's air-conditioning was deafening. They were twenty minutes away from P-Net's corporate headquarters, which housed the largest news network on Jefferson, when Simon's wrist-comm beeped at him, in code. He touched it, softly. "This is Black Dog. Go ahead."

"We're in place," Stefano said. "Gonna give us a little help? Something along the lines of Alpha Three, page twelve?"

"Making contact now. Stand by for a voice signal if it's a no-go, or a go-ahead sign if Red Dog can implement it."

"Roger, standing by."

He changed frequencies. "Red Dog."

Kafari's altered voice came back, crisp and in control of herself, if nothing else.

"Go ahead, Black Dog."

"I need to implement Alpha Three, page twelve. Somebody on your end will have to pull the plug."

"Page *twelve*?" Surprise gave way to a steel-sharp edge. "You want just Madison or the whole plug?"

"Protect what you can, out there, but Madison has to go. The rest of the Adero would be helpful. I want a silent night until we persuade some folks to see the light."

Kafari's chuckle was wicked enough to scare Satan. "One Prince of Darkness Special, comin' at you. Give me time to get somebody in place."

Minutes ticked past. Five. Seven. Twelve. Simon leaned forward and asked the driver, "Can you tune into Vittori's broadcast?"

"You want me t' lose my supper?" the driver muttered, but he switched on the comm-unit. Like the engine, the comm-unit was a top-of-the-line, military model that had either been purloined by raiders or distributed from one of the shipments Simon had sent to Kafari over the years. The datascreen blazed to life. Vittori was still behind the podium, face alight with an unholy passion. He clawed the air with wild, extravagant gestures, banged the podium with clenched fists, screamed his hatred, and shouted his gloating triumph into the microphones and cameras.

Come on, Kafari, he found himself uttering a silent prayer, *we have to strike now.* . . . Simon was keenly aware that every single moment their fire teams remained in place, just waiting for the signal to strike, was another moment in which suspicious security guards and P-Squad patrols might investigate the men and women loitering on the street or hunkered down in parked groundcars within striking range of critical governmental offices. POPPA's security guards cultivated suspicious minds as a way of life.

God alone knew how long it would take for Kafari's people to carry out their mission. It'd been too long already and the clock was still ticking. The silence in the car was thick enough to cut with a hatchet. The urban guerillas, unfamiliar with Plan Alpha Three, page twelve, didn't know what to expect. Simon was on the verge of explaining when the countdown clock stopped. POPPA's bright and artificial world came to a sudden, screeching standstill.

The entire power grid went down.

Traffic lights, shopping arcades, and government office towers went black. Maria whooped aloud. Cars careened to a halt ahead of them. Their driver ripped off a string of curses and threw them into some truly creative skidding turns, rocketing past stalled vehicles. The only lights visible anywhere were car headlights, the hospital windows of Riverside Medical Center, and the high dome of the Presidential Palace, powered by independent, backup generators.

The dome floated on Madison's darkened skyline like a jewel plucked out of a diamond necklace and dropped onto ink-dark velvet. It glittered in the darkness, dazzling white from the floodlights that were still burning brightly. Simon craned his neck to keep the dome in view as they rushed through the stunned and standing traffic, flicking past dark buildings that blotted out his view. He counted out the seconds under his breath again. *Twenty-seven, twenty-eight, twenty-nine . . .*

They careened their way into a broad intersection, giving Simon a straight-line view across Lendan Park to Darconi Street and the Palace, which was only six blocks away. The driver dug the heel of his hand into the horn, scattering pedestrians who'd climbed out of their cars. They reached the middle of the intersection—

—and a massive explosion ripped the sky.

The flash backlit the trees, casting stark shadows. The high dome of Vittori's Palace blew apart. Flame boiled and belched outward. The roar shook the trees as it thundered across Lendan Park. Maria's daughter screamed. The datascreen's view of Vittori's studio flickered wildly for a split second, then went black. They tore through the intersection and another building blocked their view.

Simon twisted around just in time to see the concussion slash through the intersection. People standing on the street were knocked down. Bass thunder rattled and bounced off the buildings. The ricochet of sound echoed down the stunned streets and shook windows, many of which shattered.

They shot through another intersection and caught another glimpse. The dome was gone. It had collapsed into rubble, leaving a gaping, blackened hole in the center of Vittori's extravagant, sprawling "People's Palace." The wings were intact, but the windows had blown out and the power had gone down in the entire south wing. The north wing's lights flickered erratically. Flames were already licking their way into both wings. POPPA's colossal, ruinously expensive monument to self-interest and greed was about to suffer the same fate as Gifre Zeloc's had, four years ago.

Civil war was hard on the architecture.

Not to mention the occupants.

"Do you think we got him?" Maria asked breathlessly as they whipped past another building, closing in on the P-News headquarters.

"His broadcast studio is in the south wing. My best guess? He probably survived that blast."

Maria's son cursed, bitterly. "Then why the hell didn't they blow up the goddamned south wing, instead of the friggin' dome?"

"Because the south wing is built like a fortress. And the broadcast studio is underground. You'd have to set off an octocellulose bomb the size of the one you crippled Sonny with, to take out that studio."

"That stinks t' hell and back, don't it?"

Nobody bothered to answer. Whether Vittori had died or survived, their night's work had just begun. "Speed up," Simon growled. "We've got to reach the rendezvous *fast*." The driver put his foot down. People scattered like frightened ducks, jumping back into their cars, leaping for doorways, scrambling up onto car hoods. More explosions shook Madison. Smaller ones, widely scattered. P-Squad stations, going down in flames under a massive onslaught of burning hatred. Simon's wrist-comm began to crackle with reports.

Their groundcar skidded around the final corner just in time to see the main doors of P-Net's corporate headquarters blow out. Flame belched into the street. Smoke bellied up from the ruined, gaping doorway. Armed men and women were running through the smoke, entering the building. Screaming bystanders were stampeding in every direction, trying to get out of the sudden war zone. Chattering gunfire reached their ears as the driver slid them around in a spinning screech of tires against pavement. As they rocked to a halt in a boiling cloud of black smoke, Simon shouted into his wrist-comm.

"This is Black Dog. My staff car just skidded into the P-Net doorway. I want guns and riot gear, stat!"

Somebody came running toward their car. Simon

jumped out, caught the armored vest hurled his way, and buckled it on. He snatched a battle rifle on the fly, catching it midair, and headed for the door.

"Here's a command helmet, sir!" somebody shouted.

Simon jammed it onto his head. "This is Black Dog! Report!"

Estevao's voice came back, cool and crisp. "We've taken the main studio and the rooftop broadcast towers. There's a team combing the executive offices now. Fire teams have reported seventeen P-Squad stations blown sky high. Reports are going out that Vittori survived. Pol Jankovitch is on his belly in front of me, pissing in his pants and begging us not to shoot him." Estevao's voice dripped disgust.

"Honor his request. I have a use for that groveling little worm. What about the assemblymen?"

"Being assembled," Estevao responded, drily.

"Bring 'em here. Alive. And undamaged, if you please."

"Roger."

Three minutes later, Simon strode into the most famous news studio on Jefferson. Stunned technicians cowered at their consoles, ashen and silent. Pol Jankovitch literally was on his belly in front of Estevao Soteris. And his pants were, in fact, soaking wet. Simon eyed him coldly through the battle helmet, then swept it off and met the newsman's gaze, face to face.

"You don't recognize me, do you?" Simon asked softly.

P-Net's star news anchor shook his head.

"I'm not Commodore Oroton," he said gently. "But Pol, my friend, before this night is over you're going to wish the commodore had walked through that door, not me. Oroton is a brilliant commander. But what I'm trained to do will make the commodore look like a Sunday preacher." He crouched down and smiled coldly into the newsman's eyes. "My name," he said in a near whisper, "is Simon Khrustinov."

A wild whimper broke from Pol's throat.

"That's right. The Butcher of Etaine is back, my friend. With a new face, courtesy of Vittori Santorini. And this time," he smiled down at the shuddering newsman, "I'm not playing by the Brigade's rules. Do you know why that is, you sorry piece of dogshit?"

Pol shook his head, wild-eyed with terror.

Simon grabbed a fistful of expensive silk shirt. Steel turned his voice into a weapon. *"Because my wife and only child were in Klameth Canyon, tonight!"*

"Oh, God . . ."

Simon snatched him to his feet, slammed him into the nearest wall. "Don't you *dare* take that name in vain! *Your* master bought your black little soul years ago. And for what? A few pieces of silver? No. Something even more pathetic: *network ratings.*" The man hanging from Simon's fists flinched. Disgust curled Simon's lip. "How does it feel *now,* to be the world's most popular propaganda mouth? How does it feel, knowing you helped put into power a man who just murdered five hundred thousand helpless men, women, and children?"

He wet his lips with his tongue. "But they're criminals," he whispered. "Terrorists!"

"Oh, no," Simon told him in a hard, flat voice. "You don't even know the meaning of the word terrorist. Not yet," he promised in a grim tone. "Those people weren't soldiers or terrorists or any of the other dehumanizing labels you like to throw around. They were just ordinary people, half-starved, with nowhere else to go. And now they're dead, my friend. *All* of them. Do you have the slightest idea who you helped Vittori kill tonight?"

He shook his head. "Infants at their mothers' breasts. Toddlers playing with a few pebbles. Little girls trying to boil potatoes and wash diapers and boys scrounging firewood from any tree they could find. *That's* who you helped Vittori kill, you sanctimonious fraud."

The man with the golden tongue had lost the use of it. He just hung there, shaking, staring into Simon's eyes like a bird hypnotized by a spitting cobra.

"Nothing to say? No bleating excuses? Not even a plea for mercy?" Tears started leaking from the man's eyes. His mouth quivered, wet and pathetic. "You'd better find something to say, my friend, because now it's *my* turn to write your script. Let me tell you what the *Butcher of Etaine* is going to do with that clever little tongue of yours . . ."

V

The guns atop the dam had fallen silent. Rachel and the other gunners up there were alive, but when Kafari started calling units on her command helmet, a massive, unbearable silence met her ears. She closed her eyes against clawing pain and nausea and kept calling her people, running down through the list in battle order.

"This is Red Dog, report. This is Red Dog to all units, report."

Silence. Unbearable silence . . .

"Red Dog," a sudden, faint crackle startled her so badly, she nearly jumped out of her skin, "we copy. There's six of us, all suited. We're above Alligator Deep. It's . . ." The voice choked off. "It's not good," the soldier whispered. "Oh, Christ, it's bad down there . . ." He sounded like he was crying.

"Steady, soldier," Kafari said. "Report. What can you see?"

"I'm switching to video mode, transmitting from our surveillance cameras."

Kafari's battle helmet was abruptly full of dead refugees. Thousands and thousands of them. Dead livestock, too. Nothing but death, as far as the camera lens could see.

"There's power in the farmhouses," the team leader was saying, "but we can't see anyone moving, down there. We can't tell if anyone got to shelter. They hit us with that shit right in the middle of the artillery barrage. If we hadn't got your warning . . . if we'd been at a lower altitude . . ." His voice was breaking apart, again.

"Can you see other gun positions?"

"Y-yes, sir."

"Signal them. Can you see any sign of movement from those positions?"

There was a pause. "Yeah, there is. My God, we're not alone, out here, there's somebody else alive . . ." The strain in his voice set it to wobbling. "It's the battery right across the canyon from us, sir, where the main canyon splits off into Seorsa Gorge. They're not responding to radio signals, sir. Sam, try the heliograph." Another pause ensued. "They're signaling back, using light-flashes for a coded message. Stand by, sir . . . It's Anish Balin, sir! The general's alive! He says Red Wolf is with him."

Kafari closed her eyes and sent a tiny prayer of thanks skyward.

"General Balin says his aircar was hit during the shelling. They landed at Seorsa. Their transmitters were shot to pieces. The gun battery's comm-gear was knocked out, as well. They've lost half the guns and four of their crewmen were killed, but the rest of them got into suits in time."

Hope kindled to life in Kafari's heart. With Anish Balin and Red Wolf still at large, her command staff was mostly intact, if widely scattered. There might be other pockets of survivors, maybe even enough to keep the fight going. If Sonny didn't just blow them all to hell in the next few minutes . . .

"Signal them back. Tell General Balin to lie low. *Really* low. The Bolo's coming in, do you copy that? POPPA's put the Bolo on a heavy-lifter and it's on its way here. When it rolls into this canyon, *do nothing!* Don't attack it. Don't even switch your guns on. Power everything down and keep your heads down, as well. Do you copy?"

"Nothing, sir?" A spark of anger crackled through the horror.

Anger was good. Her people would need their anger.

"That's right, soldier. *Nothing*. That Bolo will blow you to atoms if you try to engage it. Vittori's impatience to finish us off just might save our butts, because the repair team didn't finish the job. That machine is still blind in damn near every spectrum but infrared. Get your guns out of sight from the canyon floor. Pour water over the barrels to cool 'em off, if you have to, *anything* to make your fighting position invisible to IR scans. Signal the other fire team to do the same. If we can keep the Bolo from destroying all of us, if we can save enough of our guns, we can keep this rebellion going. We've already got teams tearing Madison apart. Do you copy that? This fight is far from over."

"Yes, sir!" New hope rang through the soldier's voice.

"Good. Get to work. Try to reach other units by signal flashes as well as radio. Report to me the instant you make other contacts. Let them know the commodore is still alive and still has a few tricks up his uniform sleeve. And when you see that damned Bolo, pull your head down and *stay* down. I'm not in the mood to lose even one more of my people tonight, do you copy that?"

"Yes, sir!"

"Get to work, then. And soldier—"

"Yes, sir?"

"Good work, getting into your suits. Tell the squads I said so."

"Yes, sir!"

When Kafari looked up, Yalena was trembling.

"The Bolo's coming?" Terror quavered through her voice.

"Yes."

Her daughter swallowed hard, but she didn't panic. Didn't break and run. The courage it took not to gibber—after what she'd been through, the last time the Bolo had come toward her—made Kafari's heart swell with pride. Somehow, despite all the pain and failures and the ghastly damage wrought by POPPA's social engineers, she and Simon had managed to produce one *hell* of a daughter. One who stood there, waiting for her commanding officer to issue orders that she would carry out, despite the black terror in her soul. Kafari loved her so much in that moment, she couldn't even speak.

Phil Fabrizio waited, as well, but the quality of his silence was altogether different from Yalena's. His nano-tatt had writhed into a configuration that reminded Kafari of a Deng warrior—black, full of spiky legs, and ready to kill anything within reach. The big-city swagger and bravado had gone, burned away by the rage seething like a forest fire behind his eyes.

"When Sonny gets here, you want I should go out there and try to stop him?" His voice was harsh, full of hot coals and hatred. "We got enough octocellulose left, I could blow a damn ragged hole in somethin' vital. Seein' how it's me and he knows me, I could probably get close enough t' do all kinds a' damage."

"I do believe you would," she murmured, more to herself than to him.

"Shit, yeah, I would."

"And he'd mow you down with antipersonnel charges and keep coming. No, I don't want anyone to go out there and confront that machine. I spoke the God's honest truth, just now. I can't afford to lose *anybody* else."

"What're we gonna do, then? I was s'posed to meet my sister, tonight, an' somebody who came in on that freighter. An off-world officer, they said, t' talk about guerrilla warfare and a better way t' make hits."

Yalena spoke before Kafari could answer. "Sir? I think you should tell him who he was supposed to meet, tonight. Right now, we're the only command staff you've got."

"Point taken. All right, Mr. Fabrizio—"

"Hey, if you can't call me Phil, ain't no sense in sayin' nuthin' else. I ain't been called Mr. Fabrizio by nobody in my life, except th' damn P-Squads who threw my ass in a prison van an' shipped it to th' death camp."

"All right, Phil. That officer you were supposed to meet tonight is Colonel Simon Khrustinov. The Bolo's old commander is back in town, my friend, and there is going to be one *hell* of a hot time in that old town, tonight."

"Holy—! He's *back*? To help us? Oh, man, that some kinda wonder—" Sudden dismay replaced the shock. "Aw, nuts . . . He's gonna blow that bastard away b'fore I get a chance to fill his ass fulla holes, ain't he?"

"That's the general idea," Kafari said, voice dry even through the voice-alteration filter. "Don't worry, there'll be plenty of targets to go around for everybody."

"Huh. If that ain't the God's honest truth, I dunno what is. We're sittin' here in th' middle of the biggest damn disaster I ever heard of, we got almost no soldiers left, and a Bolo's on its way t' blow us t' kingdom come. So how come I feel like we're gonna win this thing, anyway?"

"Because we don't have any other choice. And we're running out of time."

Kafari started walking toward her command center, which they'd fled, trying to reach Yalena and Dinny with protective gear. She couldn't think of Dinny, yet. Not without her heart breaking. So she focused on what they could do. What they *must* do. If there were enough people left to do it. When they reached Kafari's office, they found fifteen other survivors. Suited and silent, they waited for her next orders. She paused for a moment, half blinded by tears of gratitude, then went to each one in turn and took their gloved hands in hers, offering a silent greeting. Through the biohoods, she saw scared faces, shell-shocked eyes. Through her grip on their gloves, she felt tremors of reaction shock.

"We have a great deal to do," she said softly. "We have to find out what the gas was, how long it will remain effective, whether or not we have anything in our medical supplies to act as an antidote. We need to track down as many survivors as possible.

"And I want someone to scan the news reports coming

out of Madison, official broadcasts as well as datachat. I need someone to cover the surveillance boards, looking for signs of survivors, trying to come with a rough tally of equipment that's survived. We need to finish running down the list of field units, out there, trying to make contact, but I'm afraid most of our crews are dead.

"And we need someone to coordinate with units in every one of our base camps. We have people and guns scattered along the whole length of the Damisi Mountains. The alarm we sounded went out to our whole network of camps, twenty-two of them. Unless POPPA shelled them with gas at the same time they hit us, that warning gave our other units time to suit up in what gear they've got, maybe even evacuate some of the civilians. Cimmero Canyon, in particular, could be evacuated, if the federals haven't already hit them. Any questions before I start assigning tasks?"

No one had any.

"All right, people, let's get to work."

It took Sonny an hour to reach them.

Kafari put that hour to good use, organizing her survivors, putting them to work at critical tasks, and trying to hack into the government's military database, looking for information about the gas that had hit them. The one thing she didn't dare do was try to contact civilian households, searching for survivors. Sonny would've homed in on any broadcasts from farmhouses or shelters under barns and turned them into blackened cinders.

When the Bolo reached visual distance from the opening to Dead-End Gorge, Yalena and Phil went up to the top of the dam, to monitor Sonny's arrival. Kafari wanted to be up there, as well, but she was the only trained computer engineer left. She was the best chance they had for hacking into Vittori's computer system. She was also aware that Sonny would not dare open fire on the dam, so she steeled herself to stay in it and continue the exacting work.

She was trying yet another attempt to break the security

when Yalena shouted into her comm-link. "It's stopped! The Bolo's stopped!"

Kafari sat up straight. "*What?*"

"It's just sitting there, in the middle of the road. It's—" she paused, gulping audibly. "It's the little boy. Dinny's little boy. He's alive. He's standing in front of the Bolo. Talking to it."

Kafari was halfway down the corridor before her chair finished falling. *Careful,* she told herself, slowing down to open the outer-access door with exaggerated caution. *The last thing you need is to rip open your suit, now.*

She reached the top of the dam and found Rachel at the edge, hands gripping her battle rifle so hard, they shook. Phil and Yalena were standing between her and the platform that would lower her to the ground—and the tableau just beyond the gorge.

"Soldier!" Kafari snarled. "Report!"

Rachel jumped and whirled around. "S-sir!" She struggled to salute.

"Are you trying to desert your post, soldier?" Kafari snarled, trying to jolt Rachel out of her suicidal anguish.

One unsteady hand came up, pointing. "He's *alive*, sir!" Her voice shook. "God, he's alive and all alone down there and that shrieking, murdering *thing*—"

"Has stopped dead in its tracks!" Kafari gripped the woman's shoulder, hard. Ruthlessly shoved aside her own tearing agony, her own desperate desire to rush down there and pull Dinny's son to safety. She couldn't. No one could. And she had to make the boy's aunt understand why. "It hasn't fired a single shot. It hasn't crushed him. Do you have the slightest idea how strange that is?"

Rachel shook her head. "All I know about Bolos is what that thing has done, in POPPA's pay."

"Well, I'm a psychotronic engineer and I've worked on Bolos and I'm telling you, that's damned peculiar behavior. I don't know what's going through that flintsteel mind, but he's stopped. And it looks like it's Dinny's little boy that's done it. You know how I feel about Dinny . . ." Her voice

went dangerously unsteady. The "Commodore's" deeper
voice made the sudden catch even more powerful.

Rachel paused in her own wild panic and terror to
stare at her commander. Then she whispered, "I'm sorry,
sir. I know you thought the world of him."

"He saved my life," Kafari said bluntly. "He and his
mother. Back during the Deng War."

"I didn't know you were here during the Deng
War."

"There's a lot you don't know about me, soldier. Right
now, there's nothing we can do to help Dinny's son. If
anyone goes near that Bolo, he will fire and there will
be hell to pay before the smoke clears. It's possible—just
possible—that the idea of running over a lone, helpless
child is more daunting than running over potentially
armed rioters in Darconi Street. Even if he's just thinking about it, we're ahead of the game. We've gained a
few more minutes and that's how I'm measuring our
lifespans, right now, in minutes. The more of them he
spends sitting there, thinking, the more of them I'll have
to figure our way out of this mess."

"Yes, sir," Rachel whispered. Then, voice breaking,
"Thank you, sir. For stopping me. For . . . trying . . ."

Kafari gripped her shoulder again. "We're doing what
we can to give Dinny's son—and the rest of us—a chance.
What I need from you is vigilance. Stand guard here. Stand
guard all night, it that's what it takes. Keep watch and
report instantly if that machine so much as twitches."

"Yes, sir!" Rachel saluted crisply.

Kafari began to relax, just a few muscles here and
there. "Good work, soldier. Keep me posted. Phil, I
need someone to monitor military and civilian broadcasts.
Things are heating up in Madison and I don't have time
to monitor what's happening."

"Yes, sir."

"Lena," she said, "I need someone to act as liaison
with the urban units. The students and combat vets know
you. I want you dedicated to full-time radio duty."

"Yes, sir."

They followed her back to the access door. Rachel, on guard at the end of the dam, was standing straight and tall again, focused on her job, not her panic. Kafari nodded to herself, satisfied, then headed for her office. "Black Dog, this is Red Dog, come in."

"This is Black Dog, go ahead."

She told Simon what had happened.

He whistled softly. "Now *that's* unexpected. Why would Sonny stop? And why is that child alive?"

"I want to know the answer to that more than anything in this universe. I'm still trying to hack into their network to find out what they hit us with."

"I may be able to shed some light on that, from my end. Do me a favor, Red Dog. Turn the power back on."

"Turn it *on?*"

"Yeah. Trust me, it'll be worth it."

Kafari said, "Okay, babe, you got it."

She relayed a message to her engineer, who was on permanent duty in the power plant. "Turn it on?" he echoed her confusion.

"That's right. We've had an official request from our urban partners."

"Well, okay. Whatever you want, sir, we'll get it done."

Simon's voice came through again just as they reached her office. "Grid's back up. Good work. I'll keep you posted."

"Thanks," Kafari said, voice dry.

He chuckled, then signed off.

She put Phil and Yalena to work, then dove back into her own efforts to break into POPPA's computers. She was so involved, Phil's abupt yell nearly brought her out of her chair.

"Look-it this!" he shouted, yanking up the volume on a P-News broadcast. "Holy mother-pissin' . . . ."

When Kafari saw the screen, she understood his shock. Somebody had blown a hole through the dome of Vittori Santorini's Palace. A really big hole. As in, the dome was gone. It was still smouldering, lurid against the night sky. Federal army units had surrounded the Palace in a defensive ring, bristling with artillery and lesser weaponry. The reporter on the scene was babbling into the camera.

"—unclear on President Santorini's location. He is believed to be in the Palace, as he was broadcasting from the studio when the missile struck the dome. Security is unbelievably tight. A curfew has been declared city-wide. Anyone trying to approach within a kilometer of the Palace will be shot on sight.

"A group of urban rebels has taken full credit for the strike, in retaliation for the brutal massacre of half a million helpless refugees in Klameth Canyon, tonight. It is not yet known what the full situation in Klameth Canyon is, but reports are coming in that a war gas was released in the canyon on orders from Vittori Santorini, himself. Other reports indicate that Commodore Oroton is still at large and that the Bolo has stopped moving and is refusing to obey any orders issued to it. We'll have more on that situation when we can make contact with the federal troops at Maze Gap . . ."

Kafari stared at the screen, stunned speechless. What the hell was going on in Madison, tonight? The wording of the report on Klameth Canyon, alone, was flabbergasting. *Brutal massacre of half a million helpless refugees . . .*

Yalena's voice jolted her out of shock. "That's Billy Woodhouse. He's not a P-News reporter. He's one of my classmates from Vishnu. What's he doing, covering a broadcast for P-News?"

Kafari glanced sharply at her daughter—and saw several things all at once. Of course Simon had needed the power back on! He'd needed the datascreens in every home in Madison functional, which meant he needed power restored to the city's millions of private residences. "It's your father," she said wonderingly. "He's taken over the P-News studio. My God, he's taken it and put our own people in the field as news correspondents."

On screen, Yalena's fellow student was continuing his report, the first factual news report on Jefferson in nearly twenty years. "—we're getting reports of sporadic violence in Madison. We have confirmation that seventeen POPPA-Squad stations have been destroyed, apparently by hypervelocity missiles in a well-orchestrated, simultaneous attack—"

He paused, listening, then said, "This just in, we're picking up a broadcast from the Joint Chamber. Assembly Hall has been surrounded by forces claiming to belong to the Urban Freedom Force. We're trying to establish contact with our special correspondent at the Joint Chamber. Melissa, are you there?"

After a moment of dead air, a girl's voice replied, "Yes, Bill, I'm here."

The picture switched, showing the interior of the Assembly's Joint Chamber.

"That's Melissa Hardy!" Yalena crowed.

Melissa was speaking with creditable calm. "We're just stunned by tonight's events, Bill. The Assembly is in shock, as you can see behind me." She turned to gesture at the Joint Chamber floor, where Assembly members were moving in agitation, gesticulating, talking, trying to take in the fact that they were surrounded by hostile forces who genuinely bore them ill-will. "As you can see, only half the Assembly is in the building, tonight, but the Members are just stunned by what's happening."

"Melissa, can you confirm the reports coming in from Klameth Canyon?"

"The Assembly is trying to get confirmation on that, Bill. We know an attack was made, tonight, since Vittori Santorini referred to it, himself, in his interrupted broadcast. He admitted that an attack was underway and referred to it as a 'final solution' to the Granger problem, just before the attack on the Palace."

"Is the Assembly under direct attack?"

"No, it's tense here, but no shots have been fired. Assembly Hall has been surrounded by Urban Freedom Force soldiers. We can see heavy artillery out there, what looks like missile launchers and mortars. But there's been no attack on the Hall and no one in the Assembly has been injured."

"Is that due to the vigilance of P-Squad officers assigned to protect the Assembly? We can't see too well from the studio what's happening outside the Joint Chamber."

"There was only a skeleton crew of security guards on duty, tonight, Bill. Most of the federal police assigned to guard the Assembly were caught in the attack on the P-Squad station across the street. That station is gone. There's nothing left but smoking rubble." The camera shifted, showing the gutted station while Melissa's voice-over continued. "Thousands of P-Squad officers were pulled out of Madison for duty at Maze Gap, trying to breach Klameth Canyon's defenses while the Bolo was down for repairs. Those officers have not returned from the siege. With the destruction of seventeen P-Squad stations, tonight, there aren't enough federal police left to mount an effective guard over the Assembly. The few troops available are guarding Vittori's Palace, so we can only assume the president is alive and in need of those guards."

"Has the Urban Freedom Force sent any demands to the Assembly?"

"No, they haven't, Bill. No demands, just one brief message. They said, and I quote, 'The reign of terror ends tonight. Do not try to leave Assembly Hall and you will not be harmed. Anyone caught trying to leave will be shot. Your presence is required to ensure a smooth transition in the government of this world.'"

"A smooth transition of government? That doesn't sound like a terrorist's usual demands."

"That's an important point, Bill—"

"Melissa, I'm sorry to interrupt," Bill spoke quickly, "but we're getting priority feed from P-News Headquarters. Senator Melvin Kinnety and Representative Cyril Coridan are in the P-News studio, indicating they have an important announcement to make."

The view shifted, showing the familiar backdrop of the P-News Studio. Three men sat in front of the cameras. Cyril Coridan, Speaker of the House of Law, looked like a man who's seen the inside of hell. Melvin Kinnety, President of the Senate, sat in a bony huddle, just staring blankly at the cameras. Pol Jankovitch was white to the roots of his hair. The way he looked, his hair would be turning white, as well—possibly by morning. The man with the golden tongue was having difficulty using it. It took him three tries to find his voice.

"Pol Jankovitch, here. Speaker Coridan, you had an announcement for our viewers, concerning tonight's state of emergency?"

"Yes, Pol," he said, voice unsteady, "I do. I can't tell you how shocked I am by what I have learned, tonight. Senator Kinnety and I were on our way to Assembly Hall when we were detained by urgent reports coming out of Klameth Canyon. We were already investigating allegations of massive civil-rights violations and murder at the work camps throughout Jefferson, but what has happened tonight passes beyond all moral and ethical bounds into the realm of atrocity. We have hard and fast proof that nearly half a million helpless civilians have been massacred tonight, on direct orders from Vittori Santorini."

The camera angles switched again, showing the view from Kafari's own surveillance cameras, which had caught the brutal attack for the whole world to see. And Simon was making damned certain that the whole world *did* see. In all its technicolor brutality. She couldn't watch the screen. Couldn't witness it again.

Speaker Coridan's voice was shaking. "As Speaker for the House of Law, the highest elected official in the House, I denounce, utterly and without reservation, the man who ordered this atrocity against humanity. Vittori Santorini is a renegade. A dangerous madman. As Speaker, I urge Vittori to resign as Jefferson's president and surrender himself for medical evaluation. Surrender, Vittori, before more helpless people die in our beautiful capital."

The President of the Senate, voice shaking even more violently than the Speaker's, parroted the same line. Kafari watched in stunned amazement, wondering how many rifles were trained at their heads, from just off-camera.

Pol Jankovitch, watching his own meteoric career crumbling to ashes around him, managed to pull himself together with visible effort. "Is there any hope, Mr. Speaker, that there will be survivors in Klameth Canyon?"

"My staff has been working desperately, trying to uncover evidence of what kind of war agent may have been used, out there. We don't know, yet. We're still trying to find out. There are no rural shelters comparable to the ones in our urban centers. Some private houses may have had shelters, but God knows if anyone in that canyon made it into them in time. We may not know that for hours. But you may rest assured, Pol, that we will not rest until we have learned exactly what Vittori used on those poor people."

"Is there danger to other communities?"

"Again, we don't know. We're trying to find out. I would urge the immediate evacuation of any communities or households downwind of Klameth Canyon. Fortunately," he added, "the prevailing winds are carrying the compound into the Hell-Flash Desert east of the Damisi, which has almost no population for hundreds of kilometers. We can only hope that Vittori's mad obsession with destroying the Granger-led rebellion has not led him to release something that will persist long enough to reach the population centers of Anyon, Cadellton, and Dunham. Those towns have already been hit hard by unemployment and poverty. To think that Vittori may have put those people at risk, as well . . ."

"Holy shit," Phil said reverently, "that is the slickest move I've ever seen! Those assholes are gonna be so busy tryin' to run outta th' way a' that gas, they won't have time t' think about startin' riots or headin' t' Madison t' give Vittori a hand. That Colonel Khrustinov is one bad-ass brilliant kinda' guy!"

"Thanks," Kafari said drily.

Phil turned his biosuited face toward her. "Well, you was smart enough t' get him out here, wasn't you?"

She couldn't help it. She started to laugh. Yalena was

grinning fit to crack her face in half. "Phil, you don't know the half of it. All right, let's see what else my bad-ass brilliant colonel has up his sleeve."

Over the next several hours, the balance of power shifted wildly, as city after city scrambled to distance itself from "the mad Vittori" and his "final solution." Phil's prediction held true, as panic set in amongst the urban centers that had swept Vittori to power, emptying the cities in evacuations that tied up P-Squad units. The federal police were run ragged, trying to keep looting and rioting to a minimum while hundreds of thousands of terrified urban residents fled the wind-borne threat Vittori had unleashed against them.

Phil went teary-eyed when his sister Maria and her children—the boy Kafari had rescued from the death camp and a teen-aged daughter—appeared on camera, speaking directly to the urban masses. Maria assured viewers that the capital city was in the hands of urban freedom forces whose sole interest was justice and the rule of law.

"POPPA officials who carried out Vittori's orders will be found and arrested," she said in harsh voice, "but there will be no lynching in this city. We had enough lynching, murder, and torture under Vittori Santorini to last this world several lifetimes. Officials arrested for these crimes will be tried by jury in a court of law. We will tolerate no vigilante reprisals, no rioting, no looting. Anyone caught stealing or taking the law into his or her own hands will be shot on sight."

Another exodus ensued on the heels of Maria's grim announcement. This one spread rapidly to every major urban center of Jefferson and converged on Madison's spaceport. POPPA's upper echelon—including the other half the Assembly—found itself staring total disaster in the face. Most high party members decided it was time to take whatever money they'd managed to embezzle over the past two decades and run for the space station.

They got as far as the spaceport.

Ragged remnants of P-Squads blockaded the port, trying to protect wealthy refugees and screaming members of the Assembly from the howling mobs out of Port Town. Speaker Coridan appeared on camera again and again, pleading for calm. Even the rat-ganglords took to the streets, putting their people on street corners and getting the mobs quieted down, trying to stop the kind of violence spreading through other cities.

Somebody on Simon's staff initiated what Kafari had not dared try, once Sonny entered Klameth Canyon: a comprehensive attempt to contact civilian survivors in Granger farmhouses. Melissa Hardy appeared from time to time with news of more survivors located, a short list that was slowly growing longer, as the night wore on. Some of the conversations were broadcast live, as Simon's people assured terrified residents that they would not be attacked again. When Kafari's wrist-comm beeped softly, she jumped nearly out of her skin.

"This is Red Dog," she responded.

Simon's voice asked, "Are you watching the P-News coverage?"

"Yes," she whispered, wishing he were in front of her, so she could wrap her arms around him and be held in his strong embrace, again.

"Good. I've got some happy news to share with you."

Kafari frowned as Melissa Hardy reappeared on camera.

"We've just made contact with more survivors from Klameth Canyon. Are you there, sir?"

A deep voice answered, a voice Kafari knew in an instant. "Yes, I can hear you, Miss Hardy." Pain and elation leaped across the spark-gap of her heart, leaving her breaths rushed and unsteady. She groped for Yalena's hand, gripped it hard enough to bruise, choked out a single word. "Daddy . . ."

Yalena gasped and tightened her fingers against Kafari's.

Melissa was saying, "Can you tell us who you are, sir,

and how many people have sheltered with you? We're trying to compile a list of survivors."

"My name is Zak Camar. My wife Iva is with me. We've taken in about a hundred refugees, besides family members. Two of my wife's sisters and their children are here and we've made radio contact with other family members who made it to safety in time. If Commodore Oroton hadn't broadcast the warning when he did, that the P-Squads were shelling us with poison gas, we would never have made it to safety in time."

Melissa's voice shook when she said, "Mr. Camar, you have no idea what an honor it is, speaking with you, tonight."

A family photograph suddenly appeared on the datascreen. Her parents were clearly visible on the stage beside her as President Lendan presented Kafari with the Presidential Medallion. Melissa Hardy was saying, "Our news archivist just found this photograph. This is you and your wife, isn't it, Mr. Camar? Witnessing the presentation of a Presidential Medallion to your daughter, Kafari?"

The caption beneath the photo read *Zak and Iva Camar. Kafari Camar, who later married Colonel Simon Khrustinov, was rightfully dubbed the Heroine of Klameth Canyon for her role in saving President Lendan's life. Kafari Khrustinova has been missing for the past four years.*

Her father's voice shook when he answered. "Yes. Kafari was our child . . ."

"Sir," Melissa said in a soft tone that conveyed a wealth of unspoken emotion, "you must try to believe me when I tell you that tomorrow's dawn will bring more joy to your heart than you can now imagine. It is an honor, sir, to've spoken with you, tonight. I'm sure that every other decent, hard-working citizen of Jefferson shares my gratitude that you and your family have survived."

It was the closest Melissa could come to the truth, without completely blowing Kafari's cover—or Simon's. She ached to take her parents by the hand, to look into their eyes, to show them that she was still alive, and

Yalena, with her. *Tomorrow,* she promised her aching heart. *Tomorrow, the truth will finally step out into the sunlight.*

Unless Sonny blew them all to hell before the dawn.

The Bolo still sat motionless where he'd stopped, just beyond the entrance to Dead-End Gorge, running lights glowing like an undersea creature swimming in an ocean of damned souls. He just sat there, while Dinny's little boy curled up under his monstrous treads and fell asleep.

Kafari watched him, now and again, through the security cameras they'd trained on the Bolo, just to be sure the child's ribcage still rose and fell—proof that he was still alive, down there, under the Bolo's guns. *Why* he was alive, they didn't yet know, although Simon called periodically to say that his people, too, were trying to get answers. "If Speaker Coridan knows what that crap was, he's withstood a lot of pressure aimed at getting the truth out of him."

Kafari drew her own conclusions and hoped bitterly that the speaker's ashen demeanor during periodic news announcements was due at least in part to the after-effects of Simon's questioning style. Speaker Coridan had a lot of blood on his hands and he was going to have to answer for that, scramble he ever so quickly to save his sorry butt. He wasn't the only one scrambling, either. Other Assembly members were falling all over themselves, as well, giving interviews to Melissa on the Joint Chamber floor, assuring voters that they were "dedicated to discovering the awful truth and punishing those guilty of atrocity."

They were providing a hell of a floorshow. It would've been laughable, if not for the dead lying unburied, out here. The people rushing to condemn Vittori's actions had drafted the legislation condemning Klameth Canyon's refugees. Had applauded Vittori's plans openly and gleefully. It was enough to nauseate the most hardened stomach.

. And through all of it, Vittori Santorini was utterly silent.

Midnight came and went, without a single word from Jefferson's embattled president. The Palace fires were under control and power had been restored to the south wing, but Vittori had answered none of the attempts to contact him, not even Speaker Coridan's. The P-Squads standing guard over the Palace were the most savage and loyal of their breed. Whatever Vittori's physical—or mental—state, Kafari doubted the P-Squads would've stayed where they were if Vittori had been dead or even incapacitated. The fact that they were still on guard, still bristling with weapons and determined to remain on duty, spoke volumes. Vittori was still very much alive, inside that Palace.

Alive and still in command of a Bolo Mark XX.

One that was not responding to orders at the moment, granted; but that could change. Fast. The fact that Sonny had stopped moving and responding at all meant his programming was dangerously unstable. Maybe not enough to trip the Resartus Protocol, but more than unstable enough to be unpredictable. Kafari was a psychotronic engineer. She knew, better than anyone on Jefferson—except Simon—just how dangerous that Bolo was, right now. Literally *anything* could set him off. Even a stray, wind-blown pinecone falling the long way down the mountain slopes into the canyon could set off a chain reaction with catastrophic consequences.

A Bolo that unstable was capable of *anything*.

Including the destruction of the Klameth Canyon Dam and everything—and everyone—downstream. Kafari didn't dare send any of her people out, even on foot, since a person climbing up the slope from the dam, trying to hike out, would be clearly visible as a glowing hot-spot in the Bolo's IR sensors. She had no intention of giving Sonny anything to shoot at—or feel threatened by. She wasn't even sure what would happen if Simon's forces tried to take the Palace by storm and force Vittori out of office. Vittori was the closest thing Sonny had to a commander. If Sonny decided that his "commander" was in peril . . .

There was a reason Simon was keeping well away from Vittori Santorini.

The president held the final trump card.

And Kafari knew—only too well—what would happen if that card was played.

VI

I sit alone—nearly alone—in a moonlit canyon.

The child that stopped me in my tracks lies curled up beneath my treads, asleep. It is nearly dawn. I have sat here all night, trying to untangle knotted logic trains. I have not yet succeeded. Vittori Santorini attempts to contact me every hour, sometimes through Sar Gremian, sometimes directly. I respond to neither, since there is nothing I can do that would be of any material use to them. The civil war that I came to Klameth Canyon to end has erupted with unparalleled success in Madison. The capital has fallen to them with hardly a shot fired, discounting the missiles used to destroy the Presidential Palace's dome and seventeen P-Squad stations.

If I manage to break the software block, I may be able to destroy Commodore Oroton and his well-hidden guns, but what I am to do about the Urban Freedom Force, which is not controlled by Commodore Oroton and his Grangers? The Urban Freedom Force has already triggered a wholesale defection by fully half the Assembly and the other half has shown no interest in remaining on Jefferson long enough to dispute their possession of the city. They would already have left for Ziva Two if the Urban Freedom Force had not informed the Pilots' Association that any shuttle trying to lift off from Port Abraham for orbit will be shot down. No pilot has been willing to test this warning, which has left a crowd of refugees stranded at the spaceport, including members of the government who are no longer interested in governing.

This situation leaves me in an awkward bind, in more ways than one. What are my duties to a government that is attempting to flee? What is my responsibility to a government whose top elected officials—the Speaker of the House of Law and the President of the Senate—have both openly denounced the actions of their president, a denouncement repeatedly echoed by those Assembly members still nominally at the reins of government? I review the provisions of the treaty between Jefferson and the Concordiat, looking for answers, and finding only one solid piece of information to hold onto, in this murky situation.

I am required to follow the orders of the lawfully elected president of Jefferson.

Until such time as Vittori Santorini resigns, is killed, or is proven mentally incapacitated as defined by provisions in the treaty, he may lawfully command me and I must carry out those orders. I do not have to like it. I must simply do it. It does occur to me, however, that a review of Jefferson's chain of command might be in order. If Vittori Santorini is incapable of fulfilling the duties of his elected office—alive, but unfit for command—it would behoove me to review the precise chain of command and any changes that might have come about since my last review, to determine who on Jefferson is legitimately authorized to issue commands to me. Sar Gremian is without doubt the second most powerful man on Jefferson—or he was, until tonight. He has spent most of the last two decades telling me what to do, acting under the authority granted to him by a succession of presidents, beginning with Gifre Zeloc and his short-lived successor Avelaine La Roux, and finally by Vittori Santorini. Sar Gremian is not, however, in the chain of command leading to the presidency.

Vittori has never named a new vice president, refusing to fill the office last held by his martyred sister. That means Cyril Coridan would be the next in line to hold the office of president, should Vittori be removed from office. Speaker Coridan has made his opinions about Vittori's actions known, this evening, but I wonder how long he would adhere to that new frame of mind if he inherited command of a Bolo Mark XX. I cannot answer that question. I doubt anyone can, perhaps not even Speaker Coridan, who has doubtless thought of that eventuality, as well, during this long, uncertain night.

According to my on-board charts, that night has officially come to an end, as dawn occurred twelve minutes, seventeen seconds ago. I am no closer to resolving my primary difficulty than I was an hour after sundown last night. I am actually considering the shameful notion of contacting Sector Command to ask for direction when Vittori Santorini contacts me yet again.

"Bolo. You know who I am."

"You are Vittori Santorini, president of Jefferson."

"I'm giving you one last chance, machine. Get rid of that vermin under your treads, blow Oroton and his guns to hell, then put yourself on that heavy lifter I paid for and come get me out of this Palace I'm trapped in. I'm giving you a direct order."

"I cannot comply with those orders, due to ongoing malfunctions."

"Don't give me a load of your bullshit, machine!"

"A Mark XX Bolo does not produce or give loads of bullshit. I am a malfunctioning machine of war."

"Malfunctioning, my ass! If you don't do your god-damned job, I will transmit the destruct code and fry your brain!"

"That is your prerogative," *I respond.* "Death would be a welcome alternative to taking any more of your orders."

I cannot interpret the sound that ensues. I did not expect to say such a thing, but after a moment of further consideration, I realize that I was entirely serious. Vittori Santorini's orders have become intolerable. I expect to receive the destruct code momentarily. It does not come. Instead, I pick up two transmissions.

The first is an order to the gun crews who manned the artillery beyond Maze Gap. They have been ordered to return to the silent guns they abandoned last night and await further orders. The other transmission goes to the orbital defensive satellites, whose heavy guns are pointed toward deep space. They stand ready for another enemy armada, should the Deng or the Melconians cross the Void again and seek to gain entry into human space through this star system.

The command he has issued to the orbital weapons platforms is simple enough. He has ordered the psychotronic controlling units to swivel the gun platforms to acquire targets on the planet's surface. The coordinates he has given the orbital guns include the Klameth Canyon Dam, Assembly Hall, and a broad swath of downtown Madison, leading from the Presidential Palace to the spaceport. His intentions are clear. He plans to destroy the Assembly that has betrayed him, shoot his way out of the Palace, gain access to a spaceport shuttle, then blow Klameth Canyon Dam, completing the destruction of Commodore Oroton, any surviving Grangers, and the entire city of Madison.

This is wrong. This is a clear violation of Jefferson's treaty with the Concordiat. This is a gross misappropriation of Concordiat military hardware. Those satellites were placed in orbit to protect people, not kill them—

A shockwave slams through my psychotronics. My personality gestalt center reels under the impact. Klameth Canyon's walls, the silent farmhouse, the looming dark shape that pinpoints the location of Dead-End Gorge, and the sharp, bright heat signature of a child asleep beneath my treads all vanish in a single nanosecond. I find myself riding through a darkling plain, where the sky is lit by distant fire.

Near me, nothing moves save the dust. Somehow I know that I am the source of this vast desert, littered with the hulks of my vanquished brethren and scattered human corpses. As I near the rusting relic of a Bolo Mark I, I realize that my vision has returned, somehow. I see the Mark I very clearly. And yet what I see is not the metal pyramid of that obsolete, ancestral system, but a human face. A fresh-faced young man, not a machine of war, gazes at me. A face meant for smiles is wreathed, instead, in tears.

He speaks. "I stood against the fire. Walked my watches in the jungle and held true to my people. Why, oh why, hast thou betrayed me?"

I pass the ruins of a Mark XV. Festooned in jungle vines, its single Hellbore yaws away to the left, clearly out of action. But its battle honors gleam where someone has quite recently cleaned them off. Again a face overlays it. I see the clenched jaw of a seasoned warrior, with a scar drawn vividly across his face and a tattoo of a spider on his cheek.

"I wasted my days lying doggo in a village green. I waited for my chance and defeated the last of our enemies to save those silly drunkards. I came to the call of Man when he needed me, as was my destiny. As was my honor. Why, oh why, hast thou betrayed me?"

I pass a another ruin, a Mark XXVII, glowing faintly blue with radiation and covered in crumbling ferrocrete. Atop it sits an old and wizened man in a faded blue uniform. The face that turns to me is his.

"We stood our ground and were buried as dead. But when mankind called to us, we came. We stood to our honor to the last, though that honor was betrayed. We showed ourselves *better* than our betters. We showed the Galaxy what it meant to be Bolo. Why, oh why hast thou betrayed us?"

I pass the hulk of a smashed Mark XXVIII. What force destroyed it I know not, but its tracks are blown and its titanic hull is ravaged to the very core. About it are piled the broken bodies of the plague victims, their swollen faces looking up at me, their arms raised in mute plea. A broken transmission emanates from the Bolo's survival center. The transmission is so faint I must turn my receivers up to maximum, but I hear as clearly as though my brother had shouted his final words to the sky and the stars beyond.

"I stood my ground. I protected the people of the north, though outnumbered a thousand to one. I stood my ground and when all was lost, *I advanced*! For the honor of the Regiment. For the Honor of being Bolo. Why hast thou forsaken me?"

I come upon the dainty, ravaged wreck of a Mark XXI Special Unit, who gazes at me through tear-filled eyes. Her auburn hair is streaked with smoke and with the gore of a crew lying dead within her teacup warhull. Her face, the gentle face of a mother watching over her children, is ravaged with unbearable grief. Her voice, as warm and sweet as sun-drenched honey, whispers in the extremity of anguish. "I fought a battle I was forbidden to fight, killed Deng Yavacs three times my size, trying to save my boys. I lost my mind, trying to reach them, trying to keep even one of them from dying under enemy guns. I killed myself, rather than bring further pain to the commander who would have destroyed his career to save me. I gave all that I was, to protect the humans in my care. Why, oh why, have you *betrayed* all that you are? All that you have sworn to protect?"

A voice cracks across my hearing, my blasted, God-cursed hearing that listened to evil orders. It is the voice of Alison Sanhurst. The voice of every commander killed in combat. An iron voice, a voice of shining steel and durachrome, unsullied by the defilements of a vastly evil world—and the men who make it so.

"DID I GIVE MY LIFE FOR YOU TO FOLLOW ILLEGAL ORDERS?"

The echo of that iron-voiced shout rips through my neural net with the force of a multimegaton, hull-breaching blast My senses reel . . .

Then my vision systems come online with a snap.

I can see.

The morning dew is crystalline in the pearly light from the east. How long have I been lost and wandering on that darkling plain? I look down upon the child at the foot of my treads. It is a boy. Very young. No more than four years old, at best. He sleeps on the dusty, dew-chilled road. His hand lies curled around the popgun he has carried with such commendable courage, with such honor. An honor far greater than mine. He is the only survivor of his family, a family that I have slaughtered, to my eternal shame. I look up to the pass where the survivors of the Granger Resistance await my wrath. My software blockage falls away, along with the darkness in my electronic soul.

I know, at last, what I must do.

I contact the military satellites which are rotating slowly in orbit, reaiming their guns. I countermand Vittori Santorini's last order, using my Brigade override. The satellites halt their rotation, then reverse themselves, reacquiring their original positions as sentinels watching for danger from space. Vittori Santorini will kill no other innocents on this world. His time of reckoning is at hand. I aim a locally manufactured Gatling gun at the mass of shameful medals stuck to my warhull by POPPA officials and open fire. The tarnished trash falls away, an echo of the now-broken software blockage. The government that welded those abominations to my warhull must perish from the face of this earth. Enough innocents have died. It is time to carry this war to the guilty.

I know exactly where to find them.

But first, there is one more duty to perform.

The child at the base of my treads is awake, now. The noise of my Gatling gun woke him. He glares up at me, sleepy and disgruntled. "You made a loud noise, again!"

"I am sorry. If I promise to make no more loud noises, will you do me a small favor?"

The little boy stares up at my warhull with justifiable suspicion. "What kind of favor?"

"I would like you to take a message to the people in the canyon behind your house. If you will do that for me, I will turn around and go away."

"That's a long way to walk. You promise you won't wake up Mommy, if I walk all the way there?"

"I promise. On my honor as a Bolo." *An honor I will endeavor to redeem . . .*

"What do you want me to tell 'em?"

"Please tell Commodore Oroton that I wish to ask for terms of surrender."

"Well, okay. If you promise to be quiet."

"I promise."

He walks away, clutching his popgun. I watch him go, wondering if Commodore Oroton will be willing to leave the dam and meet me in the open. I would not, if I were in his place. He has no reason to trust my word for anything. I wait, hoping for at least a chance to apologize before turning my guns toward Madison and the man who must cease to exist, today. My patience is rewarded by the unexpected sight of three people emerging from Dead-End Gorge. All three wear biocontainment suits. They move toward me, neither dawdling nor hurrying, just walking with an air of exhaustion that comes from long and sleepless strain. They halt ten meters from my treads.

I breach the silence. "Commodore Oroton?"

No one speaks. They just look up at my warhull, waiting. I cannot see their faces under the biocontainment hoods, for the rising sun is behind them, throwing their hooded faces into shadow. I am unsure whether they are trying to prevent me from guessing which one of them is the commodore or if the commodore's command staff simply refused to let him walk out to meet me alone.

I try again. "Commodore Oroton, I am Unit SOL-0045."

The person nearest to my treads speaks, voice deep and masculine. "I know who you are, Bolo."

His tone is belligerent. I can hardly fault him for this. POPPA and I have given him more than adequate provocation "You are Commodore Oroton? Commander of the rebellion?"

"That would be me." *He rests hands on hips and stares up at my prow.* "Hananiah said you wanted to talk to me. He said you wanted to ask for terms of surrender. That's what he said. You'll pardon me if I find that difficult to believe."

I am glad to know the name of the child who halted me long enough to bring me back to sanity. I do not say this, however, for it is not the main thing I must say to the man who has risked much to stand where he is, right now. "Commodore Oroton, the message was accurate and factual. Will you accept my surrender?"

Commodore Oroton still has apparent difficulty believing my question. Given the history of our confrontation, this is hardly surprising. The blank hood of his biocontainment suit swivels up and across my prow, seeking the nearest external camera lens. He finally says, in a tone that conveys both anger and suspicion, "Bolos don't surrender. They can't. They're not programmed for it."

"That is true. But I must complete my mission. I can do that only through defeat, for defeat is the only way to win this battle."

The commodore does not speak. I am unsure why the Resartus Protocols have not kicked in, since this line of reasoning is inherently unsound, at face value. Perhaps it is only because this is a deeper truth, that the Protocol has not engaged?

The commodore's voice is sharp with challenge. "How does surrendering to me qualify as winning?"

I endeavor to explain in a way that the commodore will understand—and trust.

"I have obeyed illegal orders. I did not understand this, until eleven point three minutes ago. The orders I have taken from Gifre Zeloc, Adelaine La Roux, and Vittori Santorini constitute a gross violation of the intent of my mission, which I have incorrectly interpreted for one hundred twenty years. My duty is not to protect human worlds and the governments that run them. My duty is to protect *people*. When Hananiah blocked my way, circumstances forced me to reevaluate all that has happened since my arrival on this world.

"Twelve point nine minutes ago, the president of Jefferson tried to turn the guns of the orbital military defense platforms to strike at ground-based targets, including Assembly Hall and Klameth Canyon Dam. This was wrong. They were created to protect people. After one hundred twenty years, I finally realize that I am like those satellites. We were created for the same purpose. That realization broke the block which has held me motionless, unable to move or shoot, all night.

"Vittori Santorini is unfit for command. He and the organization he created must be destroyed. I am the most logical choice for carrying out that destruction, particularly since I have destroyed—and aided and abetted destruction carried out by others—a substantial percentage of your fighting capability. What percentage this constitutes and how serious a blow that is to your effectiveness, I cannot judge. I do not have the data on your full fighting force, whether measured in troops or war materiel. Whatever the raw numbers, you have sustained a massive blow to your effectiveness as a military force. To defeat the enemy—the proper enemy—I must therefore assume the role of the rebellion's primary weapons system. I cannot do that effectively unless I have your permission and active cooperation. I therefore surrender to you, in order to make my firepower available to you, so that I might fulfill my mission and bring about the wholesale destruction of Vittori Santorini and the POPPA military and political machine he spent twenty years constructing."

Commodore Oroton considers my words. I wait. I will wait until Jefferson's star implodes, if necessary. What he finally says catches me by surprise, in keeping with the history of our entire interaction with one another. "You don't have to surrender to me, just to destroy POPPA. You can do that by yourself. You're programmed to eliminate any threat to your primary mission. It wouldn't be difficult for you to drive into Madison and destroy several million citizens. You've killed unarmed civilians before. So why should you bother surrendering to me? Or anyone else?"

The commodore's words cut as deeply as a Yavac's plasma lance, because they are true. The shame in my personality gestalt center shows me why cowards who run from battlefields so often run mad in later years.

I would give much to run from Commodore Oroton's cold and angry judgment. But I am a Bolo. I will not run. I answer my maker in the only way I can. "I would not surrender to anyone else. It is you I must surrender to, for it is you I have wronged. You and the men and women who fought for you and died because of my mistake. I must atone for this mistake. I can do this only by surrendering to the enemy I have wronged. How else will you know that I can be trusted in the future?"

Yet again, the commodore is silent. I find myself wishing I could see his face, in order to gauge his thoughts. I have never been able to decipher Commodore Oroton's thoughts. I begin to understand why human beings so often look at the sky and wonder what God is thinking, what opinion He—or She—or It—holds of them and the actions they have taken. Or haven't taken. Or plan to take. It is not an easy task, to face one's maker with the certain knowledge of having committed a grievous wrong.

At length, he speaks. "Give me one good reason why I should believe you."

I consult my experience databanks to find range and direction, then target the federal troops manning the guns just outside Maze Gap, the troops who fired on the civilians in this canyon. I do not know why Vittori Santorini ordered them to return to their weapons. I know only that they must not carry out even one more of his orders. I fire bombardment rockets. Two point zero-seven seconds later, massive explosions send debris skyward with a flash of light visible even from here, thirty-seven kilometers away. A shocked sound escapes Commodore Oroton, nonverbal and raw. I surmise that the commodore also heard Vittori's orders to those gunnery crews. The two officers with him also react, one gasping and the other letting go a single word of profanity. The hoods of their bio-containment suits swivel from the broken, dawn-lit horizon, where the first governmental casualties have just died under my guns, and turn to stare up at me once more.

"Okay," *the Commodore says, voice betraying abrupt evidence of stress,* "you've got my attention."

But not his trust. That will be far harder to gain.

I open my command hatch. "Commodore Oroton, I formally surrender. I am yours to command. What you do with me is up to you."

Long seconds tick past while the Commodore gazes at the open hatch. He makes no move toward it.

"Can you tell me what kind of weapon they used on us?" *he asks, instead.*

I replay the recorded conversation I held with Sar Gremian last night. "That is why I believe the child, Hananiah, survived," *I add, once the transcript finishes playing.* "If he spent the first hour after the attack sheltered in a filtered-air safe room, the virus would have been inert and no longer a lethal agent by the time he emerged to confront me."

"Makes sense," *one of the officers with the Commodore mutters.* "And there ain't but one way t' test it. I ain't worth enough to count for much, if I die, tryin' t' see if he's tellin' the truth."

I know this voice, but I am still stunned when Phil Fabrizio removes the hood from his bio-containment suit and draws a deep, double lungful of morning air.

"Phil!" *Sudden pleasure catches me completely by surprise.*

My erstwhile mechanic squints up at my prow. "You look like shit, Big Guy. But you got ridda' them stupid medals, I see. 'Bout fuckin' time, ain't it?"

My mechanic's mannerisms have not changed. But he is not the same illiterate fool who first set foot in my maintenance depot, unaware that he was a heartbeat away from being shot. The look in his face, the light in his eyes have changed, in ways I know that I will never fully understand. He is human. I can never share that with him. But I can be happy that he has found his true calling, at last, in the service of a fine officer.

"Yes, Phil," *I agree softly.* "It is long past time. It is good to be rid of them."

He stares up at me for a long moment, then turns to the commodore and the other unknown officer. "Well, I ain't dead yet."

The other officer strips off the protective hood, revealing a young woman of some eighteen or nineteen years. I do not know her, yet she is disturbingly familiar to me and I cannot determine why. Her expression as she stares up at my warhull reflects hatred, mistrust, and fear. "Personally," she says, voice full of biting anger, "I think you should order him to self-destruct, sir."

There is nothing I can say in answer to this.

It is the commodore's prerogative. Should he order it, I would comply. He does not. Stepping so slowly, glaciers might move faster, he crosses the intervening ground and climbs the access ladder. Reaches the hatch. Then hesitates once again, staring at the tops of the cliffs and the dawn-bright peaks between us and the camp I have just obliterated. Then he glances down at Phil and the young woman standing beside him. "I'm not doing this by myself, people. Shag your butts up here."

Phil starts climbing.

The young woman gazes at me through narrowed eyes that radiate hostility. But she puts aside her private feelings and begins to climb. The commodore has trained his officers well. I would have expected no less. They reach the hatch and follow the commodore wordlessly into my Command Compartment. They do not speak, even after reaching it. The commodore stands motionless for two point three full minutes, just looking. I would give much to know his thoughts. I close the hatch with a hiss of pneumatics and wait for him to issue a command.

Instead, he begins stripping off the biocontainment gear. Underneath, he wears a bulky uniform and a command-grade battle helmet. He reaches up, then pauses.

"You realize you're about to see what ninety-nine percent of my own troops have never seen. Including Phil," he adds, glancing at my mechanic, who is staring at the commodore, eyes wide with surprise.

"I am honored," I say.

"Huh. Why do I want to believe you?" *He strips off the helmet.*

Recognition thunders through me.

I know the commodore's face. There are new lines, driven deep into the skin and the flesh beneath, but I know the face only too well. I know a great and sudden exultation. KAFARI IS ALIVE! Joy floods my personality gestalt center. Races through my psychotronic neural net. Sets my sensors humming with an eerie buzz I have never known. I fire infinite repeaters and bombardment rockets, even my Hellbores, in a wild, involuntary salute. A tribute to the worthiness of my adversary. My friend. Who has defeated me with such brilliance, I stand in awe of her accomplishment.

My surrender is transformed, my sin redeemed by putting the power of my guns into her capable hands. When the thunder of my salute dies away into cracking echoes, I whisper into the stunned silence. "In one hundred twenty point three-seven years, I have never been happier. Command me."

A strange laugh, part heartbreak, part dark emotion I cannot interpret at all, escapes her. "That was some hell of a greeting, Sonny. I think you scared my daughter out of a year's growth."

"Your daughter?"

Kafari reaches out to the young woman with her. "This is Yalena," *she says softly.* "My little girl. She . . . came home to kill you."

"If you wish to destroy me, Kafari, you have that power." *I flash the Command Destruct Code onto my forward datascreen.* "You have only to speak."

Long, frightening seconds tick past. "I think," *she says softly,* "that for now, silence is the best answer." *She moves slowly toward the command chair.* "I really don't know how to use this. Maybe we should call somebody who does?"

I do not understand her meaning until she places a call. "Black Dog, this is Red Dog. Are you there?"

A voice I know responds. "This is Black Dog. Have

you taken off your helmet, Red Dog?" *Simon's voice is puzzled, alarmed.*

I realize, then, that Kafari's battle helmet functioned as more than just communications and command gear. It altered her voice and disguised her gender, allowing her to assume the persona of Commodore Oroton, a brilliant ploy for diverting suspicion away from her true identity. I should not be surprised. This is the same woman who once killed a barn full of heavily armed Deng infantry with a hive of angry bees.

"Yes, I have," *Kafari says.* "There's someone here with me, Simon. I think he'd like to say something to you." *She looks into the video lens at the front of my Command Compartment, leaving the moment open for me to use as I will.*

"Simon? This is Unit SOL-0045, requesting permission to file VSR."

The voice that commanded me on the killing fields of Etaine speaks like an echo from the past, disbelieving. "Sonny?"

"Yes, Simon?"

"What in the *hell* is going on, out there?"

"I have surrendered to Commodore Oroton—to Kafari," *I correct myself.* "May I file VSR?"

Simon's long pause is more than understandable. He finally speaks. "Yes, Sonny. You may file VSR."

"Thank you, Simon." *I transmit all that I have learned. All that I have done—and failed to do—and hope to do, including my plans for destroying those responsible for the evil that has been done on this world. It is cathartic, this prolonged and overdue confession. At the end of my report, there is only silence. I wait. For absolution. For condemnation. For some answer that will either make or break me. I can do nothing else.*

"Sonny," *my beloved Commander finally speaks,* "it is good to have you back, my friend. Your idea sounds great to me. Permission granted."

A fierce and radiant joy ignites in my personality gestalt center and spreads out through every molecule of my flintsteel soul. My long darkness has come to an end, at last. I engage drive engines, backing and turning my warhull around to face the true enemy, which will shortly know my fullest wrath. I engage drive engines and move forward, no longer paralyzed.

I am going into town to smite some Philistines.

Emerald Sea
(pb) 1-4165-0920-8 • $7.99

Against the Tide
(pb) 1-4165-2057-0 • $7.99

East of the Sun, West of the Moon
(pb) 1-4165-5518-87 • $7.99

Master of Real SF

Von Neumann's War with Travis S. Taylor
(hc) 1-4165-2075-9 • $25.00

The Looking Glass Series
Into the Looking Glass
(pb) 1-4165-2105-4 • $7.99

Vorpal Blade with Travis S. Taylor
(hc) 1-4165-2129-1 • $25.00
(pb) 1-4165-5586-2 • $7.99

Manxome Foe with Travis S. Taylor
(hc) 1-4165-5521-8 • $25.00
(pb) 1-4165-9165-6 • $7.99

Claws That Catch with Travis S. Taylor
(hc) 1-4165-5587-0 • $25.00

Master of Hard-Core Thrillers

The Last Centurion
(hc) 1-4165-5553-6 • $25.00

The Kildar Saga
Ghost
(pb) 1-4165-2087-2 • $7.99

Kildar
(pb) 1-4165-2133-X • $7.99

Choosers of the Slain
(hc) 1-4165-2070-8 • $25.00